When a man l
and she's in j

NOW OR
NEVER

Relive the romance...
Three complete novels
by one of your all-time favorite authors

Anne Stuart has, in her twenty-five years as a published author, won every major award in the business, appeared on various bestseller lists, been quoted by *People, USA Today* and *Vogue,* appeared on *Entertainment Tonight* and warmed the hearts of readers worldwide. She has written more than thirty novels for Harlequin and Silhouette, plus another thirty or more suspense and historical titles for other publishers.

When asked to talk a bit about herself, Anne once said, "Anne Stuart has written lots of books in lots of genres for lots of publishers. She lives in the hills of northern Vermont with her splendid husband and two magnificent children, where it snows so much, she hasn't much else to do but write."

ANNE STUART

NOW OR NEVER

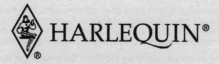

HARLEQUIN®

TORONTO • NEW YORK • LONDON
AMSTERDAM • PARIS • SYDNEY • HAMBURG
STOCKHOLM • ATHENS • TOKYO • MILAN • MADRID
PRAGUE • WARSAW • BUDAPEST • AUCKLAND

HARLEQUIN BOOKS

by Request—NOW OR NEVER

Copyright © 1999 by Harlequin Books S.A.

ISBN 0-373-20166-4

The publisher acknowledges the copyright holder of the individual works as follows:

RAFE'S REVENGE
Copyright © 1992 by Anne Kristine Stuart Ohlrogge

HAND IN GLOVE
Copyright © 1987 by Anne Kristine Stuart Ohlrogge

PARTNERS IN CRIME
Copyright © 1988 by Anne Kristine Stuart Ohlrogge

This edition published by arrangement with Harlequin Books S.A.

Visit us at www.romance.net

Printed in U.S.A.

CONTENTS

They were locked in a power struggle,
but when he turned on the charm
she wanted to surrender completely.

Rafe's Revenge

Chapter One

Rafael Starret McGinnis could smell the coffee when he stepped into his chrome-and-glass office at half past six in the morning. At that hour there was only one other person present in the rambling building that held the executive offices of Mack Movies: his partner, mentor and the smartest woman in Hollywood. "Bernie," he called out, loosening his silk tie, "I want you to bear my children."

"Too late," Bernadette Thomas said, appearing in the doorway, a mug of coffee in one capable hand. "You should have asked thirty years ago."

He poured himself some coffee. "I know I'm a stud, but even for me seven years old would have been a little young."

Bernie shook her short-cropped gray head. "Nothing's impossible for you, Rafe. Besides, there are any number of sweet young things willing to do your bidding at any hour of the day or night. You don't need me. Anyway, I made this coffee for myself. You're just lucky to get some."

"You're still a wonderful woman," he said with a smile he reserved just for her, his right arm, the woman with the secrets, who'd been in the business longer than he'd been alive. Without her knowledge, her contacts, he wouldn't be where he was, at the top of the heap, founder of one of the most successful independent studios in the history of Hollywood. Together with Bernie and a brilliant young director named Sam Mendelsohn, they'd built the company from scratch and just sold it to Pegasus Pictures for the gross national income of several South American nations. There was a saying—he who died with the most toys won the game of life. Well, he had more toys than anyone he knew of, and one of those toys was Mack Movies. Pegasus might have paid him a fortune for it, but they still had no control over it. He had the protection of one of the few solvent studios left in Southern California, and they had an adequate percentage of the money-making machine he'd created.

On top of that, he had Sam, and most especially he had Bernadette Thomas. They shared the same vision, the same dedication, and she was one of the few people who ever got her own way when it clashed with his.

"Speaking of sweet young things," she added, following him into his office, grabbing her own coffee on the way, "how was your evening with Marcia?"

"So that was her name!" Rafe said, stripping off his tie and shrugging out of his jacket. "I couldn't remember."

"Marcia Allison, twenty-three years old, three featured roles, one lead in a television movie," Bernie cited effortlessly. "I trust you didn't sleep with her if you couldn't remember her name."

"Your trust is misplaced."

"God, Rafe, how do you manage these things? Just an appropriate *darling* here and there?" Bernie said, plopping her ample frame down in a chair and watching with jaundiced eyes as he unbuttoned his shirt.

"Exactly."

"You're impossibly decadent. Does she get the role?"

He tossed the shirt in the trash. It smelled like the woman he'd spent the night with—expensive, sexual and anonymous. "I'm not a casting director," he said, reaching for a fresh shirt and shrugging into it. "It's not up to me."

"She wasn't that good, eh?" Bernie said shrewdly.

"You're a dirty old woman, you know that?" He tucked the shirt in, grabbed the silk-and-wool Armani jacket and sank into his leather chair, reaching for his coffee and stretching out his long legs.

"Or then again, maybe you weren't that good," she added.

"You aren't going to get a reaction out of me, Bernie. I'm in a bad mood, and your little sniping won't affect it."

"I noticed. Maybe I'll just add some fuel to the fire," she said sweetly.

"Oh, yeah? How do you intend to manage that?" he drawled, draining his coffee and reaching for his pack of cigarettes.

"Have you read today's paper?"

"Oh, God, what now?" he said, reaching for it as it lay on his glass-topped desk. "Who died, who's done what to whom?"

"Nothing that simple. Just the review of *Cop for a Day*."

"Damn, Bernie, you had me worried," he growled. "I thought it was something that mattered. The day I worry about reviews is the day I quit."

"It's S. H. Carlysle."

The name was enough to galvanize him. "Just what I need to make my day perfect," he said with a long-suffering sigh. "What's she saying now?"

"Read it," Bernie said, tapping the newspaper before she headed out the door, "and weep."

Tears were the furthest thing from Rafe's mind as he scanned the review, unless they were tears of rage. S. H. Carlysle had been the bane of his existence, a thorn in his side since she'd started filling in for the revered Clement Walden. Walden had been his own sort of pain—an elitist, elderly pedant who only liked films, pronounced with two syllables. Rafe prided himself on making movies, not films, and he didn't give a damn what someone like Walden said about him.

S. H. Carlysle was a different kettle of fish. The fact that she was obviously a woman was part of it. She reviewed things like a woman, he thought with a satisfyingly sexist contempt. Backbiting, hysterical, more interested in politically correct thinking than whether something worked, damn it. The review was just one more in a long line of scathing reviews that deteriorated into personal attacks on Mack Movies and Rafael McGinnis.

She'd upped the ante this time. In trashing *Cop for a Day,* the third in a line of fabulously successful action movies, she'd added that right-thinking Americans ought to boycott all Mack movies and make their significant others do the same.

"Damn," Rafe said out loud. He'd put up with her for more than a year now, and he was getting sick and tired of her cheap shots. She had every right in the world not to like the kind of movies he made. Hell, sometimes even he didn't like them. But she had no right to tell other people that they shouldn't like them.

"Can you find me a contract killer?" he called to Bernie in her adjoining office. "I want this woman dead."

"Sorry, that's not in my job description," Bernie called back. "You'll have to do it yourself."

"Love to," Rafe said, leaning back in his leather-and-chrome chair and warming his hands on the refilled mug of coffee. "How do you suggest I do that when I don't even know what the woman looks like? Except that I can guess. She's short and squat and ugly and dresses like a man."

"Watch that," Bernie warned, reappearing in the doorway, and belatedly Rafe noticed that Bernie was short and squat and ugly and dressed like a man. "If you lower yourself to attend the premiere tonight she might be there."

"I hate premieres, you know that. Last night was bad enough. I can only stand one Hollywood party a week, max," he said.

"Then it's too bad you're A-list material," Bernie said, completely without sympathy. "It's up to you. There'll be plenty of people around to let you know how things went, but if you want to touch base with the critics…"

"Why do you think I avoid these things in the first place? I hate critics. They're not worth my energy."

"It's not like you to roll over and play dead. However, if you don't mind what S. H. Carlysle says about you…"

"Do I have to have a date?" he asked with sour acquiescence.

"Rafael McGinnis is like the two-thousand-pound gorilla, he doesn't have to do a damned thing he doesn't want to do. However, if you show up unattached you're going to be bombarded by every out-of-work actress in the place, and maybe half the actors."

"You're right." He swiveled around, staring out the window into the early-morning light. The studio was coming awake, early makeup calls and scenery setups already in motion. "The sensible, mature thing to do would be to ignore the provocation, ignore S. H. Carlysle and go home tonight. Wouldn't it?"

"Absolutely. You feel like being sensible and mature for a change?"

"No," he said with a reluctant grin. "And tell Robin when she gets in to give what's her name a call. Marcia. Tell her I'll pick her up at...what time?"

"Seven. And if she can't make it?"

Rafe looked at her. "Do you really think there's a possibility of that?"

"Depends on how good you were last night," Bernie mused.

"Get out of here, woman," he said. "We've both got work to do."

Bernie moved at her own majestic pace, leaving him alone and quiet for the few minutes before his secretary, attuned to his early hours, made her first appearance. S. H. Carlysle was about the only thing that had piqued his interest in the past few weeks—he almost hated to have his curiosity satisfied. But he wasn't about to let anyone get away with the stuff she had. He needed to plan an effective revenge. And he couldn't think of a more relaxing way to spend the next half hour.

S. H. Carlysle was going to meet her comeuppance. And maybe he'd be able to concentrate a little more on the newest woman in his life, a woman whose name he could hardly remember. She'd certainly been energetic enough last night.

It was a damned shame he couldn't get nearly as excited about her as he was about the prospect of besting Carlysle. It just went to prove how completely cynical he'd become in his old age. And he wondered if he ever, just for a moment, missed his innocence.

"I'M NOT IN THE MOOD for this, Clement," Silver Carlysle said in a quiet voice.

"Dearest, why not?" countered the impossibly dapper little man sitting next to her in the back seat of a pure white Daimler. Clement Walden was an exquisite gentleman of the old school, one who believed that living well was the best revenge. He dressed impeccably, was possessed of a malicious wit that withered most human beings, and he was Silver's best and most trusted friend in the entire world. "You don't get out nearly enough, and besides, if you're going to write about the film business you need to partake of some of the social opportunities. There's nothing like a real Hollywood premiere to teach you about the artificiality of life."

"I've already had more than my share of Hollywood parties and the artificiality of life, Clement," she said scrunching back in the corner of the butter-soft leather seat. "And two Mack Movies in one week is a little more than my stomach can stand."

"I expect you to rise to new and glorious heights in your review," Clement said smoothly, touching a perfectly manicured finger to his snowy-white mustache.

"I don't see why you want me to write it. You've already seen the wretched thing in previews. I don't want to have to go in cold and come to a snap judgment..."

"Silver, darling," Clement said in a cooing voice. "You've already made up your mind about the movie, well before you've seen it. It could be the masterpiece of the decade and you'd trash it."

"Are you saying I'm unfair?"

"Not in the slightest. I'm saying I've taught you well. You know how to separate gold from dross, and if you're heading into a manure pile you know exactly what you'll find there.

Besides, I'm tired of tearing apart McGinnis in print. You provide a fresh take on the man that's charmingly nasty.''

There it was again, Silver thought, that niggling bother of a conscience. She truly despised Rafael McGinnis and Mack Movies, despised them for their cheap emotionalism, their mindless violence, their degradation of women, who were always victims, and gays, who were always caricatures. But she hated to think she had any sort of hidden agenda.

''I'm not dressed for this,'' she said, trying one more tactic, the one most likely to appeal to Clement's fastidious taste.

He wrinkled his elegant nose. ''True enough, darling. If you insist on dressing like an aging hippie, there's nothing I can do about it. I imagine other people will have the distinct bad taste to show up at the premiere in jeans and an old sweater— you won't be the only one. If only—'' he reached forward and flipped at her thick, shaggy hair ''—you could do something about this disreputable mop. I could talk to Marcel. I know he could come up with something quite extraordinary.''

''I like my hair the way it is, Clement. You've been wonderfully helpful in my work, but there's a limit to how far your influence extends,'' she said firmly, tired of an old battle.

''Is there? I wonder,'' Clement murmured. ''We're here, darling. Shoulders back, head up. Remember, you're a queen. If you insist on wearing such tatty clothes, simply think of everyone else as hideously overdressed.'' He handed her out onto the crowded sidewalk, ushering her into the brightly lighted theater with his usual solicitousness. ''We'll sit in the back and make rude comments to each other about the movie, shall we?'' he murmured in her ear. ''Maybe get some popcorn and throw it.''

''You're a devil,'' Silver said, partially reassured. The theater was jammed with people, but Clement was right. Compared to some of them, even her old jeans and cotton sweater were an improvement. Her mother would have deplored the decay in standards nowadays, just as Clement did. It was a wonder the two of them hated each other so much, when they had such a great deal in common.

She looked down at Clement from her superior height. She was six feet tall in her stocking feet, a fact that her petite mother still bewailed, and while Silver liked being barefoot, she also had a fondness for Western-style boots that added another couple of inches to her already considerable height. It would have been terrific if she'd been model thin, and when she'd been a teenager she'd starved herself, trying to achieve that gaunt-cheeked look.

In her older, wiser twenties she'd given up that notion as a lost cause. She was a healthy woman. Big-boned, curved, undeniably female. Clement might deplore her taste in clothes, but he didn't realize that part of it came from necessity. It was a lot easier to fit into men's clothes, with her long, rangy body, than into women's, even with the handicap of her curves.

There were a lot of tall men in the room, most of them self-absorbed actors looking to be seen by prospective employers. She glanced around her, dismissing them as she and Clement edged their way into the theater, when one tall figure caught her eye, and she groaned, a quiet little sound that nevertheless caught Clement's attention.

"What is it, Silver? Some old flame, risen up to haunt you?"

Clement was unfailingly nasty about her few aborted relationships, and she'd gotten in the habit of ignoring him when he was in one of his acid-tongued moods. But he was wonderful when she was hurting, a shoulder to cry on, an ear to listen, a dinner companion to ply her with exquisite wines and sumptuous foods. She'd learned to take the good with the bad.

"Nothing crucial," she said. "Rafael McGinnis is here."

"Oh, really?" Clement perked up, looking smug. "He seldom comes to these things—I wonder why he's chosen this one. Let me introduce you."

"No!" Her protest came out louder than she would have liked, causing several people around them to turn their heads and watch, ever alert for a new scandal. "I don't want to meet him," she added in a panicked whisper.

"Why ever not? Just because we despise the man's creations

doesn't mean we have to dismiss him entirely. He's really too powerful to ignore. Besides, he can be quite charming in an arrogant sort of way.''

"I'm not interested in charming arrogance," Silver said, tugging at Clement's arm.

"That's a great deal too bad, darling, because he's headed our way. And I don't think it's me he's interested in."

"Oh, God," Silver moaned, searching about her for a means of escape.

There was none. She was boxed in by the crowds, unable to move, as Rafael McGinnis bore down on them. For McGinnis the crowd parted like magic, for Silver the people remained obstinately in place. There was nothing she could do but remember Clement's words. Shoulders back, head held high, and don't cower. She just couldn't rid herself of the feeling that she was being caught by her teacher in the midst of an indiscretion.

"Clement," McGinnis said, and Silver felt an odd little shiver down her spine as she tried to hide behind the smaller man. She'd certainly seen Rafael McGinnis on television often enough, heard his deep, low voice. It was different in person. Even over the chattering crowd it had its own quiet power.

As did the man himself. He was better-looking in person, younger, although he'd been pretty potent on the tube. He was big—towering over everyone, including her. He wore a charcoal-gray suit, probably Armani, though Silver wasn't enough in tune to know for sure, and his dark hair was pulled back in a queue. His face was all planes and angles, high cheekbones, a strong nose, cool greenish eyes that looked right through you. It was his mouth that dominated his face. Large and sexy, it looked as if it could devour little girls who got in his way.

Not that she was in any way, shape or form a little girl, she reminded herself, stiffening her spine.

"Rafe," Clement said smoothly, with all his legendary charm. "How nice to see you again. And Miss Allison. Very interesting work in *Die for Us.*"

Rafe McGinnis wasn't interested in Clement's social amenities. His gaze was on Silver, and for a moment she felt caught, trapped by its intensity. "Who's your friend, Clement?"

Clement preened slightly, and Silver had the sudden, odd notion that Clement had hoped for this confrontation. "You mean my companion?" he inquired smoothly. "Or S. H. Carlysle?"

"Are we talking about two different people?" he countered, still watching her like a hawk watches a sparrow.

"I should never underestimate you," Clement said with a sigh. "Rafael McGinnis, may I present to you Ms. Silver Carlysle, my associate."

He just looked at her. Silver didn't make the mistake of holding out her hand—he would have ignored it. The gorgeous, impossibly tiny woman beside him was looking at the two of them nervously, as if caught between two angry dogs.

"I've read your work, Ms. Carlysle," he said, all that energy directed at her.

"Have you?" she countered brightly, refusing to be intimidated. "I won't ask whether you liked it or not."

"No, I would say that would be a waste of time." He took a step closer, and in the crowded lobby it was too close. "Obviously you have a problem with me, Ms. Carlysle. I can't imagine what it is—I'm considered a moderately charming individual when I get my own way, and since that's most of the time, I'm usually quite pleasant. Since you don't seem to appreciate my finer qualities, don't you think it might be better if you let someone else, someone impartial, review my movies?"

"It's not a reviewer's job to be impartial. It's to have opinions. And I don't have a problem with you—it's your movies that disgust me."

He smiled then, a wry upturning of that sexy mouth. "If you say so," he said, moving infinitesimally closer, and the closeness of his body was a subtle threat. And an odd, unsettling promise. "It just seems to me that your opinions are preformed ones," he murmured, and Silver flushed, remembering that Clement had accused and lauded her for the very same thing.

He touched her then, his long fingers brushing her face, and the heat of his flesh, the feel of his skin, was a shocking invasion, for all its insidious gentleness. "I suggest you keep an open mind, Ms. Carlysle," he added, very gently. "Or I might have to do something about it."

She stared at him, openmouthed in shock at the veiled threat. And then he was gone, moving past her, the gorgeous starlet clinging to his arm, as the crowds parted for him as they wouldn't part for her.

"That overbearing turkey," Silver gasped.

"Oh, not a turkey," Clement said, taking her arm and patting it with a paternal gesture. "We can be more creative than that, don't you think? But let's save it for the paper tomorrow." And he tugged her into the theater as she continued to fume.

Tomorrow, she thought, settling into her seat and ignoring the movie. Tomorrow Rafael McGinnis was going to be tarred and roasted and feathered. She'd never liked the man before, but it had been an artistic difference. Now, with his overt threat, it had become personal. And she was more than ready for a battle.

Chapter Two

"Any chance I could get your full attention for a moment, Rafe?" Sam Mendelsohn demanded in a long-suffering voice. "Not that my time's worth anything at all in the scheme of things, but yours is, and if you waste your time daydreaming, the gross profits of Mack Movies might drop below a hundred billion, perish the thought."

Rafe smiled faintly. "Don't give me that garbage, Sam. You know the balance sheet as well as Bernie and I do, and you know that it doesn't really matter. I'm sorry, I was thinking about something else. What were you saying?"

"What were you thinking about?" Sam Mendelsohn was the only person Rafe trusted, outside of Bernie. He was short, wiry, intense, an East Coast urbanite, just as Rafe was a deceptively laid-back Californian. The two of them, tempered by Bernie, made a powerful force in Hollywood, one that had wiped out weaker organizations without a backward glance.

"None of your business," Rafe said, reaching for a cigarette.

"Must be a woman," Sam said knowledgeably. "Bernie said you had a burr under your saddle about someone."

"Let me tell you, Sam, that cowboy slang sounds absurd with a New York accent."

"It can't be your ex-wife," Sam mused, not in the slightest bit deterred by Rafe's insult. "You haven't lost a moment's sleep since you got rid of that bimbo. And I can't believe it's that pretty little thing you had clinging to your arm last night."

"Then you'd be wrong," Rafe said. "That's exactly who I was thinking about." He hadn't slept with Marcia Allison the previous night, disentangling himself with single-minded adroitness when he'd brought her back to her house. He'd still felt restless, edgy, with no comforting sense of moral purity to alleviate it. Hell, he should have gone to bed with her after all. If he was damned if he did, damned if he didn't, he might as well do it. Then he wouldn't keep thinking about Silver Carlysle.

"Don't try to kid a kidder, Rafe. I've known you for fifteen years, through good times and bad. Marcia Allison isn't your kind of little prairie flower and you know it."

"God, not another cowboy idiom," Rafe groaned.

"Besides, Bernie clued me in on your little problem," he added.

"Sam, trust me, I have no little problem, apart from what we're going to make next."

"So what's the problem with that? We have a million ideas. *Cop for a Week,* the boxer movie, options on some of the hottest names in Hollywood. Everyone wants to work with us—we're the golden boys. Hell, we can even try a biblical epic. We have so many things in development we couldn't get around to them in this lifetime or the next."

"That's half the problem. We've got a million ideas, most of them sure money-makers, and I don't give a damn about a single one of them."

"Don't tell me you're becoming artistic on me all of a sudden!" Sam made it sound like a dread disease. "We make movies for entertainment, to make money. Not to fulfill your soul."

"I sold my soul years ago," Rafe drawled. "I'm not talking about artistic fulfillment, either. We make movies for entertainment, and they don't entertain me."

"Well, excuse me. If you don't like them then I guess we'd better find something else to do. Maybe a remake of *Heaven's Gate.*"

Rafe stubbed out the cigarette. Sam's office was a far cry

from Rafe's sterile confines. Sam's was chaos personified. Sam matched his office—tie askew, hair askew, food stains on his shirt, his jeans sagging beneath his expanding middle. He was deceptively disorganized just as Rafe was deceptively neat. Neither of them were what they seemed, and that had been part of their strength. "Maybe a Western isn't such a bad idea."

"Jeez, Rafe, did you hit your head on something? *Dances with Wolves* was a fluke. No one makes money on Westerns anymore. I mean, a tax write-off might come in handy in your income bracket, but I'd just as soon not have my name attached to a flop."

Rafe watched him for a moment. "It's up to you," he said finally. "This one'll be your baby."

Sam sank into his seat opposite Rafe. "What's the matter with you, buddy?" he asked in a softer voice. "If I didn't know you better I'd say you were depressed."

"I don't know the meaning of the word," Rafe protested, the very thought chilling him. His eyes narrowed. "You said Bernie clued you in on my little problem. How did she define it—mid-life crisis?"

"She's lived too long to make such a serious mistake," Sam said. "No, she told me about Silver Carlysle."

"I don't have a problem with Silver Carlysle." He denied it instantly. "Isn't that about the stupidest damn name you've ever heard for a female?"

"Oh, I don't know. I picture someone willowy, with waist-length blond hair and some sort of floaty dress. One that comes off with the first strong gust of wind."

"Maybe you ought to be making movies for the Playboy Channel," Rafe said. "Obviously you've never seen Silver Carlysle. She's about ten feet tall, built like a brick outhouse, and dressed from the Salvation Army."

"You're kidding. I thought she was Clement Walden's protégée. I can't imagine that old dilettante spending time around anyone who isn't as elegant as he is."

"You know more about her than I do," Rafe said. "How come?"

"You tend to ignore provocation until it becomes over-whelming. I like to look into it. She's been riding your tail for almost a year now, and I was curious as to why she had it in for you in particular."

"I hate to tell you this, Sam, but it's not me in particular. She hates our movies. She just hasn't happened to notice you exist."

Sam responded with a rude gesture. "Maybe. You're the one she usually mentions by name, though. Of course, after today's article it's all moot."

"You mean yesterday's."

"I mean today's," Sam said. "Don't tell me you've been lucky enough to have missed it."

"Where is it?" he demanded in a dangerous voice.

"I don't think your blood pressure can stand it, Rafe. Bernie must have decided to spare you." Sam was obviously amused by Rafe's reaction.

"Where's the paper?" he demanded again, rising to his full height and towering over the unabashed Sam.

"On the desk."

Rafe snatched it up, stalking toward the door.

"I guess we'll go ahead with *Cop for a Week* then," Sam called after him. "A Western. Good God, what will he come up with next?"

THERE WEREN'T TOO MANY unsuccessful screenwriters and part-time journalists who lived in Beverly Hills, Silver thought. Of course, she lived above a garage, in the former cook's apartment, and the place smelled like gasoline and car wax and boiled cabbage, but it was Silver's, and that was good enough. If it was up to her mother, she'd be ensconced in the rambling house, in her powder-pink bedroom suite with matching full bath, complete with gold faucets and imported marble. She'd lived in that room from the time she was eleven and her mother left her father to marry her stepfather.

None of that would be remarkable—it happened all the time in the modern era of disposable marriages. The only thing that made it noteworthy was that Silver's mother was Marjorie Carlysle, the minimally talented but quite lovely actress whose career was already on the skids by the mid-sixties. And her father was none other than Sir Benjamin Hatcher, the foremost British writer-director in the history of films, a brilliant, distant man who had no time for wife and daughter, and someone Silver had lost long before Marjorie had taken her and moved from the pseudo-Tudor house they'd shared, lost long before he died two years later in a car crash in England.

Her stepfather was a different kettle of fish entirely. Harry Braddock was an industrialist, with the kind of vast, steady income that was unresponsive to the vagaries of the entertainment industry. Marjorie turned her back on her career, on her old friends, without a moment's hesitation, becoming a wealthy matron, embracing that secure role with more enthusiasm than she'd ever embraced anything in her life, including her only child.

The three of them had made a decent enough family, learning to keep out of one another's way. Harry had worshiped Marjorie, and Marjorie in turn had bestowed most of her affection on the man who bought her. Silver was a ghost figure, wandering through the house, growing taller, more gangly as the years went by.

She suspected her mother had hoped she'd take up where Marjorie had left off. By the time she was five foot eleven that was clearly unlikely, and Marjorie had given up, packing her off to college with brisk efficiency.

She would have liked to find a place of her own when she finally emerged, complete with a master's degree in English literature. She'd wanted to go on for a Ph.D., anything to keep her in the safety of school for a few years longer, but Marjorie had put her foot down. It was time for her daughter to enter society, such as it was, in Beverly Hills, and decide what she wanted to do in life.

It had lasted no more than six months, long enough for Silver to renew her acquaintance with Clement Walden, the elder statesman of film criticism, long enough for Marjorie to decide she really didn't want to have a six-foot-tall daughter in her mid-twenties hanging around, reminding her how old she now was.

The funny thing was, her mother really loved her. Silver had no doubts at all about that. The woman just wished her daughter was a little more charming, a little more feminine, a little smaller.

The long-abandoned apartment over the four-stall garage had been the perfect compromise for both of them. It gave Silver her freedom without having to ask for money from her stepfather. It gave her mother a hold over her without actually having to put up with her.

So Silver had spent the past year and a half in the two rooms over the garage, fixing up old wicker furniture to make it do, spending the last tiny bit of the meager trust fund on a state-of-the-art Macintosh computer. Not for one moment did she regret the expenditure. Her father had been a spendthrift, a charming, energetic man who never worried about tomorrow, or the practicalities of life.

Silver did. She didn't like accepting handouts from her stepfather, even though Harry would have gladly bought her affection. She didn't like debt and things she couldn't afford; she preferred to make do and make her own way.

Her inheritance had paid for six very expensive years at Princeton, two of them in graduate school. She couldn't think of a better way to wipe it out than by buying something to help her write.

Silver considered herself a pragmatic person. She knew the odds against selling a screenplay were astronomical, even if she used her family connections, and she had no intention of doing that. Clement had been kind enough to give her a job, a few hours a week doing research and general office work for him. As the months had gone by he'd taken her under his wing, teaching her so much about films and the heyday of Hollywood that she was truly awestruck. She knew she was a little too reliant on Clement. On her more distant days she could see his prejudices, his little nasty ways. But he showed her more encouragement and affection than anyone had in her entire life, and she would have walked through fire for him.

He was the one who gave her her first chance. She'd happened to see a small French film when she'd been abroad, and he asked her to write a preliminary review of it before he went to see it himself. To her amazement, the review appeared in the paper one week later, complete with her byline and a check that was far more generous than first-time journalists usually received.

Since then the work had been steady. He kept most of the big films for himself, letting Silver sharpen her skills and her wits on the lesser ones. It was only her antipathy for Mack Movies' violent chauvinism in the first place, and Rafe McGinnis himself in the second, that made him decide to pass that lucrative little specialty on to her. Her antagonism amused Clement, who adored maliciousness. He was fond of quoting Alice Roosevelt—"If you don't have something nice to say about anyone then come and sit by me."

Silver flicked off the computer, rubbing a hand across her furrowed brow. This time, however, she might have gone too far. With Clement's encouragement, she had let loose with all the outrage she felt over McGinnis's movies. That would have been acceptable, if it weren't for the fact that she'd allowed her personal fury to creep in. Rafe McGinnis had always stood for everything she detested in the new Hollywood. Slick, soulless peddlers of death and sex and violence, devoid of wit or grace, they were a plague upon the land, and Rafe McGinnis, with his multimillion-dollar studio was the leader of the pack. She'd despised him from afar, but meeting him had been the final straw.

She hated aggressive men. She hated men with long hair tied at the neck. She hated men in cowboy boots and Armani suits and cool, superior expressions and smoldering sensuality that nothing could hide. She hated men with charm who used it at her expense. And there was no denying that Rafe McGinnis had a very lethal brand of charm.

Unfortunately she'd put that hatred into print. Oh, not in its raw emotionalism. She'd put it more delicately, and Clement had passed it along without comment. She'd simply made the point that moviemakers who were obsessed with sex and violence were probably beset by conflicts about those issues in their personal lives.

She really shouldn't be so nervous. She hadn't come right out and said Rafe McGinnis was unsure about his sexuality and used violence to cover it up. She'd simply suggested it. And actually, uncertainty about anything, particularly his sexuality, did not seem to be McGinnis's problem.

It was too late to change it. And she was damned if she was going to apologize for it. She was supposed to appear in the editor in chief's office in half an hour—Clement was coming to fetch her and provide moral support. If she was fired, so be it. More time for her to work on her own projects. If she had to recant, she might be able to manage it. After all, she was uneasily aware that it had been a low blow, one he more than deserved, of course, but perhaps not quite fair.

No one could sue her. She had no money, nothing of value to anyone except the trunk of her father's scripts and notes. They'd been left to her when he died, and she hadn't been able to bring herself to open it until this year. She was going through it like a miser, hoarding the discoveries, and no one even knew of its existence. Marjorie had forgotten long ago.

She heard the Daimler pull up outside, and she rose, forcing herself not to hurry. She glanced at her reflection in the mirror, but no fairy godmother had waltzed by with her magic wand. Still the same long narrow face, blue eyes that gave everything away, strong chin and nose. She looked clever and secretive beneath the thick mop of dark hair, and she felt neither. She felt like a woman in deep trouble. And Clement's doleful expression when she answered the door was no reassurance whatsoever.

''We'll fight this thing, darling,'' he announced, kissing the air beside her ear. ''We won't let them railroad you. McGinnis has gotten away with too much in this town for too long. We're not going to let him crucify you because his macho pride is offended.''

"I don't know why he'd want to crucify me," she said miserably, waiting for Clement's chauffeur to open the car door for her. "After all, no one usually reads my stuff anyway. I just fill in for you. If he keeps quiet about it no one will notice."

"I'm afraid that's not quite the case," Clement said sadly. "Your column's been the talk of the town today."

"Don't exaggerate, Clement."

"There's going to be something on *Entertainment Tonight* about it."

"Oh, no!"

"Oh, no, indeed," Clement said, climbing in beside her and waiting while the door was closed silently behind him. "So our only choice is to brazen this out. McGinnis is a barbarian, but he can't come out of this looking like a bully. Even if he doesn't care about public relations, Bernie does. She'll keep him in line."

"Who's Bernie?"

"You really are ignorant, aren't you, darling? And I thought I'd made such advances in your education. Bernie is Bernadette Thomas, one of the most powerful women in Hollywood, and you don't even know who she is."

"Of course I know who Bernadette Thomas is," Silver said irritably. "I just didn't know she was the Bernie you were talking about. She's been around since forever. Long before McGinnis and his horde made their appearance."

"I believe she was a friend of your dear father's."

"Apparently half of Hollywood was," Silver said dryly. "Was she stacked and beautiful?"

"As a matter of fact, Bernie has always been lamentably plain and dumpy."

"Then she must have been the only woman in Hollywood my father didn't sleep with."

"You've been listening to your mother again. Marjorie has

such a jaundiced view," Clement said sadly. "Your father was a brilliant man. In this life, the rules don't apply to geniuses."

Silver felt a reluctant grin curve her mouth. "Maybe that's what Rafe McGinnis thinks, too."

"That…that mongrel," Clement fumed.

"Oh, come on, Clement, that's not up to your usual style," Silver said lightly. "'Mongrel'?"

"My mind isn't working at full capacity. I'm worried for you, Silver. I'd hate to think I'd lose you because you were a bit…incautious."

"I was furious," she admitted. "Let's call a spade a spade. I suppose I could bring myself to apologize to the man. If I don't choke on the words."

"I imagine, dear heart, that any apology would need to be in print. And I don't think it's going to be that simple."

Silver glanced at him. "You think he's going to want his pound of flesh?"

Clement's faded blue eyes surveyed her with a doubtful expression. "Well, you aren't exactly Madonna, my dear, and he can have his pick of just about anyone…"

"I didn't mean that," she said, not at all stung by his disparaging opinion of her natural attractions. She was used to Clement's brutal honesty by now, and her opinion of her own beauty or lack thereof was low enough. "I mean is he going to want to nail my hide to the wall? See me cut down in my prime, never eat lunch in this town again and all that?"

"I really don't know," Clement said in a sepulchral voice. "Let's not anticipate disaster, shall we? I imagine it will find us soon enough."

"How comforting," Silver said faintly as they pulled up outside the *Los Angeles Clarion.*

"I do try to be," Clement replied.

"SO HERE'S THE DEAL, Ms. Carlysle." Jim Steuben, managing editor, pointed a short stubby finger at her. "Mr. McGinnis has decided to be magnanimous about the whole thing."

"Very magnanimous," Royal Penston, features editor, echoed.

"You will apologize in print," Steuben said.

"In print," Penston echoed.

"You will cease to even mention his name or that of any Mack Movie production in future reviews."

"Future reviews," said Penston.

"And you will present yourself, properly attired, at the Beverly Wilton Hotel tomorrow night at a party being thrown in honor of Mack Movies' sale to Pegasus Pictures."

"Outrageous!" Clement sputtered.

"Properly attired as what?" Silver said with deceptive calm. "A waiter? Does he want me to serve his guests? Or no, let me guess. He wants me to jump out of a cake. I certainly hope he can find one big enough."

"This is absurd, insulting…" Clement railed, but Steuben overrode him.

"You're to be an honored guest."

"For what purpose?" she asked warily.

"Mr. McGinnis has made it clear that he doesn't like the nasty innuendo going around, coupled with the gossip."

"If the dear boy doesn't like innuendo and gossip then he shouldn't live in Hollywood," Clement observed.

"Keep out of this, Clement, it doesn't concern you," Steuben said.

"On the contrary, it does indeed. If McGinnis insists we put on a farce as his honored guests I assure you…"

"Not you, Clement," Steuben said. "Just Silver."

There was a moment of silence. "Don't be ridiculous. She won't go, of course," Clement said.

"Yes, she will," Steuben said.

"She will," echoed Penston.

"I would think," Silver finally broke in, "that it would be up to me."

The three men turned to stare at her as if a chair had suddenly begun to talk. "Not really," Steuben said finally. "McGinnis has come up with an offer we can't refuse. You're a film buff, Silver, you should remember that quote. If you do happen to refuse, then I can honestly tell you you're finished in this business.''

"You'll never eat lunch in this town again," she muttered under her breath. "Why?"

"Oh, for a number of reasons, Ms. Carlysle," Penston volunteered in a particularly snotty tone of voice. "For one, your so-called review bordered on libelous, and we're just lucky Mr. McGinnis isn't inclined to sue."

"Well, he's certainly got you two on the run," Clement observed blandly. "How did he manage to turn you both into frightened, witless rabbits? And I'm giving rabbits a bad name."

"He threatened to pull all advertising for Mack Movies. And not just from the *Clarion*. From the entire chain of *Clarion*-owned newspapers. Do you comprehend what kind of revenue we're talking about?"

Clement waved an airy hand. "I seldom bother my head with business. Would you really have me believe that McGinnis is that powerful?"

"Believe it," Steuben said. "So here's the deal, Ms. Carlysle. You do everything McGinnis tells you to tomorrow night, the apology goes in print for the Sunday edition, and you may come out of this with your job intact."

"Only may?" Clement asked. "I'm not sure if I can consider that a strong enough guarantee."

"You stay out of this, Walden. Your nose isn't any too clean in all this. You should have checked her copy."

"I still don't think she ought to lower herself..."

"I'll do it," Silver said quite calmly.

"Don't be ridiculous, darling, I won't allow it," Clement said firmly.

"I said I'll do it. After all, it's not as if he's going to expect me to perform odd sexual acts for his friends."

"Silver!" Clement was shocked.

"I'm sure he's just going to do his best to humiliate me.

And when it comes right down to it, no one can be humiliated unless they want to. I'll be absolutely fine, Clement.''

Her elderly friend looked both petulant and extremely doubtful. ''I only hope you know what you're getting into, my dear.''

Silver thought back to Rafe McGinnis, with those cool, greenish eyes and his monumental arrogance. Tempered by a streak of truly dangerous charm. She could put up with a few hours of him if it suited her purpose, and she had no intention of losing her job if she could help it.

She'd put up with him, she'd be polite, well-behaved, her mother's daughter, and then she'd keep as far away from Mack Movies and Rafe McGinnis as was humanly possible in such a deceptively small town like Hollywood.

Because the man unsettled her. Pure and simple. And the only way to get past it was to beard the lion in his den. Face him, face her uneasiness, and learn that he was simply an arrogant suit, like so many men she'd known.

And then he wouldn't be any problem at all. Would he? She could only find that she devoutly hoped so. Clement was looking at her with a doubtful expression, one that fed her own uneasiness.

''I'll be absolutely fine,'' she said again. And she only wished she could believe it.

Chapter Three

Once the notion of revenge entered Silver's mind there was no dislodging it. No amount of common sense or latent feelings of self-preservation could make any dent in her decision. She spent that evening alone in her apartment, trying to talk herself out of it. By six o'clock the next morning she knew she was going to do it.

It took her the better part of the day to find just the right dress. Even the vintage-clothing stores didn't go in for the level of ghastliness Silver wanted, and it wasn't until she came to the Funky Fifties Resale Shop that she discovered The Dress.

It was an absolute treasure. Clearly designed for someone closer to five feet than six, it was made of bright pink chiffon, adorned with row after row of tiny ruffles that would have made the original wearer of the dress look even plumper than she obviously had to be. It was strapless, with a crinolined skirt that brushed Silver's ankles and stood straight around. It looked like the prom dress for a girl who'd never be asked to a prom, and when Silver tried it on she almost cried with laughter.

The waist came halfway up to her admittedly generous breasts, adding to the wonderfully frumpy look. The chiffon neckline sagged, making her look even more generously endowed, and the expanse of ankle beneath the frilly hem was the perfect touch.

"Costume party?" the woman with the rhinestone glasses

inquired. Silver wanted those glasses too, but she figured that might be going too far.

"You might say so," she murmured. "I don't suppose you have any silver open-toed sandals?"

"Not in your size, dearie. Try a pair of ballet slippers."

"I need heels," Silver said stubbornly, reaching for a rhinestone tiara with several of the stones missing.

"You're going to look choice," the woman said dryly.

"Let's hope so."

Her hair was a challenge. She cut it herself, in a scruffy shag she usually washed and ignored, and she knew from experience nothing on this earth would induce it to curl. She had to make do with her mother's gels and sprays, sneaking into the big house while Marjorie was out playing bridge. The last thing she wanted to do was explain her odd behavior. Marjorie did her best to keep out of the Hollywood mainstream. With luck, she'd never hear about "the hottest feud of the week," as *Entertainment Tonight* had dubbed it.

At the last minute she glanced through her mother's jewelry case. Harry regularly presented his wife with tokens of his devotion, and Marjorie made certain she got exactly what she wanted, but occasionally Harry had gotten his own way. One of the results of that was a monumentally ugly necklace made of diamonds, rubies and emeralds. It was heavy, old and very valuable, a treasured heirloom from Harry's tasteless family. Marjorie was almost pathologically possessive about it, despite the fact she never wore it. Silver held it against her smooth throat. Perfect. The rubies would clash wonderfully with the dress.

She stole her mother's Irish silk cape while she was at it. She needed to make an entrance. If Rafael McGinnis had any idea what she was about to do to him he might circumvent her, which would be an absolute tragedy when she considered all the effort she'd gone to to look deliciously ghastly for him.

At that point she stopped worrying about her job, her future in the movie industry and her ability to lunch therein, even Clement's concern meant nothing to her. She wanted to embarrass Rafe McGinnis, the powerful, invulnerable head of Mack Movies, and she no longer cared what it cost her.

He was sending a car for her, probably to make sure she showed up. He needn't have worried. She wouldn't have missed this evening for anything.

RAFE DESPISED Hollywood parties. He always had. In the old days they were simply an excuse for excess—sexual, alcoholic and everything else. Deals were made and broken at those parties, deals that never should have been conceived of in the first place. But at least the excesses had kept boredom at bay.

Bernie was right, being on the A-list had its definite drawbacks. Hollywood survived on information—gossip and innuendo included. And the only way to gather that information was at parties. It didn't matter if he was bored to tears, standing in a noisy crowd of overdressed magpies, smoke clogging his throat, alcohol numbing his brain and sizzling his nerves. He had to be there, particularly when he was the one giving the party. He stood alone and waited, inviolate, his sunglasses his only protection from the curious crowds.

Tonight was different from all those other nights. Tonight he could tolerate the sheer repetitiveness of it all because he was about to throw everyone a zinger. It had been sheer instinct that had made him deliver his ultimatum to Steuben. His rage at Silver Carlysle had been monumental, a wave of emotion that had left him shaken and curiously refreshed. For the first time in what seemed like years he felt alive.

He'd sounded very reasonable when he'd told Steuben what he wanted, but he didn't think anyone was fooled. He didn't want Silver Carlysle on his arm to convince the Hollywood gossips that there really wasn't a feud. He wanted her there to humiliate her. And he wanted her there because his furious reaction to her sanctimonious scribbling was the first thing he'd felt outside of crashing boredom in months. He wanted to savor it for as long as it lasted.

It wouldn't last long, of course. Silver Carlysle would probably either be so pedantic that he'd tire of the sport, or else she'd become annoyingly attracted to him. Women had a habit of doing that, even women who started out despising him. It had been a useful gift in the past, but occasionally it began to feel like a Midas touch. Just once he'd like a woman to stand up to him without melting. It wasn't as if he had any delusions about himself. Women didn't find him irresistible. They found his power worth lusting after.

"So where's your date?" Sam wandered up to Rafe, a drink in his hand. "Don't tell me you're going stag tonight? Has the beautiful Ms. Allison already gone the way of all flesh?"

Rafe ignored him, glancing out over the crowd. "I have a special guest tonight."

"Listen, Rafe, no one's special to you," Sam said. "At the rate you go through women there'll be no one left. Who's the virgin sacrifice for tonight?"

"You know, Sam," Rafe said in a meditative voice, lighting a cigarette, "maybe that's what I need."

"A virgin? You're in the wrong town for that, buddy."

"Not specifically a virgin. But maybe I need a good woman. A sweet, supportive little woman in an apron, to cook my meals, have my babies, give me back rubs at the end of a long day."

"Donna Reed's dead."

"I'm serious, Sam. Maybe I need a nice woman to clear my palate."

"We're talking about commitment here, Rafe, not lemon sorbet. Bernie would cut your heart out if she heard you."

"Bernie's used to me."

"So what's coming tonight? A bimbo or a fruit ice?"

Rafe's eyes narrowed behind his omnipresent sunglasses as he spotted a tall figure at the end of the room, flanked by his chauffeur. She was dressed decently enough, in a silk cape, and for a moment he felt a sudden sense of disappointment. She must be easily cowed. According to Steuben, she'd agreed to his demand without demur, and here she was, right on time, moving toward him across the crowded room. He watched her, feeling the accustomed boredom settle around him.

"Same old thing," he said to Sam, who was following his gaze.

"Maybe you'd better take off your shades, old man," Sam said dryly. "I think you've underestimated your date for the evening."

There was real glee in Sam's voice. Rafe cast him a startled look, then lifted his shades to get a better look at his reluctant partner.

"Oh my God," he breathed in a shaken voice.

"That's Silver Carlysle, I take it," Sam said. "When you go for a change of pace you don't go half measures. I think I'm going to enjoy this."

"Not half as much as I am," Rafe said, letting his glasses drop back down on his nose.

She reached him, her long legs carrying her across the room with the majesty of a sailing ship. He could see her face beneath the silk hood—the frizz of hair, the slash of bright red lipstick, the unevenly rouged cheeks. He'd had a glimpse of hot-pink ruffles beneath the cape, and he stood there, keeping the smile from his face as he waited.

"Mr. McGinnis," she said, in that throaty, damn-you voice he found himself remembering.

"Call me Rafe," he said, exerting all his charm. "Can I help you with your cape?"

So smug, he thought, watching the smile curve those ruby lips. Reaching up, she unfastened the cape, letting it fall into his chauffeur's hands.

In any other crowd her emergence would have caused a hush to fall. As it was, there was a gasp or two, a smothered giggle, and merely an increase in noise as people immediately digested the full glory of her appearance.

He grinned then. He couldn't help it. "A little predictable," he drawled. "But nice, nonetheless." He reached out with his long fingers and touched the magnificently ugly necklace around her throat. She probably thought she looked dumpy in that horrible dress. She did. But she also looked quite surprisingly luscious with that strapless neckline falling off her.

He felt it, of course. The shiver of reaction that rippled across her warm skin when he touched her. It should have bored him. Instead it fascinated him. Particularly when she looked so defiant and oblivious to the strong sensual thread that spread between them.

"I went to a great deal of trouble to look just right for you," she said, and her husky voice sent shivers down his spine.

That bothered him. It was one thing to be amused by her, fascinated by her, even attracted to her. It was another to feel such an intense pull.

"You succeeded admirably," he murmured, drawing her bare arm through his. Her skin felt hot and sleek beneath his fingertips, and he had the sudden notion that it was going to be a long night. And far too short. "Let me introduce you around. I'm certain people are dying to find out who my mysterious guest is."

It hit her then. He wondered how long it would take her to realize the magnitude of what she'd done. She'd been out to embarrass him, and she'd never considered what it would do to her own credibility.

He could take pity on her. Introduce her simply as Silver, and most people would have no idea she was the infamous S. H. Carlysle who'd trashed him so effectively in the *Clarion*.

But he hadn't brought her out to be merciful. "I know the other guests are dying to know who is my exotic companion. They'll be even more interested to find out you're my nemesis from the *Clarion*. Not to mention Clement Walden's protégée."

He felt her flinch. She hadn't thought about that aspect of it, either—that her admirably tacky appearance would reflect on the so-perfect Walden. "Uh…" she said, suddenly hesitant. "Do you suppose you could do me a favor?"

"Now why would I want to?"

She didn't look daunted, simply more determined. The effect oddly beguiling in her bizarre apparel. "I can't imagine why. Nevertheless, I'd appreciate it if you didn't mention my connection to Clement. Most people here are smart enough to figure that out—there's no need to remind them.''

"Did he approve of your little outfit?''

"He doesn't know.''

"I thought as much. I think you overestimate my guests. Most of them haven't got the brains of three maggots put together.''

"If you don't like them why did you invite them?'' she asked with a certain charming ingenuousness.

"But Silver,'' he countered gently, "you don't think I like you, do you?''

He waited for her to flinch. Instead she surprised him again by managing a rueful smile. "Good point,'' she conceded.

"Aren't you going to introduce us?'' Sam had reappeared, Bernie in tow. Bernie was looking frankly disapproving, but Rafe didn't make the mistake of thinking that disapproval was for Silver's outrageous attire. He never made the mistake of underestimating Bernie. She would know exactly who Silver Carlysle was, and assume by her apparel that she wasn't there willingly.

"Silver Carlysle, may I introduce my associates, Bernie Thomas and Sam Mendelsohn?''

"What's going on here, Rafe?'' Bernie demanded.

"Nothing at all, Bernie,'' he said blandly. "I thought I'd try to charm Silver over to our way of thinking.''

"Sure you did,'' Bernie said, glaring at him. "Don't let him intimidate you, Silver. He's an arrogant SOB, but he's not evil. I knew your father.'' She changed the subject with her customary abruptness.

The effect on Silver Carlysle was instantaneous. Wary, hopeful, pleased all at once. "Did you?'' she countered neutrally, but Rafe could feel the tension in the arm he had tucked beneath his.

"He was a good man. One of the best,'' Bernie said.

There was no mistaking the shy smile on Silver's carmined lips. It changed her whole face, softening it beneath the outrageous makeup, and the curious tightening in Rafe's gut increased. "I thought so," she said shyly.

"Who's her father?" Sam asked the question before Rafe could.

"Nobody you knew," Bernie said repressively.

Rafe didn't bother to pursue it. He knew Bernie in that kind of mood—nothing would elicit the information if she wasn't ready to give it.

Silver Carlysle was a different matter. He had the unnerving feeling that she was a Hollywood rarity—a real innocent. She wouldn't stand a chance against him.

He steered her around the crowded room, pausing long enough to give her a glass of champagne she insisted she didn't want, introducing her to a few choice people. People who wouldn't fail to make the connection, even if he didn't point it out.

She was miserably aware of it, too. By the time an umpteenth person said, "Oh, you write for the *Clarion*," and accompanied it with a knowing leer in Rafe's direction, her credibility was effectively sabotaged. He wondered whether he ought to feel the slightest bit guilty, then dismissed the notion. She'd started it, she'd upped the ante. Now it was time to pay the piper.

She held up with surprising stamina. Once she realized she couldn't free herself by tugging her arm loose, she accepted his possessive grip. She didn't know anyone in the room, another surprise, given the size and cross section of the gathering, and the fact that her father was someone who'd once been important to Bernie.

He'd caught on to that right away. Bernie was the least sentimental person he knew, and yet she still felt something for Silver Carlysle's mysterious father.

"Ready to leave?" he asked pleasantly enough a couple of hours later.

He looked down at her, caught for a moment by the deep blue of her eyes. She looked tense, exhausted and edgy, all at the same time. And he wondered what she'd look like in bed, all that edginess wiped away.

"Leave? Is the party over?" She glanced around her.

"It is for me."

"I thought I was only supposed to come to the party."

"Think again. We're going to dinner next."

"Alone?" Her voice was husky, tinged with an odd nervousness.

"In a public restaurant. You're safe with me," he said dryly.

"Why?"

"Why are you safe with me?"

"No. Why do you want me to have dinner with you? Haven't you humiliated me enough for one night?"

"Darlin'," he said, allowing a Western drawl to sneak into his voice, "I've only just begun."

SHE REALLY HATED HIM. She wasn't someone who hated easily—she tried to accept people, faults and all. She didn't care much for her stepfather, or her first boyfriend, or her physics professor in college, but she didn't hate them, or anybody else.

Except Rafael McGinnis. With his sunglasses at the dead of night and his condescending smile and his Armani suits and his strong, powerful body, she despised him from the bottom of her heart. It didn't help matters that her act of petty vengeance had backfired, causing embarrassment only to herself. It only made her detest him more.

He was watching her from behind those sunglasses, coolly, as if her response didn't matter in the slightest. She'd like to tell him where he could put his dinner invitation, but she'd come this far, she might as well go the whole way. He couldn't very well introduce her to everyone at the restaurant, maybe she still had a chance of giving him just a taste of embarrassment. Besides, she was curious as to what he'd say to her, once they no longer had an audience.

The chauffeured Bentley was waiting for them. Once more she climbed into the spacious back seat, only to find that it wasn't as spacious as she'd thought it was, when McGinnis crammed his six foot plus frame in beside her.

Apparently the evening had been planned ahead of time. Rafe leaned back beside her, as the car moved smoothly into traffic, and the smoked-glass partition kept the chauffeur well isolated.

The light was dim in the back seat, deliberately so, she knew. She wasn't a peasant, she'd been driven in Bentleys before. In just about every luxury car known to Hollywood as well. She eyed Rafe nervously as she edged away from him across the black leather seat.

"There's not that much room on the seat," he observed, making no effort to move after her. But of course, why should he? He was right, she was a captive audience.

"You don't really want me to go out to dinner with you," she said, having had enough. "You've accomplished what you set out to do in the first place. Everyone at the party knew who I was without you even introducing me."

"I shouldn't have underestimated them," he agreed. "Hollywood partygoers are like sharks when there's blood in the water. They can sniff out scandal anywhere."

"You didn't need to cling to me in such a…a friendly way," she continued. "Your plan was very successful. They assume we're sleeping together, and that my recent reviews of your disgusting movies were simply the result of personal pique."

"They do believe that, don't they?" he said, unmoved by her wrath.

"My credibility has been destroyed. People will think I let my emotions and prejudices color my reviews."

"Don't you?"

She glared at him. Not that he could see it, hidden behind those damned sunglasses. Unfortunately she wasn't able to come up with the words to refute his uncomfortable charge.

"I wouldn't worry about it if I were you," he continued smoothly. "Your credibility might be destroyed, but your career will flourish. People love scandal, they love malice, and if they think sex is behind it, so much the better."

"Sex has nothing to do with it!"

At that he lifted his sunglasses. His eyes were very dark, almost black in the dimly lighted comfort of the back seat, and they surveyed her with far too much acumen. "Sex has something to do with everything," he said. "You know, that dress backfired."

"I'm well aware of it. I'm the one who looked like a fool, not you."

"I wouldn't say that. At least you showed everyone that you weren't cowed by me. That's rare. But that wasn't what I was referring to. Obviously you chose that dress in the hope that you'd look impossibly frumpy and thereby keep my animal urges at bay. I'm afraid it's not working. The dress is remarkably frumpy. It's also surprisingly...luscious."

She stared at him in total astonishment. "You can't be attracted to me," she said bluntly.

"Oh, but I could," he murmured. "I am." And he reached for her, pulling her back across the seat and into his arms while she was still too shocked to resist.

Chapter Four

His mouth was hard against hers, hot and wet. He kissed her with a thoroughness that should have been insulting, but instead simply devastated her. He used one hand beneath her chin, holding her head still for his openmouthed kiss. The other was at the sagging neckline of her strapless dress, tugging it down.

For a moment her brain simply went numb, awash with the undeniably wonderful physical sensations of his hands and mouth. It had been so long since she'd been touched, even in friendship. So long since she'd been kissed like that. As a matter of fact, she didn't think she'd ever been kissed like that.

They used to talk about soul kisses. That's what this one was. Not simply a matter of mouths and lips and tongues. It was heart and mind and soul, it was something so powerful that it wiped out all her defenses, her judgment, her self-preservation.

For a moment the struggle was inside her, fighting against the insidious gentleness of his mouth on hers, wooing, seducing, fighting against the hands on her body, holding her but not restraining her. She lost that fight with a deep, inward sigh, giving in to the unbearable temptation to kiss him back, to let her lips soften beneath his, to touch his tongue with hers, to start on that downward slide of desire that could end in places she'd never been before.

It wasn't until she realized he was pushing her down on the

wide leather seat, until she felt the coolness of the air, the heat of his skin against her bare breasts, that her sense of self-preservation surfaced again, and this time the struggle was outward, as she realized what she was doing. And with whom.

She shoved, hard, using her hands, her knees, and he released her with a less-than-flattering acceptance. He fell back on the bench seat opposite her, and his eyes glittered in the darkness.

"Didn't you like it?" he said, his voice a faint whiskey drawl.

She wanted to slap him. She wanted to screech "How dare you?" like a proper, outraged heroine. She had the self-control to do neither, struggling to a sitting position and yanking the sagging dress up around her. "What was that for? Just to see if I'd do it?" she countered. It was just too bad that her shaky voice gave away her reaction.

He shrugged, reaching for his sunglasses on the floor, and she wanted to stomp on them. "It was worth a try," he murmured, unrepentant.

"Why? To humiliate me further?"

"No, actually, it was just spur of the moment. I wanted to." His smile was rueful, disarming. Silver refused to be disarmed.

"Stop the car."

"Oh, God, don't go all melodramatic on me," he sighed. "I swear, I won't touch you again. Scout's honor."

"Stop the car," she said between clenched teeth, "or I'll jump out of it while it's still moving."

For a moment he didn't say a word. She couldn't see his reaction behind the glasses, but she could imagine it. He rapped on the window. "Stop the car," he ordered the driver.

The huge, boatlike limousine cruised to a stately halt. Before she could leap out, Rafe was ahead of her, opening the door for her and stepping into the brightly lighted street.

To her covert relief they were on the edge of Beverly Hills, only six or seven blocks from her mother's house. She could slip off her hellishly uncomfortable spike heels and walk home barefoot in no time.

She spurned his offered arm as she stepped down from the limo, but she'd underestimated him. He caught her arm as she tried to jerk away, and she stumbled, coming up against him in the street.

"Be reasonable, Silver," he said. "Get back in the car and I'll drive you home. I'll do my best to resist my animal passions."

She could feel his heart beating rapidly beneath his shirt-front, belying the bored expression on his half-hidden face. She didn't trust him, but most of all she didn't trust herself, didn't trust what had almost happened. "I can walk," she said, yanking herself away from him.

He let her go. "Don't bother to thank me for a lovely evening," he said. "The pleasure was all mine."

"I'm sure it was." She started down the street, head held high, her mother's silk cape over one arm, when his deep, slow voice trailed after her.

"I have just one question, Silver. Who exactly is your father?"

She was glad he couldn't see her. She couldn't keep her spine from stiffening in alarm, but there was no way her face would give her away. She ignored him, continuing to trudge down the sidewalk, half expecting him to follow her. A moment later she heard the car door slam, and the limo drove off.

She turned to watch him leave, feeling curiously deflated. She hadn't wanted to waste another breath on him. For one thing, she didn't want to discuss her father, but she put no faith whatsoever in her ability to keep his identity away from McGinnis. He'd keep at it until he found out what he wanted to know.

Not that it should matter. She'd gone by her mother's name since she was twelve, when her father had agreed to let her stepfather adopt her. There was no way she'd take *his* name, and no way she'd continue to have the name of the father who no longer wanted her. Her mother was at least making an effort, and she'd been Silver Carlysle ever since, and very few people had made the connection. It wasn't as if she was petite and ravishing like her mother. She favored her father—tall, rangy, long-legged, and handsome rather than pretty.

Rafe was right, though. This was a town of gossips, a town where there were no secrets if someone was determined enough to find the truth. Her mother had been moderately well-known—if someone just put the name Carlysle together with Marjorie, the late Benjamin Hatcher would be the next obvious step.

She just hoped no one would take it. The divorce had been messy, painful, but not as bad as the fact that her father had been completely willing to let her go. He'd given her nothing but a trunk full of papers and enough money for a useless education. She wasn't about to trade on his name in a name-conscious place like Hollywood.

She turned the corner, slipping off her shoes and letting her stockinged feet wiggle on the cement sidewalk. People seldom walked in that area of town—they relied on their chauffeurs and their indoor exercise tracks. She'd probably make it back to the house without passing a single soul, but she pulled the silk cape around her anyway, tying it round her bare throat. She'd made it through the evening without it ending in complete disaster. She'd made a fool of herself, but she wasn't possessed of such overwhelming dignity that she couldn't survive it. The worst part of the evening was the end of it. When Rafe McGinnis had taken it into his head to kiss her.

She still couldn't quite figure out why. His romantic exploits had been legendary—only Warren Beatty seemed to go through more gorgeous women. She didn't for one minute believe he'd truly been attracted to her. At her best she'd fall far short of his usual standard of beauty. Dressed in frumpy nylon with frizzy hair, she'd been a disaster.

His heart had been beating fast, though. Even through her own besotted reaction she could see that he hadn't been unmoved by her. But why had he kissed her? If it was part of some grand scheme of revenge, why hadn't he done it in public?

There was no way she was going to make any sense of it.

No way she even wanted to. She needed to put his kiss from her mind. After all, it was no surprise that it was the most powerful kiss she'd ever had in her life. He'd certainly had enough experience, if the tabloids were to be believed. One had to pick up a certain amount of skill.

Her mother had guests in. Silver trudged up the driveway, her feet hurting, her dress still drooping embarrassingly low as she crept past the multitude of Daimlers, Bentleys and Cadillacs. She kept to the bushes, waving at the chauffeur who was serving as security.

Wilkers waved back, used to her by now, as she climbed to her apartment above the garage. Her answering machine was blinking, but for once she didn't succumb to temptation and rush to see who'd called her. It was probably just Clement, wanting to know how the evening went. She wasn't quite ready to tell him all the gory details. And she certainly wasn't going to tell him the truth about how the evening ended.

She dumped the silk cape on the wicker sofa and headed for the kitchen, grabbing her staple of caffeine-free cola and draining half the can. She needed a shower and a good night's sleep to put things in perspective. She was heading toward the bedroom when she stopped, unable to resist, in front of the huge mirror her mother had banished from her own bedroom before her most recent face-lift.

Luscious, he'd said. The man was crazy. Her usually thick straight black hair was frizzed around her narrow face, her blue eyes were absurd beneath the heavy makeup, her lipstick was smeared across her slightly swollen mouth. And then she remembered why her lipstick was smeared, and she put a tentative hand up to her lips.

Luscious? Absurd. Exotic, perhaps. Not quite the plain Jane as she tended to think of herself. But surely not luscious.

She didn't trust him. Didn't trust a word the man said. But still, as she ran a tentative hand across the broad expanse of bare skin that ran from her neck to the top of the silly pink dress, she thought in this case he might just be right.

"ARE YOU STILL PLANNING on dinner, sir?"

Rafe stretched out in the limo, rousing himself from his abstraction. "Not tonight, Jimmy. Drive me home."

"Yes, sir." The answer, polite as always, nevertheless suggested a certain level of disapproval. Jimmy had been driving him for the past ten years, before that he'd been employed by Pegasus Pictures to drive all their most important executives. He was as old and almost as savvy as Bernie, and he figured it gave him some privileges.

"Okay, out with it," Rafe said with a sigh, sliding the glass partition open.

"Out with what, sir?" Jimmy said stiffly.

"I can sense your disapproval a mile away. You think I'm a turkey, don't you?"

"I wouldn't put it quite that way, sir," Jimmy said. Centuries ago he'd been born in England, and he still clung to an artificially correct way of speaking that Rafe usually found humorous. Tonight, however, his sense of humor was slightly impaired.

"How would you put it?" he asked in a deceptively gentle voice.

Jimmy knew him well enough to hear the edge beneath the seeming amiability. He also knew him well enough not to be cowed by it. "A cad," he offered. "A bounder, though that's a bit archaic."

"You must have been talking to Bernie," Rafe grumbled.

"No, sir. Reading your mind."

"You're too smart for your own britches, Jimmy."

"Yes, sir."

The interior of the Bentley, Jimmy's favored mode of transportation, was silent for a moment. "Where does she live?" Rafe asked suddenly.

"Where does who live?"

"Don't be obtuse, Jimmy. Where did you pick her up?"

"She won't have far to walk, if you suddenly remembered a gentlemanly concern for her well-being."

"I can always fire you."

Jimmy's derisive sniff was answer enough.

"Does she live with Clement Walden? I know that's highly unlikely, but she is his protégée."

"Mr. Walden lives in Holmby Hills."

"If you think Steuben at the *Clarion* won't tell me, you'd better think again."

Jimmy's long-suffering sigh conveyed a world of disappointment in him. But he gave him the address in a flat voice.

Rafe let out a whistle. "Pretty fancy neighborhood."

"She lives over the garage." He pronounced it in the British manner, accent on the first syllable, and Rafe gritted his teeth, controlling the urge to remind Jimmy he'd been in L.A. for more than fifty years.

"People who live in that area don't need to rent out apartments," he said instead. "Who owns the place?"

"I couldn't say, sir."

"You're a pain in the butt, Jimmy."

"Yes, sir."

"And you know I won't be able to get anything out of Bernie, either."

"Ms. Thomas has a most excellent sense of discretion."

"And why does she have to be discreet about a second-string reviewer for a local newspaper?"

"I couldn't say, sir."

Rafe's reaction was satisfyingly obscene. Jimmy merely clucked disapprovingly in the back of his throat as Rafe slammed the dividing window shut.

Jimmy must have been put up to it by Bernie. The two of them were as thick as thieves, and whenever he saw them with their heads together his blood ran cold. It usually boded something unpleasant for him.

But what was the big secret about Silver Carlysle? Obviously she came from old Hollywood stock. Bernie had no respect for the nouveau film types, and it was clear that Silver merited her highest approval simply on account of her lineage. But the address didn't give anything away. He knew Beverly Hills very well, and no one of any consequence lived in the area where

Silver Carlysle did. There were mainly bankers and businessmen, the plutocrats of California with their manicured lawns and elitist life-style. Maybe Silver was the daughter of a banker.

No, Bernie hated bankers and businessmen as much as he did. If his associate thought she'd keep him from finding out everything he could about Silver Carlysle, then she'd certainly gone about it the wrong way. Everything she'd said and done had simply piqued his interest. He wasn't going to be able to get the woman out of his mind until he found out everything he wanted to know about her.

And he did want to get her out of his mind. Her mouth had been soft, startled beneath his, her reaction to his deliberately overwhelming kiss had been both unpracticed and disturbingly…endearing. He usually found the chase to be the most interesting part of his romantic entanglements, and he tended to get bored once things got settled.

But Silver Carlysle's hands had dug into his shoulders for a moment, and her untutored mouth had kissed him back, and he'd been more powerfully aroused than he could remember.

That was dangerous. He found his life eminently agreeable. A little boring, maybe, but that's why he had his sports car. He didn't want to take risks when it came to other human beings.

No, he wanted to get Silver Carlysle settled into a safe little niche in his mind, so he could forget about her. As long as there were unresolved questions about her, she'd linger. And she was just too damned distracting for his peace of mind.

He glanced out the smoked windows of the Bentley as Jimmy sailed through the nighttime streets of L.A. He could always lean forward, rap on the window again and have Jimmy take a detour to Marcia Allison's bungalow. Jimmy's disapproval would reach monumental proportions, but that was the least of his worries. It would get Silver Carlysle off his mind.

He had no doubts about his welcome. And that was half the problem. It wouldn't matter to Marcia that he'd just hosted a large party and she hadn't been invited. It wouldn't matter that he'd slept with her once, rejected her the second time. And it was that knowledge that kept him from rapping on the window.

He had a videotape of *Cop for a Day,* the movie Silver had trashed with stunning effectiveness. He'd sat through it on several occasions, not paying much attention, but he made a practice of having all the new releases transferred to his own personal videotape. Maybe he'd go home, pour himself a drink and watch the stupid movie. And remind himself what an elitist Silver Carlysle really was. Even if she did have wounded eyes.

But if he expected comfort he should have known better. He was a man who'd stripped comfort from his life, and there was none to be had when he needed it. His house, constantly under renovation, greeted him in dark silence when he entered. He'd bought it on an impulse, falling for its absurd Moorish outlines. It had been built sometime in the late 1920s, and it hadn't aged well. He'd been pouring money into it nonstop since he bought the place, and the end wasn't in sight. It was too small, too impractical, and about as far from the rustic simplicity of the log cabin in Colorado where he'd spent the first fifteen years of his life as he could find. And bizarre as it was, it was the only place he really felt at home.

He poured himself two fingers of single malt, ignoring the conventional wisdom that he shouldn't drink alone. Even with his mother's history as a bad example, he wasn't about to forgo his nightly drink. Especially when he had so damned much to sort through.

Three hours later he sat alone in the darkened living room. The television was a bright blue light, the videotape long ended, but Rafe didn't move.

So all right, it wasn't the finest movie ever made. It wasn't going to win Oscars or even Golden Globes, but it was going to make an obscene amount of money, millions of people were going to see it, and what the hell did it matter if a bunch of film snobs didn't find it socially redeeming?

It didn't matter, he decided finally. What mattered was that he hated it, too.

He rose, kicking over the coffee table, knocking his empty

glass to the floor, and stalked to the bay of windows that looked out over the valley. There were too many lights, too many people, too many years gone by.

He thought about his father, dead on a mountain pass in a Colorado blizzard. His mother, quietly drinking herself to death afterward. And he wondered whether it would hurt if he smashed his fist through the thick plate glass.

He turned on his heel, moving back through the darkened house with unerring instinct. The Lotus started immediately, with a throaty rumble, and he tore off into the night, not even bothering to lock his house.

He needed to drive away his demons, as fast and as hard as the highly tuned Lotus could take him. He needed to wipe out his lingering sense of depression caused by that stupid movie. Depression was for weaklings. He needed to wipe out the memory of his parents and his lost childhood. He needed to wipe out the memory of Colorado, the sweet, clean mountain air, the mountains, the stillness, both outer and inner, that you could find there. And he needed to wipe out the memory of Silver Carlysle. The last innocent in Hollywood.

"WHAT DOES THIS MEAN, 'the bizarrely costumed Ms. Carlysle'?" Clement demanded.

Silver blindly reached for a coffee, wishing she'd ignored the pounding on her door. If her head hadn't hurt so damned much she would have simply pretended to be asleep, or in a coma or in Siberia. But Clement's pounding had been fiendishly in time with the pounding in her head, and if she didn't get some aspirin she was going to die, so she'd thrown an ancient chenille bathrobe over her huge T-shirt and straggled to the door. Only to be greeted by an upraised newspaper that could only contain bad news.

"I don't know," she said wearily, tossing two pills in her mouth and washing them down. "Are you sure I can't get you some coffee?"

"Instant's only fit for pigs," Clement said with a sniff.

"Oink," said Silver weakly. She didn't dare look at her

reflection in the mirror. She'd stumbled into the shower and stood there for an hour last night, then fallen into bed. For all she knew her makeup was still streaked on her face.

"What happened last night, Silver?" Clement demanded in a slightly more reasonable voice. "Was it a total disaster? I should have insisted on coming, I know I should have."

"It was fine," she said for the fourth time since he'd arrived. Clement had seated himself on one of her wicker sofas after brushing away imaginary dust, and his expression was doubtful.

"You still haven't explained the 'bizarrely costumed' part. And how was McGinnis? I hope he had the good sense to treat you like a lady."

"He was a perfect gentleman," Silver said without a blush, remembering his cool hands against her breasts.

"Are we talking about the same man?"

"Don't, Clement," she said, draining her coffee. It did taste nasty, but she had burned out her last two coffeemakers and decided she was too scatterbrained for ground coffee.

"So he's made a convert, has he? The legendary McGinnis charm. I suppose if you like all that crude sexuality then he might have something to recommend him. And he's a very powerful man in the movie business. They do say power is the greatest aphrodisiac of all. Did you sleep with him?"

"Give me a break, Clement!" she pleaded. "Am I the sort of woman to be seduced by power? Am I the sort of woman to be seduced by someone like Rafe McGinnis, for that matter? Apart from the fact that he has the most beautiful, talented women in the world at his feet, what could I possibly find attractive about such an arrogant, soulless schlockmeister?"

"You've been reading my reviews," Clement murmured, obviously pleased. "I'm sorry I underestimated you, my dear. I should have known you wouldn't be bowled over by his tawdry sexuality. You're too much of a lady for that. Still the man does have his charm."

"Does he? I hadn't noticed," she lied.

"Didn't you?" Clement sounded skeptical. "Well, now that

you've appeased the monster, maybe we can get back to work. I was thinking of a series of articles on the modern taste for sex and violence combined. You write so well on those subjects.''

"Clement, I've promised I wouldn't write about Mack Movies anymore. And I couldn't write about sex and violence in modern Hollywood without mentioning Mack Movies,'' she said flatly.

"You didn't promise, darling. It was presented to you, and you didn't say anything one way or the other. Of course, if you're going to bow to corporate pressure, you can always concentrate on reviewing the cartoon tie-ins.''

Silver shuddered with heartfelt horror. "I haven't bowed to corporate pressure, Clement.''

"Of course you haven't, darling. Rafael McGinnis is going to forget your existence in a matter of days, if he hasn't already. You can write anything you want about him. We just have to be circumspect for a while.''

His words made a certain depressing sense. She'd definitely gone too far in that last article, and it was only her lingering sense of guilt that had made her give in to McGinnis's outrageous demand.

But that didn't mean she was going to roll over and play dead. She had every right in the world to her opinion, and if the *Clarion* wouldn't let her express it, she had no doubt she'd find another outlet. She wasn't going to let the man bully her. Not with his power, his money, his prestige.

Not with his body, his hands, his mouth.

She looked up at Clement's smooth, faintly smug face, and pushed her tangled hair back. "I'm looking forward to it,'' she said, hoping to retrieve some of her righteous anger. But all she felt was hollow inside.

Chapter Five

"You ought to be ashamed of yourself," Bernie greeted him not that many hours later when he strolled into his office.

"I've already had Jimmy read me the riot act," he said wearily. "I don't need you as well. What is this, the Preservation of Silver Carlysle Society? She can take care of herself—she doesn't need you and Jimmy as guardian angels."

Bernie was glaring at him. She had her own cup of coffee, and she was pointedly refusing to offer him any. "Did you take her to bed last night?"

"Obviously you haven't checked in with your cohort or you'd know the answer to that. And anyway, my sex life is none of your damned business." He stared longingly at her coffee. "And besides, what do you mean by 'take her to bed'? Who says I take anyone anywhere? What if we're simply talking about a mutually pleasurable experience?"

"I thought we weren't talking about it," Bernie shot back. "Did you?"

"Did I what?"

"Have a mutually pleasurable experience?"

"Not with Silver Carlysle. As a matter of fact, my time was spent both alone and unpleasantly. Have you seen *Cop for A Day?*"

"On numerous occasions," she said dryly. "It doesn't improve on closer examination."

"Is it as lousy as I thought it was?" He poured himself a cup of coffee and drained it, scalding and black and wonderful.

"No. It's stupid, mindless violence, but it's fairly good stupid, mindless violence, if you enjoy that sort of thing. It gives the public a vicarious thrill, watching people mutilate each other. So why didn't you seduce her?"

"Latent nobility?" he suggested.

"I doubt it. If you've ever had a noble urge in your life you've managed to suppress it."

He refilled his mug, then took a measured sip of his coffee as he stalled for time. "I'll tell you about Silver Carlysle," he said, "if you tell me who her father was."

Bernie didn't bat an eye. "How should I know?"

"For one thing, you know everything. For another, you told her you knew her father in my presence. So give over, Bernie. Who was he?"

"Jack the Ripper. What's on the agenda for the day?"

"Don't change the subject. Don't you want to know what happened between Clement Walden's protégée and me last night? Oh, God..." A sudden, horrific thought struck him. "Clement's not her father, is he?"

"Not likely," Bernie said dryly.

"Well, you never know...."

"In this case I do know."

"And you're not going to tell me?"

"You got it right the first time. It doesn't really matter, Rafe. He wasn't anybody you've ever met, or cared about. Just an old Hollywood legend, forgotten by most."

Rafe had known Bernie since he and Sam first arrived in Hollywood from NYU, a prize-winning independent film under their belts, looking for the right opportunity. She'd shown him the ropes, taught him all he needed to know, and when things took off he took her along with him, giving her the power and opportunities she'd always deserved. But he knew her very well after all these years, and he knew when he was going to find out what he needed to know. And when it would just be a waste of breath to keep asking.

"You knew most of the old legends, worked with them. Were you in love with this one?" he asked instead. "Is that why you're feeling so protective of his daughter?"

Bernie made a face. "If I was in love with him, and I'm only saying 'if,' then it was a long, long time ago and it no longer matters to anyone. I'm not the femme fatale type, and the man was married. What mattered between us was friendship. I trusted him, Rafe. Trusted him as a man, trusted him as a creative force. In honor of that trust I'm going to make sure you keep your cotton-picking hands off his daughter."

Rafe held up his cotton-picking hands in a gesture of surrender. "She's safe from me. Just satisfy my curiosity and I'll never even think of her again."

"If you have so much extra time on your hands I have a suggestion for you," Bernie said.

"I'll just bet you do."

"It's on your desk."

He didn't move for a moment. Bernie wasn't the type to put things in writing. She was a scrapper, a dealer, a talker, just like he was. And there was a nervous edge to her, one that betrayed the fact that whatever was waiting for him on his desk mattered to her. More than she wanted him to see.

"What is it?"

"A story treatment. From an old novel from the fifties. Pegasus Pictures bought the rights back then, and I don't think they've reverted. No one's done anything with it, it's just sitting there, waiting. You might find it interesting."

"I might," he said carefully, knowing damned well that anything that important to Bernie was interesting indeed.

"It'll be nothing but trouble for you. Production was started in the sixties and then dropped when the director died. But there was some preliminary work on it, and God knows where that is, or whether the director's heirs have any claim to it. Or whether the original writer or his heirs have a claim to it."

"Great," he grumbled.

"As I said, it wouldn't be easy. But you've been in such a foul mood I figured you needed a challenge. Go to it, sport. At least it'll keep your mind above your waist and off of Silver Carlysle.''

"What makes you think my mind's below my waist when I think of Silver Carlysle? She's not my idea of a fox, Bernie.''

"I know. But I have the utmost faith in your ultimate good taste. Leave Silver alone, Rafe. You'd be too much for her.''

He paused in the doorway, watching her. He knew perfectly well he ought to take her advice. There was nothing he wanted more than to leave Silver alone. Unfortunately the more Bernie warned him, the more stubborn he became.

He managed a tight smile. "I'll go read your mysterious proposal, and maybe I'll waste my time with it. What is it? Whodunit? Action picture? Not, God help me, a psychological drama?''

"None of the above,'' Bernie said. "It's a Western.''

"WE DO IT.''

Bernie looked up, pushing her reading glasses high on her forehead. "That fast?'' she said, but there was no disguising the satisfaction in her faded brown eyes.

"Have you ever known me to hesitate when something's right?'' Rafe said, dropping down in the chair opposite her. "You knew perfectly well I'd react this way. You've worked with me long enough, we share the same tastes. This is going to make *Lonesome Dove* look like a Saturday afternoon serial.''

"Or it's going to make *Heaven's Gate* look like a minor error in judgment,'' Bernie pointed out wryly. "You're not impervious to mistakes, Rafe, and neither am I. Are you willing to take a chance on surpassing the most notorious flop in movie history?''

Rafe grinned. "What do you think, Bernie? Aren't you getting a little tired of playing it safe?''

She just stared at him for a moment. And then she nodded. "It won't be easy,'' she warned.

"So you said before. Who says I like things easy? What's the big problem with this? The preliminary treatment says Pegasus Pictures. You've probably already got the legal department on the trail…"

"I do."

"So what's the problem?"

"Did you read everything I gave you?"

"I read enough. The treatment, started the novel, which, by the way, is terrific. I don't suppose the writer's still alive?"

Bernie shook her head. "I don't think so. He was an old recluse living out in Colorado somewhere. I imagine he's dead by now."

"And of course I noticed that Benjamin Hatcher himself was going to write and direct. I can't believe it."

"Can't believe what?" There was a careful edge to Bernie's voice, one that fascinated Rafe.

"Can't believe that a legend like Hatcher would leave behind an unfinished project and no one would pick it up. The man's one of the few truly great ones in this business, Bernie. We'll probably have film scholars crawling all over us when we do this."

"Probably."

"So what's the problem? Why didn't Pegasus ever finish the project?"

"I don't know. I have my own theory, of course. Sir Benjamin's death took everyone by shock. He died in a car accident in England, you know. When the dust settled, his papers had all been disposed of. Including the work he did on *Black Canyon*. The studio didn't have enough to go on, and without Hatcher's vision there was no one to push it through."

Rafe leaned back in the chair and propped his booted feet on her desk. She frowned at him, but she was used to it, and she didn't object. "So tell me, Bernie, my angel," he drawled. "You know a hell of a lot more about all this than you've told me so far. I remember that you were working with Hatcher when he died. You must know what he had in mind for *Black Canyon*. Why didn't you push it?"

"Who would have listened to me?" She said it without bitterness. "No one gave me a chance in this business. Except you."

"And now you're giving it to me. Why, Bernie? You must have known about this for years, thought about it for years. It's too good, too exciting to forget about."

"The time felt right. You're sick of the easy action movies, and I think the movie-going audience is ready for a change."

"Bernie," he said, entirely ready to play devil's advocate. "*Cop for a Day* just broke opening-weekend grosses. We're making money hand over fist. We'll probably take a bath on *Black Canyon*."

"Probably. Do you care?"

He didn't even hesitate. "Not in the slightest. I could do with a tax write-off. So where does this thing stand, legally? Does Pegasus own it or not?"

"Yes and no."

He shut his eyes for an impatient moment. "Stop pulling my chain, Bernie."

"Technically the option lapsed. But the book is out of print, the writer can't be traced, so it's a free project. The only problem is the work Hatcher had already done on it."

"You said it had disappeared."

"It was passed on to his heirs. I imagine you'll have to negotiate with them."

Rafe reached for his crumpled pack of cigarettes. He was down to five a day, and the last few in the pack were stale, but he didn't care. He lighted one, taking his time, and watched Bernie's nervous gestures through the haze of smoke. "Who are his heirs, Bernie?" he asked softly.

"Why do you think I'd know that?" Bernie protested weakly.

"We've already agreed that you know everything. Let's see, if my memory serves me, Hatcher wasn't married when he died. He'd been married two…three times."

"Twice," Bernie mumbled. "First to a girl in England who died in a fire. Then to a second-rate American actress who

divorced him for his infidelities and remarried a businessman.''
She stopped, waiting for the penny to drop.

"I'm sorry, Bernie, if I'm being obtuse. I haven't memorized
Hollywood lineages. What was the actress's name?'' If *Black
Canyon* wasn't so damned good he'd be bored by all this. As
it was, he was merely irritated.

"Marjorie Carlysle.''

For a moment he didn't move as everything fell into place.
"I don't like being jerked around,'' he said, very softly.

Even Bernie could be intimidated when he used that tone of
voice. "What was I supposed to do, say here's a hot prospect
that belongs to the woman you're having a very public feud
with?'' she countered.

"Yes. Then I wouldn't have wasted my time.'' He dropped
his booted feet to the floor and rose, starting for the door.

"I didn't know you were a quitter, Rafe,'' Bernie fired after
him.

He paused, looking back over his shoulder. "What's next,
Bernie? You gonna double dare me?''

"I double dare you,'' she said.

He turned, pausing in her doorway. "What makes you think
Silver Carlysle owns it?''

"She doesn't necessarily own it. She just thinks she owns
it,'' Bernie said. "The rights aren't clear.''

"What makes you think she even knows of its existence?''

"Because she's been offering her screenplay of it around.
Through Clement Walden's agent. She's offered it at Touchstone. And at Regis.''

"Over my dead body,'' he said flatly. "She'll wimp out the
men, she'll soften the violence, she'll turn it into some new-
age bullshit. And I'm sure as hell not letting Regis have it.
Have they shown any interest?''

"Rafe, I really don't know everything. The last I heard, it's
just been sitting on a desk. She didn't put her father's name
on it, and no one pays attention to a screenplay by a nobody.''

"Get legal going,'' Rafe said abruptly. "We're getting those
rights.''

"You think Silver's going to agree?"

"I don't give a damn. We're getting it. There's just one thing that mystifies me, Bernie."

She still had that wary expression on her lined face. "What's that?"

"I thought you were watching out for the poor defenseless lady. How come you're throwing her to the wolves?"

"I don't want you seducing and abandoning her, Rafe. For Benjamin's sake, I don't want to see his daughter destroyed by your powerhouse habits. But when it comes to her father's work, it's a different matter. My first loyalty is to Hatcher's artistic legacy. And to you."

"I'm glad you added that," he said dryly. "I suppose you're going to want a credit to Hatcher?"

"I want it dedicated to him," Bernie said flatly.

"You *were* in love with him, weren't you?"

"None of your damned business. I might give you a bit of advice when it comes to dealing with his daughter, though."

His eyes narrowed as he took a drag off his stale cigarette. "And what's that?"

"An old southern saying. You can catch more flies with honey than you can with vinegar."

A sudden, totally bizarre thought strayed into his mind. If he didn't know Bernie so well he'd think she was trying to throw him together with Silver Carlysle. "Are you suggesting I try to seduce the rights out of her, Bernie?"

"Hell, no. I'm just saying she might be willing to listen to reason if you behave like a decent human being for a change. You may be able to melt other women's brains, but I suspect Silver Carlysle is going to be a tougher nut to crack. She's not going to fall apart if you put your hands on her."

That was exactly what she'd done. For a brief, delicious moment in the back of his limousine. But she'd pulled herself together far too quickly for his peace of mind, just when she should have been surrendering. And if she had surrendered, this whole issue would be academic. Women seldom denied him anything.

"So let's get this straight. I'm supposed to wrest her father's legacy from her, something she's put her own work into, and I'm supposed to do it like a gentleman. I hate to tell you this, Bernie, but I don't conduct business like a gentleman."

"I have faith in you, Rafe. You can do anything, get anything, you set your mind to."

"True enough. But I won't necessarily do it your way. I don't have your patience." He pushed away from the doorjamb and headed back toward his office suite.

"Rafe." Bernie's voice called him back.

"Yeah?"

"You won't hurt her, will you?" There was sudden doubt in Bernie's voice. "Maybe we should just forget about *Black Canyon*. There are a million ideas out there..."

"Too late, Bernie," he said softly. "I want this one. And I'm going to get it. No matter what the price."

"I WISH you'd let me come up for a while," Clement said in what Silver had come to think of as his dry white whine. She usually gave in to him when he used that tone of voice. For one thing, it was extraordinarily annoying, and if she didn't acquiesce it would continue as punishment for days. For another, it always made her feel guilty. She'd been a disaster as far as her mother and father were concerned. At least Clement approved of her, supported her. She owed him her loyalty in return.

But not tonight. "I'm sorry, Clement. I haven't been sleeping well, and I'm exhausted."

"Then let me take you out to dinner. It's still early—only nine o'clock, and I happen to know for a fact that you haven't eaten anything but stale doughnuts since breakfast."

"Clement, my jeans are split at the knee, I'm not wearing a bra, and my running shoes are falling apart. Any place you'd consider worthy of patronizing wouldn't allow me into their parking lot."

"You underestimate my consequence," Clement said

blandly. "I could get you into Buckingham Palace dressed like that, if I wanted to."

She managed a tired grin at the thought as they sailed toward her mother's house in the back of Clement's Daimler. "I'm just not hungry, Clement. Give me a rain check?"

What Clement gave her was a case of the sulks, leaning back against the white leather and crossing his white-linened arms across his narrow chest. She considered giving in, then decided against it. Clement got his way far too often, and she'd be lousy company in her current state of mind.

She could always try to charm him out of his bad temper, but she didn't even have the energy for that. All she wanted to do was climb the narrow stairs up to her apartment, nuke herself a gourmet frozen dinner and tumble into bed.

"I don't know about that article, Clement," she said instead, deliberately changing the subject.

It was enough to distract him. "What don't you know, my precious? We've worked long and hard on it for the past three days, and it's absolutely splendid. The most wickedly ripe invective. You've outdone yourself."

His words just made her feel even more unsettled. "I don't know that ripe invective is my forte. Yours, perhaps."

"And yours, too, dear. You've really torn the action-movie industry apart this time, and it's been long overdue. If you're worried about your promise not to mention Rafe McGinnis, you can just leave it to me. Both our names are going to be on the series of articles. I'll just say I wrote the stuff about McGinnis."

"It's not that," she said, despite the fact that a small, edgy part of her felt a certain cowardly concern. "It just wasn't…fun anymore."

The moment the words were out she knew she'd made a major mistake. There were few things Clement Walden considered more enjoyable than slashing apart pretension and mediocrity wherever he discovered them. It was his devastating wit that had made him a household name for almost three decades.

For Silver, half the pleasure was in finding some rare jewel of a movie, or finding the gold amidst the dross, the small perfect part of a larger, weaker movie. Clement would tease her, telling her she was a disgusting optimist, but she really did find that she got more pleasure out of celebrating beauty than decrying ugliness.

And she'd wallowed in ugliness for the past three days. Ever since that disturbing evening with Rafe McGinnis, she'd followed Clement's lead, immersing herself in movies with a higher body count than the Gulf War. And every night she felt soiled, depressed and angry. And the only person she could direct that anger at was Rafe McGinnis.

As Clement had told her, he'd simply forgotten her existence. He'd had his revenge, humiliated her, forced his professional will on her and then dismissed her as he went on to pursue other things. Not that he would have pursued her, of course. That kiss in the back of his limousine was just a spur-of-the-moment impulse for him. It had nothing to do with his real taste in women, which doubtless ran to tiny blondes like Marcia Allison and away from dark-haired Valkyries like herself.

Not that she wanted him to be attracted to her. God forbid. That kiss had been disturbing enough. He knew how to get past a woman's defenses. If he could get her to kiss him back, even for a moment, then his powers were formidable indeed, and she didn't want to be exposed to them any more than necessary.

No, she was glad he'd forgotten about her, and she trusted Clement when he said McGinnis wouldn't even notice the latest series of articles.

She just wished she hadn't been quite that easy to dismiss. Silly pride on her part, of course. But alone in her apartment, late at night, there was no denying her feelings. Or at least some of them.

The Daimler slid silently up to the garage. Clement sat still, sulking, as the chauffeur opened the door before Silver could do it for herself. "You left your lights on," he said peevishly. "I thought you were so concerned about the environment."

Silver glanced up as she climbed out of the car. "Mother probably sent one of the maids down to do it. She worries about me when I'm out late."

"Your mother doesn't worry about anything but her new face-lift," Clement said waspishly.

Silver sighed. "I'm sorry, Clement," she said humbly. "Forgive me?"

He brightened an infinitesimal amount. "I suppose so. Though why I bother with you is beyond my comprehension."

"Because you love me?" she suggested.

"Hardly. Because you'll do all my dirty work and accept a pittance for a salary."

"There's that, too," Silver said, smiling. "See you tomorrow, darling."

Clement managed only an aggrieved harrumph as the chauffeur closed the door behind her. The garage was only half full when she let herself in. Her mother's limousine was out, as was her own disreputable rattletrap. Every now and then her mother tried to make it disappear, presenting something new and expensive in its place. Silver always managed to resist temptation, even when Marjorie had upped the ante to a Jaguar. She wondered what her mother would come up with this time.

There'd been a Lotus parked halfway up the driveway, but it had plates on it already. Besides, even her mother wouldn't go so far as to buy her a Lotus. Not her style at all. It had gotten to the point where she might have agreed to that other symbol of Hollywood trendy-ism, a four-wheel-drive Jeep. But her mother hadn't offered, and since Silver hadn't gotten away from the city in months, it didn't seem that dire a necessity. Maybe when Christmas drew closer she might drop a hint.

She climbed the stairs slowly, still thinking about Clement's temper tantrum and the nasty tone of the articles. Maybe she ought to have a tantrum of her own. Put a halt to the article, or at least demand a rewrite. It wasn't going in the paper for another week—she had more than enough time to tone it down, just a little.

She didn't even notice the music until she'd opened her unlocked door. Someone had turned on her CD player, and the undeniably sensuous sounds of Sam Cooke filled the apartment.

Silver didn't hesitate. Her mother had a habit of treating the apartment as her own, and she showed up at any time of the day or night, full of suggestions and advice, going through her cupboards and drawers, turning on her stereo. Though Sam Cooke was an odd choice for Marjorie.

"Mother?" Silver called, closing the door behind her.

The one light in the room had left most of it in shadows. Rafe McGinnis rose from her sofa, stretching to his full height as Silver stared in shock.

"Not exactly," he said in a wry tone of voice. "It's your worst nightmare."

And Silver, staring at him, could only agree.

Chapter Six

"What are you doing here?" Silver demanded.

"You should know better than to leave your doors unlocked," Rafe said easily. "You never know who might turn up."

Silver leaned back against the closed door, all trace of her earlier weariness gone. In its place was a kind of blazing excitement, fueled by anger, and something else she was afraid to analyze. "You must have had a pretty good reason to break into my home," she said evenly. "What is it?"

"I didn't break in. The door was unlocked, remember?" He had a drink in one hand, and he gestured toward it. "Can I get you one?"

"You can get the hell out of my apartment," she said flatly.

His smile was just a faint upturning of his mouth. "Not until we talk."

"I can call the police."

"Why should you do that?" he asked calmly, not at all distressed by her threat.

"Because I asked you to leave and you wouldn't. Think of the scandal."

"No, Silver. You think of the scandal," he said, his raspy voice only slightly threatening. "It'll backfire on you, just as your designer costume backfired on you. You really think it would do my reputation any harm? I'm a bad boy to begin with—it would only add to my legend. Whereas for you, it would be disaster.''

He was right, of course. There was no denying it. And her mother, with her passionate concern for her safe conservative life-style, would have hysterics. Besides, she didn't necessarily want him to leave. Not without telling her what he'd come for.

He certainly couldn't have come for her. She tried not to think about her disheveled appearance, but the moment it entered her mind there was no dislodging it. He was standing just a few feet away from her, and she was acutely aware of the difference between the two of them.

He was wearing jeans, too. Faded ones, that looked like they were tailored to his long legs. Not ratty ones like hers. He wore a T-shirt, a pale color that should have looked wimpy on him. It only made him sexier. And the rumpled linen jacket that hung on his frame looked like it was made to be wrinkled. Whenever she wore wrinkled clothing it looked like she'd slept in it.

Even his long hair was tied back, ridiculously neat after a long day, while hers tangled about her face in silky strands, making her look like an overgrown elf. She felt unkempt, childish and inept in front of him. And quite intensely bra-less.

''What do you want, McGinnis?'' she asked, suddenly tired again. She wanted to cross her arms in front of her chest, but she was afraid it would only draw his attention to that untrammeled part of her anatomy. ''State your business and leave.''

''There's no reason why we can't be civilized about this. Have a drink,'' he said again.

''McGinnis...'' Her voice carried a warning.

''Rafe,'' he supplied with a charming smile that she didn't trust for one moment. ''I know, it's your house. Why don't you offer me a refill?''

''I don't think you need one. I suppose your chauffeur told you where I live. I don't think the people I rent this place from will take kindly to your Lotus parked in their driveway. That is your Lotus, isn't it?''

"If your mother has any objections she can take them up with me," he said gently.

It was like a fist to her stomach. If he knew Marjorie was her mother, then it stood to reason he knew who her father was, too. Clement could never understand why she wanted that kept secret. It wasn't just an unwillingness to trade on her father's stellar reputation. It was the fact that he'd turned his back on her when she was most needy. She didn't want to accept his help when it was no longer up to him to grant or deny it.

She walked past him, into her kitchenette, and poured herself a meager glass from the bottle of scotch he'd found. She took a deep sip, forcing herself not to cough as it burned its way down her throat. There were tears in her eyes when she turned back to him, tears from the scotch and nothing else.

"All right," she said. "What do you want from me?"

She didn't believe that small, sexual smile, or the way his eyes slid gently down her body. It was an automatic instinct on his part, his stock in trade, and she wasn't going to succumb to it, even as she felt her nipples harden in reaction, even as she felt the fiery warmth in her stomach that wasn't the scotch.

"I want you to come to dinner with me."

"Forget it."

"Trust me, I'm absolutely harmless," he said, and she wondered whether the man had any acting experience. She could almost believe him, which was surely insanity on her part.

"I don't want to go to dinner with you, I don't want to talk to you, I don't want to have anything to do with you," she said fiercely.

"Why not?"

It was a simple question, impossible to answer. Not without admitting how irrationally vulnerable she was to him. Instead she settled for the obvious. "I don't trust you."

If she'd hoped to wound him she failed. He simply looked amused. "No one trusts anyone in Hollywood," he said. "It's part of our job description."

"Go away."

"I didn't get where I am today by taking no for an answer. I can be very tenacious."

"And I can be very stubborn," she shot back. "Tell me what you want and then leave."

"I have something for you," he said.

"I don't want anything from you," she parried. "Besides, I don't believe you. I've been around long enough to know the truth. You want something from me. What is it?"

He sat on her overstuffed wicker sofa again, stretching his long legs out in front of him and propping his booted feet on the scarred and battered coffee table. He looked completely incongruous surrounded by her makeshift belongings. Even the lumpy, comfortable old sofa, covered with an ancient Indian-print bedspread, looked absurdly tacky beneath his casually upscale frame. It didn't matter that he was making himself at home. He made the home surrounding him seem suddenly shabby.

"I want your father's papers."

It was the last thing she expected. Or was it? "Why?" she said bluntly, wandering around the room, nervously straightening a stack of old newspapers that she hadn't bothered to throw out in weeks. "I've had them for seventeen years, and no one's ever shown any interest in them before."

"I'm thinking of producing a version of something he was working on when he died."

"Black Canyon," she said flatly, not liking the sick feeling in the pit of her stomach. Another woman might jump to the flattering conclusion that he'd heard of her own work on the Western. Another woman might assume her big break was just around the corner. Not Silver.

"Exactly. I gather you've done some work on it yourself. Of course we'd be interested in seeing it, but I should warn you from the outset that I expect we'll be using a screenwriter with a track record. One who'd be more likely to share our vision."

"Your male vision," Silver said.

Rafe shrugged, obviously not the slightest bit uncomfortable with his outrageous demand. "I'm a man," he said. "What can I say?"

"You can say goodbye, Mr. McGinnis."

He didn't even flinch. "You're forgetting something, Silver," he said in that dangerously sexy voice of his. "Your father was working for Pegasus Pictures when he died. He was under contract. Therefore, any works in progress technically belong to Pegasus. And since I'm now a major force in Pegasus Pictures, they belong to me."

"Over my dead body."

"Be reasonable about this. You can't possibly hope to win. I've sent word to the various studios that have your screenplay, informing them there's a question of copyright infringement. You know how touchy studios can be. I expect your manuscripts will be back in a matter of days, if not hours. If you want it to be considered, send it over to my office."

"I'd burn it first."

"That might be for the best."

"Is this part of your grand scheme for revenge?" she asked, holding herself very still. "I dared insult the great Rafe McGinnis and in return I get destroyed?"

"Don't be ridiculous. I could care less about your little snipings in the paper. I admit I was irritated, but that's a minor issue compared to *Black Canyon*. I want it, and I intend to have it."

"You arrogant, ruthless bastard," she said, her voice trembling with fury. "I'll see you in hell first."

He rose then, unmoved by her fury, crossing the room to stand in front of her. "Anyone with power in this town is an arrogant, ruthless bastard," he said in a damnably calm tone. "Why does *Black Canyon* matter so much to you? If it's financial, that's easily remedied. I'm sure our lawyers could come up with something mutually agreeable."

"Money hasn't got a damned thing to do with it," she said fiercely.

"Well, it can't be out of memory for your father. The man was a genius, but he couldn't have been the finest parent. According to Bernie, he gave you up quite readily when your mother ditched him. Surely you can't think you owe him anything more than a way to make a living.''

It shouldn't have been so devastating. It was nothing more than she'd said to herself a thousand times. Coming from his cool, cynical mouth, though, it was shockingly painful.

''It has nothing to do with my father. It's mine. I put my heart and soul into that screenplay, and it belongs to me. You can't have it. I won't let Mack Movies turn it into some stupid sex-and-violence extravaganza where the women exist only to be murdered so the hero can be tormented. I won't let you have it!''

He simply watched her for a long, unfathomable moment. ''You won't have any say in the matter,'' he said finally. ''I always get what I want.''

''Not this time.''

And then suddenly she was aware of what was going on beneath the anger. She was dangerously close to the man. Her shabby apartment was dimly lighted, shadowed, and he was watching her out of hooded, unreadable eyes, eyes that saw far too much.

''Most particularly,'' he said, ''this time.'' And with seemingly effortless expertise, he put his hand behind her neck, beneath her close-cropped hair, and pulled her against him.

She tumbled, off balance, falling against him, too startled to react. And then it was too late, much too late, for he was kissing her again, his mouth hungry against hers, as his arm went around her back and held her body tight against him.

The small part of her mind that was working expected another all-out assault. That she could have combated. But this time it was different. There was no hurry, no particular demand in his kiss this time. No sensual tussle in the back seat of a limousine. He kissed her slowly, deliberately, as if he had all the time in the world to savor her mouth, to taste the trembling softness of her lips. She could taste the scotch on his tongue, and she wanted more.

And then he lifted his head, looking down at her in the

shadowy room. "I told myself I wasn't going to do that again," he said. "You have the most destructive effect on my will-power." He kissed her again, a brief, hard kiss. "But then, I seem to have the same effect on you."

"You have no effect on me whatsoever," Silver said in a tight little voice, rigid in his arms.

"Oh, yeah?" he said lazily. "Then why are your nipples hard?"

She shoved him away then, and he let her go, watching her as she scrambled back across the room. She wanted to wipe the taste of him off her mouth, but she decided that would be going too far. "I know you think every woman in Hollywood is ready to fall at your feet, McGinnis," she said in an admirably cool voice. "But I'm not one of them. I don't deny that you know how to kiss. You've probably had a great deal of practice at it. But I don't need to sleep with you to benefit my career."

His eyes narrowed, and his smile was thin. "That, of course, being the only reason for my heralded success between the sheets?"

"Oh, I expect any number of women actually find you attractive," she said. "With your masculine swagger and your arrogant cowboy manner, you might be very appealing to some people. Not to me."

He rose then, crossing the room toward her, stalking her like a predator, and Silver knew a direct streak of panic sliding down her ramrod-straight backbone. It took every ounce of courage not to take a step backward, away from him.

"You sound like Clement Walden," he said softly. "I think you've been spending too much time with him. Not that you have to worry about sleeping with him to get to the top. As long as he can control your sex life he doesn't actually need to participate. As to whether you find me attractive or not," he added, cupping her chin in one hard hand, "you'll find that life is a lot easier if you don't lie to yourself. Lie to everyone else—your boss, your mother, your tax accountant, your lover. But don't lie to yourself. You want me, Silver, and that's what scares you. You want me as much as I want you. And it doesn't make any sense to either of us. It's too soon, too illogical. But it exists, no matter how much you try to deny it.''

She opened her mouth to protest, but he stopped the words, kissing her. She told herself it didn't mean anything, didn't move her at all, as she melted against him, her breasts flattening against the hardness of his chest, her hips reaching up toward his, her mouth slanting beneath his. Even the hungry little moan must have been a moan of irritation, as his hands slid up under her loose cotton T-shirt and touched her breasts, and then she wanted it, wanted him, with a mindless ferocity that frightened her, and she knew she was going to do anything he wanted, do it there, do it then, and sanity and self-preservation had vanished with the touch of his hands and the taste of his mouth. Her hands were shaking, she could barely stand, and all she wanted to do was sink into him, lose herself with the man who was the greatest danger she'd ever faced in her life.

She heard the pounding of her heart. The pounding of his heart, against her. And the pounding on her door.

''Maybe you'd better let him in,'' Rafe whispered in her ear, nibbling on her lobe.

She stared up at him in hazy confusion. ''Who?''

''I expect it's Clement Walden,'' Rafe said with a half smile. ''Come to make sure I'm not debauching the virgin princess of Hollywood.''

She disentangled herself from his arms, his body, and the only thing that came to her mind was, ''There are no virgins in Hollywood.''

''You come damn close, honey,'' he replied. And she wondered what he'd do if she slapped him.

She didn't need to go to the door. By the time Clement remembered that she never locked it and let himself in, she was already halfway across the room from Rafe, her flaming face in the shadows.

''What's going on here?'' Clement demanded, stepping into her apartment with his usual fastidious shudder. ''Are you all right, Silver?''

"Why shouldn't she be?" Rafe drawled. "What brings you out here at such a late hour, Clement? Isn't it a little past the time for social visits?"

"I could say the same thing to you," Clement said in a bored voice. "I was halfway back to my house before I realized why that Lotus looked so familiar. For a moment I thought…well, that doesn't matter. I knew Silver was much too tired to have to deal with any unwelcome guests, so I'm here to make sure you get on your way."

"What makes you think I'm unwanted?" Rafe murmured.

"I know Silver. She's a lady, and you're a hooligan. A low-class upstart with more testosterone than brains, and she's never been fool enough to fall for your sort. If Silver wanted company she would have accepted my dinner invitation. As it is, I'm sure she'll be very happy if you'd leave."

"Clement," Silver said wearily, finally finding her voice. "I can handle this."

"You haven't been doing a very good job of it," Clement observed. "Haven't I warned you about men like McGinnis?"

"Oh, we have you to blame for it," Rafe murmured. "I should have known. Maybe your little protégée was in the mood for a hooligan. Maybe she was interested in a walk on the wild side…"

"Don't be disgusting," Clement said. "You don't know who you're dealing with. I'd like you to leave. Now."

Silver had been trying to make Rafe leave for half an hour. It made no sense that she resented Clement asking the same thing.

"We were discussing business, Clement," she said pointedly.

"Were you, indeed? Is that why your face is whisker-burned? Really, Rafe, if you're going to make out with a woman you ought to consider shaving before you show up at her apartment."

"Go away, Clement," Silver said. "And go away, Rafe. I don't have anything to say to either of you."

"But Silver," Clement began in his well-bred whine.

But Rafe had finally accepted his dismissal. He put one strong hand under Clement's arm and pulled him toward the door. "We've had our marching orders." He glanced back at Silver, standing motionless in the middle of the room. "We'll finish this later."

"There's nothing to finish. Nothing to discuss. You can't have it."

"Can't have what?" Clement said in a fretful voice. "What in heaven's name is going on here? I demand to know…"

Rafe silenced Clement by the simple expedient of shoving him out the door and locking it behind him, leaning against it to prevent Clement from reentering.

"It's not a bad question, Silver," he said, his voice a seductive murmur in the dim room. "Can't have what? The rights to *Black Canyon?* Or you?"

A cynical smile curved her mouth. "You can't have the only thing that really interests you. The rights to *Black Canyon* are mine, and you'll never get them."

For a moment he didn't move, oblivious to the sounds of Clement's pounding behind his back. "I play hardball, Silver. I always win. I fight dirty, and I'll use everything I can to get what I want. Give it up, before you get crushed."

"I'm tougher than you think."

"Maybe," he said in a meditative voice. "You're going to have to be. Don't say I didn't warn you." He moved away from the door, opening it and letting Clement stumble back in, the little man quivering in rage.

"We're out of here, Walden," he said calmly, dragging the fuming Clement with him. "I've given Silver an offer she can't refuse. She needs some time to think about it."

The door slammed behind them. Silver watched them go, then realized she was holding her breath. She let it go in a whoosh, them moved over to the windows overlooking the drive, peering through the thin-slatted blinds.

Clement's Daimler was already out the driveway. Nothing and no one but an immovable force like Rafe McGinnis could have kept Clement from hassling her further, and she knew a sudden feeling of desperation. If Clement couldn't hold out against his inexorable will, how could she?

Because it mattered too much. She wasn't going to give him *Black Canyon* and let him turn it into a piece of garbage. It was too important to her, to her heart and soul. She wasn't going to let him destroy it.

She was in for a battle, she knew that. If she was very, very lucky, that battle would be legal. Rafe McGinnis would keep away from her, letting his formidable lawyers do all the dirty work. And dirty work it would be, she had no doubts about that whatsoever. Rafe was right, he hadn't gotten where he was by being gentlemanly, decent, merciful.

But she had one thing on her side that was entirely lacking on his. A simple matter of right. And a dream. And for that right, for that dream, she was willing to fight for as long and as hard as she could. If in the end she lost, so be it. She'd make the victory taste like ashes in Rafe McGinnis's mouth.

His mouth. Damn, why had she kissed him back? For that matter, why did he kiss her? Simply because he knew how much it upset her? Even he couldn't be that ruthless, could he?

He was climbing into his Lotus, folding his long, lanky body into the tiny cockpit. At the last minute he looked up to her darkened window. He couldn't see her, she knew that, and yet his eyes looked directly into hers.

He smiled then, and it was different. Not the mocking sexual conquest. Not the cynical Hollywood grin. It was a small, rueful upturning of his mouth. As if, impossible as it seemed, he'd been caught in his own trap.

And then he slammed the door, speeding out of her mother's deserted driveway with a reckless disregard for anybody else's safety.

She watched him go. And for one mad, wild moment she wished to God that Clement had never shown up, never interrupted what had been about to happen.

Not that it would have made any difference to Rafe. It wouldn't have changed his plans for *Black Canyon,* and it wouldn't have changed her determination to stop him. But even as her mind rebelled, her body longed for him with a reckless disregard for her well-being.

Enmity was her safest choice as far as Rafe McGinnis was concerned. She had to remember that. From now on it would be war—simple, straightforward and openly declared. The lawyers would do battle, and the two of them need never confront each other again.

If only she could believe it was going to be that easy.

Chapter Seven

Rafe didn't bother to turn on the lights when he let himself into his house. Instead he walked straight through the darkened rooms, moving with unerring instinct, stripping off his clothes as he went, dropping the little package he'd never had a chance to deliver to her on the coffee table. When he reached the terrace he was nude, and he dived into the tile-lined swimming pool with one clean leap, slicing beneath the warm water without a splash.

He swam hard, lap after lap, moving through the pool at a mind-blanking pace. He didn't want to think about her, didn't want to think about what he was doing. He wanted only the water, the night sky overhead, his blood pumping, his breathing deep and measured, his body tingling with energy. And then he wanted to sleep.

But even the butterfly stroke at eleven at night couldn't keep his quicksilver mind at a comforting black. Finally he stopped at the deep end of the pool, treading water while he measured his pulse rate, and once again Silver Carlysle was back.

He leaned his shoulders against the blue tile, looking around him. The moon overhead was bright, shimmering down on his unlighted house, and in the darkness he could see the ridiculous Moorish roofline of his pretentious house. He never did understand why he hadn't picked something a little more rustic, a little more real. Some glass-and-wood cabin, with clean lines and textures instead of a romantic anomaly like this. On top of everything else, the house was in terrible shape, the tiles falling off, the roof leaking, the plumbing ridiculous, and it was too damned small. He told himself he lived there for some sort of cosmic joke, but the truth of the matter was, he loved it. And of all the people who knew his house, and were mystified by it, only Bernie understood.

He should have invited Silver Carlysle up here. Not that she would have come willingly, of course, but that was a minor issue. Once she saw this absurd place she'd be even more confused by her worst enemy. And he liked keeping her confused.

He pushed off against the tiled pool, floating on his back into the middle of the water. He knew what he was going to do. He didn't like it. Didn't much like himself for doing it. But once he'd realized the weapon he had, he knew he had to use it. Or face his own unacceptable reasons why he might be inclined to show mercy.

If you started accepting other people as vulnerable, then you started making adjustments. He'd meant it when he told Silver that anyone with power in Hollywood was ruthless and arrogant. If he showed mercy, it stood to reason he'd lose some of that power, and that was the one thing that was completely unacceptable.

He knew what he had to do. The longer he floated around in his pool, staring up at the stars, the longer it would take to put his next step into motion. He'd never been a man to hesitate. There was no reason to hesitate now.

He glanced back at the pool as he headed into the house. He was about to deliver the cruelest blow he could think of to the far too vulnerable Silver Carlysle, simply for the sake of getting what he wanted. It was ridiculously optimistic to think of her in that pool, naked, the moonlight silvering the water on her body.

But then, he hadn't gotten where he was today by accepting any limitations. Just because he was doing his best to shatter her didn't mean he still didn't want her in bed. And anger could be a powerful aphrodisiac.

He didn't want to listen to that little voice in his head that told him to leave her alone. Maybe they'd both be better off if he did. There was no way he was ever going to find out. He'd set this play in motion, and he had every intention of seeing it through to the end. He was determined to get the rights to *Black Canyon,* and he was just as determined to get Silver Carlysle. The only difference was, he intended to keep *Black Canyon.*

He flicked on the light, stepping over the debris the carpenters had left that morning, heading toward the state-of-the-art phone system in his office. It took him exactly two minutes to get what he wanted. When he hung up the phone he stood there, looking at nothing, including the sterile confines of the only finished room in the old house. And then he went in and poured himself a very stiff drink.

"YOU AREN'T GOING to like this, Silver."

Silver looked up from her computer screen. She was sitting in the little office space Clement had forced the *Clarion* to provide for her, trying to concentrate on her work, when Clement had loomed up behind her. If anyone who barely topped five foot four could be said to loom.

She turned with a sigh, deliberately darkening the screen from his prying eyes. "I imagine not," she said. "What's up?"

"I've been reading this week's edition of the *Nosy Parker.*"

Silver could feel the first tendrils of uneasiness churn in her stomach. "I'm surprised at you, Clement. The *Nosy Parker* is the sleaziest of all the sleazy supermarket tabloids. I didn't realize you had a subscription."

"It isn't a joking matter, Silver. Someone saw fit to send me an advance copy. There's no way I can soften the blow for you, my dear."

She forced herself to smile brightly. "It can't be that bad, Clement. So they've run a picture of me at Rafe McGinnis's party. I warned you I looked atrocious. And I imagine they've come up with all sorts of salacious details. If the world wants to think I'm sleeping with the man, it's hardly my concern."

"The article isn't about you and McGinnis, or at least, only marginally. It's about your family background." He dropped the brightly colored tabloid onto her desk, and she stared at it numbly, for a moment the screaming headlines not making any sense.

"Did you ever play that game, Clement?" she asked absently, staring at the paper. "The one where you make up the most absurd tabloid headlines you can think of? I won once, when I came up with 'Man Rips Out Own Heart, Stomps On It.' I never thought I'd be the subject of one." She turned away from it. "I don't think I have the stomach to read it."

"It's not bad as these things go. They haven't come up with some bizarre sex angle."

"How about my latest diet?" she asked with a lame attempt at humor.

Clement surveyed her with a critical eye. "I don't think anyone would be interested, my dear. They mainly take the tack of the impoverished daughter of a screen legend, forced to live over her mother's garage and eke out an existence as a second-string reporter."

"It could be worse, I suppose," she said glumly. "Mother's going to have a fit."

"You've stood up to her fits before. If she gives you any trouble I'll talk to her. In the meantime, we have more important considerations."

"Such as?"

"Such as the fact that the pictures of you and McGinnis leave no doubt at all that you're having the affair of the week. Such as the fact that everyone in Hollywood now knows who your father was, knows you have access to his work, knows you're trying to sell something connected with him."

"He put that in too, did he?" she said in a bitter undertone.

"The article was written by a woman."

"It was instigated by a man."

"You don't think McGinnis had anything to do with it? The man's a swine, but he wouldn't sink this low. How would the article benefit him?"

"There are no limits to how low he'd sink," Silver said. "He warned me two nights ago that he uses dirty tricks. He's merely running true to form. He wants to see me crushed and humiliated. I don't know if it's just an oversize ego demanding revenge, or whether he really wants *Black Canyon*. And I don't care.''

''Revenge I can understand,'' Clement mused. ''After all, I'm an expert at it. But we're not going to let him get away with this. I can talk to my lawyers…''

''What can I do about it?'' Silver interrupted his fuming. ''It's not libelous, is it?''

''I consider any article that says you're sleeping with a pig like Rafe McGinnis to be libel. Look at this.'' He leaned past Silver and flipped open the newspaper to the center. ''You look like a besotted tramp.''

She leaned forward reluctantly, staring at the picture. She certainly didn't look like Silver Carlysle. The fluffy pink dress rode low on her chest, her ridiculous hair looked bed-mussed, and her eyes as she stared up at Rafe McGinnis were definitely filled with emotion. Hatred, she told herself. But that wasn't what the photograph had picked up.

There was an old photo of her parents beside it, her father tall and elegant, her mother petite and beautiful, with a tiny squalling mass of humanity in her arms as she strove to look maternal. Silver had never seen that particular photo before, never seen her father looking down at the baby with a sort of surprised affection.

A lie. He'd never had time for her—he'd simply taken advantage of the publicity offered and managed to look like a doting father. It was all a damned lie.

''Don't!'' Clement protested, but he was too late, as she crumpled the paper, ripping it with cold, shaking fingers. ''It's not going to hit the newsstands for another couple of days, and we need to prepare our defense against the gossip.''

''There is no defense against gossip,'' Silver said in a numb voice. ''Nothing outside of murder.''

The telephone beside her computer buzzed, and she jumped, unaccountably nervous. ''Don't answer it,'' Clement ordered.

"Why not? I thought you said it wouldn't be out for another couple of days."

"That doesn't mean everyone hasn't already heard about it. You're not ready to deal with it. Let me take you out to lunch and we'll plan our strategy."

She reached for the telephone. "My strategy, Clement. You don't need to be tarnished by this mess."

"Silver…"

But she'd already picked up the receiver. She knew who was going to be on the other end—there'd never been the slightest doubt. "Silver Carlysle," she said, her voice husky with suppressed rage.

"I warned you."

"So you did." For some reason she didn't want the avidly eavesdropping Clement to know she was speaking to the enemy himself. "I shouldn't have doubted you."

"Who is it?" Clement demanded.

Silver put her hand over the mouthpiece. "Just an old friend. I'll come see you in a minute."

She waited, pointedly, as Clement made no move to leave her. She could be infinitely patient. She didn't mind how long Rafe McGinnis had to wait on the other end of the line, she didn't mind how long Clement stood there, frustrated. She simply waited.

"Don't be long," Clement said finally, turning on his heel and walking away.

She waited until he disappeared into his office before removing her hand. "What did you want?"

"It's nice to know I'm your old friend. I never realized you cared. I imagine that was your mentor?"

"What do you want, Rafe?" she asked again. "Haven't you done enough?"

"Are you ready to relinquish the rights to *Black Canyon?*" He sounded no more than lazily interested. She could picture him on the other end of the line, leaning back in some impossibly expensive leather chair, one custom-made to fit his body, his long legs propped up on his desk, his big hand holding the telephone, his mouth close to the receiver, his mouth...

She had to be insane to be distracted by erotic thoughts.

"Are you still there?" he drawled.

"I'm still here. Why should I give up the rights to *Black Canyon?* You've already taken your best shot, and I'm still here. Still telling you to go straight to hell."

"You think that was my best shot, Silver? You underestimate me. I can get a lot nastier if I set my mind to it. You can still walk away now, bloody but unbowed. Don't make me get really mean."

"I've got a hell of an imagination, McGinnis, and I can't fathom how you can get meaner."

"Seen your mother's necklace recently?"

She felt like she'd been blindsided. Her hand went to her neck, to the loose-knit collar of her T-shirt, as horror swept through her.

She'd never missed it. She'd clasped the ugly, outrageously expensive thing around her neck before leaving for the party, and she'd never thought about it again.

It took everything she had to keep from hyperventilating. She held her breath, long enough to quiet the first panic, and her voice was admirably cool. "I didn't know you were a thief, McGinnis."

"I'm every bad thing you can think of. It took me a moment to remember who'd worn such an outrageously ugly piece of jewelry. I almost tossed it, thinking it couldn't be real, until I found out who your parents were. And sure enough, those are real diamonds and emeralds and rubies. Does your mother know you borrowed it?"

"What makes you think it's my mother's?"

"Not your style, sweetie. Not hers, either, but her husband never had much taste. You want it back?"

"I can call the police, McGinnis."

"You wouldn't want to do that," he said. "For one thing, you'd have to prove ownership. For another, I wouldn't put up a fight, once it caused enough publicity. I just sort of thought you'd had enough of seeing your name in the paper for the time being.''

''I'm not giving you the rights to *Black Canyon* for a stolen piece of jewelry.''

''Did your mother steal it? I hadn't thought she was that kind of woman. She always seemed so staunchly Republican to me.''

''You stole it. And you're not blackmailing me into giving you the rights.''

''No,'' he agreed. ''I'm not. I'm blackmailing you into coming out to my house and picking it up.''

He wouldn't have made the mistake of thinking she'd be relieved by his suggestion. ''Why?''

''So we can discuss this. You know how these things work, Silver, even if you haven't spent much time with power brokers. I make an offer, you make a counteroffer, I sweeten the deal, you hold out for more. In the end we both get what we want. Satisfaction guaranteed.''

He was talking about *Black Canyon*. There was no reason to think he was talking about sex, except for the fact that she was momentarily obsessed with it. ''Bring it to the office and we'll talk,'' she said.

''Nope. For one thing, we'd have Clement breathing down our necks, and he's not one of my favorite people. For another, we're going to do this my way. I'm the one holding all the cards. I was ready to give it to you the other night, but you managed to distract me. Now we'll do it on my terms.''

''My apartment,'' she suggested, regretting it. Her apartment wasn't demonstrably safer than his place.

''My house, Silver. Four thousand Hemdale Drive. I'll send my car for you.''

''No.''

''No? I can always call your mother and explain the situation,'' he said gently.

''I'll drive my own car. I can be there in about twenty minutes.''

"Sorry. Some of us have to work for a living," he said, and Silver gritted her teeth. "Tonight. Nine o'clock. For dinner."

"I'd rather eat nails."

"I don't think my cook knows how to prepare those."

"I'm not coming, McGinnis."

"Then you're not getting your mother's necklace. Come on, Silver, it won't hurt you to talk. It won't hurt you to consider other alternatives to our little impasse. Nine o'clock. I'll be waiting."

He hung up before she could protest again. Not that it would have done her any good. She simply would have told him she wasn't coming. And he simply would have ignored her.

She had no choice. Marjorie loved her, in her own self-absorbed way. And Marjorie hated that ugly, expensive necklace that was doubtless covered by a very effective insurance policy.

None of that mattered. If she discovered her slightly scatter-brained daughter had helped herself to a piece of gaudy jewelry worth well into the six figures, she'd go berserk. And Silver would be paying for it, emotionally, for the next decade.

She was going to go. She wasn't some talentless actress on the make, willing to use the casting couch to get what she wanted. She was a mature adult, one who found Rafe McGinnis inexplicably attractive. That didn't mean he was similarly afflicted, even if he did have an unfortunate tendency to kiss her every time they were alone. She didn't have to succumb. This time she'd be prepared. She'd use every weapon she possessed to keep him at a distance. Because once he came close enough, her brain melted, her resolve vanished, and she'd probably give him just about anything he asked for.

"Who was that?" Clement had waited only moments before hustling back to her desk.

"No one that matters," she said. The last thing she needed was Clement interfering. She was going to have a hard enough time keeping Rafe McGinnis at bay. Clement would only complicate matters.

"What are we going to do about McGinnis?" Clement said.

Another man would have leaned against her desk, lounged in the doorway. Clement stood still, his small, spare figure upright and alert with malice.

"I don't think there's anything we can do. At least for now, all we can do is wait and see."

Clement didn't look pleased with the notion. "What's between the two of you? Is this just more revenge for your articles? I can spread the word around among the journalism community, and that man will wish he'd never interfered...."

"It doesn't have anything to do with my work. Not anymore. He wants *Black Canyon*."

Clement blinked. "How extraordinary. Not that he shouldn't, of course. It's a very nice little piece of work for a first effort, given that you started with a Western, for heaven's sake." He made it sound as if she'd worked on a comic book. "I'm simply surprised that McGinnis is that enthralled with it. It's not as if anyone has shown a great deal of interest so far. But then, where's the problem? If McGinnis wants it, you should be celebrating."

"Clement," she said wearily, "you're missing a couple of points. For one thing, we're talking about Mack Movies here. What do you think they'd do to *Black Canyon* if they got their hands on it?"

Clement nodded sagely. "A good point. Not that you'd have any guarantees anywhere else. The movie industry nowadays writes in committees, and you know what committees are like. Not much of your original vision is likely to remain in any case."

"It doesn't have anything to do with it," Silver said. "Because he doesn't want my screenplay. He hasn't even seen it. He simply wants the rights to the novel, and my father's preproduction work on it."

"How much is he offering?"

"Clement!" Silver was horrified. "Do you think I'd sell my birthright?"

"There's not much room for sentiment in Hollywood nowadays," he pointed out.

"What about honor and decency? What about matters of principle?" she said fiercely.

"Not much room for them either, darling. You're going to fight him on this?"

"What do you think precipitated the article? I'm not going to let him have it. I'll burn my father's papers before I let him have it."

"You can't stop him from getting the rights if he's determined."

"He thinks he already owns them. Father was under contract to Pegasus Pictures when he started developing *Black Canyon*. Therefore Rafe thinks it still belongs to them."

"I wonder who brought this to his attention," Clement mused. "It's not the sort of thing he'd be likely to run across unless he had a little help."

"Does that matter?"

"It might. You're right, Silver. For the time being we won't do a thing. Who knows, one of the other studios might come up with an offer if they know Mack Movies is interested. In the meantime, let me see what my contacts can come up with. We might be able to turn this thing around. I would love, simply love, to be able to put one in the eye of Rafe McGinnis."

Silver stared at the dapper little man who'd been more of a father to her than anyone in her life. She wished she could simply dump the whole problem into his hands and forget it.

But there was the problem of the necklace. And the problem of her pride. She didn't want to be rescued, much as a small, weak part of her was tempted by the notion. She didn't want Clement and Rafe making deals while she sat meekly on the sidelines.

As a matter of fact, if someone was going to do battle with Rafe McGinnis, she wanted that someone to be her.

That night, at nine o'clock, she was going into battle, fully prepared for full-scale war. She needed to be ruthless, determined and completely merciless. Rafe McGinnis was the kind of man who would take no prisoners.

She needed to be just as cold-blooded. Particularly when it came to a man like Rafe. Because the fact of the matter was, he made her blood run hot. Feverishly so.

And she had the unpleasant conviction that he knew it.

Chapter Eight

There was absolutely nothing to worry about, Silver told herself. He had a cook, he probably had a raft of servants besides, he probably lived in a house similar to her mother's. He wasn't going to go chasing her over manicured lawns. It would all be well lighted, supervised, civilized. He'd probably flirt, but then, he did that as naturally as he breathed. She didn't have to show her undeniable response.

She dressed carefully, unearthing one of the simple black dresses her mother regularly bestowed upon her. This one was demure enough, even if it showed too much black-stockinged leg, and she even searched through the tackle box that held her seldom-used jewelry and found a pair of diamond studs that had been a gift from her stepfather on her sixteenth birthday. She'd never worn them, but tonight they were just the right touch. They gave her an illusion of sophistication, of being in charge. Maybe she could trade the diamonds for the tacky necklace.

Having lived in Hollywood most of her life, she was vaguely familiar with the hilly area of Hemdale Drive. She couldn't remember any spacious estate—the houses up there tended to be smaller, more idiosyncratic, but then, with the kind of money Rafe McGinnis had made during his meteoric career, he'd no doubt bulldozed half a neighborhood and put up an ostentatious mansion.

She ought to go all out, take her mother's Rolls and chauffeur and arrive there in style. It would be one more person to turn to, if things got a little sticky.

Problem was, she didn't know if she wanted someone there to rescue her. Rafe certainly wasn't going to force her to do anything she didn't want to. There was no denying he came on to her every chance he got. Each time she'd been alone with him he'd kissed her, and it hadn't been the casual Hollywood clinking of cheekbones.

But she still couldn't really believe he wanted her. It was instinct on his part, second nature. What was that song about if you can't have someone you want, want someone you have?

If she wasn't so ridiculously vulnerable, she could steer him away from such dangerous ground. The problem was, every time he touched her, every time he looked at her, she reacted with an inexplicable longing.

Logically it made no sense. She despised everything Rafe McGinnis stood for. The violent, stupid, obscenely profitable movies, the fast-lane, indiscriminate life-style, the arrogant sexuality.

But there was something about him. Something beneath the arrogance, beneath the cool, dare-you attitude that drew her. A streak of dangerous charm, a touch of vulnerability in his green eyes. Not to mention that he was undoubtably the sexiest man she'd seen in her entire life.

But she'd spent a lifetime, twenty-nine years in fact, not succumbing to sexy men. She'd learned early on that men weren't to be trusted. Hollywood taught you that lesson early, and in the ensuing years she hadn't had any reason to change her mind. During the past few years, when she'd begun to make her way, to grow up, she'd thought of reaching out. There'd been men, kind men, gentle men, and she'd considered falling in love.

But Clement was there, protecting her best interests. If it wasn't for Clement, she'd probably be living in a bungalow in Encino, facing a life married to a very nice man who absolutely bored her to tears.

Still, she might have been happy with Tom in that bungalow.

Even if the few times they'd gone to bed together hadn't been world-shaking, she couldn't really blame him. After all, she'd been an elderly virgin, uneasy with sexuality, and he'd been patient.

Clement had hated to tell her the truth about Tom, about his ex-wife and his sleaziness with child support. Just as it had pained Clement to tell her about Dennis's managing to court her as he was trying to climb her stepfather's corporate ladder. At least in the case of Dennis it hadn't gotten as far as the bedroom.

With Rafe she knew exactly what he wanted from her. Not the perfect housewife with no demands. Not a fast track up the corporate ladder. He wanted her birthright, pure and simple. He'd do anything, honorable or not, to get it. And she'd do anything she could to stop him.

The honesty was part of what she found so refreshing in Rafe. The knowledge that the cards were on the table, along with the stakes. Winner take all. And he was so damned certain he was going to win.

She had every intention of showing him otherwise. The article in the *Nosy Parker* hadn't even hit the stands yet, but word had spread. The gossip about the McGinnis-Carlysle feud had died down just as quickly as Clement had predicted, but this would add new fuel to the fire.

She supposed there was a chance her mother wouldn't find out about it, but she doubted it. Once Marjorie's youthful face adorned the tabloids, all hell would break loose. And it would take all of Silver's emotional reserves to hold out against her.

She surveyed her appearance in the front mirror in her apartment. If there was one thing her two rooms had, it was mirrors. Marjorie was very select in her placement of mirrors, not liking to be presented with her reflection in less than flattering conditions, and she'd sent half of her collection down to Silver. Silver didn't mind being presented with her reflection every time she turned around. For one thing, she considered herself singularly lacking in vanity, for another, the mirrors lightened the area, giving it an illusion of spaciousness.

She put a hand to her close-cropped hair, ruffling it slightly. She didn't look like Silver Carlysle. For that matter, she looked more like her British father's daughter. Tall, long-legged, broad-shouldered, with her simple black dress and her sparkling diamonds, she looked like old Hollywood money. If someone was perceptive they might see the shadow of uneasiness in her wide blue eyes, the faint edginess playing around her mouth. But Rafe was hardly a perceptive, sensitive person. With any luck, he'd believe the package she presented. If anything could intimidate an upstart like Rafe McGinnis, this persona in the mirror could.

However, she had no hope at all that anyone on this earth could intimidate McGinnis. The best she could hope for was to hold her own. It was already nine, and it would probably take her a good fifteen minutes to find his house up in the hills. She'd end up making a conspicuous entrance, which would bring its own set of problems.

She climbed into her aging Toyota and pulled out into the quiet streets. Of course there was no guarantee that Rafe would have invited anyone else, but half of his strategy seemed to involve public humiliation. She could hardly be backed into a corner with curious witnesses. She'd meant it when she told him he'd done his worst. She had no other secrets to hide. No shameful affair, no sleazy business dealings, no dysfunctional family apart from the one he'd already exposed. With Silver Carlysle, what you saw was what you got. Sort of like Popeye. I yam what I yam and that's all what I yam. And if Rafe McGinnis expected something more he was going to be disappointed.

McGinnis himself was another matter, she thought some twenty minutes later as she sat in her car outside four thousand Hemdale Drive, staring at the Moorish turrets of the house that had to be his. His choice of residence made no sense whatsoever, but the Lotus parked out front, the only car in sight, proved that it was indeed.

She was certain she'd find something made of glass and wood, something starkly modern and huge. Instead the kitschy outlines of the Moorish-style cottage were small and muted against the moonlit sky. The gardens were a tangle of overgrowth, and there was construction debris littering the tiled walkway as she made her way toward the front door, moving carefully on the tallest heels she'd possessed.

The door was open. She called his name, quietly at first, afraid of what she'd find inside.

"McGinnis?" she called in a husky voice. Absolute silence. "McGinnis?" She stepped inside, stumbling slightly on a broken tile. The place had a myriad of smells: fresh lumber, the faint trace of chlorine from a swimming pool, the aroma of grilled chicken. He had to be there, lying in wait. She closed the door behind her, wondering if he was going to jump out at her and scare her.

"Rafe," she said, a little louder this time.

"That's better." His voice carried from the dimly lighted interior. "I'm in here."

She followed the sound of his voice into the darkened living room. She could see him stretched out on the couch, wearing dark clothes, his feet bare. The only light in the room came from the big-screen television, sending flickering images around the room.

She deliberately kept her gaze away from what he was watching, half expecting something deliberately erotic. He'd muted the sound and stilled the frame, but she still expected the worst. "Sorry I'm late," she said with proper carelessness. "Did the other guests go home?"

"You're the only guest, Silver." His voice was a lazy drawl across the darkened room. "We can start any time you're ready."

"Start what? I came for my mother's necklace."

"You'll get it. Eventually. When I'm good and ready. In the meantime, come and sit down."

"Why?"

"Because you're wearing the tallest heels I've ever seen, and your feet must hurt."

"They don't."

"That's probably because you put them on in my honor. How tall are you?"

She gritted her teeth. This wasn't going the way she wanted. For one thing, it was too dark in the room. She couldn't see him clearly, could only see the dark clothes and the outline of his shape against the pale-colored sofa. For another, she felt uncomfortable, exposed. She wanted to tug the hemline down on her dress, she wanted to pull the neckline up. She kept her hands at her side.

"Five eleven and a half," she answered instead. "In my bare feet."

"Those heels probably put you about six two. Impressive, but I'm six four. You're still going to have to look up to me."

"Not if I keep standing."

"Don't be a pain, Silver. You agreed to come for dinner, I agreed to hand over the necklace, and we agreed to talk business. We can't do all that if you keep standing in the middle of my living room looking like an oversize socialite."

The term rankled, and he'd meant it to. She crossed the room slowly, her body radiating elegant disdain, and sank at the far end of his sofa. Since it was the only piece of furniture in the room, she didn't have any other choice.

She kept her face averted from the screen. "What are you watching?"

His laugh was dry. "Obviously you think I've lured you up here to show you pornography. Such a dirty mind you have, Silver. As a matter of fact, this is all part of my seduction plan."

That caught her. She glanced at the screen unwillingly, and her brow knotted in confusion as she recognized it. *"Angels from Hell?"* she said in a soft voice. Her favorite of all her father's movies, though a surprisingly obscure choice for Rafe. "How did you get this? I wasn't aware that it was out on videotape."

"Pegasus owns it. I had them make me a copy a few months ago. It's one of my favorite movies."

"It was very special to my father. Though it's not my idea of an erotic movie."

"Who's talking about eroticism? You must have a one-track mind, Silver," he said lazily, stretching out beside her. "I'm not talking about seducing your body, though the notion has very definite appeal to me. We're talking about seducing you away from your elitist principles about movies versus films. That isn't a film on the screen, it's a movie. Your father made movies. I make movies. If you try to turn *Black Canyon* into a film you'll destroy it."

"It's mine to destroy."

"The hell it is." His voice sharpened for a moment, then relaxed. "The problem is, I know you. I know the kind of person you are. Deliberately, downwardly mobile. With your depressing little apartment and your ratty clothes, you're playing at turning your back on everything you were born with. Life is a game to you, Silver. You write your elegant, malicious little reviews, you rebel against your parents when you're too damned old to be indulging in such behavior, and you trail around a spiteful creep like Clement. But we all know that in a couple of years you'll forget all about it, marry some rising executive in your stepfather's business, and become the perfect conservative wife, just like your mother."

She'd almost done exactly that, with Dennis, so she couldn't refute it. "Is there a point to this?" she questioned coolly, leaning back against the cushions with a ramrod-straight spine.

"You don't need *Black Canyon*. No one else will touch it, and five years from now it won't mean anything more to you than a nostalgic memory of when you were young and foolish. Sooner or later you'll probably be ashamed of it, just as you're already ashamed of who your father was."

She could see him clearly now, in the light reflected by the wide-screen television. He was dressed in soft black pants, with a black shirt open at the neck. His long hair was tied back, his feet were bare, and he was looking at her with a kind of sorrowful contempt that lashed her soul.

"I loved my father," she shot back. "I was proud of him. I just don't like to trade on his name."

"Which just goes to prove you don't belong in the movie business. If you want to get a film done, you trade on everything you can if it'll bring in the backers. The industry isn't a place for ladies and gentlemen. You know as well as I do the rights to *Black Canyon* aren't yours. If you have some notion about seeing it produced as a testament to your father, then stop fighting me. I'm the one who'll see it produced. I'm one of the few people in Hollywood to do exactly what I want."

"Not this time."

She waited for his explosion. It didn't come, and she knew the beginnings of despair. No matter how adamant she was, he could hold out. In this battle they seemed equally matched, he by his calm ruthlessness, she by her angry determination. But one of them was going to fall, and she couldn't imagine it was going to be the mighty Rafe McGinnis.

His words echoed her thoughts with eerie exactness. "You're going to lose, Silver. Sooner or later, you're going to have to admit defeat. You can't stop me. The book exists, and even if we don't have your father's pretreatment stuff we can go ahead on our own. I have access to the best in the business. I can make it any way I damned please, and I shouldn't be wasting my time on you."

"Then why are you?"

"I really don't know. No, scratch that. One reason is your father. Your father was one of the finest craftsmen who ever lived, but he didn't make films for the likes of Clement Walden. He aimed for the masses, and he hit, time and again. If there's a living, viable part of his artistry left, then I want it."

There was a sudden silence in the room, as the unwilling thought came to her, echoed in his words before she'd even completed the notion. "But then, you're it, aren't you? The living, viable part of his talent."

"Hardly," she denied, ignoring her own sudden longing. "Don't get confused at this point, McGinnis. You don't want me. You don't even want my father's ideas—you want your own. You just want the cachet of having Sir Benjamin Hatcher's last work as part of Mack Movies.''

She didn't expect him to deny it, and he didn't. ''It gets a little more complicated than that,'' he said instead. ''You don't know about Bernie. She used to work with your father. She was obviously in love with him.''

''She and the entire female population of California,'' Silver said. ''What's that got to do with anything?'' She wiggled her foot inside the uncomfortable shoe, and realized with an element of shock that she'd snuggled into the overstuffed corner of the couch. As far away from Rafe as she could manage, so she told herself she could feel safe.

''She was the one who brought the script to my attention. She wants it made, she wants it made in his image, and she wants it dedicated to him.''

''So what does that matter? You don't listen to anybody else, why should you listen to a woman?'' She wiggled her foot again, and before she realized it he'd caught it in one hand, stripped off the shoe and sent it sailing across the room. A moment later the other one followed suit, before she could tuck her long legs up underneath her.

''Bernie knows more about the business than anyone I've ever met. Her instincts are infallible. If she wants to do something, she does it. I have complete faith in her.''

''So I have her to thank for this?'' He still had hold of her foot, holding it in one large, strong hand, his fingers massaging the silk-covered arch.

He shrugged in the shadows. ''It would have come up sooner or later. Five years ago it wouldn't have mattered, five years from now you won't care. It just happened to come up at the wrong time, when you already had a grudge against me. Be reasonable, Silver. This is the best chance for your father's final work to be produced. Bernie'll make sure it doesn't get mucked up, and you'll get a nice enough piece of change that you can move into a place of your own.''

''What makes you think I can't do that already?'' She wanted to yank her foot away. But his hand was unbelievably deft and soothing, melting her resistance. In the background the muted scene went on, reminding her of her father's passionate love for what was, undeniably, a mass-market movie.

"Your stepfather would give you anything you want, but you refuse to take it. You spent the last of your father's meager trust fund on college. That's the problem with screen legends—they weren't very good at handling their money. I'm offering you a chance to make more than most executives make in a year, plus points. Consider it your first sale. We'll buy your screenplay, burn it, and you can keep your self-respect."

"What makes you so sure you wouldn't want to do my screenplay?" He'd shifted to the other foot, and for a moment his fingers stopped working.

"Do you want me to see it?" he asked finally.

"No. I wouldn't sell it to you if you were on your knees, pleading. You sound very reasonable. But I'm not giving in. You can't have it. You can't have my father's notes, and you can't have the rights to it."

He didn't say anything more. He didn't release her foot, simply sat there as *Angels from Hell* moved to its inevitable conclusion. She didn't want to see the brief love scene, one that was nothing more than a hurried kiss in an airplane hangar and yet was somehow more erotic than any Mickey Rourke movie. She didn't want to see the battle between the aging pilot and the young upstart. It reminded her too painfully of her father's work being trashed by the brash man who still caressed her foot.

And the heroine picked up a gun, started firing it and stopped the stupid male battles. She'd always loved that part, fantasized about that part. But this wasn't an old movie. She was the combatant, not some pigheaded male, butting her head against the mightiest force in Hollywood today. And she was going to lose.

She yanked her foot away from him, pulling herself off the sofa as the credits rolled. "I came for my mother's necklace."

"You came for dinner."

"I'm not hungry."

He shrugged, unmoved by her distance. "You want to hear numbers?" He mentioned one that almost made her faint.

It didn't make her resolution waver. "No."

"Do you want a drink?"

"No."

"Do you want to go to bed with me?" The question hung in the air, shocking, abrupt. Silver knew with sudden clarity that he meant it. And that she wanted to. Very badly.

"No."

"I could change your mind."

"Not in this lifetime, McGinnis."

He rose, a sudden graceful surge that made her stumble backward, her stockinged feet slippery on the tile floor. "Is that a challenge? You'd better watch yourself, Silver. That's not the way to keep me away from you. I'm not a man who could ever resist a challenge."

She held her ground. "I want my mother's necklace," she said. "And then I want to leave."

"Certainly," he said coolly, crossing the darkened room to her side, and she kept herself from backing away with an effort. "You'll have to get it."

"Don't tell me," she said cynically. "It's in your bed."

"There goes your dirty mind again, Silver. Why are you so obsessed with my bed?"

"Where is the necklace?"

Even in the murky light she could see his wide, innocent smile. "Someplace you'll have no trouble finding it."

"I'm tired of playing games, McGinnis," she said, trying hard to keep her voice from shaking. "Don't you have any lights around here? It's weeks before Halloween, and I want to get on with my life. Where is the necklace?"

"Out there," he said, nodding in the direction of the sheltered terrace.

"Out there?" she echoed, not liking this.

"At the bottom of the swimming pool. You'll have to swim for it, Silver. Do you want a bathing suit or do you want to go au naturel?"

She looked at him for a long moment, considering, and then stared out at the shimmering, moon-silvered depths of the pool. "You're a bastard, McGinnis," she said tightly.

"Bathing suits are in the cabana," he said, reading her rage correctly. "I'll be waiting."

She wished she had the colossal nerve to call his bluff. To go out to the pool, strip off all her clothes and dive in with magnificent disdain for his schoolboy pranks. But she didn't.

She couldn't simply walk away, either. She had to get her mother's necklace back. Things were going to be bad enough when her mother heard about the tabloid—if she found her gaudy piece of jewelry was gone too, all hell would break loose.

If she wanted the necklace, she was going to have to go into the pool and get it. And she was going in decently clothed.

"I'm going to get even," she said calmly enough, heading for the terrace doors. "I want you to know that. Sooner or later I'm going to have my revenge."

She could feel his eyes on her, as physical as a touch. "I'm counting on it," he murmured.

And in the warm night air, Silver shivered.

Chapter Nine

Rafe took his time. He knew Silver Carlysle. At times he thought he knew her better than she knew herself. She was going to storm into that cabana and be confronted with a daunting choice of bathing suits. He'd seen the fury flash in her eyes, had known she'd wanted to simply pull off that elegant, unlikely little dress of hers and dive into his pool, impervious to his goading.

It was a wise thing she hadn't. She knew a predator when she saw one, even if she still couldn't quite believe he was after her. He couldn't imagine where she'd gotten such a mistaken notion of her own attractions. With her tall, rangy body, her mane of close-cropped dark hair, her wide mouth and to-hell-with-you blue eyes, she was absolutely magnificent. More woman than he'd dealt with in a long time. And she seemed to have no notion of it.

He knew who to thank for that diffidence, and it wasn't the obvious choice of an insensitive ex-husband or lover. He stripped down to his bathing suit as he followed Silver onto the terrace, grabbing a towel while he was at it. He could see Clement Walden's work in Silver's abysmal sexual self-esteem. Indeed, it made perfect sense. As long as Clement convinced Silver that sex wasn't a viable part of her life, then she'd remain his humble little acolyte, with no other man as a rival for her time and attention.

Of course it was part of her attraction. The sleeping-beauty

touch was irresistible, particularly when he was used to such
flamingly aggressive women. He should be too old and wise
to be seduced by innocence. But there was something about
her that he wanted, needed. Maybe just to wipe that innocence
away, to force her to face the world as it really was.

Flipping on the underwater lights, he slid into the warm water. The ugly necklace lay on the bottom in the center of the
pool, fully illuminated. He wondered lazily whether he'd be
able to entice her to stay in with him, surrounded by the warm,
sensual lap of the water. Or whether she was going to dive in,
grab the jewelry and run. Doing her best to drown him on the
way.

He didn't bother wondering why he'd set this up. It had all
been instinct on his part. He'd wanted her in his house, he'd
fantasized about having her in the pool. He didn't really know
what he expected to accomplish. Just to make her mad again.
And to remind her that he could make her do what he wanted.

He wasn't about to get her into bed at any time in the near
future, he'd accepted that with a certain amount of fatalism.
His assault on her stern defenses was going to be a long drawn-
out affair, and if he rushed, it would only take that much
longer. It was a delicate thing, inciting her rage while he kept
her senses stirred. She hated the fact that he got to her. But
she hadn't figured out how to make herself immune.

Of course he could always do the gentlemanly thing, he
thought, taking a few lazy strokes through the water. He could
give her back the rights to *Black Canyon*, even put in a word
at Regis or Touchstone and push it toward getting produced.
She'd probably fall into his bed in gratitude, another love slave
who'd do it for the sake of her career.

That wasn't what he wanted from her. For one thing, *Black
Canyon* had come to mean too much to him. The disillusion-
ment, the jaded cynicism had grown over the past five years,
so that he didn't give a damn about the movies he made, the
work he did. Even the money didn't matter.

Black Canyon did. It would bring his heart back, make things
matter once more, and he wasn't about to give up that dream

for anything, up to and including the most desirable woman he'd met in years.

And he didn't just want Silver Carlysle, grateful and compliant, lying on her back. He wanted her to come to him because she couldn't help herself. He wanted her to know it was the worst thing she could do, and to do it anyway. He wanted her to want him so much that common sense and all those impeccable defenses disappeared. And he wasn't going to stop until he got her.

If there'd been a door on the cabana she would have slammed it. As it was, she strode out, her body radiating a fiery rage that almost wiped out her self-consciousness. Treading water, he stared at her as she dumped her clothes on a nearby chaise longue and stomped toward the water, and he wondered whether he might have made a major miscalculation.

She'd managed to find the one demure maillot amid the various bikinis. At least it should have been demure. But it was made for a woman half a foot shorter and a lot skinnier. The silky black material molded itself to Silver Carlysle's hitherto unseen flesh, and the effect was more powerful than if she'd chosen one of the skimpy bikinis.

She had hips. Definitely she had hips, a flare of body that emphasized the smallness of her waist. She had breasts, God, she had breasts. The kind of breasts that would have ruled the world in the fifties, the kind of breasts that he knew made her self-conscious in the shapeless nineties. He'd never considered himself the kind of man to be transfixed by body parts. Maybe he was changing his ways.

And her legs. They went on forever. Long, lithe, luscious. He wanted those legs wrapped around him, he wanted her unbelievably sexy body entwined with his.

Treading water, he moved deeper, keeping his face impassive. "Coward," he taunted her softly. If she didn't look beneath the crystal clear water, she wouldn't see how even her demure choice of bathing suit affected him.

She ignored his taunt, jumping into the shallow end of the pool with a reckless disregard for her hair, her diamond earrings and the untested depth of the water. She swam toward him, with long, graceful strokes, all the time keeping her face out of water, and if she was troubled by his proximity, she managed to hide it.

"Where is it?" she demanded tightly.

"At your feet." She glanced down, looking at the plastic bag at the bottom of the tiled pool. The pool was six feet deep at that point, and the decorative tile lining made the gaudy jewels blend in a bit with the background, but he had no doubt she saw them.

What he didn't understand was why she didn't simply dive down and get them.

She moved away from him, treading water, and for the first time her concentration wasn't on him at all. It was on the hideous piece of jewelry lying within reach. Something she wanted very much, and yet made no move to retrieve.

Since she wasn't about to move, he decided to probe a little. "I take it your mother didn't know you helped yourself to her necklace," he said, moving toward her through the warm water. "Hasn't she missed it yet?"

She didn't even realize danger was moving closer. "My mother has good taste," she said absently, staring at the bottom of the pool. "She never wears the ugly thing. It may be months before she notices it's missing. I can't take that risk."

"Why didn't you ask her?"

"None of your business," she said, moving away from him in the water, backward, toward the side of the pool. "We don't necessarily see eye to eye on things."

"And she would have known you shared her same conventional good taste. The only reason you would have worn the necklace was if you wanted to look tacky." His voice was dry.

He'd managed to sting her into reacting. "I don't share my mother's taste. Besides, what's wrong with having good taste?"

"I don't believe in it. Good taste is the natural enemy of art."

"Since you don't seem to have even a passing acquaintance

with either, I wouldn't think it would matter to you," she shot back.

"Don't be predictable, Silver. I was waiting for that one." She was still retreating, he was still advancing. He couldn't figure out why she didn't simply dive for the jewels and make a run for it, but he didn't fool himself into thinking it had anything to do with him. There was some other issue at stake here, and until she came to terms with it she was going to stay in the water with him, her luscious, overwhelming body a distracting few inches away.

The moon was bright overhead, the night was as still and silent as a night in the hills of Hollywood could be. He could hear the faint lap of water against her body, the quiet catch of her breathing, and he wanted to hear her make those same sounds out of the water, when she was lying in his bed.

Damn, he was making himself crazy! This was backfiring on him—at this rate he'd be the one suffering, not her. "So tell me, Silver," he said softly, and his voice was the only soft thing about him, "what's the problem?"

She looked up from her perusal of the pool floor, momentary surprise darkening her eyes, and once again he knew he was temporarily the lesser of her worries. "Problem?" she echoed. "You mean apart from you?"

"Apart from me," he said, and he was almost touching her. If he simply let his body drift it would brush against hers. And he wasn't sure if he could simply let it drift back again. "Why don't you go get the necklace?"

"I will," she said stubbornly. "Just give me a minute."

He didn't know why he hadn't realized it sooner. "You're afraid of the water," he said flatly.

It would have been a waste of time for Silver to deny it, and she wasn't a woman who believed in wasting her time. "Yes."

"You can swim," he said. "You grew up in Beverly Hills. It's against the law for a house in Beverly Hills to be without a swimming pool."

"We had a swimming pool," she said. "We always had a swimming pool."

"Downwardly mobile, what did I tell you?" Rafe said. "So what's the problem? Some childhood trauma? Don't tell me—you nearly drowned when you were five years old and you haven't been able to put your head under water ever since."

She glared at him, and to his amusement she called him a name he wouldn't have thought she'd know. "I was seven," she snapped. "And it isn't a laughing matter."

"No, I suppose it's not. But you aren't the kind of woman who'd succumb to a childhood trauma. I can't imagine you giving in to any weakness."

"You don't even know me," she said, a touch of panic in her voice. "How can you make judgments about the kind of person I am, when you haven't the faintest idea who that is?"

"I've told you, I know you far better than you think. I know that all you have to do is make your mind up and you can face anything, including deep water and overbearing film producers. So why are you hesitating?"

She didn't move. "Don't rush me," she said. "I'll do it eventually."

That was when he realized he'd been wrong about her. It wasn't a case of self-indulgent neurosis. She was deeply afraid of the water, so afraid that his nearness, his opinion, no longer mattered. She was going to stay in his pool till her body temperature dropped, her lips turned blue, and she still wasn't going to be able to dive down and get that damned necklace.

Suddenly he felt like a fool. As long as Silver Carlysle fought back, he could revel in the battle, even knowing the outcome was preordained from the beginning. But the panic in her eyes, the paleness of her lips, the very real fear made him momentarily ashamed of himself.

He didn't like that feeling. He swore, then dived down without a word, snatching the necklace from the tile floor and surfacing again in a matter of seconds.

If he expected the light of gratitude to fill her eyes he'd deluded himself. She was watching him warily, knowing he was going to name his price.

Which of course he was. Only he didn't like the fact that

she realized it. He pushed away, moving into the middle of the pool, keeping his expression enigmatic. "All right, Silver," he murmured. "Come and get it."

She may have been afraid of water, but ravening movie producers were child's play in comparison. She came after him, her strokes strong and sure, and he knew the effort that much proficiency must have cost her. She'd conquered her terror of the water. She just couldn't bring herself to put her head under the water.

She caught up with him near the deep end of the pool, reaching for the plastic bag. He caught her wrist before she could grab it, pulling her body up against his, and she felt strong, vibrant against his water-slick skin. "Forfeit," he murmured, sliding one hand beneath her wet hair and holding her head still as he tossed the plastic bag onto the tiled walkway beside the pool.

Her mouth was wet from the water, cool and startled. He used his tongue, pushing into her, his anger and frustration overriding his better judgment.

Her hands caught his shoulders, her fingers digging in, and her eyes fluttered closed in instant acquiescence. He knew what she was doing. She was paying the forfeit, hoping to get off lightly.

He lifted his head to look down at her as they drifted into the center of the pool. "It's not going to be so easy," he muttered. And he kissed her again, his mouth covering hers, his arms wrapped around her body, as he pushed them down below the surface of the water.

She struggled for a moment, panic suffusing her body, and her fingers dug into his shoulders. But he pushed his hips against hers, held her mouth still beneath his, and she held her breath, sinking with him, letting him kiss her, letting his mouth seal hers away from the suffocating water, letting his aroused body press against hers. And then her generous breasts pressed against his chest, only that thin layer of spandex separating their flesh; and her tongue touched his, for a brief moment her terror of the water overridden by her reaction to him.

His foot touched the tile floor, and he pushed off again, rising upward, his mouth still clamped to hers, until they shot out of the water, surfacing into the moon-gilded night.

She hit him then, her fists pounding at him as she tore her mouth away, taking in deep, furious gulps of air.

But he was too strong for her, too determined. He kissed her again, pulling her beneath the surface, and her fear channeled into a rage so powerful it was a wonder the water around them didn't boil.

Up they came again, and she tried to knee him, but he stopped her, pushing her up against the side of the pool, and kissed her again. And this time when they slid beneath the pearly water she kissed him back.

The water surrounded them, a cocoon of sensation, rich and cool and velvety, caressing them, pushing them tight together beneath the surface. He could feel the tremor beneath her skin, a tremor that had nothing to do with fear, and his hands slid up her arms to the straps of the thin maillot, pulling the spandex down to her waist.

Somehow they'd moved into shallower water. When his feet touched the tile his head and shoulders were in the night air. He hauled her up against him, and she was pliant, warm against him, as he wrapped her legs around his waist.

She sank against him, her face against his shoulder, her soft breasts against his chest, and he took a deep breath, struggling for some lost remnant of control. "Do you make a habit of this?" she asked in little more than a whisper. "Drown a woman into compliance?"

He wouldn't have thought she had that much fight left in her. She startled a laugh from him. "Only if I have to," he said. He was rapidly reaching the point of no return. The sweet, heavy weight of her breasts against his chest, the sleekness of her thighs around his hips, the taste of her mouth still lingering on his, were pushing him to a point he didn't remember reaching before. He'd never been so aroused that he couldn't pull back. He was almost there now, and if he moved his hands between them, cupped her breasts, he'd be lost.

For a moment he contemplated going for it. He could have her, he knew it, despite her best judgment. He could strip off the rest of her bathing suit and make love to her in the pool, and she wouldn't even notice if they came under water.

But much as his body screamed for it, what little remained of his self-control told him no. She wasn't ready to give in completely. He could make love to her until she was a pleasured little mass of desire, but half an hour later she'd be fighting again.

He needed her acquiescence, her defeat on all fronts. If he took her body now, she'd still be able to fight back. He needed to wait until she was ready to give up everything. It was the only way he could ensure getting exactly what he wanted. And he never settled for less. He never had, he never would show that kind of weakness. Especially for a woman.

It was physically painful, releasing her, and he wondered if he was being a complete fool. But the moment his grip loosened she pushed away, and her dazed expression sharpened into awareness once more as she stumbled away from him in the waist-deep water.

"The necklace is over there." He jerked his head carelessly in the direction he'd thrown it, and watched with undimmed appreciation as she climbed out of the water.

She hadn't realized her bathing suit was at her waist. She yanked it up, her back to him, and he knew a moment's regret that he hadn't been able to see her. When he finally had her, he wanted it to be in broad daylight, on a bed uncluttered with sheets or covers of any sort. He wanted to lose himself in her glorious body. He had the strong suspicion that no one had appreciated it sufficiently before. He intended to remedy that error in judgment on the male part of the species.

She grabbed her clothes from the chaise, scooped up the wet plastic bag, and stalked toward the house. "Are you stealing my bathing suit, Silver?" he called lazily, hiding the sharp tang of need that was still eating at his gut.

"It wouldn't fit you. You're not getting *Black Canyon,*

McGinnis. And you're not putting your hands on me again,'' she said fiercely.

He pushed off, floating on his back in the pool, and there was no way she could miss how aroused he was if she cared to look. Chances are she was too upset to notice. "Don't count on it, Silver," he said. "I've told you before, I always get what I want, by fair means or foul."

"I should have listened," she said bitterly, pausing in the doorway. "I thought you'd played your dirtiest trick. I should have known you could sink even lower."

"Literally," he said in a lazy voice. "I take it you don't like the idea of being seduced into giving up the rights? Why don't you just sell them to me and I'll leave you alone? If that's what you really want."

"Sexual harassment is an ugly term, McGinnis."

"Silver, you wound me," he protested. "And I thought you liked my kisses. If you don't, you shouldn't kiss me back."

She exploded. "I hope you drown, McGinnis. I hope you die a slow, painful death. You're the most despicable, contemptible, sexist, macho turkey I have ever met in a long, miserable life, and if you smashed yourself up in that ridiculous sports car I would dance on your grave. I'd—''

He surged out of the pool, coming after her. "I wish I knew what I'd done to make you so crazy," he said dryly. "It's not my fault that I find you completely gorgeous."

"Liar."

"Am I going to have to prove it again?" he said in a silken voice, stalking her around the edge of the pool.

She ran from him. The bold, inimitable Ms. Silver Carlysle turned and ran, her clothes clutched against her, her wet bare feet making footprints on the pale tile, and it took all his self-control not to go after her.

"Later," he murmured, a promise to his needful body. "Later," he said again, when he heard the noisy muffler of her car as she tore out of the driveway, and this time he was making a promise to some deep, irrational part of him that was only partly sexual.

He ignored his own, irrational uneasiness. There was a part of him that wanted Silver Carlysle, needed her, on a level even more profound that his physical craving for her. A need that powerful was hard to shake, hard to control, and if he had any sense of self-preservation at all he'd back away, run like hell, and not even worry about *Black Canyon*. Hell, there was nothing wrong with making *Cop for a Day II*.

But he knew he wasn't going to. It had gone too far already, and Rafe McGinnis never backed down from a threat. He could get Silver Carlysle in bed, take *Black Canyon* from her, and then walk away, without even a twinge of conscience.

Couldn't he?

Chapter Ten

It was a conceptual impossibility, Silver thought. The day simply couldn't have gotten worse. Starting with that god-awful article in the tabloid, with her family history laid out in maudlin detail, only to be compounded and surpassed by the time spent with Rafe McGinnis. She had the necklace, but that was about the only triumph she was able to wrest from a day of complete disaster. She needed to keep away from him. He unsettled her, shook her to her very core, and her formidable defenses were useless against him.

No, scratch that. She wasn't an infant, to blame other people for her own problems. The issue wasn't Rafe McGinnis and whatever mystical, sexual powers he had. The issue was her weak-minded reaction to him.

She hated to admit her weakness. Hated to accept the fact that she simply couldn't deal with him. She, who'd always prided herself on her tough-minded defenses, was defenseless when it came to a man like Rafe. She despised herself for it. But she couldn't change it.

Fortunately there was no longer any reason to deal with him. She had the necklace, she wouldn't give him the rights to *Black Canyon*. Two simple issues resolved, at least to her mind. If he wanted to keep after her, he'd have to do it through lawyers.

And if only the night had ended on that firm note, she would have counted herself lucky. She should have known fate had more in store for her. Nothing could equal being kissed by Rafe

McGinnis, her body wrapped tight in his, sinking beneath the cool depths of his pool and no longer caring if she drowned.

But being stopped for speeding, wearing nothing but a too small bathing suit and bare feet, with an out-of-date license and a car with a taillight missing, certainly came a close second in the scale of disasters. It didn't help that the police made her climb out of her car and walk a straight line dressed only in that skimpy bathing suit. In the end she gave in to weakness, bursting into noisy tears, loud enough to convince the patrolman that she could drive herself home as long as she put on her spiked heels.

The problem was, once she started crying, she couldn't stop. She had to keep wiping the blinding tears from her face as she drove at a sedate enough pace through the wide, elegant streets of Beverly Hills to her mother's mansion. She didn't even bother to consider why she was crying, she who cried approximately once every eighteen months. She just knew she needed to cry, and every time she thought of Rafe McGinnis, which was far too often, she simply cried harder.

She needed a shower, she told herself as she pulled up the winding driveway and stopped outside the closed garage. She needed to wash the chlorine from her hair and skin, she needed to wash the taste of him from her mouth, the feel of him from her breasts. And then she needed to crawl into her bed, wrap the covers around her and not wake up until she damned well wanted to.

She kicked off the heels, grabbing her clothes and heading up the flight of stairs. She came to an abrupt stop on the landing, as she realized she wasn't alone.

"Uh, good evening, miss." Wilkers, her mother's chauffeur, rose from a crouching position by her door, his normally bluff face darkened with embarrassment.

Silver didn't move, as dread shot through her. "What's going on, Wilkers? I know you're not trying to break into my apartment. For one thing, you already have a key to everything here, and for another, I never lock it. So what's up?"

"Your mother."

It was answer enough. Silver climbed the remaining flight of stairs, pushing past him, into the tiny section of peace that had been the best home she'd ever had. It was empty, her makeshift furniture gone, the mirrors off the walls, the rugs rolled up. Her last remaining comfort had been ripped away, and she felt raped.

"Your mother had us bring all your stuff up to the big house. I was just putting a lock on the door," Wilkers said miserably, torn between the woman who signed his paychecks and the one who'd been his friend for the twelve years he'd worked there.

Silver didn't move. It was never cold in Los Angeles. The wet bathing suit and the night air had to be responsible for the desolate chill that swept up her spine. "Did she happen to mention what precipitated this?"

"Something about a newspaper article," Wilkers said. "She was in a rare mood, miss. She's up there, waiting for you."

Silver didn't bother to glance toward the house. "You know, Wilkers," she said in a meditative voice, "I'm not in the mood. Would you take her this?" She dropped the waterlogged plastic bag into his hand. "And tell her I'll be in touch."

"But, miss..." he protested. "You haven't a change of clothes. You can't just walk away. Where will you go?"

She managed a wry smile. "Believe it or not, Wilkers, I have possibilities. I have friends, and I have a gold credit card compliments of my stepfather that I have so far refrained from using. I'm afraid I'm going to have to lower my standards for the next month. But I'll be fine. Just fine."

"Do you want me to see if I can sneak out one of your suitcases?"

"And put your job on the line? No, Wilkers, much as I appreciate the offer. My mother can be a holy terror, and I don't want you getting in the middle. Just tell her I'll be in touch." She took one last, sorrow-filled glance around her denuded living room. "She even took my computer?" she asked in a mournful voice.

"Everything, miss."

"Well—" she forced some brightness into her voice "—I

needed to upgrade. And I needed a break from L.A.—too much smog and hot wind this time of year. Take care of yourself, Wilkers. And watch out for Mother. She doesn't like to lose battles, and she's losing this one.''

Suddenly she couldn't bear to stay in the empty apartment a moment longer. Without a backward glance she headed out, running back down the stairs as fast as her bare feet could carry her.

She didn't bother to slip on the heels again as she took off into the gathering night. Chances of her being stopped twice, even with a broken taillight, were unlikely.

She turned on the heat full blast as she drove through the wide, clear streets, and the little-used system kicked out an oily smell that turned her stomach even as it warmed her exposed flesh.

She stopped in a parking lot long enough to tug the skimpy black dress over the damp bathing suit, ignoring the fact that the straps showed.

L.A. was a big city, catering to people's whims, and it didn't take her long to find a clothing store that stayed open all night long. She bought indiscriminately, for the first time not stopping to consider price, suitability or even what she planned to do for the next twenty-four hours. She bought everything that caught her eye and looked big enough for her tall figure, using her stepfather's gold card wherever she went.

When she'd filled the back of her Toyota and her feet hurt too much to walk anymore, she gave up, heading for the nearest anonymous hotel. She hadn't lied to Wilkers—she did have any number of friends who'd put her up for the night, for the week, forever, if she asked it. Clement would be beside himself with glee—he'd been trying to get her to move into his palatial French provincial town house for the past year.

He'd ply her with Earl Grey tea and Courvoisier, he'd soothe her and murmur deliciously malicious things about both her mother and Rafe McGinnis, he'd give her back her pride and self-respect, he'd take care of her.

But she'd already had a taste of the price he'd exact from

her. Clement wanted unwavering loyalty, no diverging opinions, and a slavish audience to listen to his pronouncements. She'd had no trouble providing those requirements in the past, but in the last few weeks she'd begun to change. She still adored Clement, but occasionally, just occasionally, he could be wrong.

He'd pointed out her errors in judgment when it came to men, pointed them out in such a way that she had no choice but to turn her back on the possible relationships. She'd always been grateful he'd rescued her from making an utter fool of herself. But she was coming to the point where she was ready to risk it.

Hell, she'd done more than risk it. She had only to get near Rafe McGinnis for her brain to go into core meltdown. Clement knew it, even though she denied it to his face. If she went to Clement for shelter she'd be treated to a vicious, impossibly clever diatribe on just how pathetic Rafe McGinnis really was.

She didn't want to hear it. She didn't want to be told that the enemy, the man who was effectively destroying everything she'd worked so hard on, was unworthy. She'd imbued him with almost superhuman attributes. If he really was an ordinary mortal, then her powerlessness was that much more shameful.

She'd finished the series of articles. She had money in her account, she had a back seat full of new clothes, she had a gold credit card with a stratospheric credit limit. What she needed was a break from everyone and everything. And that was what she was going to get.

She didn't sleep well in the queen-size bed that smelled of stale cigarettes. She checked out by six the next morning, dressed in a pair of baggy black pants and a T-shirt that somehow managed to look impossibly elegant. Not that it shouldn't, when she considered the price tag she'd ripped off and thrown into the trash. The new black leather running shoes were a relief after hobbling around on high heels, but she kept her diamond earrings in. She spared herself a startled glance in her rearview mirror as she pulled into the beginnings of rush hour. Lord, even the fastidious Clement might approve.

It hadn't taken her long to decide where she was going. Or where she was going to stop along the way. She'd done a cursory amount of research into Rafael McGinnis, stopping abruptly when he became too interesting. She knew he came from Colorado originally, knew he'd gone through the University of Michigan as an undergraduate, then taken a graduate degree at NYU. He'd gotten into the movie business almost by accident, something Clement had always maintained was obvious if you saw one of his productions, and his work habits were legendary. He was at his studios by six every morning. She knew just where to find him.

She also knew going to see him one last time had to be far from the smartest thing she'd ever done. It was weakness, pure and simple, a longing on her part for some sort of resolution. Or at least a final glance.

Apparently the other employees of Mack Movies shared his zeal for overwork. The place was already busy when she pulled up to the gate at 6:45, and she paused, wondering whether she was going to have any trouble getting onto the lot to face her nemesis.

"Can I help you?" The genial gatekeeper was unlike anyone she'd ever seen in security before, with his Hawaiian shirt, baseball cap and long hair.

"I want to see Rafe McGinnis," she said, momentarily startled.

"You and half of Hollywood. I don't suppose you have an appointment?"

"I'm afraid not."

"Go home and make one."

"I'm on my way out of town. He'll see me, I'm pretty sure of it, if you could just give him my name."

The guard shook his head. "Can't do that."

Silver felt frustration building inside. Coming to see Rafe wasn't her brightest idea in recent years, but now that she'd gone this far she intended to see it through to the end. "Why not?" she demanded, trying to keep the truculence out of her voice.

He smiled sweetly. "Because I don't know what your name is."

Silver growled, low in her throat like a rabid cocker spaniel. "Silver Carlysle."

"One moment." He picked up the phone inside the booth, spoke into it briefly, and Silver knew a sudden hope that he'd come back, chastened and apologetic.

It was too much to hope for in such a casual operation. "Go ahead," he said cheerfully, raising the gate. "Second building on the right, walk in and turn left. Have a nice day."

Silver growled again, gunning the motor and zooming past him. The sooner she got out of this town, away from sun-addled surfers, the happier she'd be.

The Lotus was nowhere in sight, but she didn't let that bother her. She already knew Rafe was just as likely to be carried around by the Bentley parked outside the building, and if the man had a Lotus he probably owned several other cars besides, including the Ferrari parked beside the door.

She shoved her short-cropped hair behind her ears and climbed out of her aging Toyota. It didn't belong in such august company, but she no longer gave a damn. She was coming in for her final confrontation, and the financial inequity just solidified her determination.

The secretary wasn't any more standard than the gatekeeper. She was young, with long hair hanging to her waist, dressed in spandex biking shorts of a particularly bilious shade of green. "Miss Carlysle? First door on your left. What do you take in your coffee?"

"No coffee, thank you," she said, though the words nearly choked her. She needed caffeine even more than she needed peace of mind. The only thing more important was keeping Rafe away from her, and if she accepted his hospitality, even in a cup of coffee, she'd be giving him an advantage.

The door was ajar to his office, and beyond she could hear the quiet murmur of voices. At least he wasn't alone. If there were witnesses he wouldn't touch her, wouldn't kiss her, and she just might possibly make it through what she counted on being her final meeting with him. Taking a deep, determined breath, she pushed open the door and walked in. And then came to an abrupt halt.

Rafe wasn't there. Sitting behind his desk was a plain, age-less woman in dark-rimmed glasses, and it took Silver a mo-ment to remember her name. Bernadette Thomas. The woman who'd brought all this about.

Bernie rose with a graciousness worthy of Marjorie Carlysle at her most elegant. "We're so glad you came by, Silver," she said, her rough voice matching her no-nonsense exterior. "You remember Sam Mendelsohn, don't you?"

Silver glanced at him warily, her initial relief fading into uneasiness. "I was looking for Rafe," she said baldly.

"Damned if I know where he is," Sam said genially. "He's usually here at the crack of dawn, setting a lousy example for all of us. He must have had quite a night of it. I wonder if we have Marcia Allison to thank for it, or someone new. He goes through women so fast you need a scorecard."

Silver drew herself up to her full height, towering over the smaller man. "If that information is directed at me it's nothing I don't already know. And I certainly don't give a damn. I wanted to talk to Mr. McGinnis about a business matter."

"Don't pay any attention to Sam—he's a jerk half the time, and brilliant the other half. You're catching him in his jerk mode," Bernie said. "Let me get you some coffee."

"No coffee," Silver said again. The damnable thing was, she liked Bernie Thomas. She liked her frank manner, she liked her work, she liked everything about her. It was all she could do to summon her anger. "I gather I have you to thank for this current mess."

"I don't blame you for being angry," Bernie said wryly. "I don't suppose it would help if I said I was sorry."

"Not unless you can call Rafe off."

"No one can call him off when he's got his mind set on something," Sam said. "Besides, I don't know if I'd let him. I read the book, and it's got terrific possibilities. I'd give ten years of my life to see what Hatcher had in mind for it. The man was a legend.''

Unwillingly Silver's eyes met Bernie's. "A legend," Silver echoed stiffly. "Forgive me if I'm not that enthusiastic."

"Why don't you just hand over the papers?" Sam pushed it. "We'll keep Rafe out of it completely if you don't want to feel like you're giving in to him. I promise you, I'll treat the whole thing like the solid gold it is. You'll lose in the end, Miss Carlysle. Why don't you give in with dignity, not make this thing unbearably unpleasant?''

"I didn't come here to argue about it," she said.

"Then why did you come?" Bernie asked, with real curiosity.

"To tell Rafe that I'm going out of town. He may be one of the most powerful men in Hollywood, but I have an advantage over him. I have my father's papers, and I know where the original author of *Black Canyon* came from. I intend to find him, if he's still living, or his closest relatives and heirs. By the time I come back here there won't be any more question about who owns the rights to it. I will.''

"It's been thirty years, Silver. What makes you think you'll find any trace of him?''

Silver merely smiled. "If D. Maven is still alive, I'll find him.''

"Where?" Sam demanded.

"None of your business," she said with ultimate sweetness. "Just tell Rafe he's wasting his time."

"Don't you want to wait?" Bernie said with surprising urgency. "He'll be here any time now."

"I don't think so." Silver could feel her resolve weakening. She'd come for one reason, and one reason alone. To warn him away from her. Since he was gone, she was spared, and with luck she'd be able to return with the proof she needed.

She left the room with unruffled grace, moving slowly until she was out of their eyesight. And then she ran for it, jumping in her car and tearing out of the lot at a dangerous speed, considering the baldness of her tires.

It was a close call. His Lotus was pulling up to the building just as she was peeling away. She didn't have any illusions that he might have missed her, and she knew a moment's panic, that he might come after her. The aging engine of her poor Toyota would be no match for the Lotus, but apparently he didn't think her worthy of pursuit.

She glanced in the rearview mirror, almost sideswiping a building as she sped away from him. He was standing by the car, staring after her, dressed in black jeans and a T-shirt. And it didn't help her unsettled state of mind to realize their clothes were almost an exact match.

She was past the sprawling, endless city limits of greater Los Angeles in forty-five minutes, deftly avoiding gridlock, the army of traffic heading in the opposite direction. She had no idea how long it would take her to get to the tiny town of Elkmate, Colorado, and she didn't particularly care. D. Maven had waited for the past thirty years. He could wait another day or two.

She happened to own the only car in the greater Los Angeles area without air-conditioning. She rolled down the window, letting the fresh autumn breeze blow through her short-cropped hair, blow through her soul. In twenty-nine years she hadn't been able to break the invisible golden apron strings that had tied her to her mother's whims. Finally, thankfully, Marjorie had gone too far. And she was blessedly, completely free.

Except for the unsettling specter of Rafe McGinnis haunting her dreams. And she had every intention of exorcising that final ghost by the time she was finished in Colorado.

"WHY DIDN'T YOU keep her here?" Rafe demanded, stalking into his office.

"There's a law against detaining people against their will," Sam said from his spot on the leather sofa. "She came, she saw, she conquered, she left."

"What did she want?" He turned to Bernie, knowing he wasn't going to get a sensible answer from Sam in his current mood.

"I'm not quite sure. What's going on between the two of you, anyway?" Bernie asked. "I've never known you to be so gauche in handling women. I would have thought she'd be eating out of your hand right now. If I thought you were going to have any real trouble getting the rights to *Black Canyon* then I never would have brought it up."

"I'm not having trouble," he said with gritted teeth. "Silver Carlysle happens to be one of the most pigheaded, frustrating females I've ever met."

"Yeah, you're used to having 'em roll over and play dead, aren't you?" Sam piped up. "Maybe I ought to see if she goes for the short, rumpled type. I mean, someone in this world has got to prefer me to you."

"It's possible. But not in this case. That's part of the problem. If Silver was a man the issue would be straightforward and between our lawyers."

"I never thought to see the day when a woman would get the better of you," Bernie mused.

Rafe knew perfectly well she'd said it to goad him. It still didn't keep him from reacting. "The day she gets the better of me will be the day *Cop for a Day* wins an Oscar," he snapped. "Where was she going?"

"Out of town, buddy boy," Sam chortled. "You're going to have to sit here and twiddle your thumbs for the next few days until she decides to turn up, and then it might be too late. She says she's going after the old codger who wrote the book, and she's coming back with the deal signed, sealed and delivered."

"What are you sounding so cheerful about? I thought you were as committed to *Black Canyon* as I was?" Rafe said.

"Oh, I am. I admit, I'm torn. On the one hand, I really want to do that Western. Anything that's got both you and Bernie in such a snit is powerful stuff indeed. The book's fantastic, and the possibilities are endless. On the other hand, I really enjoy watching you squirm."

"Thanks," he said morosely. "What about you, Bernie?

You got us into this. Do you have any suggestions, or are you just going to sit around and watch me tear my hair?''

"I've got a very good suggestion," she said tranquilly. "Beat her to it."

"What the hell do you think I've been trying to do for the past few days? How can I beat her to it when I don't know where she's going?"

"Elkmate, Colorado," Bernie said.

Rafe just looked at her. Life couldn't be that twisted, could it? He stalled for time. "How do you know she went there?"

"I was in on the original development, remember? D. Maven had to be the most reclusive writer Hollywood has ever known, but I remember Elkmate. You can make it out there faster than she can, beat her at her own game."

"You got a problem with that?" Sam asked, his eyes narrowed in the early-morning light.

"Why should I have a problem with it?" he shot back.

"I don't know. You just don't look too pleased with the idea of returning to your native state. Ever been to Elkmate?"

"No."

"Ever heard of it?"

He wasn't a man who believed in exhibiting his problems. "I've heard of it. It was about thirty miles from where I grew up."

"Thirty miles away and you've never been there?" Bernie said.

He glared at her. Bernie knew as much about his childhood as anyone, and she knew enough not to question him about it. "Want to make something of it?"

She held up a hand. "I wouldn't think of it. If you don't want to go back to Colorado you don't have to, Rafe. D. Maven has probably been dead for the past twenty years, and all she'll find is an empty cabin on a hillside. You can stay right here and wait for her to come back. If she does."

"Why wouldn't she?"

"Word travels fast. Her mother heard about the tabloid article and kicked her out of the house. Or at least, that's what I was told. I don't know if she has anything to come back to.''

"Sure she does," Rafe said in a sour voice. "She has Clement Walden."

Sam shuddered. "So what's it gonna be, buddy? *Cop for a Day—the Revenge* or *Black Canyon?*"

"What the hell do you *think* I'm going to do?" he said wearily. "I'm taking the next flight to Denver."

Bernie smiled, and he never realized how sphinxlike she could be. "I thought so," she said in a deceptively tranquil voice. And once again he wondered what was going on in her razor-sharp mind.

And what the hell it had to do with Silver Carlysle. And him.

Chapter Eleven

Rafe could have taken the company plane. Even in the current economic climate of trying to scale back skyrocketing costs, Pegasus Pictures owned two Lear jets and half a dozen propeller planes. He could have commandeered any one of them, but he didn't. If he had to go back to Colorado, and it certainly seemed as if he had no choice in the matter, then he preferred to do it without a raft of witnesses.

In Hollywood he was an easily recognizable figure. Out in the real world he was much more anonymous. His height drew people's attention, but in Colorado a lot of men were tall. He'd learned early on that women tended to notice him, and he'd used that to his advantage over the years. He'd also learned how to ignore it.

When he took his first-class seat on the commercial airline several hours later, it would have taken even a Hollywood ferret like Clement Walden a great deal of trouble to recognize him. Gone was the Armani suit, the Rolex, the accoutrements of power. He was wearing old jeans, Western boots that came from Texas not some trendy boutique in Hollywood, a heavy denim shirt and a Stetson that was probably older than his quarry. His shearling-lined coat was dumped in the bin overhead, his shades covered his face, and he leaned back in his seat, one large hand around a glass of whiskey, as he shut out the world.

He didn't want to be there. He would have given ten years

of his life, half his annual income, even his beloved Lotus, not to have to go back to Colorado. The one thing he wouldn't give up was Silver Carlysle.

His grip tightened on the glass of whiskey as the silver plane carried him and a hundred others closer to Colorado. It wasn't Silver Carlysle he wanted, he reminded himself, draining the glass. At least, not more than temporarily. It was a matter of pride, a matter of power, a matter of control. He'd decided he wanted to do *Black Canyon,* and nothing under the sun, most particularly not a defensive, luscious society amazon was going to get in his way.

And if he had to go back home to do it, the one place he'd assiduously avoided for the past fifteen years, then do it he would.

The flight into Stapleton airport was bumpy but brief. It was a simple enough matter to rent a four-wheel-drive vehicle. He even could have hired a Range Rover in that moneyed city, and for a moment he was tempted. In a Range Rover he'd remember who he was, who he'd become. It was a trendy symbol of power, and it would help keep the memories at bay.

But he'd left his Armani suit behind and dressed in denim. He could have rented a Rolls and he'd still know where he'd come from. In the end he rented a four-wheel-drive pickup, taking off into the mountains while the woman behind the Hertz counter still tried to remember where she'd heard his name before.

He knew he had plenty of time. Silver was driving that rattletrap of a car—she wouldn't make the Colorado state line until sometime tomorrow, if she didn't stop to rest. He could take his time, maybe head out to Aspen to see if there was some early skiing.

He wasn't going to do that. He knew where he was headed, the pickup practically driving itself. He was going to drive over Red Mountain Pass, past the spot where his father had gone over the edge. And then he was going home.

It was almost midnight by the time he pulled up to the little cabin that had seen the first fourteen years of his life. Even through the bright headlights he could see the changes his money had wrought. During the long, intervening years, when he'd lived with his aunt and uncle, then in foster care, then on to college and making his own way, the cabin had been sold to hunters, used and abused for years, open to the weather and even stray grizzlies. When he'd made his first real money he'd bought it back, sight unseen, a lawyer handling the transaction, and he never did figure out why. Maybe because a place that had witnessed that much pain needed to be held on to. And maybe because, while he'd turned his back on Colorado, on his past, it was still a part of him. A big part.

He stared straight ahead, looking at it. His money had been spent well. Over the years high-priced contractors had fixed it up, redoing the roof, putting in new airtight windows, a sprawling addition. Inside, the amenities were all they should be, including two bathrooms, a state-of-the-art kitchen, even a hot tub. It was now the mountain home his mother had always dreamed about, the place she'd wanted to live, instead of a tumbledown shack with no electricity or running water. But she was long gone, drinking herself to death with quiet despair after his father had gone off that cliff. And Rafe had never even been back.

Why the hell did it have to be Elkmate? Why couldn't D. Maven have come from up north, around Steamboat? Or even better, how about Wyoming or Montana? Why did he have to hail from Rafe's backyard?

Not that it mattered. Mack Movies and Pegasus Pictures had resources Silver Carlysle could only dream about. Bernie had come up with a death certificate with surprising ease, once push came to shove. D. Maven had died in 1973 of cirrhosis of the liver, complicated by pneumonia, at the ripe old age of seventy-seven. He'd left no will, and no heirs.

Which meant *Black Canyon* was up in the air. No, it meant *Black Canyon* belonged to him, if he wanted it. Sir Benjamin Hatcher had negotiated for the rights. Hatcher had worked for Pegasus, Pegasus had paid the pittance a 1950s movie option was worth. Therefore, it was his.

He switched off the engine, grabbing his duffel bag from the back of the truck and heading toward the cabin as he considered how life was arranged for him. He could see a thin plume of smoke coming from the chimney, and he knew Bernie had seen to it that someone had come in, stoked the fires, turned on the heat, made sure the refrigerator and freezer were well stocked. He could remember back to the times when his mother would struggle with the fires, her hands clumsy in the cold air, her movements slowed by the vodka she was drinking in increasing amounts.

He had all the money, all the amenities, and it couldn't change the past. It couldn't make his mother's life any easier, it couldn't stop his father from going out in a blizzard, heading over a mountain pass that was treacherous even in midsummer. And it couldn't stop him from remembering.

He shut the door behind him, shutting out the autumn chill, and stared at the rustic interior. Thank God they hadn't sent a California decorator out to oversee the place. Whoever had been hired, and Rafe had never bothered to find out who, had done the job right. It looked real and solid, comfortable and homey.

And no wonder. Whether he liked it or not, wanted it or not, beneath the Indian rugs and the bird's-eye maple furniture, beneath the modern plumbing and state-of-the-art electronics, it was his home. Always had been. Always would be.

He cooked himself a frozen steak over the fancy grill in the kitchen, made himself a pot of strong coffee, nuked himself a potato and poured himself a whiskey. It didn't take much time to get the fire blazing, sending out heat into the room. He sat in front of it, kicking off his boots as he alternated between the whiskey and the coffee, and he told himself he should have brought a woman to warm the king-size bed in the master bedroom overhead. He certainly wasn't going to get Silver Carlysle in there, and he needed distraction.

He told himself he should be feeling angry, crazy, tormented by a past he'd never bothered to come to terms with. He told himself coming to Colorado was the worst idea he'd ever had in his entire life.

But when it came right down to it, with the food in his belly, the coffee and the whiskey warming him, the sound of the fire crackling, he knew a peace he hadn't felt in years. Maybe never.

And the only thing that would have made it better wasn't a faceless, inventive bed partner imported from L.A.

It was Silver Carlysle.

A DAY AND A HALF after she left Los Angeles, Silver sat in the front seat of her Toyota, her hands clenched tightly on the steering wheel. The little cabin at the end of the narrow, twisting road hadn't seen any life in maybe a decade. The windows were nothing more than gaping holes in the rough planking, the porch sagged into the dirt, the front door was long gone. The rusting frame of an old pickup decorated what might once have been called a front yard, but age and weather had made its vintage impossible to identify. It might have belonged to D. Maven, or his grandfather. Or his grandchild.

The one thing that was indisputable—D. Maven was long gone. The directions on the notes in her father's trunk were clear and precise, written in a stranger's hand, presumably one of his assistants. Or one of his mistresses. D. Maven was a recluse—he didn't have a telephone, and he despised mail. It apparently had taken all of Hatcher's legendary charm to pry the rights to *Black Canyon* out of the old codger, and it had probably required several trips and a prodigious amount of whiskey to accomplish it. Though there was no mention as to whether her father and his assistant had actually ended up making that trip.

And now his daughter had followed his path, tracking down the house where Maven had lived. Long, long ago, if the condition of the place was any indication. It had all been a wild-goose chase.

She leaned forward, sinking her head against the steering wheel. She'd told herself she should take her time, stop and rest along the way, but she hadn't. Except for a brief four-hour nap at a motel, she'd been on the road since she'd left. Reaching Denver had been straightforward enough, traveling the broad superhighways. Finding this tiny, deserted cabin, up in the stark mountainous passes was another matter altogether. Particularly when the sky had darkened into a premature black, and the rain that was just starting had a bite to it that didn't augur well for her bald summer tires.

She heard an ominous clacking sound, and she sat back, shaking herself out of her momentary torpor. Self-pity had its place in this life, but that place was very small. She'd done her best, and failed. Now the smartest thing she could do would be to get back up that narrow, twisting road and drive the hell out of the mountains.

Elkmate, Colorado was in the middle of nowhere. No towns, no motels, hardly even a gas station to enliven the mountainous region. She started the car, backing around with more speed than care, and felt the first initial slipping.

Except for her years at an East Coast college, when she hadn't even owned a car, Silver had lived her entire life in California. She had never driven through even a mild case of flurries. She looked at the wet, white stuff coming out of the early-afternoon sky, and felt a fear deep in the pit of her stomach, something that made Rafe McGinnis, her mother and even *Black Canyon* pale in comparison.

"I have a bad feeling about this," she said out loud, quoting a line used in almost every action movie since talkies began. Her only answer was the clicking sound of the freezing rain as it bounced against her windshield.

RAFE FIGURED he had plenty of time. After all, it took a certain amount of time to get from the West Coast of California to the western slopes of Colorado, and she'd have to stop along the way. He'd beaten her by taking the airplane—he could take his time before he went after Maven's cabin. Bernie's directions had been very precise, almost suspiciously so for a woman who could still manage to get lost on Hollywood Boulevard. She was hiding something, he was sure of it. But he couldn't begin to imagine what.

He slept late the next morning, in no particular hurry to do a thing. He busied himself splitting firewood and carrying some in, he drank a quart of black coffee that wasn't any particular brew, he ate steak and eggs and listened to country music on the radio and read old Louis L'Amour Westerns that some visitor had left behind.

It wasn't as if the cabin had been empty all this time. He'd always told himself he was a practical man, without an ounce of sentiment. The cabin had been available for anyone who'd asked. Sam had been out here several times, so had various friends and business associates. He'd justified its upkeep by offering it to anyone who needed a break from L.A. Some of Mack Movies' most lucrative films had been written in that little cabin. Also, some of the worst.

The air turned sharply colder, a mixed blessing. After twelve years Rafe had grown a little weary of California's endless sunshine, and the nip in the air made his blood race. On the other hand, when he strode back into the cabin with an armload of wood, the country radio station was talking about snow, sleet and freezing rain, all combined in one big storm.

For a moment his relief was overwhelming. He didn't have to go anywhere, do anything. The place was well stocked with food, coffee and whiskey, he had a telephone and a fax and a computer, enough Westerns so that he could move on to Tony Hillerman when Louis L'Amour lost his charm.

But he didn't have Silver. She was heading into those mountains, and he was willing to bet half the profits of *Cop for a Day* that she didn't know how to drive in snow. He tried to remember the car she'd driven off in, but all that he could bring back was something tinny, imported and old. She probably didn't even have snow tires.

She probably wouldn't make it past Denver tonight, if she even got that far. She'd probably wake up tomorrow morning to find herself snowed in, and be cursing a blue streak. She'd guess that he'd come after her. He'd never made the mistake of underestimating her intelligence, and he hoped she'd do the same.

He glanced out at the darkening sky, as old memories flooded him. If he'd paid attention, he wouldn't have needed the radio to tell him what he already knew. If he had to go anywhere, do anything in the next twenty-four hours, he'd better do it now. In a little while the road would be impassable.

It hadn't taken much to find out where Maven had once lived. His plan was simple enough—head out there, post the Xerox copy of his death certificate that Bernie had faxed him on the door, and leave directions back to his place. It was up to Silver what she wanted to do when she finally made it there.

But it had been more than twenty years since he'd been in Colorado, and he underestimated the severity of the storm. He was just heading down the winding gravel road to Maven's abandoned cabin when the sleet started.

He cursed, slamming the truck into neutral as he considered his options. The cabin was another mile down the narrow trail—even with four-wheel drive and good conditions the going would be slow and treacherous. With that nasty stuff coming out of the sky, there would be no telling how long it might take. The wiser thing to do would be to turn around now, before things got too bad. Storms could be treacherous this time of year, and there were some things you never forgot, no matter how long you'd been away.

He shifted in reverse, about to turn the pickup, when he saw the lights halfway down the narrow road. For a moment he didn't move. And then he began to curse, slowly.

There were headlights through the deepening gloom. And they weren't coming any closer. As a matter of fact, they were at a crazy angle, and he squinted through the darkness, knowing with both resignation and a reluctant joy that it could only be Silver.

He slammed the truck back into first and started down the path, slowly, the four-wheel drive kicking in. He could see the sleet splatting against the window, and unwillingly he remem-

bered the night he was eleven years old and his father had gone
out on the snowplow. It had started like this.

He hadn't had any choice in the matter, he'd told Rafe's
mother when she'd protested. Times were hard; he was hired
to plow the roads up over Red Mountain Pass, and he couldn't
just decide not to if he didn't like the looks of the weather.
He'd plowed it a hundred times or more each winter—he'd
make it over this time as well.

But he hadn't. He remembered his mother screaming when
they'd told her. He remembered being told that he was the man
of the family—it was up to him to take care of his mother.

They were right about one thing. He'd been a man from that
day forward, his childhood wiped out by a winter storm. But
they'd been wrong about his pretty, fragile, weak mother. He
couldn't take care of her, stop her from destroying herself. No
one could.

He was halfway down the narrow road when he saw Silver,
and suddenly he knew the meaning of that stupid phrase about
someone's blood running cold. Her car was hanging over the
ledge, and all it would take was one strong gust of wind to
push it over. At first he thought she'd had enough sense to get
out and away from danger—there was no sign of her in the
front seat.

And then he saw her, struggling to open the back door that
was balanced up high, and a moment later he saw her try to
crawl up in there.

He didn't remember stopping the truck, opening the door
and running for her. He didn't waste time calling her—if he
startled her and she jerked around it could be enough to send
her car hurtling over the cliff. Instead he sprinted across the
icy road, skidding in his leather boots, catching her legs as she
dived inside the car, hauling her out roughly, pulling her so
that she toppled over onto him just as the car lost its purchase
with a hideous grinding noise and disappeared over the edge.

For a moment neither of them moved. He lay on his back
in the ice and mud, with her on top of him, and her face was
white with shock and surprise. He wanted to reach up and hold

her tight, to press her head against his shoulder and keep her there, safe.

But of course he couldn't. He was already prepared for her rage when she shoved against him, hard, vaulting to her feet. The effect was somewhat ruined by the gathering slipperiness, and it took everything she had to keep from tumbling back down on him.

He moved more slowly, already used to the treacherous surface. "Were you trying to kill yourself?" He didn't shout, much as he wanted to, to scream out the rage and terror that had swamped him.

His bitten-off words had just as powerful an effect on her. She flinched, but stood her ground. "Do you realize what just happened?" she demanded. "That was everything, everything I owned! If you hadn't grabbed me I could have gotten my clothes..."

"If I hadn't grabbed you you'd be lying at the bottom of that crevasse, and you wouldn't be worried about clothes. You haven't got the sense God gave little green apples. How the hell did you get your car stuck up there anyway?"

"It's slippery!" she shrieked back at him in the rising wind.

"I know it is. And you should know better than to be out in this kind of weather. You shouldn't have come here at all— you belong in California, with palm trees and sunshine and your safe little life..."

"My life hasn't been safe since I met you," she said bitterly. "I should have known you'd follow me here. You've wasted your time—D. Maven is long gone."

"I know that. He died in 1973."

She just stared at him, and he knew she wanted to hit him. "How do you know that?" Her voice was low, bitter.

"I've got connections you can't even begin to imagine."

"I'm sure you do. So if he's dead, what are you doing out here?"

"Looking for you."

That stopped her. She still wanted to hit him, he could see it quite clearly in her eyes. She was also beginning to look like a drowned rat. She wasn't dressed for this weather—the cotton sweater was beaded with ice, plastering itself to her tall body, and her lower lip was beginning to tremble.

"Well," she said in a tight voice, probably to keep the shivers from it, "you found me. Now you can go back to where you came from."

He didn't move. "Are you telling me to leave you here? Alone, without a car, in this weather?"

"It's your fault my car's gone," she said stubbornly. "And I'm not going anywhere with you."

He took a deep, calming breath. For all his rage, for all his panic at the sight of her, balanced on the precipice, he felt suddenly, oddly happy. The past twenty-four hours in Colorado had been an unexpectedly peaceful blessing, the calm before the storm. Now that she was here, he was ready for anything but peace. He was ready for her. He was ready for their battles to begin again. And this time it wasn't going to end in a standoff.

"The longer we stand here and discuss it," he said evenly, "the worse the roads will get. I've got four-wheel drive and studded tires, but I don't think the truck comes with chains, and you sure as hell aren't dressed for walking. Now act like an adult for a change and get in the damned pickup."

Her eyes narrowed. "Go to hell," she said primly, and turned away from him, obviously planning on walking back to Maven's derelict cabin.

For just a fraction of a moment he considered letting her go. He had no idea what kind of condition Maven's cabin was in, but it probably still contained a roof and a fireplace. She wouldn't freeze to death, and it might teach her a lesson.

On the other hand, he had no intention of being without her for another minute. He didn't want to examine why. He just knew he wasn't going to let her go.

She slipped on the gravel road, landing on her backside with an inelegant thump. He was wise enough not to laugh, simply coming up behind her, hauling her to her feet.

She tried to yank her arm free. She was looking colder, more miserable than ever, and he wasn't too happy himself. The freezing rain had slid beneath the shearling collar of his coat, his hair was matted with ice crystals, and his hands were freezing.

"I told you, I'm not going with you," she said fiercely, tugging at his arm.

It had never come to a test of physical strength before. He'd always had the ability to cajole a woman into doing what he wanted. But this woman couldn't be cajoled, she was stubborn, furious and too damned smart. He simply hauled her up, tossing her far-from-petite body over his shoulder, and started up the slippery slope to where he'd left the pickup.

She fought him, of course. It was close to pitch-black, the sleet was coming down in earnest, and he felt a moment of real concern. "Hold still," he said, smacking her across her blue-jeaned bottom.

Her shock was so intense that she stopped fighting, rigid with outraged dignity as he battled his way up the slope, fighting for every inch. He opened the passenger door and dropped her inside, half expecting her to scramble back out again.

"Stay put!" he thundered, as she started to move.

She looked up at him, and her eyes were huge in her pale, drenched face.

"I despise you," she said.

He moved around to the driver's seat, climbed in and fastened his seat belt. "I'm sure you do," he said wearily. "Just sit back and shut up while I get us out of here, and once we get to my place you can tell me all about it in excruciating detail."

"Your place? I'm not going anywhere with you..." She reached for the door, but he simply caught her arm and slammed her back against the seat.

"I will tie you up," he said simply. "If you don't stop arguing and fighting with me, I'll strap you to the front fender like a dead deer and drive you back that way."

She looked at him for one long, startled moment, and he

could see that she almost believed him. If he wasn't so concerned about the weather he would have been amused.

As it was, he nodded. "That's better," he said. "Now let's get the hell out of here."

Chapter Twelve

At least the cramped confines of the pickup truck were warm. Silver hunched down in the seat, as far away from Rafe's tall body as she could, as she fastened the seat belt around her with shaking fingers. It was only October, for God's sake! How could they have an ice storm in October?

The heat blasted her soaked running shoes, and she could feel the prickly pain as the numbness began to recede. She tucked her hands in her armpits, shivering as the ice on her lightweight clothing began to melt in shivery droplets, soaking through to her skin. She spared a glance over at Rafe, then looked away with nervous haste. A part of her still wanted to fight, wanted to jump down from the pickup truck and stalk off in icy dignity.

Icy was the operative word here, she reminded herself. Absurd as the thought might be, she might not survive out here on her own, in weather like this. It was even remotely possible that he'd saved her life, hauling her out of her Toyota before it went over the precipice. She didn't want to think about that, either. If he'd saved her, then she'd owe him something. And there was only one thing he really wanted, only one way she could repay her debt.

She cast another brief, curious glance at him. He looked very different from the Hollywood mogul, different and yet the same. The rough denim and suede suited him, more than the Armani suits and custom T-shirts. His long hair was still tied back, and she could see the sparkle of melting ice in its dark strands. He'd stripped off his gloves, and she stared at his hands on the big steering wheel as he negotiated his way up the icy slope. She'd never noticed them before, how large and strong and capable-looking they were. The hands of a man who could do things, take care of things. Not the hands of a desk-bound dilettante.

And then she remembered the work-roughened texture of those hands, touching her breasts beneath the warm water of his swimming pool, and she shuddered.

"The heat's up full blast," he said, not looking her way as he concentrated on the driving. "Do you want my coat?"

"No, thank you," she replied in a small voice.

"You'll warm up soon enough," he said, gunning the motor as the truck went up and over the first rise. "Just keep thinking about how angry you are at me and you'll be burning up."

"I'm not likely to forget," she said, pulling her eyes away from his hands as she huddled closer to the door.

"And make sure the door's locked. I don't want you falling out into the night if we end up in a ditch."

"End up in a ditch?" she echoed. "I thought you were Mr. Cowboy, able to leap icy mountain ridges in a single bound?"

"You want to shut your mouth and let me concentrate?" he asked in a deceptively mild tone of voice. "Or do you want me to do something about it?"

Silver shut up. The white, wet stuff coming out of the sky absolutely terrified her, and while goading Rafe might take some of the edge off her panic, it might also prove dangerously distracting to the man who was supposed to get her out of there. The snow was hurtling itself toward the windshield in a mad suicide dash, and Silver leaned back, closing her eyes and swallowing the small, frightened moan that threatened to bubble up.

She lost track of time. It seemed endless, the truck moving at a maddeningly careful pace through the storm. She could feel the wheels slide on the slick surface, feel the consummate skill in Rafe's deft hands as he turned into the skid then carefully drove out of it. She'd read about that when she'd learned to drive, but the theory seemed to have no practical application. How the hell could one turn into a skid on an icy, mountaintop road?

It seemed like hours later when Rafe let the pickup drift to a halt. Silver lifted her head, suddenly hopeful. "We're here?" she asked, no longer caring that she was heading into enemy territory. She only wanted to get out of this vehicle of torture, out of the ice storm and under a roof.

"Not exactly," he said, his voice dry. "We've got one more stretch, and the road's too icy. I'm going to need your help."

She swallowed her first instinct to tell him to go to hell. Her safety depended on him, whether she liked it or not. Arguing would simply prolong it. "What do you want me to do?" she asked.

"Leave the truck in neutral," he said, reaching for his gloves, "and steer. I'm getting out to push."

"Why?" She was aghast.

"Because the ice is so bad the tires can't get any grip on the road. I'm going to nudge the car in the right direction, you simply need to steer."

"And if I start going over a cliff? Are the brakes going to work?"

"No brakes," he said. "Fortunately there are no cliffs on this stretch of road, either. The worst that will happen is you'll end up against a stand of fir trees, and you won't be going fast enough to cause much damage. Just take it slowly and carefully, don't jerk the wheel, and we should be fine."

She wanted to refuse. But he was already climbing out into the swirling storm, and she knew that there wasn't any choice. He wouldn't get out into that kind of weather unless he had to, no matter how much he wanted to terrify her. She slid across the bench seat, her fingers numb with terror, and grabbed hold of the steering wheel.

The graceful, silent glide of the truck on the surface of the ice sent a knot of fire through her stomach. She stared straight ahead, ignoring the ice that pelted in the open window as she steered the truck down the almost invisible road.

It went on forever. Her face was stinging from the icy snow, but she was too frightened to brush it away. She could only try to concentrate on steering the damned truck.

She heard Rafe shout something. Instinctively she touched the brakes, only to find the truck hurtling out of control, faster and faster, and she knew she was going to die. And then a moment later it came to a stop, slamming up against something solid.

She didn't move. The truck was still running, sending wafts of heat around her face, the icy pellets were still falling, raining in the open window.

And then Rafe opened the door, reached in and turned off the truck and the lights, plunging them into a swirl of wintry darkness. "We're here," he said.

She made a small, gulping noise as she swallowed her sob of relief. "About time," she managed in a shaky voice, trying to unfasten the seat belt. For some reason her fingers didn't work.

She felt his hands cover hers, undoing the belt, and then he pulled her out of the cab, those strong, hard hands of his surprisingly gentle. "We've got a few yards to go," he said, and his voice was emotionless. "You want me to carry you?"

"Over my dead body." She had some life left in her after all. She took a step, and for a moment her knees buckled beneath her. He caught her as she fell, but she pushed him away, using all her remaining resources to stand upright. "Lead on, MacDuff."

His idea of a few yards to go was extremely optimistic. It had to be another five minutes before the lights loomed up out of the darkness, five minutes of slogging through ankle-deep snow as the chill sank deeper and deeper beneath her skin. And then a door opened, and light and heat poured out, and she stumbled inside into safety.

"The bathroom's up the stairs to the right," Rafe said, stripping off his ice-covered coat and shaking his long hair loose. "Turn on the shower as hot as you can stand it and don't come out until you've thawed."

She moved slowly, too frozen to argue with his high-handed orders. "What about you?" she paused to ask halfway up the rough-hewn pine stairs. "You must be frozen, too."

He looked up at her, and he looked big, larger than life, and completely at home in the rustic surroundings. "Are you asking me to join you in the shower?"

"No."

"I have two bathrooms, and enough hot water for both of us. Get out of those frozen clothes."

"I'm going," she said, her teeth chattering as she continued her slow, torturous climb upward. "I don't suppose you have any suggestions as to what I can put on once I get thawed."

"Use your imagination." He had already stripped off his heavy wool sweater, and he was ripping open the snaps on his denim shirt. The fireplace behind him was huge, blazing, and even from halfway across the room she could feel the heat.

He was reaching for his belt buckle, oblivious to her watchful eyes. Or perhaps not oblivious at all. She turned and ran.

The water hurt. It made her teeth ache, her bones throb, her skin scream in pain. She leaned against the tiled wall and let the streams of water sluice down over her, as slowly, inexorably, life and awareness flooded back through her.

She didn't want to leave the cocoon of water. She didn't want to have to find something to wear, to go down and face Rafe McGinnis, knowing she was trapped somewhere out in the middle of nowhere, in the midst of a howling blizzard, with nowhere to run.

And part of her wanted to run, wanted to run quite badly. She wouldn't, of course. She was tougher than that. She just needed a few minutes to pull herself together.

But there was a limit to how long she could stay in the shower. The sooner she emerged and faced him, the sooner she'd realize she was more than capable of standing up to him.

The bathroom was flooded with steam when she finally emerged from the shower. The towels were huge and thick, and wrapping one around her tall body provided more coverage than she would have dared hope for. When she stepped into the balconied hallway she could still hear the sound of the other shower somewhere at the other end of the cabin, and she knew that for the moment, at least, she was safe.

There were two bedrooms upstairs, a smaller, utilitarian guest room with empty closets and drawers. And the master bedroom, with ice-coated skylights, a rough-hewn pine bed the size of Denver, and Rafe's clothes in the closet.

She knew a moment's pang of sorrow when she thought of her expensive new clothes lying at the bottom of some ravine, and then she forgot about it. The longer she dithered, thinking about something that couldn't be changed, the greater the chance of Rafe finishing his own shower and coming upstairs, looking for clothes for himself. It was going to take all the self-control she possessed to keep things on a professional basis. Standing in his bedroom wearing nothing but a towel wasn't the way to start.

His clothes fit surprisingly well. He was lean, but then, so was she. A little broader in the hips, a little narrower in the waist, of course, but close enough. She rolled up the hem of the jeans and ended up with a T-shirt and another heavy denim work shirt, sleeves rolled up, length reaching to her hips despite the fact that she was tall. The more layers she had, the more protected she felt, and she almost started hunting for a thick wool sweater when she realized that, wonder of wonders, she was warm.

There was still no sound from Rafe. Shoving her damp hair behind her ears, she headed back down the wide pine staircase, ignoring the huge bed and the tartan flannel-covered duvet. She hadn't seen a matching duvet in the guest room. Was she going to have to make do with blankets on such a cold, comfortless night?

He was in the kitchen, waiting for her. He leaned back against the wooden counter, surveying her, his hands cupped around a mug of coffee that smelled very close to heaven.

"You look good in my clothes," he said, and his voice wasn't much more than a low rasp.

She could have said the same thing for him, but she didn't,

moving past him and reaching for the second mug of coffee that sat waiting by the restaurant-style stove. He was wearing jeans and a black T-shirt, and for once he hadn't tied back his long hair. It hung around his face, damp, curling slightly, and she wanted to tell him he looked absurd. But she couldn't. He looked very, very sexy.

She took a deep swallow of her black coffee, then choked when the alcohol hit her. "It's half whiskey," Rafe said. "I figured you needed it."

"Not on an empty stomach I don't." She took another sip anyway, letting the liquid burn its way down, warming her from the inside out.

"I'll cook something for you. We have steak, steak, and more steak."

"You'll cook?" she echoed, astonished.

"You have no idea the range of my talents," Rafe murmured, and she ignored the wicked glint in his eyes. "Why don't you go sit by the fire and I'll bring you something."

She wanted to protest. The idea of the illustrious Rafe McGinnis cooking for her was too unbelievable, but she couldn't bring herself to offer to do the cooking for him. For one thing she couldn't cook, even if he could. For another, she hadn't eaten since the early morning, hadn't slept more than a few hours in the last seventy-two, and for the most important reason, she wanted to get away from him. The kitchen was small, hot, enclosed, and he was too big. Too warm. Too tempting.

Without a word she headed into the huge living room, sinking onto the sofa, her half-drunk coffee in her hand. She put her bare feet up on the Indian-style fabric and stared around her, wondering what was causing the weird sensation just below her heart. Telling herself it was heartburn, a reaction to strong coffee and straight whiskey. Knowing it was something more.

There were no curtains on the windows, and she could see the swirl of snow and freezing rain in the darkness, hear the constant, ominous clicking sound as the precipitation beat down on the snug cabin. The fireplace was huge, taking up a complete wall, and the fire burning brightly was probably heating the whole house. The furniture was simple, rustic, surprisingly comfortable. The rugs were old and Indian, the paintings straightforward and filled with glowing colors. She wanted to feel contempt for the place, for a Hollywood producer's version of mountain chic. Instead she felt at peace.

"I hate Colorado," she announced defiantly.

"Do you?" He appeared in the kitchen door, taking her coffee mug away and refilling it. Refilling it with whiskey as well as coffee. "The weather's not always this bad."

"Then why don't you spend more time here?"

"I have my reasons." He didn't sound defensive, simply matter-of-fact. "I grew up here."

She snuggled down in the sofa, wiggling her toes. "It's hard to believe. Where did you grow up—in Denver?"

"No, I grew up here. In this cabin. It was a little simpler then. No running water, no electricity. It does happen to have one of the most spectacular views on earth, but you can't see much in weather like this."

"Is that why your parents lived here? The view?"

He shook his head. "I doubt they even noticed. They lived here because they were too poor to live anywhere else. They would have moved to Denver in a shot. Hell, they would have moved to Australia if they'd had the chance."

"Where did they end up? Some retirement home in Florida like everyone else?" She took another deep swallow of the lethal coffee. She was beginning to like the way it burned.

"They ended up dead."

The warmth left her. This was a man who'd done everything he could to demoralize her. There was no reason why she should suddenly feel distraught.

But this was a man who'd rescued her, who'd just saved her life—a man she was foolish enough to believe was possibly just a little more vulnerable than he seemed. "I'm sorry," she said, knowing it sounded inadequate.

He didn't seem to notice. "My father died on a night like

this one," he said flatly. "The only job he could get was driving a snowplow for the road crew. He went off a mountain pass during an ice storm when I was eleven." He took a drink of his own coffee.

"What happened to your mother? Did she take you away from here?" She didn't know why she was asking. She half expected him to slap her down verbally, but he seemed oddly ready to talk.

"No, she left on her own. She drank herself to death, slowly, politely, not causing any fuss. I didn't leave here till my aunt and uncle caught up with me when I was fourteen and took me to live in Ohio." The way his voice curled around the name of that state made it sound like the worst profanity on earth.

"And as soon as you could you came back?"

"Nope. This is the first time I've been here since I was fourteen," he said, pushing away from the door. "How do you like your steak? Rare or rarer?"

"I don't eat red meat."

"You do tonight, sweetheart. Drink your coffee."

They ate their dinner in almost total silence, broken only by the hiss and crackle of the fire, the sound of the elements beating against the cabin. The steak was rare, the salad simple, and despite the fact that she hadn't eaten much at all in the past twenty-four hours, she could barely manage to eat half of the generous portion he'd served her.

He ate his own without the slightest bit of hesitation, and as she watched his strong white teeth tear into the rare meat, she had a sudden, unsettling feeling in the pit of her stomach. He was a carnivore, and she tended toward passive vegetarianism. Just how far apart could two people possibly be?

Without a word he cleared the dishes, disappearing into the kitchen, and she watched him go. Just when she thought she had a handle on who and what Rafael McGinnis was, just when her defenses were solidly in place, he'd say or do something that threw all her preconceived notions awry.

She could picture him so vividly, despite the matter-of-fact starkness of his words as he'd told her of his past. He would have been tall as a fourteen-year-old, and astonishingly self-reliant, living alone out here, with none of the conveniences everyone took for granted. His aunt and uncle might have thought he was half-savage. She knew without a doubt that he had been cool, self-contained, probably faintly contemptuous of soft suburban living. It couldn't have been an easy adjustment.

She drained her after-dinner mug of laced coffee and decided she wanted more. She rose from the sofa on slightly unsteady feet and trailed him out to the kitchen. "Did you get along with your aunt and uncle?" she asked, reaching for the pot of coffee.

She half expected him to snub her. But he seemed curiously open as he rinsed the dishes in the copper sink. "Nope. I kept running away." He reached over and poured a generous helping of whiskey into her mug. "They finally put me in foster care, and I discovered what restrictions were really like. I decided I didn't like having anyone tell me what to do, so I got a scholarship to the best college I could find, and turned my back on my past."

"Including this place," she said. "So why are you here now? Why do you still own it?"

"I didn't always. I bought it back when I made my first substantial amount of money. I must be sentimental."

"You haven't got a sentimental bone in your body."

His smile was small, mocking. "Maybe not. Maybe I just got tired of hunters trashing this place. Maybe I like to control everyone."

"There's no maybe about that," she said, half to herself.

He turned to look at her, and his eyes were cool, unreadable. "You want to have dessert before or after?" he asked.

"Before or after what?"

"We make love."

She just stared at him. She hadn't drunk that much whiskey, had she? "I beg your pardon?"

He leaned back against the counter. "We're going to, you know. You can play all the games you want, try to convince yourself and me you're unwilling, but sooner or later we're going to end up upstairs in that big bed. Things would be a lot simpler if we just accepted that fact.''

"What if I say no?"

"You'll change your mind," he said flatly.

"Or you'll change it for me?" she asked, feeling a cold dread in the pit of her stomach, warring with the hot lick of desire that spread through her belly.

He didn't say a word. He didn't have to.

"All right," she said abruptly, setting her coffee down and levering herself up on the broad counter.

The smugness vanished. "All right?" he echoed.

"I'm sick and tired of fighting with you. I don't think you're going to leave me alone until you get me in bed. I can't imagine why you'd want to—I'm hardly in your league. You only take the cream of the crop. I'm a little long on brains and short on drop-dead gorgeousness for you, but maybe you're getting bored with beauty. Or maybe you just figure that's part of how you're going to control me. That once you get me in bed I'll be so grateful for your monumental sexual prowess that I'll give you anything, including the rights to *Black Canyon,* and then bow humbly out of the picture.''

"You do have a mouth on you," he said faintly.

"So go ahead," she said, leaning back against the open shelving. "Get it over with, and then we can get back to negotiating on an even footage.''

"That's a step in the right direction," he said, not moving. "A couple of days ago you wouldn't have even admitted the word negotiation was part of your vocabulary.''

He was right, it was a major slip on her part. Particularly since she had no intention of negotiating any of the rights away.

"The only negotiating I'm interested in is getting you to leave me alone.''

"What if I promise to do that in return for *Black Canyon?*" he asked, his voice cool and distant.

She didn't even flinch. It was nothing more than she expected from him—she told herself she never had any delusions as to what he was really after. If only she didn't have such an irrational, overwhelming response to him.

"I'd consider it," she said. Wondering if she meant it.

He moved then, pushing himself away from the opposite counter, crossing the tiny area with a pantherlike grace. He came up to her, between her legs, not touching her, and his mouth was level with hers.

"The problem is," he said in a low, beguiling voice, "that I want you both. And I don't feel like settling for half."

She fought the treacherous pleasure that swept through her. "For how long?"

"I want *Black Canyon* forever. I have no idea how long I'll want you. Do you expect me to come up with a pre-coital agreement?"

She flinched. "I expect you to leave me alone."

"Not in this lifetime, Silver," he said under his breath.

He still didn't touch her. The tension in the kitchen was at fever pitch. He watched her out of still, unblinking eyes and she knew what it was like to be mesmerized.

She was a fighter, not a weak, cowering victim. "All right," she said, managing to keep her voice brisk. "Let's get it over with." And reaching up, she began to unbutton her shirt.

Chapter Thirteen

Rafe stood there, his hands braced on the counter, watching her as she calmly unfastened the denim shirt. She'd looked so damned cute when she'd come downstairs, dressed in his clothes, that he'd been half tempted to tell her so. And half tempted to rip those clothes off her.

In the end he'd done nothing, hoping to prolong the confrontation. He'd meant it when he told her they'd end up in bed together—he'd had no doubt of that whatsoever. And he knew from the faint, panicked expression in her eyes that she knew it, too. And wanted it just as much as he did.

The problem was, she just as strongly resisted it. For every ounce of desire that suffused her delectable body, there was an equal pull away from him. There was no way he could overpower her, wipe out her distrust when, in fact, it was very well founded. He could only keep pushing, and wait for the time when she was ready to give in to what they both wanted.

She finished with the last button and shrugged out of the shirt, tossing it on the wide pine floor. She was wearing one of his T-shirts, but obviously his pilfered wardrobe hadn't contained anything as utilitarian as a bra. He waited to see whether she'd pull the shirt over her head.

Instead she reached down to the jeans. She'd taken a hand-tooled leather belt and cinched it tightly around her waist—it gave her something else to dispose of before she got to the more interesting parts.

"I hope you're enjoying this," she said in a bored tone of voice, sliding the belt out of the loops and tossing it onto the floor.

"Not yet, but I expect it's about to get a lot more interesting. Do you think you could manage to put a little more enthusiasm into it?" He reached for his mug of coffee, draining it. It was cold, more whiskey than anything else, but it gave him something to do with his hands, something to keep him from touching her. Because he wanted to touch her, wanted to quite badly. And she wasn't ready.

"I'm not feeling enthusiastic," she said, unsnapping the jeans. "I'm feeling coerced."

"I'm not touching you."

Her eyes met his for a brief, heated moment. "No," she agreed, "you're not. But you're going to."

He watched as she slid down the zipper. "Yes, I'm going to," he said, his voice suddenly husky.

He could see the pale peach of his custom-made silk shorts beneath the open zipper. His fingers dug into the counter, and sweat beaded on his forehead. For the first time he had serious doubts as to who would emerge the victor in this little encounter. She was disrobing with an elegant disdain, seemingly unaffected by the sweep of desire that ran between the two of them. And he was so turned on he could barely stand.

And then he realized her blasé attitude was all a lie. Her hands were trembling as she fumbled with the jeans, her breath was coming just a trace more rapidly than it needed to, as if she'd just climbed a steep flight of stairs, and in the steamy hot kitchen her nipples were hard.

His mouth curved in a slow, triumphant smile as he leaned closer, almost touching her. "Are you going to take off the rest of your clothes?" he asked. "Or am I going to have to do it for you?"

She swallowed, reaching blindly for her coffee mug and bringing it to her lips.

He took it out of her hands. "You've had enough whiskey for now," he said, setting it on the counter beside him. "I don't want you to have the excuse of being too drunk to know what you were doing. I don't want you to have any excuses. I want you to know what you're doing. I want your eyes to be wide open, watching me, when I come inside you.''

She made a tiny, shocked sound, staring at him.

''You aren't used to having men talk to you like that, are you?'' he continued. ''They're usually polite and deferential. That's what you want, isn't it? Some tame yuppie you can ride herd on. And instead you wind up with me. I told you I was more than you can handle.''

She reached for her jeans, struggling to zip them up again, but her hands were shaking too hard. ''I'm going upstairs to bed,'' she said. ''Alone. I've changed my mind.''

He put his hands on top of hers, holding them still, and he could feel the heat of her body, the heat of her anger, the heat of her passion. ''Too late, Silver. Take off the damned T-shirt. Before I rip it off.''

She sat very still, unmoving, her eyes wide and waiting. She looked as if she expected him to hurt her. He wondered briefly if she'd been hurt before. And then he realized that it wasn't so much that she expected the worst from all men. She simply expected the worst from him.

He put his hands up, to the neck band of her T-shirt, and he watched her brace herself. Instead he slid his hand up the side of her neck, his thumb resting on her rapid pulse, as he drew her toward him, drew her unresisting face toward his mouth.

She tasted sweet, amazingly so. Her mouth was parted in surprise beneath his, and she tasted like whiskey and coffee. She was too bemused to close her mouth, and he took advantage of it, pushing his tongue inside, kissing her with a sweeping thoroughness that was overwhelming without being the slightest bit threatening.

He lifted his head a few inches to look down at her. Her eyes were wide and bright and confused. ''What are you doing?''

He smiled. It was entirely without mockery, and she reacted with wonder. He didn't feel mocking, or cynical. Her mouth was damp from his, soft and vulnerable, and he knew now how he was going to get her. Not with overpowering her. Not with dirty tricks or threats or lying promises. He was going to get her to go upstairs with him, willingly, by simply kissing her.

He did it again, partly because he couldn't believe how wonderful it had been, partly because he wanted to do it again. It was even better than the first time. He had never been particularly fond of kissing. He used it as a means to an end, a way to get a woman he wanted to want him back. He'd never had any particular affection for the practice—it was merely a skill that led to other, more intense pleasures.

But he found he liked kissing her, liked it very much indeed. He tugged her closer, so that the juncture of her thighs was resting at his belly, and he could feel the open zipper of the jeans. And he wished he could get her to unfasten his jeans, too. She was getting more enthusiastic, her hands resting on his shoulders, fingers digging in lightly, and he could feel the tension running through her.

He put his arms around her, pulling her close against him, and she came willingly enough, sinking against his chest with a sigh. It was easy enough to slip his hands under the loose T-shirt, easy enough to pull it up and over her head in one swift move, baring her breasts to him.

She tried to pull away, to cross her arms in front of her, but he stopped her, simply by catching her wrists and holding them. Watching her out of hooded eyes he said softly, "Do you have the faintest idea how much I want you?"

Now was her chance, and he knew it. She could bargain, offer him her body in return for *Black Canyon,* and in his current frame of mind he'd probably agree. He waited, holding her wrists, waiting for her to say the words that would give him permission to finish what they'd started, waiting for the words that would wipe out any last trace of compunction on his part.

She opened her mouth, but the expected words never came out. "You have me," she said. "I can't fight you anymore."

And there was a despairing, rueful expression in her eyes, and she no longer pulled against his hands.

He placed her arms around his waist, flattening her breasts against his chest, and he wished he'd had the sense to tear off his own clothes. He wanted, needed to feel her flesh against his, the heated silk of her skin caressing his. "Come upstairs with me," he whispered against her mouth. "Come upstairs and I'll give you…"

She turned her head deliberately, silencing him. Not allowing him to make the offer that he might rescind or regret, an offer that would turn the next few hours into a transaction. She slid her hands up under his denim shirt, against his skin, and the first willing caress made him shiver. He wanted her with an intensity he'd never felt before.

But something wasn't right.

He pulled away from her, out of her arms, out of her reach, leaning down and picking up her discarded T-shirt and tossing it at her.

She caught it instinctively, and the dazed, aroused expression on her face faded, as she pulled it back over her head. He watched her breasts disappear with a feeling of chagrin, and he wondered whether he had finally snapped.

"Go to bed," he said roughly, moving away from her.

He could sense her confusion. She slid off the counter, fastening his jeans around her. "I see," she said flatly.

He turned to look at her, keeping his face deliberately blank. "What do you see?"

"That you got what you wanted. Me, vulnerable, willing to do just about anything you wanted. Just to the point where I would have sold my birthright, and then you dumped me. Very effective. You were able to get me so turned on that I would have denied you nothing, all the while you were simply manipulating me. You told me you had still more dirty tricks up your sleeve, and I didn't believe you."

"You think that's why I stopped?"

"Isn't it? You never really wanted me, you merely wanted to show me the kind of power you held…"

He moved across the room so quickly she didn't have time to duck, grabbing her wrist and bringing her hand against his groin. "You think I don't want you? I hate to explain this to you, lady, but what you've got beneath your hand means that I want you quite badly. I just have no intention of taking you."

She tried to pull away from him, but he held her tightly, even though the pressure of her fingers against his erection was driving him crazy with desire. "Why not?"

"Because I'm not interested in a virgin sacrifice. You've given yourself permission to sleep with me, but you've told yourself you're doing it for the sake of *Black Canyon*. That's a pile of crap, lady, and you'd know it if you really thought about it. I want you in my bed, but I don't want that damned movie there, too."

"Then give it up," she said fiercely. "You've got a million movies to make—every screenwriter in Hollywood would work with you. Leave *Black Canyon* alone."

"And then I can have you?" he supplied the next part. He shook his head. "This is a battle, Silver, and I never, ever lose. I'm going to have you, and I'm going to have *Black Canyon*. Sleeping with me won't alter that fact, even if you think you can still be in control." He released her hand, moving away from her. "When you accept that fact, come and tell me."

"Everything has to be on your terms, is that it? You'll do me the great honor of making love to me, you'll take the only thing I've ever cared about, and you'll do it when and how you want to do it. Let me tell you something, mister," she said, moving close, in her rage forgetting how dangerous he could be, "it'll be a cold day in hell before I come to you."

He pulled her into his arms, ignoring her flailing fists. "Have you looked outside, Silver? It already is." And he kissed her, long and hard and deep, until her struggles faded, her mouth softened and a deep shuddering sigh shook her body.

His hands were gentle when they released her. He wanted to touch her, to smooth her shaggy hair away from her face, to kiss her nose, to take back the stupid ultimatum he'd issued. He should have taken her any way he could. She'd been willing, and why the hell should it matter what lies she'd told herself to come to him? He should take what she offered and run with it.

He let his hands drop to his side. He couldn't do it. Not this time. He'd slept with countless women who'd gone to bed with him for what he could do for their careers. Done it and enjoyed it, and given the women the pleasure they deserved.

For some stupid, quixotic reason he couldn't be so cold-blooded with Silver. He couldn't let her make that kind of moral bargain with herself. When she came to him, and she would, it had to be devoid of any gain. She had to come to him knowing she was risking everything. And she had to come anyway.

She walked out of the kitchen without looking back, heading up the wide staircase with all the dignity of a queen. He watched her go, then turned back to the cold coffee and the bottle of whiskey. It was going to be a long, long night.

THE BED WAS COLD. Silver piled every wool blanket she could find on it, so that her limbs felt weighted down, but she was still shivering.

Part of the problem was the fact that she'd locked and barred her door, dragging a heavy maple dresser in front of it just in case he changed his mind and decided to honor her with his sexual attentions. There were no registers in her room—the heat from downstairs stopped when it came to her locked door, and the temperature in the room was dropping rapidly.

His oversize T-shirt didn't provide much extra warmth, and she'd tried to discard it, not wanting to accept even that much from him. But lying naked in a bed across the hall from him brought its own disturbances, and even a T-shirt that had once covered his body was some protection.

She wished she could sleep. She hadn't had more than a few hours rest in recent memory, and she was bone-weary. But the cold, and her anger, kept the adrenaline pumping her system, so that she lay in that narrow bed, thrashing around, searching in vain for comfort and warmth.

Why had he done that to her? Kissed her until she was half-crazy, then turned around and accused her of being willing to trade her body for him keeping his hands off *Black Canyon*. She should have punched him in the nose.

Except for the fact that he was right. She had been willing to sleep with him for the sake of the movie.

Of course, there wasn't anyone else on the face of this earth that she'd sleep with for such a reason. And the fact of the matter was, she had talked herself into it, giving herself an excuse to do something that she'd wanted to do almost since she first set eyes on him. Definitely since he'd first set his hands on her.

And now here she was, snowbound, alone, and he was making the rules. The man's ego must be colossal, if he thought she'd abide by them. Did he expect her to beg?

What did he want from her?

She slept for a while, the sound of the wet snow pelting against the windows. When she awoke she was shivering, a faint gray light filtering through the storm-coated windows.

She climbed out of bed, her body shaking so hard she could scarcely keep her teeth from chattering. She was wearing his absurd shorts and the T-shirt, and she ought to pull on more clothes if she was going to leave the safety of her room. But what good was safety if it kept you away from what you really wanted?

The hallway was bathed in heat. His door was open at the other end, and through the darkness she could see the outline of his huge bed. Could see the glow of his cigarette as he sat there, sleepless, waiting.

It was a little past dawn. For a moment she stood there, motionless, wondering whether she should turn and run back to her room, slamming and locking the door again, locking him away from her, locking her own crazy needs away.

"Come here, Silver." He said it so quietly she almost thought she imagined it. His voice was low, beguiling, and there was no way she could resist. She moved toward the room, her long bare legs moving of their own accord.

"You have more games to play?" She stopped inside the door, one last ounce of fight in her.

"No more games," he said, stubbing out the cigarette. Her eyes had grown accustomed to the dark, and she could see him quite clearly, sitting in the bed, the duvet pulled up to his waist, his chest bare. "Come to bed with me, Silver. I'll take you on any terms you're willing to offer."

She thought about it then, the terms she could dictate. And then she knew she didn't want to think about terms. She didn't want to think about right or wrong, or her career, or her father or the future. She didn't want to think about why he wanted her. She believed him when he said he did.

"No terms," she said, crossing the room and climbing up onto the high bed. "Just you and me." And she leaned forward and kissed him.

He pulled her down on top of him, wrapping his arms around her, and his mouth tasted of whiskey and cigarettes and desire. The darkness and heat were all around them, and she closed her eyes and turned off her mind, her doubts. All that mattered was the moment. The rest would take care of itself.

He was good, she had to admit that. He knew how to kiss, how to bite at her soft lips, how to use his tongue, his teeth, his whole mouth, until the act of kissing was an erotic mating that made her dizzy with longing. He rolled her onto her back, leaning over her, pressing her down into the surprisingly soft mattress, and pulled the feather-soft duvet over both of them. And she found he was naked. And she found he was aroused.

This time when he took the T-shirt off her he did it slowly, gently. She'd never considered her breasts to be particularly sensitive—to her mind they were too big, too cumbersome, simply a source of pain at certain times of the month. But Rafe showed her new dimensions. He didn't just take them into his mouth like a hungry infant. He kissed them, breathed on them, licked them, nibbled at them, until a fire of longing burned in a direct line from her breasts down to the center of her legs.

"You like that, don't you?" he whispered in the darkness. "Do you know how long I've been wanting to kiss your breasts?'' He ran his tongue over the fiercely pebbled nipple, and she arched beneath him in dizzying response. ''I want to kiss you everywhere.'' He moved his mouth away, down her flat bare stomach, to the edge of his silk shorts.

''Oh, no,'' she said, trying to move away, but his long fingers had already slid beneath the underwear, pulling it down her legs even as she squirmed.

''Oh, yes,'' he said, his hands strong and inexorable as he held her hips, his voice gentle. ''Most definitely yes.''

The touch of his mouth against her was a shock and a wonder. She still didn't want him to do it, it made her too vulnerable, too defenseless. She didn't want to accept this from him, but he was giving her no choice.

''Stop fighting me,'' he said, lifting his head and looking at her. ''This isn't a battle anymore.'' And he slid his long fingers into her, as his mouth touched her again, and she let out a muffled sob as a small convulsion hit her.

But Rafe wasn't satisfied with small convulsions. He knew how to take each one, prolong it, until they grew, meshing together until she was trembling, awash with sensation that suddenly peaked into an explosion that shocked her. Shocked her enough to try to stop it, but her body was no longer under her control.

She pushed at his shoulders, her hands slipping against his sweat-soaked skin, and she wanted to tell him to stop, she couldn't take any more, wouldn't take any more, when he loomed up over her, moving between her legs, pushing into her with one deep, hard thrust that rocked her back against the soft mattress.

She moaned, deep in her throat, but he didn't make the mistake of thinking she was in pain. She kissed him, tasting herself on his mouth, and she wrapped her body around him, knowing this was going to be fast and hard and deep, reveling in that knowledge, needing him that way, needing him any way he cared to give her.

She never thought she'd come again. Never thought that when he reached down and lifted her hips, to deepen the angle of his thrusts, that the crazy tension would keep building, building. Until she was meeting him, her hips slamming up against his, her breath sobbing in her ear, her arms wrapped tightly around his waist as she held on until suddenly he was very still, and she could feel his warmth and life filling her, and inexplicably her body dissolved once more, lost with his.

He rolled off her almost immediately, sitting up on the side of the bed, his back to her. "Damn," he said, his voice coming in breathless rasps. "Damn," he said again. "I didn't mean to do that."

Even as her body still trembled in response, the cold overtook her. She pulled the duvet over her, shivering in the cool night air. "Didn't mean to do what?" Her own voice sounded like that of a stranger, raw and strained.

He turned to look at her, and in the darkness his expression was unreadable. "Didn't mean to lose control," he said flatly. "I didn't even remember to use any protection."

She hadn't even thought of it, she who carried condoms in her purse while pursuing a life of dedicated celibacy. "Is there any particular reason you should?" she asked carefully.

She could see the ghost of a smile flit across his face. "Nothing catching. Believe it or not, I have a sense of responsibility to the women I sleep with."

"Oh, yes, those four score and twenty."

"Not exactly." He turned around and lay down beside her again, his breathing regular, his reactions now under tight control. She missed his shaken response, regretted the return of the cool womanizer. Still, he felt so good, wrapped up against her, his body all fire and bone and muscle. "You have the most amazing effect on me. You know that, don't you?"

"No, I don't," she tried to say, but he was kissing her again, softly, his mouth nibbling at hers, and she was more interested in kissing him back than arguing. And then he moved his mouth down the side of her neck, and she realized with sudden shock that he'd done everything, everything to her. She hadn't been allowed to do more than kiss him.

The battle hadn't been left outside the bedroom after all. He was still trying to control everything, and she'd been a willing victim to his sexual thrall.

Except that she didn't feel like a victim. She felt warm, and sated and oddly triumphant. She reached up and threaded her fingers through his long hair, rubbing the silky strands against her palms. "Your hair is ridiculous," she said, nuzzling against it like a playful kitten.

She could feel his smile against the tender skin of her neck. "Your breasts are magnificent."

She closed her eyes, as his hands touched her once more. "You're not going to win," she said.

For a moment he didn't move, and she told herself she was glad she'd done it, shattered the temporary truce.

"Silver," he said, his voice low and certain in the velvet darkness, "I already have."

Chapter Fourteen

Rafe didn't make love to her again. She didn't expect it. She'd reopened the warfare between them; he'd dealt her a mortal blow. There was no way they could come together again, not with so much distrust on either side.

But she slept in his arms, her body wrapped tightly against his, slept deep and well, long into the day, and if her mind and spirit rejected him, her body had its own trust.

He hadn't said another word, simply tucked her against him, smoothing her rumpled hair away from her face, and gone to sleep. She supposed she could have left him, gone back to the sterile coldness of the guest room. But she didn't want to. She needed his warmth wrapped around her. Because she knew they were living on borrowed time, and the moment they left this bed they'd finally shared, life would come crashing down on them.

When she woke she was alone, wrapped tightly in the down comforter. Her body felt peculiar—restless, tingly, pleasured and frustrated. That was the problem with breaking a celibate streak, she thought wearily. The longer you did without it, the easier it was. Now, after one night, one occasion of admittedly powerful sex, she was already craving more.

She could fight those cravings. He'd left the bed rather than wake her and start it all over again. He probably didn't realize he'd done her a favor by giving her time to pull her defenses back around her. If she'd woken in his arms, there'd be no telling what kind of fool she would have made of herself.

That was the problem with sex. You couldn't just enjoy yourself. Your emotions had to get involved, she thought with strained disgust. You had to start thinking about stupid, impossible things like relationships, like caring, like falling in love. You started thinking you couldn't live without him, and where did that leave you? Up a very muddy creek without a paddle.

Not that this had happened to her before, Silver had to admit. Her limited experiences with sex hadn't led her to the dangerous, totally mistaken impression that she might be falling in love.

Still, the only explanation for her current state of brain-melting insanity had to be the sudden onrush of hormones. She was too levelheaded a woman otherwise.

At least when Rafe McGinnis wasn't around.

She stared at the clock beside the bed in disbelief. There was no way it could be half past one. The sunlight was streaming down on her from the skylight overhead, telling her that indeed it was. The storm was over, a new day was half begun, and she couldn't hide from it any longer.

There was no sign of Rafe as she darted into the bathroom. The hot water was as plentiful as it had been the night before, and she stayed under the shower far too long, dreading the bright cold light of day. Dreading she'd do something weak and sentimental, something that betrayed how much she'd begun to care about him.

In the daylight the rustic cabin looked bright and cheerful. She dressed in his clothes again, having no other choice, shivering when she'd pulled another pair of custom silk shorts against her skin. She needed to get away from him, from this place, as soon as she decently could. Because a strong, irrational part of her couldn't stand the thought of leaving.

She found coffee in a carafe, hot and strong and wonderful. She found sticky buns in the fridge. She devoured them all, then made herself bacon and eggs, finishing up with four pieces of toast. She couldn't remember when she'd last had a decent meal. She'd barely touched the steak he'd broiled, and last night, or was it this morning, had worked up a powerful hunger, one that food might just start to assuage.

There was no sign of Rafe. She opened the front door, expecting arctic cold, and stood there in numb surprise, enchanted. The storm had blown through, along with the cold weather, covering everything with a rime of ice that was now sparkling and dripping and melting in the bright sunshine. The air was damp and warm, almost springlike, and Silver felt a strange little tugging in her heart.

She tried to remember the misery of slogging through the ice and snow. She remembered it, all right. But she also remembered the mountains surrounding them, the limitless blue sky, the smell of the earth rather than of smog, the rough-edged beauty of it all. She was a city child, born and bred in Los Angeles, and for the first time in her life she felt as if she'd come home.

It was a lucky thing for her that Rafe hated this place. Otherwise she might start weaving all sorts of impossible fantasies. Fantasies that could never come true. He was a transplant now, a man who lived in the fast lane. It didn't matter if he seemed at home behind the big four-wheel-drive pickup truck. He didn't belong. And she had the strange, certain feeling that she did.

For the time being she had no choice but to depend on Rafe. She had no car, no clothes, nothing at all. If he wanted to stay, secluded in the remote mountains of Colorado, then she'd have no choice but to stay with him. It was a shame she couldn't work up more outrage at the notion.

She was humming beneath her breath when she closed the front door again, heading back to the kitchen to wash the dishes she'd dirtied. She froze when she heard the phone ring, waiting for Rafe to suddenly materialize from the walls and answer it.

He didn't. It was up to her, whether she wanted to face reality or not. No answering machine clicked in, as it rang four, five, six times. And then the ringing stopped, and Silver told herself she was glad.

Five minutes later it rang again. "All right, there's a limit to my self-control," she said out loud, reaching for the phone with soapy hands.

She wanted to drop it again. She wanted to come up with a fake accent, pretend she was anyone other than Silver Carlysle. But she'd inherited her mother's spectacular lack of acting skill, and when Clement's well-bred tones sounded on the other end she knew she'd have to answer.

"What do you want, Clement?" she asked wearily.

"Silver, where in God's name have you been?"

"Since you're the one calling me I'd think you'd have figured that out," she said.

"You're with that man!" Clement said in a shrill voice. "Honestly, Silver, haven't I taught you anything? I thought you were immune to that kind of mindless animal attraction. I couldn't believe it when I heard you'd gone off with him..."

"I didn't go off with him. I came out here to find the author of *Black Canyon,* and presumably Rafe did the same thing. We got caught in an ice storm, he rescued me, and the rest, as they say, is history."

"I can't believe it," Clement moaned again. "The thought of the two of you together simply boggles the mind. Haven't I taught you anything?"

"Don't waste your time thinking about it, Clement," she said in a calm voice. "It's not going to happen again."

There was a gusty sigh of relief on the other end. "Thank heavens! We may still be able to salvage something from this debacle. Things haven't been standing still since you disappeared, Silver. Your handsome stud left orders before he took off into the wilderness. While he was trying to distract you, his lawyers have been very busy."

"I imagine they have." She didn't want to hear this. She tried to pull the phone away from her ear, to hang it up, but she couldn't.

"I've told Marjorie what I think of her, of course," Clement continued, unaware of her reaction. "Locking you out in the middle of the night! Why in heaven's name didn't you come to me before things got this far? I could have used certain leverage with Marjorie, stopped her before things went too far…"

"What leverage? Stopped her from doing what? How far have things gone?" she demanded, finally giving in to her unwilling curiosity.

"Your father's papers, Silver. Technically they didn't belong to you. When Hatcher died, his old will was still in effect, leaving absolutely everything to your mother, despite the fact that she'd remarried and that you'd been born. She may have passed the trunk over to you, but technically it was hers. Everything of Hatcher's was hers, with the exception of that small trust fund."

She'd drunk too much strong black coffee. Her stomach twisted, and she wanted to throw up. She stared blankly at the wall, the receiver still to her ear. "What did she do?"

"What do you think? She sold the trunk and its papers to the highest bidder. Pegasus Pictures, of course. While you were off in his mountain hideaway, Rafe McGinnis was stabbing you in the back."

The front door was thrust open, and Rafe stood there, a load of wood in his arms. His color was high, his eyes bright, he looked healthy and oddly, irrationally happy. Until he looked at her face, at the telephone in her hand, and his expression vanished, leaving nothing but blankness in his dark green eyes.

"Is there anything I can do about it?" she asked finally, her voice raw.

"We can fight it, darling. I've got my lawyers working on it already. Your father's been dead a long time—the studio's shown no interest in *Black Canyon* until you came up with your screenplay. It doesn't matter that McGinnis doesn't actually want your work—they'll have to prove to a judge they weren't influenced by your version of it, and that would be damned hard to do. We have other options. We can break your father's will, though considering the time lapse that might be tricky. Or we can settle for a huge amount of money and a lavish apology.''

''No.''

''No?'' Clement echoed. ''I don't blame you for your fury, but we have to be reasonable about this. It's not as if it's holy writ, for heaven's sake. I've already fixed your dear mother's wagon. The *Clarion* is running my piece of the worst actresses of the 1950s, and there's a picture of dear Marjorie in her little jungle leotard as she appeared in *Swamp Queen of Africa*.''

Normally Silver would have laughed. Of all the bad movies Marjorie had made, *Swamp Queen* was the worst, her major claim to fame. It turned up on everyone's list of ten worst movies, and it guaranteed that Marjorie Carlysle would never sink into polite Republican obscurity.

But she didn't feel like laughing. ''Do what you can,'' she said numbly.

''I already have the lawyers busy earning their retainer. And Silver, come home to me. Don't let that man touch you again.''

Silver shivered. Rafe still stood in the open door, and the damp warm wind carried a sudden chill with it. ''Goodbye, Clement.''

Rafe kicked the door shut behind him, walking across the room and dumping the logs into the wood box. He left a trail of melting snow as he walked. ''So the serpent has entered paradise?'' he drawled. ''Why did you answer the phone?''

''I thought we agreed,'' she said. ''This isn't paradise, it's hell.''

He didn't touch her. Which was a good thing. If he touched her she would have shattered. Helpless with love and longing. Or in fury.

''What did Clement have to say?'' he asked after a long moment.

''That your lawyers have been successful. They managed to get my father's papers away from my mother.''

''Good for them,'' he said coolly. ''How did they manage that?''

''It was really quite simple. It turns out that my father left me nothing. The one parental gesture, of leaving his papers to me, was in fact my mother just wanting to get rid of them. Once they proved to be worth something, she's reclaimed them.'' Silver managed a brittle smile. ''And she's sold them to you.''

She didn't want to see the look of compassion that darkened his eyes. She didn't need his pity.

He had enough sense not to offer it. ''So then it's settled.''

''Don't count on it,'' she said, her voice fierce.

She expected frustration and rage from him. It couldn't be a faint trace of relief in his cool green eyes, relief that she was still fighting him. ''The battle isn't over, then?'' he asked lightly.

''Not until I win.''

''We might be at it for a long time.''

''I've got staying power.''

''So do I.''

She wanted to scream at him that they weren't talking about sex. Except that they were.

She turned away from him, staring out the window into the glorious mountains, unable to deal with him. ''I'm going to take a shower. We can talk about this when I come down,'' he said.

''There's nothing to talk about.''

''Silver…'' There seemed to be a wealth of longing in his voice. If she turned and looked at him, she'd see it in his eyes, and she'd run to him. They'd end up in bed again, and she couldn't do it. Couldn't do it to herself. She was on the narrow edge of survival—one false move and she'd topple over.

She heard his footsteps, and she braced herself. He came up behind her, and his long arms reached around her, pulling her back against his tall, strong body. His long fingers threaded through her short-cropped hair, and his mouth was at her temple. ''We can work this out, Silver,'' he said softly, and her treacherous heart cried out to believe him.

But her mind knew better. She needed to protect herself, hold together whatever small part of her still remained inviolate. She didn't move in his arms, didn't turn as she longed to. She covertly let her body absorb his heat, his strength, knowing this was the last time she'd let him touch her.

When he released her he did so slowly, reluctantly. "We'll work it out," he said again, moving away from her, up the stairs.

She kept her face to the window, waiting until she heard the bathroom door close, waiting until she heard the sound of the shower. Then she moved.

She took a pair of oversize boots from the front closet. She took a heavy sweatshirt, a couple of cans of Diet Coke, and a frozen box of muffins from the freezer. And then, quite calmly, she went outside, climbed into his huge truck and turned the key he'd left in the ignition.

It started with a throaty roar. It had the kind of dashboard that practically drove the truck itself, and she could see that the four-wheel-drive option was already engaged. Surely she could drive this boat out of the mountains. The alternative was too painful to contemplate.

At least it had an automatic transmission. She fastened the seat belt around her, put the gear into low and started off, slowly at first. By the time she'd reached the first bend in the road, she knew she could make it. And she told herself she'd had no choice at all. It was simply a matter of survival.

RAFE HAD NEVER BEEN so angry in his life. He felt like a kid, like a furious, miserable kid. He wanted to smash furniture, break windows, rip the phone out of the wall and hurl it into the fireplace. He wanted to beat his fists against the wall until they were bloody. He, who prided himself on his cool self-control, wanted to lose it completely.

He tried counting to ten. He tried counting to twenty. He stalked over to the front door and stared out into the bright afternoon light. There was no sound at all—she'd been gone for at least the ten minutes he'd been in the shower. Sound carried in the silence of the snow-covered mountains—if there was any chance he'd be able to stop her, that chance had long gone.

And he'd thought he was doing her a favor, lingering in the shower, giving her time to pull herself together. She didn't like to lose any more than he did. He couldn't really believe that she thought she'd had a chance in hell against him, but she must have thought so. Defeat had been very bitter, and he'd hoped to find some way of salvaging her pride.

Damn his lawyers! He'd told them to do what they had to do, to get those rights, but he hadn't quite realized the cost. If he'd known it would shatter Silver's tenuous faith in her father's love, would he have told them to leave it? He wished there was a way he could know.

Hindsight was always twenty-twenty. And he had to admit that there was always a solid possibility he would have told them to go ahead anyway. He'd warned her he fought dirty. And he always won.

Damn Clement Walden, the wasp-tongued little pedant! He wanted Silver as his eccentric acolyte, and he didn't care what he had to do to keep her dependent on him. He didn't want her getting involved with anyone, himself included. He probably didn't even want her working on that screenplay. The screenplay had nothing to do with the great Clement Walden, and it would therefore be unacceptable. But Silver hadn't realized that yet, realized that any form of independence would be squashed. She'd gone running back to him now, for comfort. She'd find out soon enough that Clement Walden was cold comfort indeed.

And damn Marjorie Carlysle for selling her daughter's birthright to the highest bidder. If she'd lied so long ago, why didn't she just let the lie stand? It wasn't as if she needed the money. His sources had suggested she didn't approve of her daughter's choice of career. That she wanted a junior matron.

Silver Carlysle would never be somebody's idea of a society matron. She was too stubborn, too bright, too unconventional to ever fit in with that kind of stultified society. She was made for freedom, for wildness, for fresh air and mountains and battles and love.

Damn it, she was made for him! How long was it going to take him to admit it?

And what was he going to have to pay to get her?

He picked up the phone he'd wanted to throw across the room and punched in a number. Bernie answered on the second ring, her cigarette-roughened voice sounding oddly concerned.

"I'm stuck at the cabin," he said abruptly, not bothering to identify himself. "Arrange for a car and driver, will you? Make it soon."

"Rafe, what the hell has been going on? Is Silver Carlysle with you?" Bernie demanded, and Rafe got the sudden, strange feeling that for once Bernie's concern wasn't primarily for his own tough hide.

"Why do you think my truck's gone? She took off in it about half an hour ago, and I'd assume she's out of the mountains already, heading back home. See what you can do for me, Bernie. I need to get the hell out of this place as soon as I can. It'll take someone from Denver at least three hours to get here. See if you can hire someone from Durango—they might be faster."

"I'll get Robin right on it. I need to tell you what your lawyers have done about the rights to *Black Canyon*."

"You sound disapproving, Bernie," he said in a weary voice. "I already know what they've done. Clement Walden called Silver with the happy news. That's why she took off."

There was a long silence on the other end as Bernie digested the information. "What was she running away from, Rafe?"

"I've asked you this before, and I'm asking again. You couldn't be insane enough to be matchmaking, could you?" he demanded.

Bernie had always been straight with him. "And if I was?"

"Then I'd lock you in a room with Clement Walden for a week and let you see what it feels like."

"I think there's a slight difference between the two relationships," Bernie said dryly. "We weren't made for each other."

"Oh, God, Bernie, do you have Alzheimer's?" Rafe demanded, appalled by her tacit admission. "Menopause?"

"Too late for menopause, sugar," Bernie said with her bark of a laugh. "Are you going to tell me you aren't infatuated with Silver Carlysle?"

"Yes," he said flatly.

He could hear the sudden hissing of her breath on the other end. "God, I believe you," she said, and there was no mistaking the sudden misery in her voice. "I blew it, big time."

"You certainly did," he said blandly. "You ought to consider that before you start messing with people's lives. Get me the damned car so I can get back to L.A. and see what I can do about this mess."

"Why is it a mess? You've gotten what you've wanted. She can still fight it, but it's a losing battle."

"It always was. There's just one little hitch in this whole thing."

"What's that, boss?"

"I'm not infatuated with Silver Carlysle. I'm in love with her. And I don't know what the hell I'm going to do about it."

He hung up the phone with Bernie's whoop of joy still echoing in his ears. She was a lot more optimistic than he was about it, but then, she didn't know the details about what had gone on between Silver Carlysle and the essentially bone-headed Rafe McGinnis.

Who would have thought a tough old cookie like Bernie would end up being a matchmaker? She'd given him hell when he'd made the mistake of marrying for no better reason than he'd thought it was time, but she usually kept her nose out of his romantic affairs.

But she was the one who'd brought *Black Canyon* to his attention, knowing full well it would precipitate a battle with Silver Carlysle. She'd already known he reacted more strongly to the woman than to anyone else in the past five years, including his ex-wife. Maybe it was simply that that had inspired her.

Or maybe it was her ancient relationship with Silver's father.

For a moment he allowed himself the truly horrifying thought that Bernie might be her real mother, and then quickly dismissed it. Silver looked like Marjorie Carlysle, whether she realized it or not. She had the beautiful, uncluttered features, the magnificent bone structure, the same luscious mouth and wonderful eyes.

Still, Benjamin Hatcher's daughter hadn't been a random choice. And he didn't like to feel manipulated.

But in fact, all Bernie's matchmaking would have come to nothing if it weren't for the fact that Silver Carlysle made him feel alive for the first time in years.

He glanced around him at the cabin that he'd avoided for so long. She'd even made him come home again, unwillingly, he had to admit, but he'd come. And in coming back, he'd found a part of himself that had been missing for a long, long time.

It was midafternoon already. He allowed himself a brief, chilly fear that Silver might have trouble steering the huge pickup over the melting roads, and then dismissed it. Silver Carlysle could do just about any damned thing she set her mind to. Particularly if she was mad enough.

It would take hours for a car and driver to reach him. Hours to kill. The fire was blazing, the coffee was hot, and there was a reasonable amount of whiskey left over. He could stretch out on the sofa and see if there were any more Louis L'Amours to while away the time.

But he wasn't going to do that. He was going for the coffee and the whiskey, all right. But he was going to read the one thing he'd secretly carried around with him for the past week, something he swore he'd never touch.

A copy of Silver Carlysle's screenplay. He'd had Bernie get it for him. There was no stopping Rafe McGinnis when he wanted something. He'd read the script and then he'd find whether there was any way he could salvage it and give her what she wanted. Or whether they were going to have to do it the hard way.

Chapter Fifteen

It never rained in L.A. It was raining that late Sunday afternoon when Silver drove the huge truck through the wet streets. It was probably snowing up in the mountains of Colorado again. And Rafe was probably still cursing her.

She'd grown fond of the oversize vehicle in the eighteen hours of driving. After the first two hours of sheer panic as she tried to float the boatlike thing down off the mountains, she'd learned to respect its power. The ride across Arizona was smooth and seamless, with nothing to distract her from her dark thoughts.

There was no danger whatsoever that the monotony of the landscape and the hours upon hours of driving would lull her into sleep. She'd slept long and well, wrapped in Rafe's treacherous arms. She didn't need caffeine or fresh air to keep her alert—the pain and fury in her battered heart precluded any kind of peace.

How could he have done that? How could he have made love to her, kissed her, smiled at her, all the while knowing his lawyers were doing their best to cut the ground from underneath her? She'd been a patsy, taking off to Colorado and letting herself get caught in his snare.

He'd warned her more than once, and she hadn't listened. He'd made love to her all the while he was stealing her dream.

And the final blow was that he'd stolen her father, too.

If she hadn't made the major mistake of going to bed with

him, she wouldn't be so vulnerable. But somehow the fight had gone out of her. She, who never quit, couldn't battle anymore. She just wanted to run away and hide.

There was never any question as to where she would end up. Not at her mother's mansion. Marjorie had committed the final act of betrayal, and she was self-absorbed enough not to realize how it would affect her daughter. She probably assumed that Silver would come home, move into the big house where she belonged, and become the kind of daughter Marjorie always wanted.

What Marjorie didn't realize was that Silver had tried, for years and years, to be that daughter. She'd finally come to accept who she was, accept that her mother would never be satisfied. And right now she needed to go to the one person who always gave her a shoulder to cry on, a listening ear. Clement Walden.

The heavy rain poured down on his French provincial town house, making it look like an Impressionist painting. She pulled into the circular driveway, probably the first pickup truck to enter that hallowed preserve since the house was built, sometime after the Second World War, and jumped down in the rain.

He knew her very well. He must have been watching for her, knowing she'd come to him to pour out her shame and misery. He was waiting at the open door, immaculately tailored arms outstretched.

She went into them, aware as ever of the absurdity of being comforted by a man half her size, and let him lead her into the cool, peaceful confines of his living room, all the while he murmured soothing, meaningless things. By the time she was settled on a Greco-Roman chaise, a cup of raspberry herb tea and honey in her chilled hands, she was feeling both listless and unnaturally calm.

"I hate him," she said, lying back and looking at the ceiling.

"You have every reason to," Clement murmured, sipping at his own Earl Grey. "The man's unprincipled. A liar, a swindler, an artistic cretin. How you could have thought he could be reasoned with is beyond my comprehension. I warned you, Silver, I warned you…''

"I know you did," she said, her voice soft with exhaustion and strain. "I can't explain it. There was something that drew me to him, something that called to me, no matter how much my brain told me it was crazy. I thought I saw something else in him. I thought there was a real person beneath that cold exterior, someone capable of deep, abiding love. I thought there was a wounded child…''

"And you'd be the one to heal him? Don't tell me you fell for that one, Silver!" Clement's contempt would have been painful, if only she didn't feel the same contempt already. "It's part of his stock in trade. He grew up in a nice middle-class family in Ohio, went to the University of Michigan, and then on to NYU. He didn't have a deprived childhood."

"He grew up in Colorado," she corrected him. "His father died in a snowstorm when he was eleven, his mother drank herself to death. He lived alone until his aunt and uncle came and took him to that nice middle-class family in Ohio, and he hated every minute of it. Do you realize he'd never been back to his home, not in twenty years?"

"I'm really not interested," Clement said, though the quickening in his light voice said otherwise. "I must say, this is all news to me. It's never appeared on his public bio."

"He wouldn't lie to me."

"Don't be ridiculous, Silver, the man would lie to anyone. Still, this is something quite new. I'll have to have my people look into it."

Silver sat up on the couch, a cold dread washing over her. "What do you mean?"

Clement's smile was the epitome of innocence. "Don't you want revenge, Silver? The man manipulated you, deceived and tricked you and stole the one thing that really mattered from you. Don't you want him to suffer?"

She could see him quite clearly in her mind. The distant, shuttered face, the flash of emotion in his cool green eyes. "No," she said. "I don't."

"Very noble of you, darling. Quite Christian, in fact. I never knew you were so merciful."

"You won't do anything, Clement?" She swiveled around to look at him, suddenly uneasy.

Clement smiled his wintry smile. "I wouldn't think of it, my dear."

She leaned back, closing her eyes, listening to the rain pour down outside. Thinking about the snow, and the mountains and a man's strong, talented body. "Promise?" she murmured drowsily. And she was asleep before she heard the answer.

"GOOD GOD, look at the cowboy," Bernie greeted Rafe as he stormed into the office. It was half past seven on a Monday morning, and he hadn't been in the mood for Armani. He'd jumped into the shower, dressed in jeans and denim and boots, and only eschewed his ancient Stetson at the last minute. "Where's your earring, boss?"

"Lost in a snowdrift," he replied, grabbing his coffee. "Where the hell is Sam?"

"Awaiting your presence, oh lord and master," Sam said, appearing from the inner office, rumpled-looking as usual. "What the hell have you been doing, watching too many John Wayne movies? Haven't you heard that cowboys aren't in right now?"

"Do you really think I give a damn?" Rafe said, sinking down behind his desk and surveying his office. It was odd, but it felt like home. Just as the cabin in Colorado had, just as his house in the hills had. How could a man have so many homes? So many different homes? "We've got a change in strategy."

"Lord, don't tell me that!" Sam protested, settling into one of the leather chairs. "We finally nailed Silver Carlysle, and you want to change the rules. Or is that it? It wasn't just the lawyers who nailed her, was it, buddy? How does she stack up to Marcia Allison? She's got a great set of headlights, but she looks a little too fierce for my tastes..." His voice trailed off, suddenly uneasy. "Now why do I get the feeling that I just said something I shouldn't have?"

"You usually aren't stupid for long," Rafe said in a measured voice.

"Since when have you decided to be gentlemanly and protective?" Sam asked, more curious than defensive. "After all, I usually get your leavings. Your advice has been invaluable to a lonely old bachelor like me."

Bernie had been listening to all this with a disapproving expression on her face. "I don't think there are going to be any leavings this time," she said in her gravelly voice.

"You mean you're going to do it so much there won't be anything left when you dump her?" Sam demanded cheerfully.

"Do you want to survive for the next ten minutes?" Rafe inquired sarcastically. "Because you're treading on very thin ice."

Sam laughed, unmoved by the threat. "There's not enough room in this town for the two of us, pardner," he drawled. "Don't worry, Rafe. I got the word from Bernie—the mighty McGinnis has finally fallen. I was just pulling your chain."

"You think I'm in the mood for that?" Rafe growled.

"Nope. You think I care? I just want to know if I get to be best man this time? I was out of town when you were fool enough to marry your first wife. I must say I think your taste has improved tremendously."

"You can hold my hand while I weep in my beer."

"I'd rather hold her hand."

"Boys," Bernie said sternly. "We're not getting anywhere with all this. What's going on, Rafe? If you want to settle with Silver Carlysle, you're going to have to do something about it. I gather the lawyers have worked up some conservative figures."

"She doesn't care about money," Rafe said, leaning back in his chair and propping his old boots on the teak-and-glass table that served as his desk. They looked good there. At home.

"Don't be ridiculous, everyone cares about money," Sam protested. "If she doesn't, how the hell are you ever going to get her to do what you want?"

"Maybe by asking her real nicely."

"Maybe." Sam sounded doubtful. "I don't know if she's going to be in the mood to listen."

"It depends on what she'll be listening to."

"Why don't I like the sound of this?" Sam demanded of Bernie. "We've got Miller working on the first draft of the screenplay, and not only has the man made us a fortune, he's also been up for an Oscar twice. He likes the book, he's got a good handle on what he wants to do with it."

"Just for the sake of conversation, what does he want to do with it?" Rafe took a sip of his coffee. He'd left his cigarettes in Colorado, and he hadn't bothered to get any more. This was the first time in twenty-four hours that he missed them.

"Oh, just a few cosmetic things. Tone down the girl, probably kill her off in the second act. Makes good motivation for the hero to go after the renegades, gives the audience some vicarious flesh and violence."

"What are we paying him?"

"We had to go up, of course. You know what an Oscar nomination is worth to an agent when he's negotiating a deal. But he's worth it, you know that."

"How much will he take in a kill fee?"

Sam looked at him, aghast. "You're kidding, aren't you, buddy? Tell me you're just paying me back for teasing you about Silver Carlysle. Tell me you don't mean it."

"I don't want Miller doing the screenplay. I don't care how good he is at *Cop for a Day* epics, I don't even give a damn how many Oscars he's nominated for. He's not doing *Black Canyon.*"

"Then who the hell is?" Sam snarled. "If you'll pardon my asking such a blunt question."

For a moment Rafe didn't answer, and the faint smile on his face was unreadable. "The person best suited for the job," he said finally. "Silver Carlysle."

"Oh, God," Sam moaned. "He's finally lost his mind. His brain went to his pants and stayed there, and we're all going to pay the price. Rafe, baby, no broad is worth it."

"Sam," Bernie warned, eyeing Rafe's still expression.

"You've already gotten her into bed. Anyone who's seen the two of you together knows she's crazy about you, no matter how hard she tries to fight it. You don't need to sacrifice a multimillion-dollar production just to flatter her."

"Sam," Bernie said again, her voice even stronger.

"At least let her assist Miller. No one ever writes a movie alone in Hollywood, you know that. Buy her draft, give it to Miller, and he'll see what he can salvage. He won't like sharing screen credit, but maybe we can come up with a compromise, like a story credit, or maybe 'additional dialogue' or something."

"You're missing the point, Sam," Rafe said with icy calm. "I've never made a business decision dictated by my sex life, and I'm not about to start now. I read her screenplay. There's no other word for it, Sam. It was right."

"It was right," Sam echoed, leaning back in the chair, an expression of despair on his face.

"I need you to get the lawyers in here, Bernie," Rafe continued, ignoring Sam's stricken expression. "Make it for one o'clock, that'll give Sam enough time to read the manuscript."

There was no disguising Bernie's look of triumph. "Sure thing," she said, turning to go, but Rafe put out a hand to stop her.

"You wanted this, didn't you?" he asked with sudden shrewdness. "You'd read her screenplay and you wanted us to do it. For God's sake, why didn't you just say so in the first place, Bernie?"

"Because you weren't in the mood to listen. You would have thrown the whole idea out rather than negotiate with her," Bernie said, her faded eyes defiant. "I knew that book better than anyone. I read Silver's script and I was astonished. You had the word, Rafe. It was right. It was just that simple."

He stared at her in mute frustration. "You know what kind of kill fee we're going to have to pay Miller?"

"Take it out of my share of the profits."

"If there are any profits. Westerns are problematic."

"I don't give a damn. You and I both know it's going to be brilliant. We just have to convince Sam."

Rafe turned to him. "So how about it, Sam? You ready to rise to the challenge, or will I go looking for the new Spielberg to make *Black Canyon?*"

Sam roused himself, glaring at both of them. "The script better be damned good," he said, pulling himself out of the chair.

"It's more than that." He tossed the coffee-stained pages across his desk. "There's just one thing that troubles me."

"What's that?" Bernie said warily, as Sam wandered off toward his office, muttering under his breath.

"How come you know that book better than anyone else alive?"

And Bernie only smiled.

"I THINK it might be a good idea if you came into the office," Clement said in a gentle voice some three days later. "You can't just sit around brooding."

"I'm not brooding," Silver said listlessly. "I'm swimming laps in that pool you never use. I'm catching up on my beauty sleep. I'm wearing the clothes you've been sending home for me."

She was currently dressed in one of Clement's favorites, a white linen suit that looked just a little too much like the sort of thing he always wore. She'd accepted it with a singular lack of enthusiasm, and while it made her look stylish, elegant and daring, it didn't make her look like Silver.

"You need to work. Not that I blame you for keeping a low profile. McGinnis has been looking for you."

"Has he?" she murmured, blessing the numb feeling that didn't abate at the mention of his name. "When did he get back in town?"

"Same day you did, I gather. And actually, it isn't McGinnis who's looking for you. It's his lawyers."

Even that news didn't penetrate her cocoon of numbness. "Let them look."

"Oh, I imagine they'll find you sooner or later. There are only so many places where you might be found, and our relationship is rather well known. You may as well emerge."

"In another day or so." A sudden misgiving broke through her abstraction. "Do you want me to leave, Clement?" she asked, suddenly anxious. "I don't want to impose…"

"Don't be absurd, dear girl. I love having you here, you know that. At last my little protégée is where she belongs. I just think it's getting to be time to get on with your life."

She smiled up at him. "I will, Clement. Just give me a few more days."

"Anything, darling. All you have to do is ask."

She liked being in limbo. Clement was gone during the day, and many of the evenings, too. Like Rafe McGinnis, he was on the A-list for parties, and there was always some occasion that demanded his presence. He thrived on that attention, even though he pretended boredom with it all, and the elegant, peaceful confines of his town house were Silver's peaceful haven most of the time, her solitude only broken by the occasional discreet presence of Clement's raft of servants.

And the telephone. She never answered it, of course, but she could hear it ring, almost constantly, the bell-like tones echoing through the house. Clement had instructed his houseboy never to bother Silver with the callers, but every time the phone rang she could feel her stomach knot up.

Not that Rafe would try to call her. He didn't know where she was, and he hadn't made any effort to find her, apart from siccing his lawyers on her again. She could just imagine what they wanted. Some nice discreet settlement, to ensure that she wouldn't cause any more trouble.

They didn't know her, of course. And Rafe didn't know her. She was past the point of causing trouble. She'd lost. It was that simple. He'd always told her she would, and she'd been a fool to think she could buck the system, buck someone as powerful as Rafe McGinnis, and walk away intact.

She'd paid for it. Paid for her temerity with most of the things she held dear. The last strands of peaceful coexistence with her mother. The fruits of her creativity for the last two years. Her one loving memory of her father. All destroyed, or shown for the sham they really were.

But she'd paid with something even more dear, and she'd known it was at risk early on. All her efforts at self-protection had come to nothing, though, when faced with someone as devastating as Rafe McGinnis. She'd fallen in love with the man, and that stupid act of emotional and physical surrender had made everything else lose its power over her. She'd lost her heart in more ways than one. She'd lost her heart to him, given it to a man who would never value it. And she'd lost the heart to keep fighting. Until now she felt empty and hollow inside.

It was late the next morning when the phone rang once more, pealing through the sterile house. Silver tried to pull the feather pillow over her head to shut out the insistent noise. She'd taken to sleeping as much as she could, morning, noon and night, hoping to sleep away the ache inside. She had the drugged, stupid feeling one gets after sleeping around the clock, and she stared in disbelief at the digital clock by her bed. Eleven-thirty. And she'd gone to sleep at eight the night before.

She pulled herself out of bed, running a hand through her shaggy hair. "What you have, my girl, is a clinical depression," she said out loud, over the noise of the telephone. "Now you can wander around this place, hiding out, sleeping your life away. Or you can come back to life."

The distant ringing of the phone mocked her. There was an extension by her bed, one she'd turned the ringer off but hadn't unplugged. "Life it is," she said flatly, and picked up the receiver.

"I thought you'd be there." Marjorie's voice was accusing, but even an angry Silver could hear the uncertainty beneath her deliberately arch tones. "Do you know how worried I've been? Why haven't you come home?"

Silver considered hanging up the phone and crawling back into bed. It took all her willpower not to, to remember she'd decided to face life. "I was evicted," she said in a calm voice.

"Locked out, as a matter of fact. I had no place to come home to."

"Don't be absurd, darling. Your room at the big house is just as it's always been. I've been the indulgent mother for far too long, but when your silly forays into the movie business start dragging the family name in the gutter, it's time for me to put my foot down."

"The family name wasn't dragged in the gutter, Marjorie," Silver said calmly. "Just yours. And it isn't as if you slept your way to the top. You never made it to the top."

There was a pause on the other end of the line. "Darling, perhaps I underestimated you. You do seem to have your father's way with words," she said in an acid voice. "What are you doing with Clement? Besides hiding out? He's not good for you, you know. You may think he's your champion, but Clement Walden doesn't care about anyone but himself. He's just using you to settle an old score."

"What old score?"

"I wouldn't think of passing on ancient gossip..."

"You don't talk about anything but," Silver said sharply. "Spill it, mother. What old score is Clement trying to settle?"

"Any number of them, I imagine. He's the most malicious man in Hollywood. He hates me, he hated your father, who called him a prosy old bore, and he despises McGinnis because he's everything he wants and can't have."

"What are you talking about?"

"It's really quite simple. When Rafe and Sam first turned up in Hollywood, Clement fell all over them. He called their first film the most brilliant piece of work he'd seen since *Citizen Kane*. He tried to make Rafe one of his little protégés, and you can imagine how McGinnis responded to that. He told Clement to go stuff himself, in very public, humiliating terms. Clement didn't like being rejected and humiliated by someone he'd deigned to honor with his attentions. He's been working on his revenge ever since."

"I don't believe you."

"Don't you? Ask Clement. I'll say one thing, he's usually honest about these things."

"Goodbye, Marjorie."

"Wait!" There was a sudden broken note in her voice, one her daughter knew didn't come from an excess of acting talent. Marjorie was truly upset.

"Yes?"

"I want you to come home. I know you're angry with me for letting McGinnis have your father's papers, but I checked with our lawyers and they would have gotten them in the end. We really didn't have a legal leg to stand on. It simply made sense to accept their very generous offer and get the thing off our hands. It's occupied too much of your time, baby. It's time you settled down, got married. Even—" there was a strained gulp on the other end "—have children."

Silver didn't move, deeply shocked. "You really must love me," she said finally, "if you're asking me to make you a grandmother."

Marjorie managed a choked laugh. "I didn't say you had to be in any particular hurry about it. I just want to see you happy."

"By marrying whom you want, doing what you want?"

Marjorie sighed. "I've given up on that. I want you to marry who you want, and if it's Arnold Schwarzenegger or Rafe McGinnis, I'll accept it."

"Arnold's taken."

"So he is. That leaves McGinnis. Do you love him?"

Even her uninvolved mother had seen that far ahead. "Let it be, Marjorie. This may be Hollywood, but I don't believe in happy endings. Not for me."

"Oh, baby," Marjorie said, sounding more like a mother than she had in Silver's entire twenty-nine years. "Most especially for you."

Silver sat staring at the phone, long after she'd hung up. She ought to go home, she knew that now. She needed to make her peace with her mother, who loved her despite her self-absorption. She needed to make her peace with her stepfather, a solid, unimaginative, relentlessly kind man. She needed to make her peace with herself, and hiding out at Clement Walden's town house wasn't getting her there.

It was half-past twelve by the time she showered and dressed. She knew where she'd find Clement—his was a life of unchangeable habits, and he always dined at Spago's on Thursdays, even though he decried its descent into commonness. If she hurried she'd be there ahead of him.

The rented truck still stood in Clement's elegantly curving driveway, and she knew a moment's guilt that she hadn't returned it. Except that she didn't know whom he'd rented it from. Besides, Rafe McGinnis could afford to buy that truck ten times over.

Clement hadn't arrived yet, but the maître d' knew her from previous occasions, and he ushered her to Clement's waiting table with his usual flourish. "Read your piece in the *Clarion* this morning," he said with his usual friendliness. "Nasty."

The word was said with deep approval tinged with awe, and that sudden trickling of uneasiness blossomed. She hadn't written anything for the *Clarion* in over a week, and as far as she knew, there wasn't anything on file for them to use.

She managed a faint smile. "Thanks. I don't suppose you have a copy of it lying around?"

"Someone will bring it right over," he said smoothly, and she knew he'd send a minion out to purchase one. In Los Angeles they knew how to treat their customers, especially if one was paying the kind of prices Spago's commanded. "In the meantime, may I suggest the squid ravioli in pesto sauce?"

Silver barely listened. "You decide."

She sat there, numb, waiting. Around her were faces, the famous and not so famous, and many of them were looking her way. Whispering. Sly smiles on their faces. Intimate nods in her direction.

The newspaper and the pasta arrived at the same time. She ignored the food, thumbing through the fresh paper with numb hands, the circulars already politely removed. And then she found it. Nasty indeed.

It was her byline, all right. Clement had very humbly not even taken an assistant credit. She wondered where they'd found that picture of Rafe, a tall, bony-looking teenager in a faded shirt that showed his wrists, ripped jeans that were too short, a shaggy haircut and a hurt, defiant expression on his face.

There was a grainy photograph of his mother, looking far older than her stated age, and his father, a tall, biblical-looking man with flowing beard and kind eyes.

It was all laid out for the curious in Hollywood, written in carefully malicious prose. Rich little poor boy making good in Hollywood, the American dream come true. His mother's wasted stay in a state alcohol-treatment center, a photo of the twisted wreckage of his father's snowplow. His hidden, protected past splashed all over the *Clarion* for people to gossip about.

She didn't need to feel numb with guilt. Rafe had done the same to her, of course. Worse, in the tabloid. And she was innocent—Clement had done it, Clement had concocted this mishmash of truth, innuendo and outright lies and then attributed it to her. She stared at it, the smell of the pasta rising to her nostrils, and wondered what the elegant clientele of Spago's would do if she got sick, right there and then.

Chapter Sixteen

"Silver, darling!" A woman swooped down on her, embracing her in a Poison-scented cloud. "Where have you been all this time? You're looking marvelous! I knew Clement was lying. He'd have us believe you were sitting around, sulking over a broken heart. You know how wicked that man can be. He made you sound positively pathetic. But then, Clement always has such a nasty air about him when he talks about his little protégées. I must say, you've lasted longer than they usually do. Most people see through him sooner."

"Mavis," Silver said cautiously, finally remembering the woman's name. "How have you been?"

"Just peachy, darling, just peachy. Of course, it's no wonder Clement is slightly more circumspect around you. You have a great deal more talent than his slaves usually have. That piece in the *Clarion* today is one of the most deliciously wicked things I've read in a long time. The whole town is talking about it. We never thought anyone could make Rafe McGinnis look vulnerable, but you managed. Well, as Clement said, 'Hell hath no fury like a woman scorned' and all that. You've perfected the art of revenge, darling."

Silver looked up, across the noisy, crowded restaurant. Clement was strolling toward her, his face smug, self-confident, his immaculate white suit without a wrinkle.

"Not yet," she murmured. "But I intend to work on it."

Mavis had wandered off, espying more powerful victims, by

the time Clement reached the table. "Silver, what a treat," he said, not a trace of wariness in his voice as he leaned his papery cheek down for her to kiss before taking his seat opposite her. "I was afraid you were never going to leave the house."

"Never is a long time, Clement," she said carefully. "Marc was kind enough to get me today's *Clarion*."

Her exalted opinion of Clement's intellect took a drastic plunge as her mentor smiled, not the slightest trace of uneasiness marring his genial expression. "I rather outdid myself, didn't I?" He preened.

"You did," she said. "It's a shame people don't appreciate that you're the one who wrote it."

"You needn't look so stricken about the whole thing. If you're fool enough to care about what McGinnis thinks of you, comfort yourself with the thought that he probably won't believe you're capable of writing so brilliantly. He'll probably assume I wrote it. Many people do, you know. They just assume I rewrite most of your columns for you, and I must confess, I encourage that belief. After more than thirty years I've run out of things to say. Whereas, you, my dear, are fresh and biting. I must say, in this case I really outdid myself, and you, with all your freshness and flair, can't hold a candle to an old master like me."

"Did you say 'old bastard'?" Silver inquired with deceptive sweetness.

Unease was beginning to click in. "You're unhappy with me, aren't you?" Clement said, pouting slightly. "Darling, I did it for you. The man had hurt you, and you gave me the perfect ammunition to fight back with. The man looks pathetic, and his stock in trade was his invulnerability. You should be thanking me."

Silver rose slowly, gracefully, towering over her dinner companion. "Thank you so much, Clement," she said sweetly, picking up her plate of squid ravioli, "and go to hell."

The green-speckled ravioli looked quite attractive adorning the once-pristine front of Clement's jacket. The noisy chatter filling Spago's had stopped abruptly, and all eyes were on the two of them. Clement had taken out his handkerchief and was vainly trying to mop some of the splashed pasta from his face with an air of elegant disdain. It only managed to make him appear more ridiculous.

There was a murmur as she strode through the restaurant, a murmur that swelled and rose until, when she reached the door, it erupted into an enthusiastic round of applause, sweetened by an occasional cheer. She turned, gave a solemn bow and marched out, the crowd's approval still ringing in her ears.

At least she'd left nothing behind at Clement's, only the clothes he'd bought her in his attempt to turn her into a sexless clone. She never had to go back there, never had to see him again. Her job at the *Clarion* was finished—there'd never be any choice between the Pulitzer-winning Clement Walden and a minor underling. It didn't matter.

Even *Black Canyon* no longer mattered. She'd put her heart and soul into it for two years, and now she was ready to let it go. Not because she had a sudden epiphany of mental health. But because she had something new to work on, a new idea for a screenplay, this time original, this time, of all things, a pirate epic. Now all she had to do was find a computer.

The driveway was empty when she pulled in later that afternoon. Her mother was presumably out at bridge, her stepfather at his office. She'd get settled into her room in the big house, with the ridiculous canopy bed. Maybe she'd even see if she could find one of those stupid tea dresses her mother used to keep buying for her, dresses that looked frilly and ridiculous on her long, deep-bosomed frame.

"You're a sight for sore eyes!" Wilkers emerged from the row of garage bays, wiping his hands on an oily rag. "And where in heaven's name did you get that rig?"

"It's rented," she replied with all truthfulness, jumping down from the truck. "Where's Mother?"

"Off on a mission. She'll be glad to see you home, missy. She was worried half to death about you." He tucked the rag into his back pocket. "I think herself has learned a lesson this time. Not to go interfering in her grown daughter's life."

Silver found she could laugh. "I don't think mothers ever learn that one," she said.

"Can I help you with your bags?"

"What you see is what you get." She started toward the main house, when Wilkers's voice stopped her.

"Wrong way, miss."

She turned to look at him. "You mean…"

"That's right. I told you she's seen the error of her ways. She had me move everything back a couple of days ago. I'm not sure that I set the computer up right, but I'd bet you could have it running in no time."

She flung her arms around him, kissing him loudly on his rosy cheek before racing past him, up the stairs to her loft.

Wilkers hadn't lied—everything was just as it had been. She stood in the middle of the room, confused for a moment, waiting for the peace and rightness to sweep over her. She was home at last, everything would be all right again.

Except that it wouldn't be. She still loved the place, her first piece of independence. But too many things had happened in the last weeks. She'd discovered the mountains, the peace and the cold fresh air. She'd been betrayed on all sides. And she'd made the very grave mistake of falling in love with a man who didn't know the meaning of the word.

It would come back to her, wouldn't it? The sense of rightness about the place. All she had to do was set up her computer, find a comfortable pair of sweat pants and an old T-shirt, lay in a supply of Diet Coke and coffee, and she'd find peace again.

The answer her apartment gave her was a resounding no. It was time to leave home, this time for good. While her mother's gesture of apology melted some of the ice around her heart, it wasn't good for either of them, this living in close quarters, never being what the other wanted. It was time to pack her Mac and her jeans and take off.

There was one thing she had to do before she left. She had to see Rafe once more, to try to apologize, to explain. She hadn't written the article, but she'd been fool enough to trust

Clement not to spill out things that should have been left unsaid in the first place. How could she have been so naive—not to realize what a venal creature he was?

And he'd been absolutely right—Rafe's power in Hollywood stemmed from his invincibility. He never lost, he was never vulnerable. She'd learned to her cost how invulnerable he was. But the film colony was a fickle place. The moment they scented weakness they'd be after him like sharks at the smell of blood.

He wouldn't believe her, of course. Unless, like everyone else, he'd always assumed Clement had ghosted her columns for her. In fact, it had been the other way around. Clement had grown increasingly lax about deadlines, and he'd signed her better pieces more than once. At the time she'd been immeasurably flattered. In retrospect she felt like a bigger fool than ever. It didn't matter that Clement was a past master at manipulation. She was a past master at seeing through manipulation, having lived with her mother most of her life. She should have been able to see through Clement.

It was time to get her life in order, time to move ahead. She had unfinished business to take care of, with her mother, with Rafe.

It was past nine when she set out into the brightly lighted streets of Beverly Hills in the huge pickup. She'd accomplished a surprising amount in the past five hours, including making peace with her mother, cutting the apron strings, and even getting a start on "Pirates" before she packed up her computer along with her most comfortable clothes. Her mother was willing to let her go—sad, reluctant, but accepting—and her afternoon mission had been easily accomplished. When Mrs. Harry Braddock spoke, even the *Clarion* listened with dutiful respect. A corrected byline would run for two days in the *Clarion*, starting with tomorrow's edition. Marjorie knew her daughter better than Silver realized. She knew Silver would never betray the man she loved, and she'd taken care of the matter quickly and efficiently.

The appointment with Rafe's lawyers was set for ten the next morning. She'd tried to get out of that one, returning their endless messages and telling them she no longer made any claim to *Black Canyon*. Apparently that wasn't enough for them, they wanted legal documents and all that. They wanted money to change hands too, but at that she drew the line. She was willing to give Rafe *Black Canyon*, now that she had nothing left to fight with. But she wasn't going to be bought off. She reserved that small taste of victory for herself.

All that was left was Rafe himself. She'd saved the hardest part till last. She'd considered writing a note, but the words wouldn't come. She considered saying nothing, counting on the fact that she'd be meeting with his lawyers, not him, and with luck she might never have to face him again.

But she couldn't. She wasn't a coward, and she'd never taken the easy way out. She couldn't get away with a note, or with simply disappearing. She'd run away once, in Colorado. She couldn't run away again, and live with herself. She had to face Rafe, knowing she'd be facing his contempt and disbelief, and apologize.

She drove more slowly than she'd driven since she was fifteen years old and just learning on the crowded streets of L.A. The hills were dark and still as she steered the pickup up the narrow road, and she found herself hoping, praying he wouldn't be home. Then at least she could tell herself she'd tried.

But in fact, when she reached his outlandish little house and found it dark, deserted, the hollowness inside her spread and grew. She refused to consider whether she'd had any false hopes, whether she thought there was a chance for them. She only knew that if she drove away now, she would never see him again.

She climbed out of the pickup and walked to the front door. He had one of those electronic keypads—some password would open the door, and she couldn't for an instant imagine what that password would be. She punched in several possibilities, all to no avail.

And then it came to her with stunning clarity. The most obvious choice for anyone in Hollywood. The cryptic word from the best movie ever made. She punched in the word "Rosebud," remembering the child's sleigh in *Citizen Kane*. And the door swung open into silence.

Nothing seemed to have changed since she'd been there less than a week ago. The house was still in the midst of renovation, the Moorish architecture still bizarre, absurd and ridiculously attractive. He was probably out with some starlet, she thought morosely. After all, he hadn't been trying to find her. Only his lawyers. He'd probably forgotten all about her. Until he'd seen today's paper.

She'd wait an hour, no more. She certainly didn't want to be here when he brought some sweet young thing home. If she had any sense at all she'd leave right now rather than run the risk of being thrust into such a hideously embarrassing situation.

Except for the simple fact that she really didn't think he'd do it. His romantic exploits might be legend, but she didn't think he was going to jump into someone else's bed right away. Even if she wanted to torment herself with the possibility, she simply didn't believe it.

And she'd come too far to run now. She'd wait for him, long enough to apologize, to say goodbye. And then maybe she could get on with her life.

The swimming pool drew her like a magnet. She stepped onto the terrace in the warm night air, remembering. Remembering his body drifting against hers. Remembering his mouth. Remembering, as they sank beneath the cool surface of the water, how fear left her, and only Rafe remained.

He wouldn't be home for hours, she knew that. She stripped off her clothes quickly, without giving herself time to think about it, dumping them on the chaise. She knew how to dive. She just never did.

She looked at the moon-silvered water, and thought of Rafe. And then she dived, headfirst, splitting the water like a silver arrow.

HE WAS DRIVING FAST, too fast, his booted foot clamped down on the responsive gas pedal of the Lotus. He'd let his hair hang loose, and it was blowing in the night air, whipping into his face. He was cold and angry. He was in pain, the sense of betrayal sharp and fierce, and there was nothing he could do to release it. Nothing but drive as fast as he could, hoping to outstrip the demons that rode him. But even the Lotus couldn't go that fast.

He'd spent the day watching people's faces. The smirks of those who were in his power. The compassion on the bleeding hearts. And there wasn't a damned thing he could do about it.

If he could find Silver Carlysle he could cheerfully wring her neck. He doubted that would make him feel better. It wasn't the article, with its malicious tone and cheap shots, that bothered him so intensely.

It was that he'd been so mistaken in Silver Carlysle. The woman he thought he'd fallen in love with didn't exist. Not if she could turn around and write something like that.

He pulled into his driveway, too fast, and barely avoided slamming into the pickup. The car stalled out, and he sat there, staring.

He didn't give himself time to think, to react. He jumped out of the Lotus, punched in the code on the security entrance and walked into the darkened house.

It was empty. For a moment he was horribly afraid that she'd simply dropped the truck off rather than face him. She'd never been a coward. She'd run from him in Colorado, but he knew that came more from anger than fear. She'd hidden from him in L.A. But if she was afraid of anything, it wasn't him. It was herself.

And then he knew where she was. By the time he stepped onto the terrace he was barefoot, wearing just his jeans and a T-shirt. She was slicing through the water with graceful, steady strokes, and she probably didn't even realize he was there.

He waited silently until she could feel his eyes on her. She stopped mid-stroke in sudden confusion, sinking beneath the surface, and he knew a moment's panic. And then she rose again, shaking the water out of her eyes, and looked up at him.

"You're trespassing." It didn't come out the way he'd meant it. It sounded hostile, distancing. But then, he was feeling hostile.

"Yes," she said, treading water. "I need to talk to you."

Better than nothing, he thought. Not what he wanted, but something after all. He wondered for an idle moment whether she could carry on this conversation in the nude, whether she'd manage to maintain her composure, or whether a blush of color would cover her delectable skin. And where that blush would start.

"I'll get you a robe," he said abruptly, heading into the cabana and cursing his unruly body. How could he still want her so much? How could he still think he was in love with her?

She was waiting by the edge of the pool when he came out with the thick white terry robe, her shoulders out of the water. He dumped the robe beside her and turned away, walking into the house. By the time she followed she was wrapped up tighter than a mummy, and he handed her the drink he'd poured.

"I don't..." She tried to refuse it, but he put it in her icy hand.

"Dutch courage," he said. "Besides, it's colder than you think. You might catch a chill."

"Do you care?" The question seemed to surprise her almost as much as it surprised him.

Surprised him so much he didn't answer, simply took a delaying sip of his whiskey. He hadn't bothered to turn on the lights. For one thing, he liked his house better in the moonlight. For another, he was hard as a rock, standing next to her damp, robed body, and he'd just as soon she didn't notice.

"I didn't write the article," she said flatly. "I know you won't believe me, but I didn't. Clement did. It was my fault for telling him about your past. I can't believe I did, except that I was upset and vulnerable, and Clement has a way of getting things out of people that they'd rather not say. So it is my fault, for telling him, but I didn't know he was going to use it. If I had, I would have tried to stop him."

"Tried to stop Clement Walden in the midst of a scandal?" he said. "An impossibility."

"I know you don't believe me," she said, hugging the robe more tightly around her, "but I had to apologize anyway. To try to explain. I…"

"Oh, I believe you," he said gently. "Unlike me, you don't fight dirty. That's why you'll never survive in Hollywood, why I can't believe you've survived this long. You need to learn to swim with the sharks, Silver. To use every advantage, fair or unfair, to get what you want. Otherwise you'll be eaten alive if you stay here."

"I'm not going to stay here," she blurted out. "I'm leaving."

He held himself very still. The wrong move, the wrong word, and he might scare her away forever. "Where are you going?"

She managed a rueful smile. "Back to the mountains. I'm not sure where, exactly."

"Don't go to Montana. Half of Hollywood has already moved there. Colorado's nice, and not as trendy as it used to be."

"I liked Colorado," she said in a soft, shy voice.

"You said you hated it."

"I lied."

He set his drink down, then took her untouched one from her cold hand. "When are you leaving?"

"I said I'd meet with your lawyers in the morning. I thought I'd take off after that, sometime tomorrow afternoon."

He nodded, watching her from behind hooded eyes. "That leaves tonight then," he said.

It was all he said, but it was enough. "Yes," she said, her voice a whisper of sound. "That leaves tonight." And she reached up, putting her hands on his shoulders, and kissed him.

Her mouth tasted cool and sweet against his, damp from the water in the pool. He pulled her tight against him, and he groaned deep in his throat as pleasure washed over him. She felt so right in his arms, her strong, tall body pressed against his. Couldn't she feel the rightness of it?

He loved the way she kissed him. Shy and bold, sensual and innocent, she used her lips, her tongue, her teeth in ways that were totally beguiling. Part of him wanted to overpower her, to kiss her back and scoop her up into his arms, to carry her into the bedroom and make love to her until she was a mindless mass of sensations.

But he didn't. Instinct told him not to. So he stood very still and let her use her mouth, telling himself he couldn't come just from a kiss, could he? Just from her strong hands clenching his shoulders, just from her robed body pressed up against his? Could he?

She moved away for a moment, and he let her go, reluctantly. "Where's the bedroom?" she asked, her voice husky and just faintly nervous.

It was that edge of fear that finished him. "Down the hallway," he said, smiling faintly in the darkness. "Do you want me to carry you?"

She shook her head. "You didn't even let me touch you last time. This is my turn." And she took his hand in hers and led him to the bedroom.

Her hand was icy cold, trembling slightly. She stopped by the bed and turned to him, and if there was shyness on her face there was determination, too. She began unfastening the snaps of his denim shirt, and then her mouth followed, down and down, to the buckle of his belt. She was slightly, endearingly clumsy as she unfastened it, and her awkwardness took ten years off his life, but when she finally freed him, the cool night air was a blissful relief. Followed by the shock of her mouth on him, shy, untutored, and astonishingly enthusiastic. He put his hands down, threading his fingers through her hair, needing to touch her, to hold her, as he felt his bones melt and legs tremble.

He survived as long as he could. When he could stand it no longer he pulled her upright, into his arms, kissing her full on her mouth. The robe was easy enough to strip off, his clothes a little more troublesome, and then they were on the bed, wrapped in each other's arms, rolling together until she lay on her back beneath him, her eyes shining up into his, luminous, vulnerable, her mouth damp and sweet.

She was ready for him, she was beyond ready. Her legs spread beneath him, her hips were ready to arch for his first thrust, and he wanted to so badly he was shaking. But she'd started it, she knew what she wanted, and he had every intention of letting her earn it.

He rolled onto his back, waiting for her. "Come here, Silver," he said, his voice soft and cajoling.

She stared at him, worry darkening her eyes. "I don't..." she said. "I haven't...that is...I don't know how to..."

He grinned. Not a smug, cocky smile. One of pure, masculine possessiveness. "I can't think of a better time to learn. Come here, chicken," he said, his voice gently teasing.

She came, sliding across the bed, a wary expression in her eyes. "I'm not sure..." she began again, but he simply took her and lifted her over him, so that she straddled his body.

"You wanted to be in charge," he murmured. "Now's your chance." He took her hips in his big hands, lifting her, and she sank slowly, inch by miraculous inch, as a look of sheer, primitive wonder washed over her face.

It took her only a moment to catch on to the rhythm. And then his hands left her hips, leaving it up to her, and instead he clenched the sheets, prepared for the ride of his life.

She was an apt pupil. She leaned over him, her hair obscuring her face, intent on drawing every instance of pleasure from him. She sank on him, then lifted up slowly, so slowly he groaned, afraid she'd leave entirely, and then she sank again, and it was all he could do not to grab her, to try to control the movements that were driving him to the very edge of madness.

Her body was covered with a film of sweat. She was shaking, trembling with reaction, and her smooth glides became erratic, jerky, even as he felt his own formidable control begin to dissolve. He caught her hips again, surging up into her, and she gasped, her eyes shooting open as he moved again and again and again, until she shattered around him, her body tight and convulsing, and he was with her, pouring himself into her, drinking in her strangled cry of completion.

She'd collapsed against him, her body limp, damp, exhausted. He didn't want to release her, but as her breathing slowed she began to pull away, and he knew that if he tried to hold her she'd only be that more determined to escape. So he let her move away, reluctantly, as she tried to pull some of her self-control back around her.

"We're going to have to do something about this," he said in a deliberate drawl.

She was lying on her back beside him, trying to control her breathing. She was flushed, and he could see stray tremors of reaction still rippling across her silken skin. "About what?" she said, and her voice was endearingly hoarse.

"About us. I didn't use anything this time, either, and we're playing with fire. I don't want you to have to marry me because you get pregnant."

For a moment she didn't say anything, and he wondered if he'd blown it. "No," she said finally. "That wouldn't be a good idea."

"So I think," he continued, keeping his voice casual, "that we'd better get married first. Because I don't seem to be able to think straight around you, and this is probably going to keep happening."

He wasn't sure what he was expecting. Some response, from joyful acceptance to outraged refusal. But she said absolutely nothing. She simply curled up against him, resting her head on his chest, and his fierce amazon felt very small in his arms, small and fragile.

As fragile as a mountain lion, he reminded himself. But he wrapped his arms around her, very carefully, and held her tight against him. She'd get used to the idea. Once she heard the lawyers' offer, once she knew what he was willing to do for her. She'd welcome his offer.

Unless, of course, unlike everyone else in Hollywood, she simply couldn't be bought.

Chapter Seventeen

There was never any doubt in Rafe's mind that she'd be gone when he woke the next morning. Twice during the long night he woke up and made love to her, once slowly, gently, lingeringly, the last with a wild, desperate passion, with both of them afraid it really would be the last time.

When he woke the third time he was alone. Dawn was breaking over the city, a cool, clear dawn, and the bed was empty. She was gone, leaving nothing behind but the terry robe she'd worn so briefly. He picked it up and held it against his face. It smelled like her. It smelled like the chlorine from the pool, and warm skin, and that subtle, flowery perfume she wore that was both innocent and astoundingly sexy. And he wondered what the hell he was going to do if she really left him.

He tried to swim off some of his tension, lap after lap, slicing through the water. It didn't help. He still hadn't remembered to get more cigarettes, which was just as well. The black coffee was already doing a number on him, and he wished he could even entertain the notion of spiking it with a shot of whiskey.

He couldn't, not with his family history. He had no particular craving for alcohol, no need for its varied effects, but he didn't count on that continuing. Alcohol was a mild pleasure he enjoyed—if it ever got any power over him he'd dispense with it ruthlessly.

If only he could do that with Silver. For the first time in his life he was at the mercy of another human being. If she walked away from him today he'd survive. He'd always survived.

He just damned well wouldn't want to.

He dressed in his L.A. clothes. Egyptian cotton shirt, Armani suit, leather running shoes and emerald stud in his ear. Someone told him the stone matched the color of his eyes. The thought had amused him. Now he was willing to do anything to entice her to stay with him.

The others were already assembled in the conference room at Pegasus Pictures, several miles up the road from the more down-homey atmosphere of Mack Movies. He wondered what Silver would think when she saw the phalanx of support gathered on the opposite side of the table. Would she hold her ground?

He should have told her last night, but he'd been afraid to. The great Rafe McGinnis, the invulnerable power broker who chewed up innocents and ate them for breakfast, had been afraid. Of saying the wrong thing. Of saying it at the wrong time. All he'd wanted was to take what she'd been willing to give. And wait until today to work it out.

"Back to the high life again?" Sam asked when he strode into the conference room. "What happened to Pecos Bill?"

"Leave him alone," Bernie snapped, looking pale and edgy. "We don't need your sophomoric humor today. As a matter of fact, I don't see why we need you at all. Why don't you go back to the studio and find something to keep you busy?"

"Hell, no!" Sam said. "He started it, I intend to see him finish it. And let me tell you, Rafe, if you blow it now you're in deep trouble. I would have been perfectly happy to let Miller do the screenplay until I read Carlysle's version. Now I'm not ready to compromise." He plopped his ample frame down in the seat. "You know, I think part of the power of *Black Canyon* is that it's a man's story, written by a woman. Now that I think about it, I'm willing to bet you that D. Maven was a woman, too."

Bernie spilled her coffee.

Rafe just looked at her, refusing to take it in. "You can't be serious," he said.

Bernie managed a shrug and an embarrassed grin. "What can I say? I was young once. Idealistic. Too bad I only had one story to tell."

"I'm going to kill you," Rafe announced calmly.

"Am I missing something?" Sam demanded.

"Meet D. Maven," Rafe said.

"Bernie?" Sam was aghast.

"We all have skeletons in our closet," Bernie muttered, looking embarrassed.

"Unfortunately none of this matters. We don't care about the rights to the original any longer. What we want is Silver's screenplay, and who D. Maven really was is beside the point," a well-bred voice pointed out from across the table.

Rafe dropped into one of the leather chairs and stared at Jeremiah Pinkins as he tried to absorb this latest shock. As usual, Jeremiah was eminently sensible, but then, what else would you expect from one of L.A.'s most powerful and persuasive lawyers?

Jeremiah was a man who could make Clement Walden look like a cracker. He was in the prime of life at somewhere past seventy, with a full head of flowing white hair, the voice of an orator, the stance of a patriarch and the charm of a devil. He'd headed the legal department of Pegasus Pictures for more than forty years now, and now in his well-deserved retirement he only came out when the really big guns were required. Jeremiah Pinkins was a big gun indeed, and Silver probably wouldn't even realize how desperate Rafe was.

"She's late," Bernie said, looking at her watch and taking her seat beside Rafe, the tremor in her voice betraying her uncharacteristic nervousness. "Did you see the retraction in the newspaper? Walden really wrote that article."

"I hadn't noticed," Rafe said absently, concentrating on the walnut door to the outer office.

"Didn't notice? Someone spills your dirty laundry all over the feature page of the *Los Angeles Clarion* and you don't

notice?'' Sam said. "I suppose we have Jeremiah to thank for
the clarification.''

"No, you don't,'' Jeremiah announced in his wonderfully
rounded tones. "Though I did have my people check with the
Clarion. It seems Clement Walden has been a naughty boy.
Signing the wrong name to various pieces. Nothing illegal
about giving credit away, but he's also come close to plagia-
rism more than once. Perhaps overstepped the bounds. Apparently he's going on a long sabbatical. To write the definitive
book on film criticism, supposedly.''

Bernie snorted with contempt. "The definitive book on ped-
antry, you mean. What about Silver?''

"It was hardly my people's place to ask,'' Jeremiah said.
"However, I was given to believe they'd welcome her if she
chose to fill Clement's shoes.''

Rafe didn't blink. He didn't know whether that was good
news or bad news. If she took the job she'd still be in L.A., at
least part of the time. Which meant she'd be close enough for
him to keep working on, if she turned her back on him now.
On the other hand, he wanted to take her away from all this,
for at least part of the long future he envisioned. Up into the
mountains, to make babies and movies and love.

"Do you think she's going to show?'' Sam drawled, loosening his already disreputable tie.

"I don't know,'' Rafe said honestly, thinking of the light in
her expressive blue eyes, the softness of her mouth, the strength
in her body. Gone, run away from him. "I really don't know.''

The two buzzes on the intercom startled them all into silence.
"I guess they're here,'' Rafe said unnecessarily. He buzzed
back, and a moment later the door opened.

He'd expected she'd come with her own battalion of lawyers.
With Clement Walden hovering at her shoulder, her powerhouse of a mother lurking behind, and all the legal firepower
her wealthy stepfather could afford. Instead she stood alone,
and despite her height she looked small and fragile.

She'd dressed for the occasion, in some sort of soft knit dress
that rested delectably on her curves. She hadn't done it on

purpose, he knew that. She probably just wanted to look professional. Instead she looked so good he wanted to clear the room and throw her down on the table and make love to her until she couldn't fight him anymore.

He didn't move, a muscle ticking in his jaw. "Silver," he greeted her, sounding calm and almost bored. "Where's your lawyer?"

She closed the door behind her, and he could see the nervousness in her movements. "I don't need one. I spoke to Mr. Pinkins's office yesterday and tried to explain. I'm not contesting ownership of *Black Canyon* anymore. It's yours. I won't fight you. I'll sign anything you want me to sign, give you what you want. I just don't want to deal with it anymore."

Rafe started to say something, but Jeremiah cleared his throat, forestalling him, and the sound was deafening in the conference room. "That's exactly why you need a lawyer, Miss Carlysle. Making rash statements like that will only get you into trouble. I doubt that you have any idea what Mr. McGinnis wants from you, so if I were you I wouldn't be quite so ready to hand it over without a certain amount of negotiation."

She smiled then. A mischievous crinkling in the corner of her mouth, that made his body go rock hard beneath the table. "I imagine I can guess," she murmured. "He can have the rights to *Black Canyon*—I won't contest his ownership. Therefore he doesn't have to pay me anything, and it's all settled."

"On the contrary, my dear," Jeremiah intoned. "He doesn't want the rights to *Black Canyon* alone. As a matter of fact that's no longer an issue. He wants to use your screenplay."

Rafe didn't know what he expected. Tears of joy. Silver flinging herself across the table at him in love-filled relief. Something. Anything.

She didn't move. "How much?"

Pinkins was used to dealing, and used to reading the emotional temperature in the room. He named a figure, just below the top price Rafe wanted to pay, well above the amount he'd planned to start with.

Silver didn't even blink at the sound of more money than most people make in their lifetimes. "No," she said flatly.

Rafe sat bolt upright in the leather chair. "No?" he echoed. "Why not?"

She moved across the room, graceful, sexy, determined, and leaned over the table, the others in the room forgotten. "Because," she said, very calm, "you can't buy me. You can have the Western, you can do anything you damned please with it, but you can't have my screenplay. God, you're even willing to fork over a ridiculous amount of money just to salvage my pride. You don't need to. My pride is just fine, thank you. I can turn and walk away, and it won't hurt at all. You won, Rafe. You told me you would, and I didn't believe you. You proved it, in no uncertain terms. Don't try to throw the game at this late date because you feel sorry for the loser. I didn't lose. I'm letting go. It's not worth fighting for anymore."

"Sit down, Silver," Rafe said in a deceptively gentle voice. She didn't move. "Sit down," he thundered, and everyone in the room jumped. Everyone but Silver.

She took the seat, however, but there was no missing the defiance in her eyes.

God, it was the defiance he loved. Along with everything else. "We won't do *Black Canyon* without your screenplay," he said flatly. "Isn't that right, Sam?"

"Right," Sam piped up immediately, obviously fascinated by all this.

"You won't do *Black Canyon* with it," she said flatly.

They stared at each other across the table for a long, silent moment. And then Rafe leaned back. "That settles that."

"I suppose it does."

"If I might say something…" Jeremiah Pinkins began, but Rafe very calmly stopped him.

"We're finished here. Bernie, would you give Jeffrey Metzger a call at Regis Pictures. They've been doing their damnedest to get a look at Silver's screenplay ever since we got it away from them. Tell them they have first shot at it."

"Wait a minute!" Sam protested.

Rafe glanced at him, then sighed. "They can borrow Sam for director, and you too, Bernie, if you want to go. Jeremiah can negotiate." He rose, walking away from the table, not looking at Silver's stunned figure.

"Rafe!" Bernie protested. "You're handing it over to your strongest competitor, just like that?"

He paused at the door, looking back into Silver's shocked eyes. "Just like that," he said. And walked out the door.

THE ROOM WAS PANDEMONIUM after Rafe dropped his bombshell. Silver sat in the chair, unmoving in her disbelief. He'd outdone her, and for a moment she sat frozen in shock.

And then she began to laugh. Absurd as it was, she couldn't help it. She sat back in the chair and laughed until the tears ran down her face, until the others in the room stopped their bickering and stared at her in shock and consternation.

She'd been ready to give him everything, to make the final sacrifice, as some doomed act of love. And instead, like some cockeyed version of "Gift of the Magi," he'd made the same sacrifice, leaving her own grand gesture effectively trashed. There was nothing she could do but laugh.

It took her a moment to compose herself, with the aid of Bernie's unexpectedly feminine lace handkerchief and what little was left of her self-control.

"He always does win, doesn't he?" she said weakly.

Bernie stared at her. "Does that mean you agree?"

"Do you think I can let him make that kind of sacrifice? Give up what he's been fighting for? Give it up for me?" She sighed, not sure whether she was close to tears or laughter again. "Of course I agree. Whatever terms you want to come up with, Mr. Pinkins."

"I've warned you, Ms. Carlysle..."

"It really doesn't matter," Silver said. "He's going to be paying my bills anyway."

Bernie still stood there, her craggy face creased with concern. "It'll mean a great deal to all of us," she said. "We all believe in the project. And I wanted to do it for your father's sake.''

Silver looked up at her, at the plain, horsey woman who was twenty years older than her mother. "You broke up my parents' marriage," she said, out of the blue.

Bernie flinched. "Yes."

"Marjorie could overlook the starlets and the one-night stands. She simply couldn't tolerate the fact that he could sleep with someone he respected, someone…" Her words trailed off.

"Sleep with someone so old and ugly," Bernie supplied wryly. "Your father loved my mind. He loved your mother's face, he loved a hundred women's bodies. I was just the final insult. He would have left her if it hadn't been for you. He loved you, Silver. Even if he wasn't smart enough to show it."

"Not good enough," she said fiercely. "I want a man who isn't afraid to show he loves me."

"Then for God's sake go after him," Bernie said. "Before he gets away."

Rafe was standing in the parking lot, between the two vehicles. On the one side was his Lotus, fast and sleek and very California. On the other was the rented Colorado pickup truck, mud still clinging to its axles. He stood in the middle, waiting for her.

"Did I hear you laughing in there?" he asked, sounding no more than casually interested.

"You did. You told me you always won, and I never really believed you." She came up close to him, not touching, tilting her head back to look up into his face. He was wearing shades again, and he looked very California. "I just didn't realize that we could both win. Which car are we taking?"

He didn't touch her, and she wanted him to. "The truck belongs in Colorado," he said. "The Lotus in L.A."

"Does it snow a lot in Colorado in October, or was that just a fluke?"

"It snows a lot in the mountains."

"I love the mountains."

"I love you," he said, pushing the sunglasses up on his forehead, and she didn't for one moment doubt him.

She smiled then. "Let's get snowed in," she said, "and we can spend our time arguing about it."

He put his arms around her then, drawing her tight against his strong, hard body. "Be glad to," he said, his mouth hovering over hers. "But let me warn you, I always win."

"I'm counting on it," she said. "Because so do I." And threading her fingers through his long, wavy hair, she kissed him, giving him her heart and soul and love.

Bernie stood watching from behind the thin-slatted blinds in the front office, a radiant expression on her wrinkled face. "Ain't love grand?" she murmured out loud. "This one's for you, Benny." And she let the blinds drop closed again, turning back to the conference room, secure in the knowledge that her job was done.

They had two things in common—
they both had deep, dark secrets and
they were both falling in love...with each other.

Hand in Glove

Prologue

"Judith?" The voice was tear-filled, raw and shaky.

Judith let out a small, desperate groan into the telephone receiver. "Lacey, it's three o'clock in the morning!"

"I know, I know, Judith. It's just that—" Lacey's voice caught on a strangled sob "—I'm frightened and I don't know what to do."

Judith was too tired to keep the long-suffering sigh to herself. "Lucy, you're always getting yourself into messes. I don't want to hear about it. I don't want to hear how good Ryan Smith is in bed. I don't want to hear about his angry wife. I don't want to hear how you've made another mistake and you want me to bail you out."

"You've got it all wrong."

"Have I?"

"For one thing, Ryan Smith isn't married. For another, he's lousy in bed."

"It still sounds like you've made another mistake."

"Judith, I think he's trying to kill me."

Slowly, deliberately, Judith counted to ten. "I don't think so, Lacey," she said patiently.

"No, I mean it. Someone's been watching me, following me around...."

"Well, then, get out of there. Go back to Manhattan. If Ryan Smith isn't any good in bed, you won't be missing anything," Judith said, getting cranky.

"I'm not ready to leave."

Someone new in the wings, Judith thought. "So what do you want from me?"

"I didn't say that I wanted anything from you...."

"Lacey, you never call me unless you want something. Okay, Ryan Smith is trying to kill you." And who can blame him? Judith added silently. "What do you want me to do about it?"

"You have connections there at the paper. Couldn't you pull a few strings, arrange an interview with him? That way you could show up, check out the situation and see whether I'm imagining it."

"I don't need to drive up to the Hudson River Valley to know you're imagining it, Lacey. And people who write syndicated fix-it columns do not do interviews with world-famous puppeteers. Sorry, I can't help."

"Judith, didn't you hear what I said? I think he's trying to kill me!" Lacey sounded more affronted at her friend's lack of sympathy than actually frightened.

"Then get out of there," Judith said flatly. "Call me tomorrow. And for once in your life, make it before midnight."

"Judith..."

Slowly, carefully, Judith replaced the receiver. With a weary sigh she slid back down in her bed, pulling the covers over her head and consigning the latest melodramatic fantasy of one of her oldest friends to the garbage heap it deserved. Someone was always out to get Lacey. Her persecution fantasies were almost as numerous as her delusions of grandeur, and Judith had learned long ago to discount them. She discounted them now, praying that Lacey wouldn't call back and disrupt the first good night's sleep she'd had in weeks.

Lacey didn't call back. Twelve hours later her body was found enmeshed in the hydro system of Ryan Smith's Puppet Factory on the banks of the Hudson River. And Judith wondered if she'd ever sleep through the night again.

Chapter One

It was too damned hot for only the middle of May. The sun was beating down overhead, turning the interior of Judith Daniels's 1957 gull-wing Mercedes into an oven. She opened the window, delivering her perfect curtain of hair to the four winds, and pressed her leather-shod foot down harder on the gas pedal. She had unaccustomed knots in her stomach; the sweat on her palms was from nerves, not from the ninety-plus temperature; and her brain was busy with second, third and twelfth thoughts. She had to be out of her mind.

Who did she think she was, some bizarre cross between Nancy Drew and Brenda Starr? What made her think she could infiltrate the very sacrosanct premises of The Puppet Factory and solve a mystery that was probably nothing more than an accident and not the murder she alone suspected? And what would she gain by learning the truth? Were her motives all that pure? Did she want to find out what really happened to one of her best friends, or did she want the long-elusive byline?

She'd always prided herself on being brutally honest, unflinching when it came to her ambitions. But right now Lacey Hollister's death and the probable cover-up were foremost in her mind, and she was too much of a journalist to ignore the potential if what she suspected had happened turned out to be the truth.

The Hudson River Valley was in full flower, with the rich, leafy green of new growth turning the two-lane highway into

a winding tunnel of color. Five miles till Miller's Junction, the
tiny town on the east side of the Hudson. Five miles till she
reached the converted mill that now housed The Puppet Factory.

She was traveling at fifty-seven miles an hour, despite the
twists and turns of the road. At that rate she'd be there in about
six minutes, which was all the time she had left to change her
mind. She and Lacey hadn't been close in years, so why should
she owe her anything? It was only nostalgia and guilt that were
preying on her mind. And morbid curiosity.

During the last few years their relationship had consisted of
late-night phone calls, with Lacey complaining to Judith after
each love affair had fizzled. When you came right down to it,
Lacey had only herself to blame. Her sexual habits were downright dangerous. Time after time Lacey set her sights on some
unattainable male, and nothing would stop her until she got
him. And of course, once she got him, the prize lost its appeal.
Then she'd be crying on Judith's shoulder again, ignoring the
broken marriage and murderous fury she'd left behind. Sooner
or later she'd been bound to move in on the wrong man, the
wrong relationship, and it looked as if that was what had happened.

She'd chosen Ryan Smith this time, the reclusive, brilliant
puppeteer, and taken dead aim at him, worming her way into
the world-famous Puppet Factory, worming her way into his
bed. And as usual, she hadn't been happy with the results.

They'd found her body caught in the elaborate hydro system
of the refurbished mill. There'd been an investigation, and Judith had used her sources at the *Philadelphia Mirror* to keep
close tabs on its progress. But in the end Lacey's death had
been ruled an accident, and Ryan Smith had gotten off scot-
free. And Judith couldn't rid herself of the suspicion that his
seldom-used money and power had engineered that comfortable verdict at the inquest.

She didn't have much on which to base that suspicion. But
a hysterical late-night telephone call and her reporter's instincts
told her it wasn't the accident the rest of the world thought it

was. Lacey had hated heights and detested being alone. So why had she been hanging over a balcony in the middle of the night with no one around? There was no way that Lacey could have fallen without any witnesses present.

It was all too circumstantial for Judith even to mention to anyone. Judith would follow her nose and try to find some hard evidence. If Lacey's paranoid hysteria had been right, if Ryan Smith had really been planning to kill her, Judith wouldn't let him get away with it.

Her fix-it column at the *Mirror* was on hold, her job in abeyance. Not that anyone knew what she was doing. As far as the editorial staff was concerned, Judith Daniels was on a long-deserved two-month vacation. And when she returned, exclusive in hand, she could kiss the fix-it column goodbye and concentrate on what she'd wanted all along—investigative journalism.

The idea had seemed so simple when she'd first thought of it. Lacey had managed to get hired as a sort of glorified gofer, a cross between clerk-typist and apprentice puppeteer. If they had hired Lacey, who had had no qualifications other than her luscious figure and bubbly good nature, then they could hire Judith. She'd passed the first test—her job interview was scheduled for this morning. All she had to do was convince Mrs. Elvira Carter, and presumably Ryan Smith himself, to hire her.

Judith had never been denied any job she'd applied for. Only the lofty heights of investigative reporting had escaped her, and that state of affairs wasn't going to last much longer.

She swung the Mercedes into The Puppet Factory's parking lot, pulled it in beside the raft of Japanese and Swedish imports and switched off the engine. Her palms were still sweaty, the heat was still blistering, but her doubts had, for the moment, been dismissed. She owed Lacey something for the good times they'd shared, and she owed herself this chance at escape from a stifling job. She'd find out just what had gone on inside this old mill. If Lacey's death had been nothing more than a bizarre, incomprehensible accident, she'd accept that fact and go back to her fix-it column with the knowledge that at least she had tried.

The converted textile mill was built into the side of the riverbank and stood five stories above the water. Its ancient wood frame was stained a warm mahogany, the new windows and trim blending with the original structure. From the parking lot, which was opposite the river, only two and a half stories were visible. There were maybe a dozen cars parked there, with nothing more exciting than an aging Toyota station wagon. Judith's exotic Mercedes was by far the flashiest vehicle, and once more she regretted her decision not to rent an anonymous American sedan.

At least Ryan Smith couldn't be there. A man with his undoubted money would certainly drive something a little better than a Datsun. Hell, he probably had a Rolls and a chauffeur; Lacey had always been attracted to the trappings money could provide. So for now all Judith had to do was persuade Mrs. Carter to hire her.

The cream linen suit was barely wrinkled despite her long drive, and Judith slid the jacket over her ivory silk blouse with only a passing regret for the steamy weather. Although the wind had blown through the open car window, her hair was reasonably subdued; and she started up the bank of stairs to the entrance of the factory, assured that she looked like a normal, neatly dressed job applicant.

Her looks had worked against her more than once, smoothing the way when she'd rather have earned it, greasing the wheels, making people expect the wrong sort of things from her. But there wasn't much she could do about that.

Judith Kennedy Daniels was the daughter of an extremely old, extremely wealthy Irish Catholic family from the Main Line of Philadelphia, and every inch of her long, leggy body, her flawless complexion, her blue, blue eyes, her silky blond hair and her perfect features proclaimed that lineage. She resembled a tall young Grace Kelly, elegant and untouchable. Until one looked deeper into her eyes and saw the streak of mischief; until she changed from her silk and linen into the more usual baggy jeans and T-shirts, her hair pulled back with a bandana and a streak of grease across one high cheekbone.

But right now she looked like a refugee from the jet set, from her handmade leather pumps to her perfect pageboy, and she entered the fourth floor business office in the ramshackle old mill as if she were royalty.

There were two women in the well-lit, spacious office. One was a bespectacled female in the shady area between forty and sixty, hunched over a computer screen, barely daring to cast a furtive, curious glance in Judith's direction before returning her attention to the machine in front of her. That left the other occupant, and Judith turned to her, summoning her most charming smile.

Mrs. Elvira Carter was not impressed, and Judith could only be glad she hadn't held out her hand. Doubtless the woman would have refused to shake it.

She was in her sixties, a squat, sour-looking creature with colorless eyes, a thin, pursed mouth, gray hair the texture of steel wool and probably a heart of flint. Her eyes swept over Judith's figure, and she emitted something that could only be termed a snort.

"Mrs. Carter?" Judith inquired in her smooth, warm voice, determinedly unruffled. "I'm Judith Daniels. I have an interview—"

"You won't do."

"I beg you pardon?"

"I said you won't do. We need someone who's willing to work for a living, not a debutante," the woman said, her flat, Midwestern accent expressionless.

Judith didn't let a trace of irritation cross her features. "I'm a hard worker. My references—"

"I trust my own judgment, not someone else's," Mrs. Carter snapped. "Your references were fine, but you won't do. That's that. Goodbye."

Judith stared down at her, controlling the urge to turn on her heel and stalk from the room. For Lacey, she would try one more time, even if it meant groveling before this unpleasant woman. "I've driven a long way this morning," she said gently. "Don't you think you owe me the courtesy of an interview?"

"I don't owe you anything," Mrs. Carter said, eyes becoming beadier, thin mouth harder. "If you don't..."

Judith heard the door open behind her, but years of self-discipline kept her from turning to look at the recent arrival. Whoever he or she was, the person was enough to stop Mrs. Carter in her tracks.

"The air conditioner on two is broken again," a deep male voice said in an exasperated tone. "The damned place is an oven. Try calling Matthews again and see if you can get him out here."

Judith allowed herself a brief, curious glance behind her. The man was tall, dark-haired and dressed in rough denims. He looked more like a carpenter than someone who controlled a multimillion dollar corporation. Ryan Smith didn't have his picture taken very often, but during her research Judith had managed to dig up a photo that was more than five years old. He hadn't changed much since then. He was still tall, rangy and surprisingly attractive.

"What kind of air conditioner?" she asked.

For the first time he looked at her, from a height that must have topped six feet four, and his green-gray eyes were both startled and slightly amused. She'd definitely worn the wrong clothes, she thought with a sigh.

"It's a Roberts 450," he said finally. "It's brand-new and it's never worked right, and we can't get the damned repairman out for love or money. Why?"

"I can fix it."

The slight amusement broadened to a disbelieving grin. The grin was a revelation in his narrow face, lighting it with a breathtaking beauty that left Judith momentarily shocked. And then the smile was gone as quickly as it had come, and his craggy, austere features resettled into a distant expression.

"Sure you can," he drawled, his eyes running from the tips of her leather pumps up her designer linen suit, past the silk blouse to her clear, perfect features. "Call Matthews again, will you, Ma?"

Judith was somewhat bewildered at hearing the sour Mrs. Carter referred to as "Ma." "I can fix it," she said again. "I've worked on a Roberts 150, and the newer model shouldn't be that different. It won't do you any harm to let me try."

"Who the hell are you?"

"My name's Judith Daniels—"

"She's here for a job interview," Mrs. Carter intervened. "I told her she's not what we're looking for."

Ryan Smith studied her again. "You should be wearing short white gloves and a pillbox hat," he said.

Judith felt an unaccustomed red stain her cheeks. "They taught me to dress properly for a job interview."

"Who taught you?"

"Bryn Mawr College," Mrs. Carter supplied, in a tone that suggested the school was something close to a brothel.

"And what do you think Bryn Mawr taught you that would come in handy in a puppet factory?" Ryan Smith asked Judith skeptically.

She'd caught his interest—at least that was something. "They didn't teach me how to repair air conditioners, if that's what you're wondering. I picked that up on my own."

"Call Matthews," he ordered again. "I'm sorry, Miss Daniels, but I trust Ma's opinion."

"It wouldn't do you any harm to let me try. Even if Matthews will come, it'll take him some time to get here. And I'm already here."

He paused. "So you are. All right, Miss Bryn Mawr. Follow me."

"Ryan…" Mrs. Carter began.

"Don't worry, Ma," he said from the door. "If Matthews can't even fix the damned thing, I doubt the princess will. Say goodbye to Ma, Miss Daniels. I don't think you'll be seeing her again."

"What if I can fix the machine?" Judith demanded stubbornly, not moving.

He looked at her out of those distant eyes, and once more a slow smile crossed his face. "If you can fix the machine," he said, "you're hired."

Judith grinned in return. "Then you've got yourself a new worker, Mr. Smith."

If he was surprised she recognized him, he didn't show it. "Ryan," he corrected. "Say goodbye to Ma."

Judith gave Mrs. Carter a smile that was greeted by a stony glare. "See you later, Ma." And she followed Ryan's tall figure out into the stairwell.

HE COULD HEAR her trotting along behind him, those ridiculous shoes going tap, tap, tap on the metal staircase leading down to the lower levels. He'd been a fool to agree to let her near the air conditioner; he should have trusted Ma's judgment. Still, she was more than overprotective, and there was something about the lady trailing him, a determined look in those sky blue eyes of hers that made him think there might be a chance in hell that she could fix a complicated piece of machinery that had stumped even the experienced dealer.

But that wasn't all. She was familiar, damnably familiar, yet he couldn't place her. The name, the face, the very look of her sparked some well-hidden snippet of memory, and he prided himself on his ability to remember even obscure details. If she walked out of the factory now, it might take him ages to recall where he'd seen her and heard of her. Until that happened, he wouldn't be able to concentrate on his work.

"You from around here?" he questioned lightly, his long legs eating up the flights of stairs.

"No."

"What made you apply for work at the Factory? It doesn't seem like your sort of job." He kept his voice neutral. He had nothing against the woman. After all, princesses had their place in this world. They just didn't have any place in The Puppet Factory or in his life.

"I like puppets."

Simply said, and somehow he believed her. He probably

shouldn't, not when there was that nagging familiarity teasing his brain. She must have another reason for being here, and as soon as he remembered who she was, he'd have the answer. But he could believe that she really did like puppets, no doubt just because he wanted to.

"I don't need any more puppeteers," he said. "The job would involve grunt work. Making coffee, working on costumes, helping Ma out in the office."

"I could do it."

"Don't you think you're a little overqualified?"

"Isn't that up to me to decide?" she countered.

"Hell, no, princess. I'd be the one signing your paycheck. It's up to me to decide." He looked over his shoulder at her. That pale, generous mouth was set in a stubborn line, her eyes were nothing short of furious, and her body radiated determination. Wait till she got a look at the mess Matthews had made of the Roberts 450 last time he was here, Ryan thought smugly. She'd turn that well-bred tail and run.

He could see the wheels spinning in her brain as she asked, "It wouldn't involve the puppets at all?" She was trying to sound diffident.

"You'd have to talk to them. Everyone does—it's part of the scene around here."

"Mrs. Carter talks to them?"

He allowed himself a small grin. "Ma keeps out of the lower levels. She has trouble enough being pleasant to humans, and the puppets are sensitive."

"How is this place set up?" Judith glanced around curiously, seemingly unruffled by the oppressive heat that only increased as they descended the next flight of stairs. "Not that it's any of my business, since you're about to send me packing," she added, forestalling him.

He shrugged. "Who knows? You may be able to fix the air conditioner after all. Stranger things have happened. To answer your question, this used to be an old textile mill. There are five stories. The first floor—or basement—is used to store supplies, old costumes, puppets, wood. The second floor is a workshop, where we design and assemble the puppets. The third floor is the creative level. That's where we work, experiment, play around. It has a very sophisticated video system—most of what we do there is taped for future study. The fourth floor is the business level, where Ma and Bessie hang out. There's a conference room that's never used, and still more storage space."

"And the top floor?"

He hesitated only a moment. "Nothing to speak of. We have a freight elevator that goes up there, but no stairs. It's not used much."

"And where's the air conditioner?"

They'd stopped on the second floor landing. He pushed open the door, and a blast of heat wafted over them. "Right in here, princess," he said. "It's all yours."

The designers and crafters, usually some twenty strong, had all headed up to the cooler, air-conditioned floors. The huge space was deserted, projects scattered about, half finished. The Roberts was sitting in the west wall, making ominous, grumbling noises while sending out miserable blasts of heat. Ryan glanced at Judith, waiting for her reaction.

"Got any tools?" she said, stripping off her jacket and tossing it on a workbench.

"Everything you could want."

She advanced on the monster and rolled up her silk sleeves, a determined look in her eyes. "I'll need a Phillips screwdriver, medium size, a regular screwdriver, wire strippers, small vice grips and maybe some wire nuts."

"You expect me to get them for you?"

"I don't see anyone else around, do you?" she said patiently. "What did you do, spray paint it with lube oil?" she asked in disgust, squatting in front of the machine, oblivious to her skirt trailing in the dust.

"If you're too squeamish…"

"I'm not. How come you didn't put central air conditioning in when you redid the place?" Her voice held no more than idle curiosity as she switched off the machine and started poking around.

"I should have. I was hoping it wouldn't be necessary. I hate artificial air."

"Can you imagine what it would have been like in the 1800s when this was a working mill?" She began pulling green, yellow and red wires out of the heart of the Roberts seemingly at random. "It must have been very close to hell."

"It doesn't usually get this hot." He set the tools down beside her, noticing with fascination that she already had a streak of grease across her forehead and over the right shoulder of her blouse.

"It would with machinery running. Hand me the vice grips, would you?"

He did so, and as her hand brushed his, she left a trail of black grease on his fingers. "Sorry about that," she muttered, rubbing her filthy hand across her skirt. "It's what I suspected."

"What is?" He squatted beside her, fascinated in spite of himself as he watched her deal with the arcane complexities of modern machinery.

"He wired it wrong. Roberts air conditioners are tricky. It's easy to reverse the—" She stopped in midsentence. "Do you know what I'm talking about?"

"No."

"Do you care?"

"Not really. Not as long as it's working."

She grinned, and there was a spot of grime on her nose. "It will be. Give me five minutes."

Slowly he rose to his full height, staring down at her as she continued to fiddle with the recalcitrant air conditioner. He'd finally placed her, and he wished to hell he hadn't.

That woman, Lacey, the one who'd been stupid enough to fall into the hydro system and get herself killed. That silly little creature who'd followed him around, panting at his heels like a bitch in heat with her nonstop prattle. Part of that nonstop prattle had been about her friend Judith, the reporter. She'd even shown him a picture of the two of them in college, ten years earlier. Bryn Mawr, he thought with a grimace. No wonder Judith Daniels looked familiar.

And she hadn't said a word about her friend Lacey. She'd come up here just because she liked puppets, had she? God, he'd had enough reporters around the past few weeks to last him a lifetime!

She shoved the wires back in and turned the switch. Instead of the ugly grinding noise he had come to expect, there was a quiet, satisfied purr. Cold air began to pour around his ankles.

Judith rose, pushing her hair back and leaving a trail of grime. She looked like a chimney sweep, and immensely pleased with herself.

"Well?" she said.

"Well," he said. "You've got yourself a job."

Chapter Two

The moment the words were out of his mouth he seemed to regret them. Judith couldn't figure out why. After all, she'd fixed his air conditioner in no time flat, and she was young and presentable. Maybe he was scared of Ma's reaction. No, scratch that. For all his quiet demeanor, Ryan Smith didn't look as if he'd be scared by anyone or anything.

"Great," she said quickly, not giving him a chance to renege. "Do you have a place where I can wash up?"

Once more a trace of amusement danced through his eyes, then vanished just as swiftly. "Next floor up. There are showers and a kitchen for employees."

"All the comforts of home?"

"It's tax deductible," he said flatly, denying any charitable motives.

The swinging door slammed open and a whirlwind rushed through. "Ryan, where the hell have you—" The whirlwind stopped, resolving itself into an extraordinarily handsome young man. "Good God, it's actually cool down here! Did Matthews finally accomplish the impossible?"

"Not Matthews, Steve," Ryan said. "Meet our new miracle worker. Judith Daniels, Steve Lindstrom."

"Hel-lo, pretty lady." The man moved closer, like a bird dog scenting a nice plump partridge, and Judith got a good look at him: wavy blond hair, dimpled chin, broad shoulders, muscular body, Nike-shod feet. "Where did Ryan find you?"

"She found us. I still haven't quite figured out how," Ryan said.

Judith cast him a quick glance. So he wondered about her, did he? Not half as much as she wondered about him.

"Well, you're a welcome addition to The Puppet Factory," Steve said, all but panting over her. "Ryan doesn't hire women for their looks, and, lady, you're the best thing I've seen in years."

"Down, boy," Ryan murmured. "She's here to work, not to provide mattress duty."

"Ryan!" Steve appeared distressed. "Just because you're inhuman doesn't mean the rest of us aren't interested in the basic biological functions of eating, sleeping and sex."

"I'm more interested in the basic biological function of work. Which is why Judith is here. Isn't it?" There was a deceptively silky tone in his voice as he turned to her.

Steve thinks he's inhuman, she thought, putting that piece of information away in her brain for further study. Steve Lindstrom was a little too human for her tastes, but he certainly seemed talkative enough. If he were as indiscreet as he was loquacious, he could prove helpful indeed. As long as she didn't mind dealing with someone who had all the earmarks of an octopus.

"I'm here to work," she agreed. "When do you want me to start?"

"As soon as you're ready. Why put off the inevitable?"

"Ryan, you sound as if you don't want her here," Steve protested, moving closer. Judith was glad she was covered with grease. If she'd been relatively clean, Steve would have had his hands all over her by now.

Ryan looked at the two of them. "I'm not sure that I do," he said.

If only it weren't for Lacey, she thought. If only she had the nerve to throw the damned job back in his face. Let him wait for Matthews to fix his air conditioners!

But she couldn't do that. She was here for a reason, and she couldn't let pride or temper interfere. "I can start as soon as I find a place to live."

"No problem," Steve said. "Micki's looking for a room-mate."

Ryan snorted. "Micki and the princess? Now there's an odd couple."

"Who's Micki?" Judith asked.

"The Bronx Bombshell." Steve must have decided Judith was worth the mess, for he draped an arm around her shoulder and led her back toward the hallway. "Lemme explain the hierarchy around here, Judy."

"Judith."

"Whatever. Ryan, the man who's following us and glowering, is numero uno, the chief honcho, the boss man, the big cheese. Franz Himml is number two. He's been with Ryan forever and he's a sweet old buzzard. Very mittel-European, old-school, traditional sort of guy."

"He's also technically the best puppeteer in the business," Ryan said mildly enough.

"Maybe," Steve said. He smelled of spicy after-shave. Judith hated men who wore after-shave. She smiled at him, wondering if she could duck under his arm, drop back and put Ryan Smith's arm around her shoulders. Good heavens, what had made her fantasize about that? Either of these men might have murdered Lacey. She'd have to learn to be less trusting if she was going to get anywhere.

"Anyway," Steve continued, "after Franz comes yours truly. What I lack in traditional approach I more than make up for in youthful exuberance."

"*Time* magazine said that," Ryan put in. "Steve memorized every word."

"Well, it was apt," Steve replied with mock defensiveness. "Then Micki's moving fast to number four. She's got a way with the Green Goddesses that no one else does, and she's getting better and better with Billy and Fafnir."

Judith stopped in her tracks, deftly twisting out of Steve's embrace. "I thought you did Billy and Fafnir," she said to Ryan in a semiaccusing tone.

"Doing your research, Judith?" he inquired. "I used to. Right now we're working on having everyone be able to do every puppet. I don't want to do any more Las Vegas nightclubs or Broadway shows."

"That way we can go wherever we want," Steve said, trapping her unwilling body once more and ushering her up the stairs. "We'll have a lot more freedom, and Ryan can concentrate on what he does best."

"And what is that?"

"Why don't you let Miss Curiosity figure it out herself, Steve?" Ryan said from directly behind them, and there was no mistaking the thinly veiled order in his voice.

"Yes, sir," Steve answered with a show of docility as they stopped before another set of swinging doors. "Prepare yourself, Judy. You're about to discover the most important part of the The Puppet Factory."

"More important than Ryan?"

"Definitely," Ryan said, opening one door and letting the cacophony spill out around them.

"I can do the honors," Steve said. "You don't need to waste your time, Ryan."

Ryan smiled, that small, sexy smile. "I wouldn't miss it for the world. Come along, princess."

Judith pulled herself away from Steve's possessive grip. "Let's get one tiny thing clear," she said firmly. "My name isn't Judy, and it sure as hell isn't princess. My name is Judith, or hey you, and that's all I'm going to answer to."

There was silence in the hallway, a silence almost drowned out by the noise beyond the open door. She could see Ryan watching her, weighing his options. She'd given him reason to fire her if he wanted to be hardnosed about it, and she knew all along he wanted that reason. She opened her mouth to apologize, then shut it again. She wasn't going to spend the next few weeks listening to that mocking voice calling her princess every time she turned around, not even for an ill-defined debt she owed Lacey.

Steve cleared his throat nervously. "I'll go see if I can find Micki." He vanished into the workroom, leaving her to face Ryan's enigmatic expression.

He looked austere, disapproving, and his green-gray eyes were cool. He was going to tell her the job wouldn't work out after all, and it was all her fault. She stood there looking up at him, mutely defiant, forgetting the streak of grease down her face, her filthy suit, her tangled hair and general air of disreputability.

"Princess," he said deliberately, "I'll call you anything I damned well please."

"Over my dead body." The moment the words were out of her mouth she choked. She could feel her face turn pale, then red, but there was nothing she could do about it.

Damn him, he smiled, a cynical, sour little smile. "So you know about that, too. How much else did you discover in your research?"

"It only makes sense to find out everything you can about a prospective employer," she said finally.

"They teach you that at Bryn Mawr? They told you to wear suits, and look where it got you." He reached out one deft finger and traced the streak of grease across her shoulder. "If I were you, Judith Daniels, I would learn discretion. If you know about the accident, then you might guess that people are very jumpy around here. It makes them nervous when someone dies like that. If you want to get along with everybody, you'll need to exercise a little caution." His voice was calm.

"And if I don't?"

"If you don't," he echoed softly, "you'll regret it."

She looked up at him fearlessly, only a distant part of her brain noticing how nice it was to look up at a man for a change. "Is that a threat?"

"Take it in the nature of a little friendly advice. My insurance rates have already skyrocketed. I don't want to jeopardize them any more."

"Is that what that woman meant to you?" she couldn't keep herself from asking. "An increase in your insurance rates?"

Once more his face was shuttered, unreadable. "I don't think that's any of your business. Are you certain you want this job?"

She glanced past him into the noisy, crowded workroom. "I'm certain."

"Then, *princess*," he said deliberately, "after you." And he gestured her inside.

It was bedlam. Noise and color, heat and light; voices talking, singing, laughing, crooning; the voices of puppets surrounding her in a wave of sound. The third floor of the puppet factory was, like the workshop below it, one large room, with a wall of windows overlooking a wide balcony that stretched above the river. There were video cameras angled from the ceiling like a security system gone haywire; there were video monitors all over the place; there were platforms and booths and stages of every size and description. And there were people, predominantly young and casually dressed, with puppets in their hands, the soft, malleable glove puppets for which The Puppet Factory was famous.

"Hey, you," a low, sexy voice growled in her ear. Judith jumped, startled, and turned to look into a pair of eyes made from Ping Pong balls. They resided in the middle of a purple fur face, above a waxed mustache that would have done a villain proud, and a long, forked tongue slithered between furry jaws. "Hey, you," the voice said again. "What a babe. I didn't know they let good-looking chicks in this place."

"Don't call her a chick." A plaintive, gentle voice admonished the creature, followed by the appearance of a little boy. Except that the little boy had a pair of glasses for eyes, orange yarn for hair, and a soft cloth face that looked downright wistful. "Women don't like to be called chicks; it's demeaning," the puppet told his friend. He turned to Judith. "Please excuse him. Fafnir doesn't know much about the proper behavior between the sexes. He's only a dragon, and there aren't men and women dragons. There are only dragons.'' The puppet waited expectantly for her reply.

Judith felt like a complete and utter fool. Every eye in the place was trained on her; she could feel Ryan Smith himself directly behind her, watching her reaction to his offspring. She cleared her throat nervously. ''How do they make baby dragons, then?'' she managed to say, trying to look straight at the puppet.

Fafnir sunk his head down low on the stage. ''They don't,'' he offered mournfully. ''That's why we're almost extinct. A thousand years of celibacy can get to a creature—it's no wonder I'm a little preoccupied with sex.''

''You're obsessed,'' the other puppet said sternly, then turned back to Judith. ''Allow me to introduce myself. I'm Billy. Do you work here?''

Not for long if I don't get the hang of this, she told herself. ''Yes,'' she said.

Billy sighed. ''That's nice. We don't have enough women here. The only ones I get to see are Ma Carter and Micki, and neither of them has enough time for me. Micki's always too busy, and Ma's as mean as a snake. No offense, Fafnir,'' he added.

''None taken,'' Fafnir murmured.

''So we're delighted you've come,'' Billy continued, his face contorting into an expression of shy pleasure. ''Aren't we, Faf?''

''We are, indeed. I'd sure like to see what's under that—''

''Fafnir!''

By this time Judith had recognized the subtleties of Steve Lindstrom's voice beneath the puppets' familiar tones. And suddenly she relaxed, reaching out and rubbing Fafnir's furry head. ''I'm glad I'm here,'' she said softly.

Fafnir butted against her hand, purring happily like a contented kitten. ''Better watch out,'' he said. ''Billy'll fall in love with you.''

For a moment she was startled. All her research had told her that Billy was Ryan's alter ego, and for a moment she thought… But no, it was Steve behind Billy's figure right now, Steve coming on to her as he had done since he met her.

"He'll survive," she said wryly.

"Go away, boys," a rough, New York-accented female voice broke through, and for a moment Judith expected another puppet to surface beside the dragon. But when a hand tapped her shoulder, she whirled around to meet a pair of cheerfully malicious black eyes set in a pale, narrow face that bore the reminiscent scars of acne. The eyes were human eyes, full of sparkle, and the face was framed with lanky black hair, not with yarn. "I'm Micki Verrenger," the woman said, eyeing Judith up and down with the same glint of amusement that everyone at the damned place seemed to share. "I hear you're looking for a place to stay."

"News travels fast," Judith murmured. The puppets had vanished from the stage, the other workers had gone back to their own concerns, and Ryan Smith was nowhere to be seen. "I'm going to be working here."

"So I've been told. Taking over Spacey Lacey's job. I hope you have more sense than to take a nosedive into a turbine," Micki remarked cynically. "Ryan doesn't want to have to keep replacing the help."

Judith opened her mouth to protest, then shut it, unable to come up with a civilized response.

"You look like you have brains, anyway," Micki continued, nodding. "Despite that stupid outfit you're wearing. Why the hell do you want to be a gofer in a place like this?"

Judith tried the same line again. "I like puppets."

Micki snorted. "So do I. But then, I don't look like Grace Kelly in her prime. What's your name?"

"Judith Daniels."

"Well, Judith Daniels, I have an ugly little ranch house about ten miles from here. I smoke nonstop when I'm not at work, but I keep it confined to my bedroom and the kitchen. I'm a lousy housekeeper and I like to stay up late and blast Phil Collins on the stereo. I like junk food and cheap red wine and minding my own business. Think we've got anything in common?''

"No," Judith said.

"Want to room with me?"

"Yes."

Micki nodded. "Aren't you going to ask about the rent?"

"How much is the rent?"

"What's your salary?" Micki countered.

"I didn't ask about that, either," Judith confessed.

Micki's outspoken reflections on Judith's brainpower and ancestry were obscene and imaginative. "Find out, for God's sake, and we'll work something out. I don't care if you were born with a silver spoon in that prissy little mouth; we'll pretend you have to live off your salary and deal with it from there. I'll get you the keys and draw you a map, and you can go settle in. I'm sure Ryan wants you working as soon as you can—yesterday at the latest, and there's no use putting it off."

"Sounds good."

"And one more thing," Micki added.

"Yes?"

"Just so we don't step on each other's toes. You've met Steve? The one coming on to you in the puppet booth?"

Judith nodded, glad to have her suspicion confirmed.

"I sleep with him sometimes," Micki said. "When neither of us has anything better to do."

"I'll keep my hands off."

Micki shook her head. "No, that's not it. He's yours for the taking. We don't have any claims on each other and we don't want to."

"Okay," Judith said.

"Ryan's a different matter."

"You're sleeping with Ryan?" Somehow she'd missed this complication. Lacey had usually complained about whomever she'd had to supplant, but Judith had gathered that when Lacey had snared Ryan, he'd been unattached.

"No," Micki said. "He doesn't believe in bedding the em-

ployees. He made one exception, and he's been regretting it
ever since.''

"And?"

"And if he decides to make another exception, it's going to
be with me, not you. Understand?''

"Perfectly."

Micki nodded. "Then we'll get along just fine." She held
out a small, tough hand. "Welcome to The Puppet Factory."

It was the only welcome Judith had gotten so far. She put
her larger, grease-covered hand in Micki's and shook it.
"Thanks."

"Cozy," said a familiar voice. Fafnir was once more leering
over the side of the booth. "You realize, dear Micki, that your
entire conversation is on videotape?''

Once more Micki's language was impressive. "I keep forgetting it's like Big Brother on this floor. Next thing you know,
he'll be putting cameras in the john."

"What makes you think he hasn't?" Fafnir asked.

"Because he's not a voyeur. More's the pity. You'll magic
that tape, won't you, Faf, sweetie?" Micki wheedled, rubbing
her pert nose against Fafnir's waxed mustache. "Make it disappear?''

"For a price. What are you doing after work?"

"Getting Judith settled. Maybe she'd be interested in your
scaly advances."

Judith looked into those Ping Pong-ball eyes for a startled
moment as Fafnir's malleable face moved in a pantomime of
lust and despair.

"No," Fafnir said. "I don't think so. Billy'd kill me."

"Suit yourself," Micki said, completely at ease conversing
with a cloth dragon.

"But remember, princess," Fafnir added, "I saw you first."

To Judith's amazement, Micki jumped from the dragon as if
she were burned. "How'd you do it?" she demanded. "I didn't
even see you."

"Do what?" Fafnir said, Ping Pong-ball eyes staring. And

with a sudden shock Judith recognized the difference. It was no longer Steve behind the booth, it was Ryan himself.

Micki had gotten over her momentary jolt. "Well, Fafnir, old buddy, you aren't going to tell your maker about this, are you? Not that it's anything he doesn't already know."

"Your secret is safe with me. Take care of the princess."

Judith moved past Micki's still figure, coming up close to the booth, and once more she reached out to pat Fafnir's furry head. She could feel the shape of Ryan's hand beneath the soft cloth; the sensation was oddly intimate and strangely erotic. "If you call me princess again," she murmured, "I'll rip your forked tongue out."

Fafnir flipped over on his back in ecstasy. "I love it when you talk dirty."

Micki reached out and shoved Fafnir down behind the stage. "You gotta watch your step around here, Judith," she said, pulling her toward the door. "You never know who might be listening. And Fafnir's too damned cheeky."

"You do know the difference between fantasy and reality?" Judith asked in a strangled voice as they stepped out into the hallway.

"The line gets a little blurred sometimes. Deliberately so. Don't let it get to you, kid. You'll fit in just fine. Anyone who can threaten to rip out Faf's tongue has it made."

It took Judith several minutes to shake the disorienting effects of the past half hour from her brain. "I hope so," she said, thinking of the disparity between the lustful dragon and the distant, reserved puppeteer. Somewhere in that disparity might lie the answer to what had happened to Lacey. "I surely hope so." And she allowed herself a tiny, nervous shiver.

HE WAS ALONE in the room, and no one knew he was there. It was small, dark and claustrophobic. No windows, no light but the bright square of the video monitor. His eyes watched the screen, intent, murderous, unblinking. Waiting. Waiting. Waiting....

Chapter Three

Micki's ranch house was just as ugly and tacky as she'd said it was. It stood in the midst of a development that had its origins in the postwar boom of the fifties; and like a tawdry beauty, the house was aging badly, with paint peeling and stucco cracking. Suburbia was now the victim of neglect, just as the cities had been three decades earlier. Despite Micki's assurance that she kept her chain-smoking to the bedroom and the kitchen, the entire house smelled stale and musty, like old ashtrays. The oppressive heat didn't help matters, but at least Micki had an air conditioner. Judith thought that maybe the artificial climate Ryan Smith despised would help clear the smell of cigarettes from the air along with the steamy warmth.

It hadn't taken her long to carry in her stuff from the Mercedes to the small, square bedroom in the back of the house. The mattress on the single bed looked as if it had had rougher use than any mattress ought to, and the windows were painted shut and coated with grease and an orangey film that was probably cigarette smoke. The gray wall-to-wall carpeting was stained and ratty; the one armchair had ripped, faded upholstery and broken springs; the narrow chest of drawers had to have come straight from either the Salvation Army or a penitentiary. Gray, limp Cape Cod curtains barely covered the grimy windows. A faded Indian-print bedspread lay across the mattress, and the door was missing from the closet.

"Home sweet home," Judith muttered, dumping her bags on the floor. "Yuck."

If Micki Verrenger was expecting a rent commensurate with Judith's salary for this dump, she was sadly mistaken, Judith thought as she stripped off her suit and blouse and dumped them in the already overflowing wastebasket. Ryan Smith was more than generous with salaries and benefits: a gofer-cum-clerk typist at The Puppet Factory was paid the equivalent of a managing editor's salary, and another very fat sum was deposited at regular intervals into an untouchable profit-sharing plan. Judith's suspicions had been aroused when a hostile Ma Carter had started naming large amounts of money, but it soon had become clear that, despite the generosity of her salary, Judith would still be the lowest paid employee there.

Clearly Micki could afford to do better with the house. A stack of Phil Collins records was lying scattered about a living room that was only slightly more inviting than the guest bedroom, and the other bedroom door revealed a huge, rumpled waterbed and air so thick with stale cigarette smoke that Judith started coughing.

A month, she promised herself. She could stand it for a month; she could stand anything for a month. For the years of comradeship with Lacey that had preceded the years of distance and irritation, she could live in decaying suburbia.

But there was no reason why she had to live in filth. A glance at her thin gold wristwatch told her it was only a little after noon. She had more than enough time to clean her room and the bathroom and to stock the mildewed refrigerator with something other than Diet Coke, hot dogs and twenty-seven kinds of mustard. Then, once her landlady returned home, she could start finding out more about Ryan Smith and The Puppet Factory.

It was a nice thought, but difficult to carry out. The bedroom improved with clean windows, a vacuumed carpet and no curtains. The bathroom appreciated having the lime and rust deposits removed from the cracked porcelain fixtures, and even Judith enjoyed raspberry yogurt and Tab for lunch. But Micki

Verrenger didn't bother to come home that evening, so Judith's investigation got exactly nowhere.

Tomorrow, she promised herself, falling into bed at the unaccustomed hour of ten o'clock, too exhausted to wait up any longer. Tomorrow she'd start work; tomorrow she'd start finding out what enemies Lacey had made at The Puppet Factory. Other than Ryan Smith. And Micki. And Ma had already proved she was nobody's friend. Three suspects so far, with probably more to come. Just because Lacey had suspected Ryan didn't mean Judith could afford to dismiss any possibilities. Lacey had never been a reliable observer. And never had a byline seemed so remote.

JUDITH COULD TELL by the smell of freshly brewed coffee and freshly lit cigarette that Micki had returned sometime during the night. Even the sagging mattress hadn't kept Judith from sleeping, and if her muscles felt cramped, a few stretches would take care of that.

After throwing on a faded pair of baggy jeans and an oversize olive-drab T-shirt, she stumbled barefoot into the living room, carrying her bright red Reeboks with her. Micki was already up and dressed, a cigarette dangling between her lips, a gooey pastry on a napkin in front of her. Her greeting was somewhere between a snarl and a moan, and Judith knew immediately that Micki Verrenger wasn't a morning person.

"I don't like to talk before my second cup of coffee," Micki said in a raspy monotone.

"Okay," Judith replied in a docile enough voice, pouring herself a cup of coffee. She could feel Micki's speculative eyes running over her rumpled figure, but she didn't say a word, just leaned against the counter and took a deep gulp. And promptly proceeded to spit the liquid into the sink.

Micki grinned. "Don't you like my coffee?"

"I have never tasted anything worse in my life," Judith said flatly, reaching into the fridge for one of the cold Tabs.

"I don't think there's room for your Tabs and my Diet Coke," Micki said, clearly spoiling for an argument.

"There'd better be."

"Getting feisty in your old age? At least you don't look like a Park Avenue matron this morning. And what the hell is that thing in my driveway? It looks like a prehistoric DeLorean."

Judith washed the bitter taste of the coffee oils from her mouth. "That's an apt enough description. It's a gull-wing Mercedes. They were built for a few years in the fifties; mine's a '57 and I love it with a consuming passion. I have to, considering the time I spend working on the thing. It's not exactly the most reliable mode of transportation."

"I suppose we could ride to work together," Micki said, draining her coffee without a shudder. "What my Escort lacks in dash it makes up for in dependability."

"Will our hours be the same?"

Micki shrugged. "Who knows? There is no such thing as a regular working day at the factory. We start as soon as we can get there and we work until we're finished. The business office is a little more structured, but if I'm working later I can always get a ride back with someone while you take the car. Jimmy and Melvin live three blocks over, and Franz drives right by here every night."

"Jimmy and Melvin are...?"

"Two of the apprentice puppeteers. They were part of that horde milling around yesterday that Ryan didn't introduce you to. They were the ones wearing puce sweat suits and Reeboks." Micki eyed Judith's shoes with a speaking expression. "You haven't met Franz yet, of course. He's been down in the city working on a science fiction movie."

"Steve said Franz was the second-best puppeteer around."

"That's right."

"Ryan said Franz was the best in the world."

Micki grinned, stubbing out the unfiltered cigarette she had smoked down to a mere ember. Stubbing it out in the gooey pastry. "Ryan's humble. Franz is very inventive, technically flawless and impossibly dedicated. He's the only one of us who really believes in the puppets. But he hasn't got Ryan's vision or genius. As far as I'm concerned, Ryan Smith is the best puppeteer alive today, maybe the best of the century.''

"But then you're not really impartial, are you?''

"What do you mean by that?'' Micki snapped.

"You're in love with him.''

"Bull,'' she said inelegantly. "I admire him, I respect him, and I want his body. That doesn't necessarily mean true love. God, you can take the debutante clothes away from you, but you can't get rid of that head-in-the-clouds mentality. Grow up, Judith. Sex doesn't mean love.''

Judith finished her Tab, rinsed out the can and set it on the countertop. "You can educate me on the way to work. And you can also tell me about the girl who died.''

A wary expression immediately crossed Micki's face. "Spacey Lacey? What do you want to know about her for?''

"Just curious. Ryan said everyone was edgy since she died. I'd like to know why.''

"Ryan said that? Listen, Judith, Lacey was a pushy little space cadet. She showed up here and pushed her way into everything, talking nonstop about the most boring and inconsequential things.''

"What'd she push herself into besides Ryan's bed?''

"You remember me telling you that, do you? She was getting tired of Ryan.'' Micki lit another cigarette and dropped the match in her coffee cup. "She'd started going after Steve, and you know Steve. He wasn't running too far. She was good buddies with Franz, too, though I don't think she was sleeping with him. And she tried to cozy up to me. Wanted to move in when my last roommate moved out, but I told her no way.''

"Then why did you let me move in?''

Micki grinned, exhaling a long stream of smoke. "Just a sucker for your upper-class looks, I guess.''

Judith moved away from the sink and leaned over Micki's smaller figure with only the suggestion of intimidation. "You'll find that looks can be deceiving, Micki,'' she said. "I can be just as much of a dirty in-fighter as you can.''

"What are we fighting over? Did you come here for Ryan, too?"

In a way, Judith thought. If he murdered my friend, I want his head on a platter. "The last thing in the world I want is to sleep with Ryan Smith," she said aloud.

"Then why are you here? It sure as hell isn't because of a love of puppets."

For a long moment Judith studied her. She was sorely tempted to confide in Micki. It would make things a whole lot easier if she had someone to talk with, someone to share her suspicions with.

But Micki had already come up with several motives. She hadn't liked Lacey, and Lacey, with her usual hapless self-absorption, had gone after the two men Micki was involved with. No, Micki wasn't the person to talk to—at least not until Judith could rule her out.

She straightened up. "It's a long, boring story that you really don't want to hear. It involves an ex-husband, a boss who couldn't keep his hands to himself and a nosy family. I wanted to get away and do something new."

Micki nodded, swallowing it whole. "You're right, it sounds boring as hell. Let's get to work. I want see how Ma likes you in your new incarnation."

"Am I allowed to comb my hair?"

"What, and spoil the effect?" Micki sighed. "Okay, but make it snappy. Franz is due back this morning, and he promised to help me work on my Madame Rinaldi."

Judith had had more peaceful drives in her life. On the empty roads of Miller's Junction, Micki drove as if she were on an L.A. freeway, proving the tinny little Escort had more power than one would have imagined. Judith gritted her teeth, dug in her feet and held on for dear life. While Micki careened around corners and raced up hills, Judith tried to concentrate on what she'd accomplish on her first full day in The Puppet Factory.

There was one unpleasant aspect to the entire thing. She was lying to everyone, being sneaky and dishonest, and no matter how pure her motives were, the fact remained that only one person deserved her deception. The rest of them were taking her at face value, and she felt like the worst sort of slimy liar, tricking these people.

It must be hell to be a spy or an undercover cop, she thought, gripping the vinyl edge of her seat as Micki squealed around a curve in the road. And when all your waking hours were consumed with living a lie, what kind of havoc would that wreak on your personal life?

Lucky for her that right now she had no social life. Her parents were living in Hilton Head and weren't expecting to see her till the weather got cooler. Her brother was at Stanford, her sister was in Minnesota, and it had been too damned long since she'd been in love. Months had turned into years, the men she dated were childhood friends, and there were times when she'd felt as if her life were as extreme in one direction as Lacey's was in the other.

You couldn't will yourself to fall in love, and you couldn't go looking for passion without running the risk of having it explode in your face—as it had done in Lacey's. But Judith's life often seemed arid and lonely, and she would have given anything for a dose of mindless, heartbreaking passion.

Well, it would come, sooner or later. And heaven only knew, now wasn't the time for it. She'd be far too busy during the next month or so, finding out the truth about Lacey's death. When that was over, when she was safely back in Philadelphia, ensconced in her new job on the news desk, then she could concentrate on her empty love life. For now, she had a job to do.

Ma Carter didn't like her jeans and T-shirt and braided hair any better than she'd liked her linen suit. But Judith had ascertained quite early that Ma Carter didn't like a damned thing, with the probable exception of Ryan Smith.

She certainly didn't waste any time demonstrating her disapproval to her unwelcome helper. Judith was set to work filing box after box of correspondence, receipts and bills that had been sitting in storage on the top floor for more than a year, papers going all the way back to the start of Ryan Smith's career in the mid-sixties, when he was still in college and working part-time at a local television station.

For the first three hours she was fascinated, certain she'd find clues, hints, evidence that would point her in some useful direction. By the time she'd finished the solitary lunch Ma had insisted on and gone back to the dusty papers, she was bored, restless and irritated.

It would have helped if she'd been allowed downstairs to the employee lunchroom. But Ma had decreed that the filing, which had been sitting around for as long as twenty years, couldn't sit twenty minutes longer. Judith had eaten her raspberry yogurt and gone back to the file cabinet without even the surcease of a few moments' conversation. Bessie, the other office worker, did no more than offer her an occasional shy smile as she continued her fascination with the computer screen, and Ma stalked around, glowering, nipping any friendly overtures in the bud.

Judith hadn't quite realized how desperate she was until Ryan walked in the door. She sighed, leaning back against the cabinet and pushing her hair out of her face, trying to squash down the irrational rush of pleasure that swept over her. Instead of engine grease, she left a trail of dust across her lightly tanned face. Not that it mattered. Ryan didn't even glance in her direction.

"Call Richardson," he said abruptly, bending over Ma's desk.

Judith took long enough to notice the imperceptible softening of Ma's granite countenance before she pushed herself away from the filing cabinet and stretched to her full height.

"Not Matthews?" Judith questioned.

Ryan turned to look at her, slowly, as if just realizing she was there. Which was all an act, Judith thought. He was as aware of her presence as she was of his. And for his own reasons he was just as suspicious of her.

"Not Matthews," he said finally, his eyes opaque. "The air conditioner is still working."

"Fancy that," she said with a grin. "What needs fixing now? I could do with a break from filing."

"If you don't like the job, Miss Daniels…" Ma began in a dangerous tone.

"I love the job. It's just hard on the eyes and the back to file for—" she checked her watch "—five hours straight. What's broken?"

"One of the VCRs in the control room," Ryan said, ignoring Ma's glower. "It's got a tape stuck inside. I want it taken out without damaging it. It's too important to lose."

"Piece of cake."

"If you destroy the tape," he said gently, "I'll wring your neck."

Judith looked down at his beautiful, deceptively strong hands. She hadn't seen him or talked to him since that odd confrontation in the puppet booth, when she'd stroked those hands that had been hidden inside Fafnir's furry body. Had Lacey's neck been wrung before she was tossed over the balcony? Had those beautiful hands done the wringing?

"I'll fix the VCR," she said in an even voice, not giving away any of her dark suspicions. "And I won't damage the tape. But if I do, I know how to mend them."

"Is there anything you can't do, Judith?"

No mocking "princess" today, she noticed. It was hard to call someone in jeans and a T-shirt a princess. "I can't cook," she said. "And I can't sing." And I can't fall in love, she added silently.

His eyes were narrowed, speculative. "Just be grateful you live in an age of microwave ovens and compact disk players."

"Both of which I can fix."

He shook his head. "Come with me. Don't worry, Ma," he said, forestalling Ma's cry of outrage. "The filing has waited this long, it can wait a few years more. Let's see if Judith can do what she says she can."

"I don't like it, Ryan," Ma said.

Was there a note of warning in her voice? Judith stood there, mesmerized, listening for the faintest nuance, the slightest hint.

Ryan smiled in a wry sort of way, and Judith waited for him to tell her to go back to her filing. "Sorry, Ma," he said, regret and something else roughening his voice. "But she's mine now."

And Judith, seeing his distant expression, felt a little frisson of fear run down her backbone. One that felt strangely like excitement.

They descended the stairs in silence, a silence Judith was loath to break. Ryan Smith unnerved her—there was no way she could deny it—and part of that unsettling feeling came from the very simple fact that she found him attractive. He was different from the men she was used to, so much more complex. Besides, it wasn't unusual for her and Lacey to find the same man attractive. Ten years ago, when they were in college, they'd always been interested in the same men.

It had been a problem then. Lacey's entire life had run in patterns, and those early patterns had been difficult for Judith to deal with. She'd meet a man, start dating him, begin to fall in love, then make the mistake of introducing him to Lacey. And open, enthusiastic Lacey would, of course, like any man who caught Judith's eye. Her cheerful friendliness would slip into an affair that neither she nor the hapless man could help, leaving Judith hurt and confused and finally inured to it by the third time it happened. She had stopped introducing her dates to Lacey.

Maybe it was just the remnants of hurt that made her look at Ryan Smith in ways she shouldn't be looking. Maybe she was sick enough to want revenge for a decade-old wound. Or maybe Ryan Smith was merely a deceptively attractive man, and she'd better watch her step.

The control room was on the blissfully cool second floor, just off the workshop. "In there," Ryan said, not bothering to show her the way. In fact, he seemed almost eager to abandon her. At least, Judith thought gloomily, the odd attraction wasn't mutual.

"What about tools?"

"In there. It's the middle VCR, the Panasonic. For God's sake, be careful."

"I always am," she snapped, nettled.

He looked at her for a long, reflective moment. "I hope so," he said. And she had the odd feeling he wasn't talking about repair work.

The control room was a narrow, soundproofed box of a room, with long tables and shelves covered with a myriad of electronic equipment, primarily videotape players and monitors. There was only one Panasonic, and Judith spent a few moments studying it. She had the machine unplugged and the metal covering half off when the door opened, and a little gnome of a man stepped through.

He looked like one of the puppets. He had a wispy shock of grayish-white hair that was standing straight up all over his pink skull, shaggy eyebrows, a thick, untidy mustache and soft, wistful eyes that could have belonged in Fafnir's face, surrounded by purple fur. He was short, slightly stooped with age, but his small, square hands looked very strong. He gazed up into Judith's curious blue eyes, and a smile of welcome wreathed his face, making him appear even more like a cherub.

"Fräulein Daniels, I presume? Micki has been telling me all about you." He moved forward, taking her hand and bowing over it in a parody of a Prussian officer. Except that he was absolutely, touchingly, serious. "We are delighted to have you here. Particularly if you can make some sense of these machines."

"And I am delighted to be working here, Herr Himml," Judith said with equal formality, rising to her feet and towering over him. "I've long admired your work."

The little man shrugged. "Please, call me Franz. We're very casual around here. You really understand these machines?" He eyed the VCR with a look of uncomplicated dislike.

"I understand them."

"*Sehr gut,*" he said, nodding. "Very good. I will leave you to your work, then. You will be careful, Fräulein Daniels?"

"Judith," she corrected with a forced smile. "Why should I need to be careful?"

"There has been…an accident. We would not like anything to happen to you." He was very earnest, very charming, and if he'd been thirty years younger and two feet taller, Judith would have fallen in love.

Instead she smiled, touching his arm with a reassuring gesture. "I'll be careful. You too, Franz."

"Oh, he won't hurt me," said Franz absently. And before Judith could say another word he vanished from the control room, leaving her staring after him as a core of dread formed in her heart.

Chapter Four

Judith was uninterrupted for the remaining ten minutes it took her to extricate the tape, remove the label that had managed to come off and stick itself to the VCR innards and reassemble the offending machine. It was lucky the job was so simple; at that moment she could spare no more than a quarter of her concentration on the task at hand.

Whom had Franz been talking about? "He won't hurt me," he'd mumbled. Who wouldn't hurt him? Had it been that easy to have her suspicions confirmed? One day on the job, and his good friend had condemned him?

She pushed a loose strand of hair back, frowning at the VCR as she cautioned herself against jumping to conclusions. Who was to say Franz had been talking about Ryan Smith?

Of course, she could always ask him what he meant. That had the benefit of being simple and direct, with the disadvantage of possibly tipping her hand far too soon. If Ryan had the slightest inkling of why she was really here, if he knew she was connected with Lacey, she'd be out on her tail so fast that her head would spin.

No, a simple, direct question wouldn't do at all. But that didn't mean she couldn't be devious, perhaps sit next to the old man during lunch sometime—if Ma let her out of the claustrophobic office to eat. That way she could pump him about all sorts of things, gently lead the conversation back to his obscure muttering and find out what Franz really thought.

So why did she feel like such a piece of slime for contemplating this course of action? Why didn't she feel dangerous and devious and very clever, instead of like a cheat and a liar?

Because to everyone but the killer she *was* a cheat and a liar. If there even was a killer. The sooner she accepted that fact, the sooner she could get on with her mission. And get back to her life at the *Mirror* and her comfortable smoke-free apartment.

The cool second floor was deserted when Judith left the control room. It was just after four, but the only sound was the quiet hum of the smoothly operating Roberts 450 air conditioner. Judith allowed herself a brief, smug smile.

There was a balcony on the river side of the building, a twin to the one on the third floor. It stretched over the water, catching the late-afternoon sunlight. Judith noted with surprise that a couple of picnic tables were shoved in a corner beside a pile of lumber, sawhorses blocked the entrance and the double glass doors had a chain looped around them.

Her talent with machines extended to locks. The padlock wasn't complicated, more for show than for force, and she spent less than a minute unfastening it with a slender screwdriver. She dropped the chains silently, undid the next set of locks and stepped out onto the wooden decking.

A strong, wet breeze blowing off the river ruffled through her hair. She took a deep, appreciative breath, part of her reluctantly agreeing with Ryan's assessment of artificial air. The dampness of the river, of things growing and the warmth of the sunlight beating down had it all over climate control.

She climbed over the row of sawhorses and moved toward the railing, realizing that this balcony had a better view than the one above it. There were benches built into the railing; and the decking, though badly stained in a few places, looked like redwood compared with the pine boards that were piled next to the picnic tables. Clearly Ryan was planning on replacing the old flooring. Judith rocked experimentally, but the terrace was sturdy, immovable. Why wasn't it in use?

She peered over the railing, down, down into the swirling

river. The turbine sat below her, deep in the water, a huge, nasty bit of machinery if ever there was one. If Ryan thought she'd work on that thing, he could guess again. Although she'd yet to meet an engine whose workings eluded her, Ryan wouldn't know that. She would simply insist that a power turbine was beyond her capabilities. Not for anything would she crawl around in something that had turned her friend into hamburger.

Of course, it wasn't the machine's fault, she reminded herself. Lacey had fallen, with or without somebody's help, possibly from this very balcony. Maybe that was why it had been blocked off. A sudden chill swept across her heated skin, and she backed away from the edge, trying to stifle the frisson of nerves that erupted as the unexpected reality of death and suffering forced its way into her consciousness. Her masquerade was no longer a game.

"What the hell are you doing here?"

She was glad her back was toward him. That gave her an extra minute to compose her expression, to turn and face her employer with her usual grace and calm. "I wanted a breath of fresh air," she said easily. "Is that a crime?"

Bad choice of words, she thought, but kept her pleasant expression firmly in place. Ryan didn't even blink. He was watching her out of those unreadable green-gray eyes, and his mouth was set in an unsmiling line that was disapproving. He stood there with his hands stuffed in his pants pockets, waiting for an excuse to move, she thought.

A moment or two was all he needed to take his hands out of his pockets and throw her off the balcony, she estimated. She'd keep an eye on those hands; if they started moving, she would, too. And if she kept her eyes trained on his pockets, she would have no choice but to concentrate on the general area, which Bryn Mawr had taught her was not proper behavior in an employee. With a sigh she lifted her head and met his gaze.

"Not anymore."

"I beg your pardon?"

"It isn't a crime to be out here," he said patiently. "The police took the barricades down last week. I'm the one who locked the place. Why did you pick the lock?"

When in doubt, lie. "It wasn't locked," she said. "The padlock was open and the chain was hanging loose. I figured if the balcony was dangerous, a sign would be posted."

"It's not dangerous."

She stepped forward, across the stained planking. He wasn't about to toss her over the terrace. At least, not right now. "Then why isn't it being used?"

"I didn't want anyone out here until I had the decking replaced."

Judith looked down at the darkened boards beneath her Reeboks. "You don't have to replace the redwood," she said. "I know of all sorts of things that can get stains out. A mixture of oxalic crystals and—"

"They're bloodstains."

Judith stared transfixed at her feet. Nausea rose swiftly, joined by a dizziness she was desperate to hide. Very carefully she inched away from the stained wood, over to the side of the balcony, and with her last ounce of grace she sank onto one of the built-in benches. "Oh," she said.

Ryan still hadn't moved; he just watched her. "You remember the woman who died, don't you?" he prodded, and she thought she was imagining that his voice sounded slightly mocking. "When the police found her body caught in the turbine, they brought it up here and set it on the deck.

"Oh," she said again, her voice faint.

"I figured having picnic tables out here might be a little unappetizing," he continued. "Carpenters are coming in next week to replace the decking. If you want to see if you can get the stains out in the meantime, feel free to try."

She was going to throw up. She was going to have to turn around, lean over the railing and throw up in the Hudson River. And here they'd been fighting pollution for so long, she reminded herself, trying to fight the nausea with a strained bit of humor. Slowly, determinedly, she swallowed the bile, then looked up at Ryan. "No, thanks," she said.

"I didn't think so. In the meantime, I suggest you stay away from this balcony. I had it locked on purpose, to keep people away. We don't need any reminders of what happened."

"No, I imagine you don't." She rose to her feet, not even swaying. She met his gaze. "Maybe you'd better find out who left it unlocked."

He didn't bat an eyelash. "Maybe I'd better do that," he agreed. He watched her as she climbed over the sawhorses, reaching for the door. "The bathroom's on your left," he added.

She stopped for a moment. Ryan Smith saw too damned much—she'd have to remember that. "Thanks," she murmured, and let one of the heavy glass doors swing shut behind her, shutting away Ryan and the sight of the balcony.

HE SHOULDN'T HAVE DONE THAT, Ryan thought. She looked white, shaken, despite that deliberately calm smile. He hadn't had to be so gory, telling her the mangled remains of one of her best friends had been placed on the deck where she'd stood.

But he didn't like liars. And he didn't like that determined innocence of hers, coupled with those searching eyes. She'd unlocked the padlock—he'd just checked it when he'd found the VCR on the fritz. She'd been snooping around, and it served her right to come up against something unpalatable. She was probably puking her brains out in the bathroom at that very moment.

What the hell did she want from him? It hadn't taken more than a couple of phone calls last night for Ryan to find out all he needed to know about Judith Kennedy Daniels. The *Philadelphia Mirror* certainly wasn't on the level of the supermarket tabloids, so it wouldn't have any interest in trumped-up stories based on circumstantial evidence and overimaginative reporters.

Lacey Hollister's death had been a freak accident. There was nothing mysterious or sinister about it. It had been just an unfortunate occurrence that had the possibility of mushrooming if too many people like Judith Daniels came snooping around. He'd always kept a low profile, but that didn't mean he wouldn't make good copy. The puppets of The Puppet Factory were world famous, and the name Ryan Smith, though less well-known, would sell papers if it was connected with a grisly murder.

But, dammit, Lacey hadn't been murdered. Not that half a dozen people wouldn't have liked to strangle the silly creature, himself included. But he hadn't; no one had. She'd fallen and died, and that was that.

Not if Judith had her way, however. Maybe he should kick her out right now, tell her he knew what she was doing. He could even call on the security people whom he'd hired for a short while after the accident, just to make sure the princess didn't sneak back onto the premises.

But he knew reporters, and he already knew Judith. The more obstacles he put in her way, the more determined she'd be to overcome them, the more certain that he was covering up something. Hell, he had nothing to hide. No one did. At least, not as far as Lacey was concerned. Let Judith snoop; let her ask questions; let her poke around to her heart's content. Sooner or later she'd have to give up, go back to her lonely-hearts column or whatever it was and leave him alone.

And it couldn't happen any too fast for his peace of mind.

Of course, he had to admit there was the added complication of his finding her completely delectable. He wasn't one to let his glands get in the way of his better judgment, though, and his better judgment told him to keep away from Judith.

But if she'd been gorgeous yesterday, with her silk and linen and grease-stained nose, she was bordering on irresistible today in that shapeless, rumpled T-shirt, baggy jeans and tied-back hair. He'd seen her come in with Micki, and then spent the entire day fighting the urge to break the air conditioner just so he could get her downstairs again. When the VCR had screwed up, he'd been relieved and delighted, enough so that Steve had commented on his uncharacteristic smile as he'd headed for the fourth floor.

It had to be a midlife crisis come just a little bit early, he told himself, pulling the sawhorses back into formation. At three years shy of forty, he must be approaching a second adolescence. Come to think of it, he hadn't had much of a first one. He'd grown up too soon, too fast. Maybe he was just getting around to being a libidinous teenager.

Well, Judith was the wrong person to start with, even if she looked like every teenage boy's prom-queen fantasy. An odd thought struck Ryan: she probably suspects me of murdering Lacey. But she wasn't about to get involved with a murderer, and he wasn't about to get involved with someone who thought him capable of killing.

So there they were, he mused, fastening the padlock again, noting the tiny scratch marks from Judith's screwdriver with a wry smile. The only thing he could do was let her snoop until she grew tired of it and everyone here and went back to her old life. In the meantime he could watch old Grace Kelly movies on the VCR and pretend they were two other people, in another place and another time.

"There you are, Ryan." Micki was bounding down the stairs in her high-top basketball shoes. "Ma says to tell you Josiah Greenfield called and it's urgent."

"Lawyers," Ryan said bitterly. "What does he want now?"

"Haven't the faintest idea. Have you seen Judith? I'm going home, and if she wants a ride it's got to be now."

Ryan was already heading toward the stairs. "She's in the bathroom throwing up."

"Oh, yeah?" Micki was reaching for a cigarette, then put it back as she met his disapproving glare. "Why's she throwing up?"

"I told her what caused the stains on the deck."

"Nice guy."

"Mr. Sunshine," he agreed. "Keep an eye on her, will you?"

"Why?"

He shrugged. "I don't know. Just let me know if any-thing…interesting happens."

"I thought you didn't mess with employees. You did once, and look where it got you."

"I don't want to mess with her, Micki," he said, lying. "I just don't want any more trouble."

"And you think she's trouble?"

He hesitated. He wasn't a man to give his trust easily, but Micki was one of the few people who'd earned it. Still, there was no need to share his suspicions. "You know me, Micki," he said. "I think everything is trouble. Just watch out for her, will you?"

"Just what I need. Baby-sitting," she said disgustedly. "Which bathroom?"

"The nearest one. Is Ma still upstairs?"

"Waiting for you and getting grumpier every minute."

"How can you tell?"

Micki laughed. "I don't know why you keep her around, Ryan. It's not as if you like her any better than anybody else does."

"What can I say? I'm a nice guy," he replied.

"An absolute prince. Speaking of which, I better get to your latest victim. How detailed did you get?"

"Not very. She must have a weak stomach."

"Maybe," said Micki. "Maybe."

JUDITH SAT BACK on her heels, pushing her hair away from her damp, sweating face. At least the bathrooms in The Puppet Factory were kept spotless. There was nothing worse than throwing up in a public rest room.

Well, she'd gotten rid of her yogurt, her Tab, and anything else residing in her stomach, and she used every ounce of her self-control to keep from dry-retching. She rose on trembling legs and headed for the sinks.

Splashing cool water on her face helped; rinsing her mouth out helped; slapping her pale cheeks helped. But nothing could wipe the vision out of her mind. The blood-stained wood had brought Lacey's death gruesomely home to her. Before, it had been removed, a distant, polite grief. Now it was real. If Judith had ever had any doubts about what she was doing, they'd finally vanished.

"There you are." Micki lounged in the doorway, a cynical smile on her face. "Ryan said you were in here throwing up. Want a ride home?"

Judith allowed herself one brief glance in the mirror. She looked pale, drained, like something the cat had dragged in; and Micki's face behind her looked smugly satisfied.

"Sure," Judith said. "But if you smoke all the way home or drive like you did this morning, I'm going to throw up all over your vinyl seats."

Micki already had a cigarette out, ready to light up. There was a strict no smoking rule at The Puppet Factory, and she was allowed to smoke only in the bathrooms and out on the balcony. Judith swallowed, waiting for Micki to tell her to walk the three miles home.

Micki put the cigarette back in its rumpled pack, tucked it into her shirt pocket and nodded. "Okay," she said. "Just to prove I'm not always a bitch."

Judith breathed a sigh of relief. "Thanks."

"And in return you can do something for me," Micki continued, a malicious smile on her dark, narrow face.

"Anything," Judith said rashly.

"You can tell me why Ryan wants me to spy on you."

HE SAT WITH THE DARKNESS all around; warm, moist darkness that provided safety and comfort. No prying eyes; no one to see, to know. Just the darkness, like a mother, protecting, nurturing, holding.

But the brightness lay beyond. The colors, the lights, the noise and sound and wickedness that must be punished. Sinners, all of them. The woman had returned. Already she was busy, and already Ryan had been enmeshed. He needed protection; he didn't understand these women. He had to be protected.

She'd looked different. She'd looked sweet and innocent, and for a moment he had hoped it would be all right.

But no. She was like the other ones. She was a whore, like the other whores, and she must be punished. Someone had to right the wrong.

His gaze dropped to his hands stretched out in front of him, clenching and unclenching, as if around an imaginary neck. Hands covered with bright green fur. And he closed his eyes in the warm, sweet darkness.

Chapter Five

"Damn, it's hot," Micki said, pushing a limp hank of black hair away from her scarred face. "I'm sweating like a pig."

"You'd be cooler if you weren't sitting in the sun," Judith said in her most prosaic tones, looking up from the cassette player she was taking apart.

"I'd also be the same pasty white color you are," Micki shot back, shifting her bikini-clad body on the plastic chaise longue. It was just before noon on a Saturday, five days after Judith had moved to Miller's Junction, and the heat had continued unabated. While Micki worked on her tan and smoked cigarettes, Judith sat in the shade and fiddled with the car stereo that hadn't worked in the eight months since it had eaten Micki's favorite Phil Collins tape.

She looked down at her legs, exposed by the khaki hiking shorts that she never wore hiking. "I'm not pasty white," she said calmly. "And I do have a tan. It's just subtle."

Micki blew out a long stream of thick smoke in her direction. "Could have fooled me."

"If you want your tape player fixed, you'll show a little more tact."

"I want my tape player fixed, my portable phone fixed and my garbage disposal fixed."

"And I want your clean-air machine fixed," Judith said, concentrating on a tiny screw.

"If you don't like my smoking…"

"Micki, I love your smoking. It makes me appreciate my lungs."

"God, you and Ryan make a perfect pair," she said in a disgusted voice. "There's nothing worse than an antismoking fanatic."

"I don't think so."

"Don't think there's nothing worse?"

"Don't think that Ryan and I make a great pair," Judith replied evenly. "You told me yourself that he wants you to spy on me, though heaven only knows why. I haven't seen him since my first day at work except in passing, and then he glares at me."

"Good."

"I told you, Micki, I'm not interested in poaching on your territory. I have no designs on Ryan Smith. You can have him."

"Don't I wish," Micki said, lighting a fresh, unfiltered cigarette from the stub of her last one. "The only woman who's going to have him is someone like Eleanor Bellows."

The screwdriver slipped, gouging a tiny piece of skin from Judith's hand. "Who's Eleanor Bellows?"

"She was his fiancée. They were together… God, it must have been four or five years. They even bought a house—which she decorated—set a wedding date and everything."

"And what happened?"

"To Eleanor? She must have changed her mind. First thing we knew, the wedding was off, Ryan was living in that suburban mansion alone, and Eleanor was getting married to somebody else. I think he was a television producer like her father. You must have heard of J. F. Bellows. He's the one who produced all The Puppet Factory specials. That's how Ryan and Eleanor met."

"And the girl, the one who got killed," Judith said carefully. "Did she break them up?"

"Oh, no, Ryan and Eleanor separated more than a year ago. Spacey Lacey wasn't poaching on anyone's territory. Except mine," Micki added pointedly.

"You don't have to remind me," Judith said, snapping the metal covering over the cassette player. "I know when to keep my hands off and mind my own business."

"Do you?" It was Fafnir's gravelly voice posing the question, and Judith didn't even look up. She was used to Micki's facility with the puppet voices and her odd moments of using them. She wasn't crazy about waking up to the sound of Madame Rinaldi singing in an off-key coloratura, but she'd quickly ascertained that the more she objected, the more Micki would persevere.

"Yes, I do," she said, screwing the tiny screws shut. "I'm here in Miller's Junction to work, nothing more."

"Sure you are," Fafnir's lecherous voice drawled. "Next thing I know, you'll try to sell me the Brooklyn Bridge. Listen, princess, why don't we drop all the pretense and you can tell me why you're really here?"

"Listen, you…" Judith began, raising her head. The irritated words died on her lips as her wrathful gaze met Ryan Smith's even expression. He was standing there in the tiny little yard, watching her, and his mirrored sunglasses hid any reaction he might have had to their conversation.

Micki had a satisfied smirk on her face. "I wondered how long it was going to take you to notice. Ryan has a bad habit of sneaking up on people. Comes from years of slipping in and out of puppet booths."

"Did anyone ever tell you that it was an unnerving habit?" Judith demanded, wishing she had sunglasses of her own to hide behind, wishing she'd worn baggy pants and a bra.

"Yes," said Ryan in his own voice. "Micki told me I should put taps on my shoes."

Judith glanced at his feet. Long, narrow feet, in keeping with his body. "I don't think they'd work with Nikes."

"Probably not." He didn't move, just lounged there, looking cool and at ease in the hot noontime sun. "Don't you answer your phone?"

Micki shifted on the chaise, and the sound of her greased body sliding across hot plastic hung in the steamy air. "The portable one's broken, and Judith hasn't fixed it yet. Anyway, I don't suppose you're here to see me,'' she said with just a trace of petulance as she stubbed out her cigarette in the overgrown grass. ''If you want me to work today, you can forget it. I need the sun.''

''Not you, Micki. Your roomie.''

Judith's head jerked up in surprise. He'd been ignoring her for days, so this sudden craving for her company unnerved her. ''Something broken?''

''One of the television monitors. I must have knocked against it and didn't realize it. I can't work without it.''

Judith uncurled herself from her sitting position. ''It'll take me only a minute to change.''

''There's no need. Those are as good working clothes as anything. Unless you want your linen suit again.'' His voice was just slightly mocking, and she didn't have to look behind those opaque sunglasses to know that his eyes were sweeping over her bare legs, her unbound breasts beneath the loose cotton shirt. At least she was relatively compact in that area. If she were as voluptuous as Micki, she wouldn't have dared walk past Ryan without clutching her arms around her torso. As it was, she couldn't begin to guess his opinion of her, and she didn't know that she wanted to.

''All right. I'll get my keys—''

''I'll drive you.''

''I'd rather have my own transportation.''

A slow smile lit his face. ''And I'd rather have you ride with me so I can explain what's broken. It'll save time.''

''But then you'll have to drive me back,'' she said stubbornly.

''Franz or Steve can drop you off.''

She kept her shoulders from sagging in relief. ''They're working, too?''

''They're working, too. You're safe from my lecherous designs.''

She grinned. ''It's not you I'm worried about. It's Fafnir.''

''Billy'll keep him in line,'' Micki said, leaning back on the chaise and closing her eyes. "Bring back some beer, willya? And if you get real inspired, maybe a pizza. With lots of anchovies."

"No anchovies," Judith said firmly.

"And get some good, cheap American beer, none of that imported crap. And another carton of cigarettes while you're at it."

"Forget it."

"I'll pay you back."

"I'm not transporting cigarettes in my car, Micki," Ryan said. "If you want coffin nails, you can stir your lovely body and get them yourself."

Micki grinned up at him. "Thought you'd never notice, boss."

"No employees, Micki," he said.

"Keep that in mind, Ryan," she shot back, nodding in Judith's direction.

Judith could feel his eyes on her, and even though she couldn't see them, she knew his gaze was brooding and troubled.

"Don't worry, Micki," he said. "I don't repeat my mistakes."

There was a quiet, unmistakable snort from Micki's recumbent figure. Again Judith opened her mouth to say she'd drive herself, and again she closed it. She hadn't been able to get within ten feet of Ryan all week, and once she began to work on the monitor, she probably wouldn't see him afterward. This was a heaven-sent opportunity to find out more about him, whether he was the man Lacey had thought he was. She was a fool to give in to her uneasiness.

"You ready?" Ryan inquired politely. "Or have you got some other excuses?"

Judith's smile was only slightly forced. "I'm ready."

Without another word he took off around the corner of the dilapidated ranch house, leaving Judith with no choice but to follow like a dutiful Muslim wife, ten paces behind her lord and master.

She'd already learned that Ryan Smith didn't go in for chauffeured Rolls-Royces, even though he could well afford them. His serviceable Toyota station wagon had seen better days. The cracked vinyl seats were blazing hot to Judith's bare legs, and she watched Ryan with a mixture of curiosity and awe as he folded his large body into the narrow confines of the driver's seat. He took off into the early afternoon heat without a word, his sunglasses still shielding his face, his fingers draped over the steering wheel..

He had beautiful hands. She looked away, out the passenger window at suburbia fading into countryside, looking anywhere but at those hands of his. She didn't want to be aware of him as a man, even to think of him as a fellow human being. Not until she could absolve him of complicity in Lacey's "accident."

Because to be aware of him as a man was to be attracted to him. Stuffed into the cramped confines of the Toyota, with his denim-covered thigh perilously close to her bare one and his body heat adding to the warmth of the air, she couldn't avoid acknowledging that she found him fascinating. Something about him pulled her, drew her toward him, and if she gave in to that attraction, it would signal the end of her investigation. There was no way she could try to prove a man guilty of murder when all the time she was falling in love with him.

Of course, falling in love was a bit extreme at this stage, she reminded herself. So the man had beautiful hands. And a sexy mouth. And bony shoulders that were almost irresistible. And eyes that were enigmatic and enchanting. And the most gorgeous smile, on the rare occasions he used it. And…

She shifted uncomfortably in the seat, mentally slapping herself. First things first. Find out how Lacey died, and then you can fall in love. Princess, she added to herself in Ryan's mocking tones.

She stiffened her backbone, stretched out her legs and turned to look at Ryan's distant profile. "Are you this charming with all your employees, or do I get preferential treatment?"

He glanced at her then, and one beautiful hand lifted the

sunglasses to expose his eyes. He grinned. "What's this? The first shot fired on Fort Sumter?"

It was a lot easier being truculent when he didn't smile, she thought morosely. "I don't like being ordered around," she muttered.

"Then don't work for a living. I don't think you really have to, do you, Judith? It doesn't take someone from *Women's Wear Daily* to recognize the price of your clothes. And while your car may be almost thirty years old, it has to cost a fortune to maintain."

"I fix it myself," she said hotly.

"I'm sure you do. But a gull-wing Mercedes is a rare and glorious thing, expensive as hell to begin with. The parts alone must run up a huge bill."

"I can afford it."

"And if you owned a Ford like Micki does, you wouldn't have to answer to unreasonable bosses like me."

"You pay me a lot more than what it costs for the upkeep of my car. You pay a lot more than anyone I've ever worked for," she added. "Why? Guilty conscience?"

He'd settled the sunglasses back down on his nose. Without taking his attention from the road, he cast her a small smile. "What do you think I'm guilty of, Judith?"

He'd stopped her on that one. "Making too much money?" she countered.

"I didn't know there was such a thing."

"Every household in this country has a Billy puppet or a Fafnir toothbrush or a Madame Rinaldi tricycle. Or sheets, or a game, or a music box, or posters, or…"

"We've licensed the puppets 927 times," he said. "If you're going to name everything that's connected to the puppets, we'll be at it till Monday."

"And you make money every time one of those puppets is sold."

"And the sheets, and the posters, and the underwear, and dolls. Money keeps pouring in, and I can afford to pay people well. Is it my fault that American children have an inexhaustible need for brand-name things?"

She couldn't miss the lashing of contempt in his voice. "Don't you like children?" she questioned, shocked.

Once more he looked at her, and now his smile was tinged with bitterness. "Not much."

"But you spend your life with the puppets, making children happy—"

"The puppets are just as much for adults as they are for kids," he interrupted. "That's what makes them work so well. I don't give a damn whether I'm making some grubby-faced little urchin happy. I do it for the money."

Something didn't ring true in that cynical declaration, but Judith was too angry to figure out what it was. "As long as you're happy," she said coldly.

"Sublimely," he replied. "And if you're such a tender hearted, motherly type, why don't you take your substantial salary and give it to the orphans of the world? Better yet, trade in your Mercedes and donate that money."

She was just about to snap at him when it occurred to her that Ryan Smith had been one of those orphans he'd scathingly denounced. The research she'd done on him had been full of his childhood. He'd started with the puppets as a kid, entertaining the other children in the institutions and foster homes where he'd grown up. She shouldn't leap at everything he said. He didn't trust her; he'd made that more than clear. And she'd be a fool to take him and his cynical remarks at face value. Maybe he really hated kids. Or maybe he was goading her, trying to get her to lose her temper and tell him why she was really there.

Could he guess? And was she in danger if he did? She'd have to be more careful. In her quest for the truth she'd been overlooking the fact that she might be risking her own safety by prying into things better left hidden.

"I'll keep the Mercedes for now," she said evenly. "And my salary."

"I thought you would." He pulled to a stop in the middle

of the deserted parking lot. No sign of Steve's Mazda RX-7; no sign of any other car. Maybe she was about to take a swim from the balcony, after all.

He extricated himself from the cramped driver's seat and stood there waiting. "Are you coming?"

She considered it. She could always lock the doors and wait for someone to rescue her. Or she could brazen it out. If she were on her guard, he wouldn't be able to sneak up on her. She was probably faster than he was.

She certainly wasn't stronger. His chambray shirt sleeves were rolled up to his elbows. and she could see the wiry, corded muscles in his tanned forearms. If he wanted to wrap those hands around her throat, there wouldn't be much she could do about it.

"Ryan, for heaven's sake, get in here!" Steve called from the open doorway. "We've been waiting for ages."

Judith climbed out of the car with all the insouciance she could manage. She moved ahead of Ryan, but his hand reached out and caught her arm, pulling her up short, proving her correct in her assessment of his strength. Not that he was rough; just forceful, and very, very strong.

"Feeling safer?"

She blinked. "Was there ever any reason not to?"

"You tell me." His hand was still on her arm. The sunglasses continued to shield his expression, and he didn't move, didn't let her move, but simply stood there, waiting.

Honesty, or a semblance thereof, was the best policy. "Listen, Ryan," she said with disarming frankness. "Some young woman met a nasty death in your Puppet Factory less than a month ago. And she died on a weekend, when the place was deserted. I'd have to have nerves of steel or be very stupid indeed not to be a little apprehensive about the place."

His expression, or lack thereof, didn't change. "Maybe," he said. "But I don't think you're afraid of the Factory."

"No? What do you think I'm afraid of?"

Once more that small, bitter smile lit his face. "Me," he said, releasing her arm. "Let's go, princess. You have a video monitor to fix.'' And without a backward glance he strode into the building.

RYAN DIDN'T LOOK BACK to make certain she was following. He knew she would be. He wasn't convinced that she didn't have nerves of steel or that she was very stupid.

He was sorry Steve had come out on the landing and called to him. It would have been interesting to see if he could have gotten her inside while she believed the place was empty. She'd given him one of those brief, sidelong glances that had convicted him on the spot, and the set of her delicate jaw had suggested that she was expecting him to turn into Mr. Hyde the moment the steel door closed behind them.

If they'd been alone, he would have been half tempted to have proved her right. Not by tossing her over the balcony her friend had slipped from, but by slinging her gorgeous body over his shoulder and carting her up to the top floor like a modern-day Quasimodo. She wasn't wearing a bra, a fact she was trying to ignore, and her long, bare legs filled him with thoughts erotic enough to put a damper on his anger.

But the anger was still there, simmering. And no matter how delicious he found her, he wasn't going to lay a finger on her. He was in enough trouble as it was—he didn't need to go messing with a reporter out to get him. Hell, he wouldn't put it past her to sleep with him for the sake of her damned story.

It was becoming very clear to him that that was why she was here. Not to find out the truth behind Lacey's accident. She'd already decided on the truth. She'd picked her villain; now she wanted proof. She wouldn't stop until she found it.

She couldn't be having too good a time in the process. He knew human nature well enough to recognize even the subtle signs. Judith Daniels thought he'd murdered her friend in cold blood and then covered it up. And Judith Daniels was just as attracted to him as he was to her.

It must be an unpleasant feeling, to want to sleep with a murderer. Well, it was no more than she deserved.

He wasn't going to do anything to convince her of his innocence. For one thing, as long as she was being so damned devious he couldn't very well bring the subject up. For another, he knew that Lacey's death had been nothing more than a ghastly accident.

No, he wasn't going to convince her. As a matter of fact, he was tempted to do just the opposite. To let her believe he was some sort of crazed killer and that she might be the next victim. It would serve her right.

Of course, if he confronted her with the truth, she'd have no choice but to leave. If he strung her along, acted suspicious, she'd cling like the tenacious bulldog reporter he'd already figured she was. His choice was simple and he made it. Whether it was wise or not, he wasn't ready to let go of Judith Daniels. Not quite yet.

THE BUILDING ECHOED. His eyes watched. His mouth curved in a travesty of a grin. Death lurked, execution for crimes committed, for crimes still only dreamed of. Justice, steeped in the rich red smell of blood. Waiting for them all.

Chapter Six

"There you are, sweet cakes," Fafnir greeted Judith as she walked into the cool, spacious third floor. "Love those legs. Lemme tell ya, babe, you should never wear long pants. Va-va-voom!"

Judith grimaced. She could recognize Steve's come-on beneath this Fafnir's familiar tones, and she mustered all her self-control not to snarl at him. For all Steve's self-vaunted talent, there was something unpleasant about his interpretation of Fafnir's lustfulness. When Ryan was doing it, the leers were somehow charming. When Steve did it, she wanted to rip Fafnir's tongue out.

"Now, now, Fafnir, my child," Madame Rinaldi scolded in her typically arch tones, "leave the poor girl alone. She doesn't need you drooling all over her. Do you, Judith?"

"Not much," she muttered self-consciously. Madame Rinaldi was not one of her favorite puppets. The only prominent female puppet, the good Madame with her bleached blond pompadour was vain, captious, self-serving and incredibly manipulative. It said something for Ryan that his major foray into the feminine consciousness had turned out to be so shallow. "Where's Ryan?"

"He's gone into the green-and-yellow booth," another gruff, cheerful voice announced. "You want I should call him for you?"

Hideous Harry the Hippo was a different matter. With his

green fur, Ping Pong-ball eyes and wistful expression, he generally made Judith forget her self-consciousness. "That's all right, Harry. I'll find him."

"I'm here." Ryan stepped out from behind one of the larger booths that dotted the open space of the third floor.

She crossed the room reluctantly. "I thought you were Madame Rinaldi," she muttered, moving past him into the booth.

"Not this time. That's Franz." He followed her in, closing the door behind them, and Judith felt her breath catch in her chest.

"What about Harry?" She tried to sound nonchalant. The green-and-yellow booth was one of the largest, with room for three puppeteers and a ten-inch color monitor, not to mention puppets hung on pegs on either side of the enclosure. There was more than enough light filtering through the transparent curtain that shielded the puppeteer from the audience's eyes, but she felt imprisoned in the compact booth.

"Franz, too. Harry and the Madame are Franz's prize creations. Harry's one of the easiest puppets to do, but only Franz can do Madame Rinaldi justice. Micki's making great progress with her, though, and sooner or later she might almost reach Franz's level."

"You didn't create Madame Rinaldi?" Judith looked up at him in the half light of the booth.

"Nope. Does that surprise you?"

Damn, he was so close. "Why should it?" she countered evenly, determined to be unmoved.

"Because Madame Rinaldi is by far the most popular of all the puppets," he said. "There are more Madame Rinaldi toothbrushes and nightgowns sold than any of the others."

"So? Don't you get a piece of the action, anyway?"

"I do."

"Then what does it matter who created her?" Judith ignored the fact that she was obscurely pleased that Ryan wasn't responsible for the disagreeable Madame. "Show me what's wrong with this monitor so I can go back to enjoying my weekend."

"I'd think the problem would be obvious. It doesn't work."

"I can see that." The monitor was clamped to the bottom of the stage, its small screen dark. Judith tapped it, and it swung loosely. "Should it move like that?"

"Nope. It's supposed to be fixed at a level where I can see it without having to move around too much. I think I knocked it loose."

"And pulled the wires out." Judith discovered the culprit. "It should take me about ten minutes. Why don't you go get a cup of coffee while I deal with this?"

"Stop trying to get rid of me. I need to be here to make sure you get the monitor at the right level."

"You can do that after I rewire it."

"I want to watch you work."

"I can't work with you breathing down my neck."

"Try it," he suggested, his affable tone not masking the direct order.

She considered storming from the booth. She considered telling him what he could do with his monitor and his job. Then she shook herself. For some reason Ryan Smith wanted to get to her. And that was the last thing she would allow to happen. He wasn't about to strangle her in the compact fastness of the puppet booth, nor was he about to have his wicked way with her, not with two witnesses nearby.

"Okay, then you can make yourself useful. I need wire strippers, two screwdrivers and a flashlight."

"I'm way ahead of you. Look on the shelf to your left."

Every tool she could want was waiting for her. She wasn't going to get rid of him that way. With a long-suffering sigh she knelt on the floor and began pulling the wires out, then immediately regretted her action. Kneeling on the rough floor of the puppet booth brought her eye level with Ryan's waist. Mouth level with his zipper. Judith promptly dropped the wire strippers.

"Hey, what are you two doing in there?" Fafnir's voice called out from across the room. "Looks pretty kinky to me. Speak to me, Billy. Are you all right in there?"

"Shut up, Faf." Billy's voice came from directly above Judith. "You know Judith—she doesn't like smutty talk."

"How about smutty behavior?" Fafnir countered, unrepentant. "Come on, Billy. Send her over to my booth. I can keep her busy."

She could feel Ryan's eyes on her from up above, watching her as she fumbled with the wires. It was taking her much longer to fix the monitor than it should have, and she refused to consider the reasons for her unaccustomed clumsiness. Probably just a normal reaction to being closeted with a murderer, she told herself, wrapping the yellow wire around the terminal and screwing it down.

"If you don't watch it," Billy said, "she'll rip your tongue out."

"Empty threats, Billy."

"She's the woman to do it, Faf."

"Children, children!" Madame Rinaldi entered the fray. "Don't fight over the girl. She's not the usual low-class creature you men like to hire. Treat her with respect."

"Oh, I don't know, Madame," Harry's voice replied, and it took Judith a moment to realize that both those voices came from Franz's talented throat. "She might be just like all the other ones. You never can tell...."

The monitor crackled and came back to life as she screwed the last wire down. She was confronted with a vision of the front of the puppet booth. Billy was out there, looking troubled. She glanced up, way up Ryan's body to his puppet-covered arm stuck out before the curtain. *Puppets,* she told herself. *They're only puppets.*

"It's fixed," she said unnecessarily.

He looked down at her, abstracted. "Tilt it up a bit. A bit more to the left...no, that's too far. Up a bit more. Perfect."

She tightened the bolt that held the monitor in place, then let out a deep sigh of relief, releasing the tension as she did so. "Am I reprieved?"

He'd lost interest in her. Billy was on the screen, looking

around, and Ryan was busy watching him. "Go ahead. Someone'll give you a ride home in an hour."

"What am I supposed to do in the meantime?" She rose to her full height, thankful to be away from that subservient, distinctly erotic position at his feet. He still towered over her, but his interest in his unwelcome repairwoman was nil.

"Talk to Madame Rinaldi."

"No, thank you. I noticed some light bulbs were out in the lounge. Maybe I'll replace them."

"Suit yourself." He dismissed her. "Hey, Fafnir," Billy's voice shouted across the room. "How about those Mets?"

THERE WAS ONE THING to be said in Ryan's favor, Judith thought as she wandered back toward the employees' lounge. He was scarcely even aware of her proximity. She'd knelt at his feet, getting all hot and bothered, and all he'd noticed was his damned puppets.

And thank God for that, she reminded herself. The last thing she needed was for Ryan Smith to be aware of her as a woman. Her current situation was complicated enough, but it would be untenable if her most likely suspect suddenly made a pass at her. Especially since she wasn't completely sure she'd be able to resist it. And him.

The lounge was cool and deserted. She walked past it and out onto the balcony. The sun was brilliant in the hazy blue sky, beating down on the Hudson River Valley. The scent of water and growing things was strong, and a light breeze stirred the air around the old mill. It was a day for lying in the sun, for walking in the woods, for sitting and dreaming. It wasn't a day for the memory of murder.

But she had no choice in the matter. Much as she'd like to stretch out on the balcony and soak up some of the sun, she couldn't forget that just below her lay the balcony that had held Lacey's body. And beneath that was the rushing river and the turbine.

She shivered in the hot sunshine and moved away from the railing. Brooding wouldn't help. Action would. There weren't any burned-out light bulbs in the lounge—the regular janitorial crew made sure of that—but it had been a good enough excuse. Ryan was too wrapped up in his puppets to notice such mundane things. Instead she would quietly and systematically search through the custom-made teak lockers allotted to the employees of The Puppet Factory, looking for something, anything, incriminating. Starting with Ryan's.

Of course, figuring out which locker was the lord and master's was the first step. The lockers were numbered, not named. Number one clearly belonged to a female, and it didn't take a brilliant mind to notice the smell of stale cigarettes and figure the locker had to be Micki's. The next four held absolutely nothing of interest. Judith recognized the matching puce windbreakers belonging to Micki's neighbors, Jimmy and Melvin; she also recognized the smell of Franz's pipe in the old wool sweater with fuzzy green fur clinging to it. But it wasn't until she reached the eighth locker that she found anything remotely suspicious.

This was Steve's locker. She could tell by the bottle of sickly sweet cologne, by the large mirror on the door, by the three changes of clothes and the large leather carryall that on a less dedicated Casanova might resemble a purse. And in that purse/carryall was a stack of papers dotted with cryptic scribbles of dates and amounts. Amounts that were very large indeed. If Judith were any judge of the matter, she was holding a stack of gambling IOUs in her hand.

She slipped one of the crumpled pieces of paper in her shorts pocket and put the carryall back in the locker, careful to leave it just as she'd found it. She closed the door, casting a furtive glance around her in case any of the three puppeteers decided to come in search of her, and breathed a sigh of relief. The lounge was still empty. That odd prickly feeling at the back of her neck, that peculiar sensation of being watched, had to stem from a guilty conscience.

Steve's locker was the last in that row. Judith moved down the shiny hardwood floor to the next bank of lockers. There were boxes piled on top of them, and her curiosity was aroused.

She didn't dare go looking for the ladder and investigate right now; the risk was too great that someone would catch her in the act. Of course, she could always say she was looking for light bulbs. No, that wouldn't work. The light bulbs were in plain sight in the compact kitchen area. She'd have to come back sometime when Ryan and his cronies weren't working and investigate further.

But that might be easier said than done. As far as Judith could see, the man was a full-fledged workaholic. Then she remembered that Ma had said he had to go down to the city sooner or later—papers needed to be signed and people needed to be met. She could wait until then.

In the meantime, she had time for one more locker. And if luck was with her, it would prove to be Ryan's.

The door was locked. For a moment she stared at it, unbelieving, and shook the brass handle. It didn't move. She shook it again. The locker had to be Ryan's—who else would bother to lock it? And there had to be something incriminating inside. No one would lock away sweaters and running shorts. One last time she shook the recalcitrant handle, so intent on it that she didn't notice the prickling sensation had increased to mammoth proportions. The spicy scent of after-shave filled her nostrils.

And then the teak locker was falling toward her, the darkness was closing in around her, and somewhere in the back of her mind she could feel the heaviness of pain. She was falling, falling, and the locker was falling, and she cried out, a short, sharp cry for help. And that cry was "Ryan."

WHERE THE HELL was she now? Ryan wondered irritably. Probably going through Ma's desk, if he was any judge of character. At least he had the dubious satisfaction of knowing she'd have a hell of a hard time finding her way up to the fifth floor. Any secrets up there would be kept far away from her prying eyes.

He could hear Madame Rinaldi and Fafnir arguing in the background. He knew he should rouse himself and join in as Billy, the peaceful mediator, but he couldn't bring himself to do it. And that was Judith Daniels's fault. One more thing to blame her for.

He couldn't work with her around, at least not with the single-minded dedication and efficiency he expected from himself. And her absence was almost as distracting as her presence. He hadn't needed that monitor fixed. There were more than half a dozen booths on the floor, not to mention stages, sets and various other paraphernalia for puppets to play in. He could have used any one of them and let Judith spend the weekend immersed in Micki's cigarette smoke. But no, he'd had to leave Franz and Steve, just when things were beginning to develop, and drive over to confront his nemesis.

Maybe he should fire her. Tell her he knew who she was and what she was doing, and to take her sweet little butt out of there. He'd do it, too, if he thought getting rid of her would wipe her out of his mind. But he knew it wouldn't. There was something between them, something more than her ridiculous suspicions and his errant moments of lust. If he sent her away, it would only postpone the inevitable.

Damn, where was she? There were no burned-out light bulbs in the lounge. The maintenance crew was too good and too well paid to let that happen. She was looking for an excuse to snoop. He stepped out of the booth, half his mind still attuned to the other puppets.

Madame Rinaldi was singing an aria in thrilling accents. Her falsetto wavered between slightly sharp and slightly flat. The melody was Puccini and the words were Lewis Carroll. An errant grin lit Ryan's dark face. There was no one, absolutely no one, who could match Franz's genius for sheer nuttiness.

Fafnir was watching from another booth. He seemed lifeless, and for a moment Ryan wondered whether Steve was even there. But then Fafnir lifted his shaggy head, pursed his lips and whistled insultingly.

"Where ya going, boss?" he queried.

"Looking for Judith."

Madame Rinaldi stopped in midnote, peering at him. "You

living room, so Judith had no idea whether Steve had taken his leave or taken the surprisingly unwilling Micki to bed. She really didn't care. All she cared about was getting back to sleep.

Still...she couldn't rid herself of the suspicion that Steve hadn't come for Micki's lush charms. But what else could he have wanted?

She was just drifting back to sleep when she remembered the steno pad, with her suspicions all written down in fairly legible handwriting. The note pad probably had the words *Philadelphia Mirror* emblazoned on it.

"Hell and damnation," she muttered, throwing back the covers and climbing wearily out of bed. She tiptoed across the room and opened the door a crack. With her luck, Micki would have changed her mind and be writhing on the living room floor atop Judith's incriminating note pad.

Whether Micki had changed her mind or not, the living room was deserted. With all the stealth she could muster, Judith headed back out to the sofa and reached for her note pad.

It was gone.

Chapter Seven

The heat wave continued unabated. Judith spent Sunday in bed, thanking God for air conditioners and nonprescription Ibuprofen. Micki had been spectacularly unsympathetic, Phil Collins was turned up to ten, and cigarette smoke seeped under Judith's tightly shut door. Only a few more weeks, she promised herself, burying her aching head under her pillow.

Micki made no mention of the note pad, and Judith didn't dare ask. If Steve had ended up spending the night, he was long gone by the time Judith dragged herself out of bed, and there was just as good a chance he was the one who had taken the notes. She had no choice but to wait and see what happened.

Monday wasn't much of an improvement. Judith's headache had subsided to a dull throb, but the heat and humidity were so thick that she could scarcely breathe. Micki's coffee made her nauseated, the Mercedes wouldn't start, the toilet overflowed, and every piece of clothing Judith owned was dirty, her headache having taken precedence over a trip to the Laundromat. Despite the general messiness of her job, there was no way she could show up to work in grease and mud-stained jeans, and no way she'd wear the other linen suit she'd brought with her. She was still living down comments about her haute couture on the day she'd arrived.

Which left a baggy pair of cutoffs and an oversize white T-shirt for her to wear. What they lacked in coverage they more than made up for in coolness, and even Micki's cheerful contempt didn't daunt her.

Her roommate sat at the kitchen table, puffing one of her interminable cigarettes, drinking her ghastly coffee, her fresh layer of golden tan turning her slightly yellow in the fluorescent lighting of the small room. She was immersed in a copy of the weekly newspaper, deliberately ignoring Judith's pacing. Finally she flipped the paper back and fixed her unblinking black gaze on Judith.

"If you're in such a goddamned hurry," Micki said genially, "you can always call a taxi. Or hitch. Or fix your stupid car."

Judith threw herself into the kitchen chair opposite her. "I'm in no hurry," she lied. "I'd just like to get there before Memorial Day."

Micki smiled sourly, dropping her cigarette stub in her half-finished cup of coffee. It hissed for a second, then went silent. "You'll get there soon enough. I've just been reading about your predecessor."

Judith kept her expression bland. "Anything interesting?"

"Only that she came from the same neck of the woods you did. The upper-class environs of Philadelphia. I hear that high society is a pretty small world. Are you sure you didn't know her? You two were about the same age."

"What was her name?"

Micki's lip curled. "You know her name, Judith. It was Lacey who was spacey, not you."

Judith wouldn't budge an inch. "Lacey who?"

"Lacey Hollister."

"Never heard of her. I don't know any Hollisters."

Micki picked up her coffee cup, her eyes intent on Judith's expression. "I don't think I believe you."

Please let her drink, Judith begged silently. Give me that much to make my day.

But Micki set the cup down, and the cigarette stub floated cheerfully on the waves, spreading tobacco crumbs on the oily black liquid.

Judith smiled blandly. "Do you have trouble keeping room-mates, Micki?"

There was a long, strained silence. And then, to Judith's surprise, Micki laughed, a raw sound, rusty from disuse. "As a matter of fact, I do. How long do you think it'll take me to drive you out?"

"I don't think you can do it. Not until I'm ready to go."

"Maybe not," Micki said, picking up the cup again. "But I wouldn't bet on it. Unlike the old cliché, I'm not pretty when I'm angry."

Judith grinned. "I am."

"Hell, you're always pretty. Why do you think I hate you so much?" She set the cup back down, rising to her full five feet three inches and stretching.

Judith didn't move. "Do you hate me?"

"Naaah," Micki murmured. "But I sure as hell don't like Ryan calling up to find out how you're doing."

Judith didn't have time to consider what her reaction to that interesting piece of information was. All she knew was that she was reacting, and quite strongly. "What did you tell him?"

"Wouldn't you like to know?"

Judith tapped her fingers on the Formica table. "As a matter of fact, I would."

"I told him you were fine. A little bash on the head isn't going to slow you down."

"Thanks a lot."

"You're welcome," Micki said with a grin. "Okay, kid. I'm ready."

Judith watched with sour satisfaction as Micki drained her cigarette-laced coffee.

IF RYAN HAD BEEN CONCERNED about Judith's condition, her schedule for that day didn't reflect it. Ma Carter started her on enough filing to give anyone a headache; then the ribbons needed changing in the two printers and the three electric type-writers. The Roberts 450 was now working too efficiently, freezing everyone out of the second floor. Judith spent a messy half hour adjusting it, before moving on to a malfunctioning video camera, three dead audiocassette players, a hurried lunch of her perennial raspberry yogurt out on the upper balcony, and more filing. It wasn't until late afternoon that she had a chance to go back to the employees' lounge. The refrigerator had grown schizophrenic, melting the ice cream in its freezer and freezing the rest of the contents.

The carpenters were one flight below, rebuilding the deck on the lower balcony, removing any lingering trace of Lacey's death. The pounding and sawing drowned out any quieter sounds, and it took all Judith's wavering courage to edge her way back to Steve's locker, one eye alert for falling boxes or similar blunt objects.

She half expected his locker to be locked, too. But it opened easily enough, and the leather carryall was still hanging from a brass hook. Breathing a small, silent prayer of relief, she unfastened the buckle and slid her hand inside.

The damned bag was empty.

Nothing, not a scrap of paper, not a comb, not an errant penny or a particle of dust. And no note pad from the *Philadelphia Mirror* filled with incriminating doodles. The satchel was empty; the pockets in his clothes were empty; the floor and the shelf of the locker were empty. Hell and damnation.

She gave the door a satisfactory slam when she shut it. Then, with only a cursory glance over her shoulder, she marched to the locker Ryan had designated as Lacey's, the locker that had signaled Judith's downfall on Saturday.

There were no boxes overhead, waiting to clobber her. The narrow teakwood closet opened easily enough. And, of course, it was just as empty as Steve Lindstrom's leather purse.

"Looking for something?"

She hadn't heard him over the noise of the carpenters below. And since she was standing in front of the open locker, she couldn't deny she'd been snooping. She turned and looked up at Ryan.

"I wanted to see if there was anything in this locker that

would make it worthwhile for someone to knock me unconscious," she said.

"I don't think the boxes had any malicious intent," he said, reaching out and pushing the door shut. He was very close, but she stood her ground, not moving even as the closing of the door brought him within inches of her.

"You didn't find anyone on Saturday?"

"Not a soul. You're looking for crimes where they don't exist, princess," he drawled, and for a moment she wondered if he meant anything more than Saturday's accident.

But no, he couldn't. He had no idea who she was or why she was really there. It was mere coincidence on his part. Or a guilty conscience.

"Maybe," she muttered. Why did he have to stand so close to her? Why did he have to be so tall, when she was used to being eye level with men? There was something unsettling about having to look up into a man's eyes. Something threatening and faintly, perversely, arousing. She concentrated on his shoulder, but that wasn't much better. He had very nice shoulders beneath the denim shirt. Broad enough, but not too broad, slightly bony, strong but comfortable looking.

She backed away, into the teak locker, no longer caring if it looked as if she were retreating. She was. He's lousy in bed, she reminded herself. Lacey had said so. But what the hell did Lacey know? She had been voracious enough to overwhelm any man. Judith had the sudden, uncomfortable suspicion that in this instance Lacey had been dead wrong. And then she shivered at the macabre direction of her thoughts.

For a long moment Ryan stood there without moving, looking down at her out of faintly hooded eyes. Then he shook his head in mock defeat. "Stay out of other people's lockers, Judith, or I'll have to warn them about you." He moved away, releasing her from the momentary thrall in which she'd been caught. "Check in the workshop before you leave," he said, suddenly distant and businesslike. "There's been some trouble with another one of the monitors."

She held herself stiffly, watching him leave, and then she

sank back against the unyielding dimensions of the lockers. It had been a close call. She'd gotten away with it this time, but his forbearance was unlikely to last. Sooner or later he would catch her snooping again and fire her on the spot. Unless, of course, he actually had killed Lacey. In which case, she might be lucky to escape with her life.

She was crazy to be here. Crazy to be snooping around, looking for clues, conversing with a murderer. If it wasn't Ryan, it had to be someone else at The Puppet Factory. On the other hand, maybe one of Lacey's old lovers had shown up. Or a spurned wife. There were any number of people who owed Lacey a debt of ingratitude. Perhaps her past had simply caught up with her.

Judith went over to the partially dismantled refrigerator, dismissing that wishful thought. Something was going on at the Factory. There were undercurrents of anger and sickness that Judith couldn't begin to recognize but could feel with that half-developed reporter's instinct of hers. She couldn't turn her back on it until she found out what those undercurrents signified and how they were involved in Lacey's life and death. She'd ignored Lacey's final cry for help, and there was no way she could live with that guilt without doing something about it.

The third-floor work area was still crowded when Judith finally finished with the refrigerator. Micki was deep in conversation with Franz, sparing Judith only a brief glance before returning her attention to the rumpled little man. He managed to grant her a shy smile, and Judith smiled back. If there was one person she felt comfortable with in this place, one person she trusted, it was Franz, with his baggy old sweaters and his pipe and his benign countenance. He looked like one of Ryan's creations, a lovable old codger with a charming accent and an endearing manner. Rather like Hideous Harry the Hippo, the shaggy green puppet that now rested in Franz's right hand.

Steve wasn't anywhere in sight, hadn't been all day, and Ryan was thankfully absent. Then Fafnir reared his purple head from behind Steve's usual puppet booth, his long forked tongue slithering over his woolly jaws. "Hi, babe. I see ya took my advice about short pants."

Judy grimaced. She could feel the eyes on her, from Franz's gentle ones to Micki's frankly cynical gaze. At least Ryan was nowhere around to watch and judge while she conversed with his horny little dragon.

She walked over to the puppet booth. "They were the only clean clothes I had, Fafnir," she said sternly, wondering what would happen if she started talking to Steve, the puppeteer, instead of to his mouthpiece.

"Whatever," Fafnir said. "I love it. I'll tell you what I'm looking forward to. The Memorial Day picnic out at the boss's. You'll wear a bikini, won't you, honey cakes? Please tell me you'll wear a bikini."

"Only if you do." God help her, the chatter got easier as she went along. Here she was, talking to a purple cloth dragon as if it were a rational human being. Which in fact, the man behind him was. Maybe. With Steve she couldn't be certain.

"Listen, babe, for you I'd do anything. Breathe fire, terrorize maidens, make toast..."

"Terrorize maidens?" Judith had a sudden, uneasy suspicion. "When did you last terrorize a maiden?"

Fafnir cackled. "Last time I found one. That must have been in 1753. Maybe it was 1754. Haven't met a maiden since then."

"Cut it out, Fafnir!" Billy appeared beside the dragon, his little face pinched in a look of concern. "I've told you, Judith doesn't like that smutty talk."

Steve was getting better and better at doing Billy, Judith noticed absently as she found herself smiling at the little-boy puppet. She could hardly tell the difference between his voice and Ryan's.

"How do you know?" Fafnir responded. "What you know about women you could put on the head of a pin. Women like smutty talk and they like smutty action even better. Don't you, babe?"

"Fafnir, your lechery wears a little thin after a while," Judith said firmly.

To her horror Fafnir flopped over on his back, his jaws crumpled in an expression of grief. "I know," he said contritely. "I know. But it's all I've got." And with that he disappeared behind the booth.

"Don't look so worried, Judith," Billy said, edging closer to her. "He'll be okay. Someone needs to tell him to cool it every now and then. There's no need to feel guilty."

Judith controlled the little start of surprise that swept over her. Steve was good, and far more observant than she would have guessed. "Must be the white man's burden," she said. "Guilt, that is."

"There's a lot of that going around," Billy agreed.

Judith stared at him, then mentally shook herself. She was trying to read a puppet's expression, for crying out loud! "Who feels guilty about what?"

Billy shrugged. "Micki feels guilty about smoking and sleeping around. Steve feels guilty about gambling, Franz feels guilty about his past, and no one knows what it is except maybe Hideous Harry. Ma feels guilty about Ryan. Ryan feels guilty about Ma feeling guilty. Matter of fact, Ryan feels guilty about a lot of things. About Lacey's accident, for example."

"Why should he feel guilty about Lacey's accident?"

"Because he thinks the railing should have been higher, that he should have known how spacey she was, that he could have done something to prevent it. That's crazy, of course, but who says guilt is rational?"

Judith could feel a reluctant smile spread across her face. "Who says?" she echoed.

"Hey, Judith." Billy dropped his voice to a low-pitched, cajoling note. "Come here."

"I am here."

"No, I mean closer. Closer." He gestured with one tiny gloved hand, and Judith found herself moving closer. "I want to tell you something," he whispered. "If you can promise to keep a secret."

"Of course." She dropped her voice to a conspiratorial level.

Billy scrunched up his cloth face into an amazingly effective expression of anxiety and longing. "Fafnir's not the only one with lustful thoughts," he whispered in a breathless rush.

Judith almost laughed. But she didn't. She was caught up in the magic of the puppets, and she was terribly afraid that if she laughed she'd wound Billy beyond mending. Dignity in children and puppets was a hard-won commodity, and at that moment she didn't want to jeopardize it.

"That's okay, Billy," she said gently. "A few lustful thoughts keep us healthy."

He dropped his head onto his gloved hands in an attitude of despair, then lifted his face to peer at her. "But, Judith," he said in a curiously rough little voice, "it's you I want."

Judith stood absolutely still. For the moment, everything around her receded—the watching eyes, the puppet booth, the man beyond the little cloth doll.

Billy moved closer. "I want to be your lover," he said, his voice a small, seductive croon. "I want to kiss your eyelids, the small of your back, your shoulder blades. I want to taste your tears. I want to feel you wrapped around me, shuddering, shivering, crying. I want your body, Judith. I want your mind and I want your soul. I want your love." And without another word he disappeared behind the puppet booth.

The last conversation had been carried on at such a quiet pitch that none of the eavesdroppers could have heard. But they could see her incomprehensible reaction. She could feel the heat in her face, in her breasts, between her legs. She could feel the tight knot of longing that was uncurling in her stomach, and she knew her hands were shaking.

She'd just been seduced by a master. Forget that a cloth puppet had done the talking. She'd been turned into a melted little pool of longing by someone who knew exactly how to do it. She'd been a complete fool to underestimate Steve.

She turned on her heel and stalked from the room. She couldn't trust herself to hold a rational conversation with anyone—she needed a few minutes to compose herself. Then she would go back, find Steve and tell him never to do that to her again.

The nerve of that man, she thought as she stepped out into the comparative cool of the upper balcony. How dared he come on to her like that, using the puppets, sneaking past her reserve! He had to be the one who'd removed the tell-tale pieces of paper from his carryall—had he removed the one she'd slipped into her shorts pocket? Had he taken the steno pad from Micki's house? Had he seen Judith snooping and banged her over the head?

But that didn't sound like the Steve she was rapidly coming to know too well. He was cheerful, friendly and surprisingly adept at manipulating emotions. Yet he didn't strike her as a killer.

For that matter, neither did Ryan Smith. And where was he when she needed him? Steve would never have dared pull a stunt like that if Ryan had been around.

"Ready to go?" Micki strolled out onto the balcony, lighting a cigarette as she came.

"In a minute. First I have to have a little conversation with Steve," Judith said in a determined voice.

Micki laughed. "That's going to be a little difficult. Steve's in Las Vegas."

Judith turned to stare at her, dumbfounded. "Then who was in Steve's booth?"

"Who do you think? Ryan, of course. What the hell were the two of you talking about, anyway? It looked fascinating."

Judith pushed past her. "Where is he?"

"Ryan? He's gone. The moment you left the room he walked out. I expect he's on his way home." Micki tossed her just-lit cigarette over the balcony into the Hudson. "So what did he say to you that got you all hot and bothered?"

The anger she'd felt toward Steve was dissipating into a fractured confusion that was part rage, part regret. What the hell had Ryan been doing to her?

She looked into Micki's curious face. "Not a thing, Micki," she said. "Not a thing."

HE KNEW EVERYTHING.

Evil. Whores, all of them; evil, filthy whores. And they must be punished. She must be punished. Ryan was too innocent, too trusting. He would be contaminated by her evil, as he had been by the last one. He must be protected, no matter what the cost.

Evil must be punished. Justice must prevail. His fist struck the table; furry green feet shuffled across the floor. And evil would be punished. Soon. Very soon.

Chapter Eight

"Get your things, princess," Ryan Smith said. "It's going to take us at least two hours to get into the city, and we're running late."

"I beg your pardon?" Judith was sitting cross-legged on the floor in front of a partially dismantled dehumidifier, the pieces lying scattered around her like flower petals. It was just after ten o'clock on a Thursday morning, and she hadn't seen her employer since her unsettling encounter with the puppets on Monday. She opened her mouth to confront him, then shut it again in unexpected embarrassment. In three days she hadn't been able to wipe the erotic images from her mind. And since she couldn't calmly bring up the incident without turning beet red, she had no intention of giving Ryan Smith that satisfaction. "What city?" she said instead. "And what's it got to do with me?"

"Manhattan." He reached down and took the vice grip from her hand. "And you're coming with me." His fingers wrapped around her wrist and tugged, pulling her to her feet. She was dressed in cutoffs again, and another baggy T-shirt, but at least she hadn't had time to get really dirty.

Judith's immediate response was, the hell I am, but she swallowed it. Some deference ought to be shown to a boss, even if she suspected that boss of brutal, cold-blooded murder. "Why?" she inquired politely enough.

His small grin acknowledged her restraint. "I need someone

with secretarial skills to make notes while I drive. I need a mechanic in case my Toyota breaks down. It's been temperamental recently. And I need someone who's observant, who can notice things I might miss. You're observant, aren't you, Judith? You have an inquiring mind, don't you?''

''I have a normal amount of curiosity,'' she said stiffly.

''Oh, I'd put it a bit higher than that. Anyway, I'd rather take one person than three, and you're that one person. We'll swing by your house so you can change and get your things—''

''Things?'' she repeated.

''We'll be spending the night at Steve's apartment.''

''I want to feel you wrapped around me,'' he'd told her in Billy's ingenuous voice. There was no sign of any such desire right now, but Judith felt her stomach tighten. ''Is Steve back from Las Vegas?''

''I don't expect he'll be back until he runs out of money. No, princess, we'll be staying in his apartment alone. You in the bedroom, me on the couch. Just to prove I have my gentlemanly moments, after all.''

''Couldn't someone else go? I'm really involved right now....''

''No one else can make intelligent notes and fix a Toyota. Don't worry, you're safe from my lecherous clutches. I have no intention of jumping your bones.''

''That's not what Billy said.'' There, it was out in the open.

He didn't look the slightest bit chagrined, merely amused. ''Billy may want to. So does Fafnir. But I'm not the puppets. Stop bitching, Judith. You're my employee, and as such you're supposed to do as I tell you. I promise you, I'll control my baser instincts.''

''What if I say no?''

''I could always fire you.''

''Would you?''

''Maybe.''

She stared up at him. He wouldn't dare murder her—everyone would know she'd gone off with him, and he'd have no way of covering it up. She didn't have to worry about unwanted advances, either. While she considered him to be an alarmingly sexy man, he wasn't someone who couldn't control his appetites. He wasn't like Steve Lindstrom, coming on to anything in skirts. And she could find out a great deal if she could only put the time to good use.

"What about this mess?"

"Leave it. We'll be back by tomorrow afternoon—you can finish then. Any more excuses?" He looked bored, impatient, as if he actually might fire her if she gave him one more argument.

"None," she said, making up her mind. "Just let me tell Micki where I'm going."

"I've already told her."

Score one for him. He might have told her, or he might not have. If he hadn't, then no one would know where she'd gone, and he could throw her off some bridge with no one the wiser. "I had some things to tell her."

"You can leave her a note at the house."

"So I can," she murmured, relieved. "I'll do that."

His cynical smile was definitely unsettling. "You do that," he agreed. "Come on, princess. We're due at the lawyer's by one. Then we go to the Metropolitan Museum and on to a club in the Village."

"Why?"

"We go to the lawyer's to sign papers. We go to the Metropolitan Museum to see an exhibition of puppets. We go to the Dead End to see a couple of new puppeteers who might work with us."

"Why can't we drive home after that?"

"Because it'll be late and I'll be tired, and no, I don't trust your driving."

"It's a damned sight better than yours."

"Judith, Judith," he said with a mock sigh. "I'm your boss, remember? You're supposed to be deferential."

She quickly salaamed. "Yes, my lord and master."

He merely smiled that damned cool, secretive smile and said nothing at all.

RYAN WAS DRIVING SLOWLY and carefully, not because he wanted to, but because she might kick up a storm of protest if he drove as hard and as fast as his temper warranted.

God, she absolutely infuriated him! Whom did she think she was fooling? She looked at him as if he were Bluebeard and Ted Bundy combined, and somehow she expected him not to notice. It would serve her right if he was a crazed killer. She wouldn't make it as far as the city limits.

He'd expected more of an argument from her over his trumped-up excuses. For all his reasons for taking her to the city, they boiled down to just one; he wanted her with him.

He'd kept as far away from her as he could the past few days. Ever since he'd let his fantasies get out of hand when he'd had Billy talking with her, he couldn't get her out of his mind. So he'd cooked up a bunch of reasons to get away from The Puppet Factory, most of which could have waited till a later time. Maybe if she saw him away from the scene of the so-called crime, she might view him in a more rational light.

Aside from that, he knew he shouldn't put off seeing his lawyer any longer than he had to. Josiah Greenfield had more common sense than most of his breed, plus a built-in sense of self-preservation that extended to his clients. Ryan needed to talk with him about Steve's little problem. About Lacey's unfortunate accident. And about Judith Daniels's presence.

Chances were that Josiah would tell him to fire Steve and kick Judith's pretty little butt back to Philadelphia. He wasn't about to do either of those things. Then Josiah would give him some good, solid advice for dealing with the problems the two of them were causing.

Probably all he needed was time. Time for the memory of Lacey's accident to fade; time for Judith to realize there was no crime, no criminal, only a tragedy. Steve might require more than time, but his problem wasn't crucial. Unless he'd been the one to club Judith on the head last Saturday.

It was another damnably hot day. The air conditioner in the Toyota had long ago given up the ghost, but at least the hot breezes blowing in the open windows cooled things off a tiny bit. He spared a glance at his unwilling passenger. She looked cool and unruffled, the perfect princess in her linen suit, neatly coiffed hair, thin-strapped leather sandals and stockings.

He'd almost forgotten she could look like that. He'd gotten used to her dirt streaked face, her bare legs, her baggy T-shirts that hinted at a compact lushness underneath. It wasn't the princess he was attracted to, and he suspected she knew that and had dressed accordingly.

"Aren't you hot in that jacket?" he inquired lazily, one arm resting in the open window as they barreled down the highway at a more than respectable speed.

"No."

He controlled a sigh. She really was a lousy investigator. If she knew what was good for her, she'd exert a little more of the charm he suspected she had. She'd flirt with him; or, if she couldn't bring herself to do that, she'd at least be a little more civil, instead of glaring at him when she thought he wasn't looking.

Sooner or later he would reach his limit. Josiah's office was only minutes away now. He could hold out long enough to get some legal advice on how to deal with the spy in the ranks. But another twenty-four hours were not going to pass without his confronting Judith with her suspicions.

He parked in the basement of Josiah's building, herded Judith upstairs and left her in the spacious waiting room outside the lawyer's office. He looked back at her before closing the door, noting sourly how well she blended with the elegant furnishings. She sat on one of the sofas, neatly shod feet together, staring up at the huge poster of Hideous Harry the Hippo in all his furry green splendor. Josiah made a great deal of money from The Puppet Factory, and he didn't mind advertising it. A poster of Billy hung in his private office, one of Madame Rinaldi in the ladies' room.

"So you're still in a mess," Josiah observed from behind his spotless walnut desk.

"Still in a mess," Ryan agreed, stretching his legs out in front of him. "I think Steve's embezzling. I can't be sure, but it looks like he's in debt up to his ears. I wouldn't be surprised if Lacey had helped him. She had access to the financial records and could easily have covered up for him.''

"What makes you think it's Steve?''

"He's the only one in trouble. His gambling's gotten worse and worse. Besides, he was sleeping with Lacey before her accident.''

"Do you think he was involved in her death?''

"It was an accident,'' Ryan said firmly. "And, Steve was in Atlantic City when it happened. There's no question about his alibi.''

"Who thought he needed an alibi?''

"No one did. For God's sake, Josiah, I'm not on the witness stand,'' he snapped. "How many times do I have to tell you that Lacey Hollister's death was an accident?''

Josiah leaned back in his chair, his homely face benign. "I guess until you convince yourself, Ryan,'' he said.

"Damn you,'' Ryan replied without rancor.

"How much is missing?''

"About fifty thousand dollars.''

Josiah shook his head. "Why don't you just free up his profit-sharing money? He must have close to ten times that much salted away.''

"The profit-sharing plan is supposed to provide for people's futures. If he got hold of it, he'd just piss it away.''

"That's not your problem, Ryan. You're not responsible for Steve's future. You pay your employees more money than they have any right to expect, and you cut them in on a piece of the action with all your licensing. You've more than done your duty—you don't have to take on their moral well-being and their future along with everything else.''

"So what do you suggest I do?''

"Fire him.''

"I can't do that. For one thing, I can't turn on him when he's in trouble. For another, I need him. Franz can't take on any more than he's got already, and the others simply aren't at Steve's level.''

"Then get someone in to tighten up your books. Make it impossible for him to get any more, swallow the loss and don't let it happen again."

Ryan grinned. "I knew I could count on you."

"I still think you should fire him," Josiah grumbled. "So what else is new? Do I dare ask you if anything's come up concerning that girl's death?"

"In a manner of speaking."

"Damnation! The district attorney was supposed to get in touch with me directly if—"

"It has nothing to do with the district attorney. As far as the town of Miller's Junction and the county are concerned, the cause of death was accidental."

"Humph," said Josiah, still skeptical. "Then what's the problem?"

"A reporter."

"The one you had me check on? What was her name—Davis?"

"Judith Daniels."

"That's it. She writes a fix-it column for one of the Philadelphia papers. I wondered why you were so interested."

"She was Lacey Hollister's roommate in college. She showed up asking for a job, not saying a word about her newspaper credentials, pretending she'd never heard of Lacey."

Josiah just stared at him. "And I bet you hired her."

"You know me too well."

"You want to give me one good reason why you didn't send her packing?"

"I can give you several. First of all, while she's there I can keep an eye on her. The more she snoops the sooner she'll realize that nothing's going on. I just want to make things easy for her."

"Give me another reason."

Ryan grinned. "She can fix a Roberts 450 air conditioner. Not to mention videotape recorders, car radios, dehumidifiers, refrigerators and anything with a motor."

"Is that it?"

"Not quite. She's sitting in your waiting room. Take a look at her and see if you can come up with another reason."

"Ryan, you're asking for trouble."

"I don't need to ask. It's taken to following me around."

"So fire Steve, get rid of the reporter and then go on a long vacation, maybe a cruise around the world. You've been a workaholic too long. You need some time off, some peace and quiet."

"That's what I'm looking for. And that's what I need Steve for. Franz can't do it alone, and Micki's not good enough yet. A couple more months, tops. In the fall I can go."

"You said that last year, and every year since I've known you."

"Maybe I didn't relish the idea of going alone."

"And this time you don't think you'll be alone?" Josiah asked, rising from his desk. "Who've you got in mind? Anyone I know?"

"You're about to meet her."

"Good God, not the reporter?"

Ryan rose, too. "I never said I was overburdened with common sense."

"You're one of the most hardheaded men I know. I can't wait to meet this paragon. You sure you know what you're doing?"

Ryan shrugged. "No."

Josiah stared at him. "Well, if you can admit that much, there might be some hope for you. Let's see your Mata Hari."

JUDITH SQUIRMED IN HER SEAT. There was no reason why she should feel uncomfortable. The perfectly groomed regulation British secretary was engrossed in paperwork, the waiting room was cool and gracious, and it didn't look as if Ryan had any intention of clubbing her on the head. She'd spent the two-hour trip into Manhattan taking notes, trying to distance herself from Ryan's ideas while she kept track of them on paper.

It had been an uphill battle. No matter what she thought of him personally, there was no denying he had a brilliant mind.

While she'd busily written down his plans for an operetta involving puppets and live performers, she'd done everything she could not to get involved, not to make her own suggestions, not to tell him how astonishingly inventive he was.

He didn't need to hear that, especially from her. Ryan Smith knew perfectly well that he was the best.

She squirmed again. There was something about the posters that unnerved her. The bright splashes of color on the umber walls should have been cheering. Indeed, she found Fafnir's familiar countenance amusing.

No, there was something about the poster of Hideous Harry—an expression in his Ping Pong-ball eyes, his green fur mouth, something that made the hair on the back of her neck stand up. It was patently ridiculous, of course. It had to be a trick of lighting, or a product of her own overwrought imagination. There was no way a blown-up photograph of a cloth puppet could look malevolent.

She didn't hear the door open to the inner office, but then she didn't need to. She'd developed a sixth sense as far as Ryan was concerned; she knew where he was almost before he got there, a fact that should serve her well if ever he turned a murderous rage on her. The man beside him was short and stocky, looking more like a bantamweight boxer than the lawyers she was used to.

She rose, and Josiah Greenfield gave her a long, measuring glance from head to toe. "Now I understand," he muttered obscurely.

"I thought you might," Ryan said, making the introductions without giving Judith any explanation of his enigmatic exchange with the lawyer. "Come up to the Factory soon, Josiah. I'm sure Micki would be happy to see you."

"I'm not so sure of that," he said morosely. "She threw her tape deck at me last time I was there."

"Don't worry," Judith said. "I fixed it."

"That won't keep her from throwing it again. Nice to meet you, Miss Daniels."

She nodded politely. She would have given ten years off her

life to have listened in on their hour-long conversation. She had no doubt whatsoever that it concerned her, and common sense told her it had to have involved Lacey. Ryan suspected her; she knew that much. At times she was amazed that he didn't fire her and have done with it.

He simply turned his distant, handsome face to her, and there was no hint in it of what had just passed between the two men. "Let's go."

And, dammit, she had no choice but to follow.

JUDITH HAD A HARD TIME keeping up with Ryan as he moved swiftly through the busy city streets. She'd always prided herself on her fast pace, but she was a piker compared with Ryan. Of course she was hampered by her high heels. Ryan was still wearing Nikes, she noted peevishly. It would serve him right if in her hurry to keep up with him she fell and sprained her ankle.

Actually it would be her own just deserts. Ryan would finally have a good excuse to fire her, and she'd have no choice but to go to the police with her farfetched suspicions.

"Slow down," she said, trying to keep the snappishness out of her voice.

He stopped, looking back at her over his shoulder. "Do you want to take a taxi? The museum's only five blocks away."

"No, I don't want to take a taxi," she said crossly. "Nor do I want to break land-speed records getting there."

"All right. We'll walk slowly and decorously and talk about the weather," he drawled.

"We can walk at a decent pace," Judith said, "and you can tell me why you keep a disagreeable old bitch like Ma Carter on the staff."

A long, dead silence greeted this outburst, and for a moment Judith wondered if she'd blown it. He turned his back on her and started walking again, but this time the pace was reasonable, and after a moment's hesitation she caught up with him.

"She hasn't done anything, has she?" he asked suddenly, keeping his eyes trained on the sidewalk.

Judith nodded. "I do."

The woman handed her a boxed VHS tape. "God, it must be terrific! Don't you just love it?"

"It has its moments," she drawled, with his fingers on her back and his amusement showing clearly on his face.

"Is he as sexy as they say he is?" the damned woman continued.

Judith controlled the urge to slam an elbow into the stomach too close behind her. "I don't know," she said. "How sexy do they say he is?"

"Well," said the clerk, snapping her chewing gum, "I've heard that he looks like a cross between Robert Redford and Clint Eastwood. I've also heard that he was horribly deformed, and that's why no one ever sees him."

Judith laughed with delight. "Pretty on the outside, ugly on the inside," she replied, moving away from the counter. "Thanks."

Ryan didn't say anything until they reached the broad expanse of sidewalk on Fifth Avenue. "Why didn't you tell her who I was and let her decide for herself?"

She hesitated. "Why didn't you?"

"Because I don't like crowds, and I don't like to be recognized and fussed over."

She nodded. "I know. And that's why I didn't tell her."

There was real surprise on his face. "A genuine act of kindness, princess? I didn't know you had it in you."

Judith's warmer feelings began to ice over. "Where do we go next?"

"For a walk. We're not due at the Dead End till nine. So lighten up, Judith, give me your hand and we'll stroll through Central Park like normal people. Like friends."

She didn't move. He was standing there, his tall frame silhouetted against the bright sunlight streaking his dark brown hair. His eyes were solemn, patient, with just a trace of humor lingering in their depths. Unlike her, he hadn't dressed for the city; he was still wearing faded jeans and a soft cotton shirt. There were lines bracketing his mouth, and they weren't from smiling. He was austere, handsome and very remote, and he was holding his hand out to her.

She put her hand in his. His fingers closed around it, imprisoning her, and for a moment she almost pulled away. But she let her hand stay there.

"Okay," she said. "We'll walk through the park."

"Like friends?"

She nodded. "Like friends."

And with that truce, the last of her suspicions were relegated to Miller's Junction. When she got back she'd think about it; when she got back she'd watch him some more. For now, she was going to enjoy her day, even enjoy the sweltering heat of Central Park during this unseasonably warm spell.

It shouldn't have surprised her, the attraction that grew, that threatened to overwhelm her. She'd had hints of it before, and she wasn't a self-deluding fool. As for Ryan, he didn't seem prey to the same feelings. He was exerting an amazing amount of quiet charm, but if it covered a layer of lust, only he knew about it. She could have been Micki or his lawyer; she could have been anyone walking through the park with him, eating dinner at a sidewalk cafe in SoHo that had sinfully wonderful Italian food, sitting at a nightclub table, drinking Bloody Marys and wondering if he was going to touch her again. The small of her back still tingled; her hand still remembered his grip. Was this why Lacey had chased after him so mercilessly?

No, Lacey had chased after countless men, most of them complete losers. And though their taste hadn't overlapped in years, Judith suddenly found herself questioning how bad Ryan could possibly be. Maybe he just hadn't found the right woman.

The act at the Dead End was two puppeteers, a young married couple named Burkholtz, and they were very good indeed. They were dressed in black, with their glove puppets on their hands, and they neither used a booth nor made any attempt at ventriloquism.

There was no question of the Burkholtzes not recognizing Ryan Smith when he was in their presence. At the end of their act they came over to the table, shy and stammering, like the gawking groupies Judith was sometimes afraid she resembled.

Once more Ryan surprised her. He bought them drinks, charmed them, praised them, even gave them a subtle suggestion or two that left the couple gushingly grateful and Judith amazed that he possessed such tact. He certainly never used any around her.

Then they were out on the street, Ryan's long stride eating up the sidewalks, Judith once more just barely keeping up with him. "They're very good, aren't they?" she managed to say when he'd slowed his headlong pace.

He spared her a brief glance. "Very good."

"So what's the problem?"

He stopped still in the middle of the crowded sidewalk. Even though it was after midnight, the city heat still hung heavily around them, and the people who pushed past them were hot and bad tempered. "With the Burkholtzes? Nothing at all. If I'm lucky they'll come to work at the Factory."

"Then why are you practically racing down the sidewalk? In a hurry to get somewhere?"

Ryan grinned suddenly, and Judith felt that treacherous reaction inside her. "I'm in a hurry to get to Steve's apartment."

"Any particular reason?" Her voice was very cool, but her heart was hammering.

"Because I'm tired, Judith. Nothing more sinister."

"I wasn't expecting anything sinister."

"Weren't you? What were you expecting?"

Unbridled lust, she thought. "A good night's sleep," she replied.

"I can't guarantee that. Steve's apartment is in a noisy section of SoHo, so there's not much peace and quiet. That's why he spends most of his time in Miller's Junction."

"Why does he keep the apartment?"

Ryan shrugged. "It's rent controlled and cheap enough. It gives him a place to escape to if he's had enough of suburbia. And it gives me a place to bring women to."

"Have you?"

Ryan laughed. "You haven't seen it yet. Believe me, I can afford something a little more conducive to romance if I were so inclined."

Romantic it wasn't. It was a fourth-floor walk-up in a very old building that smelled of urine, marijuana and boiled cabbage. Judith half expected a rat to come scuttling along the stairs as she trudged up behind Ryan.

The apartment itself wasn't much better. It consisted of three rooms, furnished mainly in Indian print bedspreads, posters and mattresses strewn here and there. The bedroom had a conventional bed big enough to hold an orgy, and the African masks adorning the wall, though mildly malevolent, didn't give her the uneasy feeling that the poster of Hideous Harry the Hippo had.

Ryan had followed her to the bedroom door, standing too close. "No air conditioning. You'll have to settle for an open window and street noise or a closed window and suffocation."

"Difficult choice."

"Do you want anything? Coffee? A drink?"

Coffee, tea or me, Judith's mind said irreverently. "No, I'm fine. What time do you want to leave tomorrow?"

"As soon as you can pull yourself out of bed."

He hadn't moved. If she just swayed slightly, she'd be touching him. And she wanted to sway. She was hot, tired and a little dizzy from one too many Bloody Marys. If she'd had one more, she would have crossed those few inches, put her arms around his neck and pressed her mouth against his.

She blinked, banishing the sudden fantasy. "Okay. See you tomorrow."

His smile was slow, secretive, and a trifle too knowing. "Tomorrow," he said. And he shut the door behind him, leaving her alone in the room.

The open window didn't help the stuffiness much. She changed, made a quick trip to the bathroom and then climbed in the huge bed, forcing herself not to consider what sort of insect livestock might be lurking. Cockroaches like the one crawling in the bathroom sink were probably the least of her worries. She slid down beneath the obligatory satin sheets and turned off the light, willing sleep to come.

Sleep wasn't obliging. She could feel the streetlights shining on her eyelids. She could hear the voices, the rumble of cars, the sounds of doors slamming and babies crying and people pressed in around her. And she could hear Ryan, moving about in the other room, and each footstep, each muffled sound, vibrated in her stomach.

She had no idea when she finally fell asleep. And she had no idea when she woke up, sweating, in a complete, uncontrollable panic, with Hideous Harry looming over her, his furry hands reaching for her, death and madness and destruction and...

"Wake up, Judith," Ryan snapped, his voice at variance with the concern in his eyes. He was sitting on the bed, his arms on either side of her shivering body. "You've had a nightmare. Wake up."

He'd turned the light on at the wall. The low wattage provided little illumination, but there was enough to see that the man beside her wasn't about to strangle her.

He was wearing his jeans and nothing else. His arms and chest were bare, with smooth, honey-colored skin, delineated muscles and just a trace of hair. For once his expression was clear—she could see it in his eyes. He wanted her; he wanted her as much as she wanted him. Desire hung heavily in the stuffy night air. They were inches, moments, apart. She scarcely dared to breathe, waiting for Ryan to make his move.

He rose, his body silhouetted in the dim light, the moment gone so quickly that she thought she'd imagined it. "You okay?" he murmured, his voice expressing distant concern.

"Yes," she said, cursing herself for her frustration. "It was just a nightmare. I'm fine now."

"Then we'd better try to get some more sleep," he said. "You want me to leave the light on?"

"Please." The door closed silently behind him. She fought the last tremors that shook her body, irritation wiping out her nightmare-induced panic. How could he be so damned immune to her, when all he had to do was come close to turn her into a pile of marshmallow fluff?

Except, she thought, remembering his silhouette, he hadn't been immune, had he? There'd been unmistakable physical evidence that he'd reacted to her, at least on one level, as she'd been reacting to him.

Damn the man, she muttered to herself, climbing out of bed. How could she be so attracted to a man she thought capable of murder?

The answer was blissfully clear. She couldn't be. Ergo, Ryan Smith hadn't killed Lacey. Someone else had.

And if Ryan Smith wasn't the villain, then her task had shifted dramatically. She no longer had to snoop and lie and prowl around to prove him guilty. She had to snoop and lie and prowl around to prove him innocent.

She walked over to the window, staring out into the almost deserted city streets. There wasn't a puff of wind, the temperature had dropped only a few degrees, and the heat that had baked into the sidewalks during the day wafted upward in a great thermal mass. There would just be time enough for a cooling off before the sun rose and everyone started sweltering again.

She was turning back to the bed when her bare foot stepped on something sharp. She bit down on her outcry before it escaped her lips. She didn't need Ryan Smith coming back in here to investigate, with his bare chest and his jeans riding low on the sexiest pair of hips she'd ever seen. She didn't need any more temptation or frustration, let alone more chances to make a stupid move.

Leaning down, she picked up the offending object and stared at it for a long, breathless moment. A silver earring. The design was unique, a blend of swirls and angles with a lapis lazuli set in the middle. The last time she'd seen that earring, Lacey had been wearing it.

Slowly Judith's fist closed around the piece of jewelry. It would be so convenient for her to pin everything on Steve. Circumstances were pointing in his direction—he'd make a perfect scapegoat. But despite the fact that she'd found a hard piece of evidence, Judith couldn't rid herself of the conviction that Steve was no more guilty of murder than she was.

Which led her back to Ryan.

"Hell and damnation," she muttered. And limping slightly on her sore foot, she climbed back in bed, the earring still clutched tightly in her hand.

HE DIDN'T FORGET. Even though he couldn't see her, couldn't have her, he knew she was there, evil, waiting to be punished. Punished like the others, like all the others. And in that punishment would come purity, and purification, and she would be glad. As the others had been glad.

His Ping Pong-ball eyes searched the darkness around him. Monster, they called him. Lovable, furry monster. But he wasn't a monster, he was justice. He was the avenger. Hideous Harry the Hippo, shuffling in the darkness, waiting to be called.

Darkness all around. Heat and damp and darkness. Waiting for another to join them.

THEY LEFT EARLY the next morning, fetching the Toyota from Josiah Greenfield's parking garage and heading out into the traffic before the desperate heat could envelop them.

They didn't say much. Ryan seemed lost in thought, grunting over the ghastly instant coffee Steve's apartment had provided, murmuring vague responses to Judith's lame attempts at conversation. Finally she gave up altogether. It wasn't as if she didn't have as much on her mind as he did. Perhaps more.

The earring was burning a hole through the pocket of the loose-fitting linen pants she was wearing, still in deference to city fashion. Clearly Lacey had moved from Ryan's bed to Steve's. Apart from Judith's curiosity about Lacey's abysmal lack of taste, this opened a whole new can of worms.

Would Steve murder someone he was sleeping with? Would Ryan? Had Lacey really been murdered, or had she fallen, and was Judith just a final victim of Lacey's paranoid self-absorption?

The last was always possible. Anything was possible. But her instincts, which she had learned to trust over the years, rejected that comfortable conclusion. And until she could find some sort of proof that Lacey's death had been an accident, or proof that it hadn't been, she would have to keep digging.

She allowed herself a brief glance at Ryan's profile. He was wearing dark glasses against the early morning glare, and his large, well-shaped hands were clasped tightly around the steering wheel, betraying his tension. Beautiful hands, Judith thought. She hoped her new instincts were right, and that those hands hadn't wrapped themselves around Lacey's neck.

With a sigh, she slid down farther in the worn front seat, concentrating on the shimmering heat rising from the roadway. It was going to be another scorcher. For one brief moment she thought longingly of her desk at the *Mirror,* of the air-conditioned chaos of the newsroom. Then she dismissed that image. Right now, despite her doubts, despite the silence from the man beside her, she was exactly where she wanted to be. Damning her own foolishness, she shut her eyes and tried to catch up on some of the sleep that had eluded her the night before.

Ryan looked over at her. He should do as Josiah had suggested, he knew. He should kick her out of The Puppet Factory and out of his life. The longer he was around her, the more involved he became. Involved? *Obsessed* by a woman who suspected he was a killer! He'd made some stupid moves in his life, but this one had to take the cake.

But even as he contemplated firing her, he also knew he would do no such thing. It was already too late for that. He didn't think he could let her go once she gave up her idiotic quest.

But that wasn't the problem right now. The problem now was to get back to the Factory and away from her before he jumped her. His hands tightened around the steering wheel, and he ground his teeth and drove faster, away from the teeming city.

WHEN THEY RETURNED to Miller's Junction two hours later, the last thing Judith felt like doing was working. She was cranky and out of sorts from her sleepless night, and the fitful nap in the car hadn't been much help.

Having to deal with Ma didn't help, either. Most of the workers left right before lunch on Friday, but Ma and Bessie were still hard at it, and Judith knew she had no choice but to join them in the chilly office. If she had felt hostile toward Ma before, that emotion was nothing compared to her feelings now. It didn't do any good to tell herself that if Ryan didn't hold a grudge, she certainly shouldn't. It wasn't Ryan she was feeling defensive about, anyway; it was a twelve-year-old rejected by the only family he'd ever known.

Was that enough to make a man a murderer? Not likely. If he wanted to kill anyone, it would have been Ma Carter, not Lacey. Judith spent a few pleasant moments planning the older woman's demise, then dismissed the fantasy. Whatever her crimes were on this earth, she was already paying for them.

Ma looked at Judith, still dressed in her city clothes, and sniffed disdainfully. "You might as well go home," she said. "You aren't needed here."

Bessie looked up from her computer, the sunlight glinting off her glasses. "What about the message?" she asked in her plaintive little voice.

"She's not dressed for work, Bessie," Ma snapped, no more amiable to her dogsbody than she was to Judith.

"That's all right," Judith said hastily. "What message?"

"One of the switches is out in the basement," Ma told her. "It can wait. You wouldn't want to wreck your fancy clothes."

"I'll fix it," Judith said sweetly.

"You aren't needed."

"I'll fix it." She bit off the words, controlling the urge to glare. "Who reported it?"

"Don't know," said Ma, turning away from her. "If you can't find it, we can get someone who can."

"I'll find it." Judith's words were just short of snappish now.

Ma sat back at her spotless desk, shuffling neat papers. "You do that," she said.

Judith didn't like the basement. It was dark and dank and musty smelling, despite the bank of dehumidifiers that were kept going constantly. It was a rabbit warren of small, windowless rooms, some filled with old costumes, some with boxes, some with junked video systems and the like. She could only be glad there wasn't much down there that ever needed repair.

The hydro system that was housed in one corner of the ground floor was beyond even her expertise, but a simple light switch she could manage. She stopped on the second floor and grabbed a few tools, then went down the last flight of stairs, her high-heeled shoes making a noisy little tap-tap sound.

God, she hated the bottom floor. She especially hated it right now, with the dimness, the shadowy shapes of stored puppets and costumes, the eerie sense of discarded lives. The first light switch she turned on worked, though a surprising number of the bulbs were out. The custodial crew hadn't done its usual exemplary job down here.

Judith wove her way through the narrow aisles toward the hallway bisecting the basement. It was getting progressively darker, and her leather shoes on the cement floor made an odd sort of shuffling sound, one that seemed to echo and repeat itself in the cluttered basement.

She should have brought a flashlight. The light was so faint that she could barely make out the switch on the wall. She could see the cover plate half off, and she reached out for the switch, planning to flick it and see if this was the culprit.

Something, some hidden presentiment of danger, stopped her hand in midair. She looked down at the cement floor. There was a pool of water at her feet, unheard of in a place so ruthlessly climate controlled. She looked at the light switch again, and in the dimness she could see the cracked plastic of the switch, the bare metal just discernible.

She took a deep, shuddering breath and stepped backward, away from the switch, away from the unlikely pool of water. Her leather shoes would have provided little insulation from the electric shock. It probably wouldn't have killed her, but it would have given her a hell of a jolt. She stood there, shivering all over in deep, horrified panic.

There was a perfectly reasonable explanation. Someone must have knocked against the switch plate, breaking the plastic. Never mind that it looked as if it had been done with a hammer and with great deliberation. Never mind that there was no possible reason for the water to be pooled in just that spot. Everyone would have said it was just another accident.

She was chilled and shaking all over as she walked back through the crowded basement. The shadowy, huddled shapes looked even more menacing, but this time she was too frightened to care. All she wanted to do was get the hell out of there. No one was going to be working this weekend. When she came back on Monday, she could check the switch again, equipped with insulated glove and shoes. Then she could fix it.

In the meantime, she was damned well going to find out who had reported the problem, who had sent her down here to a possible nasty death. And then she'd go to the police, and to hell with her sacred byline.

HE WATCHED HER GO. She was too smart, too cunning. But he could be smart, too. It was only supposed to have been a warning, a small, effective threat, but she'd been too clever for him.

She wouldn't be the next time.

Chapter Ten

The May heat wave continued unabated. Records were broken all over the country, but particularly in the Northeast, where air conditioners were overloading all the available power sources, and tempers grew short indeed. Husbands beat their wives, wives murdered their husbands, violent crime increased by twenty-five percent and gun sales doubled.

How anyone had the energy to commit murder was beyond Judith's comprehension. Surely the sane thing to do during such blistering, oppressive weather was to take to one's bed with an ice pack, not attack one's husband with an ice pick. However, there was no accounting for tastes. She'd begun to avoid the living room while Micki listened to the mounting toll of violence on the local television news. Even so, she couldn't escape some of the more particular horrors—the children kidnapped; the fire that swept through a tenement and wiped out twenty-three lives; the young woman found strangled, her body tossed into an abandoned quarry.

The channel Micki liked to watch seemed to enjoy that particular disaster. The reporters went into great detail about the unfortunate young woman, apparently a random victim, who'd been found wearing a skimpy halter and shorts. The only clue was an odd amount of green yarn beneath her broken, bloodied fingernails. Apparently she'd put up a fight, and the police were looking for someone fool enough to wear a green sweater during a heat wave.

At that point Judith had walked out of the room, disgusted with Micki's morbidity. The moment she'd lost her audience, Micki had switched the channel to *Wheel of Fortune,* turning up the volume loud enough to follow Judith into the bathroom.

Judith stared at her reflection in the mirror. She had circles under her eyes, her usually smooth blond hair was thick and wavy from the extreme humidity, and her mouth was pale. She thought she looked haunted. Haunted by Lacey? Or haunted by her growing attraction to Ryan Smith? At this point she wasn't sure.

The incident with the light switch had unnerved her. All weekend she'd brooded about it, trying to decide whether to go to the police, whether to confide in Ryan, in anyone. First thing Monday morning she'd headed back down to the basement with a loudly protesting Micki by her side, only to discover a dry floor and an undamaged light switch.

Micki hadn't been reticent about voicing her opinion of Judith's idiocy, so she was glad she hadn't confided her real worries to her caustic roommate. Of course, no one admitted to having reported a broken light switch, and Judith gave up asking when people started looking at her oddly. She decided to continue on as if nothing had happened. And to be very, very careful.

MEMORIAL DAY TURNED OUT to be another scorcher. Judith had been looking forward to it with mixed emotions ever since she started working at The Puppet Factory. This was the day when the puppeteers and their mates and co-workers converged on Ryan Smith's home for swimming, partying, beer and a barbecue. For the first time since they'd returned from the city, Ryan wouldn't be able to disappear, not in his own home.

It wasn't at all what she expected, but then she wasn't sure what would have suited him. Certainly not this massive suburban mansion with its pseudo-Colonial architecture, carefully landscaped grounds and powder-blue wall-to-wall carpeting that blanketed the living areas. The interior decoration had been

done by a master, with taste and discretion, and Judith vaguely
remembered Micki's telling her that Ryan's fiancée had decorated it before dumping him for a television producer. Clearly
the house was her style; just as clearly, to Judith at least, it
wasn't Ryan's. The marriage would never have lasted, she told
herself. He needed some place a little less frilly, a little less
self-conscious.

"There you are, Judy." Steve materialized at her elbow as
she followed the crowds of chattering people through the house
to the back terrace. "I was wondering when you were going
to show up. I hope you're wearing a bikini underneath those
shorts."

"I'm not," she said briefly.

He shook his head. He was wearing the male equivalent of
a bikini, a ridiculously tiny scrap of black cloth that clung to
his not-that-impressive assets, setting off his well-tended tan
and his sleek muscles. He had a great deal of golden-blond hair
all over his body, and a smug smile on his face. He'd be a
very handsome man, Judith thought fairly, if he just weren't
so convinced of that fact.

"Have a good time in Atlantic City?" she murmured, ma-
liciously pleased to see some of the smugness vanish. He'd
returned from Las Vegas for three days, worked like a madman,
then taken off for Atlantic City, promising to return in time for
the picnic. He'd kept that promise, probably because he'd lost
as badly there as he had in Nevada.

"Peachy," he grumbled. "Hey, babe, I was sorry I wasn't
around to entertain you when you stayed in my apartment.
Ryan's not the most jovial fellow at the best of times. I could
have kept you company in that bed of mine."

"No," she said, "you couldn't."

"You can't imagine how distracting it was," he continued,
unabashed. "I got back and found my sheets smelled like vi-
olets. Like you, Judy."

"I'm sorry I didn't have time to change them."

"Oh, no, I liked it. Even if it was a little too…stimulating.
But you have that effect on me, Judith."

She dropped her eyes to the definitely unaroused condition of his bathing suit. "Do I?" she murmured sweetly. "I hadn't noticed." And she walked away from him, pulling her T-shirt over her head as she went.

She'd worn a simple black tank suit that covered the length and modest curves of her, made for swimming and attracting a modest amount of sun. She slid her shorts off, dropped them on one of the chaise longues and headed straight for the crowded crystal blue of the huge swimming pool. She hesitated for a moment, feeling someone's eyes watching her. It was a feeling she'd forced herself to become used to, ascribing it to her rapidly burgeoning paranoia. When she'd least expect it, the back of her neck would prickle and she'd look up, trying to pick out which of her co-workers was staring at her. She'd never caught anyone with a hostile look in his eyes.

This time was different. She looked up, knowing it wasn't hostility in the gaze that impaled her, but a hot, wanting stare that would be Ryan's.

He was across the pool, talking with Franz, a drink in one hand, his attention seemingly on the old puppeteer while his eyes watched her. He was dressed coolly enough, in khakis and a white open-necked polo shirt, and Judith briefly regretted that he wasn't wearing the same excuse for a bathing suit that Steve had. It would have been interesting to see whether he was any more impressive than his womanizing assistant.

She couldn't blame the sun for the heat that suffused her body. It was her own, errant thoughts that were to blame. Averting her gaze, she dived into the pool, slicing through the cool, chlorinated water. When she came up for air, Ryan was gone. Then one of the assistant puppeteers splashed her, she splashed back, and she pushed her host out of her mind. Or at least away from the forefront. He was never gone completely.

If the day was a scorcher, it was nothing compared to that look he'd sent her across the blue expanse of the pool. If Judith had had any doubts before, she had them no longer. Ryan Smith wanted her with a white-hot intensity that terrified her.

And the most terrifying thing of all was that she wanted him just as intensely.

She climbed out of the pool, shaking the water from her sleek body, and almost went after him when she spied her nemesis. Ma Carter was standing guard over the barbecue, her face shaded by an oddly frivolous hot pink *Miami Vice* sun visor. Her long-sleeved cotton shirt was buttoned at the wrists and throat, her denim wraparound skirt flapped in the hot breeze, and her stubby, square feet were encased in white anklets and lime green espadrilles. In honor of the festive occasion she'd painted a slash of bright orange lipstick across her lips, and that odd note of feminine color only made her seem more unwelcoming.

Judith had more than enough of Ma during working hours, what with her silent disapproval and the grunt work that was loaded on Judith's not fragile shoulders. But because so many repairs were needed from time to time, she hadn't had to do penance in Ma's fourth-floor office very often. If it ever got to the point that she was desperate to escape, she could always ask Franz to break something deliberately and call on her for help.

Franz was her favorite person in the factory. She wished she saw more of him. He tended to work alone, or with Ryan, and kept away from the lively, chattering people who thronged the three lower floors of the renovated mill. But he was always scrupulously kind, even gently flirtatious when he happened to meet Judith over a broken video camera or a malfunctioning piece of equipment.

When Ryan disappeared, he'd left the elderly puppeteer behind. Meeting Judith's troubled gaze, Franz carefully skirted the edge of the swimming pool to reach her side. "How is the head, Judith? No aftereffects?"

Judith smiled at him. "No aftereffects. Just a hell of a headache."

"There could be worse things," he said solemnly, perching on the edge of the chaise beside hers. He was dressed in loose-fitting trousers and a white shirt buttoned high. A Fafnir baseball hat shielded his high domed forehead from the blistering sun.

"Aren't you going to swim? It's miserably hot," Judith said.

"I never learned, I'm afraid. And I came to talk to you. We never seem to have time at work, and here, with all this partying, I thought we could be more private in a crowd, so to speak."

Judith held herself very still. "You have something private to say to me?" Franz had been nothing but studiously polite since she'd arrived at The Puppet Factory. Maybe he'd seen more than anyone realized.

"I want you to be careful, Judith," he said in his heavy German accent. "I worry about you. I wonder that a pretty girl like you would be happy in the dirt and oil and machinery."

"I like it at the Factory," she protested, startled to realize she was telling the truth. She loved the noise and color and constant flow of creativity, and she genuinely liked her fellow workers, from Micki's caustic tongue to Franz's vague kindness to Steve's impartial lechery. And most of all, she liked Ryan Smith. If "like" was the operative word.

Franz shook his head. "You don't belong there, *fräulein*. You shouldn't have to put up with Ma's bad temper, or to fetch and carry for everyone. You belong in a city, with young men your own age."

"Steve's my age."

Franz made a dismissing sound. "He is as much out of the question as Jimmy and Melvin are. Or Ryan himself. No, Judith, you are young and healthy. You need to find a man and have babies, and you won't find that man here."

"But Ryan..."

"Ryan is not the man for you. You know that as well as I do. Think about it, Judith. Life is too short and precious to waste."

She stared at him. She had a thousand questions, a hundred protests, but there were too many people around for her to voice them. "I'll think about it, Franz."

He leaned over and patted her hand. "I know you will, *fräulein*." Then he rose and headed toward the house.

Judith watched him disappear. She had little doubt that he and Ryan would end up in some air-conditioned blue-carpeted room, talking about their puppets, ignoring the merriment around the swimming pool. With a sigh Judith flopped back on the chaise, offering her lightly tanned body to a brief bout with the sun. She'd burn in about an hour, but in the meantime she could at least dry off and observe her co-workers behind her sunglasses.

Micki was surrounded by men, and it was no wonder. She was once more wearing that neon yellow excuse for a bikini, her darkly tanned body was oiled and glistening, and her over-size sunglasses shielded the malicious glitter that always lurked in her eyes. Steve was one of her coterie, and Micki was enjoying herself immensely. Nothing to be learned there, Judith thought, unless Micki was jealous of Lacey's undeniable ability to attract the opposite sex. But no, Micki wasn't the killer. Judith's instincts couldn't be that far off.

"Enjoying yourself, Miss Daniels?" a familiar voice said in her ear. She turned to see Josiah Greenfield sink into the chaise beside her. The lawyer was wearing a pair of swim trunks that were a little more discreet than those which currently adorned Steve's private parts, and his compact, muscular body had a solid layer of tan.

"I am. I didn't realize you'd be here."

"Ryan always invites me to these parties. I like to make sure everything's going well, that he's not running into any legal problems, any dangerous situations." He smiled blandly, and Judith was reminded of a shark. "How are you coming with your work? Any results yet?"

All Judith's defenses were roused. "What is it you think I do here, Mr. Greenfield?"

"Please, call me Josiah. I haven't been called Mr. Greenfield by anyone since I was a third-year law student. And I don't know what you do. Some sort of PR work, isn't it? You strike me as a writer of some sort."

Judith smiled thinly. "Looks can be deceiving. I'm a handyman. I fix things—air conditioners, Toyotas, VCR equipment." Light switches, she added silently.

"Oh, really?" he replied. "I had no idea. Now where could I have gotten the impression you wrote?"

"From Ryan?"

Josiah shrugged, an equally thin smile on his face before he turned to brood in Micki's direction. "I doubt it. I must have gotten my signals mixed."

Judith had seen that look before, or at least a variant of it. Josiah Greenfield was looking at Micki in much the same way Ryan had looked at Judith a few minutes ago. Micki, who always noticed a new man, was studiously ignoring him. Curiouser and curiouser, Judith thought.

"Micki doesn't have anything to throw this time," she said, remembering their previous conversation.

"You're right," Josiah agreed, no longer interested in pinning Judith to the chaise and pulling off her wings. He rose and began to wander toward Micki without a backward glance. Judith saw her roommate spare a quick glance at her oncoming suitor and then deliberately focus her attention on Steve again.

Idiot, Judith thought without rancor. People around here seemed peculiarly lacking in taste. That Micki could prefer Steve to Josiah's honest, though less than subtle, worth; that Lacey could have preferred Steve to Ryan...

The smell of roast chicken mingled with the chlorine and suntan oil as the day wore on. The temperature, already unbearable, climbed higher still. Judith spent most of the time in the pool and continued watching everyone as pitcher after pitcher of Bloody Marys disappeared. She drank sparingly, keeping her eyes on Ma as she presided over the barbecue; on Josiah as he cornered Steve Lindstrom and murmured something that made Golden Boy turn pale; on Micki as she played Steve off against Josiah; on Ryan himself as he still managed to elude her.

His elusiveness could be to her benefit, she thought, pulling herself out of the pool in midafternoon. He'd keep away from wherever she was heading. She could develop a sudden blinding headache from the intensity of the sun and go in search of some aspirin. It might take her a while to find some; she might blunder into the wrong rooms, the wrong bathrooms. Heavens, she might discover all sorts of interesting things on her pain-blinded quest.

She could feel Ma's eyes on her as she stepped through the sliding glass doors into the thickly carpeted hallway. Ryan had seen her going in this direction, and he'd immediately gone the opposite way and was now deep in conversation with Josiah. No one else would be wandering around upstairs. If she were fast, and discreet, this could be a heaven-sent opportunity.

She had just put her bare foot on the first step when a strong hand gripped her arm.

"Where do you think you're going, missy?" Ma demanded. The bright orange lipstick had worn off, and her unadorned mouth was thin and harsh.

"I've got a headache," Judith said, stifling the tiny start of nervousness that spiked through her. Ma wouldn't, couldn't hurt her, not with fifty witnesses close at hand. "I was going to lie down for a while."

"Go home and lie down."

"It's not that bad a headache. I'm sure if I lie down for just half an hour I'll be fine."

"Go home and lie down," Ma repeated.

"My head hurts too much for me to drive."

"If it hurts too much to drive, the headache won't be better in half an hour. Go home, and don't come back." Ma's fingers were digging into the tender flesh of Judith's upper arm.

Suddenly Judith's hold on her temper snapped. "Go to hell, Ma. And don't come back." Yanking her arm from the woman's grip, she continued up the stairs.

She stopped once she was out of sight, letting her heart resume its normal pace, not moving until she was certain Ma wasn't going to follow her up to the deserted second floor. If she'd ever had any doubt before, that doubt was gone. Ma Carter was her enemy, and the gloves were off.

Judith shrugged. She'd learned nothing new. In the meantime she'd better make good use of her time. Ma was more than likely to go straight to Ryan and tell him that his princess was snooping again. Dammit, she'd better hurry.

She moved swiftly and silently through the carpeted hall, into each perfectly decorated, completely uninhabited bedroom. It didn't seem as if anyone had ever used them, and Judith found herself wondering if Ryan ever had guests, family... No, he was an orphan, wasn't he? The only family he could boast, such as it was, was Ma Carter.

Maybe he just had a cleanliness fanatic for a housekeeper. No, it was more than that. Once more Judith's reporter's instincts were coming into play, and she just knew that no one had ever spent the night in these rooms.

Clearly she hadn't found the master bedroom yet, and that had to be the most important room. It would have been nice if she'd conveniently discovered the twin to Lacey's earring underneath a bed, or one of Micki's Phil Collins tapes, or maybe all those pieces of paper from Steve's carryall. But one couldn't always count on luck; one had to keep plugging along.

The last door, at the end of the hallway, had to be to Ryan's bedroom. Finally she'd find something, some sign of human habitation, some clue to the thoughts and life-style of its occupant.

For a moment she thought she'd washed out again. It was the master bedroom all right, with a sumptuous bathroom, too. The blue carpeting was spotless; no one had tracked sawdust, paint or yarn from the puppets in here. The king-size bed looked positively virginal; the doorknobs of the row of closets, spotless. The silk shades on the windows were at just the right level. If Ryan Smith lived in this luxury suite, he did so without touching anything, even the floor.

The closets had clothes in them. Suits, even a couple of tuxedos, clearly tailor made for a very tall, lean man. They looked as if they'd never been worn. Bending down, she picked up one of the leather shoes. The sole had never touched anything harsher than carpeting, if that.

Thoughtfully she shut the closet doors and went into the bathroom. The black porcelain decor had the same unblemished look as the rest of the house. If anyone had ever used the huge shower or shaved above the sink, all traces had been ruthlessly eradicated.

Judith opened the medicine chest and received another shock. It was crammed with prescription drugs. Bottle after bottle after bottle, all for Ryan Smith. Some were as much as three years old, and all looked full. She stared into the cabinet as a thousand confused thoughts fluttered through her brain. Who was the man downstairs? Why would he get all this medicine and never take it? Why would he have clothes he never wore? Why would he own a huge, elegant house and never live in it? Was this all some tangled Alfred Hitchcock plot, with the real Ryan Smith locked away and some fiendishly clever impostor taking his place?

No, that was impossible. Looks could be faked, but not his talent. No one could do the puppets as well as Ryan—she'd seen it for herself. But what in God's name was going on?

She reached for the bottle of Motrin. By this time her head really was beginning to pound, and the prescription was only a few months old. She was half tempted to grab one of the untouched bottles of tranquilizers for good measure.

"Enjoying yourself?"

She dropped the open bottle of Motrin in the sink, and the bright orange pills spilled out against the black porcelain. Ryan Smith was lounging in the open doorway, blocking it and her escape. She could see over her shoulder that the bedroom door was firmly shut. No witnesses.

She began scooping the pills up. "I had a headache. I was looking for something to take."

"You found more than you bargained for, didn't you?" he inquired in a mild enough voice. "Why didn't you use the downstairs bathroom? There's a first-aid kit down there, aspirin, Tylenol, anything you could want."

"I...I felt dizzy. I wanted to lie down." She kept scooping up the pills, and suddenly his hand shot out and caught her wrist. The pills dropped back into the sink as she slowly raised guilty eyes to his.

"There were plenty of bedrooms, Judith. Your feet were wet from the pool. You left a very discernible trail as you went from bedroom to bedroom."

"Would you believe Goldilocks and the three bears? The first bed was too soft, the second was too hard, and the third..."

"Button it, Judith," he snapped, his hand still tight around her wrist. She'd be no match for his strength, if he chose to use it. "I'm not in the mood for jokes."

What are you in the mood for, she thought but didn't ask. Now was not the time to tweak the dragon's tail. "I...I'm sorry," she said weakly, dropping her gaze. "I didn't mean to intrude on your privacy."

"Judith, you didn't shut one of the closet doors completely. You were pawing through my medicine chest. *I want to know why.*"

Her fingers were beginning to feel numb. He was very tall, looming over her. Usually she could stand up to him, but now, with guilt and bare feet and her bathing suit making her feel about two feet tall, all she wanted to do was cower.

But Judith Daniels didn't cower, and she didn't admit defeat before she absolutely had to. "I suppose I'll have to confess," she said, raising her head and looking him in the eye. To her astonishment, she saw more than anger in his eyes. There was surprise, something that looked oddly like hurt, and the lingering embers of desire still glowing.

"I suppose you'll have to," he agreed. The grip around her wrist loosened slightly, but he didn't release her.

Judith shrugged. "I'm curious."

"No kidding."

"I mean it. I'm the sort of person who always looks inside people's refrigerators when I visit their houses. I always check out the medicine chest when I go to the bathroom. I look at the mail when it's left lying around. I eavesdrop on phone conversations. I'm just nosy. It's a human enough failing. I'm not proud of it, but it's not criminal. It's usually completely harmless. Unless, of course, someone has something to hide,'' she finished fearlessly.

He just stared at her, his face unreadable, and she couldn't tell whether he swallowed that story or not. It was close enough to the truth. She was a curious person, though she did her best to control the more antisocial aspects of that trait.

''I hate to be unoriginal,'' he said in his slow, sexy voice, ''but curiosity killed the cat.''

''Is that a threat?''

''A warning, princess. If you go around stirring things up, you might stir up a hornet's nest. And you'll be the one who'll get stung.'' He released her wrist, and the blood tingled as it flowed back through. She'd have bruises tomorrow, she thought. Of course she bruised easily, but she'd have to make certain he noticed the marks he left on her. He deserved some guilt for frightening her like that.

He moved back into the bedroom, and she had no choice but to follow him, edging around him toward the door. He watched her furtive movements with a distant amusement she couldn't begin to understand, until she put her hand on the unsullied brass doorknob.

The door was locked.

Chapter Eleven

She considered throwing herself on the white paneled door and kicking and screaming. At least that would give the pristine room a more lived-in look. She considered calling for help; she considered flinging herself on Ryan Smith and scratching him until he let her out. But after one furtive glance at her captor, she decided against that alternative. Ryan would like nothing more than to have her fling herself on him. And if she did, the battle wouldn't last very long.

With all the dignity she could muster, which was considerable, she turned away from the door and regarded him coolly. "Isn't this a little extreme?"

To her irritation and relief he laughed. "Princess, you are a treasure. Only someone with generations of blue blood could be so composed in circumstances like these."

"I wouldn't know. I've never been in circumstances like these before."

"You mean no one's ever caught you snooping? That surprises me, given your uncontrollable curiosity. I would have thought you'd come up against an outraged host before now." He dropped down on the bed, which looked a great deal smaller with his body stretched out across it. Smaller, and a lot more inviting.

She didn't want to move any closer, but her bare feet were ignoring her brain's directions. Why the hell hadn't she stopped long enough to pull on a T-shirt? It was unnerving to be dressed in nothing but a swimsuit whose discreet lines suddenly seemed revealing indeed as Ryan lay back, fully dressed, and watched her out of hooded eyes.

"I'm surprised you followed me," she countered. "The way you've been avoiding me the past week, I figured if you saw me enter the house, you'd head in the opposite direction."

He didn't try to deny it, she noticed. "That's exactly what I did. And then my own curiosity got the better of me when I noticed how long you were gone. So I thought I should make sure you weren't running off with the silver. I mean, I don't really know that much about you, do I? You've been working for me only a little more than two weeks, and I didn't bother to have Ma check the references you gave her. Maybe I should have."

"They were all impeccable." She'd spent days seeing to that.

"I'm sure they were," Ryan said with a silky smile. "Which is why I didn't bother. Come here, Judith."

His softly murmured instruction took her completely by surprise. "What?"

"I said come here."

"Don't be ridiculous. I'm not going to sleep with you to get you to unlock the door," she said in a waspish tone. "You forget, I can fix anything. I'm sure I can find a way to unfasten the lock. Or if worse comes to worst, I can take the door off the hinges."

"You don't have any tools."

"I can find something around here that will work."

"Not in this bedroom. You've snooped enough to notice it's singularly ill equipped. Almost as if no one really spent any time in it. Or did you overlook that?"

"I didn't overlook it."

Ryan shoved a couple of pillows behind his back, and if the seductive menace hadn't vanished, it had lessened considerably. "Relax, princess. Your chastity is safe. Sit down." He saw her instant refusal and added, "On the chair, Judith. Not on the bed. And then we can have a little talk."

"Talk?"

"We'll have a trade. I'll answer any question you want. But you'll have to answer one of mine."

"I don't see what good it will do to trade lies," she said boldly enough, moving toward the damask-covered slipper chair that belonged more properly in a lady's boudoir.

"No good at all. We have to promise to answer truthfully. Come on, princess. A question for a question, a truth for a truth. That's fair enough."

"Fair enough," she agreed. He wouldn't lie. For some reason she knew that. Whatever she chose to ask him, he'd answer truthfully. But what did she dare ask him? Did you murder my best friend? Do you know who did?

"You first," she said. Her bathing suit felt damp and clammy in the air-conditioned atmosphere. Hadn't Ryan said he hated artificial air? Why had he chosen that environment for his house?

"Okay. Do you want to go to bed with me?"

Whatever she had expected, that wasn't it. "Is that your question," she said, "or is that an offer?"

"A question," he replied. "Requiring a truthful answer."

She just stared at him. There were so many other things he could have asked her. She knew perfectly well that he was as suspicious of her as she was of him. He had to wonder why she'd shown up out of the blue and talked her way into a job at The Puppet Factory; he had to wonder about her incessant questions about Lacey and why he'd caught her snooping again. And he had to know the answer to his question was yes.

"No," she said.

He smiled faintly. "Cheat. You're supposed to tell the truth."

"What made you pick that question?"

"I know the answer to the others."

"What others?"

"You know them as well as I do," he said. "What's your question? And I'll answer it honestly."

Did you kill Lacey? Who did? She opened her mouth, but

the wrong words came out. "Why do you have a medicine chest filled with prescriptions that no one's ever taken? Why is your closet filled with clothes that have never been worn? Who are you?"

He lounged there on the bed, perfectly still for a long moment, and then he threw back his head and laughed, the last trace of his lingering reserve vanishing in his amusement. "Judith," he said weakly, "you are absolutely priceless! What if I told you I was a zombie, come back from the dead? Or a werewolf? It sounds like you're expecting something suitably melodramatic."

Judith was not overly fond of being laughed at. "I'm expecting an answer."

"The answer is Ma."

"I beg your pardon?"

"In case you hadn't noticed, I'm something of a workaholic. I stay up all night working, I forget to eat, I don't dress warmly enough in winter—all those things. So I get run down, I get insomnia, I get colds and fever and walking pneumonia. And Ma makes doctor appointments for me, ignoring my protests. When I don't go she has them make house calls, following me all over the mill. So now when she tells me she's made an appointment, I go. I pick up my prescription and put it on the shelf and ignore it. That way she's happy, and I lose the least amount of time."

Judith found that she believed him. "What about the clothes?"

"Ma, too. She thinks I should dress better. Instead I dress the way I always dress and probably always will. So she orders clothes and has them delivered, and I put them away in the closet and forget about them."

"But this house has such an…unlived-in quality. How can you live here and still have it feel like a hotel? Or do you live here at all?" she asked suddenly.

Ryan sat up, swinging his legs over the side of the bed. He was suddenly very, very close. "You've had your question,

Judith. And you had your truthful answer. All I got from you,'' he said softly, ''was a lie.''

''Is it so hard to believe that a woman wouldn't want to go to bed with you? You're acting like Steve.'' She tried to sound cool and unruffled, but her voice came out strained, husky, and she wished there were some graceful, unobtrusive way to move away from him.

He ignored the insult. ''I don't find it hard to believe a woman wouldn't want to go to bed with me. I find it hard to believe that *you* wouldn't.''

''Why?'' Dammit, she was trembling.

He smiled with a peculiar sweetness. ''I'll show you.'' And before she realized what he had in mind, he slid his hands around her waist and pulled. She was on the bed, on top of him, her bare legs tangled with his khaki-covered ones, her breasts pressed against his chest, her hands pushing against his shoulders as she stared down at him out of startled, momentarily defenseless eyes. Her heart was hammering wildly, as if she'd just run a marathon, and her body felt hot and trembly and achingly ready. She stared at him, wide-eyed, imprisoned by the hands on her waist and the legs wrapped around hers, and waited.

It was suddenly very still and silent in the room. From the distance they could hear shrieks of laughter, splashing from the pool, noise and merriment that was oblivious to the battle being waged on the huge bed.

It was a battle of wills, not of strength. It was a battle she fought with herself, not with Ryan. It was a battle she wanted to lose.

If she stayed there even ten seconds longer, chest to chest, heartbeat to heartbeat, she'd be lost. She had to make him let her go. His mouth, his sexy, unsmiling mouth, was so close, so very close, and she wanted that mouth, she wanted the hard, aroused body beneath her, more than she wanted anything in her life; and if she gave in to that wanting, she'd be throwing away her honor, her career, possibly her life.

She looked down at him, at the hooded eyes, the waiting mouth. "Did you kill Lacey Hollister?"

He moved very quickly. One moment she was lying tangled on top of him; the next, she was an ignominious heap on the floor. Without a backward glance Ryan strode across the room and unlocked the door. He turned around, waiting, his expression shielded, his eyes averted, polite and slightly impatient.

She pulled herself to her feet, rubbing her bruised butt but making no move to leave the room. The door was open—someone would hear her scream. "Did you?"

"Get out, Judith," he said evenly.

She walked to the door, no longer afraid of him, and paused beside him. "Did you?"

"I don't ever want you in my bedroom again, unless you get an invitation. And at this point that's highly unlikely."

"I'm devastated," she said coolly. "Did you?"

His eyes narrowed. "What the hell does it matter to you?"

She smiled, and that composed smile took every last ounce of effort. "You've already had your one question, Ryan." She went down the hallway, her bare toes digging into the thick blue carpeting.

He didn't try to follow her, and she wished to God she weren't wearing a bathing suit. She knew perfectly well it didn't ride up in back, and she still wanted to tug at it. A moment later she was down the stairs and out of sight.

Halfway down she stopped, leaning against the wall to catch her breath. She was hot and cold and trembling all over, and now that she had no witnesses she could allow reaction to set in. It had been a close thing, a damned close thing. And instead of feeling relief and triumph at her escape, all she could feel was regret.

She heard a tiny sound and looked up, to the top of the stairs, directly into Ryan's enigmatic eyes. He could see everything, see what her self-control had cost her. For a brief moment he could see her reaction to him, the inexplicable wanting that ignored her suspicions and fear. Then she pushed herself away from the wall and headed the rest of the way downstairs, out into the sweltering heat and the laughing, jostling crowds.

Ryan watched her go. He'd almost had her. She'd almost shut away that damnable distrust and gone with her feelings. He'd felt her reaction as he'd held her, the heat and warmth and excitement building in her. And he'd felt her fighting it, resisting it, when all the time she'd wanted to cross the few inches that separated them.

Her question had taken care of any chance of that. She must have been in a panic to have blurted it out. And it had been more than effective. Never in his life had he been so angry. If he really had a murderous streak, she would have seen evidence of it there and then. A good solid twenty-five percent of him wanted to hit her, hard, for thinking him capable of such a thing.

But the other seventy-five percent held sway. He hadn't hit anyone in anger since he was twelve years old and Ma Carter had brought home the curly-headed five-year-old who was going to take his place after seven and a half years of relative security. He'd hit Toby as hard as he could, and Toby had screeched like a banshee. Pa Carter had dragged Ryan out to the woodshed, and when Ryan had returned, disgraced, to the state home the next day, he'd been covered with bruises that had taken almost a month to disappear. That was the last time he'd hit anyone, and the last time he'd been hit.

It might have been the last time he'd been so angry. He wasn't used to feeling such raw, overpowering emotions. He thought he'd become more civilized in his old age, removed from anger and passion and rage, distant, safe from pain. That was exactly what Eleanor had complained about during their years together. Not his physical intimacy, but his lack of emotional involvement. They'd slept together, lived together, made love together with a quite acceptable passion, but he'd never let her get close to him, he'd been no more than startled and slightly depressed. And that reaction had passed quickly.

But with Judith Daniels his shield of safe distance was vanishing as if it had never existed. He wanted to grab her and

shake her; he wanted to yell at her; he wanted to throw her
down on the spotless blue carpets and rip her clothes off and
make love to her until they couldn't fight any more. And then,
after they regained their strength, he wanted to do it all over
again.

He'd made love to Eleanor in that big bed she'd chosen,
never anyplace else. And he'd had sex with Lacey Hollister
when she'd crawled in with him one night—short, unsatisfac-
tory sex that had left him feeling slimy and used the next morning.

When the time came, and there was no "if" about it, he
wasn't going to make love to Judith in that damned bed. On
the rug, in the black bathtub, in the swimming pool. Maybe,
just maybe, in his own bed. But not here, with all the ghosts
around.

Damn her to hell, anyway. If only there were some way he
could prove to her how wrong she was—that Lacey had fallen,
that there was no conspiracy, no murder, just a careless, stupid
accident.

He'd have Josiah do some more digging. He'd wait it out,
wait for Judith to give up and admit she was wrong, then come
to him and admit who she was and what she was doing. But
he didn't know how much longer he could wait.

HIDEOUS HARRY THE HIPPO shuffled through the deserted mill,
his furry feet curiously quiet. He liked it best when he was
alone. No one could bother him; no one would laugh at him.
He could think, and plan, and make decisions.

He needed to make those decisions soon. She would have to
be punished, he knew that. He'd tried to warn her with the
light switch, but she hadn't listened. He hadn't wanted to hurt
her, because he'd hoped she'd be one of the good ones, one of
the pure ones. But he'd seen Billy and Fafnir, he'd seen Ryan,
and he'd known.

He wouldn't have to do it alone. His friend would help him.
She understood his mission, understood what they must do.

She'd helped him before. She understood women and their weaknesses; she knew the best way to catch them.

He didn't like to hurt them. He didn't like them to struggle. They had to be punished, but it was best done quickly, painlessly. A simple execution.

And the women were becoming more frequent. There was that evil whore who'd worked here, who'd sullied Ryan and laughed at them. And then, just last week, there was the stranger, the girl in the halter top and shorts. She'd pretended she wasn't interested, but he'd known she was coming here, coming after Ryan; he had seen it in the sway of her hips and the curve of her pink lips. And he'd decided not to let her get that far.

When the new girl had gone, what next? The forces of evil and wickedness were getting stronger, and Harry was growing old and tired. The more vengeance he had to dispense, the more energy he lost.

But if he could do no more, he could send his friend out. And if she tired, there was Fafnir. And Billy. Someone would always take his place.

He shuffled over to the balcony, staring across the terraced expanse to the slightly churning river below. Judith would follow Lacey, he thought. Judith would be purified in the water. And she would thank him, when she knew. Yes, she would. She'd be happy and at peace.

Shuffling onward, he moved back down toward the basement, and his cold, dark home.

Chapter Twelve

It was a cool, misty morning. At 6:00 a.m. the blistering sun hadn't had time to bake off the dampness from the night before, and the air was actually breathable. Judith slid from the seat of her Mercedes and inhaled deeply. She should start getting up earlier every day, at least until the heat wave broke. One needed to remember what it was like to be able to breathe the air.

The parking lot at The Puppet Factory was deserted, as she'd expected it would be. People would still be recovering from yesterday's revels. If they showed up at all, they'd be straggling in sometime after ten o'clock, or maybe not till the afternoon. She had plenty of time to make a last-minute adjustment on the Roberts 450 air conditioner, to see that the refrigerator was chilling and not freezing everybody's yogurt, and to search the areas of the five-story-high building that she'd yet to investigate. She would have to force herself to go through the basement again. She'd been avoiding it since the incident with the rigged light switch, and if she gave in to her cowardice, she'd continue to avoid it. But she couldn't afford to do that. She was going to have to face up to her fears and make certain the answer to Lacey's death didn't lie hidden in that jumbled cellar.

And she'd seen the top floor just once. There were no stairs leading up there, or at least, none she could find. The open-sided freight elevator provided the sole access, and though Judith wasn't particularly frightened of heights, the flat, moving platform gave her the creeps. But she'd only been in the store-room at the end of the fifth-floor hallway. She'd passed locked doors on the way, doors that could hide answers.

Well, she had more than enough time now to search the place from top to bottom. Something had to turn up to further her seemingly fruitless investigation. So far she'd found more questions than answers. Just a sign, a small piece of evidence, she requested of an indifferent providence. Some clue that proved Ryan innocent.

The heavy steel front door was locked, but Judith had the keys. She'd taken them from Micki's dresser, not even both-ering to leave her a note. Micki hadn't come home last night, and Judith hadn't the faintest idea who was enjoying her en-thusiastic favors. Steve? Josiah Greenfield? Ryan?

The building was dark and silent, and as the door clanged shut behind her, Judith had to suppress a small start of ner-vousness. Lacey had been alone in the building when she'd died. The coroner had figured she'd gone over the balcony and died sometime Sunday morning.

Today was Tuesday, not Sunday, and there was no murderer lurking ready to drop Judith into the Hudson River by way of a turbine. She was safe, and much faster on her feet and more observant than Lacey had ever been. If someone or something came after her, she could outrun it. Even if it had very long legs.

"Stop it." Her voice sounded firm and determined in the stillness of the building. "You have a job to do, princess," she added, using Ryan's mocking sobriquet on purpose. "Stop looking for trouble."

She headed down the stairs, looking over her shoulder only three times. And each time the shadowy stairwell was deserted. When she reached the bottom she looked back one last time. Nothing, no eyes staring down at her, no ominous figure. That odd sense of being watched had to be her imagination.

The Roberts required a simple adjustment, and the refriger-ator on the third floor was working fine. It was just after seven when Judith climbed the stairs, having given in to her cowardice for the time being. She told herself it would take forever to search through the basement. Anything could be lurking amid the jumbled clutter, bodies and clues could have been stashed in every corner, and she could overlook them in all the mess. There was no way she could find anything before people started arriving, she rationalized, and she promised herself that the next time things slowed down, she'd suggest to Ma that she start organizing the ground floor. She could just imagine what Ma might suggest in return.

Ma Carter wasn't the type to appreciate helpful suggestions, or indeed, anyone's ideas but her own. Anyway, the basement was probably too cool and damp to present ideal working conditions for Ma's least-favorite employee. She was far more likely to send Judith to the fifth floor, where the shimmering heat probably turned the top of the building into a potter's kiln.

Which wouldn't be a bad idea. Judith was having more than enough trouble getting up there on her own, without Ma's sanction. The steel stairwell ended at the fourth floor, and if there was another, smaller flight of stairs leading to the top, it had to be behind one of the narrow locked doors that Ma had insisted were closets.

Judith stared at one of them. The lock was solid, probably pick-proof to someone of her limited talents. While opening a locked door was something she'd covered in her fix-it column in answer to questions from parents whose toddlers had locked themselves in the bathroom, she herself had never managed to master that particular art. Her breaking-and-entering abilities extended only to padlocks. For doors, she much preferred brute force, taking them off the hinges. The locked doors on the fourth floor had hidden hinges.

There was always the freight elevator. It was on the third floor right now, and didn't possess anything as sophisticated as a call button. She could screw up her courage and head down there again. It wouldn't be difficult to figure out how to run the elevator. Her worst problem would be gritting her teeth and riding the damned thing.

The hour was approaching eight o'clock. Ryan had called

himself a workaholic, and he'd disappeared after their confrontation in his overdecorated bedroom. He wouldn't have a hangover or a sunburn—the day's sun had only added to his tan. Would he have postcoital depression?

No, he'd partaken sparingly of wine, women and sun. He'd be here, working, long before anyone else bothered to straggle in. If she was going to try to get up to the fifth floor, she'd better do it now.

Franz had left early, too. He'd be the second person to show up, and then the rest of the puppeteers would wander back to work. If she were drawn into a conversation with Fafnir or Madame Rinaldi, she had little doubt it would be in the form of a peacemaker between contentious puppeteers acting out their aggressions. Could puppets commit murder?

God, what a creepy thought! she chided herself as she went down to the third floor and the waiting freight elevator. As if one of those furry, lovable creatures could be violent! It would be as silly to suspect Mother Teresa of cold-blooded murder as to suspect Billy. Or Hideous Harry.

The air conditioner was humming away, and as she walked through the seemingly deserted expanse of puppet booths and stages that littered the third floor she could smell the enticing scent of fresh-brewed coffee. Damn! Someone—Franz? Ryan?—had already arrived.

"There you are, hot stuff." Fafnir poked his furry head over the lip of the stage. "I heard that ridiculous car of yours and wondered when you were gonna show up. Whatcha been doing?"

Judith stopped, and for the first time she didn't take the time to wonder who was behind the puppet. She responded to Fafnir, not to the puppeteer. "None of your business, Fur-face," she said, rumpling the purple yarn at the top of his head.

"Come on, Judith. I won't tell anyone. It can be your secret. Don't you want to share secrets with me, Judith?" His voice dropped to an enticing low note. "Come on, sweetmeat. Tell me."

"Don't trust him, Judith." Billy shot up beside him, his little cloth face intent. "He'll just take advantage of you."

"Come on, Billy," Fafnir whined. "I was just starting to make some progress with the babe here. I don't need you interfering."

"She's not a babe, she's the woman I love," Billy replied in a dignified voice.

"Well, she's the woman I want to—"

"Don't say it," Billy warned.

Judith moved closer to the booth and put a restraining hand on Billy's head. "Stop fighting, guys," she murmured. She reached out and stroked Fafnir's jaw, and he flopped over on his back, purring ecstatically. "There's enough rotten stuff going on..." Her voice trailed off.

She was standing there, embracing two creatures made of cloth and Styrofoam, talking to them as if they were human. Beneath Fafnir's furry throat she could feel the shape of a hand; beneath Billy's yarn-covered head she could feel long, deft fingers, the harness and strength of human bone and muscle. Ryan.

"Damn you to hell, Ryan Smith," she said, ripping Billy's limp cloth from off his hand and flinging it to the ground. "How *dare* you do this to me?"

Fafnir slowly withdrew behind the semitransparent curtain. And then Ryan stepped out from the booth, the furry purple puppet still on one arm, his face reserved and distant.

"Do what to you?"

He was wearing faded jeans and a loose white T-shirt, and his tanned, muscular arms hung at his sides, as if in waiting.

She wouldn't allow herself to be intimidated. She wouldn't allow herself to react to his nearness, to the warmth and enticing scent of him. She wouldn't let herself think how those arms would feel around her, how that thin, unsmiling mouth would feel on hers.

"You know perfectly well what," she said in a low, furious tone of voice. "You've done it before, using the puppets to come on to me like that. Using them to pimp for you. It's degrading, disgusting, cheap and rotten! And how you could *do* such a thing—''

''Judith, they're just puppets,'' he cut in, his voice eminently reasonable. ''They're dolls, with no personality or thought other than what I give them.'' He pulled Fafnir off his hand and held up the puppet, an empty purple husk. ''There's nothing sacred about them—they just reflect me. If they're coming on to you, it's because I'm coming on to you, and you won't hold still long enough to let me do it myself.''

Judith looked at Billy's crumpled figure on the floor, at Fafnir's limp body, at Ryan's distant face. The face of someone she wanted but couldn't trust. She felt herself ripped in a thousand directions. And suddenly the frustration was too much.

She lunged at him, lunged for Fafnir's lifeless body as it dropped on the floor beside Billy. Ryan's hands caught her tight on her bare arms, and he hauled her up against him, his fingers digging into her tender flesh, his face inches away from her furious face.

''I think we've put this off too long, don't you?'' he said. And his mouth covered hers.

Her arms were trapped between their bodies as he tipped her head back, and she struggled, pushing him, fighting him. But her mouth opened for him even as she fought, and he kissed her, long and hard and deep, an overwhelming, passionate kiss that allowed her no chance to respond, only to accept. And when he freed her arms she moved them around his waist, her hands sliding up under the T-shirt to caress the smooth, sleek skin on his back.

He was startled as her flesh met his, she could tell. Suddenly the kiss changed, his grip on her loosened, his tongue cajoled and enticed. It no longer invaded, and his lips and teeth bit gently into hers. His hands—those deft, clever hands—pulled her cotton shirt up and began to caress the bare skin of her back, drawing her closer, into the sheltering heat of his body.

She could feel his arousal pressing against her stomach, against his pants. She could feel her nipples, hard now, pushing through her clothing, leaving him in as little doubt about her

arousal as she was about his. She wanted to drop her hands
and slide them beneath the waistband of his jeans; she wanted
to sink to her knees in front of him and take him into her
mouth; she wanted him, all of him, and she no longer wanted
to think about the consequences.

They both heard the heavy steel door slam shut. They both
heard the clatter of footsteps heading in their direction. And it
was no longer up to Judith to fight what was happening between them.

He released her, and she stepped back. She could feel the
wetness of her mouth, the hardness of her nipples, the rasp of
her breathing in her throat and the pounding of her heart. She
stared at him for a long moment, at his enigmatic expression,
at his chest heaving rapidly, at the unmistakable bulge in his
faded jeans. And then she turned and ran.

IT WAS A HELL OF A WAY to start a week, Ryan thought, staring
after her. But then nothing had been simple or right for months
now. The uneasy feeling had started with Steve and the missing
money and had come to full flower when Lacey had fallen over
the balcony.

And Judith Daniels, with her snooping, her questions, her
very presence, seemed to be bringing it all to a head.

Hell, now he was getting spooked. Squatting, he picked up
the discarded figures of his creations, wiping some of the dust
off Billy's white face, untangling Fafnir's yarny hair.

"Sorry, guys," he murmured, slipping Billy onto his hand.
"She seems to bring out the worst in me."

"I don't know," Billy said. "Maybe it's the best."

Ryan grinned down at the puppet. "Maybe you're right.
There are times, Billy, when you have a hell of a lot more
brains than I do." He tossed the puppets onto the open stage
of the booth and went in search of some coffee. Never once
noticing that the omnipresent video cameras were turned on.

IT WAS A HELL OF A WAY to start a week, Judith thought, still
sweating lightly despite the frigid temperature on the fourth

floor, where Ma kept the air conditioner turned up full blast. Bessie sat huddled in a heavy sweater, staring intently at her computer screen. She looked up long enough to offer Judith a secretive smile, then went back to her work.

There was Ma Carter, glowering at Judith. That was enough to wipe the most erotic experience from one's mind. And Ryan's kiss might well be just that, Judith thought, shaking herself mentally.

"I didn't think you'd bother to show up," Ma said with undisguised disapproval. "Most people aren't going to drag themselves in today, so why did you?"

"Devotion to duty?" Judith suggested cheerfully.

Ma snorted. "You think I haven't noticed," she said in a growl that couldn't reach Bessie's ears. "You're chasing after him, just like the other one. But it won't do you a speck of good. He's not interested in you."

Judith, her mouth still damp from Ryan Smith's kisses, looked calmly into the older woman's beady little eyes. "What other one?" she asked.

"You know perfectly well what other one." Ma's voice was rushed as tension and hostility spewed forth. "She died."

"Why did she die? Was she being punished?"

Ma looked startled. "It was an accident," she said firmly. "Accidents happen, and they can happen to you. Leave Ryan alone. He doesn't want you and he doesn't need you. Go back to where you came from." The anger and dislike emanating from her were so strong that they were almost overpowering.

But Judith had stood up to furious editors, overbearing publishers and condescending college deans. She wasn't about to quail before a bad-tempered Ma Carter. Much as she wanted to.

"Sorry," she said evenly, ignoring the nervous pounding of her heart. "I can't do that."

Ma's jaw clamped shut, reminding Judith of a jail door slamming closed. "Then watch your back," she said thinly. And marched over to her desk, ignoring Judith's shocked expression.

Bessie looked up then, her face composed. But her dreamy, bespectacled eyes had a different look in them, as if she found the confrontation vastly amusing. As soon as it had appeared, the expression was gone, and she resumed typing industriously.

And Judith, knowing when she was outnumbered, turned and ran for the second time that morning.

Micki straggled in sometime after noon, looking hung over and oddly pleased with life. Her mouth was swollen and she had a whisker burn on the side of her neck. Judith could just imagine what the rest of her body looked like, and had to fight back a twinge of envy. It had been years since she'd looked or felt like that. If ever. Offhand she couldn't remember a man who'd made her feel that way, and she wondered who had done the honors with Micki.

Not that she was about to ask. Micki dreamed her way through the afternoon, snapping only once. But since Ryan ignored Micki just as thoroughly as he ignored Judith when their paths happened to cross, and since Micki didn't even seem to notice, Judith could at least be sure that Micki hadn't yet had her wicked way with her employer. Judith's mood lightened a fraction.

THE PUPPET SAT BACK and stared at the tiny color monitor. He'd seen the tape countless times, but somehow he couldn't keep himself from rewinding it and replaying it, over and over again. It had gotten so that he didn't even have to play the tape; he could see it clearly in his mind, goading him, telling him what he must do.

But he still didn't know how he should do it. That would come to him later—it always did. Something would give him a sign, let him know the best way to punish her. Leaning forward, he concentrated on the flickering images in front of him. Of Ryan, his body pressed against the woman's, his arms holding her, his mouth devouring hers. And of the woman's hands, pulling up his shirt, caressing his back. Voracious, wanton hands.

Hideous Harry looked down at his own hands. The green fur was shaggy and worn in places. Slowly he clenched his fists. Maybe he should use his hands.

Chapter Thirteen

Judith didn't find the tape until Thursday afternoon. She was just getting ready to meet Micki in the parking lot when she noticed the shards of black plastic on the floor beside the overflowing wastebasket. She was in the deserted control room, and the people who were still working were one flight up, on the third floor. With a surreptitious look around, Judith dived into the wastebasket, pulling out papers and empty yogurt containers and racing sheets and ratty green yarn. The green yarn struck an obscure chord in her memory, one she quickly dismissed. There was green yarn on half the puppets, and they all had a tendency to shed. She delved further, past the crumpled packs of cigarettes that could only have belonged to Micki.

And there it was. A Beta tape, or rather, what was left of one. The plastic box was crushed to smithereens; the ribbon of tape was drenched in yogurt and heaven only knew what else. She stared down at it in disgust, about to drop the papers back over it, when she reconsidered the matter.

No one ever threw out tapes at The Puppet Factory. Not with Judith around to splice and fix them, not with machinery for editing and rewinding and all sorts of arcane uses. Certainly no one ever smashed them.

It would have taken considerable force on someone's part to have inflicted that much damage on the tape. She'd dropped any number of tapes in her life, but they simply didn't shatter or even tend to chip. Someone had gone to a lot of trouble to make sure the tape was destroyed. Assuming the destruction was willful. The other possibility was no less palatable. Whatever was on the tape might have been so infuriating that it had driven the watcher into a destructive rage.

Regardless of the reason, Judith wasn't about to let the tape be tossed out in the trash that evening. Scooping up the sticky mess, she stuffed it into her knapsack that nowadays doubled as a purse. Then she quickly refilled the wastebasket and headed up the stairs, confident no one had seen her.

Micki wasn't thrilled about being kept waiting. She sat sweltering in the late-afternoon heat, tapping her short fingernails on the steering wheel of the Escort, glowering as Judith approached.

"Sorry," Judith murmured, unrepentant. "Let's go."

Micki merely snorted, peeling out of the parking lot with a squeal of tires. Their relationship had improved somewhat over the last few days, Micki's good humour lasting an inordinate amount of time. It hadn't taken Judith long to discover that Josiah Greenfield was the man who'd been enjoying Micki's favors, or to hear the intimate details of their on-again, off-again relationship. Despite its drawbacks, Micki seemed pleased.

The house smelled stale when they arrived home. Judith went straight to the kitchen and began to clear off the metal table. Puffing away on one of her incessant cigarettes, Micki hoisted her butt onto one of the counters and watched Judith set to work on the scrambled tape.

It was a messy, tedious job. Cleaning the tape was only half the battle; the other half included splicing it, opening and emptying one of Micki's unused tapes, ignoring her roommate's cries of outrage and demands for reimbursement, and winding the old tape onto the new reels.

By ten o'clock that night she had a blinding headache, a growling stomach and trembling hands from the precision work. But the tape was ready to be viewed.

"This better be something, Judith," Micki warned, opening a can of beer and taking a deep swig. "You worked on this instead of my clock radio, and it's going to be your fault if I don't wake up in time tomorrow. I'm expecting *Gone with the Wind* on this tape.''

"It's from the Factory," Judith said absently, searching the refrigerator for something edible. The best she could come up with was half a Sara Lee orange cake, and for a moment she considered burying her face in it. She controlled her hunger long enough to get a fork, and proceeded to finish the cake right out of the aluminum-foil tray.

"You don't look much like Bryn Mawr with your face full of cake," Micki said with cheerful malice.

"I'm downwardly mobile."

Micki laughed. "Okay, let's see the tape. Maybe we'll get some homegrown porn. Like Ma Carter and old Franz doing it. That would be a sight to see."

"Not for me." Judith inserted the tape in Micki's newly reconditioned machine and turned on the color television set. Could she have been laboring over pornography? And had someone with puritanical tendencies destroyed it?

For a long while just the gray-white fuzz of unrecorded tape appeared on the screen. Micki had long ago lost the remote control, and Judith was too weary to get up and fast-forward it. She sat slumped on the overstuffed sofa, with Micki sitting cross-legged on the floor nearby, staring at the snowy screen.

"Not very exciting, Judith," Micki drawled, draining her beer can. "This is what you went to all that trouble for? It was probably just a defective tape, and no one wanted to go through the hassle of returning it. You know Ma—she makes everyone fill out reports and memos in triplicate. Someone must have figured it wasn't worth dealing with."

"Maybe." The hum of the air conditioner and the buzz of the empty tape had a soporific effect on Judith as she lounged there, half mesmerized.

Suddenly the screen was no longer empty. It showed The Puppet Factory. As a matter of fact, the shot had been filmed from the camera trained on Ryan's booth.

Nothing happened for a long time. The booth wasn't

empty—Judith could see the curtain rustle. A sudden, sickening feeling began to grow in the pit of her stomach, and it wasn't from the Sara Lee orange cake.

"This is incredibly boring, Judith," Micki said, rising to her feet. "I'm going to turn on Phil Collins...." Her voice trailed off as Fafnir appeared in front of the puppet booth.

"There you are, hot stuff," he said, looking to the left. "I heard that ridiculous car of yours and wondered when you were going to show up. Whatcha been doing?"

Judith made a dive for the television, but Micki was ahead of her, surprisingly strong for someone much shorter than Judith. "We'll watch it," she said grimly as Judith's figure appeared on the screen.

Judith could have struggled. She and Micki could have gotten involved in an undignified wrestling match on the stained gray carpet. But what would that accomplish? With a short nod, she pulled away, back to the sofa, watching.

Watching as she conversed in a low voice with the puppets, caressing them. Watching her own anger, and Ryan's appearance from behind the booth. Watching as Ryan reached for her.

"We've put this off too long." His voice came from the stereo speakers of Micki's state-of-the-art video equipment. And she watched as he kissed her, his back to the camera, her hands reaching up under his loose white T-shirt and caressing his tanned back.

The tape proved one thing, she thought miserably. She hadn't imagined the erotic power of that kiss. It came across on the TV screen just as vividly, and she sat there, angry and embarrassed and aroused all over again.

As she watched her videotaped image run away, she leaned forward, curiosity winning out over other emotions. She saw Ryan looking after her, picking up his puppets with surprisingly tender hands.

"Sorry, guys. She seems to bring out the worst in me."

And as he walked out of camera range, the screen turned back to gray fuzz.

Micki rose. Her compact body was quivering with rage.

"So," she said in a small tight voice. "*Gone with the Wind,* it ain't. I'm getting out of here."

"Micki…"

The door slammed behind her. Moments later the angry rumble of the Escort engine faded into the distance. Judith just sat there, staring at the fuzzy black screen, trying to still the sense of disquiet that was washing over her.

Who had destroyed that tape? Who had watched it and then smashed it in a wild fury? It came as no surprise to her that their brief, torrid kiss had been filmed—those damned cameras were on most of the time, anyway. She should have thought of it herself, gone and double-checked to make sure nothing incriminating had gotten on tape.

But the scene had been immortalized and someone hadn't liked it one tiny bit. Judith couldn't be certain, but she suspected that it had been viewed more than once. The wavy lines and slight skips in the tape might have come from the damage inflicted on it, but they also were in keeping with tapes she'd seen in which certain parts had been replayed again and again.

The person responsible couldn't have been Micki. She'd been no more than marginally interested in Judith's attempts at reconstructing the tape. And her anger at the kiss was real and new. She'd had no idea what they'd find on that tape.

What about Ryan himself? He would have been the one most likely to realize he and Judith were being filmed. Could he have taken the tape, watched it and then destroyed it?

Somehow Judith didn't think so. For all the questions she had about him, he didn't strike her as a disturbed personality. She couldn't picture him sitting in the dark, watching the tape, smashing it. If he had found it he would have simply erased it. If he'd reacted as strongly as she had to its contents, he wouldn't have replayed it. He would have come in search of her and kissed her again.

But that left a number of people who could have ruined the tape. Ma Carter, for one, except she never went down to the control room. The same held true for Bessie. Jimmy, Melvin,

Franz, Steve and all the other puppeteers had the opportunity. Yet why would any one of them bother?

Unless it had been the murderer. Unless the murderer had killed Lacey because she'd slept with Ryan. That same person with a sickly jealous mind could have smashed the tape. But if so, where did that leave Judith?

She got up and turned off the tape. For a brief moment she was tempted to rewind it, to watch again, in the solitude of the darkened living room, those moments in Ryan's arms. But she pushed the Eject button instead, then carried the refurbished tape into her bedroom and hid it under her thin, lumpy mattress. She wouldn't put it past Micki to enact her own instant reply of the tape's initial destruction, and there were too many questions left unresolved.

Despite the air conditioning, the house felt damp and muggy. Suddenly Judith had to have some exercise, a taste of what passed for fresh air during this continuous heat wave. The Mercedes had overheated and was still on the blink, but the semisuburban neighborhood surrounding Micki's ranch house was safe and moderately well lighted. She'd go for a brisk walk around the block and see if she could make sense of all this.

It was after ten-thirty, and the air had only slightly cooled off. There was no sign of Micki's car, and Judith would probably end up having to hitch to work. She could always call Franz—he lived nearby. Or she could stay home and watch the tape again and again, just as her secret watcher had done.

She shivered in the warm night air as she set off down the cracked sidewalk. The whole situation with the videotape gave her the most unpleasant feeling, of someone peeping in her windows, invading her privacy. She felt violated, her skin crawled, and it took all her self-determination to shake off the feeling of still being watched.

Micki's house was part of a development that had run out of money halfway through construction some ten years ago. There were four more houses past Micki's, and then the buildings just stopped, leaving a block of empty lots and scraggly undergrowth. The sidewalk continued beyond, and the ugly little houses continued on the other side of the street. Judith's pace slowed as she approached that strangely menacing tangle of bushes and weeds. Maybe she was being stupid. After all, one of her oldest friends had been murdered, she'd already been conked on the head once, someone had tried to electrocute her, and someone didn't like the fact that she'd been kissing Ryan Smith with surprising abandon. Maybe she shouldn't be out walking alone in the dark, in a deserted neighborhood.

She heard the sound of a car behind her and felt relieved. She wasn't alone, after all. Maybe it was Micki, coming back to yell at her. Or at least some late-returning neighbor, another pair of eyes to watch and make sure she was safe.

It was odd, though. The sound of the motor had started up rather abruptly. She hadn't noticed anyone parked down the street when she'd set out.

She turned and looked over her shoulder. The car had its bright lights on, blinding her. It was accelerating swiftly, too swiftly, and the headlights seemed to be coming straight at her.

She began to run, telling herself she was foolish, that she should stand her ground and the car would drive by. Her feet felt leaden beneath her, her heart was pounding so hard that it slammed painfully against her chest, and her mouth was dry with terror. She raced down the sidewalk, certain that the car was about to swing straight at her. She stumbled, barely managing to keep her balance, and risked a quick, terrified glance as the car bore down on her.

She had a jumble of images: a large, anonymous American sedan, blinding headlights, a face twisted with rage. Conscious thought vanished and sheer instinct took over. She dodged, rolled and scrambled into the underbrush, crawling on hands and knees like a crazed spider searching for safety. She ended up in a little ditch surrounded by bushes and lay there unmoving, her breath rasping silently in her lungs, a cold sweat covering her body.

The headlights were spearing through the bushes, over her head. She held herself very still, ignoring the stones digging into her ribs, listening with dread for the sound of the car door opening, for heavy footsteps coming in search of her.

The sounds never came. Another set of headlights split the darkness as a newer, throatier engine joined the idling rumble of the first car.

"Anything wrong, mister?" a voice called out.

Judith waited to hear someone speak in a normal, concerned voice and say he thought he might have hit someone.

There was no answer. Instead the first voice came again, rich with anger and tinged with fear. "Are you out of your mind? It ain't Halloween, y'know, buddy!"

She didn't dare move. She listened instead to the squeal of tires as one car sped away. She listened as the second car drove off. She lay there, concentrating, until she was certain that the sounds had faded, that the cars were truly gone. Then she sat up and brushed the dirt from her face.

She remained seated for a long moment as waves of remembered terror washed over her. But she didn't dare sit there too long. He might come back. The sooner she got safely back to the ugly little box of a house, the better off she'd be.

If she didn't run the equivalent of the four-minute mile, she came damned close. There was still no sign of the Escort, and Judith slammed and locked the front door, shoving a chair under the doorknob and fastening the chain. If Micki decided to return that night, she could wake Judith up. Not that Judith expected to enjoy a good night's sleep after almost becoming part of the cracked pavement.

She made a quick check of the house to be sure all the windows were locked and that no one was lurking under the bed or in a closet. She poured herself a full glass of Micki's apricot liqueur, the only alcohol in the house, and then climbed into the shower, fully clothed, to let the cool water sluice down over her trembling body.

She was covered with scrapes and dirt from her roll in the bushes. When she finally felt clean, she stepped out, dumping her wet clothes on the floor and putting on a pair of shorts and a shirt. The scratches were long and red but not dangerously deep. Enough to show the police when she called them.

She paused with her hand on the telephone. Of course, there were definite drawbacks to reporting this incident. For one thing, she had no proof. For another, her background was bound to come out. She could no longer stay at the Factory once Ryan Smith realized who she was and why she was there. It would be up to the police to continue with the investigation, and they'd bungled it once before. Chances were they'd bungle it again and Judith would be left with no satisfaction, no answers and no byline.

What could she tell them, anyway? That a large, dark car had tried to run her down? It could have been a drunk driver. It could have been her own paranoia. After all, the driver hadn't come after her. If someone had been intent on killing her, he could have waited for the second car to go by, followed her into the bushes and tried to finish the job. But what the hell had the second driver meant by his crack about Halloween?

She was just getting close. Things were happening and tempers were getting frayed. Someone had smashed that tape; someone had possibly tried to kill her. Someone was on the verge of tipping his or her hand, and the wrong move might scare that person back to safety.

She took her hand away from the phone. She wouldn't call the police. Not yet. She'd be very, very careful. She'd watch her back, as Ma Carter had so kindly suggested. She wouldn't give anyone another chance.

Micki didn't return that night, but she was sitting in her car, leaning on the horn, at seven-thirty the next morning.

Judith hesitated before opening the passenger door. The night had brought only broken sleep and fitful dreams, nightmares really, that had left her wide-awake and sweating in remembered terror. The last dream had been the worst. Through the blinding headlights she'd looked at the driver as he bore down on her. And before she'd jumped to the side, she'd had a glimpse of a face twisted in ugly rage and hatred, and she'd known what the man had meant about Halloween.

The face had been green.

Chapter Fourteen

Micki didn't say a word when Judith slid into the car beside her. Her expression was grim, just this side of sulking, and she kept her gaze averted as Judith fastened the seat belt and clutched the vinyl seat in preparation for Micki's usual driving skill. Then she turned and ran her cold black gaze over Judith's apparel. Her lip curled in contempt.

Judith could well imagine why. She was wearing a pair of baggy pants to cover the long scratches on her legs and an oversize dusty rose cotton shirt to hide the bruises on her arms. There wasn't much she could do about her face. Her body and hands had taken the brunt of her roll in the underbrush; the faint scrape on her cheekbone would be missed in dim light, and Judith was determined to stay in the dim light all day. She'd even left her blond hair hanging loose in the vain hope that it might cover the mark on her cheek.

"What the hell happened to you?" Micki demanded in a gruff voice.

So much for hoping no one would notice, Judith thought. She hadn't had time to think of a plausible excuse, so she just shrugged. "Do you care?"

"Not really," Micki said. "Just so long as it hurt."

Judith's fingers curled a little more tightly around the vinyl seat. "You don't want him, you know. You just think you do."

"Do tell," Micki said in a sugary tone.

"For God's sake, Micki, you've had every man in the place crawling at your feet. You don't need him, too."

"He's the only one I really wanted."

"Don't give me that crap," Judith snapped. "You just don't like hearing the word no. You aren't cut out to be a victim, no matter how hard you try to convince yourself."

Micki's attempt at pathos vanished abruptly. "You'll find out how easy it is to be a victim," she snarled, slamming the car into reverse and speeding out into the roadway, nearly colliding with a passing car.

"What do you mean by that?" Had Judith been wrong all the time? Had she been living with Lacey's murderer and not even realized it? Micki was livid with jealousy and rage. Was it a murderous rage?

"You come here," Micki said tightly, "with your Bryn Mawr smiles and your Grace Kelly looks and charm every goddamned man around, including Ryan, who's old enough to know better. I'm sick to death of upper-class bitches slumming. I'm sick to death of Ryan falling all over people like you and ignoring someone who's been waiting for years for just a moment of his attention—" Her voice broke, and to Judith's amazement, she dashed away a faint trickle of tears. Tears of rage, tears of frustration, or real tears of sorrow over an unrequited love?

Guilt swamped Judith. "Micki, I'm sorry—"

"The hell you are!" Micki swung out into the traffic, ignoring oncoming vehicles, stop signs and common sense. "I'm warning you, Judith. Keep out of my way."

"Does that mean you want me to move out?"

There was a long, tense silence in the car. "No."

"No?" Judith was incredulous.

"No," Micki said again. "He's going to tire of you very quickly. He only wants you because you're something he's never had. He grew up in foster homes and orphanages, usually on the wrong side of the tracks, and he's dazzled by your socialite beauty. But he's not a stupid man. Sooner or later he'll realize he belongs down here with the common folk."

"Common folk like you?"

"Common folk like me. Don't forget it, Judith. You're nothing more than a symbol for what he never had. And Ryan knows how empty symbols are."

Micki was good at deflating egos—Judith had to grant her that much. If she'd been fool enough to entertain daydreams, they were gone now. Doubtless Micki was right. There was nothing Judith could do to keep from looking exactly like what she was, the privileged daughter of a privileged class. Modified combat sportswear, grease-stained hands and ratty, braided hair didn't change matters. Hell, she could be shoveling manure in her underwear and still look like a lady.

And Ryan, with his deprived, lonely childhood, wanted that lady. Probably just to prove to himself that he could have her. Once he'd had her, he'd discard her. As he'd discarded Lacey?

But Lacey had tired of him, hadn't she? Maybe Ryan hadn't liked being rejected. Maybe he'd gone after Lacey and…

No! Absolutely, unequivocally, no! He hadn't killed Lacey. Someone else had, and she had to keep that thought firmly in mind.

Lord, she could almost thank Micki. Maybe she had been allowing herself to fantasize, just a tiny bit. Micki's rough words had brought her back to reality with a thud. Ryan Smith wasn't for her. But that didn't make him a murderer.

She had to find out who was; who had tried to run her down last night; who had smashed the tape; who had hit her on the head. And once she did, once she proved Ryan's innocence and uncovered the guilty party, then she could leave. Secure in the knowledge that not only had she learned the truth about Lacey, but she'd exonerated someone she felt far too deeply about. And there was always the article she'd write. It might even be the first step to a Pulitzer.

Somehow that fantasy didn't work its usual magic charm. She didn't want to be making an acceptance speech. She wanted to be back in Ryan's arms, princess or no.

IT WAS NOT the most pleasant of days. She decided she didn't trust a soul in the place. Not Ma with her veiled threats; not

Micki with her overt ones. Not Bessie with her sly eyes; not Steve with his heavy-handed flirtations that somehow rang false. Not even Franz, with his sweet, absentminded gaze and his brilliance with the puppets. And not Ryan. Dammit. No matter how much she wanted to, she couldn't trust Ryan.

For once nothing broke down. Every single piece of machinery was working in tip-top condition. As usual Ma could be counted on to find something unpleasant with which to keep Judith busy, but even her malicious imagination failed her. Judith was kept busy cleaning out a supply closet, one of the two locked doors she'd figured led to the fifth floor. That left one other possibility, a possibility Judith flatly planned to breach when she got the first chance.

In the meantime she spent the day in the closet, alone, sorting through empty and half-filled boxes, consolidating supplies, and thinking about Lacey. And Ryan.

The closet was at the far end of the suite of offices; the hum of the machines, the quiet clatter of the IBM Selectric that Ma still preferred and the murmur of voices were a pleasant buzz in Judith's head. She lasted through a Spartan lunch of raspberry yogurt and Tab, but even the caffeine was useless in light of her sleepless night. Sometime around two in the afternoon she curled her knees under her on the thickly carpeted hall flooring, leaned her head against the closet wall and fell soundly asleep.

SHE WAS SUDDENLY, instantly, awake. Her skin felt cold and clammy, her neck stiff, her eyes gritty, every muscle in her body sore and cramped. Pushing herself up and away from the wall, she peered through the shadowy corridor. There was no longer the beneficent hum of machinery, the quiet sound of voices, the measured footsteps, the distant clatter of creativity from the lower floors. She glanced at the thin gold watch she'd worn ever since she graduated from Bryn Mawr, and felt a nervous clutching in the pit of her stomach. It was a quarter to seven, and she was alone in The Puppet Factory.

Or at least she hoped she was alone. The window at the end of the hallway showed a deserted parking lot. Micki hadn't bothered to wait for her, hadn't come looking for her when she didn't show up, and probably wouldn't notice when or if she came home that night. Scratch that ''if'' Judith told herself nervously. She'd simply call a taxi, then wait for it out on the front steps, as far away from the balconies as…

Whom was she kidding? Here was her golden opportunity— she'd be a complete fool if she blew it now. She wouldn't bother with trying to jimmy the lock on the other closet door; she'd screw up her courage and go find the freight elevator. It wouldn't be more than a minute, albeit a long, endless one, to move the elevator to the top floor, even if the contraption was down in the basement. And once she got to the top floor, she could find out what was kept such a deep, dark secret at the otherwise open Puppet Factory. What was Ryan hiding up there?

Her running shoes made little sound as she headed toward the lower floors. In the distance she could hear the ominous rumble of thunder. The sky was unnaturally dark for early evening, and Judith allowed herself a small, silent prayer that the heat wave was finally about to break. What they needed was a hell of a thunderstorm to wash away the muggy, blistering heat, water the parched earth and dissipate everyone's tension.

What they'd get instead would be more heat lightning. The weather had been full of false promises, even an occasional drenching rain, usually in the middle of the night when no one could appreciate it. All it did was add to the humidity. No, this was bound to be another dud.

The shadows were eerie in the old mill. The heaviness of the air, the grumbling thunder in the distance, everything added to her uneasiness. She paused outside the third-floor entrance to the work space. The lights were off, but she could see the freight elevator over at the end, waiting. For one last time she considered turning around and running back up to the front steps, maybe even hitchhiking home. There was a pay phone half a mile down the road at a small convenience store; she could either call Micki or a taxi from there.

Lightning streaked across the sky outside the bank of windows, followed by a sharp, violent crack of thunder, and Judith knew she wasn't about to take a stroll down a tree-lined highway. Gritting her teeth, she pushed one of the swinging doors and walked into the workroom.

The booths and stages were dark and threatening shapes. Judith cast a suspicious glance up at the video cameras, but no little red light signaled they were working. She didn't know whether to be relieved or not. At least, if she had any reason for her sense of unease, there'd be a film witness.

She could feel a pair of eyes burning into the back of her neck beneath her hair. The clammy feeling was there again, covering her skin like a coating of ice, and her heart began to pound. She peered around in the semidarkness but saw nothing. It was just her overactive imagination. But why the hell hadn't she bothered to turn on the lights? She was in the middle of the room now—the light switches were behind her, and there were shadows in the way, shadows and...and noises. Snuffling, shuffling noises.

"Who's there?" Good Lord, her voice sounded strong and defiant, not at all like the quivering coward she was. She stood motionless, listening to the sounds move closer. "Who is it?" she demanded again, and the anger in her voice was unfeigned, an equal partner to her terror.

Maybe it's rats, she told herself, her feet glued to the hardwood floor. *Maybe it's Micki, trying to scare me.*

She could see nothing in the shadowy darkness. She could only stand there and listen as those odd muffled sounds grew louder and louder, almost as loud as her terrified heartbeat.

If it was Micki, she was doing a damned effective job. Judith tried one last time. "Who is it?" By now her bravado was wearing thin, and her voice had a definite quaver in it. No answer; just the creak of floorboards as someone, something, moved up on her.

Lightning streaked across the sky, turning the darkened room blue-white for a brief moment. Judith screamed, panic finally winning out, and she raced back toward the door, the stairs, the parking lot and the dubious safety of the thunderstorm.

Noises were echoing around her head: the thudding of her heartbeat, her rasping breath, the delayed report of the thunder, the sound of pursuit. The swinging door slammed back at her as she ran through, and she ignored the glancing blow, storming up the stairs, tripping once and slamming her shins against the metal steps. Then she was on her feet, running, running, the terror behind her, safety ahead of her, running—

He absorbed her impact far better than the door or the stairs had. She barreled into him, unseeing, and his hands reached out and caught her, holding her steady against him. She looked up and saw Ryan, and she knew she was safe.

She put her head against his shoulder, her arms around his waist, and held on, letting the pounding of her heart sink into his flesh, letting the terrified clamminess of her skin be warmed by his heat. She stood there in the darkness, listening to the steady beat of his heart, to the distant rumble of thunder. There were no snuffling sounds, no footsteps in pursuit. The Puppet Factory was silent, empty, with just the two of them embracing on the stairs.

Only for one moment did she consider that he might have been her pursuer. As soon as the thought entered her mind, she dismissed it. Whatever had been after her, if it was something other than the building settling and her overactive imagination, that something had been evil.

She felt his hands grip her arms gently, the long fingers caressing her flesh. Slowly he moved her away from him, just far enough so he could look into her face. A streak of lightning illuminated him in the dimness, his eyes filled with emotions she could only begin to recognize.

"What's going on?" he said finally. "What are you doing here so late? Why were you running?" There was no disapproval in his voice, no curiosity. He sounded detached, as if he were waiting. Waiting for what?

"I…I fell asleep," she said, and she no longer had even the

semblance of self-possession left in her shaky voice. "When I woke up, everyone was gone."

"What were you doing on the third floor?"

Lie, she ordered herself, wanting to confess. "I thought Micki might still be around. Or Franz. I don't have my car here and I needed a ride home."

He pushed her a little bit farther away, though his hands still held her, and she dropped her arms to her sides reluctantly. She missed the comforting feel of his flesh against hers, but she didn't dare tell him the truth.

"And why were you running?"

She looked up at him, at his implacable face. *Because a monster was chasing me. Because Lacey's murderer was after me.* "I'm afraid of thunder," she said out loud.

He closed his eyes briefly as an expression of something that was vaguely akin to pain washed over his face. Then he opened them again, and there was no mistaking the disappointment and anger on his face.

"For God's sake, Judith," he said wearily, "why do you always lie?"

His words cut through her like a knife. "All right," she said. "I thought I heard something in the workroom. It spooked me and I ran. And I really don't like thunder very much."

He was suddenly intent. "What did you hear?"

She shrugged. "It was probably just my overactive imagination. Just some sort of muffled noises. Footsteps, that kind of thing."

"It could have been me."

"It probably was," she said, wishing she could believe it. She pulled away, and he let go of her arms. He was wearing khakis and a white polo shirt, and she suddenly had a blinding vision of the videotape, her hungry hands pulling at his T-shirt, traveling up his back....

She shook her head to banish the memory. "Anyway, you can't blame me for being a little spooked," she said with an attempt at reasonableness. "After all, that girl was killed here just a little more than a month ago. It's enough to make anyone edgy.''

He held himself very still in the darkness. He was tall and slim and straight, and Judith wanted to wrap herself around him, to huddle against him for protection.

''What girl?'' he asked slowly.

Judith looked at him in amazement. ''You know what girl,'' she said, exasperation breaking through her studied calm. ''The one who fell over the balcony. I don't remember her name.''

The moment the words were out of her mouth, she regretted them, though she wasn't sure why. They seemed to galvanize Ryan. He moved closer to her, almost as if he were stalking her. She wanted to back up against the wall, but she stood her ground.

''Think hard, Judith. You'll remember if you try,'' he said bitterly.

''Was it Lacey something?''

His smile was definitely threatening. ''Not bad, Judith. Do you have this much trouble remembering the names of all your college buddies?''

She felt as if someone had shoved a fist in her stomach. She could feel her face turn pale, but she didn't move. It would do her no good to deny it. ''How long have you known?''

''Since the day you showed up here. Lacey used to talk about her good buddy Judith, who worked on a newspaper and wanted to be a big-time reporter. Is this how you're going to do it? Using your friend's accidental death to further your career?''

She kept herself from flinching. His accusation was a low blow, but no more than she sometimes felt she deserved. ''Was it an accident?''

He smiled grimly. ''That's the sixty-four-thousand-dollar question, right? I'm convinced it was; you're convinced it wasn't. So you came here to lie and spy and use us and her, all for your own rotten gain.''

She absorbed the words like blows. ''Then why did you hire me?''

"Better the devil you know than the devil you don't," he said. "If it hadn't been you, it probably would have been someone else. At least with you I could keep an eye on what you were doing."

"And knock me over the head if I got too close."

"No one knocked you over the head. Not that I haven't been sorely tempted to during the past few weeks."

"Is that the only reason you hired me?"

"Hell, no. You can fix a Roberts 450. I don't take that lightly." Anger was crackling between them, and electricity, like the heat storm outside.

Judith's body began to tingle with the anticipation, the excitement, the rage and the frustration. "Is that all?" she said, looking up at him.

"Not quite," he said. "There was always this." He pulled her into his arms, and his mouth came down on hers.

Chapter Fifteen

Judith fought for a moment, simply to prove a point. And then she began to kiss him back, her mouth opening beneath his, her tongue reaching for his marauding one, her hands tight on his waist. He felt warm and strong and solid beneath her hands, far removed from the nebulous threat that had stalked her through the dimly lit caverns of the third-floor workshop, and she stood on her toes to press her body closer to his.

He made a low sound of approval, snaking an arm around to her shoulders to move her closer still, catching her jaw with his hand and holding her steady for his kiss. She closed her eyes, reveling in the sense of him, the scent, the taste, the warmth, the softness of his polo shirt and the bone and muscle beneath it. No more, she thought distantly. No more arguments, no more defenses, no more rationalizations and rejections. She wasn't going to fight him any longer. If he wanted her, he could have her, and to hell with the repercussions.

He broke away, looking down at her, his eyes smoky and unreadable. ''Isn't this where you're supposed to slap my face and say, 'How dare you'?'' His voice was low and husky, unbearably seductive.

Judith considered her alternatives. ''No,'' she said.

''No?'' he echoed, puzzled.

''No,'' she repeated. ''Or maybe what I really mean is yes.''

He was suddenly very still. His long fingers still held her chin, lightly, his thumb gently caressing her jawline. She waited, hoping to hear some acknowledgement, an avowal of undying love or at least mild enthusiasm. Instead he nodded, coolly enough, and now was the time that Judith wanted to slap him and say, How dare you?

"What were you doing on the third floor?" he said instead.

She broke away, and he let her go, with no satisfying bit of reluctance. Her immediate instinct was to lie, and then she reminded herself that she no longer needed to. He knew everything. Almost. "I was looking for the freight elevator. I wanted to see what was on the fifth floor."

He nodded. "Of course. I'm surprised you didn't pick the lock on the fourth-floor stairs."

"I'm not much good at B and E."

"Pity," he murmured, taking her arm. He looked a little brutal in the dimly lit hallway, and the flashes of heat lightning alternately illuminating his face weren't reassuring. She considered pulling away from him, then decided it would be childish and possibly a waste of energy. She'd made her decision, hadn't she? She could live with the consequences.

At least she could if her instincts were right. If they were wrong, if she was mistaken about Ryan Smith, she might not live at all.

"Second thoughts?" he murmured, waiting, his hand on her arm, on the long sleeve that covered her scrapes and bruises.

He would let her go; suddenly she knew that. And it would be her last chance. Her last chance at many things.

"No," she said, lifting her head and looking him directly in those distant eyes of his. "Are you going to show me the fifth floor?"

"Bluebeard's chamber? It would be my pleasure." And he led her down into the expanse of the third-floor workshop.

If something had been there earlier, stalking her, it was long gone. No longer did she feel those eyes boring into the back of her neck. The room was silent, with only the crackle of the lightning and the sound of their feet on the old hardwood floors making any noise at all.

He passed in front of the open-sided freight elevator. "You still think someone was chasing you?"

"Someone," she said, "or something." She eyed the elevator with dislike. "Couldn't we use the stairs?"

"Nope. If you want to see the fifth floor, you'll have to do it the hard way. Are you afraid of heights?"

"Not particularly. I just don't like freight elevators."

"Tough," he said leading her onto the platform and releasing her arm. As he punched the buttons with a certain savagery, Judith moved to the center of the elevator, bracing herself as it began its ascent.

For the start of an affair, this was lacking a certain jungle charm. Ryan was standing to one side, half glaring at her, and she was cheerfully heading up to a deserted area with someone who might be a murderer. Well, perhaps not cheerfully, she had to admit. If only he'd kiss her again. When he kissed her she forgot about common sense and justice and reasonable suspicions; all she could think about was Ryan.

The freight elevator ground to a halt. There was a narrow hallway, a flight of stairs doubtless leading to the locked door on the fourth floor, and two sets of doors. Ryan went to the first one and unlocked it, not bothering to check whether Judith was following.

She stepped off the platform and moved up behind him. "What do you keep in here?" she questioned in a deceptively even tone of voice.

He cast a brief glance at her. "The bodies of my victims. Lacey got away, unfortunately, but the rest—"

"Stop it!"

He leaned back against the unlocked door, blocking it. "You want to tell me you don't think I murdered Lacey?"

"I don't think you murdered Lacey."

A brief, cynical smile danced across his face. "Now why don't I believe you?"

"Ryan, if I didn't trust you, I wouldn't be here with you now," she said. "If I thought there was any chance you killed Lacey, I'd be taking my life into my hands, wouldn't I?"

He considered that for a moment, and she thought she could see some of the tension leave him. "But you still think she was murdered?"

"I'm convinced of it. I just don't know who did it, or why."

"And you think the contents of the fifth floor are going to help you figure out the answers to those questions? I don't think so." Opening the door, he gestured her inside.

Judith looked around her, oblivious as he closed and locked the door behind them. "This explains it," she said.

"Explains what?"

"Why your house didn't feel lived in. You don't live there at all, do you? You live here."

"I live here."

It was one huge room, half the expanse of The Puppet Factory, with shiny hardwood floors, white walls and a minimum of furniture. She could see a utilitarian kitchen in one corner, a white sofa, piles of books everywhere, but not a puppet in sight. Nor a video camera, thank God, or even a television set. The heat lightning was still crackling outside, sending shafts of light snaking across the unlit room, from window to window, briefly illuminating the shadowy proportions. There was an extra-long twin bed against one wall, next to a small chest of drawers with a reading lamp on top of it. The entire effect was spare, almost austere, but oddly restful.

"It looks like a monk's cell," she said, blurting out the first thing that came to her mind.

"Does it?" He seemed unconcerned, moving past her toward the kitchen, and she followed him. "You want some coffee?"

"No."

"You want a drink?"

"No."

They were standing in the open kitchen. There was a café table with one chair, the only chair in the place. "Don't you ever have any guests?" she asked.

"If I do, I have them at the house."

"No one comes up here?" she persisted.

"No one even knows I live here. Ma suspects, but even she doesn't know for certain."

"Why?"

"I like my privacy," he said simply.

"I didn't mean that. I mean, why me? Why did you bring me up here?"

He dropped into the chair. "I thought you'd caught on."

"You could have taken me to the house. I would have gone," she said.

"I didn't want to take you there. I wanted you here, where no one's been. I didn't want to make love to you in the bed where I screwed Lacey."

Judith paled. "She told me you were lousy in bed."

He laughed with real amusement. "And you still came upstairs with me? Trust, indeed, Judith. You'll have to judge for yourself." Catching her wrist, he tugged her, gently, down onto his lap.

She went willingly, curling up against his big, warm body. He threaded his fingers through her sheaf of hair, tilting her head back for his kiss, and his mouth was teasing, gentle, biting and arousing on her mouth, her lips, her cheek, her ear. He'd never kissed her like that before, soft and enticing; it had all been anger and fiery passion, and Judith felt herself growing damp and warm and shivery all over. She put her hands on him, resting them lightly on his shoulders, and she could feel his wiry strength, the tension, the wanting. His hair was damp, he smelled of soap, and Judith realized he must have showered just before he'd come down and found her running for her life. As his mouth traveled down the line of her throat, she began to explore his skin, his eyelids, the strong line of his nose, as her hands smoothed back his hair and held him against her.

He was unfastening the buttons on her oversize shirt, doing it deftly enough. And then the shirt was hanging loose around her, and he'd unfastened the front clasp of her bra. She looked down, at his long, dark fingers against the whiteness of her breast, and felt a cramping surge of desire between her legs. She'd forgotten what it was like to want someone this much.

Or maybe she had never wanted someone as much as she wanted Ryan Smith.

"Tell me what you want," he murmured against her ear, his breath warm and moist and arousing. "Show me."

In answer she pressed her body harder against his hand, arching against him, and her greedy hands were once more tugging at his polo shirt, sliding underneath to his sleek, smooth flesh.

He moved away, far enough to help her pull the garment over his head, and then he pushed her shirt and bra down her arms, dropping them on the kitchen floor. The sky outside the bank of windows had grown blacker still, and the wind rushing through the room carried the scent of dampness and the ozone of a storm.

Ryan ran his hands up her bare arms, his fingers delicate on her bruised and scraped flesh, and the shadows in the cavernous room darkened his face.

"What happened to your arms?" he asked, but her mouth stopped him, her arms slid around his neck, her sensitive breasts pressed up against the muscled smoothness of his bare chest, and there was no more time for questions as the last of their restraints fell to the floor with their discarded clothes.

His kiss held a hint of desperation, warning of the insoluble problems surrounding them. She kissed him back, clinging to him, wanting to absorb him into her very pores.

He surged to his feet, still holding her, carried her across the shadowy room and dropped her on the bed. He stood over her, his eyes hooded as he stepped out of his pants, and she knew a moment's regret that he hadn't let her help him, discover him.

She could feel tendrils of anxiety pulling at her. First times were always a little frightening, and this wasn't casual sex after a dinner date. This was dark and dangerous, not the scratching of a hormonal itch. It wasn't something she could chalk up to experience and forget about if it ended in disaster. It was too important, too desperately important, and it terrified her.

Some of her reactions must have been mirrored on her face. Ryan sank down beside her on the bed, his hands deft on the drawstring of her loose-fitting pants. "You don't need to look so worried," he murmured in a conversational tone. "I'm not really bad in bed."

She managed a faint smile. "That's not what I'm worried about," she said, her voice rusty. His hands were warm and strong and far too practiced as they slid her pants and underwear off her hips and down her legs, leaving her naked, exposed, vulnerable to his heated gaze.

"Then what is it?" He didn't touch her. He just sat there, his beautiful body inches away. "What are you afraid of?"

There had been enough lies between them. "I'm afraid I'll fall in love with you," she said in a voice so low that he almost couldn't hear her. "I'm afraid I already have."

Whatever he'd been expecting, it clearly wasn't that. A tremor rippled across his body, and he gazed at her with an unreadable expression in his eyes.

Lightning sizzled outside the open windows; thunder rumbled around them as if in an angry warning. And then she was in his arms, his mouth fiercely possessive on hers, and her fears fell away.

There wasn't room for the two of them on the bed, but it didn't matter. Half covering her with his larger body, he slid his hands up her narrow rib cage to cup her small, aroused breasts. His mouth followed, his tongue flicking the tiny bud of one nipple, and she moaned, pressing against him, her hands threading through his hair and holding him against her.

His skin was like silk beneath her hands, the muscles taut and tense, the texture and scent of him filling her senses and washing away any lingering trace of common sense. She was on fire, burning for him, aching for him, and she bit her lip to keep from crying out her need.

One of his hands moved lower, across her flat, quivering stomach, down to the juncture of her thighs; and instinctively, foolishly, she tightened against the touch she was longing for. He raised his head to look at her, his mouth damp, her breast wet and glistening in the shadowy half light, his hand resting lightly on her. "Still fighting it, Judith?" he murmured. "Open your legs for me."

And she did. His fingers slid lower still, reaching the sensitive core of her, and she shuddered in reaction, digging her fingers deeper into his shoulders.

He made no complaint but dropped his mouth down to capture her other breast while his fingers began a slow, delicious invasion. She whimpered, lifting her hips toward him, and he withdrew, leaving her momentarily bereft. But it was only to stroke her, before he returned to fill her aching emptiness.

Slowly, wickedly, he alternated that rhythm, the deep, pulsing entry, the sure, teasing caresses, until she had to bite back the screams, until her head was thrashing back and forth on the pillow and her body was arching, shuddering, shimmering and clenching around him.

He waited, long enough for the initial wave to crash over her and subside; then he replaced his hand with his body, a steady, merciless invasion that was like nothing she had ever experienced. She was still damp and shuddery from the strength of her climax, and now he was calling forth new, even deeper responses.

Their bodies were slippery with sweat, and the storm-laden breeze made no difference to the heat flaming between them. He put his hands beneath her buttocks, drawing her closer still, and she moaned with an odd combination of pain and pleasure as her body stretched to accommodate him. Her eyes blinked open for a moment, to look up into his, and the expression of dazed, fierce pleasure on his strained face was enough to shatter the last of her control.

She wrapped her legs around him, pulling him in deeper. Her hands clutched his shoulders and her mouth caught his. He began the ancient movement of retreat and advance, and each time she was sure he was filling her with more than she could bear; each time she was sure she'd never be so empty.

Conscious thought was vanishing. Never had she felt this way, lost, straining, found, attaining. Emotions washed over her, wrenching her, inside and out, and she felt him stiffen in her arms, heard the strangled gasp that was her name tumble from his mouth, and then suddenly she was lost once more, a blue-white streak of heat lightning in a storm-darkened universe.

Ryan collapsed against her, a heavy tangle of limbs and skin and hair. She held him close, her mind floating as the tremors still racking her body faded into nothingness.

For a moment she wondered if he'd sleep like that. Even if he crushed her body, she wouldn't mind. She didn't want to risk losing anything of what had just passed between them; she didn't want him to move and break the spell.

Slowly he lifted his head, shifting some of his dead weight off her, and she breathed a surreptitious sigh of relief before she dared look up to meet his gaze.

"'One small step for man, one giant leap for mankind,'" he quoted in a shaky voice. He looked as shell-shocked as she felt.

She smiled up at him. "You think you just landed on the moon?"

"It feels like it. About as close to heaven as I'm likely to get." He stared down at her, his expression both somber and infinitely tender. "I'm crushing you."

"No, you're not."

"No more lies, Judith."

"Well, just a little," she admitted, then regretted it. He moved away from her, breaking that wonderful joining, hovering for a moment above her.

And then he slipped off the side of the bed, pulling her with him, tumbling to the floor in a welter of limbs and sheets and rekindled desire.

She lay sprawled on top of him, their eyes laughing into each other's, when the darkness clamped down around Judith's heart with the suddenness of a summer storm. All the questions, the problems, the danger came crashing back into her consciousness.

"What is it?" He could see her pale face, her sudden panic.

"I just remembered," she said. She could feel her eyes fill

with hot tears. She, who seldom cried, was about to burst into a demoralizing bout of weeping.

He held her close against him, cradling her in his arms with a tenderness he hadn't ever shown her. He stroked her tangled hair and flushed skin as she wept against him.

"Why can't it be like this?" she whispered against his damp chest when the tears had finally abated. "Why does it always have to be so damned complicated?"

He reached a hand up to tilt her chin toward him, and his eyes were both bleak and loving. "Because life is like that," he said. "And the best you can do is take your happiness when you can find it, and let tomorrow take care of tomorrow."

"I don't believe that," she said.

"I'm not much good at things like this, Judith. I had a lousy childhood, and that's something that gets pretty deeply ingrained. I don't let myself care. I don't let myself open up to other people. I don't think I'm very good for you."

She lay there looking at him. "I don't suppose you are," she said.

"Maybe we'd better end this."

"Maybe we'd better."

"It's a mistake."

"Probably." She still didn't move.

"Well," he said finally. "I've made worse mistakes in my life." And once more he began to kiss her tear-damp mouth.

FOR A BLACK, desperate moment Hideous Harry was so angry that he nearly rushed out after them. Yet he watched them, watched the freight elevator move slowly upward. It didn't matter that they hadn't touched, that they had seemed angry with each other. He knew what they would do when they reached the top floor, the apartment only he knew about. He knew, and he shook with rage and disgust.

He had failed. He had to protect Ryan, and once more he had failed. But he could retrieve the situation. He could punish her, as she deserved to be punished. And he wouldn't wait any longer. The next time he found her alone, he would finish her sinful life, and the crushing darkness would leave his shoulders, leave him in peace. For a while, at least.

But there would always be others. Sinners—evil, wicked whores. And he must punish them, too.

But first Judith. As soon as he possibly could.

And with a nod of satisfaction and newfound determination, he shuffled off into the darkness.

Chapter Sixteen

Ryan sat in the car, watching her go. It was just after seven in the morning, and the sun was already blazing down on the Toyota, turning it into a furnace. Last night's heat and lightning might never have existed, because the few hours of soft breezes had stalemated back into blistering heat.

He ran a weary hand through his hair as he watched Judith head up Micki's sidewalk. Someone was looking out the window, watching Judith's approach just as he watched her leave.

If she were anywhere near as tired as he was, she wouldn't be in the mood to face Micki. And she had to be as tired—she'd been just as busy.

They'd made love again on the floor of his loft. And then they'd gotten very silly, determined not to think about the ramifications of why she was there in the first place. They'd gone out and eaten too much pizza and drunk too much beer, then ended up at his swimming pool.

He'd made love to her on the steps of the pool, surrounded by the gentle lap of shallow water. She'd made love to him on the chaise, her hands and mouth hot and eager and quick to learn. They'd made love in the sauna and had almost made love in the front seat of the Toyota on the way back to Micki's house. But they hadn't made love in that damned, haunted bed.

She had a beautiful back, he thought, slumping down and staring after her. And a determined walk that was belied by the almost imperceptible sway of those luscious hips. And her legs, her long, gorgeous legs, wrapped around him....

He straightened up, cursing. He couldn't afford to sit there mooning after her, nor could he afford to spend time being obsessed by erotic memories and fantasies. She'd been completely open and honest with him during the long hours of last night and this morning, and despite his denials, an uneasiness lingered. Something didn't ring true, something wasn't right. He had to find some answers before he could prove to Judith that her suspicions were groundless.

For a moment niggling fear swept over him—that Judith was right, after all, that Lacey had been murdered. If that were the case, it opened up a whole Pandora's box of trouble, one that he simply refused to face. She had to be mistaken, dammit. She had to be.

Judith stopped with her hand on the door, turning to look in Ryan's direction. He could see her expression quite clearly, those wide, suddenly vulnerable blue eyes, her kiss-swollen mouth, her defiant chin. She smiled at him, an unsure little smile, and lifted one hand. Who would have thought a princess would be unsure?

He almost bolted out of the car after her. He didn't want her in that depressing little house with Micki cross-examining her. He wanted her with him, now, always. She'd told him she was afraid she'd fallen in love with him. He was afraid, too. Afraid of emotions he couldn't lock away anymore, afraid of caring too much and having her abandon him, as he'd been abandoned too many times.

Maybe he should end it right now, while he still could. Looking at her motionless figure by the door, he knew it was already too late. He couldn't—wouldn't—give her up.

But he could find the answers to her questions. And maybe those answers would be his answers, too.

He raised a hand in an answering salute. Then he leaned forward, started the car and drove away from her in the early-morning haze.

"HAVE A GOOD TIME?" Micki was sitting in one of the chairs, puffing on the stubby end of a cigarette. The ashtray by her side was overflowing, the air was blue with stale smoke, and cigarette butts floated in the three half-empty cups of coffee on the floor beside her.

Judith shut the door and leaned against it, weary beyond belief. While her body still glowed with remembered pleasure, her mind was once again twisting into doubts and questions. The last thing she wanted was to face Micki's accusing glare. "Yes," she said, waiting for her roommate's explosion.

Micki nodded, blowing out a stream of smoke. "Are you in love with him?"

"Yes," Judith said again.

"And is he in love with you?"

Micki certainly had a way with words. "Not that I know of," Judith replied. "Does that help?"

Very deliberately Micki leaned over and put out her cigarette. "I've been thinking about it," she said. "Thinking about it all night long. And I'm coming to the conclusion that it doesn't really matter."

Judith sank down on the lopsided sofa, surprise undermining her determination to go straight to bed and stay there. "What doesn't matter?"

"Well," said Micki, lighting another cigarette, "Much as I hate to admit it, you may be right. I may want Ryan simply because I can't have him." She shrugged. "I'm not sure, mind you. And you're not off the hook yet. But I'm considering the possibility. I think Ryan might be a little too complicated for me. I can think of a number of men who let themselves enjoy life."

"And Ryan doesn't?"

"What do you think? He has scars that run pretty deep. Too deep for me. Maybe I'm better off with Jos—with someone else."

"Maybe you are," Judith said abruptly, rising to her feet. "I'm going to bed."

"Don't you want to find out whether I forgive you?" Micki looked affronted.

"At this point I'm too tired to care. I want some sleep. I don't think I'm going to talk you into it one way or the other, so I might as well not waste my breath. You can tell me when I get up."

"Pleasant dreams," Micki said, a sour expression on her face.

They weren't. They were god-awful nightmares, erotic, frightening, death-filled nightmares. In her dreams she'd be making love to Ryan, almost reliving his touch on her skin, when he'd suddenly turn into a monster. A fire-breathing dragon, with none of Fafnir's lustful charm, ready to devour her. A vicious, knife-wielding harridan instead of Madame Rinaldi's overblown egotism. Even the Green Goddesses were terrifying, strangling Judith in their alfalfa-sprout hair.

But worst of all was Hideous Harry. Just when Ryan was carrying her out of the swimming pool in her dream, his face became distorted and turned into green yarn, twisting into a murderous rage. And instead of placing her on the chaise, he held her helpless body above the pool, ready to plunge it into the suddenly bottomless depths.

Judith woke up sweating and shaking, panic beating around her ears like the flapping wings of a thousand angry birds. Green yarn. Suddenly it was making horrible sense. The young woman found in the quarry had green yarn underneath her fingernails. The face of whoever had tried to run her down was made of green yarn. And there was only one possible answer.

Someone was dressing up as Hideous Harry, someone who'd murdered an innocent young woman. Someone who'd tried to kill Judith. It didn't take a great leap of deductive reasoning for her to know that same someone had murdered Lacey.

She sat there in the stifling room and continued to shiver. It still made no sense at all. What did Lacey and a stranger and Judith Daniels have in common? They were young, they were female, but that was about it.

She needed to talk to Ryan, to tell him what she'd figured

out. Maybe he could make better sense of it, come up with some solid answers.

The digital clock beside her bed read 4:30 p.m. in glaring red letters. Judith stared at it in patent disbelief for a long moment before leaping out of bed.

She was supposed to meet Ryan at six-thirty. That would give her enough time to shower, change her clothes and satisfy her suddenly overwhelming hunger. Before she found Ryan and satisfied an even more overwhelming hunger.

Micki was nowhere in sight; the Escort was gone. Judith ate everything in the refrigerator that wasn't growing mold, showered, dressed, then headed out to the Mercedes, crossing her fingers that the recalcitrant beast would start. She should call Ryan and tell him she was coming early, but if the car started, she didn't want to risk having it stall on her. And if it didn't start, she'd be spending at least another forty-five minutes fiddling with it.

She slid into the driver's seat. She was wearing a pale blue halter sundress, with no underwear at all, and she couldn't wait to see Ryan's reaction. She wouldn't tell him about her green-yarn theory—that someone was impersonating Hideous Harry—until later. For the moment all she wanted was his arms around her, his smooth warm skin next to hers.

The Mercedes started on her first try. She cast one last, meditative glance back at the ranch house, weighing the chances of the car idling smoothly while she ran back to call Ryan. She lifted her sandaled foot off the gas pedal, and the engine began to sputter and die.

Immediately she replaced her foot and shifted into reverse. So she would get there half an hour early. He'd welcome the surprise.

If possible, the day was even hotter than the preceding ones. As she drove through the haze, the open windows blasted warm air through her still-damp hair, and the sundress clung to her skin. She couldn't wait to get it off.

There was no sign of the Toyota in the mill's parking lot, but that was to be expected. She hadn't learned where Ryan parked during off hours, but it definitely wasn't in the main lot. On impulse she drove back out again, parking down the road at an abandoned gas station and walking back. No need to give any weekend worker ideas, she thought.

She took out the key Ryan had given her and slipped it into the lock of the heavy steel door. The building was cool and dark, with no sign of life anywhere. Had it been half an hour later, he would have been waiting for her. As it was, she had no choice but to seek out the freight elevator and make her way to the fifth floor.

She went down to the third floor and peered through the inner glass door into the shadowy corridor, then breathed a tiny sigh of relief. The freight elevator wasn't there. It wasn't until then that she dared admit that she was very happy she wouldn't have to cross the haunted expanse of this floor. Even if she'd convinced herself that those odd noises yesterday had been a result of her imagination, she didn't want to put herself to the test. The second, fourth or even bottom floor would be far preferable.

The freight elevator was waiting on the second floor, just past the control room with its silent collection of advanced technology. This time she didn't make the mistake of leaving the lights off. The hell with electric bills. The Roberts 450 was humming along, anyway, using a lot more power than a few light bulbs.

It was with a horrifying sense of déjà vu that she heard the sounds, the same snorting, snuffling sounds she'd heard the day before. They were coming from beyond the open door of the control room.

If she had any sense she'd simply march up to the door and look inside. Maybe Melvin and Jimmy had had a fight, and one of them was weeping his heart out in private. Maybe it was some wild animal, trapped inside the old building, looking for a way out. She'd feel like a complete fool when she found the harmless answer to the mysterious noises, but she wouldn't mind that at all.

She inched forward slowly. Sheer, primitive terror held her

viselike on the threshold of the open door, unable to step inside. And then she heard a new noise—the shuffling of footsteps.

Her paralysis dissolved as a cold sweat broke out over her skin. She turned and ran, too terrified to notice the clatter of her high-heeled sandals on the bare wood floors or the noise of the door swinging shut behind her. She had to get away, as far and as fast as she could.

She raced up the stairs, past the third-floor landing and up the next flight, her head filled with the sound of labored, heavy breathing, moving in on her with a rapidity that was horrifying. She reached the steel front door and shoved against it. It wouldn't budge.

She wasted desperate moments shoving it, pounding on it, before she gave up. There was no place to hide on the fourth floor—Ma always locked the office. She made it back down the stairs, allowing herself a quick glance over her shoulder as she dived for the swinging doors of the workroom. In the darkened stairwell all she could see was a tall shadow moving toward her, covered with green yarn.

She didn't have much time; she half crawled, half fell into one of the booths halfway across the room, pressing herself flat against the flimsy wall, cramming a shaking fist into her mouth to try to stifle the sound of her breathing. For a moment she heard only the blessed safety of silence, and she permitted herself the small hope that he, or it, hadn't noticed where she'd gone.

That hope was dashed when she heard the quiet hiss of the door swinging shut. Then the footsteps, slow, determined, shuffling footsteps, moving across the hardwood floor toward her. And then, most horrifying of all, came the voice.

It belonged to Hideous Harry the Hippo.

"Judith," he crooned. "I know you're here. I saw you, Judith. You shouldn't hide from me. I'll find you, you know. You can't hide forever."

She pressed herself flatter against the wall of the booth, willing her very bones to melt. She knew that voice, that sweet, cartoonlike voice. But she couldn't even begin to guess who was behind it.

Harry's was one of the easiest voices to duplicate. They all were adept at it—Ryan, Steve, Franz and Micki. Even the majority of the apprentice puppeteers had mastered it. Anyone could be calling to her, calling her to death.

She held her breath as the footsteps approached, willing her heart to stop beating.

"Don't fight it, Judith," he said in a singsong voice. "It won't do you any good. Come out. Don't make me find you." The footsteps moved past her, away from her, and she risked a tiny, shallow breath.

The sounds were receding toward the river side of the building. She would wait, she would count to twenty, and then she would run for it.

But where in God's name would she run to?

And then she heard a new sound, smooth and metallic, followed by hot air swirling through the air-conditioned room. He'd opened the door onto the balcony.

It flashed through her mind in a microsecond—a vision of Lacey's body hurtling off the balcony into the murderous machinery of the turbine below. She could see her own body falling, the blue sundress billowing out around her. She had to peer out, make sure he was far enough away, and then run for it.

Slowly, imperceptibly, she leaned forward, and a silent breath of terror escaped her. She could see him quite clearly, silhouetted by the double glass doors. Moving back, directly toward her.

He was a life-size version of Hideous Harry, with furry green yarn roped around his body. He was tall, very tall—perhaps six and a half feet. There was only one person at the Puppet Factory who was almost that tall. Ryan Smith himself.

She sank back and closed her eyes. If she didn't breathe, didn't move, he might not find her. There were any number of booths in the room—it would take him a while to get to her. And he couldn't be sure she was in here, could he?

"Judith. Oh, Judith." The voice was low and sweet and beguiling, calling her to death. A lover's voice. *Her* lover's voice?

Tears of panic and despair began streaming down her face as she listened to his approach. A small, suicidal part of her was tempted to step out of the booth, to end the desperate waiting, the listening, the terrifying advance. But she held herself as still as a statue. Then she sensed him moving past her, and she drew a deep, shaky breath.

Dead silence reigned for countless moments. Harry had disappeared, waiting for her to make one wrong move. She wondered where he could have gone.

Arms snaked around her neck suddenly, thick, burly green arms, cutting off her strangled cry. She kicked back in desperation, but he seemed impervious to pain, impervious to her. The arm tightened across her throat, choking her, stopping her breath, and still she fought as the darkness closed around her and her lungs threatened to burst. She couldn't lose consciousness, she told herself. If she did, she'd never regain it.

She slammed her elbow into the soft green yarn behind her. There was a muffled grunt of pain, a word that she almost heard, and then everything darkened further.

Desperately she tried to swim out of the encroaching blackness. She was being dragged along the floor, over the threshold, out onto the rough decking of the balcony. She could hear the water flowing beneath them, the ominous noise of the turbine. With one last effort she yanked herself free, rolling away from him.

But it was too late. He caught her as she tried to crawl, hauling her up into his arms with superhuman strength, holding her over the balcony, the grinding machinery. And then he heaved her, and she was falling, falling, falling, to her death in the river below.

Chapter Seventeen

Judith could feel the wind rushing past her; she could hear the scream being torn from her lungs. She was clawing the air in panic, kicking and reaching out for some tiny piece of solidity, when her hands caught something, caught it and stopped, stopping the free-fall with a jerk that almost tore her arms from their sockets.

She hung there, eyes shut, breath sobbing in her throat, for an endless moment. Judith was strong; her arms were more than capable of supporting her weight, and for a long moment she just rested and thanked God she'd overcome her prejudices and gone to a fitness center. She could do push-ups, chin herself—and hang from a ledge with no more than a minimal amount of strain.

She opened her eyes. It wasn't a ledge she was clinging to; it was the floor of the lower balcony deck that she'd caught on her way down. Relief coursed through her. As soon as she got her screaming muscles under control, she could swing her leg up and crawl onto the decking. But then where would she go?

She heard the rumble of the turbine beneath her. And then she felt the balcony shake as someone walked—no, shuffled—out onto it.

"Judith," Hideous Harry's eerie voice called. Her hands were slippery with sweat, her terror so intense that she almost let go of her lifeline. He was on the far side of the terrace, but she could tell by the tiny tremors beneath her hands that he was moving. All he had to do was look over on the north side and he'd see her.

"Judith," he crooned again. Slowly, carefully, she edged herself toward the building. She'd landed about halfway out on the deck, dangling over the river, and the building side might offer some haven. At least protection from Harry's eyes.

Shit, Harry's eyes were made of Ping Pong balls! The whole situation was unbelievably macabre. What in God's name was going on?

"Judith." The singsong notes came again, rippling across her backbone like a rusty razor. She moved faster, hand over hand, hoping against hope that the sound of the turbine would drown out any noise of her scrabbling toward safety. There were orange iron supports holding up the balcony. If she could just reach them, she could crawl underneath the base of the balcony and hide there, pressed up against the building.

In her panic one sweaty hand slipped. She was dangling by a rapidly weakening hand over the deadly turbine and the water below. Had Lacey gone through this? Or had her death been quick and clean, a free-fall to eternity?

Lacey had been a born victim. Judith was a survivor, dammit. She wasn't going to fall into that hydro system; she wasn't going to let a puppet murder her, for God's sake. She was going to make it to safety and hide there until Ryan showed up to save her.

She swung her body, reaching up, but her hand missed the decking. The creature was at the western edge now, calling her. She swung again, and this time her fingers caught, so that once more she had two hands supporting her weight. And then she moved, hand over hand, as fast as she could to the iron supports.

The muscles in her arms were screaming with agony when she finally released her grip and scrambled onto one of the supports. She tucked herself in, huddling on the narrow metal beam, just as Harry's voice floated down above her. "Judith," he crooned. "Princess."

It was uncontrollable, the small whimper of pain and despair that came from her mouth before she clamped her bruised hands over her face. No one called her princess, no one but Ryan. Ryan should have been in the factory, waiting for her. Despite her superstitious terror, she knew perfectly well that the creature on the balcony wasn't a huge, animated puppet, but a human, hiding in a costume. She'd seen full-size costumes at the museum exhibit. Doubtless there were others stashed away.

There was only one person at The Puppet Factory who was as tall as the monster stalking her. No one else even came close. No matter how much she wanted to deny it, how many excuses she tried to come up with, the answer was clear and unavoidable. Ryan Smith had tried to kill her. Ryan Smith was a deranged murderer.

It was unavoidable and unacceptable. She couldn't be in love with a man who had seduced her with such intensity and skill, and then find herself his victim the next day. It was too perverse, too cruel even to contemplate.

She was suddenly very cold. The narrow steel could support her, but just barely, and only if she curled herself into a very small piece of humanity. She needed to do that. She wasn't going anywhere until she was certain she'd be safe. If that meant waiting until working hours on Monday, so be it. She'd survive. She always did. Even if right now she wasn't completely sure that she wanted to.

She drew a deep breath, willing the fight back into her ravaged soul. And then she wrapped her arms around her shivering body, dropped her face against her knees and prepared to wait.

WHEN RYAN WOKE UP, it was with only the distant memory of pain. The loft was dark with evening shadows; the old-fashioned wind-up alarm clock by the bed read seven-thirty. An hour past the time he was supposed to meet Judith. At least he'd had the forethought to give her a key. But why hadn't she braved the freight elevators and woken him up?

Damn. If only he hadn't had that headache. He should have

sweated it out, not resorted to the minipharmacy inside his medicine chest. He should have settled for aspirin, but he didn't have anything that mundane, and he hadn't realized Demerol would pack quite such a wallop. It left him fuzzy-headed, with strange, shadowy nightmares flirting with the edges of his consciousness.

She was probably fuming. Except that Judith didn't fume, didn't sulk, thank God. She might very well punch him, but she wouldn't sulk.

He hopped over to the window as he pulled his second sneaker on. No sign of her Mercedes, but she'd been having trouble with it. Maybe she'd come in a taxi.

She was probably down on the second floor tinkering with the Roberts 450. Or messing with one of the VCRs. Her talent for machinery fascinated and enchanted him. When it came to anything more complex than turning on a radio or driving a car, he was a hopeless idiot. All those knobs and wires and motors made perfect sense to her, just as the complexity of the puppets was second nature to him.

The freight elevator had a call button on the fifth floor only. He pushed it, edgy and impatient.

Nothing happened. He pushed it again, cursing slightly under his breath, bouncing from one foot to the other. He wouldn't blame Judith for being livid if the freight elevator had chosen today, of all days, to give up the ghost. It had always run smoothly, one of the few pieces of equipment that was reliable, but he'd found you couldn't trust anything mechanical.

But if the elevator was broken, Judith would probably have fixed it. Or at least have taken it apart and be in the midst of tinkering with it. He'd told her he was taking her out somewhere special for dinner, so she'd probably be wearing one of her Grace Kelly dresses. And it would be covered with filth, she'd have that omnipresent streak of grease across one patrician cheekbone, and he might very well have to strip her clothes off and make love to her until neither of them even thought about food or restaurants or elevators.

The elevator was definitely not working. He bounded down

the steps, unlocked the door and stepped into the deserted fourth-floor hallway, then paused for a moment. A strange whispering shivered across his soul, a warning of danger, disaster, despair. As quickly as it had come, it disappeared, leaving him shaken. And then he dismissed it. For now he wasn't going to worry about it. He wasn't going to worry about anything. He was going to concentrate on loving Judith, and tomorrow would be time enough for the ever-increasing possibility that Lacey Hollister hadn't fallen accidentally from the balcony.

Judith wasn't anywhere in the building. He'd expected to find her working, but the air conditioner was humming smoothly, the control room was dark and silent, and there was no sign that anyone had been around in the past few hours.

The double glass doors to the balcony were ajar, letting the hot air swirl inside, letting the expensive, climate-controlled air out. Ryan glared at the smoothly running form of the Roberts 450. He could almost hate the damned thing, if it weren't for the fact that it had brought Judith into his life. No, Lacey's death had brought Judith into his life, he reminded himself grimly. But the air conditioner had given her the opening she'd needed.

He didn't dare turn it off. Even though he hated the artificial air, even though there was no need to cool the room on a weekend when no one but he planned to work, he left the machine running. The last time he'd tried to turn it off, Judith had spent hours getting it to work again. She was going to be mad enough already that he'd inadvertently stood her up.

He headed back upstairs and went out on the front steps. Maybe she'd come, hadn't found him and gone to the house to see if he was there. Or maybe she'd driven back home in a rage. Either way, he was determined to find her, and if she was furious they could fight. And then they could make up.

There was a wry smile on his face as he headed down the steps and across the parking lot to the small storage building that served as a garage. It felt good to open up to someone, damned good. It felt good to have finally won her trust. At last she knew he didn't have anything to do with Lacey's death, accident or no. She trusted him, and that trust was very, very sweet.

He was whistling as he drove out of the deserted parking lot. Never once did he look back at the dark monolith of the converted mill.

IT WAS COLD, so bitterly, bitterly cold. Judith huddled on the iron support and shivered, telling herself they were still in the midst of a heat wave, telling herself it couldn't be any less than seventy-five degrees, telling herself she was warm, dammit, as the moisture from the river condensed on her skin. It had to be after nine o'clock. The sky had darkened completely.

She'd heard the sound of a car driving away and wondered whether she dared try to climb out from under the balcony and make her escape. But she hadn't moved. Some half-defined instinct warned her that her nemesis was still in the building, waiting for her. Clearly Harry hadn't been convinced she'd fallen to her death. He'd spent at least half an hour shuffling around, calling to her, leaning over the balcony to peer into the swirling current below.

What had he expected to see? Her body, floating. Blood, as she got sucked into the huge turbine Ryan had installed for manufacturing their own power. Whatever Harry had looked for, he hadn't seen it. He'd kept shuffling and calling her name in that eerie singsong voice. A voice she connected with songs about the alphabet and cookies and rubber bath toys. And monsters. How could she forget that? Hideous Harry was the foremost monster in The Puppet Factory. She had been incredibly stupid to ignore the obvious.

Finally the shuffling had stopped, and silence, thick and smothering like the air, had settled around her. Later, she couldn't tell how much later, the terrace doors had been closed, and she was alone out there. Or had they been closed behind Harry, and was he right now sitting on the deck, motionless, waiting?

Sooner or later she was going to have to move. For one

thing, her legs were falling asleep. If she didn't do something to improve her circulation, she'd fall right off the beam into the water, completing Harry's mission. And she had to go to the bathroom. Too much tension made her consider risking death for the sake of a flush toilet. The water lapping beneath her didn't help matters, either, and she spent a good hour contemplating how to accomplish such a delicate task while balancing on an iron beam.

She managed, almost falling off in the bargain, and spared only a momentary regret for the antipollution crusaders of the Hudson. And once the blissful physical relief had passed, she chalked up one more grudge against Hideous Harry.

She couldn't, wouldn't think of him as Ryan. It wasn't Ryan who had tried to kill her, who had picked her up with superhuman strength and tossed her over the balcony. It was some sick, twisted part of him, hidden deep inside, that took on the persona of Hideous Harry. Ryan was her lover. Harry was the killer.

She must have slept. She never would have thought it possible, but the hours passed, dragging so slowly that she thought she'd go mad. She was too tired to notice that the sky was slowly lightening, too tired to do more than cling to the support like a leech, counting on her muscles to do what her mind could no longer order.

The sun began to rise, reaching even underneath the balcony, and the icy dampness of her skin turned to baked sweat. One more hour, she told herself numbly. She could take it for one more hour, and then she'd climb out and face anything that awaited her.

Judith didn't hear the sound of cars driving into the parking lot on the far side of the building. She didn't hear the distant clang of the front door, or the footsteps on the upper balcony. But she did hear the double doors open on the lower balcony and felt the tremor of the decking as someone strode out onto it.

But not with Harry's shuffling pace. This person was strong, determined, and she stirred, opening her mouth to call for help.

"Judith?" Ryan's voice came from directly above her. He must be staring down into the water, she thought distantly. Looking to where they'd found Lacey. Wondering why they hadn't found her. "Judith?" His voice was filled with panic. Surely not the voice of a murderer.

She opened her mouth again, but nothing came out. Not a syllable, not a sound. She just sat there, huddled beneath the balcony, and listened. Listened as his footsteps receded; listened as tears flowed down her face, silent hot tears of despair and betrayal.

It might have been half a minute later—or perhaps half an hour—when she heard the voices. Two of them—no lone madman intent on destruction. She immediately recognized who was speaking.

"Do you think she went over the side, Sergeant?" an earnest voice inquired as heavy footsteps clomped over her head.

Another set of footsteps. "Don't see any blood, do you? She might not have even made it here last night. Remember the girl in the quarry? This one could be another victim. We'll have to set up an APB..."

Judith tried to call out, but still no sound came. She tried again, and a hoarse, croaking sound issued forth, barely audible.

"What was that?" the first voice said.

"I'm under here," she said weakly. She scrambled off the support, clinging to the underside of the balcony as she edged her way along it. "I'm here."

And then strong, capable hands were hauling her up over the railing and onto the balcony floor. Her knees gave way beneath her, and she collapsed on the decking. New decking, she thought dazedly. With no bloodstains marring the narrow planking.

"Are you all right, miss?"

All she could do was shake her head. The deck was firm and solid beneath her, and for a moment she was tempted to press her body into it. She remained in a sitting position, shivering in the early morning sunshine.

"Someone tried to kill me," she said in a raw, rusty voice.

"Who? Did you get a good look at him, miss?" The policeman's solicitude rapidly became intent curiosity.

"Yes," she said. "It was Hideous Harry." Even to her own ears that sounded absurd. "I mean, it was someone dressed up like one of the puppets. He…he chased me around the factory. I hid in one of the puppet booths, but he dragged me out of it and threw me off the balcony."

"There was no sign of a struggle, miss." Doubt was more than clear in the younger policeman's troubled voice.

"Then he must have cleaned it up!" Judith said in a high-pitched voice. "I knocked over the booth when I was struggling—I'm sure I did. They're flimsy enough. If you look harder you'll probably see some damage."

"We'll do that, miss. What were you doing under the balcony?"

"I told you, Harry…whoever it was threw me over."

"And you just managed to catch yourself." The sergeant was openly skeptical now. "Fortunate for you, miss."

They heard him coming. A cold hard knot of dread formed in Judith's stomach, and she gathered all her waning determination to pull herself to her feet. She was standing, unsteadily enough, when Ryan stormed through the double glass doors.

He stopped short, and for once his expression wasn't the slightest bit enigmatic. She had no trouble at all reading his emotions. Astonishment and joy came first, and he took a step toward her, ready to fold her into his arms.

She couldn't help it. She flinched, and the light went out of his eyes. He halted, staring at her, knowing she must have heard him calling her, knowing she hadn't answered but had stayed hidden, hiding from him. His face closed up, and he became the Ryan she had first met, austere and distant. The pain that sliced through her was worse than her doubts, worse than her suspicions.

She took a step toward him, but it was already too late. He'd withdrawn in on himself, shutting her out. "Princess," he drawled, and she remembered the crooning voice calling her that. "Should they be reading me my rights?"

Chapter Eighteen

The policeman beside Judith couldn't help but laugh. "Read you your rights, Ryan? You gotta be kidding. This is the young woman?"

"This is the young woman," he agreed in a cool voice. "What happened?"

"She claims she was thrown over the balcony by a puppet," the older policeman said in the tone of someone sharing a good joke.

Ryan's eyes narrowed. "Which puppet?"

"Hideous Harry," Judith said defiantly. She was feeling less and less vulnerable, and more and more furious with the obvious doubt of her rescuers. "He chased me through the building, calling my name, and when he caught me he tried to throw me into the river."

"Quite a story," the sergeant said. "Who does—what was it, Horrible Harry?"

"Hideous Harry," Ryan corrected. "And most of us can do his voice—he's one of the easiest."

The sergeant scratched his head. "Has Miss Daniels worked here for a long time? Is her testimony reliable?"

Judith's jaw dropped in astounded fury. This was how Lacey's death had been glossed over. The local police were so awed by Ryan, so determined not to inconvenience him, that they'd ignored a murder on their doorstep. Just as they seemed bound and determined to ignore an almost murder.

"She's been here three weeks," Ryan said. "She's a reporter looking for a story."

"A reporter, eh?" the older policeman said in a tone of heavy disapproval. "I've just about had my fill of reporters during the past two months."

Judith looked at the three of them, the two sour-faced policemen and the distant Ryan. "Tough," she snapped, anger giving her renewed energy. "Someone tried to kill me, and you're damned well going to try to find out who. Now, are you planning to take my statement here, or shall we go to police headquarters?"

"Whatever you want, Miss Daniels," the older man said, not the slightest bit intimidated. "Joe can take your testimony right now, if you're sure you want to push it."

"I'm sure." She started off after the younger man, but Ryan's voice stopped her.

"Where's your car?" He sounded no more than casually interested.

"Parked down the road." She wouldn't meet his eyes. She couldn't bear to see the madness lurking there.

"When you've finished I'll give you a ride to it."

"No." Her refusal was automatic and rude.

He only smiled, and Judith felt that too-familiar wrenching inside her. He'd been testing her, giving her one last chance to trust him. And she'd failed.

But what if she was wrong? What if it hadn't been Ryan in that costume, shuffling after her in the deserted building? But no one else came close to Ryan's imposing height. No one else called her princess.

"I'm sure the police can give me a ride to my car," she said.

"I'm sure they can," he replied evenly. And he turned his back on her and walked away.

It took the policeman forever to take her statement. Everything she said they questioned and requestioned, with those dubious expressions on their faces. Finally Joe slapped his book shut. "We'll be in touch, miss."

"I certainly hope so," Judith snapped. "Don't you think it's just a little too suspicious, with one woman dying here only a month ago and another one found in a quarry?"

The sergeant was suddenly all attention. "What makes you think there's a connection between the quarry murderer and your so-called puppet killer?"

"What makes you think there isn't?" she countered.

He sighed. "Come on, Joe. Let's drop this reporter—" he made "reporter" sound like a nasty word "—off at her car and get back to the station." He glared at Joe's report book. "Damned paperwork," he muttered under his breath.

They dropped her at the car as if they couldn't wait to get rid of her. The Mercedes was where she'd left it, unlocked and with the key in the ignition. Of course the wretched thing chose not to start, but Judith just sat there, turning the key, until finally the engine sprang to life. She took off with a spurt of gravel, speeding down the road with a complete disregard for the policeman following in her wake.

She didn't want to think, didn't want to feel, didn't want to do anything but stand in a hot shower, eat a hot meal and climb into bed. She couldn't face the doubts, the guilt, the consequences. Right now all she wanted to do was hide.

Micki's Escort was gone from the driveway when Judith pulled in, and she breathed an uncertain sigh of relief. On the one hand, she didn't want to have to launch into detailed explanations and answer numerous questions. On the other hand, she didn't particularly feel like being alone. But she had no choice in the matter. For one childish moment Judith longed for her parents, for her apartment in Philadelphia, for the comfort and safety of home. But her parents were in Hilton Head, her apartment was closed up, and now wasn't the time to turn and run. She had to see this thing through to its conclusion, even if she didn't think she could bear the results.

She'd left her purse under the seat during her sojourn at The Puppet Factory, and she reached for it now, pulling it out into the sunlight.

She could feel the scream start in the back of her throat, and she clamped her teeth down on her lips to keep from letting it out. Wrapped around the leather strap was the empty husk of one of the puppets. Hideous Harry.

RYAN STOOD LOOKING OUT his fifth-floor window as Judith followed the police to their patrol car. She didn't bother to look back; she couldn't feel his eyes staring at her as she walked away.

He wanted to dwell on his sense of betrayal, his rage at her lack of trust. He wanted to brood on the injustice of it all, on the tragedy of having finally found someone he could love, only to have his tentative emotions thrown in his face.

But he couldn't do it. Later he could view himself as the noble, misunderstood hero. Right now there were more important things to worry about. Such as whether he'd been a fool all these years. Whether his blind loyalty was indirectly responsible for the death of who knew how many women. And what the hell he was going to do about it.

He couldn't jump to any conclusions. He'd let the police do that, by assuming Judith was lying to create a marketable story. And she might have been doing exactly that. She'd been devious and manipulative before; maybe this was all part of her master plan.

But, unlike the police, he didn't really think so. There were too many questions, too many unexplained happenings, that were finally falling into place. Yet he wouldn't take any action until he had proof.

He moved away from the window and headed for the telephone. He needed some answers, and he couldn't afford to wait any longer for them. He reached for the phone book, and a moment later he was dialing.

HARRY SHUFFLED across the basement floor. They'd finally left, Ryan had gone back to the top floor, and he was alone once more.

He'd failed. He'd somehow known that he had. He'd missed

that sense of satisfaction, of release, that should have come when Judith died. But there'd been no sign of her. He'd waited all through the night, listening, hoping, but she'd been too clever for him. It wasn't until the others had come, and he had gone back into hiding, that she'd appeared.

He'd been too far away to hear anything, yet he knew she'd left with the police. Maybe she'd leave Ryan alone now.

But even if she did, that still wouldn't earn her a reprieve. She was a sinful, evil whore, and she must be punished. She knew that now. She'd seen him, and she'd find him following her. Under the seat of her car, in her bedroom, wherever or whenever she least expected it, she'd find him watching her. And the next time she wouldn't escape.

JUDITH SLEPT almost twenty-four hours straight. Micki came home sometime during the night, tried to wake her up and failed. The phone rang, and Judith tossed in her sleep, nightmares haunting her, covering her in a cold sweat but never waking her.

It was nine-seventeen when she finally opened her eyes. She lay there for a long moment, trying to decide what to do. She could go to work, pretend nothing had happened, and wait for Ryan to make his next move. She could run like hell, leaving the whole filthy mess up to those incredibly dense policemen to untangle when the next woman was murdered. Or she could turn over, bury her head under the pillow and go back to sleep.

The last option seemed preferable. Her whole body ached from her night on the iron beam. Her arms felt like lead, the muscles stretched and pulled from supporting 135 pounds from a balcony deck. Her head ached, the back of her neck was stiff with tension, and her legs were cramped.

The door of her room slammed open. "You awake yet?" Micki demanded.

"I would have thought you'd left for work already," Judith said, dragging herself into a sitting position and reaching for the Motrin.

"And miss all the juicy details of the attack of the crazed puppets? Not on your life. I got dibs on the movie rights."

"Micki," Judith said wearily, "there are times when your sympathy unmans me."

"That's exactly what I'd like to do." Micki came into the room and perched on the sagging bed. "Unman you, that is. So who do you think did it? Ryan? Sweet old Franz? My money's on Ma Carter."

Judith glared at her housemate's cigarette, but Micki was unabashed. "I didn't realize anyone believed me. Anyway, how did you hear about it?"

"We all know. Ryan's called a meeting for ten o'clock this morning—he had Bessie phone everyone to tell them to be on time, for once. She told me the juicy gossip. So come on. What really happened? Did you get raped? Was Hideous Harry green fur all over?"

"Micki, get the hell out of my room. Or I'll sic him on you."

"Sure thing. You can fill me in during the drive." She rose, stretched her lithe body, then paused. "What's that doing here?" she walked over to the battered armchair and held up the lifeless form of a Hideous Harry puppet.

Judith stared at it in numb dismay. "I thought I threw that out," she said in a low voice. "I didn't bring it in here yesterday morning—I'm sure I didn't."

For once Micki said nothing, just looked at her curiously. She walked out of the room, the puppet under her arm. Less than a minute later she returned, her olive skin a sickly ashen color. "You mean this one?" she said, holding up a second puppet.

Judith began to shake. "This isn't your sick sense of humor, is it? It isn't funny, not in the slightest."

Micki shook her head. "I wish it were. Because this means someone was in here, and that makes me very uncomfortable. Unless you really are lying, trying to get a story."

"You heard about that, too?"

"Everybody knows everything—that Spacey Lacey was

your old college buddy and that you're a hotshot reporter who infiltrated the ranks, looking for a story."

"I'm not a hotshot reporter," Judith said. "I write a syndicated fix-it column. Judith the Jack of All Trades."

"Fancy that. I've heard of you. Did you find what you were looking for?"

"I don't know. The police and Ryan seem to think I made it all up. What do you think?"

Micki watched her out of dark, unblinking eyes. "As a matter of fact, I think you're telling the truth. And I'm not sure that Ryan doesn't think so, too." She stared down at the puppets in her small, capable hands. "You know, I never really liked Harry. He always gave me the willies. I wish Franz had never invented him."

"I forgot that he was Franz's creation. He's been a part of The Puppet Factory for so long that I keep thinking he was Ryan's."

"No, he's Franz's, even though the old guy doesn't do him too often anymore. It's too easy for the rest of us to fill in." Micki shook her head. "There's one suspect you can rule out. Franz Himml is the nicest guy in the world. He'd no more hurt a living being than he'd fly to the moon. He's almost like one of the puppets himself. And he's the only one who really believes in them, just a little. As the rest of us become more jaded, he becomes more idealistic. I tell you, the man's turning into a saint."

"I don't think it's Franz, Micki." Judith climbed out of bed and stripped off her clothes, knowing it was useless to plead modesty and order Micki out.

"Geez, willya look at those bruises!" Micki exclaimed. "Did you show them to the police? I bet then they'd believe you."

"I didn't feel like doing a striptease," Judith said, putting on clean underwear. "Besides, the way they were acting, they probably thought I'd done it to myself."

Micki leaned against the doorjamb. "So who do you think it is? If it's not Franz, who's your leading suspect?"

Judith tugged a voluminous cotton shirt over her head, taking an unreasonably long time with it. When her face finally emerged, her expression was blank. "I have no idea."

She shouldn't have underestimated Micki. The woman stared at Judith, a slow-burning anger filling her dark eyes. "You think it's Ryan," she said in an accusing voice. "You sleep with the man, tell me you're in love with him, and then decide he's a murderer. I guess your sense of loyalty began and ended with Spacey Lacey."

Judith sighed. "Micki, I don't know what to think. All I know is the Hideous Harry that was stalking me was about six and a half feet tall. There's no one at The Puppet Factory who comes close to that height. No one but Ryan."

"You bitch," Micki said in an unemotional voice. "I'll be more than happy to prove you wrong. And I can tell you one thing—your stupidity has wrecked anything between the two of you. He must know you suspect him."

Judith nodded, keeping her misery banked down.

"Then it's over, lady. And that's fine by me. We'll go back there today, and I'll help you find out who threw you and your airheaded buddy over the railing. After that, you just might want to do the honors yourself."

Judith stared at her. She wished she could summon up the energy for righteous indignation, for a spirited defense of her suspicions, for something to say. But she couldn't. She felt as low and slimy as Micki considered her to be. And all her doubts and justifications, no matter how rational they were, sounded hollow in her own mind.

"I'd appreciate your help," she said softly. "All I want is the truth."

"We'll find it," Micki promised. "And then you'll get your elegant little tail out of here, right? Back to Philadelphia? Because you can be damned sure Ryan won't want you around anymore."

"I'll leave," Judith agreed.

"Then I'll help. Get moving, Judith. We're going to be late." She tossed the empty puppet forms on the unmade bed.

JUDITH HAD GEARED HERSELF UP for nothing. It had taken all her self-possession and not a little courage to walk back into The Puppet Factory, where she found herself the center of everyone's curious attention. Everyone's but one.

Ryan was gone. Steve was sitting on a table in the lounge, charming and at ease as he outlined the new company policy. Until the current "incident," as he termed it, was cleared up, no less than three people should be together at all times. No one was to go anywhere with only one other employee, not until Ryan returned.

And that was that. Judith sat there, an odd mixture of relief and unhappiness washing over her. Ryan had believed her, after all, enough to institute this precaution. Maybe Micki was right; maybe she'd been incredibly wrong.

It was a strange, uncomfortable sort of day. Franz was very quiet, working with one of the young puppeteers on mastering Madame Rinaldi. Steve was bouncing off the walls, all brilliant charm and a look of desperation in his eyes that only a fool could miss—and Judith was no fool. Micki ignored her; the rest of the people watched her obliquely, until Judith had no choice but to retreat to the quiet of the fourth floor. There she had to face only two pairs of curious, disapproving eyes.

She wasn't even sure Ma would let her in, but the woman merely looked up, frowned and returned to her paperwork.

"Is there anything I can do?" Judith asked hesitantly, standing in the doorway.

Ma pursed her lips and glared. "You can get the hell out of Miller's Junction and leave us alone," she said flatly, pushing her chair away from the desk. "Or next time maybe you won't be so lucky." Then she rose and strode out of the office, shoving Judith aside as she went.

A dead silence prevailed. Bessie looked up from her computer, a sly, excited expression on her face. "You mustn't mind Ma," she said in her soft little voice. "She's so worried about Ryan. He wouldn't tell her where he was going, and he's never done that before."

"No one knows where he's gone?"

Bessie smiled. "I didn't say that. I made a few phone calls. I know exactly where he went. He went to Nevada."

Nevada, Judith thought. Gambler's paradise. There was only one gambler in The Puppet Factory, one person with a crushing addiction and a desperate manner. Oh, God, could it possibly be Steve and not Ryan, after all?

She knew her dismay showed on her face, but she couldn't summon the effort to hide it. "Thanks," she said numbly.

Bessie smiled again. "My pleasure," she cooed.

Chapter Nineteen

It wasn't until two days later that Judith and Micki remembered the basement. They had ignored Ryan's edict; keeping three people together all the time wasn't feasible when two of them lived together. An uneasy truce had sprung up between the women fostered by their shared determination to find out exactly what had happened.

There was no sign of Ryan, no word from him, but policemen kept appearing in odd corners of the factory. Sometimes it was Joe and his sour-faced sergeant; sometimes it was a different, less skeptical pair. No direct questions were asked, but the police were definitely watching. And Judith had the ironic satisfaction of knowing they were there because Ryan had summoned them.

"Why would there be full-size puppet costumes?" Judith asked, spooning up the last of her yogurt. She and Micki had remained behind in the lounge while people drifted back to work. Franz, Jimmy and Melvin were over in the corner, out of earshot. Micki lit up her third cigarette with a trace of defiance.

"There are a whole bunch of them. The Ice Follies had several sets made for their show in '84. The American Ballet Theatre used some for a ballet just last year. And full-size costumes were used for television specials and the theater. Billy, Fafnir and Madame Rinaldi are big business."

"Where would the costumes be now?"

"Down in the basement along with everything else." Micki blew a stream of smoke in Judith's face. "Wanna go look?"

Judith waved the smoke away. "I want to do something. Every piece of equipment in this place has been working perfectly, Ma Carter just threatens me if I show up on the fourth floor, and I'm going quietly crazy."

"Not that quietly," Micki observed.

"If only the damned heat would end. I bet the murder rate rises during this kind of weather."

"I imagine it does. Well, you sure you trust me? Just because I haven't strangled you yet doesn't mean I haven't been sorely tempted."

Judith grinned sourly. "I think you'd have a hard time picking me up and heaving me over a balcony. I outweigh you by about thirty pounds."

"I thought madness gave one enormous strength."

"That's right." All Judith's cynical humor vanished. "He'd have to be crazy, wouldn't he?"

"I expect so. In the meantime…"

"Ladies." Franz appeared beside them, his gentle, lined face creased in worry. "You're not supposed to be just two together. We must all be careful, very careful."

Judith smiled up at him. "Don't worry, Franz. We'll be fine. We trust each other."

He shook his head, his shaggy eyebrows waggling. "Sometimes trust is not enough," he said heavily. "Be careful, ladies. Please." And he shuffled after the retreating figures of Jimmy and Melvin.

"He's such a dear," Micki said with a sigh. "This is all very hard on him. It probably reminds him of his childhood."

"I beg your pardon?"

"Franz comes from Minolte, in Alsace-Lorraine."

"Minolte? Why does that sound familiar?"

Micki stubbed out her cigarette. "Because it was the scene of a horrible Nazi atrocity. The male population had gone to war after Germany invaded, and the women remained at home. Naturally they formed the resistance. But they went too far.

When one of the German officers raped a young woman, they killed him. And in retaliation the Nazis shot every so-called decent woman in the town, no matter what her age was. The only people who were left were boys and old men. And the town whores. I guess the Nazis weren't into cutting off their noses to spite their faces.''

"And Franz was one of those boys?'' Judith asked, her heart aching for him.

"Franz was one of them. He was about thirteen years old, and he had to help bury his mother and three sisters.'' Micki shook her head. "It's no wonder he likes to lose himself in the puppets. What a childhood for someone to survive! But I bet you don't know anything about that kind of life. You've been pampered and protected all your life.''

"Cut it out, Micki,'' Judith said. "I'm not about to justify my existence to you or anyone else. Are we going to look for those costumes, or do you want to sit here and snipe at me?''

"We're going to look for those costumes,'' Micki replied, rising. "Do we take anyone along with us?''

Judith shook her head. "I don't think so. What if we pick the wrong one? The creature that threw me over the balcony was more than capable of dealing with both of us.''

"I thought you were convinced it was Ryan. As far as I know, he's still in parts unknown.''

"At this point I'm even ready to consider Franz as the killer.''

"That's an improvement, at least. Though I don't know if Ryan will thank you for suspecting his closest friend.''

"Ryan's not going to thank me for anything but getting out of here. And I'm going to do exactly that, as soon as I find out who murdered Lacey.''

"I know. Why do you think I'm so eager to help you? I want you out of here just as much as Ryan does. We'll find the answers. We might find them in the next hour, if we're lucky.''

"If we're lucky,'' Judith echoed, getting to her feet. "Or maybe we'll only find more questions.''

The basement hadn't improved since Judith's last visit there. It was still a jumbled, disorganized mess. The two women worked diligently, pawing through artifacts of twenty years of puppetry, always with an eye over their shoulder for an errant monster or two. No one bothered them.

The search took more than an hour. The costumes were in the northwest corner of the basement, next to the compact power plant. Judith could hear the water rushing outside and the muted roar of the turbine as it turned the flow of the Hudson into electrical energy. She looked down at her shaking hands in wry disgust. It would be a long while before she got over the events of last weekend, the hours spent huddling on an iron beam, staring down into the murderous swirl of the lower Hudson.

She almost screamed when she saw the Ping Pong-ball eyes. After her initial hysteria had subsided, she managed to push the boxes out of the way, then call Micki in a calm voice as she pulled the yards of purple fur free.

It was the empty form of Fafnir, the forked tongue slack in the furry jaws, the long arms hanging loose, the tail dragging on the floor. She tossed the puppet to Micki, then reached for the others, for Billy and Madame Rinaldi and the Green Goddesses. There was no sign of Harry.

"This must be where it came from," she said, pointing at the pile of lifeless costumes on the floor.

Micki was holding up Fafnir, peering at the puppet curiously. "Those were the television costumes worn by dancers during a production number. I remember they had a hell of time trying to see."

Judith grew very still, staring at the limp, oversize puppet. "Where do their eyes go?"

"In the neck, of course. People can't very well look through Ping Pong balls, can they? The wearer's head goes in the neck, and the head of the puppet is sort of like a hat..." Micki paused, meeting Judith's stricken eyes. "Oho," she murmured. "And it makes people of average height almost seven feet tall. That's what you were basing your suspicions on, wasn't it?

The Harry who chased you was tall, and you thought he had to be Ryan.''

''Put the costume on, Micki.''

''I don't have to. None of these would fit him. If he wore a puppet costume, he'd end up being the size of a Kareem Abdul Jabbar. And your murderous Harry wasn't that big, was he?''

Judith shook her head. ''He was only about six and a half feet tall.''

''You really blew it this time, Daniels,'' Micki said with malicious glee. ''Ryan's the only really tall person working here. It's usually too hard to fit big people into a booth. So the one person it *couldn't* have been was Ryan.''

''He called me princess.''

''Who did? The puppet? That doesn't prove anything. Half the people here have heard Ryan call you that. Face it, Judith. When you screw up, you don't do it halfway. What are you going to say to him?''

''I don't know. Somehow I don't think 'I'm sorry' will sit too well,'' Judith said, stepping over the pile of puppets.

Micki tossed Fafnir on top of one of the Green Goddesses, the bean-sprout hair fanning out around them. ''No, I don't think it will, either,'' she said, her voice rich with satisfaction.

''But one thing I can do,'' Judith said. ''I can have the police come and see these puppets. They thought I was crazy when I said a full-size puppet was chasing me. At least this provides an explanation. Maybe they can even find fingerprints....''

''I doubt it. Anyway, the police left just before lunch, and it's now—'' she checked her Swatch ''—a little after four. You'll have to call them to come back.''

''It'll be worth it. Finally there's some proof.''

''Such as it is,'' Micki sniffed. ''You'd better call from the fourth floor. You don't want anyone to overhear you.''

''What about Ma and Bessie?''

''It might make sense to suspect everyone, but I doubt either of them could throw you over a balcony, much as they'd both like to. Don't worry, I'll keep you company. If it comes to a battle between Ma and Bessie and you and me, I'd put my money on us anytime."

Neither of them felt the eyes that watched them leave the jumbled corner of the basement. There was a dark, nearly empty room there, hidden behind a pile of old scenery, its only source of light the unblinking glare of a video monitor. Neither of them heard the minute shuffling sound, the muted cough, the odd, snuffling noise.

Harry watched them go, his hands clenched so tightly that the cloth covering them threatened to rip. Sinners, both of the women. He could wait no longer. First Judith, tonight.

And tomorrow it would be Micki. He had hoped to spare her, but not after this. He had no choice now. She was a whore like all the others, and she must be punished. Destroyed, as the others had been, and sent to meet her justice.

He hoped God would give him the strength for these awesome tasks. He was growing weary, and his mission was growing larger. He just needed enough energy for the last two. Then he could rest.

Until the call came to him again. And he would have to rise up and meet it, dispensing judgment and vengeance as he was told to do. To somehow make the past right.

In THE END Judith had to brave the fourth floor alone. She and Micki were passing the third-floor workroom when Jimmy and Melvin signaled to Micki. "Keep us company, will you?" Jimmy begged, his large brown eyes shadowed. "Franz had to go make a phone call, and you know we're supposed to be at least three together at all times."

"Jimmy," Micki said in an exasperated voice, "you and Melvin live together. You spend anywhere from twelve to sixteen hours together, and neither of you has killed the other."

"We want to do everything Ryan asks," Melvin said in an aggrieved tone. "And if he wants three of us together, then that's what we're going to do." He grabbed Micki's wrist. "Come on—we can do the Green Goddesses for a while. I'll even let you be Roka. You always looked good in blue. Jimmy'll be Riviera, and I'll do Catalina again.''

Judith waved her on. ''I'll be fine. Bessie and Ma will make my threesome.'' As Micki hesitated, Judith said, ''Don't tell me you're worried about me?''

That was enough to move Micki. ''Check with me after you call,'' she muttered, following the puppeteers into the noisy clatter of the workroom.

The final flight of stairs to the fourth floor was open and well lit. There was no place for a murderous puppet to hide, no spot in which danger could lurk. She was perfectly safe, Judith told herself firmly. Perfectly safe.

Ma had the air conditioning up on ten against the renewed fervor of the heat wave. Bessie was huddled over her computer, a thick cardigan sweater covering her thin arms, and the brief look she cast up at Judith was both shy and sly.

''Speak of the devil,'' Ma said, hanging up the phone. ''I was just going to come looking for you.''

''Were you?''

''I've got a message for you. From Ryan.''

Judith's heart slammed to a halt, and then began a slow, heavy beating. ''Yes?''

''He's back,'' Ma said. ''He wants you to meet him out at the house.''

''Did he say why?''

''Nope. And I wasn't about to ask him.'' Ma stared at her out of flinty eyes. ''Are you going?''

''When did he want me?''

''As soon as you can make it.''

Judith just stood there, considering her options. Unlike Ma, she knew perfectly well why Ryan had sent a message for her to meet him at his deserted house. He was giving her one last chance to trust him. And there was no way in hell she was going to blow it this time.

Her proof of his guilt had been circumstantial; her proof of his innocence was equally so. She'd be a fool to go. She should call the police and ask them to search the basement, comb through everything. With half a dozen people working on it, they should come up with something that would lead them to the killer.

But she wasn't going to do the wise, sensible thing. She was going to leave without saying a word about the basement, show up at his house and hope and pray that she was finally right to trust him. And if she was wrong, she wasn't sure she minded the consequences.

She looked out the window. The sky was unnaturally dark, with black, roiling clouds churning overhead. A break in the weather had been promised for days, but it had failed to materialize. Now it might finally arrive, in the guise of one hell of a storm.

"I'll leave now," she said. "If you see Micki, tell her where I've gone."

The two women sat in silence and watched her go.

"Don't you think you should have told her where that message came from?" Bessie said finally. "Just in case?"

Ma glared at the younger woman, her usual hostility tinged with an unexpected trace of guilt. "If I can't trust Franz," she said, "who can I trust?"

"No one at all," Bessie replied. Her eyes met Ma's in a long, knowing look. "Maybe you'd better tell Steve." She turned back to her keyboard.

With a heavy sigh, Ma Carter reached for the phone.

JUDITH COULD FEEL the eyes watching her as she walked out to the car. She stopped and stared back at the wall of windows at least three times, not caring if that reaction demonstrated her paranoia. There were no faces in the windows, no shadows brooding over her.

It had to be the weather. Once more lightning was shimmering through the sky, followed by the sullen rumble of thunder. They needed a storm, a drenching, cleansing rain to wash away the evil and the dread. Tonight they just might get one.

Her car door was unlocked, as usual. Sitting on the driver's seat was a Hideous Harry doll, its long arms wrapped around the throat of Madame Rinaldi. But that puppet wasn't wearing Madame's normal silks and satins. Instead it was dressed in faded denims and khaki. And despite the brassiness of the hair and the painted-on florid makeup, it bore an uncanny resemblance to Judith.

During the two days Ryan had been gone there'd been no more puppets. Now that he'd returned, another reminder had been left in her possession. Judith yanked the dolls from the front seat and threw them across the parking lot. They lodged under a rusty Datsun, and she sincerely hoped the bald tires would squash them.

She started the car, just as another streak of lightning snaked across the sky. Her hands shaking, she grasped the leather-covered steering wheel. He isn't the killer, Judith told herself with an attempt at remaining calm. I know he's not. I always knew it, deep in my heart. I couldn't have fallen in love with a disturbed murderer. And even though I'm scared spitless, the only way I can prove I don't think he did it is by showing up at that damned mansion with no one to protect me.

The killer had to be Steve. While the puppeteer was splendidly muscled, he was definitely a few inches shy of six feet. He could wear one of those costumes and easily tower over her.

Ryan had gone to Las Vegas, obviously to check out Steve's gambling problem. Judith couldn't begin to imagine the connection between high-stakes gambling and the murder of young women, but one must surely exist. And Ryan must have found that connection.

She drove slowly through the darkening afternoon. Rush-hour traffic, such as it was in the mainly rural area of Miller's Junction, had begun, and the oncoming cars had their lights on against the unnatural darkness. She reached over and flipped on the radio, but all she could get was static from the electric storm, so she turned the radio off, cursing the fact that she'd never bothered to put a cassette player in the car. She would have given a great deal for some soothing music just then. Brahms, perhaps. Or Todd Rundgren.

There was no sign of Ryan's aging Toyota outside the massive front door of his estate, but Judith hadn't expected to see it. He usually kept it behind the house. He was a man who valued his privacy, his aloneness. He'd let her in for a little while. Would he do so again?

The house seemed dark and deserted, even though Judith knew he must be inside. She sat in her parked car for a long moment, marshaling her reserves, trying to decide on the proper opening statement. Such as, "Hi, there, I didn't really think you were a crazed murderer," or the more direct "Let's go to bed."

Neither of them seemed quite right. Maybe she should simply keep her mouth shut and listen for once in her life.

The first drops of rain were spattering down when she got out of her car. She ran across the crushed white stone of the driveway, prepared to pound on the door for Ryan to let her in.

The door was already opening as she reached the front step. She dashed inside without looking and wiped the rain water from her face. The door shut behind her, plunging the hall into darkness. She peered around, ready to thank Ryan for letting her in.

The figure in the shadows was too short and too broad to be Ryan. Panic swept through her, holding her motionless, as Franz Himml stepped out of the darkness.

Chapter Twenty

He was staring at her, his eyes bright with concern, his gray-white hair shining in the eerie, storm-laden light filtering through the windows above the front door.

"You shouldn't be here, Judith," he admonished. "You especially shouldn't be here alone."

Judith felt almost weak with relief. "God, you scared me for a moment, Franz. I thought you were… I mean, I thought…"

"You thought I was the madman who's been stalking you," he said gently. "I almost wish I were. Because I would never hurt you, you must know that. If it were me, you'd be safe. As it is…" He let the sentence trail meaningfully, and Judith could barely suppress a shudder of apprehension.

Quickly she stifled it. Steve was back at the Factory—he had no idea she'd come out here. "Where's Ryan?"

"I don't know. I had a message to meet him here. You too?"

Judith nodded, reaching for the light switch by the door. Despite her relief that it was only Franz, her peace of mind would improve tenfold if the house had a little illumination.

Nothing happened when she threw the switch. "The storm must have knocked out the power," Franz said. He looked over his shoulder. "It's getting very dark."

"Yes, it is. Why don't we look for some candles or a flashlight? Better yet, why don't we look for Ryan? He must be here somewhere."

"I shall look for Ryan," Franz said in his formal way. "You can find candles?"

Judith shrugged. "I imagine they're in the kitchen." She paused, not quite knowing how to phrase her next words. "Where was Steve when you left?"

There was no mistaking the look of surprise and regret that moved across his face. "He was busy with the green booth. Something wasn't working right, he said. Why? Do you think he might have something to do with this horrible thing?"

"Oh, no," Judith lied.

Franz nodded grimly, unconvinced. "I'll look for Ryan. You can find the kitchen in all this darkness?"

Thunder rumbled in moody counterpoint to their conversation. "I expect so. If I have any trouble I'll scream for help."

"An odd choice of words," Franz said. "You'll have no reason to scream."

"No, I'm sure I won't."

The kitchen, with its one long window overlooking the pool, was brighter than the hallways. Judith leaned against the sink, staring out at the now torrential downpour, watching it turn the pool into a miniature ocean of angry waves. A strong wind whipped through the trees, scraping them against the house, and the sound of rain pouring on the roofs was oddly nerve-racking. Usually she found the sound of summer rain on a rooftop to be one of the most soothing sounds there was. Not today.

She turned her back on the window and stared around her. Everything was perfect in here, from the restaurant stove to the walk-in refrigerator to the wine closet with its key still resting in the lock. Now where in the hell would someone keep candles in a kitchen as well equipped as this one?

She was bending over a drawer, rummaging through it, when the back door opened. It took her a moment to notice, so well oiled were the hinges, so well hung was the door. But the swirl of rain-wet breezes blew against her legs, and she whirled around.

Steve Lindstrom's face was hidden in the shadows of the

room, but there was no mistaking him, even in the bright yellow slicker and with his hair plastered down by the rain.

"Thank God you're here," he said simply. "What the hell did you think you were doing, coming out here alone? I couldn't believe it when Ma called me."

Judith remained very still. A pair of gardening shears was in the drawer behind her, but she didn't fancy reenacting *Dial M for Murder*. There was always the strong possibility she wouldn't even slow Steve down, even if she managed something as distasteful as lodging the shears in his throat. She allowed her glance to slide toward the wine closet; then she met his gaze with a bright, innocent smile.

"Why should Ma call you? And I'm not alone. Ryan's here," she said.

"Ryan?" He began stripping off his rain gear. The rugby shirt he wore more than emphasized his muscular build, and Judith knew she'd have no chance at all if it came to a physical battle. "I'm glad about that. I hadn't realized he was back. What are you doing out here in the kitchen?"

"Looking for candles. In case you hadn't noticed, the power's out."

"It's out all over the place," he said, coming closer. She ordered herself not to move, not to flinch, as she took a quick look at his hands. They were broad, square-fingered and probably very strong. Hell, she already knew they were very strong. She'd felt them wrapped around her throat. "Any luck with the candles?"

"I think they're in the wine closet," she said. "Feel like taking a look for me?"

He didn't even hesitate. "Sure thing." And reaching for the door, he stepped inside.

Two seconds later she slammed it shut behind him. She hadn't waited quite long enough, and the door banged into him, knocking him over. Agonizingly long moments went by before her shaking fingers could lock the door and pull the key out, while she tried to ignore his pounding, his shouts, his no-doubt murderous rage.

And then she ran through the darkened house screaming for Franz, the key clutched in her hand. She tripped and sprawled on the pale blue carpet, and the key went spinning from her hand. She didn't bother to look for it; she just surged to her feet and kept running.

She couldn't find Franz. He seemed to have disappeared, and as for Ryan, she had strong doubts as to whether he'd been there at all. Steve had admitted that Ma had called him. He must have set the whole thing up, convinced Ma that Ryan had left a message for Judith and Franz. They both were doomed to be his victims this time, and only pure chance had saved them.

The library was deserted, as were the living room, the den and the dining room. Where the hell could Franz have gone to? He might hear Steve pounding for help and let him out, not realizing that he was the killer. She had to find Franz and explain everything to him. Franz was such a sweet, trusting soul that he might not even believe her. But she'd make him believe her, before they called the police.

She started up the stairs. It was very dark in the windowless stairwell, and even darker at the top. Judith had to summon every ounce of her common sense to keep herself moving. The danger was locked in a closet in the kitchen. She was safe.

He was waiting for her in Ryan's bedroom. He was sitting calmly on the bed, his eyes filled with sorrow, his face illuminated by the ever-increasing flashes of lightning outside the windows. He looked up at her, his expression gentle and concerned. "I've been waiting for you." And he spoke in Hideous Harry's voice.

"For God's sake, hurry, Ryan!" Micki shrieked in his ear.

"I've got the goddamned pedal to the floor," Ryan said between clenched teeth. "We're doing eighty-three miles an hour and we're keeping only two wheels on this road. Shut up and let me drive."

"Why the hell does it have to rain now?" Micki moaned. "And so much of it. The road's practically flooded."

"The road *is* flooded," he snapped back. "How the hell could you let her out of your sight? You knew she was the one who was in the most danger. How could you have done that?"

"How could you have taken off without warning anyone of your suspicions?" Micki shot back.

"I had to have proof. I couldn't just accuse my best friend of being a murderer without some proof."

"And you found it in Las Vegas?"

"I found it in Las Vegas. And in London. And God knows where else—and all the time I never even suspected. As far as I can piece things together, it used to happen about once a year. On the anniversary of his mother's death, someone would die. A young girl. He used to pick prostitutes, women with shadowy pasts and no one to care if they died. Hell, he might have killed twice as many women as they suspect he did, maybe three times as many. And then he got worse. There was a college student in Los Angeles, a secretary in Miller's Junction. And there was Lacey."

"Let's not forget Lacey. Watch out!" Micki screeched as the car slid halfway across the road. It took Ryan precious moments to regain control, and then he was building speed again. "Listen, don't kill us getting there. Ma will have called the police—they'll probably make it there before we do."

"And that still might be too late."

Micki was silent for a moment. "You're right. Step on it."

JUDITH STARED at Franz in numb horror. "I am in deep trouble," she said out loud, not moving.

He rose and walked toward her with a slow, shuffling gait not too unlike his usual pace. Why hadn't she noticed before? she berated herself.

"I won't hurt you," he said in that eerie half croon that was totally devoid of his German accent. "I don't want to hurt you. But you must be punished. You know that. You'll thank me. You don't want to live a sinful life. And you know there's no escape but death. Death will be a release, a blessed release. It's what you've wanted, what you've been praying for," he intoned gently. "Don't run, Judith. Let me help you."

Her Reeboks were glued to the baby-blue carpet. She watched, paralyzed, as he shuffled closer, flexing his strong workman's hands in readiness. "Steve..." she managed to croak.

"Is locked in the closet. He'll never know what happened. Because you won't make a sound, will you, Judith?"

"Don't count on it. And you're lying. I know you are. You're going to kill him, too."

"Of course not!" Franz looked shocked. "We only kill the women."

It made her skin crawl to watch the face of the man she'd trusted and to hear the sweet, cartoonlike voice of a murderer coming from his mouth. She tensed her muscles. She'd have only one chance, and she'd better use it wisely. "Franz..."

"Franz isn't here," he said simply.

"Where is he?"

"He's gone. He doesn't know what I do. He couldn't live with it. But someone has to right the wrong that was done so many years ago. He can't live with that, either, with the injustice. So he lets me do it, and pretends he doesn't know what's happening. But I think he's beginning to suspect. He's been taking sleeping pills and tranquilizers so I can't get free, but I threw them away. I think I'll tell him. It's not fair that I should have to do it alone. I'll tell him after I take care of Micki."

"For God's sake, why would you want to hurt Micki?"

"I told you," he said in a tone of great patience. "I don't want to hurt anyone. But she must be punished. She's a whore, just like you, and the whores must be punished."

"But, Franz..."

"Franz isn't here, I tell you. I'm Harry." His shuffling footsteps were bringing him steadily closer, and his hands were reaching for her, stubby fingers outstretched. "This will only take a moment."

Her paralysis finally broke. "The hell it will." And she took off down the dark hallway.

He caught her at the top of the stairs, his strong hands wrapping themselves around her throat and pressing. She kicked out, breaking free, and rolled down the long flight of stairs, tucking in her head and relaxing her muscles as she'd learned to do years ago in gymnastics.

After she'd landed in one piece, she got up and didn't waste any time looking behind her, but kept running. He'd catch her in the house; as big as it was, it was too small to hide in. If she could just get outside, she'd have a chance. The rain was a heavy curtain of water, and visibility was practically nil. The lightning that was coming closer and closer was preferable to Franz's determined madness.

She spared only a reluctant glance at the wine closet. Steve was still shouting, still pounding, but the key was lost somewhere in the house, and Franz would reach her before she found it.

Judith had made it to the kitchen and was halfway through the back door when Franz caught up with her. This time her struggles did her no good. He threw himself at her, knocking her down, half in and half out of the doorway. The rain was covering her torso, feeling like warm blood, and his hands closed around her neck once more. She screamed, beating him with desperate hands, rolling in the pooling water beneath them, fighting for her life.

"Harry. Oh, Harry."

Judith thought she must be dying. That voice calling him sounded like Madame Rinaldi's arch tones. Franz lifted his face into the streaming rain, suddenly alert, and the pressure on Judith's throat lessened an infinitesimal amount.

"Harry, for heaven's sake," Billy's voice said in an irritating tone. "Get off her, willya? Don't you know she's my girl? You don't want to hurt her."

"Besides," the good Madame said, "you were supposed to be faithful to me. I tell you, Harry, my boy, that position looks completely suggestive. Get off her, or I'll be extremely cross with you."

Slowly the hands loosened, releasing her, as Franz sat back, his weary face confused. "She's been bad," he said in his Hideous Harry voice.

"We know, dear," Madame Rinaldi said soothingly. "But we mustn't punish her. The police are coming. They'll take care of her."

"The police? I don't want the police here."

"Come on, Harry," Billy said, "be a sport. We don't want to have blood on our hands, do we? If she's been bad, it's up to the police to take care of her."

Franz looked over his shoulder into the kitchen, his eyes narrowed. Judith could just barely make out the figures in the dim light, and for one horrid moment she thought there were two full-grown puppets in there. Then the lightning streaked again, illuminating Ryan and Micki, the desperation on their faces, and she breathed a sigh of relief.

Franz shook his head. He gazed down at her, his eyes bulging slightly, looking uncannily like Ping Pong balls. "She has to die," he said. Suddenly there was a knife in his hand, and Judith couldn't imagine where it had come from. She waited, mesmerized, as the cold steel moved closer.

"Harry!" Fafnir's voice stopped the descent of that shining silver weapon. "We've been buddies since the beginning. Don't do that to the princess. No matter what she's done, I still love her."

Franz looked back, up into Ryan's desperate eyes, and the knife pressed against Judith's throat. "I'm sorry, old friend," Harry's voice crooned. "But I have to protect you." And he placed the blade against her jugular vein.

"Franz, no!" It was no longer Billy or Fafnir. It was Ryan, loud and angry and full of command.

Another streak of lightning sizzled across the terrace outside, followed by a roar of thunder that shook the entire house. The lights flashed back on, flooding the kitchen with a bright white glow. Franz blinked, staring down at Judith's supine figure and the look of sheer terror on her face. Then he turned to look at Ryan and Micki. The knife dropped on the tile floor beside Judith, and he buried his face in his hands.

"Mein Gott," he said in his normal voice, "what have I done?"

That was the last coherent thing Franz said. Ryan drew him slowly away from Judith and took him out of the room with a touching gentleness. And then Micki was all solicitude and surprising efficiency, wiping the rain off Judith's stunned face and the trickle of blood from her neck, all the while keeping up a low, insulting monologue that was enough to distract Judith from the shock of what had just happened.

"You don't have the sense of a raw turnip," she said, pulling Judith's shirt over her head and replacing it with her own. Micki's shirt was much smaller and clung to her damp skin, and Micki looked even more absurd in the soaked, oversize cotton blouse, but Judith was still too overwhelmed to say anything. "What the hell did you mean by taking off like that? Don't you know better than to trust anything Ma says? At least she had the sense to warn us. And by the way, where the hell's Steve?"

"In here, dammit." Steve's muffled voice filtered out of the wine closet, and Judith giggled. The laugh was slightly tinged with hysteria, but it was a laugh nonetheless, and she felt slightly more human.

"I lost the key," she said in a slightly strained tone.

"How the hell did he get in there?"

"I locked him in. I think granting me the intellect of a turnip might be overstating the case. I thought he was here to murder me, so I trapped him in there and went to tell Franz."

"Maybe the brains of a slug," Micki agreed. "Sorry, Steve. We'll have to find the key."

A string of obscenities issued forth. "Is everyone okay?"

Micki's glance met Judith's, and she shrugged. "As well as can be expected. Open yourself a bottle of wine. It may be a while."

"I'm already halfway through a California Cabernet. Take your time."

Micki turned back to Judith. "Do you want to see Franz?"

Sheer terror swept through her before she could stamp it down. "Do you think he's safe?"

"You weren't in any position to hear, but the police and an ambulance were right behind us. I'm sure Franz won't be able to hurt anyone again."

"I don't want to see him."

"No, I don't expect you do. What about Ryan? Don't you owe him something?"

"What? An apology for thinking he was a murderer? A thank-you for saving my life? I think the best thing I can do for him is to leave."

Micki uttered a short, succinct word. "I thought we agreed you had the brains of a slug. Maybe we ought to go lower still. For heaven's sake, Judith, the man needs you. Stop thinking of your pride and think of him."

At Micki's sharp words the last of Judith's anxious self-pity vanished. "You're giving up, eh?"

"What can I say? You belong together—if you'd both show enough sense to do something about it."

"Where is he?"

"I think he took Franz into the library."

"I'll go to him."

"Do that."

But Ryan wasn't in the library. There were more than half a dozen policemen, including the two abashed-looking cops who'd first doubted her. There were three white-coated paramedics, and there was a little old man in a straitjacket, a lost, confused look on his face.

He glanced over at Judith, and his face twisted into an expression of misery. And then he spoke.

Judith's body was covered with a cold sweat. The voice that came from Franz's talented throat was a young boy's voice. And he spoke in German.

"What's he saying?" a policeman inquired, only mildly interested.

Judith was excellent in French, lousy in Spanish and passable in German. "He's asking for his mother," she said quietly.

Chapter Twenty-One

"So who hit me over the head?" Judith demanded three days later. She'd packed her clothes, loaded the Mercedes and called her apartment superintendent in Philadelphia to warn him of her imminent return.

"Steve. He wanted to get his IOUs away from you, and he thought you were after him."

"Bastard," Judith muttered genially, curling up for the last time on the lopsided sofa. "After him for what?"

"Steve's intellect isn't much better than yours. He was in hock up to his ears to some rather nasty types. When Lacey realized Ryan wasn't her Prince Charming, she turned to Steve, and together they figured out a way to embezzle money from The Puppet Factory to cover some of his debts. When Lacey was killed he thought the mob had done it, as a warning to him. And he thought you were part of the mob, out to finish the job."

"He thought I was a hit woman?" Judith stared at Micki, amused and astonished. "You're right—he *is* more of an idiot than I am!"

"But he's a very good puppeteer. Second best, now that Franz is out of the picture. At least he was sorry for hurting you. That's why he showed up in the middle of the night that time. Not for me at all, but to see whether you were okay. He said he didn't mean to hit you so hard. He just wanted to stop you."

"Great," Judith drawled. "Did he take my note pad?"

"Uh-uh. I did."

"So you knew all along that I wasn't here just to work?"

"I knew the moment I laid eyes on you. The note pad just gave me the proof."

"Well, you could have said something sooner," Judith said crossly. "I could have used someone to talk with."

"I wasn't about to do you any favors." Micki stared at her for a long, silent moment, and then her voice softened. "Are you going to see Ryan before you go?"

"I doubt it. I don't think he'd see me. He's been holed up on that top floor for the past three days. I think it's clear that I'm part of a very unpleasant memory. With Franz in the hospital, too sick even to come to trial, I'm the last reminder. Once I'm gone he can go on to more important things."

"Slug," Micki muttered. "If you don't see him, you're a coward and a rat."

"Listen, I'm leaving him for you," Judith protested lightly.

"Don't do me any favors. You leave Ryan the way he is now, and he won't be any good to any woman for decades. And then we'll all be too old to care. He's alone there, Judith. And he needs you."

"He doesn't need me. He doesn't need anybody but his puppets."

"That's because everyone abandoned him *but* the puppets. Just like you're about to. Or was this merely some sort of society girl fling? Screw the puppeteer and then go back to real life? You're more like Lacey than I thought."

"Micki," Judith said, "I couldn't bear it if he said no."

Micki just looked at her. "Well, you'll never know unless you ask. If you'd rather live the rest of your life not knowing, then you'll never be any good as a reporter."

"I'm a damned good reporter," Judith protested.

"Yeah, and I can't wait to see what you're going to write about this."

"Nothing."

"What? And blow your big chance? You *are* into maso-
chism today, aren't you?"

"It's the only thing I can give Ryan."

"No, it's not."

"Micki…"

"Get the hell out of here," Micki demanded, waving her
cigarette and glowering. "Stupidity makes me grouchy."

"Life makes you grouchy," Judith said, rising with her customary grace. She had her linen suit on again, and her hair and
face were flawless. No one would ever know she could take
apart a Mercedes engine and put it back together again in less
than an hour. "Goodbye, Micki. See you sometime."

"Goodbye, Daniels. See you tomorrow."

I'M NOT GOING to see him, Judith told herself, driving down
the narrow, twisting roads of Miller's Junction. He doesn't
want me, it's too late for anything and it's a waste of time. I'm
not going to see him.

The parking lot was deserted when she pulled up in front of
The Puppet Factory. Ryan had closed the place down for the
week, to give everyone some time to recover from the shocking
events of the past few weeks. No one had seen him or spoken
to him. But Micki had known Judith better than she knew herself. She wasn't going to go away without seeing him.

The heat wave had finally broken. The storm three nights
ago had washed away the thick, sultry air, the dampness and
the hundred-plus temperatures. It was in the seventies today,
with a soft breeze, low humidity and the smell of summer in
the air.

The metal door was locked, but Judith still had the key. She
entered the building and paused for a moment, letting herself
remember, poking the memory of terror as if she were prodding
a sore tooth, to make certain it still hurt. It didn't.

Franz was a very sick man, mentally and physically. He only
spoke German now in that little boy's voice, and physical tests
had revealed cancer riddling his body. He wouldn't live long,
which was a blessing to everyone. Particularly to Franz.

Judith still didn't like freight elevators. She found it on the second floor. The Roberts 450 was silent. Someone had ripped the wires from it in a fury. Ryan, of course. He never could figure how to turn the damned thing off.

At first she thought the elevator wouldn't move. But it did, slowly, grudgingly, carrying her up to the fifth floor. She braced herself in the middle of the platform, braced herself for the coming confrontation. She didn't even know what she was going to say or what she expected to accomplish. She only knew that Micki was right. She wasn't going to give up so easily. Some things were worth fighting for.

To Judith's surprise, the huge loft area looked deserted. The glare of the bright midmorning sun bounced off the bare white walls. And then she saw him.

He was stretched out on the white couch, wearing a loose cotton shirt and white drawstring pants, his bare feet hanging over one side. He stared at her with that distant, blank expression on his face, and his green-gray eyes were opaque as they drifted dismissingly down her formally dressed body.

"What are you doing here?" His voice was flat, bored.

"I'm not quite sure."

"You want to apologize for not trusting me? Fine. Apology accepted. You want to thank me for saving your life? Fine. Thanks accepted. Goodbye, Judith. Take your Ralph Lauren suit and your Bryn Mawr education and leave."

"You can take your attitude and—" She bit off the retort, willing herself to be calm. Fighting with him wasn't what she wanted. Was it?

Maybe it was. She crossed the room to him. "So you're sitting there feeling guilty," she said.

He ignored her remark. "If I'd been a little more observant, I might have seen something years ago. Countless women died because I let loyalty blind me."

"Great," Judith said, dropping down on the foot of the couch. He moved his legs out of her way, but just barely. "So you're taking on the guilt of the world. Why don't you blame yourself for Nazi atrocities while you're at it?'' She kicked off her high-heeled white sandals.

He just stared at her. ''Maybe I'm experiencing other emotions besides guilt. Maybe I'm grieving for the loss of my closest friend.''

''Maybe you're sulking.'' She slipped off her white linen jacket and dumped it on the floor. ''I hate to be crass, but it seems like Franz was a friend you can afford to lose.'' She began unbuttoning her blouse.

Ryan was watching her in fascination. ''Am I allowed to be concerned for the reputation of The Puppet Factory?''

''Nope. You don't care about things like reputation or people's stupid gossip. The Puppet Factory will weather the scandal, and so will you.'' She slipped the blouse off her shoulders and dropped it on the floor. She was wearing a sheer silk camisole with no bra, and her nipples were erect beneath the soft material.

''What the hell are you doing?'' he demanded irritably. He could have pulled himself away, could have ordered her from the place. He hadn't, so she took that as a sign of encouragement and unzipped her skirt.

''I'll give you two guesses,'' she said, standing up and letting the skirt fall to the floor. Her bikini panties weren't much more than lace and ribbon, and she hadn't bothered to wear stockings. She stood there, looking down at him. ''I'm not leaving you, Ryan.''

A small, wry smile tugged at the corner of his mouth, and suddenly Judith knew it was going to be all right. ''Not dressed like that, you aren't,'' he said.

''Not dressed like anything,'' she replied, dropping back down beside him and applying herself to the buttons of his shirt. ''It's very simple. I love you and you love me and we belong together. We don't have a lot in common, but I'm willing to work on it. As long as we don't have to live in that damned house. This place is big enough for us, for now. But we'll have to get a bigger bed. You can work with the puppets and I'll keep all your machinery in working condition and we'll be very, very happy.'' She looked at him expectantly. "All you have to do is ask me to stay.''

"Who says I love you?''

She'd finished unbuttoning his shirt and was now applying herself to the drawstring of his pants. She was already happily aware that he was reacting in a very positive manner to her improvised striptease, but his hand shot out and caught hers in a crushing grip before she could continue.

She met his gaze fearlessly. "You told Franz when he was holding a knife at my throat.''

His other hand reached up to gently stroke the deep scratch mark Franz's knife had left at the base of her jaw. "That was Fafnir,'' he said. "And Billy. They're puppets, they're not me. I never told you.''

She was very still. "Then tell me now,'' she said in a quiet voice.

His hand slid behind her neck, tugging her closer. "I love you,'' he said, his mouth reaching for hers. "Don't ever leave me.''

And she put her arms around his neck, following him down on the sofa. "I won't, Ryan,'' she said. "I won't.''

Was he a con man...a gigolo?
All she knew was that she wanted him—
no matter what.

Partners in Crime

Chapter One

Alexander Caldicott yanked off his tie and sent it sailing across the room. It was supposed to land on the lumpy double bed but it fell short, ending up on the stained wall-to-wall carpeting. An ignominious fate for Brooks Brothers' best silk knit tie, and Alexander didn't give a damn. He rolled up the sleeves on his Egyptian cotton dress shirt and sank down in the one chair the sleazy hotel room had to offer. The chair wobbled beneath him, threatening to collapse under Alexander's well-muscled one hundred and seventy-five pounds, but then held still.

Alexander, better known as Sandy, cursed out loud, a solemn, profane curse that was more at home in the Princeton Pike Sleep-a-While Motel than silk ties and Egyptian cotton shirts and a burnt-out lawyer named Alexander Caldicott. It was the worst day in a long line of miserable, depressing days, and even the thought of the Canary Islands wasn't enough to cheer him. It would be more of the same. More forced camaraderie from his fellow man at play, more casual, careful sex from the determinedly attractive female of the species. His travel agent knew just the sort of thing he liked, and had dutifully provided it year after year, with only the settings changing.

But Sandy was sick of it. Sick of hearty friendships from people he'd never see or hear from again, sick of instant relationships that never lasted. He was bored with his apartment in New York, wary of his family in New Jersey, dreading autumn, tired of his MGB, frustrated with his law firm, and sick unto death of everything in his life, up to and including the latest professional triumph that had culminated just that afternoon.

If he hadn't been so burned-out, Sandy thought, he would have known Jimmy was lying. Anyone known both personally and professionally as Jimmy the Stoolie should have been approached with a little circumspection. But Sandy hadn't been paying close enough attention. He'd been too busy trying to get Jimmy off the charges of arson and conspiracy to notice whether Jimmy was being straight with him. He'd been too involved with trying to get through the trial and head for the expensive vacation he now found he was dreading. He'd been too damned self-absorbed to do more than pull off a full acquittal of the charges, only to have Jimmy take him out for a celebratory drink and then inform him he'd been lying all the time.

If you lie down with pigs, Sandy told himself, you were bound to get pig droppings all over you. Maybe he should leave criminal law, head for the nice, clean world of corporate shenanigans. What was the lawyer's line from *The Big Chill?*— "All my clients rape is the land."

Even that sounded deadly right about now. Maybe he'd leave his partnership at MacDougal and Sullivan and never come back. There was nothing keeping him there. No wife any longer, and his family would scarcely miss him. The only people who would mourn his departure would be the mechanic he supported with his temperamental old MGB. Him and maybe a bartender or two.

If only things weren't so damned predictable. If only his life hadn't turned out to be just what was expected of him. Prep school, Princeton, Yale Law School, a partnership in a firm that boasted a social conscience. He'd even had his perfect blond wife, and if Margery hadn't lasted, well that was to be expected too, given today's statistics.

He slid back in the uncomfortable chair, stretching his long legs out in front of him. Maybe he should have asked Beverly to come along. She was always good for a laugh, and maybe she would have kept him from his self-absorbed brooding.

But even Beverly had gotten predictable and tiresome. No doubt she found him just as boring. What he needed, Sandy thought, was something to shake him up. To knock him out of his depression and malaise, something to care about. Anything.

The traffic from Route One almost drowned out the sound of the knock on his door. He sat there for a long moment, unmoving. Not many people knew he was there. He'd deliberately chosen a small, run-down motel instead of one of the big ones that were rapidly dotting the area just outside of Princeton. He wanted to keep a low profile during the three-week trial, and he was sick to death of anonymous hotels. At least the Princeton Pike Sleep-a-While Motel had character. All of it bad.

The knocking came again. Someone was definitely at his door, and the only person who knew where he was staying was Jimmy the Stoolie. The last thing Sandy felt like doing was having another heart-to-heart chat with the little sleaze. Besides, Jimmy should be on his way back to the city by now, an undeservedly free man.

The damnable thing about all this, Sandy thought absently, was that he wasn't upset about a professional criminal cheating the system and getting out when he so richly deserved a few years locked away. As a lawyer it was Sandy's duty to provide the best defense to anyone, guilty or innocent. No, it was the fact that Jimmy had lied, and had pulled Sandy into aiding and abetting those lies, that rankled so badly. It had taken all his willpower not to smash his fist into Jimmy's smiling mouth. If it was Jimmy at the door right now he might very well let his willpower go out the window.

He pulled himself out of the chair. Whoever was outside the peeling door of the motel room wasn't about to go away. The knock was brisk, authoritative, demanding a response. Hell, it sounded just like his mother.

Bright autumn sunlight flooded the dingy room when he threw open the door. For a moment his eyes narrowed against the glare, and then he realized the woman standing there was about as unlike anyone he could have imagined.

She was short, and he liked tall women. She had mousy brown hair, and he was partial to blondes. Her eyes were brown, too, and partially obscured by wire-rimmed glasses that gave her a faintly startled look. Her mouth was too generous, and so was her nose, and her clothes were drab, boring, the sort of things worn by a Midwestern librarian. She couldn't have been much older than thirty, or much younger, either. He stood in the doorway, looking down at her, trying to summon up at least an ounce of polite interest.

"I suppose you'll think this pretty rude of me," she said abruptly, and there was a rasp of nervousness in an otherwise melodious voice, "but I'd like you to help me commit arson."

For a long moment Sandy didn't move. And then he slowly stepped back, gesturing her into the room, and shut the door behind her.

HE WASN'T AT ALL what Jane Dexter expected, but then, a confidence man would have to be attractive, wouldn't he? It would certainly help him in his schemes. And she'd seen the photograph, the elegant, austere blond man with his sleazy-looking lawyer. The evening paper had given the details of the three-week trial, and Jane, too depressed and fractious to concentrate on anything more intellectually strenuous than "*Different Strokes*" reruns on the motel's black-and-white TV, had resorted to reading every single word in the article, drawn by a face she'd recognized.

She'd been staying at the Princeton Pike Sleep-a-While Motel for almost ten days, and she could hardly have missed the beautiful man three doors down. When she hadn't been so involved in her own problems she'd wondered about him, why someone who was clearly so prosperous would hole up in such a down-and-out motel. The royal-blue MGB parked outside his room could either be considered a wreck or a classic, depending on your attitude, but there was no question that the man was used to better things.

Jane had found herself making up stories about him to help distract her when things got to be too much. He could fit any number of roles she fashioned for him. He was tall, a bit over six feet, and beautifully coordinated. His shoulders were just broad enough, his legs long, his hands, from what she could see from a distance, were well shaped. His hair was blond, probably lightened from hours on the deck of a yacht or racing around a tennis court, and his remaining tan set off features that were just this side of perfection. She hadn't gotten close enough to see his eyes, but she knew they had to be perfect Aryan blue. His mouth was thin but sexy, his teeth very white, his cheekbones and jaw chiseled. He even had a perfect nose, damn him.

Jane's favorite fantasy was that he was a deposed Balkan prince, trying to reclaim his family's estates. Failing that, he was the long-lost heir to one of the big industrial families around. He could be a famous football player, but that didn't really fit his regal grace. Or he could be a soap opera star hiding out from voracious fans. The last thing she expected he'd be was a professional criminal, with an arrest record longer than the Brooklyn Bridge. Arson, extortion, and a host of lesser crimes had been thrown against him, and nothing had stuck. He'd gotten off this time, thanks, according to the reporter, to the brilliance of his attorney rather than his own innocence. Jane had looked at Alexander Caldicott's weasely little face in the paper and searched for signs of brilliance in the shifty-looking eyes. It would have been much easier to believe he was the hardened criminal, not Golden Boy.

But the picture's caption identified them quite clearly. Besides, what would a hot-shot lawyer be doing at the Princeton Pike Sleep-a-While Motel? No one in their right mind would stay there if they had any other option, she thought, ignoring the fact that she was doing just that. There was an empty apartment less than ten minutes away just waiting for her, and she'd chosen this decrepit motel, rather than surround herself with depressing memories.

But the man three doors down wouldn't have her reasons.

There was no question about it, the astonishingly handsome man she'd been covertly studying for days was nothing more than a professional criminal, ready to sell out to the highest bidder. And he was exactly what she needed.

He was looking at her with an odd, slightly bemused expression in his eyes. On closer inspection they weren't blue at all, they were a deep, unfathomable, smoky gray. And that thin mouth of his was even sexier close up, though he clearly couldn't have thought she was much of a temptation. Jane had no illusions about her charms. If she'd had any, they'd been wiped out two years ago in her ruthlessly amicable divorce. Squaring her shoulders, she looked up into Jimmy (the Stoolie) Calvin's enigmatic eyes, and repeated her opening gambit.

"I'd like you to help me commit arson."

"Would you really?" His voice was deep, unaccented. "Let me fix you a drink and you can tell me why you chose me for such a proposition. Scotch all right?"

"Do you have any coffee?" She looked around the room uneasily. It looked just as bare, just as tattered as her own room. At least she'd managed to brighten her own cubicle with fresh flowers, but Jimmy the Stoolie had added nothing more than a bottle of Scotch to the depressing confines.

"Just Scotch. Besides, this sounds like a Scotch-and-water discussion, not a coffee discussion. Take a seat. I wouldn't trust the chair if I were you. Better sit on the bed."

"Uh…where are you going to sit?"

It wasn't an unpleasant laugh, but Jane flushed anyway. "I'll risk the chair. Don't worry, I'm not about to jump on you."

"I didn't think you were," Jane lied, sitting gingerly on the sagging bed.

He had his back to her, and a very nice back it was. He was wearing a white cotton dress shirt that clung to his shoulders and back. The linen trousers fit quite nicely too, and Jane had to control an absent, completely irrational sigh of regret.

"Not that you should walk into strange motel rooms," he added, handing her a glass of whiskey that was far too dark.

"It's not a strange motel room," she said. "I've been sitting in one exactly like it for the last ten days."

"You're staying here, too? I hadn't noticed you."

"No." Jane took a sip of whiskey and shivered delicately. "I'm not exactly noticeable."

He didn't make the usual protests, and for that Jane was grateful. He lowered his body into the chair opposite her, and she watched it creak ominously. His own glass of whiskey was even darker than hers, and she wondered, not for the first time, if she'd made a very grave mistake in coming here. She hadn't allowed herself time to think. She'd been so mad, so desperate at the events of the last few days, that she'd thrown down the newspaper, slipped on her shoes, and marched down the walkway before she could have second thoughts. She was having far too many of them right now.

"So tell me," the man said, "who are you, and why have you chosen me to commit arson for you?"

"I'd...I'd rather not give you my name right now." She took another sip of the whiskey, wishing it were coffee. "Not until we see if we can come to an agreement."

He really smiled then, not the small wry upturning of his mobile mouth but a full-fledged grin. "We'll call you Madame X then," he said solemnly. "Shouldn't you be dressed in black, maybe with a veil covering your face? You look more like a Midwestern librarian."

"I *am* a Midwestern librarian," Jane said, coming close to hating him for a moment.

"Sorry," he said. "I'm a smart aleck sometimes. Why me?"

"I read the newspaper tonight. About your trial."

"Did you? I didn't bother."

"It was very interesting."

"It must have been, if it sent you to me."

Jane took a deep breath. "It made it clear you were really guilty."

"I beg your pardon?"

"The article made it clear that you were a professional crook, and that only your lawyer's brilliance got you off."

A strange, half-pleased, half-disturbed expression crossed his face. "My lawyer?"

"His name is Calderwood?"

"Caldicott," he corrected absently. "Alexander Caldicott."

"Anyway, he managed to get you off. Though I must say he didn't look that brilliant in the picture."

"Looks can be deceiving."

"Yes," she said, looking at his handsome, patrician face, "they can. So anyway, I have need of an arsonist. That is, if you're looking for work. I would think you'd be at loose ends. After all, you didn't know till this afternoon whether you'd be going to jail or not, so you probably haven't made too many long-range plans."

"No, I hadn't. Caldicott is a very great lawyer," he said with a small grin, "but even he isn't infallible. I thought he'd probably get me off but I couldn't count on it. There's one thing you haven't taken into account, though."

"What's that?"

"Suppose I've decided to mend my ways? Go straight, live a life beyond reproach."

She tried to keep the stricken expression from her face. "That would be wonderful," she managed.

"Liar," his voice was teasing, soft, dangerously beguiling. "Don't worry, Madame X. I have the suspicion that my criminal career is just beginning."

When Ms Jane Dexter left his room forty-five minutes later she was weaving slightly. Sandy had plied her with Scotch, watching with fascination as she began to relax and expand under the influence of Cutty Sark. She'd given him her name within ten minutes, though he had to admit he preferred Madame X. Not that Jane didn't suit her. Plain Jane, the librarian from Baraboo, Wisconsin, back in her hometown of Princeton, New Jersey, looking for an arsonist.

Sandy shook his head in disbelief and poured his half-filled glass down the stained bathroom sink. He'd have to get a copy of that paper. The caption must have gotten their names reversed. It was the first time in his life he'd ever been mistaken for someone of Jimmy the Stoolie's ilk, and the experience was novel enough to be entertaining.

He should have told her, of course. He'd meant to, but she'd looked at him with such wonderful awe and distrust that he couldn't resist stringing her along. For the first time in months the deadly lassitude had left him. That odd little encounter might be enough to make his trip to the Canary Islands entertaining after all. Anytime he got bored he could think back to little Ms Jane Dexter and laugh.

She would wonder about him when he didn't show up for dinner tonight. They were supposed to meet at the steak house in the mall, the most anonymous place he could think of, and there she'd outline her plan. He almost wished he could make it. His flight was at ten o'clock tonight—if he missed it he'd have to go back to New York and that was the last thing he wanted. If they'd picked a decent restaurant he could have sent her flowers and a graceful note of regret. He couldn't see managing that in the cafeteria-style steak house he'd assiduously avoided in the past.

No, she was going to have to wonder about Jimmy the Stoolie. She'd probably figure he went back to his life of crime in the bowels of New York. He wondered if the paper would correct its error. He wasn't about to bring it to their attention, and he doubted Jimmy would. So Ms Jane Dexter would have to make other arrangements, always wondering what happened to her first-choice felon.

Sandy stripped off his clothes and headed for the rusty shower stall. He should be delighted to get away from his self-imposed exile, to immerse himself in the luxurious surroundings that would be provided for him. The memory of Jane Dexter's offer of employment would keep him going. Who knows, when he got back he'd probably find she needed a lawyer. Maybe he could offer his services.

Now if he had even an ounce of decency left in him, he would fight his way through the hordes of teenagers that crowded into the mall and meet Madame X long enough to tell her the truth. If he had any conscience at all he'd warn her against committing the felony of arson, or even conspiring to. They'd laugh over her misunderstanding, admit to the error of her ways, and he'd head off to Newark Airport in plenty of time to get his flight, secure in his own nobility.

He cursed as the hot water turned abruptly icy, and jumped out of the shower, banging his elbow and knee as he went. That's what he'd do. He'd make the time to stop there and meet her, out of pure decency and love for his fellow man. And he'd do it because if he didn't, he'd go absolutely crazy wondering why a conventional-looking creature like Ms Jane Dexter wanted to commit arson. So much for noble motives.

The phone rang as he let himself out the door. He paused for a moment. Apart from Jimmy the Stoolie, only the chief legal clerk of MacDougal and Sullivan knew where he was. Right now he wasn't interested in last-minute details, in the law, in anything at all but getting out of this motel. He'd check in with them once he got to the Canary Islands. In the meantime he was going to settle up his account and head for Quaker Bridge Mall and a woman of mystery. And he found himself whistling as he shut the door behind him.

Chapter Two

Sandy had to park half a mile away from the entrance to the sprawling structure of Quaker Bridge Mall. It was a Wednesday night, hardly peak time for shoppers and browsers, but it might as well have been the height of Christmas shopping instead of a balmy evening in mid-October. He cursed under his breath as he crossed the wide expanse of the parking lot. He'd have to remember to take this hike into account when he left Madame X. He didn't want to miss his plane.

It took him even longer to thread his way through the crowds wandering aimlessly around the enclosed mall. He'd miscalculated where the steak house was, and had chosen the parking lot and entrance farthest away. Once he found the coy, Old English facade he had to wait again, shuffling through the cafeteria line like a bag lady, eyeing his purported strip sirloin with deep misgivings. He knew just what his librarian would be doing: munching politely on a salad, eating barely enough to keep a bird alive. While he, for the first time in months, was famished. It didn't matter if it was strip loin of urban rat, he'd eat it, and the microwaved potato, and the limp salad, and the grease-soaked roll. It took him a while to find Jane in the crowded dining room, and he wondered for a moment whether she'd turned the tables and stood him up. Finally he spotted her over in a dark corner, hunched over her tray, and made his way across the room, only to stop in amazement and stare at her dinner.

He'd never seen so much food in his life. She had the Lumberjack Special, the largest steak the place offered, and it was covered with mushrooms, onions, and green peppers. She had a mound of limp french fries, a half-eaten roll, two desserts, and what looked like a small bathtub of some sort of soft drink. He sank down in the chair opposite her, placing his own more discreet tray on the table, and he wished he'd succumbed to the violently pink strawberry shortcake the place served. Maybe Jane would offer him some of hers.

"Are you pregnant?" he asked abruptly.

It was the second time he'd seen her blush. The first had been when he told her to sit on his bed. He didn't realize women still blushed, particularly women over thirty.

"No, I'm not. Why do you ask?"

"Pregnant women eat a lot."

"So do I," she said defiantly.

"You don't look like you do."

She blushed again, and there was just the tiniest bit of a smile behind the wire-rimmed glasses. Not so plain Jane after all, he thought, biting into his greasy roll. "I thought maybe you wanted to torch the father," he added lazily. "Seduced and abandoned and all that."

The smile left her eyes. "He's not the one I want you to torch."

They ate in silence for a few moments. "You want to tell me who he is?" Sandy said finally.

"Who? The man who seduced and abandoned me or the man I want you to torch?" She managed to sound flippant through the strawberry shortcake that she showed no inclination to share.

"I hope you aren't actually suggesting I set a person on fire," he said plaintively. "I do buildings, not people, and I have an excellent safety record. No one's ever been hurt in one of my fires, not even a fire fighter." Now why was he repeating Jimmy's words to her when he should be telling her the truth, making her see the error of her ways? But if he told her, she might very well get up and walk out, and he'd never know who she wanted to sabotage.

"It's a building. A corporation, as a matter of fact." She'd managed to eat everything on her tray and drain the gallon of soda besides, and Sandy looked at her with new respect.

"I'm listening."

"Ever heard of Technocracies Limited?"

He had, but Jimmy the Stoolie wouldn't. "Can't say that I have."

"It's a research and development firm here in Princeton, run by a man named Stephen Tremaine. It's run along simple enough lines—he provides the space and the funding for research scientists, and they come up with all sorts of things and split the patents. New kinds of baby formulas, new kinds of rocket boosters, new kinds of nail polish."

"And?" he prompted as her recitation came to an abrupt halt.

"My brother worked for Tremaine. He developed a revolutionary process for coating tools and metal machine parts with titanium. It's usually very expensive, but it makes the tools last practically forever. Richard figured out a way to do it cheaply."

"Sounds innocuous enough."

"It should have been. Richard, my brother, has always been intensely idealistic. If there's been a cause he's followed it. He's spent more time in jail than you have, protesting the war in Vietnam, nuclear power, the exploitation of migrant farm workers, environmental polluters, everything. He had very strong principles."

"Had?" Sandy prodded gently.

"He died a little over a month ago," she said bleakly, pain still shadowing her eyes. "He was in a freak car crash in upstate New York. And now Tremaine's planning to take his titanium coating process and sell it to the highest bidder. Do you know who the highest bidders are?"

"I can imagine."

"It'll either be the Defense Department of this country or

one even worse. And that would betray everything Richard ever believed in. I can't let Tremaine do it, I just can't!''

"What did Tremaine say?"

"The same old garbage he's always said." Her voice was bitter. "That he understands my feelings in the matter but there's nothing he can do about it. He insists Richard never signed a contract restricting the use of his inventions to peaceful applications. And he says as soon as things get settled he'll take the best offer he can get."

"Hold on a minute," Sandy protested. "What things does he have to settle? I'd think it would be a fairly straightforward transaction."

"I would have thought so, too. But something's holding it up. He wanted access to Richard's apartment, but of course I refused. Not that there's anything useful in there, but I wasn't about to give him anything."

"Who's Richard's heir?"

"I am. Our parents are dead."

"Then anything in his apartment should legally belong to you."

She gave him an irritated look. "You've been hanging around your lawyer too long. I thought of that. Don't you think I've checked into every possible legal alternative? Richard's possessions belong to me, Richard's work belongs to Technocracies. I have no legal claim on the formula."

"If Richard did sign a contract stipulating his work was only to be used for peaceful purposes, wouldn't there be a copy of it among his private papers?"

"I've searched through everything a dozen times. Richard wasn't the most practical of men. He probably wrapped the garbage in it or something. Not that he was practical enough to even wrap his garbage."

Sandy had long ago forgotten to look at his watch. "So what is it you want to torch?"

Jane took a deep breath. "Richard's lab at Technocracies. I'd rather have no one use the formula than to have it get in the wrong hands, and I know Richard would agree with me.

You're good at that sort of thing, aren't you? Minimizing the damage, making sure no one gets hurt.''

"It would be a waste of time. For one thing, the lab is on Tremaine's home turf. Anything useful in the place would have been gotten out long ago. You'd just be destroying useless information.''

"You have any alternatives?''

"Of course," he said, leaning back in the uncomfortable little chair. "We can find out what's holding up the sale of the formula. It must be a damned good reason. There are rumors that Technocracies Limited is in financial trouble. Tremaine would want a fresh infusion of money as soon as he can get it. We might also be able to find a copy of your brother's contract with the stipulation that his inventions be used for peaceful purposes.''

"I thought you'd never heard of Technocracies?''

Sandy didn't even blink. "The name didn't ring a bell until you started describing it. Er…my lawyer mentioned something about their troubles. If we can find out what's holding up the sale we can turn it to our advantage.''

"You aren't, by any chance, talking about blackmail?'' She was carefully folding the crumpled paper napkin on her tray, refusing to meet his eyes, and he watched her hands, the short, well-shaped nails, long, graceful fingers, narrow palms. There was no sign of a wedding band, but he suspected that hadn't always been the case.

"You think blackmail's worse than arson?'' Sandy countered. "We'd just use it to keep Tremaine from doing what he shouldn't be doing. Of course we could always see if we could get something for our trouble on the side.''

"No!'' She looked up then, her eyes intent. "I don't want anything from Stephen Tremaine. I just want to keep the formula from falling into the wrong hands.''

"All right. There are legal ways of doing it, if you're prepared to take a chance.''

"I'm not," she said flatly. "Besides, what do you know about the law?''

Sandy grinned. "I've picked up some useful knowledge over the years. In my line of work you spend a fair amount of time with lawyers and judges."

"I'll bet."

"No snotty cracks, Madame X," Sandy warned. "Or I just may refuse to help you."

"You're going to help me? What's in it for you?"

"Presumably whatever was in it for me to torch Technocracies Limited. You were planning on paying me, weren't you? In my profession I don't need to get too involved in pro bono work."

She looked startled at his use of the technical, Latin term, and he cursed his slip of the tongue. If he wasn't going to tell her the truth he'd better make sure she didn't guess on her own. And to his surprise it didn't seem as if he had any intention of telling her the truth.

"No," she said slowly. "I suppose you don't. Only lawyers and doctors have to worry about dedicating part of their working hours for the betterment of mankind without payment. I suppose it's lawyers and doctors who have to worry about the tax breaks. Do you even pay taxes?"

"Not if I can help it. What've you got against lawyers? Apart from the fact that no one could help you with this problem."

"What makes you think I've got anything against lawyers?"

"The way your nose wrinkles when you say the word, not to mention that subtly delightful curl of your upper lip," Sandy said.

"I was married to one," she said flatly.

"Not the one who seduced and abandoned you?"

"The same."

"Well, at least he made an honest woman of you in the meantime."

She just stared at him, her dark expression making it clear that the subject was closed. "How do you suggest we go about finding what's going on at Technocracies?"

"My naturally devious turn of mind," Sandy said. "I have all sorts of ideas."

"Such as?" she prompted.

He glanced down at his watch. His plane was leaving Newark for the Canary Islands in twelve minutes. Considering that the airport was forty minutes away, he wasn't going to make it. He looked across the Formica-topped table at his dinner partner. If he had any sense of decency at all he'd tell her who he was. She said she'd checked with lawyers, but clearly she hadn't found one with any brains. There were all sorts of ways to deal with the likes of Stephen Tremaine, and Sandy or any one of his partners could probably put an abrupt halt to Tremaine's machinations. A restraining order at the very least could keep any sale of technology tied up for years.

He should tell her who he really was, what he did for a living, and pass her on to one of his partners to deal with the matter while he arranged for a later flight. They could handle it all in an efficient, businesslike way, just as he could, and there'd be no need for subterfuge, deviousness, or excitement.

He opened his mouth, prepared to confess. "Such as," he said, "infiltrating their ranks. A little industrial spying can go a long way if you have the knack of it."

She was looking at him with a combination of awe and apprehension. "And you have the knack of it?"

"Hum a few bars and I can fake it," he said cheerfully. "How are your secretarial skills? Do you think you could get a typing job?"

"Maybe. As long as I don't run into Uncle Stephen."

"Uncle Stephen? Have I missed something along the way?"

"Stephen Tremaine is my godfather," she said gloomily. "Richard's, too."

"Nice guy," Sandy said. "Scratch that idea. I never really liked it in the first place. I guess we'll have to go directly to plan number two. That is, if you're willing to put yourself in my hands."

She looked daunted, and he wanted to reach over and pull those wire-rimmed glasses away from her doubting eyes. He kept his hands in his pockets, tipping back in the chair and watching the silent struggle that shadowed her face. "Of course, we could always try a more honest approach," he added. "I could find you a lawyer, a better one than you've had before, and he might be able to put a spoke in Tremaine's wheels. What it lacks in verve and imagination it makes up for in respectability."

That word tipped the scales. "I'm sick and tired of being respectable," Jane Dexter said. "I'm tired of being reasonable and seeing other people's points of view and always doing the *proper* thing and not the *right* thing. My brother believed in certain things, and he suffered for those beliefs. I'm not going to allow Stephen Tremaine to destroy his legacy, and I don't give a damn if I end up in jail. I'm going to do anything and everything I can to stop him, and if you won't help me I'll torch the building myself."

Her words tumbled to a stop. She was breathing heavily, and Sandy noticed absently that there were breasts beneath that drab jacket. Nice ones, rising and falling rapidly in her agitation. Her eyes were sparkling with determination and anger, her mouth was soft and tremulous with emotion, and her hands were clenched around the napkin. And suddenly Sandy forgot about Beverly, forgot about leggy blondes and the Canary Islands.

"We won't start with arson," he said mildly enough, resisting the impulses that were sweeping through him, most of them indecent. "We'll begin with breaking and entering."

Jane Dexter looked panicked. Startled, frightened, wary. And then she smiled, a wide, beautiful smile that reached her eyes and lit her face with a warm glow that was effectively destroying any defenses Alexander Caldicott had left. "I'm in your hands," she said simply. And he hoped to God she meant it.

SHE WAS A FOOL, Jane thought as she headed through the crowded walkway, dodging teenagers and senior citizens and infants in strollers. What in heaven's name had possessed her to follow a noted criminal into his motel room, set up an assignation, and then agree to commit a felony with him? She hadn't agreed, she'd encouraged him. Practically demanded that he break the law. She had only herself to blame when she realized she was to be part and parcel of that criminal act.

She shouldn't look at it that way, but a lifetime, almost thirty-one years, of careful consideration prevented her from doing otherwise. She'd always been cursed with the ability to see the other person's point of view. She could sympathize with the migrant workers, but understand the boss's problems. She could hate the war in Vietnam, but worry about the threat of communism. She could detest American involvement in Central America, but wonder about the freedom in the so-called democracies. She could dislike nuclear power but wonder about the alternatives.

She could even see her husband's point of view when he left her. She couldn't even be angry with him. Eminently reasonable as always, she simply gave him his divorce and let him walk out of her life.

But that fairness, that willingness to see the other side of a question, was degenerating into a wishy-washy inability to make a commitment. Just once in her life she had to change. She had to make a stand—it was all she could do for a brother she'd never really understood or been comfortable around. Idealists were hard to live with, and brilliant idealists were even worse. So while she'd loved Richard, as she'd loved their parents, she hadn't liked him very much. All she could do now was respect his memory, and do this one last thing for him.

Even if this one last thing meant meeting someone most inappropriately named Jimmy the Stoolie at a sleazy motel and heading out for a night of crime. It was the least she could do, it was all she could do. And if the thought of her sober, intellectual parents spinning in their grave was an added fillip, then every cloud had a silver lining. And with a sudden grin, she headed on out into the warm New Jersey night.

SANDY WAS FOLLOWING HER at a discreet distance, careful to keep out of her way. Part of him still couldn't quite believe this small, conservative-looking woman was really eager to embark on a life of crime. Part of him couldn't quite believe he was going to aid and abet her. He'd worked long years for his law degree, passed his bar exam with flying colors, practiced for six years with quite remarkable success. If he was caught breaking into Technocracies Ltd. he could very well be disbarred.

But that wasn't going to happen. For one thing, he wasn't planning to get caught. For another, if worse came to worst Jane had told him enough to put pressure on Tremaine to drop any possible charges.

If he didn't help her he had no doubt at all that sooner or later she'd be storming the slate gray building out on Route 206 with a bucket of kerosene and a book of matches. And while it was none of his business, it hadn't taken him long to realize that he didn't want Jane Dexter locked away, out of his reach. He still wasn't quite sure why. Keeping her safe for now would do until he figured it out.

He hated answering machines, hated the high-tech one MacDougal and Sullivan had bullied him into buying, but now and then they had their uses. Heading toward a bank of public phones, he punched in a few numbers, punched in a few more, and began to record a new outgoing message.

"This is Alexander Caldicott. I'll be out of touch for the next two weeks, soaking up sun in the Canary Islands. If you need to get in touch with me please leave a message with my secretary at MacDougal and Sullivan and someone will help you."

He hung up the phone, grinning. He'd made the break. Now he just had to make sure he survived the next two weeks while he kept Madame X out of jail. Somehow he had the feeling his restless boredom was just about to disappear. Had disappeared, in fact, the moment Jane Dexter had walked into his motel room and asked him to commit arson.

Some days you eat the bear, some days the bear eats you, he thought. Right now he felt as if he'd had a very satisfying dinner of bear meat. And things were only going to get better.

Chapter Three

It was after eleven that night when Jane heard the peremptory knock on her door. She'd spent the past few hours moving from bed to chair to bathroom to bed, unable to settle anywhere. She'd searched through the meager belongings she'd brought east with her, looking for something suitable for a breaking and entering. The best she could come up with was an old pair of jeans and a heavy cotton sweater. The sweater was a dark beige, the jeans so faded they were almost baby blue, but it was all she could manage on such short notice.

She practically flew to the door, expecting a cat burglar. Jimmy the Stoolie had changed from his elegant suit, but the smoke-gray running suit wasn't what she'd imagined an experienced crook would wear. He was looking her up and down with an amused light in his eyes that was becoming all too familiar. Why he should find her so amusing was beyond her imagining, but she didn't like it.

Jane took the offensive. "Is that your idea of the sort of thing to wear when we're breaking into a building?"

He strolled in, closing the door behind him with a quiet little snap. "I was tempted to ask you the same thing," he said, "but I decided to be polite."

Jane flushed, determined not to back down. She didn't like Jimmy the Stoolie, she didn't like his patrician good looks or his East Coast aristocratic manners. It didn't matter that the manners were phony, they still reminded her of all the golden men who'd never really had time for her. "I don't have to be polite," she said sweetly. "I'm the boss."

"Actually I meant to talk to you about that." Sandy dropped down onto her bed, making himself completely at home. "If you're going with me tonight you're going to have to do as I say."

"I'm going with you," she said determinedly. "And I haven't the slightest intention of doing what you tell me."

"Then you aren't going," he said flatly, stretching out on the bed. "You seem to forget, I'm the one who's experienced in these matters. I wouldn't think a librarian would have much experience with 'B and E.'"

"I read a lot." Her voice was ridiculous, defensive, and the man's eyes crinkled in a wry smile.

"Reading isn't good enough. You're going to have to trust me, trust me enough to know what's best. When I say duck you'll have to duck, when I say run, you run. No questions asked, no arguments, no democratic decisions. If you can't accept that then the deal is off."

Jane stood there watching him, chewing her lip in frustration. What he said made absolute sense, but the last thing in the world she wanted to do was give him any sort of power over her. Her self-esteem, her peace of mind were too precarious to entrust to this charming con man.

On the other hand, if she didn't do as he said she had no doubt at all he'd walk out and refuse to help her. When it came right down to it he probably did know best about such things, much as it galled her to admit it.

She was asking him for help, she'd have to learn to accept it. "All right," she said finally, "we'll do it your way. This time."

He moved swiftly then, coming off the bed in one fluid, graceful movement and reaching her side. She backed away quickly, coming up against the door, and he reached a hand out to steady her, the laughter fading from his eyes. "Don't be so nervous, Jane," he said softly. "I'm not going to hurt you."

She drew herself upright. "You startled me. And I think it's understandable that I'd be edgy. I've never broken into a building before.''

He nodded, sober for once. ''The first time is always the hardest.''

She looked at him curiously. ''What was your first time like?''

He shook his head, a smile once more curling the corners of his mobile mouth. ''You wouldn't want to know,'' he said softly. ''You'll do as I tell you?''

''Yes.''

''Don't sound so sulky, Jane. I may very well save your life.''

She had to stop the sudden clenching of her heart. ''It's not going to be that dangerous, is it?'' she demanded.

''I made a few calls. Tremaine favors armed guards and patrol dogs.''

''What?''

He shrugged, grinning that disarming grin. ''This wouldn't be any fun if it was too easy. Trust me, Jane. Do as I say and we'll be just fine.''

''And if we're not?'' she said, resisting that charm stonily.

''Then I know a heckuva lawyer.''

And Jane, remembering the weasely little face in the grainy newspaper photo, snorted derisively before following him out into the brightly lit New Jersey night.

THEY DROVE through the sparse nighttime traffic in the blue MGB. It ran a little rough, and Jane gave it a doubtful look as her companion sped down the wide roads. ''Are you sure this is the car to take? I'd think we'd want something reliable for a quick getaway.''

''This car's reliable,'' he said, clearly stung. ''It's in classic shape—you don't see many like this nowadays.''

''Amen,'' muttered Jane. ''It needs a tune-up.''

''It had one three days ago.''

''Doesn't hold it long, does it?''

He glared at her. "Suddenly you know about cars, too, Madame X?"

"I read a lot."

He managed to hold the glare for perhaps fifteen seconds longer. And then he laughed, a short bark of humor that lessened the tension filling the car. "Now is not the time to pick a fight with me. We've got a challenging night ahead of us—we don't need to be at each other's throats."

"It keeps me from being nervous." She slid down in the leather seat, stretching her legs out in a useless effort to relax.

"Well, it makes me edgier. Cut it out." Without warning he cut the wheel to the left, pulling into a narrow, vacant lot and stopping the car behind a billboard advertising Tanqueray Gin. Jane had a sudden, intense longing for a tall glass of the stuff, forget the tonic, as Jimmy the Stoolie bumped to a halt, flicking off the key with one well-shaped hand.

"Am I allowed to ask questions?"

"Feel free. I need blind obedience, not silence," he replied, pulling on a pair of leather driving gloves that he hadn't bothered to wear before. "Look in the glove box. There should be another pair in there."

"Why don't I just promise not to touch anything?" Jane suggested brightly.

"Put them on." There was no room for argument in his tone of voice. "Your pal Tremaine's building is just beyond that vacant warehouse. We're going to walk from here."

Jane opened her mouth to protest, then shut it again. All she could do was trust this stranger and do as he ordered. Six hours ago she'd never spoken a word to the man, now she was in the midst of committing a felony. The Baraboo Board of Libraries wasn't going to tolerate a felon in their employ, nor were most libraries in her experience. They tended to be a conservative bunch, quick to condemn and slow to understand. No, if they were caught her career was down the tubes.

She could tell Jimmy the Stoolie she'd wait in the car. She could tell him forget it, she'd changed her mind. After all, Uncle Stephen doubtless thought he was doing the right thing.

He must have good reasons for believing he had the right to sell the process to whomever he chose.

But he was wrong. And she couldn't let Richard's life mean nothing. She pulled herself out of the car, taking a deep breath of the night air. It tasted of damp earth and autumn and the tang of exhaust. "I'm ready," she said, meeting her companion's curious gaze.

If only he didn't have such beautiful gray eyes, she thought. If only his smile wasn't completely bewitching. He smiled at her then, and it took every ounce of effort to keep from melting. "Good girl," he said. "Keep your head down and follow me." And Jane followed.

Technocracies Ltd. was a sprawling complex of buildings on Route 206 just north of Princeton. In the daylight it was beautifully proportioned, perfectly landscaped, a spacious, elegant place to work. At night, that moonless night in particular, it was a dark, ominous huddle of buildings. The decorative shrubs hugged the building, menacing shapes to add to Jane's already terrified state of mind. The parking lot was empty, but somehow she failed to be reassured. The guards, and she truly believed her accomplice when he told her there were guards, must have parked somewhere.

Jane did as she was told, following her companion's tall, well-built figure as he approached the building, hiding in his shadow as he in turn hid in the shadow of the building. He moved with unerring instincts, directly to a bank of doors, and stopped in front of one of them.

"Are you going to use a credit card?" she whispered. "I've never seen anyone jimmy a lock."

"Shhh." He pulled something out of his pocket, and she leaned forward, curious to watch a lock pick at work.

Her companion held up a key, inserted it in the lock, and opened the door, gesturing her inside. She went, stopping dead still inside and turning an accusing glare on him.

"Where'd you get that key?" she demanded in a fierce whisper. "And don't tell me it's a skeleton key—I know better."

"I wouldn't think of telling you any such thing. Where do

you think I got it?'' He stood there looking down at her, patient, amused, and she was sorely tempted to kick him in the shins.

''From my godfather? Maybe you figured you could get more money from him if you strung me along and reported to him.''

''You do have a devious mind.'' He was clearly admiring rather than offended. ''I never even thought of that. The idea has merit, but it's full of holes. Tremaine doesn't sound like the sort who'd appreciate my offer of assistance. He'd probably just turn me in to the police and double the security. Guess again.''

Her nerves were at a screaming pitch, her palms damp and slippery inside the over-large pair of driving gloves he'd forced her to wear. ''Now isn't the time to play games.''

''Why not? It eases the tension.''

''For you, maybe. Not for me.''

He took pity on her, his gloved hand cuffing her chin lightly. ''Cheer up, Madame X. If you're going to embark on a life of crime you'll have to be cool, calm and collected. I got the key off your key ring.''

''Mine?'' He surprised her into a little shriek, and the hand that had cuffed her chin immediately covered her mouth, pushing her against the wall.

''Not that cool,'' he muttered in her ear. ''We aren't supposed to be here, remember?'' He removed his hand. ''You had a set of keys lying on your dresser. Presumably your brother's? Everything was nicely marked—apartment, beach house, Vermont house, L-1, L-2, Techno. It didn't take a great criminal mind to figure the last key would get us in here without having to resort to credit cards and jimmies and the like.''

''I should have thought of it myself,'' she said, self-recrimination warring with another, less acceptable emotion. He was standing close enough for her to feel the body heat emanating through the expensive gray sweat suit. The feelings he aroused in her were disturbing, unacceptable, and inescapable. She was reacting to him as a woman reacts to a man she wants, and she was a hundred times a fool to do so.

"That's all right," he said, still not moving, too close, too damned close. "All part of the service."

"Service?" The word was breathless. She could lean a little closer in the darkened hallway and be touching him again. It was tempting, very tempting.

"Jimmy the Stoolie's Rent-a-Crook."

It was enough to break the hypnotic spell. "Are we going to search this place or not?" she snapped, remembering to keep her voice to a whisper.

"I suppose we'd better. It's now—" he checked the ultrathin gold watch on his strong wrist "—eleven fifty-three. Tremaine uses Foxfire Security Systems, which means two men, two Dobermans, and probably two guns, will be here sometime after one o'clock. They have three stops before this one, and it depends whether any of my colleagues have chosen tonight to break into one of Foxfire's other clients' offices. I don't expect we'll be so lucky, so we'd better be out of here no later than quarter of one. Okay?"

She stared up at him. "How do you know all that?"

"Professional secret. Quarter of one okay with you?"

"Fine," she said, fighting back the distrust.

"Then let's go."

It was damned lucky she was gullible, Sandy thought. He couldn't very well tell her he'd called a colleague who'd called a client who'd called a friend to find out how Technocracies Ltd. handled security. She probably didn't want to know the sordid details, anyway. She'd rather believe he had some sort of criminal osmosis.

The keys had been a stroke of good luck. They'd get through the night with similar luck, if his sources had been correct. As they moved through the empty hallways he wondered what the real Jimmy would have done if Madame X had shown up at his motel room.

Tried to seduce her, for one thing. And while that reaction

hadn't been Sandy's first, it was becoming more and more appealing.

Except that prim and proper Jane Dexter wasn't the sort to fall into bed with a professional criminal. He'd have to overcome all her misgivings, all her doubts, all her very strong defenses.

The thought was challenging. Could he make someone want him so much she'd be willing to turn her back on years of security and ethics? The question had never come up before. The women he met knew he was a well-paid, unmarried lawyer of healthy habits and well-mannered disposition. They were running no danger at all getting involved with him.

With Jane it was a different matter. If she ever went to bed with him she'd be taking untold risks. If she went to bed with him it would be an act of faith and trust such as he'd never experienced. The more he thought about it, the more he wanted it.

"This is it," Jane said abruptly.

For a moment he didn't know what she was talking about. And then he looked at the heavy walnut door in front of them, the raised bronze lettering announcing the executive offices. "In there?"

"Where else? You told me there wouldn't be anything in Richard's lab, and I expect you're right. Uncle Stephen's office is the best place to start."

Uncle Stephen's office, he thought glumly. He'd been hoping to back her into a corner in some empty little lab. "All right," he said easily, reaching for the doorknob. The heavy brass handle didn't budge.

Jane was watching him, her eyes steady and curious behind her wire-rimmed glasses. "I don't suppose you brought a key for this one?"

"No sarcasm," he uttered. "We'll have to be inventive." The idea of breaking into an office with his gold American Express card would have appealed to his sense of humor if he had any kind of assurance he'd be successful. He pulled the thin sliver of plastic from his wallet, squatted down, and tried to look as if he knew what the hell he was doing.

It didn't help having Jane breathing down his neck. He could catch a slight trace of the perfume she was wearing, something faintly flowery that was nevertheless more sensuous than innocent. He spared himself a brief glance over his shoulder at her intent face. Plain Jane indeed. He wanted to push her over onto the too-expensive carpeting that lined the hallway and forget about her damned brother.

He turned his attention back to the task at hand. He heard the little click, and ignored it, refusing to believe it would be that easy.

"You did it," Jane whispered, reaching past him and turning the handle. The weighted door swung open.

"Of course I did." He rose to his full length, towering over her, hoping it was too dark for her to notice his astonishment. "Of course it took me a little longer than usual."

"I'll start with the receptionist's desk," she cut in. "Why don't you check out Uncle Stephen's office?"

The moment he saw the bank of teak filing cabinets he knew why she'd given him the good part. He had no hope whatsoever that the files were unlocked, and one desultory little yank proved him correct. Jane Dexter probably expected him to use his much-abused American Express card on each one of those file cabinets, something he wasn't about to do. It had been dumb luck the first time. He had no faith at all in his ability to repeat that particular miracle.

He didn't have to. Tremaine hadn't locked his desk, and sitting in the top drawer was a small gold key ring. The man was either innocent of wrongdoing, or supremely self-confident. From what little Sandy had heard of Stephen Tremaine, he had a very good notion it was the latter.

He was halfway through the files when Jane joined him. She sat cross-legged on the floor, leafing through the folder he'd handed her, her head bent like a studious little girl. She must have felt his eyes on her, for she looked up, directly into his face.

"You're awfully good at this sort of thing," she said. "The files were locked, weren't they?"

"Yes." He felt no need to enlighten her further. Better to have her think he was almost omnipotent. "It all comes with practice," he added modestly.

"You know, you just don't look the type." She closed the folder and reached for another one.

"What type?"

"Oh, you know. Hardened criminal and all that."

He considered making a crude joke, but resisted the impulse. While he might consider the past few hours in the nature of an adventure, Jane Dexter took it much more seriously. "We've already agreed," he said solemnly, "looks can be deceiving. You, for instance, look like a very conventional middle American. Instead, beneath that mild exterior hides the heart of an adventuress."

"Beneath my mild exterior hides a panic-stricken woman," she said tartly. "We're getting nowhere. There isn't even any mention of Richard's name in the personnel files. No contracts, no insurance packages, nothing."

Sandy nodded. "You're right. Which in itself is a sign we're on the right track. There should be some trace of your brother, some mention. How long did he work here?"

"Seven and a half years."

"Someone has carefully expunged all trace of him from the records. The only way to get his files will be through the computer." He eyed the silent screened monolith in the outer room with deep misgivings. "I don't suppose it would hurt to check. We don't have much time left. I'll clean up in here and you can see what the computer has to offer."

"See what the computer has to offer?" she echoed. "I don't know a thing about computers."

"Why not? I thought you read a lot."

"Not about computers, if I can possibly help it. I'll clean up and you try the computer."

Sandy sighed. "It would be a waste of time. I don't know anything about computers, either."

She just looked at him for a long moment. And then to his surprise she laughed, a deep, throaty chuckle at complete odds with her prim exterior. "We make pretty inept spies."

"But I'm hell on wheels at breaking and entering."

"You're hell on wheels at finding keys," she corrected. "Better put Uncle Stephen's back in his drawer."

She didn't miss much, he had to grant her that. For a moment he wondered how long it would take her to realize the newspaper made a mistake, that she wasn't consorting with a dangerous felon but a mild-mannered lawyer. And what would her reaction be when she did find out? He thought he might prefer the Dobermans.

"We'd better get out of here," he said suddenly, remembering. "It's ten of one, and those guys might be early."

Together they slammed the teak file drawers shut. Sandy almost forgot to relock the outer office, but Jane reminded him, and then they were racing down the hallway, their sneakered feet silent on the heavy carpeting. He didn't know whether the sound of traffic from 206 had gotten louder, or whether it was his own overstimulated heart roaring like that. The heavy glass door clicked shut behind them, and they were outside in the damp night air.

Headlights split the darkness as someone pulled into the parking lot, and he grabbed Jane's hand, pulling her along, panic and adrenaline rushing through him. She went with him, her gloved hand tight in his, and moments later they were off the property, heading toward the highway. The streetlights were bright, too bright, illuminating their figures, and Sandy could hear the slam of car doors, the muffled growl of ferocious canines as the two of them slid down the embankment, landing in a tangle of limbs.

They'd been seen. A flashlight shone in their direction, more like a spotlight, and a rough voice called out. "Hey, what are you two doing down there?"

Sandy didn't have much choice in the matter. The dogs were coming closer, the strong beams from the spotlight circling over their heads. He ripped off his gloves and stuffed them in his pocket, noting with approval that Jane had done the same thing without having to be told.

A dog snarled. A tightly leashed dog, Sandy devoutly hoped. A few more feet and they'd be seen. He looked at Jane's panicked expression and did the only thing he could think of. Yanking her onto his lap, he shoved one hand down her sweater and set his mouth on hers.

Chapter Four

It was the last thing Jane expected. Her heart was pounding wildly, her breath coming in tortured gasps, terror and a twisted sort of excitement were racing through her body. The feel of his hand on her breast, even through the lacy bra, shocked and aroused her. His mouth was on hers, wet, hot, seeking, his tongue and lips taking complete, unquestioning control of her and overwhelming any ounce of restraint she might have had. Too many emotions were batting at her, too much adrenaline, too much stimulation. She snaked her arms around his neck, pressed her breast against his hand and kissed him back, wanting nothing more than his mouth on hers, that desperate, erotic claiming that was shaking her to the very marrow of her bones.

Dimly she heard the dogs barking. Lights were flashing over her head, and for a moment she thought it was the force of his kiss making her see stars. Then she thought it was lack of oxygen causing the lights to go on in her brain. He tore his mouth away, gasping for breath, and she realized those celestial lights were flashlight beams.

"Helluva place to bring a lady, buddy," a voice called from above them. Her companion was looking at her, eyes glittering in the artificial light, and his breath was coming as rapidly as hers. Then he turned his head toward the intrusive beam of light.

"What can I say? We were out jogging when we decided to…er…take a little break. You wanna turn those lights off?"

His voice was disgruntled, a man interrupted in the throes of passion.

"Better pick someplace else, pal," another voice said, less amused. "This is private property, and you're trespassing."

Slowly the man beside her uncoiled his body and rose, shielding her from the light. "We'll do that. Sorry to bother you."

"No trouble. Just be glad I didn't unleash the dogs." An exuberant snarl punctuated that flat statement, and Jane shivered.

Jimmy the Stoolie was playing his part to the hilt. He put an arm around her shoulders, pulling her trembling body against his, and started down toward the road. She could feel the inquisitive, unsympathetic eyes following them, and she shivered in the warm night air.

"Do you think we fooled them?" she whispered under the noise of the traffic.

"Probably." They were back at the car by then, and he released her, too quickly, the action reminding Jane it had all been part of a very efficient charade. "You're quick," he said, his voice approving. "For a moment I thought you were going to hit me."

"The thought crossed my mind," she lied. Hitting him had been the last thing she'd contemplated. "All in a day's work."

THEY DROVE BACK OUT to Route One in silence. It was well past one in the morning, and traffic had thinned to a muffled roar. Jane's heart had slowed to a dull, steady throb, her hands were dry, her stomach in knots. She glanced over at her companion. Jimmy the Stoolie seemed lost in thought, his gray eyes intent on the driving, his strong hands gripping the leather-covered steering wheel loosely. One of those hands had cupped her breast. That practiced deftness must have been pure instinct on his part. He couldn't have consciously caught the tiny bud of her nipple and teased it into swollen arousal with attack dogs and armed guards looming overhead. An accident of nature, Jane decided, sinking gloomily in the seat.

''What next?'' he asked as he pulled in front of her peeling motel-room door.

Tension shot through her body. ''What do you mean?'' She couldn't deny the pseudo embrace in the ditch beside 206 had aroused her, but she certainly wasn't about to jump into bed with a professional arsonist and con man. Particularly when she'd known him for less than twelve hours.

Again that slow smile, as if he read her mind. ''What do we do tomorrow? Unless you're ready to call it quits.''

''I'm not. Even if tonight was a total washout that doesn't mean there aren't other possibilities.''

''I wouldn't say tonight was a complete failure. The fact that your brother's personnel file was missing suggests there's something going on...''

''I *told* you something's going on.''

''So you did. But one has to consider all the possibilities. And you might have been racked with paranoid delusions due to unresolved grief over your brother's untimely death.''

''Do you hang out with a lot of pop psychologists along with lawyers?'' she questioned sweetly.

To her surprise he flushed. ''Just worth considering,'' he said. ''You're still determined to go through with this?''

''Still determined. With you or without you. Are we going to torch the place?''

''No, we're not going to torch the place,'' he said wearily. ''Violent little creature, aren't you? I've got a few tricks up my sleeve.''

''Such as?''

''Leave it to me,'' he said mysteriously. ''I'll give you a call tomorrow morning and we'll make our plans.''

She was being dismissed. She breathed a sigh of relief, but felt disappointed that she wouldn't have to fight him off. She hadn't really expected to, but after the tangle in the ditch she couldn't help her mind from considering such things.

It was a waste of time. People who looked like her companion were never interested in plain Janes, and people who lived as she did weren't interested in compromising themselves with professional criminals. They were nothing more than partners in crime, and unless they ran across more Dobermans and armed guards he wouldn't have to touch her again.

He reached over and caught her willful chin, his long fingers cool against her heated flesh. "Earth to Jane, come in please," he murmured.

"Sorry, I was distracted." She was still distracted, by the look, the scent, the heat, the touch of the man beside her. She pulled back, and his hand dropped too readily. "Tomorrow," she said, climbing out of the car and locking it behind her.

He was coming with her. She couldn't read his expression in the artificial light, wasn't sure she even wanted to. "There's no need to see me to the door," she said hastily.

"I'm not. I've got the room next door."

The darkness covered her embarrassment quite nicely. "Since when?"

"Since this evening. I'd already checked out when you came up with your charming proposition. When I reregistered I had them move my room. I thought it might come in handy."

I'll just bet you did, Jane thought, then wiped out the fantasy. Why in the world was she so paranoid about the man's intentions? He'd said and done nothing to suggest he had any physical interest in her. For all she knew he might even be gay. No, scratch that. The man standing tall and straight in the lamplight was definitely, distressingly heterosexual. And even if her instincts told her he wanted her, her intellect assured her that fantasy was nothing more than wishful thinking on her part.

"Tomorrow, then." Her voice was steady, showing none of the tangled thoughts racing around in her weary brain.

"Tomorrow," he agreed, standing by his door as she fumbled for her key in her back pocket.

He waited until her door closed behind her, waited until he heard the distinctive sound of bolts being shot into place. "Damn," he muttered to himself, opening the peeling green door that was a twin to Jane's. "How do I get myself into these things?"

Of course the answer to that, he thought, pouring himself a

generous shot of Scotch and dropping down on the bed, was that he didn't. This was the first time he'd ever gotten involved in a situation rife with such lies and complexity that it simply boggled his mind.

He'd had more than a few bad moments that night, starting with the locked file cabinets and ending with her crack about pop psychologists. That was exactly what Beverly did for a living, and her conversation was dotted with phrases like "meaningful relationships" and "getting in touch with yourself." He'd always been revolted by her psycho-babble, and then to find he was doing it himself...

He drained the whiskey, stretching out on the lumpy mattress that was even worse than the one in his previous room. He considered turning on the TV—Princeton was in range of both New York and Philadelphia and even without cable there was always something on. The Princeton Pike Sleep-a-While Motel's only cable channel was an x-rated one. Clearly the place was misnamed—here people didn't usually rent rooms just to sleep.

Dirty movies were the last thing Sandy needed. He could still feel Jane's light, strong body beneath his, taste the surprising enthusiasm of her soft mouth. He was beginning to think he'd been mistaken in chasing after Amazons for all these years. He was rapidly growing partial to small brunettes, a Jane who wasn't very plain after all.

He cursed out loud, a nice, rounded obscenity he'd picked up from a teenage nephew, and was about to say it again when he heard a rapping on his wall.

"Is something wrong?" Jane's voice was muffled but unmistakable. He wondered what she was wearing, and he groaned.

"It's nothing." He sounded admirably calm. "I just stubbed my toe."

"Oh. Good night, then. Pleasant dreams."

Pleasant dreams, he thought cynically. Who would be innocent enough to wish a stranger pleasant dreams? Only a Midwestern librarian who was totally ignorant of how she affected him. He was going to have dreams, all right. He was going to dream about that slender, warm body of hers wrapped around his, he was going to dream about that soft, lovely mouth and those surprisingly generous breasts of hers. And he was going to have nightmares about what she was going to say when she found out who he really was.

He turned over on his stomach, shoved his face into the foam pillow that smelled of stale cigarette smoke and moaned. It was going to be a long night.

IT WAS TEN THIRTY-FIVE in the morning when Jane finally surfaced. She blinked sleepily at her watch, then sat bolt upright, jumped from the bed and raced to the window. Pushing the sickly green curtains out of the way, she saw in relief that the MGB was still in place. He hadn't taken off in the middle of night, never to be heard from again.

Not that it wouldn't have been a good thing, she thought as she rushed through her shower. If Jimmy the Stoolie were gone she'd be on her own, and sooner or later she'd have to give up in defeat. With a professional by her side the possibilities were endless, and so were the risks.

She had her morning ablutions down to a science, one that usually lasted seven and a half minutes. Today, in a hurry, it took her twelve, making sure the minimal mascara and liner were just right, even bothering with a slash of tinted lip gloss and a pinch of color on her pale cheeks. She braided her wet hair, tossing it over her shoulder, and grimaced at her reflection. She wasn't doing it for him, she reminded herself. The opinion of her partner in crime meant absolutely nothing to her. No, she did it for her own flagging sense of self-esteem.

By five of eleven there was still no sound from next door, no knock on her door, no jangling telephone. She considered her options. She could bang on the wall, but that seemed a little intimate. She wouldn't have done it last night, but that curse floating through the thin walls had a desperate edge to it, and she'd been afraid he'd hurt himself.

She could walk out into the bright sunlight and knock on

his door. But what if he were still asleep? She didn't fancy having him stagger to the door in rumpled pajamas, or even less.

She picked up the phone and dialed the desk. For a moment her mind went blank, forgetting his last name. She could hardly ask the bored-sounding clerk for the room of Jimmy the Stoolie, could she?

Calvin, that was it. Jimmy Calvin.

"No one by that name," the gum-popping voice replied, and the phone slammed down.

Jane counted to ten, dialed 0 once more, and said in her sweetest voice, "I know he's registered. He's in the room next to me."

"Then why don't you go and knock on his door?" Slam.

Jane counted to fifteen, dialed 0 and said, "Because I don't want to disturb him. Could you please ring his room for me?"

There was a long-suffering sigh on the other end of the line, accompanied by a loud snapping of gum. "There's no one in 4-A, and the man in 6-A isn't James Calvin. He's registered as Alexander Caldicott."

SOMEONE WAS CHASING after him, someone with a huge mallet, twice the size of an average man, and that person was slamming the mallet down on the ground, causing a major earthquake. It was Yosemite Sam, his red handlebar mustache bristling, shouting and cursing as he slammed the mallet down and the entire landscape hopped. It didn't hop as fast as he did, and he realized without much enthusiasm that he was Bugs Bunny.

The pounding continued, the dream faded, and Sandy sat bolt upright in bed, realizing he wasn't Bugs Bunny racing through a Southwestern desert, he was Alexander Caldicott in a motel in New Jersey.

The flimsy door was trembling with the force of someone's fist. "Wake up," Jane Dexter said fiercely from the other side and Sandy had one more realization. He was neither Bugs Bunny nor Alexander Caldicott, he was Jimmy the Stoolie. And he sank back into the pillow with a groan.

"Go away," he said weakly. It was too early and he was too hung over to face her and the truth he knew would have to come out. He'd have to tell her—sometime during the sleepless night he'd come to that conclusion. He'd take her out somewhere, not a cafeteria like that godawful steak house but someplace restrained and elegant, where she wouldn't dare throw a scene. She'd be embarrassed at her mistake, but he'd be charming, and they'd both end up laughing about it.

She didn't sound like she was laughing right now. "Wake up, Jimmy!" she said, still pounding. He could see the cheap panel vibrate, and he knew she wouldn't give up.

"I'm coming," he groaned. He'd resorted to finishing the bottle of Scotch around four-fifteen, when sleep had still eluded him. He didn't know whether he'd finally drifted off or blacked out, but the end result was the worst headache he'd had in his entire life.

He stumbled to the door, yanked it open, and stood glaring into the sunlight. Jane was glaring just as fiercely. "It's about time." She bit off the words, stepping into the room. He reached beyond her and shut the door, shut out the blinding sunlight that was threatening to split his skull. "I have something to ask you." And then her voice trailed off as she noticed what he was wearing.

Sandy ignored her, collapsing back on the bed. The weakened frame shook beneath the force of his body, but he didn't care, just lay face down in the tangled covers as he waited for Jane to pull herself together.

It wasn't as if he was stark naked. He'd slept in his briefs and T-shirt—both were a sedate navy blue, and if she'd been married she'd been bound to see someone in a lot less. Hell, there was more to his underwear than he usually wore swimming. God damn all librarians and people who pounded on his door demanding answers when he had the world's worst headache...

"Why are you registered under the name Alexander Caldicott?"

All self-pity vanished, and he stared down into the creased

white sheets, his beleaguered brain working overtime. He'd always had the ability to think fast, particularly in crucial situations, and now wasn't the time to come up with the truth. She'd probably break a chair over his head.

He rolled onto his back and eyed her calmly. Her normally pale face was still slightly pink, and she kept her eyes fastened above his neck. For a moment he had the sadistic wish that he had slept in the nude. If she was going to react like a Victorian virgin she might as well have something real to panic about.

"I'm registered under Caldicott's name because he's responsible for my bills," he said blithely, obscurely pleased that he wasn't actually lying.

"Why?"

"Part of a deal we worked out. He'll be reimbursed. It just helps with record keeping and all that."

She looked doubtful, then guilty. "Actually, I suppose I should be paying for your room."

"I draw the line at being a kept man," he said in his most solemn voice, and her cheeks flushed pink again. He wondered if he could get her to come a little closer. If he could just manage to trip her, get her onto this too soft bed with him, she might very well respond as she had last night.

Speaking of response, he thought with a silent groan, rolling onto his stomach once more. She might not have noticed if she kept her gaze on his face, but he had the suspicion it was taking every ounce of concentration she possessed to keep from letting her eyes drift lower.

"I didn't mean to offend you...you're teasing me, aren't you?"

"Yes."

She sighed, sinking down into the powder-pink vinyl chair that was the one improvement this room had to offer. "I'm too gullible."

He grinned at that. "Very true. And no, you don't need to pay for my room. We'll work out the finances later."

"But I don't even know if I can afford..."

"You can afford me. And if you can't, I may be into doing a little pro bono work after all."

"I couldn't accept that," she said stiffly.

"We'll work something out." He still didn't dare roll over again. She was having the most amazing effect on his senses, and she wasn't even a blonde. "Listen, let me grab a shower and then we'll head on out."

"Head on out where?"

He grinned. "Back to Technocracies, of course. Breaking and entering netted us very little, so it's back to plan one. It's time for a little industrial espionage."

Chapter Five

"This is an incredibly stupid idea," Jane hissed as she trailed Sandy down the same carpeted corridor they'd traversed less than twelve hours ago. It looked different in the daylight, bland and professional and distinctly unthreatening.

Neither of them bore much resemblance to the two burglars of the night before. She could scarcely recognize Jimmy the Stoolie. His wheat-colored hair was slicked back and parted in the center, his aristocratic nose was marred by a pair of glasses, he walked with a stoop-shouldered slouch, and his tie was knotted badly. For such minor changes the results were considerable, turning the golden prince into an attractive nerd.

She didn't know if her own transformation was as effective, though her companion had assured her it was. She'd gone in the other direction, fighting him all the way in the confines of his sleazy hotel room.

"Haven't you got anything livelier to wear?" he'd demanded, eyeing her sensible khaki suit and white blouse with disgust.

"No."

"Didn't that lump of a jacket come with shoulder pads?"

"I threw them out."

He snorted derisively. "I believe it. We'll have to wad up some tissues. We need to give your clothes some shape."

"It has quite enough shape, thank you."

"Stop arguing." Before she'd realized what he was doing

he'd reached out and unfastened the top two buttons of her white oxford shirt. She batted at his hands, but he ignored her, yanking at the material until his critical eye found something to approve. "One would never know you had breasts under those clothes," he muttered.

Outrage and amusement warred within her, and for once amusement won. "I think people are supposed to take it on faith." She jerked away from him, taking the wadded up tissues from his hand. "I can manage from here, thank you." She turned to the mirror, tucking the tissues under her bra straps to form makeshift shoulder pads. "They'll probably slip and I'll end up looking like the hunchback of Notre Dame."

He came up behind her, and his fingers were deft in her tightly braided hair. "They'll be too busy looking at your cleavage." He spread her damp hair around her shoulders, fluffing it slightly, gazing at her with an expression she couldn't quite fathom.

"Satisfied?" she demanded, turning to face him and instantly regretting it. As usual he was standing too close, and he'd touched her too much already for her peace of mind.

He wasn't through touching. "Almost. Change the sensible shoes to something a little spikier, put on more lipstick, and these—" he reached out, unwound the curved stem of her wire-rimmed glasses from her ears and pulled them off "—have got to go."

"Mr. Calvin," she began fiercely.

"Who?"

"Calvin. It's your last name, isn't it?"

He had the grace to look slightly flustered. "It's an alias."

"I'm not surprised."

"So is Jimmy." He peered through her glasses, shaking his head and blinking. "Call me Sandy."

"Sandy?" she echoed.

"Short for Sandor Voshninsky," he said blithely. "That was my favorite alias and I haven't used it for a while. You don't need these glasses."

"I get a headache without them."

"Join the club. I already have one." He reached up and settled her glasses on his own classic nose, peering through them. The transformation was instantaneous. He looked nearsighted, slightly wimpy and suddenly approachable. Jane found she didn't like that approachability one bit.

"I don't think we're going to fool anyone." She reached down to button her shirt, but he caught her hand, stopping her, holding it far too long. "If Uncle Stephen hadn't left for Europe I wouldn't even consider it. It's a lucky thing we met at his house and not at the office. I know his executive assistant never forgets a face, and once she sees me..."

"We don't have to fool them for very long. Listen, this is a simple scam. I know they'll hire me—I can talk anybody into anything."

"I believe it," she muttered.

"And you only had to look at the cluttered desks around there to know they're behind on their clerical work. You show up with the proper credentials and they'll jump on you like fleas on a dog."

"Charming figure of speech."

"Good help is hard to find nowadays. Everyone wants to be a chief, no one wants to be an Indian."

"How come I got elected to be the squaw? Why don't I tell them I'm a research scientist and you're the typist?"

"Because you don't have the experience to carry it off," he said bluntly. "I do. All you have to do is smile and lean over."

"Sexist pig," she said mildly. "How do you know the person hiring me is a man?"

"I don't. You'll have to adapt. If it's a man, you flirt very, very discreetly. Show him those terrific legs you try so hard to hide. If it's a woman, pull your skirts down and come on strong and subdued. Play on the sisterhood angle, but don't let her feel threatened."

She stared at him for a long moment, trying to ignore the flush of pleasure that had swept over her when he mentioned her terrific legs. She did have good legs, but she hadn't expected him to notice. "You have the most devious, manipulative mind," she said.

He leaned closer, and for a brief, startled moment she thought he was going to kiss her. Instead he reached under her jacket and adjusted the wad of tissue. "Thanks," he said cheerfully. "But you're showing great promise yourself."

Right now she didn't feel the slightest bit promising. Jimmy, no, Sandy had called Technocracies Ltd. And apparently the company was in dire need of temporary secretarial help. She didn't even understand half of what Sandy said about himself. All that mattered was the end result. Sandy had an appointment with the chief of personnel, Jane was to be interviewed by the other end of the corporate ladder.

"Cheer up, Madame X," he murmured at the door of the personnel office. "You'll do fine."

To her amazement she did, though she had a few schizophrenic moments. Charlie Pilbin, a harassed-looking middle-aged man, interviewed her, and she dutifully hiked her skirt up, leaned forward, and spoke very seriously of her interest in word processing. She hadn't a snowball's chance in hell of being hired if she admitted she knew nothing about computers, and she'd managed to pick up enough information in her job at the Baraboo City Library to sound knowledgeable. She could only pray Sandy rescued her before she actually had to confront one of the electronic beasts.

There she was, being as subtly seductive as she could possibly imagine, when the door opened and a woman walked in. Jane didn't need an introduction to know who the newcomer was. Richard had been loud and hostile about Elinor Peabody, and the vivid word pictures still lingered.

Stephen Tremaine's executive vice-president was a stunningly attractive woman in her late thirties. From the tips of her leather-shod feet to the top of her silvery-blond hair, a distance that encompassed almost six feet, the woman emanated poise, intelligence, and the kind of ruthless determination that had always given Jane a headache. Some people were so sure of things in this life, and nothing ever swayed their intense certainty.

Whereas Jane was far too likely to view all the possibilities and have a wretchedly hard time choosing which one was the least of all evils. She rose politely, looking up at Elinor Peabody, and knew one thing without any doubt. The woman was trouble.

"Is this the new temp?" Ms Peabody inquired abruptly. Jane was too nearsighted to be sure, but it seemed as if the woman's icy gaze took in Jane's appearance, not missing a detail, and found her wanting.

"It is." Charlie Pilbin clearly didn't like being interrupted, and he didn't like Elinor Peabody. Jane didn't need glasses to ascertain that—his tone of voice made it very clear. "Judy Duncan, meet Elinor Peabody, Stephen Tremaine's executive assistant."

"Executive vice-president," Ms Peabody corrected him. "The promotion went through last month, remember?" She nodded at Jane, a curt greeting. "You're familiar with IBM computers and software?"

"Yes," Jane lied.

"Elinor, I haven't finished interviewing her yet..." Charlie complained, but Ms Peabody sailed right over his objections.

"You don't need a life history for a temporary employee, Charlie." She was using a "be charming to the subordinates" voice that Jane found fascinating. She could hear Charlie Pilbin's teeth grinding. "I'm sure Judy will be able to catch on quickly enough, and you can finish up the paperwork later."

"But..."

"Thanks, Charlie." She put a hand on Jane's arm and swept her from the room with a backward glance. "It doesn't do any good to be wishy-washy about these things," she announced. "If you find a home at Technocracies Limited, you'll soon learn that Stephen Tremaine's creed is fast decisions and deal with the consequences. You seem *reasonably* well-equipped. I have no doubt you'll do just fine."

Jane began to grind her own teeth, but Elinor Peabody was

too caught up in her own master plan to notice. Five minutes later she found herself plunked in front of a computer screen, staring at blinking amber blips and trying to wish away the cold sweat that had broken out on her forehead.

At least Ms Peabody had turned it on for her. Jane leaned forward, peering desperately at the letter *A* flashing back and forth and praying for guidance.

"Are you nearsighted, Ms Duncan?" Peabody demanded abruptly.

Jane kept staring at the screen, then belatedly realized the woman was talking to her. How could Jimmy…no, Sandy keep his aliases straight?

"I have new contact lenses." The lie came so easily Jane was secretly horrified. She'd always prided herself on being scrupulously honest and completely straightforward. She'd slipped into the shadowy life of half truths so easily she wondered if she'd ever make it back out again.

"You shouldn't let vanity get in the way of efficiency," Elinor Peabody intoned, and Jane swallowed a retort. Elinor Peabody was born with the kind of beauty that very little could tarnish. Perfect bone structure combined with an indomitable will left nothing to chance. If she ever needed glasses she'd probably order her eyes to improve. Doubtless those china blue eyes of hers would comply.

"I won't, ma'am," Jane muttered, reaching out and pushing a key. The damned machine beeped at her, and once more Elinor Peabody raised her head.

She rose and circled the wide teak table that served as a desk, coming to loom over Jane's unevenly padded shoulders. "Sorry, I forgot to let you into the file. You need two passwords, and I'm not about to give either one of them out." She leaned past Jane and began tapping on the keys, and Jane got a full dose of her perfume. Poison, by Christian Dior. Wouldn't you know it, Jane thought with a sigh, cursing her partner in crime for getting her into this mess.

"There you go." Ms Peabody moved back. "It's certainly

a simple enough task. Just enter the new tax information for each employee, then go on to the next one.''

"Simple enough," Jane muttered, peering at the screen. Personnel files at her fingertips, if she could just manage to move from one name to the next.

God bless them, the creators of the software provided a help file at the top of the screen. Holding her breath, Jane pushed a key. To her amazement, a personnel file appeared in bright amber. Adamson, George Social Security #156-42-5917.

She pushed another button. Allman, Gregory. Astor, Jacob. Her face was flushed with triumph, and she pushed her irritating mop of hair away from her eyes, hunching closer. Computers were easier than she'd ever imagined. What a fool she'd been to be terrified of them. Bachman, Joyce. Ballard, Alice. Butler, Charles. Cashill, Patricia. Davis, Alexander. Debrett, Piers. Dunbar, Glenn. Eddison, Larry....

She stopped, perplexed. The personnel files held records for all employees, past and present. Larry Eddison had retired four years ago, Alice Ballard had worked as a consultant for three months in 1978. Where was Richard Dexter's file?

She looked up at the Help file, but this time the programmers let her down. They refused to tell her how to go back, only how to move forward. All she could do was forge on ahead and hope the damned files would start all over again when she got to Z.

Fairbanks, Robert. Kellogg, Roger. Peabody, Elinor. Sullivan, Nancy. Tremaine, Stephen.

That answered one question. The files covered everyone, from corporate head to mail clerk. Richard's file must have been deliberately deleted.

Xanatos, Grigor. Zallman, Yeshua. And then a blank screen, with nothing more than a blinking, taunting letter *A*.

She allowed herself a brief glance over at Ms Peabody, but her golden head was bent over her spotless desk, the bright sunlight gilding it. Jane managed a silent snarl and went back to the screen. It had been fairly simple so far. All she had to do was punch a few buttons and the program would reappear.

It had been remarkably easy when Ms Peabody did it, and despite Jane's deep-rooted feelings of inferiority she told herself that anything Ms Peabody did, she could do.

The computer disagreed. For long minutes it sat there sullenly, flashing that bright *A* at her while she pushed keys and combinations of keys. And then suddenly it went wild, letters and numbers and figures that looked like they were part of the Greek alphabet began hurling themselves onto the screen. The damned thing began buzzing, a rude, grating noise, mocking her, and then, just as Ms Peabody rushed to her side, the entire screen shuddered and went blank.

Dead silence reigned in the office. "Move out of the way," said Ms Peabody. The words were bitten off, and Jane moved.

The older woman sank gracefully into the chair Jane had vacated, bowed her head in what appeared to Jane as silent prayer, and set her fingers on the keyboard. Jane held her breath.

But even the indomitable Ms Peabody couldn't coax life from the recalcitrant computer. After long, fruitless moments she moved away, icy rage vibrating through every cell of her elegant body. "Twenty-three years of personnel records lost, Ms Duncan," she said in a deceptively mild voice. "I think, I'm afraid, that you won't do for Technocracies Limited."

Her very calm was terrifying. Jane managed a weak smile, wondering whether she ought to plead, ought to protest. She decided she'd be lucky if she escaped with her life. "I'm terribly sorry…"

"Just leave," said Ms Peabody, sweeping past her and heading for the phone. "Marcus," she said into the receiver, "bring me that new computer genius you hired. It's an emergency."

Jane was still hovering by the door. Ms Peabody fixed her with an icy stare. "You can leave anytime," she said, then looked over her shoulder at the opening door. "There you are, Marcus. Let's hope your new wonder boy is all he's cracked up to be."

Marcus turned out to be a middle-aged man complete with nerd pack and pot belly. In his wake came Sandy, a Band-Aid wrapped around one corner of *her* glasses. He was stooping just slightly, his coat flapping around him, and as he passed Jane he reached out and pinched her backside, well out of view of the other two people in the room.

"What seems to be the trouble, ma'am?" His voice was nasal, just this side of an adolescent whine, and it took all Jane's willpower not to giggle.

Ms Peabody opened her mouth to speak, then spied Jane still lingering at the door. "Go!" she thundered. Jane turned and ran.

THEY'D TAKEN BOTH CARS, and Jane couldn't rid herself of the suspicion that Sandy hadn't had much faith in her chance of success. It was understandable—she didn't have much faith either. She drove home through the early-afternoon traffic, muttering under her breath, replaying the scene in her mind and coming up with alternatives that cast a more flattering light on her efforts.

She slammed into the room, yanked the tissues from underneath her bra straps and squinted into the mirror. Her cheeks were flushed, her thick brown hair tangled, and she couldn't see without her glasses. It had been dangerous enough driving home, peering through the windshield of her Escort. It would be foolish indeed to go out again.

She flopped down on the bed. She was starving, she was edgy, she was tired, and her head ached. Surely Richard wouldn't demand this kind of sacrifice on her part. He was dead, surely he was past caring.

He might be, but she wasn't. As tempting as the thought might be, she couldn't turn her back on her responsibility. Today had taught her a lesson, however. Subtlety wasn't her strong suit. When Sandy came back she'd ask him about pipe bombs.

The spiky high heels he'd made her wear hurt her arches. She kicked them off, reaching up to fasten her blouse, then dropped her hand. *The hell with it,* she thought tiredly, rolling onto her side and curling in on herself. There'd be time enough to change later.

She always hated sleeping in the middle of the day—her worst nightmares came then. She dreamed she was in a car, rolling over and over down an embankment and then bursting into flames. But the fire smelled of pepperoni and onion, not of gasoline, and the brightness wasn't the bright glow of fire, it was the meager bedside light. And that wasn't Death leaning over her, it was Sandy, squinting through her glasses, holding a square white box that could only contain pizza in front of her nose.

Jane looked up at him. "I'm not going to ask how you got in here without a key," she said in her calmest voice. "I simply want to know whether there are anchovies on that pizza."

"What if there are?"

"I'll scream for help."

He grinned at her, flipping open the lid. "No anchovies. I guess our unholy alliance continues for a bit."

Slowly, wearily Jane pulled herself into a sitting position. Sandy had plopped himself down on the bed beside her, helping himself to a generous slice of pizza. Reaching out, she pulled her glasses off his nose and settled them on her own. The metal frame was warm from his body heat, and she wished she'd let him hand them to her.

She touched the white Band-Aid that was wrapped conspicuously around the frame. "Did you have to break them?"

"Don't worry—the Band-Aid is for effect, nothing more. You certainly screwed up their computer." He finished his slice of pizza, crust and all, and reached for another.

Jane decided she'd better move fast or she'd starve to death. "I told you I didn't know anything about computers. Neither do you. What happened when they found you couldn't fix it?"

"They still don't know. The PC in Ms Peabody's office is completely out of whack. They think I'll be there first thing tomorrow morning to pull the personnel files from its bowels."

"Oh, God," Jane murmured.

"Is that 'Oh, God' in response to the splendor of the pizza

or the destruction of the computer?'' Sandy had put his long legs up on the bed, his tie was off, and he'd rumpled his blond hair into a spiky punk look.

''Both,'' she said, reaching for another slice. ''So neither of us gets to go back.''

''Just as well. Your boss of five minutes found out who you are. By tomorrow they'll tumble to the fact that we were hired together.''

The pizza began to feel like lead in her empty stomach. ''How'd she find out?''

''Who else but your beloved godfather?'' Sandy said, kicking off his shoes and making himself comfortable. ''Eat that last piece and you die.''

She eyed it wistfully. ''It might be worth it. How did Uncle Stephen know?''

''He had an anonymous tip that you broke into the place last night.''

''How in heaven's name did he know that?'' she demanded, horrified.

''Very simple,'' said Sandy. ''I told him.''

Chapter Six

Plain Jane looked absolutely adorable sitting there with her blouse gaping open, the Band-Aided glasses perched on her nose, her lips red from the pizza. "You did what?" she demanded.

He smiled sweetly, ripping apart the last piece of pizza, and handed her the smaller portion. "I gave Uncle Stephen an anonymous tip. I thought it would be useful to see how he reacted—whether he called the police or went to ground."

"And...?"

"No sign of cops anywhere around the place. Ergo, he's trying to cover up something. Unless he has a soft spot for you and doesn't want to get you in trouble." He frowned suddenly. He hadn't thought of that possibility until now, but if it had been up to him he wouldn't have turned Jane in.

"Uncle Stephen doesn't have a soft spot for anything without a bottom line. Don't you think you were taking a big risk? They may have connected us sooner than you hoped. If he had called the police you would have been back in jail so fast your head would swim."

"Back in jail? I wasn't in jail before."

"What about the arson and conspiracy charges? Didn't they arrest you?"

Thank heavens for his ability to think fast. "You forget, Alexander Caldicott is one of the world's great lawyers. He got me out on bail before they even locked me up." Not strictly true, Sandy thought. The real Jimmy the Stoolie had spent an uncomfortable night in custody before he'd managed to spring him on his own recognizance.

"I still think you were taking too great a risk." Jane sat up and tucked her feet underneath her. "I didn't find anything I didn't already know. Richard's personnel records have been deleted from the files."

"Everybody's personnel records have been deleted, thanks to you."

"Don't be pedantic. Before my little mishap I went through all the employees. They had everyone listed who'd ever worked there, from Stephen Tremaine on down, and no mention of Dick whatsoever."

"Dick?" Sandy echoed, momentarily diverted. "As in Dick and Jane?"

"Our parents weren't very imaginative." Her narrow shoulders were hunched defensively.

"I don't suppose you have a younger sister named Sally?" He knew he shouldn't push it but he couldn't resist.

"Living in Dubuque with her second husband and three children," she said gloomily. "Could we get back to the subject?"

"Not yet. Where is sister Sally during the grand quest for your brother's legacy?"

"They never got along. Dick wasn't that easy a person to be around. People with such high principles seldom are. He didn't have much patience for compromise, or for people he considered his intellectual inferiors. Which included just about everybody."

"Did it include you?"

"Oh, me most of all," she said with unfeigned cheerfulness. "I was anathema to him. The little peacemaker, with no more conviction than a willow tree, swaying with each strong breeze. He was right, I'm afraid."

Sandy had a sudden swift desire to punch Dick Dexter in the teeth. "Your brother sounds like an intolerant, pompous idiot."

If he expected an argument he wasn't about to get one. "I'm

afraid he was," she admitted. "But I loved him anyway. And I mourn his death, though not as much as I should. I suppose that's why I feel so guilty. I just…can't really comprehend that he's gone. I don't believe it." She sighed. "I suppose that's a fairly common reaction to untimely death. Sooner or later it'll sink in. In the meantime, I have to do what I can to preserve his memory."

"Urrmpphh." Sandy knew the sound from his throat was uncompromising, and he didn't care. He wasn't motivated by any great liking for Richard Dexter. His motivations were pure and simple—keep Jane out of trouble. And have the undisputed pleasure of moonlighting as a con artist while he was doing it.

"We're not making much progress," she added. "I've been thinking—Uncle Stephen has to sell the process because Technocracies is in such big trouble. If we burn the place it would render the situation obsolete. Either he'd be out of business entirely and we won't have to bother, or he'll get so much from insurance it'll solve his cash flow problems. You can do that, can't you? Torch an entire building?"

"Don't look so eager," he growled. "Yes, I can, and no, I won't. You're not thinking clearly again. If the place is destroyed and Tremaine is out of business he'll cut his losses and sell anything negotiable to the highest bidder. We've already ascertained that we don't know where the process is."

"Oh," said Jane, disappointed.

"And I beg to differ with you. We're making more progress than you realize. I spent an inordinate amount of time in the executive washroom trying to clean computer grease from my hands. Ceramic tile is excellent for carrying sound. Your godfather put off his trip to Europe, and for a very good reason."

"Which is?"

"He can't sell the process if he doesn't have the process," Sandy said triumphantly.

"He doesn't have it?" Jane shrieked. "Who does?"

"No one. At least, no one has all of it. Your brother didn't work exclusively at Technocracies Limited. He had at least one private lab, and maybe more, and your buddy Tremaine hasn't the faintest idea where they were. All he knows is that when Richard died there was an important piece of information missing from his work at Technocracies. Without it the process is useless.''

He was unprepared for her response. Unprepared for the blazing smile that lit her face, turning her from passably attractive to a raving beauty. He was unprepared for the whoop of joy, unprepared for her to launch herself at him, flinging her arms around his neck and kissing him soundly on the cheek. And he was unprepared for her immediate withdrawal. He reached out, trying to capture her arms and keep her tight against him, but she'd already slipped away.

''Our troubles are over,'' she said, her eyes alight.

''No,'' he said, ''they're not.'' He hated to disillusion her, but she'd figure it out sooner or later, and he didn't trust her without his restraining presence. She was too damned bloodthirsty. ''Tremaine isn't going to give up. They're hiring private investigators to find Richard's laboratories. Sooner or later the information is going to turn up, unless you think he would have destroyed it.''

She shook her head. Her hair was still loose from her earlier transformation, and it tangled appealingly around her narrow face. ''He wouldn't do that. He was too egocentric to destroy anything he'd invented.''

''And of course he'd have no reason to do so, would he?'' he prodded. ''It was only a coincidence that a vital part of the process is missing. Wasn't it?''

Jane was lousy at dissembling. ''Not exactly.''

''Not exactly,'' he echoed. ''What have you neglected to tell me? If we're going to be partners in crime we can't keep things back from each other.'' He didn't suffer more than a slight twinge at the thought of all he was keeping from her.

''I didn't think it was that important. Dick was always paranoid—I just thought it was part of his persecution complex.''

''What was?''

She made a face. ''He called me a couple of days before he died. He must have had some sort of premonition. He said if anything happened to him I had to make sure Uncle Stephen didn't misuse the titanium coating process.''

''Was that a premonition?'' Sandy asked. ''Or did he know he was in danger?''

Jane sat very still. ''You think it wasn't an accident?''

''I don't know what to think. There's a lot of money at stake, and Stephen Tremaine is not known for his ethical restraint. You know the man better than I do. Do you think he'd balk at murder?''

''Absolutely,'' Jane said. And then a moment later, ''At least, I think so.''

''Thinking's not good enough. I think we're going to have to be extra careful. If he's killed once there's nothing to stop him from killing again.''

''This is ridiculous. No one's killed anybody. You sound like some sort of murder mystery. People don't go around killing other people.''

''Yes,'' he said gently, ''they do.''

The dingy motel room was silent, with only the sound of the traffic from Route One filtering through the thin walls. In the distance Sandy could hear the sound of a television set turned up too loud, the noise of a shower two rooms over. And the sound of Jane's steady, troubled breathing.

''Have you ever killed anyone?'' she asked finally.

''No.'' He could say that both for himself and for the real Jimmy the Stoolie. Though of course he shouldn't have taken Jimmy's word for it—the man was a pathological liar. But in his years of practicing law he'd learned to tell, not necessarily who had and who hadn't committed murder, but who could and who couldn't. Jimmy definitely fit in the hadn't and couldn't category.

But Jane Dexter was a question mark. Common sense told him a civilized Midwestern librarian wasn't about to go around wreaking havoc, but her frustration level was high. And if it turned out that Stephen Tremaine really had murdered her brother, he had no idea what her reaction might be.

''We have several options open to us,'' Sandy continued.

"We can drop everything, hope that Tremaine never finds the missing part of the formula, and go our merry way. Or we can try to outfox him and find the rest of the formula before he does. After that it's up to us. We could always sell it to the highest bidder ourselves…"

"No."

"Just a thought. Or we can destroy it. Or just salt it away someplace until we make up our minds."

"Or we can torch the place."

Sandy shook his head. "Jane, Jane, you must curb these violent impulses. It wouldn't do any good at all. Tremaine's no fool—he'll have copies of the formula."

"Then I guess we really have no option at all. We'll have to find the rest of the formula before he does. That way we can blackmail him into selling it to someone we approve of, and Richard will be satisfied."

Richard won't care, Sandy wanted to point out, but he tactfully controlled himself. "Personally I approve of the highest bidder, but I bow to your wishes." He shifted on the bed, moving imperceptibly closer. Jane was so caught up in her plans that she didn't even notice.

"How much does Uncle Stephen know? Does he have any idea where Dick's labs might be?"

"I'm not sure. He and Peabody got a bit…distracted, and gentlemanly restraint forced me to stop eavesdropping."

Jane snorted. "I hadn't noticed you plagued by gentlemanly restraint. Are you telling me Uncle Stephen is sleeping with Ms Peabody?"

"I don't think they were sleeping."

Jane shook her head. "The swine."

Sandy shifted closer, so that his thigh pressed against hers. "Some men are," he said innocently.

"They are indeed. We'll go back to Dick's apartment," she said decisively.

"Now?" While the bed they were sitting on wasn't terribly comfortable, it had the undisputed merit of being readily available.

"Tomorrow. I went through that place with a fine-tooth comb but I might have overlooked something."

Sandy nodded. She smelled like flowers and pizza and soap—an undeniably erotic combination. "It would help to have a fresh look at the place."

"And you're exceedingly fresh. Move your leg."

He didn't. He looked at her for a long, thoughtful moment. She didn't blink, though he could tell she wanted to, she didn't fiddle with her blouse, though he knew she wished to hell she'd rebuttoned it. She just looked into his eyes with an I-dare-you kind of glare, and Sandy Caldicott couldn't resist a dare.

He shifted, smoothly, gracefully, so quickly that she didn't have time to squirm away. In seconds she was sprawled on the bed, beneath him.

"I didn't know you numbered rape and assault among your crimes," she said through gritted teeth. His face was inches away from hers, and behind the wire-rimmed glasses her dark brown eyes were blazingly angry and not the slightest bit frightened.

"I'm not going to rape or assault you," he said in his most reasonable voice. "I'm just going to kiss you."

"I don't want to be kissed."

He was holding her hands down, his hips were pinning hers, and her breasts were pushing against him. "Tough. I deserve something for combat pay. Not to mention the pizza." And he dropped his mouth down on hers.

She tried to jerk away, but he let go of her hands and caught her jaw, holding it in place for a long, leisurely kiss. He could feel her hard little fists pounding at him, but he ignored them, lost in the sweetness of her lips. She bounced her hips, trying to throw him off, but it only aroused him more. And for all her fight, for all the anger in her hands, her mouth was soft, pliant, and opening to him.

She was no longer beating at him. Her arms had slid around his neck, her tongue had reached out to touch his, and her body was softening beneath him as his was getting harder and harder. She made a little noise in the back of her throat, half a moan, half a whimper, and he wanted to hear more. He wanted to hear her crying against him, wanted to feel that surprisingly lush body wrapped around his, he wanted to turn off the lights and shut out the depressing little motel and lose himself in Jane Dexter's wonderful body.

He paused for breath, lifting his head to look down at her through passion-glazed eyes. She lay there, panting, her lips slightly swollen from his kisses, her eyes closed behind the glasses. Beneath the closed lids, hot tears were pouring down her face.

Sandy jumped away as if he were burned, cursing loudly and profanely as guilt swamped him. "For God's sake, Jane, it was only a kiss!"

She opened her eyes and to his disgust and amazement she grinned at him. "Neat trick, eh?" She pulled herself to a sitting position, rebuttoned her blouse almost to her neck, and stood up, keeping well out of his reach. "It's my one accomplishment. I can cry any time I want to."

He just stared at her. No longer did he have any desire to push her back on the bed. There was nothing he hated more than tears—like most people he couldn't deal with them, could do nothing but feel guilty. He felt tricked on the most fundamental level, and his temper was fraying around the edges.

"I'd be more than happy to give you something to cry about," he snarled.

"You would."

"I beg your pardon."

"You would give me something to cry about," she said calmly, moving over to the wavery mirror and wiping the tears off her cheeks. "You'd give me nothing but trouble and misery, and I'm not about to let myself in for it. I've had enough misery in the past couple of years to last me for a long time, and I'm not going to make any more mistakes when it comes to men."

"And I'd be a mistake?"

She met his eyes in the mirror. "The biggest," she said, sighing. "So we'll keep this as a business partnership, all right?

I'm sure you can find someone who's more your style. Some leggy blonde who's not into commitment.''

"They're all into commitment," he said gloomily, ignoring the little shock he'd felt at her words. How did she know he liked leggy blondes? Hell, who wouldn't? Except right now he had no interest in leggy blondes whatsoever. He was only interested in petite, bespectacled ladies with rumpled brown hair and tears still glistening in their eyes.

Crocodile tears, he reminded himself. "I think," he said, "I've had enough for one day. I'm going to bed."

"Good night." She was cool and unmoved, watching him as he headed for the door.

Sandy considered sulking. He considered slamming the door, he considered telling her what he thought of her phony tears. And then his sense of humor surfaced. "It's not going to work," he said, opening the door and standing there in the cool night air.

"What isn't?"

"You're not going to be able to keep from making mistakes."

"I can try."

"Yes, you can. But it won't do you any good. And next time I kiss you I won't mind if you're awash in tears."

She glared at him. "There won't be a next time."

"Oh, yes, there will." He shut the door behind him, stepping out into the night. And through the thin walls he heard her voice.

"Yes, there will," she said out loud. And Sandy, his good humor totally restored, headed back to his own room.

RICHARD'S APARTMENT didn't look any different from the last time Jane had been there, three days ago. The boxes she'd packed were still neatly stacked in the hallway, the curtains were drawn, everything exactly where she'd left it. She stepped into the musty smelling apartment, waited until Sandy closed the door behind them, and announced, "Someone's been here."

"How do you know?" He wandered past her into the boring, box-shaped apartment. "Is anything missing?"

They'd gotten along fine, eating breakfast together and being very careful not to touch each other. Now, alone in the closed-up apartment, Jane was remembering the night before, the brief, overwhelming moments on that concave mattress, the feel of his body on hers, the lean muscle and sinew and bone that had felt unbearably delectable covering hers.

Quickly she wiped out that thought. If Sandy remembered she'd seen no sign of it—his temper had been cheerfully un-impaired that morning. Maybe he'd gone out and found a leggy blonde. No, she would have heard it. The walls were paper thin between their rooms.

But those few moments on her bed were probably more commonplace to someone like…like whatever name he chose to use at the moment. While for her they were a shattering revelation.

"Jane?" Sandy prodded.

"I can't tell. I just get this feeling that someone's been snooping around."

Sandy shrugged. "Either you're as paranoid as your brother was or Tremaine's detectives have been both efficient and un-scrupulous. Your guess is as good as mine." He crossed the dull beige wall-to-wall carpeting and peered behind the curtain into the parking lot below. "When were you last here?"

"Three days ago. Plenty of time for someone to come in and search the place." She stared at the neatly piled boxes with a sense of oppression. She'd spent days packing everything away. She could only hope Sandy wasn't about to suggest they unpack everything.

Apparently Sandy had something else in mind. "Well, if someone broke in while you were gone they didn't find what they were looking for."

"What makes you say that?"

He let the curtain drop and turned to face her. "Because Stephen Tremaine and two suspicious-looking characters just drove up. And unless I miss my guess, they're heading up here to give the place one more look.''

"We've got to hide.''

"No, we don't. You have every right and reason to be here. I, on the other hand, ought to make myself scarce. I'll be in the bedroom while you get rid of them.''

"But what do you expect me to do? Sit here and twiddle my thumbs while they break in?'' she demanded, both frightened and furious.

"If they have any experience at all they'll ring the doorbell,'' he said calmly. "That's the first rule of 'B and E.' Make sure the place is deserted. All you have to do is answer the door and send them on their way.''

"And if they won't go?''

He grinned, that disarming, golden-boy grin that didn't belong to someone known as Jimmy the Stoolie. "We'll deal with that when we get to it.'' Right on cue, the doorbell rang, and Jane jumped.

"Get the door, Madame X,'' he prompted, disappearing into the bedroom. "Time for Act Two.''

Chapter Seven

Jane stood in front of the door, wiping her damp palms on her khaki trousers and taking a deep, calming breath. The doorbell rang again, and the doorknob twitched, suddenly, suspiciously. For half a moment she was tempted to let them break in, just to see their reaction when they came face to face with her. And then she thought better of it. She had no desire to initiate a confrontation—the past thirty-six hours had been far from blameless on her side as well as theirs.

"Coming," she called, and heard the thud as someone jumped back from the door as if burned. "Just let me fiddle with these locks," she said cheerfully, making a great deal of noise before swinging open the door. She looked directly into her godfather's flinty eyes and flashed him her widest, most guileless smile.

"What the hell are you doing here?" Stephen Tremaine demanded gruffly, striding into the room with his two goons at his side. He was a short, barrel-chested man in his late fifties, with a shock of carefully tended white hair, a perpetual tan, and small, unsentimental slate-blue eyes that he used to stare down competition. He didn't believe in wasting time on social amenities, and he stood there in his beautiful suit, staring at Jane, tapping one perfectly shod foot in a blatant demonstration of just how impatient he was.

"How nice to see you, Uncle Stephen," she almost cooed.

"You just saw me last week," he snapped. "What are you doing here?"

"Packing Dick's stuff away."

"You already did that."

There was no way Stephen Tremaine would know that, if he hadn't already been in the apartment. Jane felt a sudden surge of satisfaction at having trapped him, whether he knew it or not. Maybe she was developing a talent for intrigue. "I had a few more things to take care of," she said calmly. "Speaking of which, why are you here? And who are your friends?"

"They don't matter," Tremaine said, walking past her and peering at the stack of boxes. "I hope you realize that anything pertaining to Dick's work legally belongs to Technocracies?"

"Of course." Her tone was dulcet. She wouldn't ask him again, she'd wait.

He poked one stubby, well-manicured finger at one of the boxes, snorting audibly. And then he moved on, prowling around the apartment like a caged beast, his two goons standing silently by the door. As long as he didn't head for the bedroom she would let him poke and pry all he wanted to. If he found anything interesting, all the better for her.

He stopped at the window, whirling suddenly. "Where were you yesterday?"

She didn't bat an eye. "Here, packing. Where were you?"

"At work. We had trouble with some temporary workers. Some fool woman messed up our computer system, and a so-called hotshot destroyed one of our terminals." His eyes were accusing.

"It's so hard to find good help nowadays," Jane said with a sympathetic sigh.

Tremaine just looked at her. She knew what he was thinking, as clearly as if he'd spoken his thought out loud. He was trying to decide whether or not to accuse her of infiltrating Technocracies. She knew by his tiny nod that he'd chosen not to. "Yes," he said, "it is."

"We all have our problems," she said vaguely, wishing he'd leave.

He was suddenly solicitous, moving back toward her and taking her damp, cold hands in his hot, hard ones. "But it's you I'm worried about, Janey. This has all been too much for you, losing Richard and then having to come east and pack up everything. I know Princeton doesn't hold very many happy memories for you. Why don't you let me finish things up for you? I have a staff who can handle these matters. They'll finish packing, ship the stuff back to you, and close up things. You've been through too much already. Go back to Wisconsin and let me do this for you."

Damn, he was good, Jane thought, letting him squeeze her hands and look earnestly into her eyes. He was about as earnest as a tarantula. "You're sweet to offer, Uncle Stephen," she said. "But I've got some time off, and it helps me to be here."

His tough little hands tightened painfully on hers. "I think you're making a mistake. I think you should go back and leave things to me."

"No." The word was only slightly ragged, and she met his eyes fearlessly, not quailing before the sudden flare of rage in them. "No."

He dropped her hands, stepping back a pace or two, and then he smiled once more, displaying small, sharp teeth. "All right, Janey," he said. No one ever called her Janey. "Suit yourself. I only wanted to save you needless grief."

"I appreciate the thought."

He nodded. "Then we'll leave you to it. I'll just use the little boy's room before I go…" He was heading toward the bedroom, and Jane felt her heart leap in panic.

She opened her mouth to stop him, to protest, then shut it again. There was nothing she could say that could possibly sound reasonable. She shut her eyes, listening to the sound of the bathroom door closing, waiting for Tremaine's exclamation of surprise.

There was no sound at all but the noise of running water. Jane opened her eyes, to look into the blank, emotionless faces of Tremaine's prepossessing escort. She managed a shaky

smile. "I left the bathroom sort of messy," she said in explanation. Neither of the goons said a word.

Minutes later Tremaine was back, anger in his eyes, a smile
on his mouth. "We'll be going now, Janey. That is, if you're
sure I can't help?"

"I'm sure, Uncle Stephen. You've done more than your
share already."

The smile vanished. "Don't count on it." And he was gone,
the two henchmen following closely behind him.

She stood there, sagging against the wall, as she listened to
the sound of their footsteps receding into the distance. Her
hands were still shaking, her forehead was covered with a cold
sweat, and she wished to God she could go back to Baraboo
and forget about any lingering familial debts.

She crossed the room to the window, watching as Uncle
Stephen got back in his Mercedes. "Sandy?" she called out,
not moving from her vantage point. "Are you still here?"

"Still here," he said from directly behind her, his advent
silent on the thick beige carpeting. "Your godfather's a curious
man."

"Where were you hiding?"

"In the bathtub with the shower curtain drawn. Fortunately
your brother favored navy-blue shower curtains, and Tremaine
didn't think to check. I was able to watch him without him
seeing me." He leaned forward and stared at the window, and
for a moment she watched his profile, that perfect, chiseled
line, the strong nose, the beautiful eyes, the rumpled blond hair.

Jane sighed absently. "You watched him? You pervert."

"What was I supposed to do, stare at the grout? Besides,
Tremaine didn't do anything one usually does in a bathroom.
He checked the medicine cabinet, under the sink and he even
lifted the back of the toilet and looked in the tank."

"Why?"

"I imagine he was looking for something. Whatever it was,
he didn't find it."

"So where does that leave us?"

He shrugged. "We'll just have to take up the search."

"Even though we're not sure what we're looking for? It might not be the formula."

"Even though we're not sure what we're looking for," he agreed. "Let's start with the boxes."

She looked at him with complete, utter loathing. "I just spent days packing them."

He leaned forward, and to her shock he brushed his lips across hers. "Then we'll just repack them," he said sweetly. He moved away before she could react, before she could hit him, before she could twine her arms around his neck and kiss him back. "Let's get started."

THE PARKING LOT outside Richard Dexter's lakeside condominium was brightly lit. All the Hondas and BMWs and Saabs gleamed in the artificial light, radiating a glow of financial well-being. Some of that glow penetrated the shambles of what had once been a spotlessly organized apartment, illuminating the littered floor. Sandy looked across the room at his partner in crime, just barely suppressing a grin.

Jane was sitting, shell-shocked, in the midst of a mountain of papers, her eyes glazed behind her wire-rimmed glasses. "I cannot," she said faintly, "look at one more piece of paper."

"It's probably a lost cause," Sandy agreed. "Whatever Tremaine is looking for isn't here. It would help if either of us knew the faintest thing about chemical engineering. None of Richard's notes makes sense to me, even the shopping lists."

"I know," Jane said wearily, stretching out on the mounds of paper. She was wearing pants for a change, and the crumpled khaki fit her long legs and delectable rear quite nicely. "No one could ever read Richard's handwriting. Maybe Uncle Stephen has the missing part of the formula and he just can't decipher it. Maybe we've read a dozen copies of it and not known what it is."

"Maybe, but I don't think so. Your brother doesn't sound like he was a very subtle man. Would he be likely to hide it among similar stuff so no one would notice?"

"Nope," Jane said, taking off her glasses and closing her

eyes. "He'd put it somewhere obvious. He probably thought no one could ever find his secret lab and he's left it locked in a file cabinet. Maybe he didn't even bother to lock it." She sat up, pushing her tangled hair out of her eyes. "We've got to find the lab, Jimmy."

"Sandy," he corrected absently. "Do you think we'll have any better luck recognizing it there?"

"No. We'll just have to burn the place down."

"Not again! The trick to a life of crime, dear heart, is only resort to violent action when you've used up all the alternatives," Sandy said reprovingly. "We've still got a lot of options left."

"Such as?" There was a delightfully pugnacious tilt to her chin. Even in her overtired, underfed state she still had a blood-thirsty streak that never failed to enchant him.

"I can't give away trade secrets," Sandy said, wondering how long he was going to be able to stall her. "In the meantime, I think I'd better feed you. You get nasty when you haven't eaten."

"Anything," she said longingly. "Just so long as it's hot and there's a lot of it."

"Burger King?"

She smiled beatifically. "Heaven," she replied. She scrambled to her feet, slipping on a precarious pile of papers.

He was there to catch her before she could catch herself. He could have just caught her arm, but he couldn't resist sliding his arm around her and pulling her upright. She looked up at him, startled, and he heard her sudden intake of breath, felt the tension and undeniable awareness in her body as it rested lightly against his.

She bit her lips, and he wanted to do the same thing. He didn't. "Why are you looking at me like that?" he asked quietly, not releasing her.

"I just wondered why you do what you do."

He felt his mouth curve up in an involuntary grin. "What would you think I'd do for a living?" he countered.

"I would have thought you'd be a gigolo."

He released her quite abruptly. "Why?" he demanded, insulted.

She was so tired and hungry that she'd lost half her defenses. "Well, I don't know..." she floundered helplessly, "it's just that you're so damned good-looking, and I wouldn't think you'd have much chance to use your looks when you're torching buildings."

He tried to reach for her again, but she'd moved out of reach. *Later,* he promised himself, watching her pick her way across the floor. "You forget," he said evenly. "I'm a con man on the side. Looking like I do, I manage to convince people I'm Princeton and Harvard Law School and a silver spoon, and they'll buy anything I sell them."

She nodded. "I can believe it. What are you going to try to sell me?" The question was lightly spoken, but Sandy wasn't fooled. She didn't trust him, on a very basic level. He shouldn't expect her to, he'd done everything to foster her belief in him as a sleazy crook. It shouldn't bother him in the slightest.

"Nothing you don't want to buy," he said.

Her smile was slightly lopsided. "That's just what a con man would say."

He wanted to tell her the truth, but that would only brand him a bigger liar and far less trustworthy than he'd proven so far. For the time being he had to keep his mouth shut. "Be nice to me," he warned, "or I won't take you to Burger King."

It was the right thing to say. She smiled, the shadows leaving her eyes. "I'll hitchhike if I have to."

"Don't worry, Madame X. I have to keep my partner in good working condition." He'd reached her by then, and he kept himself from touching her.

"What about all this?" She gestured to the mess.

"What would happen if we just left it for a few days?"

Her smile turned into a full-fledged grin. "Sounds good to me. Maybe I'll take Uncle Stephen up on his offer of assistance. Can you picture Elinor Peabody repacking these boxes?"

"It boggles the mind. Come on, partner. It's fast food time,

and then maybe we'll see if *The Untouchables* is playing anywhere. We could use a few pointers on how to be real criminals.''

''Aren't you a real criminal?''

Damn, he had to watch every word he said. Even exhausted
and starving, Jane Dexter was too damned sharp. ''There's always room for improvement,'' he said cheerfully, snapping off
the light and plunging the trashed room into darkness.

Within minutes they were crammed into his MGB and heading toward Route One, the engine coughing and jerking and
sputtering. Neither of them noticed that Stephen Tremaine's
goons were watching them from the front seat of an anonymous
sedan. Or that the American car pulled out and followed them
into the warm October night.

''WAKE UP, LAZYBONES.'' The voice was coming from a spot
unacceptably close to her ear. Jane reached up and batted at it,
pushing her face deeper into the pillow.

But the irritating voice wasn't the sort to be easily routed.
''Wake up,'' it said again, and as Jane slowly struggled up
from the mists of sleep she recognized it as Sandy's. Beside
her. On the bed.

Her eyes shot open and she flipped over in sudden outrage.
She would have taken the sheet with her, but Sandy's body
was keeping it in one place. She ended up sitting there, wearing
nothing but an oversize T-shirt that had ridden too high on her
thighs, glaring into her felonious partner's smoky-gray eyes.

''How did you get in here?'' she demanded. ''And don't tell
me you picked the lock. I've seen you in action—you do much
better with a key.''

''We have a connecting door,'' he said, unchastened. ''I took
the precaution of unlocking it last night.''

''Take the precaution of locking it, buster,'' she snarled.
''And get off my sheet.''

He moved, reluctantly, and while he kept his expression suitably sober, she could see the light of laughter lingering in the
back of his eyes. ''You're grumpy when you wake up.''

"I'm grumpy when I'm woken up," she corrected. "What time is it, anyway?" She peered out at the sunshine filtering through the threadbare curtains. "We didn't have anything planned, did we? You were just going to get in touch with a few of your underworld contacts and see what you could dig up."

It must have been her nearsightedness that made him look so peculiar for a moment. Almost guilty. She reached for her glasses, settling them on her nose, and his expression was as bland as ever.

"It's after ten. And the situation's changed."

She pulled herself up, wrapping the sheet around her body, suddenly alert. "What's happened?"

"Your godfather took off this morning for parts unknown."

"And just how do you know that?"

"I don't sleep till all hours of the morning," he said in a lofty tone. "I woke up at six, went running, and then decided to kill some time waiting for you to emerge from your beauty sleep. So I staked out Tremaine's house. I got there just in time to follow him and his two henchmen to the Mercer County Airport."

"Where's he going?"

"I couldn't very well walk up and ask him, now could I?"

"You're supposed to be a con man," she grumbled. "Why didn't you con it out of the flight controller or whoever they had working there?"

"I thought I'd con it out of Tremaine's wife."

Jane sat back, running an absent hand through her sleep-tangled hair. "We could certainly try."

"What's this we? You don't run a con on people you know," he said severely.

"Of course you don't. But I've never met Annabel Tremaine."

"Why not?"

"She wasn't home the other day when I met with Uncle Stephen. She's his second wife—the first one dumped him when she got tired of his playing around. I imagine Annabel will do the same when she finds out about Elinor Peabody. Particularly since Annabel was Uncle Stephen's administrative assistant when he was married to Aunt Alice.''

"Sounds like *Dynasty*," Sandy drawled.

"Uncle Stephen has the morals of a reptile. So how are we going to con Annabel?"

Sandy looked blank for a moment. "Give me a minute. It'll come to me."

"Door-to-door salesmen?" Jane suggested. "Religious fanatics?"

He shook his head reprovingly. "We wouldn't even get in the door. What about environmental activists? Save the dolphins and that sort of thing."

"Uncle Stephen probably eats dolphins for breakfast. We need something more esoteric."

"Loons?" Sandy suggested.

"Loons," she echoed. "I like it. They have a summer place in Maine on a lake with loons. That should appeal to Annabel enough at least to let us in. Once we do that, it's up to you to get the information out of her."

"Why up to me?"

"You're the professional crook around here," she said. "Aren't you?"

For some reason Jimmy the Stoolie alias Sandy looked abashed. "So I am," he said with the air of one making a discovery. "So I am."

Chapter Eight

It was just after one when Jane's rented Escort pulled up in front of the Tremaine's home on Cleveland Lane in the heart of old Princeton. Jane sat behind the wheel for a long moment, admiring the stately grace of the huge old house, with its ancient boxwoods, its perfect landscaping, its beautiful flagstoned walkway up to the wide front door. When she looked more closely, though, she saw signs of decay that she hadn't noticed in her earlier visit. The boxwoods needed trimming, the red paint on the front door was faded and just beginning to peel, the dead leaves of autumn lay scattered on a lawn that hadn't been cut. The signs weren't obvious, just the subtle warning signals that all was not well with the Tremaine finances.

"Nice place," Sandy said in a neutral tone of voice.

Jane shrugged. "I grew up in a house very much like this one. A little smaller, a little more haphazard looking, but the same general idea."

"Was your father a captain of industry like Tremaine?"

"Not exactly. My parents were college professors."

"I didn't think even Princeton paid its professors well enough to afford this kind of life-style."

"Princeton doesn't." Jane stared out the window, trying to fight the old sense of inadequacy that was settling down around her. "They came from an older class of moneyed educators. They inherited enough to enable them to indulge themselves in teaching. My parents were so impractical they couldn't have survived if they had to do anything as simple as follow a budget and live on their salaries.''

''Your brother didn't sound very practical, either.''

''He wasn't. But I am,'' she added with a trace of defiance. ''Sensible Jane.'' The plain was left unspoken, but she knew he had to be thinking it.''

''How'd you get along with your parents?''

''Sandy, they've been dead for more than seven years now. They were killed in a plane crash when they were on their way to a conference. It's not the issue right now.''

''Maybe,'' he said, ''maybe not.''

Jane allowed herself a weary sigh, answering him anyway. ''I got along with them about as well as I got along with Richard. In other words, they basically ignored my existence.''

''Why?''

''Richard was enough of a challenge for them. He was extremely gifted, even from the start. He could read by the time he was three, solve algebraic equations when he was five, balance mother's checkbook when he was eight, which was the most impressive feat of all. In comparison I was just a normal little girl, walking when I should, talking when I should, playing with dolls and reading Nancy Drew books. My parents must have thought I was a changeling.''

Sandy just looked at her. ''What about your sister? Was she one of the brilliant ones?''

Jane shook her head. ''Sally went the other route. When she saw how things were she decided to be stupid. She was always in the lowest classes in school, got rotten report cards, and simply refused to try. The funny thing about it, though, is that in certain ways she's much smarter than my parents or Richard ever were. She just hides it.''

''So we've got the brilliant Dexters, the slow one, and ordinary old plain Jane. Is that it?'' His voice was just slightly taunting, and she turned from her perusal of the old house to stare at him in outrage.

''How dare you...?'' she began.

''Isn't that what you've been calling yourself? All your life, even now, when you should be years removed from the slights of childhood, you go around dressing like plain Jane, thinking like plain Jane, acting like plain Jane. Maybe you should learn to lighten up.''

"Maybe you should learn to—" she stopped the obscene sentiment before she uttered it, replacing it with something safer "—should learn to mind your own business. I'll be whoever I want to be.''

"Exactly. And you've chosen to be plain Jane.''

Outrage and hurt had vanished long ago, to be replaced by a simmering, bristling anger. "Well, honey, you're a fine one to talk. You've decided to be Jimmy the Stoolie, Sandor Whatsisname, among other names. How many aliases do you have?''

He blinked for a moment, like a lizard facing bright sunlight. "At least I have a little variety in my life.''

"I like constancy.''

"Do you ever find it?''

"Not in someone like you,'' she snapped.

"Were you looking for it?''

That silenced her. He was sitting very still in the passenger seat of the stripped-down Ford, his thick blond hair rumpled over his high forehead, his tanned, beautiful face composed and no more than slightly curious. He was wearing a suit that was far too conservative and far too expensive for either a conservation fund-raiser or a felon, but she had to admit he was absolutely gorgeous. And completely out of reach.

"No,'' she said. "I wasn't.'' But even though she knew better, she would have liked to have found constancy of any sort in the man beside her.

"Are you sure?'' His voice was soft, beguiling, teasing at her senses. *He's a con man,* she reminded herself. *He knows how to use people.*

"This conversation is going nowhere,'' she said abruptly. "Are we going to talk to Annabel Tremaine or aren't we?''

He smiled at her, that brilliant, heart-stopping smile that she knew would haunt her. "We are. Actually, I am. You're going to stand by and look serious and concerned while I pitch her. Think you can handle that?''

''I can handle anything you dish out.''

The golden smile broadened to a grin. ''I'll hold you to it.''

It took a while for someone to answer the door. Jane could hear the melodious chimes echo through the house, but there was no sound of life, or scurrying footsteps. ''No one's home,'' she hissed. ''Let's get out of here.''

''Tremaine went alone, and someone kissed him goodbye,'' Sandy said, pressing the doorbell again. ''And that BMW was in the driveway this morning and it hasn't been moved. She's home.''

''You're wasting your time.''

''You can always wait in the car, Jane,'' he said, not bothering to look at her.

''The hell I…''

The door swung open, and a slender, willowy figure stood in the darkness of the hallway, peering out into the bright autumn sunlight. Jane watched in utter fascination as Sandy smiled at the shadowy figure. He knew just the right level of wattage to turn on. Not too overwhelming—the shy creature hiding from them would have probably run. Not too subdued, just enough to coax Annabel Tremaine out of hiding.

''Hi,'' he said, his voice warm and soothing and just faintly tinged with a Southern accent. ''I'm Ashley Wilkes and this is my wife Melanie. We're representing the Northeast Conservation Alliance for Saving the Loons. James MacDougal suggested you might be interested in helping us in our quest. We tried to call before showing up like this, but there was no answer.''

Jane allowed herself a cautious, curious glance at her companion. She had no idea who James MacDougal was, but apparently Annabel Tremaine did. She also hadn't read *Gone With the Wind* very recently. She opened the faded red door wider, exposing herself to the brutal sunlight, and smiled up into Sandy's beautiful gray eyes, ignoring his putative wife completely.

"This is rather a bad time," she said vaguely, running a slender hand through a carefully styled mane of silver-blond hair. "My husband's away right now, and I'm afraid I'm between maids, but if you want to come in…"

"We'd love to," Sandy said firmly, turning his back on his beloved Melanie and putting one strong hand under Annabel's elbow. Jane followed in their wake, allowing herself the brief, totally satisfying treat of sticking her tongue out at his beautiful back.

Annabel Tremaine must have been between maids for quite a while. The house was very dark—all the curtains were drawn, shadowing the disarray. Their hostess picked her way with exaggerated care over the piles of clothing, magazines, and dishes, dropping down on a damask-covered sofa and pushing a chintz comforter onto the floor.

"Could I offer you a drink?" she cooed, and everything clicked into place for a confused Jane. At eleven o'clock in the morning Annabel Tremaine was well and truly sloshed.

"It's a little early," Jane said, sinking down on a chair, jumping back up again and removing an empty wineglass before reseating herself.

"It's never too early," Annabel said cheerfully, blinking at them. "What about you, Mr. Wilkes?"

"Not right now," he said.

"You wouldn't mind getting me something, now would you?" Annabel purred.

"How about a cup of coffee?" he suggested calmly.

"Mr. Wilkes, I've been drinking since eight o'clock this morning, since my husband walked out the door. Why should I go and spoil such a carefully acquired state of bliss?"

"You don't look very blissful," Sandy said in a gentle voice.

Annabel blinked again, and slow tears ran down her beautiful cheeks. She was perfectly preserved, anywhere from forty to sixty, with wide, slightly dazed eyes, neatly coiffed hair, beautiful clothes, and makeup applied to her perfect features with a master's hand. Her advanced state of inebriation didn't even put a dent in her physical beauty. Clearly she didn't make a habit of drinking all day, or it would have begun to take its toll on her exceptional looks.

"I'm not blissful," she agreed with a trace of petulance. "I don't want you to think I'm a drunk. I only do this when my husband goes out of town. He's just been doing it a little too often, and I know he's seeing her, and I don't care. Not one tiny bit," she added defiantly.

"I'm sure you don't. How about some coffee?"

"How about some vodka?"

"It's all gone."

"Damn." Annabel had slumped sideways a bit, but she pushed herself back into a sitting position, crossing her shapely ankles. "I'll have to send out for more. I only hope we still have credit at the liquor store. Stephen's been closing all my accounts. He's put me on a budget. Would you believe such a thing? I'm sure he hasn't put Miss Goodbody on a budget."

"Miss Goodbody?" Sandy echoed. He hadn't taken a seat, he was hovering in the doorway, and Jane suddenly realized his problem. He didn't want to take advantage of the woman. It would have been a simple matter to mix her another drink from the bottle of vodka that was, in fact, half-full, and then pry any information he wanted out of her. Instead he wanted to sober her up. Jane's partner in crime had a conscience. The notion was startling and yet, not really surprising.

"My husband's mistress," Annabel said tearily. "Oh, he calls her his vice-president or something like that, but I'm not fooled. How do you think I got him in the first place? Back then they didn't have to make their mistresses executives—they could keep them as secretaries until they dropped them."

"He didn't drop you," Jane said.

Annabel looked crafty. "I was too smart for him. I'm too smart for Miss Goodbody, though she doesn't know it."

"I'm sure you are."

Annabel's fine blue eyes squinted at her. "Who are you?" she demanded suddenly. "What are you doing here?"

"We're here to save the Loons," Jane said somewhat desperately, as Sandy still stood silently by.

"It won't do you any good," Annabel said firmly. "My husband shot a loon two years ago. Nearly went to jail for it. He hates the damned things and their awful noise."

Trust Uncle Stephen to shoot an endangered species, Jane thought. "When will your husband return? Maybe he'd like to assuage his conscience by making a donation."

"My husband has no conscience," Annabel snorted. "And I haven't the faintest idea when he'll be back."

"Where's he gone?" Jane demanded bluntly, when Sandy still said nothing.

Annabel focused her rapidly blinking eyes on Jane. "Why do you want to know?" she said belligerently. "And what are you doing here?"

"We're representing the Save the Loons Foundation," Sandy finally spoke, moving into Annabel's wavering line of vision. "Perhaps we should come back when your husband returns."

"I don't know when he'll return," she said fretfully. "He's gone off to upstate New York and I haven't the faintest idea why. But I can guess who went with him. Elinor Goodbody."

"Peabody," a dulcet voice corrected from behind Sandy. She'd entered the house so silently no one had heard her coming. Elinor Peabody looked much as she had two days ago—perfectly groomed, perfectly collected, perfectly angry. Rather like a sober version of Stephen Tremaine's wife.

Annabel had struggled to her feet, weaving slightly. "Elinor," she purred, suddenly all affability. "What brings you here?"

"I promised Stephen I'd check in on you. He was worried you might get too lonely. But I see you have visitors already." Her eyes met Jane's, bright with mockery, and Jane waited for the boom to fall.

"They're from the…what did you say you were representing, dears?" Annabel inquired dazedly.

"The Save the Loons Foundation," Sandy said.

Elinor's eyes ran the length of Sandy's cool, elegant body, and Jane followed that gaze with an odd tightening in her stomach. One she called uneasiness, refusing to give another, more elemental name to it. "And I imagine you're their resident computer whiz," she murmured silkily, gliding over to him.

"Actually I'm not very good at computers," Sandy replied in a low, caressing tone of voice that had Jane clenching her fists. "I'm better working with people."

"I'm sure you are."

Enough was enough, Jane thought, rising from her chair. "We'd better be going," she announced abruptly. "We'll come back when Mr. Tremaine returns from his trip."

"That would be nice," Annabel said vaguely.

Ms Peabody turned an amused gaze back to Jane. "In the meantime, the two of you devoted conservationists might pay me a little visit. I have a great interest in saving loons."

Jane just stared at her. Sandy broke in, smooth and unruffled as ever. "We'd be more than happy to accept any help you have to offer, Ms Goodbody." He let his eyes travel her elegant, voluptuous length just as she had surveyed him. Jane growled low in her throat.

"Peabody," she corrected gently. "Why don't you come by my place tonight around eight? I'm sure we can be a great help to each other."

"We'll be there," Sandy said.

Elinor's mouth turned down in a sour little smile of acceptance. "If that's necessary. In the meantime, why don't you leave Mrs. Tremaine to me? She does this every now and then, just to punish Stephen."

Jane looked back at her hostess, startled, and discovered Annabel sound asleep on the sofa, snoring slightly. "Maybe he deserves it," Jane said.

Ms Peabody's smile broadened. "Maybe he does. Tonight at eight. My address is in the phone book—I imagine two resourceful people like you can find it."

"I imagine we can," Sandy said. He moved slowly, easily over to Jane and took her arm in his. He had to feel the clenched muscles, the tension vibrating through her, but he said nothing, just patted her hand gently. "Till tonight."

Neither of them said a word as they walked through the darkened house. Only when Sandy shut the peeling red door behind them did Jane finally speak. "Do you suppose Annabel is safe with that she-wolf?"

Sandy smiled. "Don't you like Ms Goodbody?"

"She's a snake."

"A snake who seems willing to help us. I don't imagine there's much Elinor doesn't know about Stephen Tremaine's affairs."

"Then you don't know Uncle Stephen," Jane said, climbing into the Escort. "He doesn't know the meaning of the word indiscreet. Anything Ms Peabody knows she had to worm out of him."

"First she's a snake and now she's a worm," Sandy said, sliding in beside her. "You didn't mind her all that much before. Why all the sudden hostility?"

She paused in the act of starting the car, turning to look him directly in his guileless gray eyes. Except, she reminded herself, she'd never known anyone so full of guile in her entire life. "I don't like what she's doing to Annabel. I don't like the fact that while she's busy ruining one woman's marriage she seems ripe for a fling with you. I don't trust her willingness to help, and I don't trust..." The words trailed off, and she turned her attention to the dashboard of the car.

"You don't trust me," he finished for her, quite gently.

"Is there any reason why I should?" she muttered.

"Yes." His hand covered hers before she could start the car, pulling it away, and she had no choice but to look at him. "You should trust me because we're partners, Jane."

"Partners in crime."

"Whatever," Sandy dismissed her cavil. "We're in this thing together, and if we can't trust each other, if you can't trust me, then we may as well give it up right now. Is that what you want?"

She looked at him, at his stern, unsmiling mouth, his stormy eyes, his unflinching expression, and she was ashamed of herself. "I trust you, Sandy," she said. "I do trust you. For a crook you're very honest," she added, hoping to coax a smile from him.

There was no answering lightening in his face. "Or for an honest man I'm very crooked," he said. "Let's get out of here. This place depresses me."

Jane looked back at the subtle signs of decay around the beautiful old house, thought back to the beautiful woman passed out on the damask sofa. "Me too," she said. And she put the car in gear.

SANDY SLUMPED DOWN in the uncomfortable bucket seat, pulling his sunglasses out and propping them on his nose. Not for one moment longer could he meet Jane Dexter's trusting gaze, not for one moment longer could he even stand to see his own reflection in the glare of the windscreen.

The names he was calling himself were so obscene he almost blushed. He had no excuse in the world—if he were any sort of decent human being he'd put a stop to this charade right now. He'd tell Jane Dexter who he really was, that he'd never broken any more laws than the average liberal college student growing up in the early seventies had broken, and that he'd do everything legally in his power to help her.

He believed her when she said she trusted him. That made it all the worse. He'd taken her very rational distrust of men, of him, and turned it around so that she was starting to open up to him. Sooner or later she'd find out the truth, whether he had the guts to tell her or not. And worse than her rage, worse than her justifiable fury, was the thought of seeing those trusting brown eyes clouded with hurt and betrayal.

"What was that?" Jane questioned, her eyes trained on the early afternoon traffic clogging Elm Road.

"What?"

"Did you say something? I thought I heard you groan."

Sandy scooted upright in his seat, shoving his sunglasses back up his nose. Now was the time to tell her. Before things got any worse. "Just clearing my throat," he said, flashing her his most charming smile, the one that could melt the heart of the stoniest judge.

And Jane, bless her poor, gullible heart, smiled back at him, and he started calling himself those names all over again as they headed back toward Route One.

Chapter Nine

It was a cool, clear night in October. The smell of burning leaves still lingered in the evening air, the dampness of a late rain mingled with the scent of autumn closing in. Outside the Princeton Pike Sleep-a-While Motel the air was filled with exhaust from the ever-busy Route One. By the time they reached Elinor Peabody's cozy little stucco house in the Riverside section of Princeton the more soothing sights and scents took over, reminding Jane of her childhood, of Halloweens spent trudging the broad, beautiful streets around her parents' house and collecting chocolate bars that she'd never eaten.

Dick had never bothered going out on Halloween, even when he was little. He preferred to stay home, reading, to dressing up in outlandish costumes and racing around the usually staid residential streets. By the time Sally was old enough for trick-or-treating, certain people had taken to putting razor blades in apples, and Halloween in the suburbs came to an abrupt halt. Jane still missed those earlier times, especially on a night like this, when the sights and smells of her childhood came rushing in on her, leaving her absurdly vulnerable as she hadn't been in years.

Elinor Peabody's house was a pale peachy color with aqua trim, carefully landscaped grounds, and an inground swimming pool in the back. Years ago Riverside had been one of the newer sections of town, a place for young couples and tacky houses. Sandy had casually informed Jane that the house was now on the market, and Ms Peabody was asking four hundred and fifty thousand for a place not much larger than her parents' garage. She'd probably get it, too.

The MGB coughed to a halt outside the well-tended walk-way. At least with Ms Peabody there was no sign of imminent decay. "You want me to wait in the car?" Jane finally broke the silence that had lasted since Route One.

His face was shadowed in the car. "You might have a long wait," he said, his voice giving nothing away. "Ms Peabody had a lean and hungry look. If I go in without you I might not escape with my virtue intact."

Jane discovered the sheltering darkness could be beneficial as well as frustrating. There was no way he could see the dismay on her face. "Well," she said finally, "if you're willing to make that sacrifice for the cause I shouldn't stand in your way." Her voice was stiff and unhappy.

He leaned across the front seat, his face inches from hers, the warmth of his breath brushing her mouth. "I'm not," he said softly.

She couldn't keep the relieved smile from wreathing her face, and this time he was close enough to see it. His eyes were sober, watching her, and his mouth drew closer until it feathered her lips.

And then he pulled away. "Besides," he said in a more normal voice, "we decided that despite my gorgeous looks I'm not a gigolo. Now wouldn't be the time to start. Unless you feel like supporting me yourself?" He didn't wait for an answer to the astonishing question, merely climbed out of the low-slung car and moved around to open her door.

If Elinor Peabody was disappointed to see Jane accompany Sandy, she was masterful enough to disguise it. She was also masterful enough to maneuver Jane into a hard chair some distance away, and Sandy into the overstuffed sofa beside her. She was dressed for success that night, in a flowing aqua jumpsuit that complemented a cleavage well-hidden in her daytime uniforms. Her silky blond hair was a tawny mane down her back, and Jane was knowledgeable enough to recognize the subtle difference in her makeup. Ms Peabody was on the prowl, and she wasn't going to let someone of Jane's caliber stand in her way.

Jane stiffened her back in the uncomfortable chair, listening with only half an ear to the idiotic pleasantries about the balmy fall weather and Princeton traffic. This time she wasn't going to give in without a fight. She'd caved in too many times, in her childhood, in her career, in her short-lived marriage. She was through with being understanding, with sitting back and letting other people have their way.

She rose from the chair, crossed the room and sank down gracefully in an overstuffed chair to the left of the sofa, stretching her legs out in front of her, inches away from Sandy's. Her legs were better than Ms Peabody's, even if she didn't have a model's figure and tawny hair and perfect eyesight.

"Why didn't you tell Annabel who we were?" she demanded bluntly, breaking through the polite fencing. She was prepared for Sandy's disapproval of her precipitous question, but he said nothing, leaning back against the cushions with the air of a man about to enjoy himself.

"Annabel wasn't in any condition to comprehend anything, Ms Dexter," Elinor replied sweetly. "I didn't want to confuse her any more than necessary."

"You're the reason she was in that state in the first place." Jane went on the attack.

"No, I am not." Elinor leaned forward, forgetting her languid pose, forgetting Sandy. "No one's responsible for Annabel's drinking but Annabel herself. And maybe Stephen helps a bit. But you've got to realize Annabel doesn't do that very often. Just every few months when she's angry with Stephen and feeling sorry for herself. She doesn't have a serious drinking problem."

"Yet," Jane said.

"I didn't invite you here to discuss Annabel Tremaine's domestic problems." Elinor carefully recovered her composure. "As a matter of fact, Ms Dexter, I didn't invite *you* at all."

Sandy finally stirred himself. "I don't go anywhere without my boss," he said lazily.

"Your boss? I wondered how you two fit together. Somehow I didn't imagine you were lovers."

Jane swallowed the growl that threatened to erupt. Instead she leaned forward, putting a predatory expression on her face that would have done Ms Peabody proud, and placing a possessive hand on Sandy's knee. She felt the slight quiver of surprise beneath her hand, and then he was still, watching all this with great curiosity.

"You haven't impressed me as someone with much imagination," Jane cooed. "Sandy is my...associate. We're in this together. In every sense of the word." Sandy's knee twitched again, and Jane suspected she'd pay for this later.

But Ms Peabody merely nodded, her sultriness turned off, all business despite the flowing loungewear. "I'm prepared to help you."

"Why?"

Ms Peabody's smile was quite frightening. "Let's just say I have a score to even up with Stephen Tremaine. I'm a firm believer in looking after my best interests. But I don't think my motives concern you. I think what matters to you is what happened to your brother."

Jane's languid self-control vanished. "I beg your pardon?"

"Was I wrong? I thought these elaborate charades were connected with your brother's death."

Jane had the eerie sense of things swinging out of her tenuous control. "Uncle Stephen wants to sell Richard's titanium coating process for defense purposes, either to this country or to another, hostile one. I owe it to Richard to keep him from doing that."

"Do you now?" Ms Peabody murmured. "How are you planning to stop Stephen?"

"Part of the process is missing," Jane said. "You know that as well as I do. If I can find it before Uncle Stephen does I'll destroy it."

"And your brother's life work at the same time? You're very severe, Ms Dexter."

"He would have wanted it destroyed, rather than have it used for military purposes," Jane said firmly.

"I imagine you're right. Your brother always was a royal pain." She rose, crossing the pretty pink chintz room and pouring herself a drink. Straight vodka, and she didn't offer them anything. "I'm afraid I can't tell you where the missing part of the process is. I don't know any more than Stephen does. He thinks it's in Richard's private laboratory, and we don't really know where that lab is."

"Neither do we," Sandy drawled, finally entering the conversation. "Where did Tremaine go today?"

"Upstate New York. He's gone to the area where Richard had his accident."

"Does he think he'll find some clue there?" Jane demanded. "Richard was just passing through, heading for Vermont when his car went off the road. I wouldn't think he'd learn anything there."

"Maybe not. All I can tell you is he isn't any farther along in his quest than you are. He hasn't the faintest idea where the lab is, and all his private detectives aren't helping. Is that what you are, Mr...?" She let it trail, eyeing him over the rim of her glass of vodka.

"Just Sandy," he replied modestly. "And no, I'm not a private detective."

"Then just what are you?"

Time to intervene again, Jane thought, rising briskly. "We appreciate your help."

Elinor shrugged. "It wasn't much."

"You could keep in touch. Let us know if Tremaine comes up with anything."

"I could. We'll see how I feel."

Jane headed down the hallway, Sandy strolling casually along beside her, when she turned to look at Elinor's still figure. "I just wish I knew why you were willing to help us."

Elinor's smile was icy. "Let's just say I didn't bargain for getting involved in murder."

"HE COULDN'T have been murdered," Jane insisted for the twenty-seventh time. She was sitting cross-legged on her motel bed, her hair shoved behind her ears, her glasses slipping down her generous nose, her blouse unbuttoned lower than she doubtless realized. Sandy looked at her and controlled a wistful sigh.

"Why not?" They'd repeated this conversation too many times for him to remember. "Do you think Stephen Tremaine is incapable of murder?"

"Not necessarily. But I can't believe he'd risk it. I wouldn't think the stakes would be high enough. Damn that woman! How could she just say something like that and refuse to explain?" Jane fumed, bouncing on the bed in her agitation.

"Ms Peabody knew exactly what she was doing. She wanted to get you riled up and not thinking straight." He was lounging against the wall by their connecting door, trying to decide how he could get beside her on the bed without having her throw a major fit.

"She succeeded. Do you suppose that was why she did it? That this was all part of Uncle Stephen's plan to get us so confused we went off in a thousand directions?" Her eyes were swollen with unshed tears. He knew she'd shed tears in the darkness on the long drive home, but she'd refused to cry in front of him.

"It's always a possibility." He managed a casual stroll over to the front windows on the pretext of looking out into the artificially lit parking lot. That little maneuver got him a few feet closer to the bed and kept her off guard. If only she'd start crying again he'd have an excuse to comfort her. He'd been on fire since she'd made that phony pass at him earlier—he could still feel the imprint of her hand on his knee and hear the very real possessiveness in her voice.

Jane shook her head. Her thick brown hair was coming loose from the braid down her back, and her glasses were slipping down on the end of her nose. "I don't think so. There was real hostility in her voice when she talked about Uncle Stephen. I think she's definitely out to get him. I just don't know whether getting him involves lying or not.''

Sandy crossed to the bed, leaning over her and resting his hands on the sagging mattress. ''If she was telling the truth, if Richard really was murdered, then this isn't a game anymore. It's a matter for the police.''

''Is that what it's been to you? A game?'' Her voice was tight and throbbing with tension, and she was so angry she didn't realize how close he was, didn't comprehend the possibilities when he sat down on the bed beside her.

''No,'' he said, pushing a strand of hair back from her flushed face. ''But it wasn't a matter of life and death, either.''

''I keep forgetting,'' she said bitterly, not moving beneath his hand.

''Forgetting what?'' His voice held no more than mild curiosity as he reached out and pushed the glasses back up her nose. He would have liked to have taken them off her, but he decided that would be pushing his luck.

''That you're an amoral criminal, selling your expertise to the highest bidder.''

He wasn't even affected. He looked down at her, a gentle smile on his face. ''But at least my body's for free,'' he said, and kissed her.

He more than half expected the reaction he got. For a moment her mouth softened beneath his, her whole body radiating warmth and desire. The next moment he was shoved away, the stinging imprint of her hand on his jaw as he toppled off the bed and onto the threadbare carpet.

He looked up at her from his ignominious position, sprawled on the floor. She was kneeling on the bed, holding her hand and staring down at him in shock and dismay. Her hand must hurt her a good deal, he thought, because it sure as hell hurt his face.

''I've never hit anyone in my life,'' she said, her voice dazed. ''Not since I was eight years old.''

He kept a straight face for a moment longer, then grinned

up at her. "Maybe you should have hit your ex-husband," he said, sitting upright on the hard floor. "Not to mention your self-centered brother."

"Don't. He's dead."

"That doesn't mean he wouldn't have benefited from a good wallop," Sandy said gently.

She stared at him for a long moment. "God, Sandy, what am I going to do?" she said finally.

There were a number of possibilities, most of which she'd find completely unacceptable. He'd already mentioned the police, and clearly she hadn't liked that idea. He'd tried another pass, and while she'd been more amenable, common sense had reared its ugly head. That left only one possibility. The real Jimmy the Stoolie and his impressive underworld connections.

"What we're going to do," he corrected gently, "is get a good night's sleep. I'm going to make a few phone calls, see what I can stir up, and tomorrow we'll head into the city."

"Why?"

"Because if Stephen Tremaine really was responsible for your brother's death, you can bet your cookies he didn't do it himself. He hired someone. And in New York we can find out exactly whom he hired."

"How?"

"I have friends," he said modestly. "Friends in low places. We can even stay in my lawyer's apartment while we're checking out leads."

"Your lawyer pays your bills and lends you his apartment?" Jane said, mystified. "Why?"

Sandy shrugged. "What can I say? He likes me."

"Are you blackmailing him?"

This being a criminal has its drawbacks, Sandy thought, swallowing his outraged protest. Righteous indignation had no place in his scheme of things. "No, I'm not blackmailing him," Sandy said patiently, with only a slight edge. "He owes me a few favors, I owe him a couple. It all works out."

"So the glorious Alexander Calderwood owes favors to a

gangster," Jane mused. "Remind me not to hire him if we get caught torching Technocracies."

"Caldicott," Sandy corrected, the edge coming out. "And you couldn't ask for a better lawyer."

"I could ask for a more honest one."

He just managed to keep from growling. "Besides, I'm not a gangster. I'm just a minor talent."

"True enough. You can barely manage to pick a lock."

Enough was enough. Sandy's romantic mood was thoroughly banished by now, his jaw was throbbing, and Jane was looking decidedly cheerful. "We'll go tomorrow."

"Fine," she said, lying back on the bed, seemingly unaware that her skirt had ridden up her thighs, exposing those beautiful legs of hers, that her glasses were sliding down her nose again, and that no matter how mad he was right now he still found her absolutely delicious. "I don't think we'll find anything, but it will help matters to know for sure."

"You've decided Tremaine didn't kill your brother?"

"I don't think so. Call me irrational, but I think I'd know. I trust my intuition about people, and I just don't think Uncle Stephen could have done it. It had to be an accident."

Sandy had made it to the connecting door, but he stopped for a moment. "You trust your intuition about people," he echoed. "What does your intuition tell you about me?"

He would have given ten years off his life to have been able to read her mind right then. Whatever she was thinking, it was powerful. Her eyes widened, her mouth grew soft and tremulous, and for two cents he would have crossed the room and landed back on the bed with her.

And landed back on the floor, no doubt. Within seconds she'd wiped the incriminating look from her face, tightening her mouth and narrowing her eyes. "That you're nothing but trouble," she answered. "Good night."

That was true enough, he thought. But he wished he knew what else she'd been thinking for that brief moment before her defenses shuttered down again. "Pleasant dreams," he said, hoping they'd be lustful ones.

There was no question that his would be.

THE WHIMPERS WOKE HIM. It was sometime in the middle of the night—the Princeton Pike Sleep-a-While Motel didn't supply digital clocks to succor the insomniac, and he could only peer at his thin gold watch and guess that it was after three. The fluorescent lights from the parking lot glared into the room, and he lay in the uncomfortable bed, his ears straining for the sound that had pulled him from a deep sleep.

Maybe the sparsely populated motel had rented the room on the other side, and right now some energetic couple was being slightly vocal in their endeavors. Or maybe some stray alley cat was lurking outside, prowling along the cracked cement walkway, looking for a juicy mouse. Or maybe, he thought, as the sound came again, his partner in crime was crying.

He pulled himself out of bed, and headed for the connecting door, grabbing for his bathrobe as he went. Not that she hadn't already seen him in his underwear, but in her current fragile state he didn't want to do anything to alarm her further.

He wouldn't have put it past her to barricade the connecting door, but it opened easily, silently at his touch. He expected a shriek of outrage when she realized he'd faked locking the door, but all that came from the narrow figure on the bed was another muffled whimper.

The eerie blue-yellow light from the parking lot outside cast gloomy shadows in the shabby room. He could hear the distant roar of trailers barreling down Route One, but Jane slept on, oblivious, lost in her own nightmare world of misery.

He should leave her alone, he knew that. He should go back to his own room, slam the door loud enough to wake her out of her tear-laden sleep, and let her work out her problems by herself. What the hell did he have to offer her but more lies?

The bed sank beneath his weight as he sat down beside her. He touched her shoulder, gently, hoping just to jar her out of the nightmare but let the sleep continue.

Her eyes flew open, staring up at him, dazed, myopic, filled with unshed tears. "What are you doing here?" she demanded in a husky voice.

"You were having a nightmare," he said softly, reluctantly pulling his hand back.

"I was dreaming about Richard and the car crash. I was in the car with him, falling down the embankment, rolling over and over and over." Her voice shuddered to a halt.

"You're safe," he said, knowing how lame it sounded. He wondered how he was going to be able to touch her again. He'd probably end up on the floor.

"I suppose I am." Her eyes narrowed as she looked up at him. "What are you wearing?"

"A bathrobe," he replied, startled.

"A F C." She reached out and traced the telltale monogram. "Don't tell me you stole your lawyer's bathrobe?" There was more weary amusement than indignation in her voice.

"Of course not," Sandy said, glad the darkness hid his expression. "I just borrowed it."

"You're an unregenerate scoundrel, Sandy or Jimmy or whoever you are."

"I'm afraid so," he agreed, feeling suddenly very guilty. Maybe now was the time to tell her, now in the timeless hours between midnight and dawn. The longer he waited the worse it would be. "Jane," he began earnestly, steeling himself.

"Good night, partner," she said, interrupting him gently but firmly.

"But I wanted to…"

"Good night."

He had no choice. At least he could comfort himself with the knowledge that he tried. Not hard enough, but he did try. He sat on the bed, looking down at her.

"Good night," he said. And without another word he went back to his room, closing the door silently behind him.

Chapter Ten

"I wouldn't trust Elinor Peabody further than I could throw her," Jane said, huddling deeper into the leather car seat as they sped toward New York.

"Neither would I," Sandy said reasonably enough. "That doesn't mean she can't be useful."

Jane gave her clothing a look of disgust. The artfully streaked and tattered jeans had clearly seen better days, the top resembled something Geronimo might have worn. At least it covered her. Beneath it was a metal studded leather bra that Sandy had presented with a flourish. She wouldn't have worn it at all if the feathered shirt hadn't provided a few desperate gaps, and she would have given anything to be able to wrap her underdressed body in a nice, enveloping raincoat.

Her hair was even more absurd, but by the time she'd attacked it she'd become reckless, getting into the spirit of the thing. It stuck out every which way, aided by mousse, styling gel, and the kind of teasing she hadn't seen since her brother went to the senior high school prom with Rita Di Angelo in a fit of teenage lust never repeated in his noble manhood.

But the hour-long, cramped ride into the city in Sandy's MGB was giving her more than enough time for second thoughts, and every time she glanced at her reflection in the mirror she cringed. The blue, purple and pink streaks radiating above her eyes were visible even without her purloined glasses, and the black lipstick made her look like the bride of Frankenstein. She shivered delicately, looking out over the New Jersey Turnpike, and hoped her left earring wouldn't catch in the feathers. She'd closed her eyes when Sandy had inserted the diaper pin in her right ear, and she still couldn't bring herself to look closely at it.

It was long past dusk, an early autumn chill was in the air, and the smell of New Jersey exhaust penetrated the closed windows of the little car. Jane had drawn the line when Sandy had tried to douse her with some sort of musk that smelled more like pesticide, but maybe that would have been better than the sulphurous fumes rising from the sprawled-out megalopolis surrounding Newark.

"You could have stayed home," Sandy said gently.

"I wouldn't exactly call the Princeton motel home," Jane said, allowing herself another, surreptitious glimpse of Sandy's spiked blond hair and torn T-shirt and swallowing the sigh of part disgust, part lust. While she looked like a cross between Cyndi Lauper and Vampira, Sandy managed to look like a punk Don Johnson. Certain things in life weren't fair.

"What would you call home?"

"The second floor of a run-down Victorian house in Baraboo, Wisconsin. I used to live in a boxy apartment but it drove me crazy."

"Somehow I don't see you as a Victorian."

"Don't you? I've been called prudish in my time." She knew her voice sounded raw, but she hoped he wouldn't notice.

Sandy noticed everything. "Who called you prudish? Your ex-husband?"

"Yes."

"Does he have anything to do with your Victorian lifestyle?"

Jane sighed. "I wish you wouldn't be so damned nosy. Why don't we change the subject?"

"Lovely weather," he said obediently enough.

There was a long silence. "You really want to know about my marriage?"

"Only if you want to tell me."

"If I wanted to tell you I would have brought up the subject myself."

"Yes, I want to know about your marriage," Sandy said, dropping all pretense.

"All right. It doesn't take long to tell. I met Frank at the University of Wisconsin. I was taking a night course in Japanese Socialism and he was rebounding from a messy divorce."

"Japanese Socialism?" he echoed in a voice of horror. "Why in the world would you willingly choose to study something that dry?"

"I thought it was time to try something new. I'd already had enough arts and sciences to keep me going. Do you want to hear about my academic career or my marriage?"

"We're getting near the turnpike exit. Which takes the shorter amount of time?"

"Definitely the marriage. Frank was teaching the course, which was unspeakably boring. He'd just been divorced by his wife of five years—apparently she needed to find herself and he'd been holding her back. So he cried in my arms for a while, then figured there probably wasn't much of me left to find, so he proposed, and I was fool enough to accept."

"Why?"

It was a good question, one she hadn't considered in a long time. She gave the unrepentant Sandy her most severe look. "Because I was in love with him," she said firmly.

Sandy, of course, wasn't cowed. "Really?"

She didn't hesitate. "At this point I don't know anymore. Maybe I married him because he looked like Dustin Hoffman and he was man enough to cry. I should have realized one should never marry a man who's crying over another woman."

"What happened?"

"His ex-wife found herself, Frank got over his rebound and went back to her. It was all very civilized and decent, everybody was terribly sorry about the whole bloody mess."

"Did you put up any kind of fight?"

"Are you kidding?" Jane tossed her frizzy mane over her feathered shoulder. "I'm much too reasonable a person. I'm cursed with seeing everybody else's point of view. They both made a mistake and they'd suffered too long for it. I bowed out gracefully and flew to Mexico for a fast divorce so they could get remarried on their old wedding anniversary.''

"Nice. What did you give them as a wedding present?"

Jane glared at him. "What makes you think I gave them a wedding present?"

"You'd already been such an incredible sucker I'm sure you didn't stop there. I bet you refused alimony."

"Of course."

"What about community property?"

"Stop sounding like a lawyer. We'd only been married seventeen months. We hadn't had time to accumulate much more than a car and a time-share in Bermuda where we spent our honeymoon."

"What happened to them?"

"I gave them up. I don't like Saabs and I never want to go to Bermuda again."

"Did he give you any compensation?"

"Sandy…"

"Didn't you have a lawyer?" He was sounding positively incensed.

"Of course I did. A friend of Frank's took care of the details."

"A friend of Frank's shafted you."

"I didn't want anything," she said, anger and desperation making her voice tight and hard. "I just wanted my freedom."

"You didn't get anything else." Sandy didn't look at her, concentrating instead on the heavy evening traffic as he headed for the Lincoln Tunnel. "Not even your self-respect."

If she hit him they'd probably swerve into another car and die. Still, the thought was tempting. With great difficulty she swallowed her rage. "My self-respect doesn't depend on material possessions."

"That's good. Let's just hope it isn't influenced by being screwed by people who once cared for you." His voice was tight with anger, and that emotion finally stirred Jane out of her own fury.

"What does it matter to you how I'm treated? If *I* don't mind why in the world do *you*?"

"Are you trying to tell me you don't mind?" he countered.

She thought about it, carefully, prodding at the remembered pain like a tongue prodding a sore tooth. "I mind about me," she said finally. "I mind that I made a fool of myself. Apart from that, it's all ancient history."

He didn't have to say anything, his skeptical expression was reaction enough. She tried to shove a deliberately careless hand through her teased and tangled mane, but her fingers stuck in the rough mass. "All I know," she added sweetly, "is that I'll never let a man make a fool out of me again."

His derision vanished. "Good idea," he muttered, turning his attention back to the narrowing road.

YOU'RE GETTING MORE *and more foolhardy as time goes on,* Sandy berated himself as he maneuvered the car down the crowded, narrow streets of the Lower East Side. He'd had plenty of chances to tell her the truth, plenty of times when he could have set things straight and then sat back and let others take over this incredible mess. Instead here he was, wandering around places he shouldn't be seen, looking for people he shouldn't even know existed.

He wouldn't have done it if Elinor Peabody hadn't called up with a name. A name he knew. Anyone else and he would have left it alone, but the coincidence made it unavoidable.

Years ago, when he was first practicing, his partners had handed him a case too dirty for them to soil their patrician hands with. When Gregory Matteo had shown up in his office all Sandy had known was that he was squeezed into a thousand dollar suit too small for his fat, sweating body. After talking with him Sandy had watched the contradictions mount. The man had an income and a title ill-suited to his meager intellect, combined with a bullying attitude that irritated Sandy enough to look further into the man's background. He'd been accused of assaulting a police officer. He'd actually been beating his girlfriend, but she'd refused to press charges, so only the policeman who'd tried to stop him ended up going to court.

He'd gotten him off on a technicality, a maneuver that required no great brilliance on his part, but Matteo had been almost pathetically grateful. And he'd made a firm promise: if Sandy had ever needed anything, he had only to send word to his notorious father, Jabba Matteo himself, and that wish was granted. And as Sandy had watched the man waddle away he'd wiped away an icy sense of relief that it was over so quickly.

Jabba Matteo was so powerful, so dangerous and so rich that his very existence was almost a secret. The media that didn't hesitate to stake out presidential campaigners and malign anything that moved seldom mentioned his name, and then only in the most circumspect manner. Even Sandy didn't know the extent of the senior Matteo's activities, and he didn't care to. All he knew was that one of his quasi legitimate forms of employment was arms dealing, and that Matteo owed him one. Once Elinor Peabody mentioned his name, the die was cast.

Getting in touch with him had proven the major challenge, one that Sandy had chosen to meet in typically brazen style. Three blocks away, their guide to the underworld was waiting in Ratner's delicatessen, probably stuffing his ratty little face with strawberry cheesecake. The real Jimmy the Stoolie was waiting for them, and it was going to take all of Sandy's quick thinking and mental juggling to keep Jane and Jimmy at arm's length.

"So how come your lawyer hangs out with godfathers?" Jane queried as he pulled up beside a boarded-up building and switched off the car. "I didn't think Alexander Caldicott was a hireling of organized crime."

"He isn't. He knows a friend of a friend. I should have thought of him myself. If anyone in New York knows anything about arms dealing, Jabba's the man. He'd also be likely to know if anything...unpleasant...happened to your brother."

"Something unpleasant happened to him, Sandy. He died."

"I know," he said hastily, trying to keep from staring in

total fascination at her streaked and painted face. He could barely see the normal, so-called plain Jane beneath the gold and purple stripes, the spiky, tangled hair and garish mouth. He still wanted to kiss that mouth, black lipstick and all, and he was still far too partial to what lay beneath the metal-studded leather bra, but for the present he struggled to keep his mind on business. He'd explained the situation to Jimmy, and the little weasel had promised his full cooperation in exchange for a break on his legal fees, but Sandy wasn't fool enough to trust him. If Jimmy thought he could get some sort of advantage out of his information he'd try to, and the next few hours would prove harrowing indeed if Sandy wasn't extremely careful.

"Isn't that your lawyer?" Jane murmured, reaching for the door handle.

Jimmy the Stoolie was sauntering toward them, a smarmy smile on his rodentlike face. Sandy just watched in growing dismay. He'd told Jimmy to borrow a suit from his wardrobe— they were close in size and the doorman would let him in. Needless to say Jimmy had chosen the best one he owned—a Giorgio Armani he kept for special occasions. Jimmy had already dripped a faint trail of strawberry on one lapel, and that was probably the trace of whipped cream just beside the pocket. Sandy bit his tongue in outrage.

"There you are, Jimmy," the real Jimmy said, displaying his prominent teeth in a condescending smile. "I wondered when I'd see you again. Not in any trouble are you, my boy?"

"None at all," Sandy said between his teeth. "It was good of you to meet us."

"Not at all, Jimmy, not at all. After all, you've kept me busy these past few years. It's no trouble to lend you a hand." He put his newly manicured hands on the car, leaning down to leer at Jane. "You must be Jimmy's little friend. Do you realize what sort of man you're hanging out with, Miss…?"

"No names," Sandy snapped, getting out of the car and fiddling uselessly with the lock. He hadn't been able to lock the MGB since 1978, but he always made a pretense of it in case someone happened to be looking.

And Jimmy was looking very carefully, his attention torn between the leather bra and the exterior of the MGB. "He's a pretty unsavory character," Jimmy continued, opening the door for her and watching with undisguised admiration as she slid her luscious legs out. Those tattered jeans did nothing to disguise their long, graceful length, and Sandy was on the edge of shoving Jimmy out of the way if he didn't stop drooling.

"Then why do you do so many favors for him?" Jane asked sweetly.

"Favors?" Jimmy echoed, mystified as well as entranced.

"Pay for his motel, cover his bills, even lend him your monogrammed bathrobe," Jane said innocently. "How do you know he won't run off with all your things?"

"Don't forget the apartment," Sandy piped up helpfully. "It was very decent of you to lend us your Park Avenue apartment since you're going out of town."

"You know," Jimmy mused, leaning forward and peering beneath Jane's feathers, "I may stay in town after all. There's plenty of room for you at my place anyway, but I might as well be a good host."

Sandy came over and slung a friendly arm around Jimmy's shoulders, grinding his bones with just enough pressure to make his accomplice turn pale without actually groaning in pain. "We appreciate the thought, Alexander, but we know how important that Baltimore case is. We'll just have to let you go."

Jimmy smiled weakly. Baltimore held a great many unpleasant secrets, most of which Sandy knew. "You're right, Jimmy," he said. "We'll have to do it some other time."

Sandy released his crushing grip, carefully moving Jimmy out of the way and taking Jane's arm in his. "Where's Jabba? Does he know we're coming?"

"He knows," Jimmy said, and Sandy couldn't miss the uneasiness in his voice. "I'm not sure your friend is going to like the company."

"My name's Jane," she said, and Sandy could feel the tension beneath the feathers. "And I'm used to him. How bad could things get?"

Jimmy laughed, a high-pitched, nasal giggle. "Used to him?" he echoed, looking at Sandy's thinly disguised patrician profile. "Honey, you ain't seen nothing yet."

"Sandy?" He could hear the beseeching note in Jane's husky voice, and he placed his hand on top of her arm, pressing slightly.

"You don't have to come," he said. He wished there was some way short of the truth that could keep her miles away from Jabba Matteo. But Jane Dexter was nothing if not a determined woman, and even the outlandish costume he'd provided hadn't deterred her.

"I'm coming," she said, her momentary hesitation gone.

He looked down into her somber eyes, surrounded by the rainbow streaks. She didn't trust him, and she was wise not to. But the one thing she could trust him with was her safety. Tonight, for possibly the first time in her life, he was deliberately leading someone into a dangerous situation beyond her own control. He had to count on the hope that it wouldn't be beyond his.

He managed a casual shrug. "Suit yourself," he said, ignoring Jimmy's admiring expression. "But remember to keep your eyes down and your mouth shut. We're heading into a patriarchal society, and no one's interested in equal rights around here. Understand?"

"Understood." She tried to pull away from him, but he held fast, his fingers tightening on her arm. The more he held on, the more she tugged, and in another moment they would have been involved in a wrestling match in the middle of the Lower East Side, when Jimmy decided to intervene.

Sandy was so startled he released her, and Jimmy took her arm with more graceful aplomb than he'd shown in his entire misspent life. "I'll take care of her, old boy," he murmured. "You just take care of yourself." And he started off down the littered, crowded sidewalks, Jane walking meekly enough beside him.

Sandy didn't move for a long moment, staring after his best Armani suit on Jimmy's stooped shoulders, watching Jane's magnificent legs and that absurd tangle of hair. Others were watching, the curious, sullen eyes so prevalent in a domain of criminals. Watching Jane and Jimmy's progress, watching Sandy, watching the MGB that couldn't be locked. Sandy gave it one last worried glance. He loved his aging, impossible-to-tune car with a passion he reserved for nothing else, and he couldn't rid himself of the miserable possibility that when he returned it would be gone.

But it was a choice between his car and Jane. And to his surprise there was no question at all which one mattered. Without another glance at the shiny blue finish, he hurried down the sidewalk after his former client. He could always buy another car.

Chapter Eleven

What in the world am I getting myself into, Jane thought as she moved along the broken sidewalks. She was in a part of New York her parents had always warned her about, and she was on the verge of meeting people she scarcely believed existed. The only protection she had was her own somewhat limited abilities, a felon who looked like a prince, and a lawyer who looked like a felon. Between Sandy and his lawyer there wasn't much choice, and if she had any sense at all she would have stayed at the motel in the first place instead of dressing up in such outlandish gear and walking the streets of the Lower East Side.

Her sense of uneasiness had been growing by the day, by the hour, compounded by the sudden intensity of the situation in which she found herself. Something bothered her about Sandy, and she couldn't quite pinpoint what it was. Something that didn't ring true, and every time she felt she was coming close to understanding it he'd do something distracting like kiss her. It had an amazing power to cloud her mind, but she couldn't afford to let it happen again. She'd managed to keep her own raging reactions under control, but it was a close call each time. Next time she might not make it.

The lawyer beside her didn't seem right either. She knew his suit was worth a small fortune, but the shoes didn't match. They were too shiny, and the black and white patent clashed with the muted colors of the suit. His hair was badly cut—

more for flash than for style, and the diamond ring on his pinky simply didn't look Princeton to her. But times had changed, and there was no question that her family had been elitist snobs. Maybe large diamond pinky rings were more in vogue than she remembered.

"Not far now," the unlikely lawyer said, guiding her around a corner and down a poorly lit alley where the debris underfoot was even thicker. He smelled of expensive cologne, but it was a brand Jane particularly disliked. Sandy was following behind them, not close enough, and for a moment she regretted struggling with him. She'd rather have his hand under her elbow. His fingers wouldn't be squeezing and stroking in a nasty, encroaching sort of way.

The alley was a dead end. There was a brick wall in front of them, windowless, doorless buildings on either side, with garbage heaped around a decrepit looking dumpster. The lawyer released her, heading straight for the rusty dumpster, as Sandy came up behind her.

"Second thoughts?" he inquired gently, the soft voice at odds with the punk appearance.

Jane watched with deep misgivings as the side to the dumpster swung open, spilling forth light and noise into the alley way. She considered lying, but it would be a waste of breath. Already Sandy knew her far too well. "And third and fourth and fifth thoughts," she said. "Do I really have to walk into a dumpster?"

The sleazy-looking lawyer was beckoning them toward the narrow stairs inside the camouflage garbage container, and as Jane moved closer she noticed that every attempt at authenticity had been made. The metal bin stank of rotting garbage.

"Too late to turn back now," Sandy said, his hand replacing his lawyer's on her befeathered elbow. And she'd been right—it was strong, comforting, the human warmth enabling her to duck her teased head and step into the narrow flight of stairs.

She went down slowly, following the Armani suit, Sandy directly behind her. As the smell of garbage faded, another scent replaced it, one of expensive, musky perfumes and colognes, whiskey and humanity. Not the rank sweat of the subway, this was expensive, freshly washed sweat. When she reached the bottom of the steps she stopped, absorbing the feel of Sandy's body as he bumped into her.

It looked like an odd combination of Chinese brothel, upscale nightclub and Soho loft. The place was packed, though nowhere could Jane see anyone she'd particularly like to socialize with. Feathers, chains, leather and hardware abounded. Jane was instantly grateful Sandy had taken her glasses. She had the distinct feeling she wouldn't care to see anyone here more closely, and she followed Caldicott blindly through the thick smoke and haze, her eyes downcast, as ordered.

"Hey, Jimmy," a man's voice called out, and she could feel Sandy's hand tighten reflexively on her elbow. She waited for him to respond, but Caldicott did it for him.

"Where's Jabba, Crystal?"

"He expecting you?"

"Would I be here if he wasn't?"

"Who knows?" the husky, cheerful voice responded. "Maybe you've brought some fresh talent. Who's your little feathered friend?"

"Ask Jabba," Caldicott replied cheerfully, as Jane bit back a tiny moan of sheer panic and claustrophobia.

"You ask Jabba. He's in the back. I'll tell him you're here." Jane allowed herself a brief glance at their interrogator, and then wished she hadn't. The voice had been basso profundo, the hair a Dolly Parton wig, the dress Ralph Lauren ruffles. She dropped her gaze to a thick pair of ankles and size twelve spike heels as they disappeared toward the back.

"Great guy," Caldicott said cheerfully. "Lucky we ran into him. I might have had a hell of a time finding Jabba."

"I thought this was prearranged," Sandy said, and Jane turned to look back at him in surprise. Her easy-going partner in crime sounded downright dangerous, and Caldicott reacted with uncharacteristic nervousness.

"It's as prearranged as things get with Matteo. I explained what was going on," Caldicott said uneasily. He had a prom-

inent Adam's apple above his silk knotted tie, and it was bob-
bing in agitation.

"You'd better have," Sandy said softly, his voice a very
definite threat. He caught Jane's fascinated gaze, and immediately smiled at her. "You look like you've seen a ghost."

She wet her lips, tasting the strawberry flavor of the purple-
black lipstick. "I just suddenly realized how dangerous you
could be," she said, her voice faltering.

He seemed equally as startled. "Only to low-lifes like him,"
he said. "Never to you."

She managed a weak smile in the noise and smoke. "You
call your lawyer a low-life? What does that make you?"

His expression was instantly veiled. "An entrepreneur," he
said. "And your partner in crime, in case you've forgotten."

"I haven't." She was too nearsighted to tell if everyone was
watching them, but she couldn't rid herself of the feeling that
countless hostile eyes were following their every move.
"Sandy," she said, her voice low and beseeching, "I think I'm
frightened."

If everyone was watching them that fact had no effect on
Sandy. He pulled her into his arms, feathers, leather bra and
all, and he was hot and strong and safe around her. She hid
there, her face pressed against his shoulder, the noise and lights
swirling around them, as she slowly pulled her strength back
around her. He held her just as long as she needed holding,
and when she felt strong enough to move away he released her
instantly.

"Feel better?" he inquired in the most casual of voices.

She managed a tremulous smile. "Yes."

"Don't worry. I won't let the bad guys get you."

"They wouldn't want me, would they?" she countered seriously.

"They'd be fools not to."

"This way." Caldicott was back between them, his cologne
overpowering the other, more suspect smells of the crowded
rooms, and Jane had no chance to respond. The lawyer had her
hand caught tightly in his, tugging her through the maze of

chattering, bright-eyed people toward a door in the back, and she followed, certain that Sandy was right behind her.

The silence of the next room was thick and shocking after the cacophony before, and the filtered light only compounded Jane's myopia as the lawyer drew her to a halt. Sandy was beside her, his hand caught her other one, and slowly she lifted her eyes to the figure in front of them.

She had never seen a human being so immense in her entire life. He seemed to fill the end of the narrow room, and in the gray filtered light he seemed an amorphous blob of semihumanity, larger than three normal people put together. He was dressed in some sort of gray suit, but his abundant flesh spilled around him. His skin was pasty gray, his eyes dark little raisins in a face of suet, his mouth was small and cruel and pink. He was smiling at them with that mouth, and he waved a fat, balloonlike hand in greeting.

"Welcome, friends," he said, and his voice was another surprise. She would have expected something low and rumbling from that mountain of flesh, but instead it came out in a high-pitched wheeze, barely carrying the length of the empty room. On second glance Jane noticed the room wasn't empty at all. Stationed at strategic points along the bare walls were studiously casual men, their loose jackets concealing their weapons. Jane shuddered, and she could feel the cool dampness of the hands in hers. Both Sandy and his nefarious lawyer were just as scared of Jabba Matteo as she was.

"How nice to finally meet you, Mr. Caldicott," Matteo purred, his voice lilting his amusement. "I've been hoping for a chance to repay the favor you did me and mine so long ago, and now that time has come. And as I live and breathe, this must be Jimmy the Stoolie. Come closer, young man, and tell me how I can assist you and this surprising young lady."

Sandy's hand clenched more tightly around hers, but his elegant profile gave nothing away. The man on her left was pale and sweating profusely, and she was glad she didn't have to count on him to defend her in court. At least Sandy could keep his head when things got difficult.

"We appreciate your seeing us, Mr. Matteo," Sandy said, his voice steady and deceptively casual. "Caldicott probably explained our problem to you."

"Your lawyer did mention something. And please, call me Jabba. Such formality distresses me. Old friends such as we shouldn't stand on ceremony. Come, come, Jimmy. Bring the little lady closer."

It was Jane's turn to be startled. She lifted her head, against Sandy's previous orders, and stared defiantly into Jabba's pig-like eyes, and then wished she hadn't. For all the comic-book trappings, the absurdity of place and time, the eyes of the huge man in front of her were pure evil.

"We want to know about Stephen Tremaine." Sandy angled his body to shield her an almost imperceptible amount. "You know everything in the world of arms dealing. What is Tremaine up to?"

Jabba chuckled, a high, wheezing sound. "Why limit it to arms dealing? I know everything worth knowing, or I can find it out in minutes. Stephen Tremaine is trying to sell an advanced titanium coating process to the highest bidder he can find. Libya has already backed down—the asking price is much too high. Chile is interested, but has yet to make an offer, Chad wants it but is also too poor, and Iran doesn't want to wait. At this point it looks like he's going to sell to the President of Salambia."

"But he's a madman," Jane said, horror overriding her common sense.

Jabba's evil little eyes smiled on her. "Indeed he is, dear lady. A very wealthy madman, and one of my best customers. You mustn't judge him too harshly, dear lady. You've lived too sheltered a life."

"Shut up," Sandy hissed at her, his strong hand grinding the bones in her wrist.

"But let the little woman speak, Jimmy the Stoolie." He accented the name, as if he and Sandy shared a secret joke. "I'm not used to such innocence, and it amuses me. She's the one who wants to know, isn't she? Let her ask the questions."

Jane ignored Sandy's warning hand, pulling away from him and confronting Matteo with deceptive fearlessness. Her knees trembled, her stomach churned, and she could only hope she could ask her questions and escape without throwing up on the red Oriental carpet beneath her feet.

"Does Tremaine have the entire formula?" she demanded. "Or is he still missing a crucial part of it?"

"Dear me," Jabba said, fanning his pale basketball-size head with a copy of *Fortune* Magazine. "I hadn't realized what was causing the delay. How delicious. He went to all that trouble to silence your brother and now he's unable to profit from it. Maybe that has something to do with his interest in a certain property in Bay Head. I do love irony, don't you, Ms Dexter?"

The room was utterly, completely still. She no longer felt Sandy's restraining hand, was completely unaware of Caldicott's terrified stance. She moved forward, so close she could feel the heat and danger emanating from the mountain of flesh in front of her. "Did Stephen Tremaine have anything to do with my brother's death?" Her voice was raw with emotion, and she was no longer frightened.

Jabba's grin revealed two rows of tiny gold teeth. "Dear child, I don't know. I can assure you he didn't hire any professionals before yesterday. I would have heard if he did. But I couldn't say whether he opted for an amateur hit. The man is desperate, and your brother's death was very convenient."

Jane just stared at him numbly, listening to the words she didn't want to hear. "What do you mean before yesterday?"

Jabba chuckled. "Word has it he's retained the services of a notable knife artist named Lenny the Rip. I didn't bother to check, and sometimes any information can be…premature. If he has, I expect you'll find out sooner or later." He'd finished with her, turning his attention back to Sandy. "Was there anything else you wished to know?"

Sandy glanced over at her, then shook his head. "That about covers it."

Jabba nodded, his row of chins quivering. "Then my debt

of honor is repaid. I will have to make sure my son doesn't incur another such debt."

Sandy said nothing, simply inclining his head graciously. The lawyer was still sweating in the cool room.

"And I think," said Jabba, "that you might make me a small gesture to ensure your good will and discretion."

She could feel the tension in the room. It was a palpable thing, and once again she had the eerie sense that all eyes were on her, from Jabba's evil dark ones to the deadly cold emotionless ones of the men lining the wall.

Again Sandy nodded, this time with less grace. "I'd be more than happy to oblige."

Jabba giggled. "I thought you might. Why don't you leave me Ms Dexter for the night? I can promise her an interesting time, and we'll return her in one piece."

The lawyer beside her swore, casting a desperate glance over at Sandy's immobile face. The army lining the room had straightened, clearly expecting some action, and Sandy's face was carved in stone. Jane could see his gray eyes flicker as his brain struggled for some way out of their current mess, and she resisted the impulse to start screaming in utter panic. Instead she waited, forcing herself to be calm.

Sandy shrugged. "I'd love to oblige you, Jabba. Shall I come back and fetch her or will you send her home?"

Jane's moan of outrage was drowned out by Jabba's laugh. "I'll send her home when we've finished with her. It's been a long time since we've seen such an innocent. Her costume only makes her naïveté more apparent."

"I'm rather fond of it myself," Sandy said, lifting one of the feathers and letting it flutter down. "I do trust you don't actually wish to touch her?"

"Trust away, dear boy," Jabba said with a smirk.

"Because I should warn you that much as I adore the young lady, she's not terribly...healthy." The pregnant pause said it all. "It's nothing fatal, but the results could be quite uncomfortable, if you know what I mean."

Jabba recoiled faintly, his smile fading. "I don't believe you," he wheezed.

Sandy only smiled. "I may be lying," he agreed. "But how will you know?"

Jabba stared at them, long and hard, and Jane held her breath, waiting for the ax to fall, waiting for the slit-eyed army to draw weapons and put an end to their impertinent existence.

And then he began to laugh, the sound coming from deep within the rolls of fat surrounding his body, bubbling out, shaking his huge frame until Jane thought he might choke to death in front of her eyes. Tears poured down his rosy cheeks and caught in the folds of his chins, his gold teeth glinted in the lamplight.

"Philadelphia lawyer," Jabba chuckled breathlessly. "It's just as well. My honor is compromised enough as it is. In this case I'll keep it intact."

"I thought you might see it that way," Sandy said smoothly.

"But I suggest you leave the back way. It wouldn't do my reputation any good to have it known I let you walk away without paying any duty. And I don't think you'd care for that sort of attention either, not in your line of work."

"A con man can't be too careful," Sandy said.

Jabba chuckled, dabbing at his tear-streaked face. "If you're a con man what do you call your ailing young lady?"

Sandy looked over at her, and there was a fiercely possessive gleam in his blue eyes. "My partner in crime," he said. "What else?"

JANE RAN BLINDLY, stumbling through the dark streets after Sandy, too terrified to even think. The pounding of her heart and the rasping of her labored breathing drowned out any possible sound of pursuit, but she could imagine a horde of those grim-faced men chasing after them through New York's mean streets.

She had no idea how far they'd come when Sandy pulled to a stop, dropping her abused wrist and leaning against a building to catch his breath. She could feel the cool evening air dry the sweat on her face, she could smell the exhaust and the fear that had surrounded them back in that dark, hot room, and she shivered.

"Was it worth it?" Caldicott whined. He'd ripped the Armani suit during their mad dash, and Sandy was eyeing the tear with nothing short of outrage.

"No," said Jane.

"Yes," said Sandy at the same time. "We know we're in trouble and we know Tremaine is dangerous."

"We already knew that," Jane pointed out, stripping off her black lace half gloves.

"But now we know who he's negotiating with. And we know he's still a ways from finding the rest of the formula. We have some time."

"We don't know how much," Jane said.

"At least we have a night's sleep."

"And we know where we're going tomorrow."

Sandy looked at her with deep apprehension. "All right, I'll bite. Where are we going tomorrow?"

"Bay Head. My brother inherited a house on the ocean. Tremaine must think the formula is there."

"And what do you think?"

"I think it's a good possibility. Richard used to go there and refused to invite any of the family. It would be the perfect place for a lab, and it's less than an hour from Princeton."

"All right," Sandy said wearily. "Tomorrow we go to Bay Head. Tonight we go back to the apartment."

"I was thinking I might join you after all," Caldicott began, half bravado, half edginess. "Jabba's spooked me good and proper…"

"Too bad, old man," Sandy said firmly. "But you're going to be busy with the police."

"I didn't do anything!" the lawyer declared instantly, sounding for all the world like either a criminal himself or a very naughty little boy.

"I didn't say you did," Sandy said, reaching out a long arm and hailing a taxi. The yellow cab pulled up beside them, and

Sandy opened the door. "But you're going to be busy filing a stolen car report."

"Not the MG?"

"The MG," Sandy verified with only a wince of sorrow. "All in a good cause, though. Thanks for the use of the apartment, old boy. See you in court." And he slid in beside Jane, slamming the door in Caldicott's pinched little face.

The real Jimmy the Stoolie watched them disappear into the night, a mournful expression on his face. He stood there for a long time, not moving, until a skinny, ratlike figure scuttled up to him out of the darkening shadows.

"Here's the key, Jimmy," he rasped, dropping it in his outstretched hand. "But boy, that MG needs a tune."

Chapter Twelve

For all Alexander Caldicott's sleaziness, there was no denying he lived well. The taxi dropped them uptown, on East 66th Street, and the uniformed doorman was as elegant as he was discreet, ushering Sandy in with a "Good to see you again, sir" that was the epitome of understated tact.

"You spend a lot of time here?" Jane whispered as they were passed on to an equally circumspect elevator operator.

"More than Caldicott does," Sandy replied innocently. "Half the people who work here think I *am* Alexander Caldicott."

"I'm sure they had a little help in that assumption."

Sandy merely smiled. Sure enough, the elevator operator murmured, "Welcome home, Mr. Caldicott," as they exited the small gilt and walnut cage on the sixth floor. Even in her advanced state of shock and exhaustion Jane didn't miss the passing of paper money.

The apartment had the dry, musty smell of uninhabited places, and Jane stumbled into the elegant foyer with only a tenth of her usual curiosity. She wanted to ask him where Caldicott had been the past few days, but she didn't bother. Instead, she asked the question that was uppermost in her mind.

"Where's the shower?"

"Straight down the hallway. You want some clean clothes? I'm afraid your suitcase was in the MG, but I think I can come up with something."

"Anything," Jane said with a shudder.

"I'll leave something outside the door," he promised. "Though I'll miss the leather bra."

"You try and wear it," she offered, heading toward the bathroom. She stopped halfway down, turning to look at him with the last ounce of curiosity in her weary body. He was standing in the entrance, staring after her, his spiky hair rumpled.

"What is it?" he questioned softly.

"Matteo was bluffing, wasn't he? He didn't really want me?"

Sandy shook his head. "Don't count on it. You were in deep trouble at that moment."

"What if he hadn't given in? Would you have left me?"

The dim light cast eerie shadows on his face, and she remembered the steel in his voice when he'd threatened his lawyer, the danger radiating from him when he'd confronted Jabba. "What do you think?" he asked, not giving an inch.

Jane thought about it. "I think Jabba was lucky he decided to let me go," she said finally, turning back toward the shower.

The sun was rising over the canyons of New York when Jane finally emerged from the shower, her towel-dried hair dripping onto her shoulders, an oversize black sweat suit presumably belonging to Caldicott enveloping her body. At least it didn't smell of that awful cologne. The apartment was huge, with a living room, formal dining room and three bedrooms, each one the size of a studio apartment. She found Sandy in the kitchen, laying out thick sandwiches and imported dark beer.

There must have been two showers in the rambling old place. Sandy's hair was still spiky, though this time it was wet from the shower, and he was wearing faded jeans and nothing more. The jeans were zipped but not snapped, and Jane noticed that somehow in between his bouts of criminality he must have found time to work out. He'd already made it clear he'd never soil his hands with physical labor, so his smoothly muscled chest and shoulders had to come from something slightly more elitist.

"Do you want anything to eat?" he inquired, padding across the tile floor on bare feet.

"I think I just want a bed," she said in a small voice. She backed up as he advanced. She was in no condition to fight off any errant advances, in no condition to fight her own desires. He kept moving closer, and his body was even more beautiful as he drew near, and she wanted to burst into tears.

She did. He stopped within a foot of her, not moving closer, and even without her glasses she could see the skepticism in his face. "Is this part of your act?" he asked. "Or are you really crying this time?"

"You can tell when I'm really upset," she said between choking sobs, "my nose gets red and I get the hiccups." She punctuated that watery statement with a noisy "hic," and her sobs increased.

"Proof enough," he said, crossing the distance between them and pulling her into his arms. She was beyond thinking, beyond caring, and she went willingly, grateful to be enveloped against a strong, warm chest, a soundly beating heart, a male body that had protected her. So many emotions had swept over her during the past few hours that she could no longer summon the energy to fight. The rage and terror, the outrage and determination had vanished with their escape. All that was left was a shimmering desire washing through her, and all her rational, logical doubts vanished. What she wanted tonight was comfort and oblivion, and her partner in crime could provide just that.

She slid her arms around his waist, his skin firm and hot to her touch. She tilted her head up, just slightly, waiting for his mouth to claim hers, for the demand that this time she'd respond to.

His hands threaded through her wet hair, holding her still. She waited for his mouth, but he moved no closer. The tautness of his body told her he wanted her, but still he did nothing about it. Slowly, reluctantly she opened her eyes a crack.

"No," he said gently.

Her eyes flew open the rest of the way. "No, what?"

A small, self-deprecating grin lit his sexy mouth. The mouth she wanted on hers. "No, thank you."

She tried to pull away from him then, but he wasn't about to let her go. "I think I've just about lost my sense of humor, Sandy," she said in a raw voice. "Let me go."

"I don't want to."

"Make up your damned mind!" she said desperately, struggling. It was a waste of energy.

He took her shoulders and shook her, a hard, brief shake. "Listen to me, Jane. I could have you tonight, and you're not so naive that you don't know that's exactly what I want, what I've been working for since the moment you walked in my door and asked me to commit arson for you. And I'm going to have you, sooner or later, and I hope for the sake of my sanity that it's going to be sooner. But not tonight. Not when you're tired and frightened and vulnerable, not when you've been through so much that you'd go to bed with anything that moved just to blot out the last few days. When we make love I want you to know what you're doing, I want you to want me enough to trust me, to look at me, to know that it's me you're making love to and not some faceless soporific. Do you understand?"

He still hadn't released her. His long fingers were biting into her slender shoulders, and the tension running through him put her own anxiety to shame. His mind might have bought what he just said, his body was putting up a hell of a fight.

Still, she'd had enough time to come to her senses. "What makes you so sure it's going to happen? How do you know you aren't blowing your one and only chance?"

"Lady," he said wearily, "I don't sleep around. When I go to bed with someone I do it because she matters, not just to scratch an itch. And I expect my partner to feel the same way. If it's not going to be that way, it's not going to happen."

She stepped back, and this time he let her go. "The last thing I expected from you is a lecture on morals," she said, but there was a faint resurgence of humor in her voice.

"We all have to have some standards," he said, running a weary hand through his wet hair.

He was still impossibly beautiful. And she still wanted that lean, tough body pressed against hers through the long hours of the early morning. But she'd come to her senses, and next time she wouldn't be so vulnerable.

"So where do I sleep?"

"Take your pick. The back bedroom is the quietest, the front one's got the most comfortable bed."

"You've tried them all?"

"I spend a lot of time here."

"How come Caldicott has such a huge apartment that he never uses?" she asked with her last ounce of curiosity.

"It's a condo he inherited from his parents. I guess it's cheaper than a lot of studios."

"So he can afford to run a flop house for con men?" Jane asked.

"If he wants to."

"Why would he want to?"

"Why don't you ask him next time you see him?"

"Am I going to see him again?"

"Jane," he said wearily, "it is five-fifteen in the morning, and we've been through a hell of a night. Stop cross-examining me."

"Just trying to keep you in practice in case we get caught. You sure you won't change your mind?" She was teasing now, in control and marvelously self-assured. He wanted her, he wanted her as much as she wanted him, and yet she was deliciously safe.

"Go to bed, Jane," he growled. "I can always change my mind."

It was tempting, but she'd gotten her second wind. "I'll take the quiet back bedroom. See you in about six hours."

"Eight."

"Six. We have to get to the Jersey shore before dark."

"Six," he groaned. "I should have left you with Jabba."

There were sheets on the narrow bed in the back bedroom.

The room was plain and austere—she could see the darker patches on the wallpaper where pictures had once hung. Children's books were piled in haphazard rows in the lateral bookcases, an old orange-and-black Princeton pennant still decorated one wall, and the musty smell was heavy in the air. It took all her strength to pry open the window to let in the cool morning air, and then she dragged her weary body to the little bed and tumbled in. When she woke up she'd think about Richard, about Stephen Tremaine and his nasty double dealings. When she woke up she'd think about Sandy and what in the world she was going to do about her overwhelming attraction to him. For now all she needed was sleep.

SANDY LEANED against the wall and breathed a sigh of relief. It had been a close call. Granted, she'd been in the shower almost half an hour, but the apartment in which he'd been raised was littered with family memorabilia, including silver-framed photographs in almost every room. He'd raced from one end of the apartment to the other, shoving pictures in drawers, under beds, between mattresses. If he'd had any sense at all he would have taken her up on her half offer, carried her to bed and made sure her brain was no longer working well enough to notice anything.

But he couldn't do that to her. He couldn't take advantage of her fear and exhaustion, he couldn't take advantage of the wanting he knew burned beneath her strong defenses, not when those defenses were down. And he couldn't make love to her when he was busy living a lie.

When it came right down to it she might very well be right— it might have been his only chance. But maybe, just maybe, when the manure hit the fan, she'd remember and give him credit for his self-control and forbearance. Or maybe she'd be too mad to think.

He needed a decent night's sleep. He needed to sit Jane down and tell her the truth, no excuses, no more lies, just the facts, ma'am. And while he was at it, he ought to call in the theft of his beloved car. For some reason the recalcitrant MGB had lost its importance in his life. While he regretted its loss, he knew it wasn't a sensible car for a married man.

What the hell was he thinking of? He must be getting punchy. Too little sleep, too much excitement. What he needed was eight hours of solid sleep in his own bed. Jane was only going to allow him six, and that would have to do. Maybe once he told her the truth she'd leave him to sleep forever.

He was sorely tempted to tiptoe down the hallway and check on her. He wanted to watch her sleep, her defenses gone, her face absurdly young and vulnerable. He wanted to take the chance that she might still be awake, that he could forget his peripatetic principles and join her in his narrow boy's bed.

He'd already taken one shower. Maybe another cold one would put a halt to the temptation. Why, he asked himself, did he have to be so damned noble?

SHE SLEPT FITFULLY in the strange bed, and her dreams were bizarre, confused ones, laden with doomed sexuality, pervaded with longing and despair. No one was as he seemed. Jabba kept metamorphosing into his Star Wars counterpart, Sandy and the sleazy Caldicott kept changing persona. Stephen Tremaine wandered in and out of her life, and sometimes he was her father, sometimes himself, always disapproving.

She herself was the most confused, alternating between martyr and avenger, virgin and whore, victim and criminal, until she woke up covered with a cold sweat, blind and terrified.

There was no clock in the room, and Sandy had confiscated her watch along with her glasses. She had no idea what time it was, no idea where Sandy was. All she knew was that she had to find him, had to find the peace and comfort only he could give her. It didn't matter that he'd turned down her tentative offer once—he'd regretted his nobility the moment he gave in to it, and it would take nothing, a glance, a smile, to have him banish his finer instincts.

She didn't care whether it was right or wrong. She didn't care whether she was making the worst mistake of her life. She needed someone, she needed Sandy, and his past no longer mattered. He couldn't have committed any more foolish mistakes than she had in marrying Frank and then relinquishing him so easily.

He'd taken the middle bedroom, but the queen-size bed was empty, the sheets pulled apart, the pillows tossed here and there. She could hear the sound of the shower in the background, and leaning over, she squinted at the digital clock. Nine-thirty—she'd slept a grand total of four hours.

She wondered if Sandy was taking a cold shower. If he was it would be a complete waste. She considered stripping off the black sweat suit and climbing naked into his bed, but she didn't quite have the nerve. Instead, she kept her clothes on, climbed into the bed and pulled the navy-blue sheets around her, awaiting his return.

He was a long time in the shower. She sat there, her nerves getting the better of her, waiting for him. She reached for a magazine from the pile stacked beside the bed. *Princeton Alumni Weekly*, she noticed. What scintillating reading material. She was about to toss it down when she noticed the photograph on the cover. There stood Sandy, surrounded by three very Princetonian looking gentlemen, and her curiosity was aroused. Why would Sandy be posing for the Princeton Alumni Weekly with a bunch of yuppies?

The caption was mistaken, of course, but then, captions often got screwed up. The men on the cover were identified as Gregory MacDougal, '73, Elroy "Max" Sullivan, '72, Alexander "Sandy" Caldicott, '75, and Jonathan Cohen, '77. All partners in the law firm of MacDougal and Sullivan.

She stared at the caption for a long moment, then turned back to the picture. Sandy was wearing the Armani suit she'd seen destroyed the night before.

It wasn't a conscious realization, a mental leap, but more like a sudden clearing in her previously befogged brain. The knowledge was surrounding her like a cold, nasty blanket of truth, and for countless moments she sat in his bed and shook.

He'd left his wallet on the dresser. The picture on his driver's license wasn't flattering, but it was definitely Sandy. The top drawer was jumbled with old photographs of Sandy and a family that looked exactly like him. Pictures of Sandy at Princeton, pictures of Sandy skiing. All the evidence of an elitist life spent far from the bowels of New York and a life of arson and petty crime.

She started hunting for a blunt instrument. Her rage was so total, so overwhelming, that violence came immediately to mind. Never mind her pacifist ideas: right now her fury was so strong that she was ready to kill.

But Alexander "Sandy" Caldicott was still locked safely in the shower. Fond thoughts of *Psycho* danced through her brain, but she dismissed them as calm slowly, painstakingly returned. He'd made a complete and utter fool of her. Like it or not, she was too civilized to kill him. She'd have to settle for revenge.

She stood there in the doorway to his bedroom, a cold, evil calm settling over her, as she listened to the shower end. She waited, prepared, as he stepped into the room, knotting a towel around his waist.

He didn't see her at first. When he did he jumped, startled, and then flashed that beautiful, ingratiating grin. "I couldn't sleep," he said, coming toward her. "Must be the strange bed."

"Must be," she said gently, ignoring his beautiful body that was still glistening from the shower.

"Are you all right?" He bent down, looking into her distant face, his wonderful gray eyes worried.

"Fine," she said. "I'm just anxious to get to Bay Head."

He smiled at her, his head ducked down, and she knew he was going to kiss her again. She considered letting him, but at the last moment she chickened out, backing away from him before his mouth could brush hers. If he actually touched her she might forget her noble resolve and strangle him with her bare hands.

"Can we get coffee on the road?" she murmured.

He looked at her for a long, puzzled moment. "Sure," he said finally. "It'll take me a few moments to get dressed. Think you can wait that long?"

"Oh, I'm very patient when I know what I want," Jane said evenly, visions of Sandy's head on a platter dancing in front of her eyes. "Take your time."

And Sandy, an uneasy light in his eyes, was ready to go in three minutes flat.

Chapter Thirteen

Sandy didn't know how he was going to explain his sudden acquisition of a late-model Audi from the basement garage, but for once Jane wasn't asking any questions. She still had that pinched, peculiar expression on her face, she wouldn't meet his eyes, and the tension vibrating through her slender body was so intense he found his own fists clenching in sympathetic response.

It was an Indian summer Sunday in New York, beautiful, and the city was practically empty. He drove through the park on the way to the tunnel, hungry for a taste of cool green after the heat and squalor of the night before. He'd been hoping to talk Jane into a leisurely brunch at one of his favorite restaurants, but one look at her averted profile and he had abandoned the idea. It was just as well—he was known by name at most places, and he'd already been pushing his luck by taking her home to his apartment.

He was used to thinking on his feet in court, and his experience had served him well when he'd come face-to-face with Hans the elevator operator who'd known him since adolescence. But Jane was a smart lady—it had been sheer luck that she hadn't tumbled onto all the amazing coincidences so far.

It was more than luck. He knew from observing human nature in and out of the courtroom that people saw what they expected to see. Once Jane got it into her head that he was Jimmy the Stoolie it would take a great deal to convince her of anything different. If he were reasonably circumspect he'd be safe.

"Penny for your thoughts," he said as he headed the Audi into the Lincoln Tunnel.

Jane turned slowly to look at him, her eyes unreadable behind the wire-rimmed glasses. "You wouldn't want to know them," she said.

"That bad, eh? I'm glad I'm not Stephen Tremaine. I wouldn't care to have your fury directed at me."

Her smile was cool. "Oh, I'm very rational and civilized. I'm not one to let my emotions overwhelm me."

"And if we find that Stephen Tremaine actually did have your brother killed, what then? Won't your emotions get the better of you? Won't you want your revenge?"

"First things, first," she said, continuing before he could ask her to explain that enigmatic statement. "I haven't been to the Jersey shore in years."

"I don't think it's changed much. It was already built up as much as it could be, and the real estate is worth so much that when things start disintegrating new money comes in and buys the old places up. How come your brother owns a place in Bay Head and you don't? A research scientist, even one at the top of Tremaine's payroll, wouldn't make enough to buy one."

"Especially not one like Richard's," she said, her voice losing some of its tight, strained quality. "It was left to him by an eccentric bachelor uncle. One who hated women. He hadn't been in the place in decades, but he'd had it kept up, and when he died he left it to the one relative who least wanted it. Typical of Uncle Oscar."

"What did Richard do with it?"

"Not much. I gather he'd come down weekends occasionally, when Princeton got too crowded. In fact he came down here the weekend before he died. I hadn't thought it made any difference, but if it really wasn't an accident..." She shuddered, her hands pleating and repleating the khaki shirt Sandy had found in a back closet for her. "I was going to come down here sooner or later, but I knew he'd never cared much for the place so I couldn't believe he would have had his private laboratory here. Maybe I was wrong.''

"What are you going to do with the place?"

"I beg your pardon?"

"You inherited it, didn't you? Are you going to sell it?"

"Why?" Jane inquired sweetly. "Were you interested in buying it?"

"I don't make that kind of money with my penny ante schemes."

"Maybe Alexander Caldicott would buy it for you. He seems to be bankrolling everything as it is.''

She was looking out into the early-afternoon traffic, so he couldn't see her expression, but her tone of voice had been downright caustic. She couldn't have found out... No, it was impossible. Jane wasn't the kind to take that information quietly. If she found out he'd been lying to her she'd be more likely to rant and rave. Wouldn't she?

"Don't you like Alexander?" he probed gently.

She turned then, her brown eyes limpid and innocent, and he breathed a sigh of relief. Jane wasn't that practiced a dissembler. "Of course I do," she said. "He keeps you out of jail, doesn't he?"

"Does that matter to you? Whether I'm in jail or not?"

"I wouldn't get very far in my life of crime without an experienced crook like you, now would I?''

Something was definitely wrong. Maybe it was as simple as a delayed reaction to last night, or distress about her brother, or concern about the time it was taking to get to the bottom of it. One look at her delicious, thoroughly stubborn lower lip and he knew he wouldn't find out anything more until she was good and ready to tell him.

"I guess not," he said.

Without another word she flicked on the radio, tuned it to Bruce Springsteen, and turned up the volume loud enough to preclude conversation, as they headed toward the New Jersey Turnpike.

THE MAN BESIDE HER was right, the Jersey shore hadn't changed much in the last fifteen or so years. In this transitional off-season, the streets, while not deserted, were more reasonably populated, and there were no signs of urban decay as there were in the inland cities.

Suddenly Jane was transported back to her teenage years, when a bunch of kids would pile into someone's old Beetle and drive to the shore for a day of sunburns and junk food and very little sea water. It had been a wonderful time, spent hidden behind prescription sunglasses, stuffed into a bikini she blushed to remember, playing WNEW-FM too loud and irritating everyone else on the beach. She had very few memories of such innocence—those times had been few and far between during her ordained quest for academic excellence. It wasn't until she flatly announced to her parents that she was refusing Stanford, Harvard, and Princeton in favor of a small liberal arts college in the Midwest that she once more experienced that heady feeling of youthful joy and power.

The old house on the ocean hadn't changed much. Unlike its neighbors, it hadn't been freshened with a new coat of paint, the shingles were streaked and weathered, and weeds were poking out of the cracked walkways. She'd been there once since Richard inherited it, and with him had made the tour of rusty pipes, outdated wiring, cheap furniture and rattan rugs. The house had smelled of boiled cabbage and dead fish, and four years later it smelled the same. There was no apparent sign that Richard had been back in the past few years.

The first thing Jane did was open all the windows. The second was to check that the power and phone were working. The former was, the latter wasn't, but that wouldn't matter for one night. Not unless she murdered the man with her and then wanted to turn herself in.

She couldn't think of him in terms of anything but a pronoun or a four-letter word. It didn't matter that she'd been calling him Sandy, clearly an often-used nickname for Alexander. It didn't matter that she knew him as Caldicott—she still thought of that little weasel as his lawyer, not as his client.

"We're spending the night here?" the creep inquired as he came back down the stairs.

Jane turned off the rusty tap water and turned to face him. "You can go back to your lawyer's apartment if you want," she said sweetly. "I'm staying here."

"I'll stay. Though what you think we'll find is beyond me. It doesn't look as if anyone's been here in years."

"Richard wasn't the type to settle in. He probably just brought a suitcase and ate out. That doesn't mean he wouldn't leave some sort of sign. He left directly for Vermont from here. Chances are we'll find a reason."

"I don't see any sign of a laboratory. Not unless it's hidden behind fake walls or something." He shoved the sleeves of his rugby shirt up to his elbows and peered into the empty refrigerator.

"The wiring hasn't been upgraded. He couldn't have had a lab here. His work requires some sophisticated instruments and a decent power source."

He shut the refrigerator door and leaned against it, staring out the grimy kitchen window at the ramshackle garage. "So we've come to a dead end."

"Not necessarily. That's what comes from being on the other side of the law, Jimmy," she said with just a touch of malice. "You don't have to put your energies into discovering things, you have to put them into keeping from being discovered. It's different when you're the one who's looking. There's trash in the wastepaper baskets, there are papers and envelopes less than two months old in his desk. He left his McDonald's wrappers here—we'll be able to look at it and see whether he was alone or whether there is enough trash for two."

"You do have a devious mind," he said admiringly.

"I'm probably better suited to a life of crime than you are, Jimmy."

"Call me Sandy," he said with a trace of irritation.

"Sandy's too bland and innocuous a name," she replied sweetly. "I prefer to think of you as Jimmy the Stoolie. After last night's encounter I have no doubt at all that beneath that wishy-washy exterior lurks the soul of a completely sleazy liar, but it's easy to forget and think you're a decent, upstanding citizen.''

He just stared at her, at a complete loss for words, and she watched him with limpid delight. He couldn't very well insist that he wasn't a rotten liar—after all, he'd gone to a great deal of trouble to convince her that was exactly what he was. He couldn't very well insist what she termed his wishy-washy exterior was the real thing, that bland and innocuous Sandy was his real name. All he could do was glare at her from across the large, old-fashioned kitchen.

''It's always nice to know what my partner in crime thinks of me,'' he said finally, pushing away from the refrigerator and moving toward her.

Jane eyed him warily. No matter how furious, how outraged and murderous she felt, she couldn't rid herself of the irrational, utterly degrading attraction she still felt for him. ''Why don't you go out and find us something to eat,'' she said, forestalling his steady approach, ''and I'll make a start on the trash?''

''That sounds like an offer I can't refuse.'' He stopped his headlong advance. ''Wouldn't you rather go out for dinner?''

''I'd rather get started. The longer we take the greater the chance that Uncle Stephen will find the missing part of the formula first. We've wasted too much time as it is.''

He didn't reply to the indirect criticism. ''Do you want to make a list?''

''See if you can find a place with take-out fried clams. We'll also need some instant coffee and maybe something for breakfast.''

''No instant coffee. We get ground coffee or we go without. I think I'll see if I can find a bottle of Scotch, too. Something tells me it's going to be a cold night.''

''It's Indian summer,'' she pointed out.

''I wasn't talking about the temperature. Anything else?''

Enough rope for you to hang yourself, she thought sweetly. ''Anything that strikes your fancy, Jimmy.''

''Let's leave it at wishy-washy old Sandy, okay?'' he said,

his voice just short of a bark. "I'm used to it by now." The door slammed behind him, the Audi screeched out of the driveway, and Jane stood at the kitchen door, trying to fight the burning feeling of anger and tears that had lodged in her chest since early that morning.

"Damn you, Alexander Caldicott," she whispered, trying the name on for size. It suited him, all right. How could she have been so blind and stupid?

She hadn't bothered to mention to him that the house already contained a bottle of Scotch. Her brother's one human weakness in his entire austere life had been a fondness for the best Scotch he could buy, and he could buy the best. There was bound to be a bottle of Cutty Sark or Pinch somewhere around in the dusty old cupboards. And that was exactly what she needed, right then and there.

She found it under the sink, next to the rusty can of Drano. The ice cubes in the freezer were dry and shrunken, the rusty water unappealing, so she poured herself a goodly portion, neat, and stepped out onto the screened-in back porch.

Most of the screens were ripped and shredded, but thankfully the mosquito season was well past. The house sat smack on the beach, and while its stretch of white sand leading down to the churning gray water was ostensibly private property, no one had abided by that edict. Jane noticed the charred remnants of a campfire, several cans and bottles, but nothing that couldn't be cleaned up in a few minutes.

She sank down gingerly on an aging lounge chair, propped her feet up, and took a deep sip of the warm Scotch. Despite the unseasonable warmth of the day a fresh breeze had picked up, and the strong salt scent of high tide teased her senses. The sun was setting, the purples and reds of a brilliant sunset reflecting over the ocean. It never failed to work out that she was on the wrong coast at the wrong time. The only time she'd spent on the Pacific she'd been involved in a seminar that included rising at dawn and being locked away in meetings during sunset. Here she was on the East Coast, finally able to watch nature, and the sun was setting out of sight. And she had no intention whatsoever of being up early enough to see the sun rise.

She had more than enough time to drink her whiskey, watch the tide ebb, and think about the future. She'd have to find Richard's lab on her own, without any help from her so-called partner in crime. Though she was beginning to lose interest in the chase. Richard made his life a monument to high principles, but that didn't mean she had to waste months and months trying to follow in his footsteps. She'd always felt like such a cop-out compared to Richard's high-flown standards, but maybe she'd been too harsh on herself. Maybe it wasn't such a crime to be able to see the other person's point of view, no matter how distasteful it might appear.

She toyed with the notion, as she toyed with the glass of rapidly disappearing whiskey, considering various occasions when she might have been too understanding. While she was an old-fashioned liberal, she understood the fears that drove conservatives. While she enjoyed an occasional whiskey or a glass of wine, she realized the dangers certain people ran in indulging even marginally in such social drugs.

And what about Frank? He'd made a mistake, divorcing his first wife and then marrying Jane on the rebound. He hadn't excused it, or tried to blame anyone else, he'd been terribly sorry about it. Had she been wrong to forgive him? To understand?

Jane drained her whiskey, setting it down on the smeared glass-topped table with a snap. Yes, she'd been wrong. Because she hadn't really forgiven him. She'd kept her hurt and anger and sheer outrage locked inside, tamped down beneath her well-nurtured civility, and it had done nothing but eat away at her.

Damn Frank, damn Richard and damn Alexander Caldicott. Damn all men everywhere. Revenge, sweet revenge was the answer. When she got back to Baraboo she'd see if she could find one of those companies that delivered a cream pie in the face of specified victims. It was the least she could do for the happy couple.

But more important was Sandy Caldicott. She needed him to make as big a fool out of himself as she had of herself. She still hadn't quite figured out how to do it, but she wouldn't sleep until she had. And once she'd gotten rid of him, she could concentrate on finishing her business in Princeton.

Richard didn't deserve her vengeance, but Stephen Tremaine did. Enough of this messing around—tomorrow morning she'd head back to Princeton, alone, buy whatever seemed ultimately inflammable, and torch Technocracies Ltd. If she couldn't stop Tremaine from selling the formula she could certainly make a mess out of his business.

She should get moving and go find some clean sheets, make up a bed. While she wasn't sure she wanted to stay here alone in this big, empty house, she definitely didn't want Sandy around for longer than it took to wreak a considerable amount of havoc.

Embarrassment would do it, she thought, wanting to head for another glass of whiskey but not daring to. She hadn't eaten anything all day and that first glass had hit her like a mallet. She needed to keep her wits about her if she was going to outfox her accomplice.

She was too tired to think of how she was going to do it. She'd simply have to play it by ear. Draw him out into a long, incriminating conversation, and then let him have it. Maybe simply bash him on the head and have done with it. She hadn't been thinking ahead—she'd end up being stranded here without a car. Still, it would be worth it, just to see the look on his face when she calmly, evenly, told him to go to hell.

In the meantime, she'd better get to work. There was a decent amount of old paper trash in the kitchen—she could go back there, dump it on the floor, and begin sifting through it for any sign of where Richard hid the formula. And she could help herself to just a tiny bit more of the whiskey.

IT TOOK SANDY too long to find the only open grocery store, and he had to give up on the Scotch. He'd forgotten it was Sunday, and there were still certain things you couldn't buy on a Sunday. He was getting to the point where he'd kill for a glass of Scotch.

The sun had almost set by the time he pulled the Audi back into the cracked driveway, but as far as he could see no lights had been turned on in the house. He tried to quell the sense of uneasiness that had been plaguing him all day. He'd never had any psychic ability, but all day long he'd been dogged by the feeling that something was very wrong.

He forced himself to move slowly, fetching the groceries from the back seat and walking deliberately toward the kitchen door. He saw her the moment she walked in. She was seated in the middle of the floor, surrounded by garbage. There was a smudge on her cheek, he hated to think of what, her wire-rimmed glasses had slid down her nose, and she was clutching a McDonald's bag in her hand. He could still smell the memory of the onions.

She looked up at him, and for the first time that day her expression wasn't wary, defensive, on edge. In the dim light of the kitchen he could see her cheeks wet with tears, and her mouth trembled with a vain effort at control.

"Stephen really killed him," she said in a broken voice, and without hesitation he crossed the room and sank down beside her, ready to draw her into his arms.

Chapter Fourteen

His arms felt so good around her, his body warm and strong, and for one weak, desperate moment Jane absorbed the comfort, the sheer loving presence that radiated from him. And then she remembered.

She shoved with all her might, sending him backward among the McDonald's wrappers and then scrambled to her feet. Normally she wouldn't have been strong enough to do it, but she took him off his guard. He lay sprawled there, staring up at her, a bemused expression on his too-handsome face.

"I take it you finally figured it out," he said.

If he hadn't said the word "finally" she might have kept her temper under control. That word was like a red flag to a bull, reminding her just what a deluded fool she'd been. All the frustrations of the past few years washed over her in a haze, and she reached for the first thing she could find. It was a tin pitcher that had once held iced tea, and she hurled it at his head.

He dodged, rolling over in the garbage, but she'd already followed it with the bag of groceries and the bottle of Scotch. He struggled to his feet, half laughing, half terrified, as he held his arms up to ward off the barrage.

"Calm down, Jane," he said, backing out of the kitchen. "If you'd just think about it you'd realize it was funny."

"Hilarious," she snarled, flinging a ceramic lamp at his head. "Just a complete riot." Her glasses were slipping down her nose, her hair had come loose, and she felt like an avenging angel.

"Come on, Jane, it wasn't my fault," he said, ducking the lamp and dodging behind a chair. "You were the one who decided I was a criminal."

"You *are* a criminal. You're a cold-hearted, lying, manipulative bastard." She hurled an antique copper fire extinguisher, a copy of *Shakespeare's Complete Plays*, three glass ashtrays and a box of matches. One of the ashtrays connected quite smartly with his forehead, eliciting a yelp of pain, and the matches bounced off his nose.

"Jane, I have been helping, even if I didn't admit who I am," he said. "If you'd just…put that down…listen, you'd realize…ow!" She'd gotten him with a brass hurricane lamp, and he went down into a heap, hidden behind the chair.

She was reaching for the fire poker when the silence penetrated her rage. The house was still. From outside the open windows she could hear the muffled thunder of the surf, the sound of intermittent traffic. But inside, behind the chair, all was silent.

Her sense of horror and remorse was as sudden as it was overwhelming. "Sandy?" she said, her voice weak as she dropped the poker on the ancient, sand-embedded carpet. "Say something," she pleaded. "Curse, moan, anything."

There was no sound, not even the rustle of clothing as he lay out of sight. Her last ounce of mistrust vanished, and she shoved the chair out of her way and sank down beside his prostrate body. His forehead was bleeding, his face was pale, and his taunting, teasing gray eyes were closed. Perhaps forever.

"Damn you," she said desperately, picking up one lifeless hand. "Don't you dare be dead." He didn't move, his eyelids didn't flicker, and as she reached up to touch his face he made no response. His skin felt icy beneath her hot, shaking hands, and she thought back to all the things she'd ever read about head injuries. She should pull back his eyelids and check to see if his pupils were unevenly dilated, she should take his pulse, listen to his heartbeat.

The last seemed the easiest thing to do. She pressed her head against his chest, her hair fanning out around her, and was rewarded with a slightly accelerated thumping. Not too fast to worry about, and it proved he was still alive. She sat back up, missing the hand that was just reaching to touch her, and pulled his inert body into her arms, cradling his bleeding head in her lap.

"Damn it, Sandy, wake up," she moaned. "I didn't mean to kill you. I just wanted to hurt you a little. Please, Sandy, don't die. You can't die! I can't live without you." As stupid as the words sounded, she realized with sudden shock that they were true. She didn't want to live without Alexander the Stoolie Caldicott.

Her dying lover's eyes shot open, his eyes clear and curious. "Why not?" he inquired calmly.

She considered dropping his head back on the hardwood floor, but she had vented her violent rage enough for one night. "I take it you're not dying," she managed with admirable nonchalance.

"Just mortally wounded. Why can't you live without me?"

"Don't you think you're pushing your luck? The iron poker is still in reach." She tried to pull away, but he'd somehow managed to get an arm around her while lying in her lap, and short of actually dumping him back on the floor she had to stay put.

"You're not going to beat me to a bloody pulp, Jane," he said softly. "You can't live without me, remember?"

She stared down at him for a long moment. The room was sinking deeper and deeper into shadows, with only the light from the kitchen illuminating the darkness. A wind had picked up, sweeping through the open windows, bringing the dampness and scent of the ocean around them. "I've already drawn blood," she said, her voice husky as she reached out and touched his forehead with gentle fingertips, bringing them back wet and sticky.

He winced, whether from pain or the sight of blood she couldn't be sure. "Well, then," he said, his voice not much more than a low, sexy growl, "kiss it and make it better."

She thought about it for a moment, then, leaning forward, she kissed his mouth instead, her own lips pressing softly, questioningly against his hard ones. He still felt cool against her fevered skin, and then his mouth opened, his arm slid up around her neck, pulling her down to him, and he was as hot as she was. Suddenly the darkness was all that mattered, the darkness and his body next to hers, his mouth hungry, claiming, this time taking only yes for an answer.

Moments later she was on the floor herself, the scratchy rush matting beneath her back, Sandy Caldicott above her, his body lean and hard and pressing her into the floor. He was no longer a comic-book felon or her partner in crime, he wasn't even a burnt-out yuppie lawyer. He was darkness, powerful, sexual, wiping out the terrors of the night and the anguish of loss and betrayal, he was life and heat and desire, and he was everything she ever needed.

His hands were wondrously, infuriatingly deft, sliding up her leg, beneath the khaki skirt, along the finely muscled line of her leg. Her own hands were far less practiced, pulling at the rugby shirt, ripping the buttons, needing his cooperation to strip it over his head. And then his chest was warm and bare against her, the chest she'd spent far too many moments eyeing with surreptitious longing. He was smooth-skinned, with only a smattering of golden hair in the middle of his chest, and the tactile sensation of his golden flesh beneath her fingertips was unbearably arousing. She whimpered with longing, back in her throat, and he swallowed the sound, his mouth hot and devouring on hers.

While she'd been fumbling with his shirt he'd managed to strip her of her skirt and sweater with such expertise that she'd scarcely been aware of it. When he lifted his head to look down at her with such fierce, heady desire she suddenly realized she was stretched out on a scratchy rug in nothing but her thin scrap of bikini underpants and lacy little bra. All her exposed flesh was tingling with desire, with heat and hunger that she hadn't known she could feel. All the while her heart and soul were longing for him, and her brain was screaming no.

Her mouth was connected to her brain. "I don't want this," she said clearly. "I don't want to feel this way."

For a long moment he didn't move. "If I had any sense of honor or decency I'd back off," he said finally. "But we've already proven that when it comes to you my honor and decency get shot to hell. Too bad if you don't want to feel this way—you do. You want me as much as I want you. And I'm not about to give you time and space to come up with a dozen lame excuses that will keep us both in the state of advanced frustration we've been suffering through for the last few days." He dropped his mouth back onto hers with a brief, savage kiss that left her dazed and breathless. He pulled away, and that look of fierce possession was back on his face.

With one graceful movement he stood up, pulling her with him. She swayed for a moment, hoping to keep out of his arms, but she couldn't fight both him and her own deep-rooted desires. When he swung her up into his arms she went willingly, closing her eyes in dizziness as he headed for the stairs.

"Don't do this," she muttered when he kicked open the bedroom door at the top of the stairs. The house had only twin beds, but it didn't seem to daunt him. He dropped her on the bed, then reached for his belt.

"Give me one good reason, Jane," he said, kicking off his shoes. "Just one."

She didn't bother trying to climb off the bed—he'd stop her and she didn't really want to go. "If you leave me alone I might learn to trust you, respect you."

He unzipped his pants and stripped them off. "Sorry, Jane. Tonight I don't want trust and I don't want respect. I want love."

She tried one last time. "Isn't that a euphemism?"

"Maybe for you, lady. Not for me." He climbed onto the bed beside her, pulling her into his arms.

It was close enough to a declaration on that windswept Indian summer evening. He'd left the door open, and the only light in the cavernous second floor of the old cottage was the fitful shadows bouncing off the water. There was no one to watch, no one to listen, no one to judge. For now, for tonight, she would do what she knew she shouldn't. She would do exactly what she wanted.

His hands slid down her body, beneath the thin bands of her panties, pulling them off and tossing them away from the bed. Her bra came off with equal simplicity, and then she was naked beside him, her long legs sliding, twining with his rougher ones.

She felt as if she'd been running, running, and she didn't know if it was from something or to someone, maybe a little bit of both. She wanted the darkness to close around her, to wipe out the shadows and half-light, she wanted anonymity, to be alone in bed with a man she couldn't even call by name. Alone with a man she shouldn't want, but did.

She kept her eyes tightly closed, savoring the possession of his mouth on hers, savoring the feel of his deft, arousing hands on her body, simply wanting to lie back and be pleasured by someone else who had taken control. It was no longer her responsibility.

He pulled his mouth away from hers, and she waited for its fiery possessiveness to travel down to her aching breasts, waited for the seduction to continue.

It was a long wait. Slowly, reluctantly she opened her eyes and looked up into Sandy's wary gray ones.

"I thought I told you," he said, his voice husky with strain, "that I don't provide sexual Valium and instant forgetfulness. I'm not a dream lover, Jane, here to fulfill your fantasies while you lie back with your eyes closed. This is a game for two players, lady. Ante up."

His fully aroused body was half on top of hers, holding her captive as she tried to pull away. This time he was expecting it, and clearly he had no intention of letting her go.

"Listen, buddy, I don't even want to be here," she said fiercely.

"Liar."

"I don't want you."

"Liar."

She tried to hit him, but he caught her wrist, forcing it down on the mattress and holding it there. "You're the liar," she said in a furious undertone. It didn't help that she was intimately aware of every square inch of flesh pressed against her, it didn't help that her desire, rather than abating in the face of her justifiable outrage, was only growing to unmanageable proportions.

"Maybe," he said. "Who's being honest now?"

The room was very still. She could hear the rumble of the surf, the keening of the wind through the old windows, the pounding of her lover's heart still pressed against her own, the steady, labored breathing of two people beyond the limits of stress. She looked up at him, keeping her own expression carefully blank as she tried to read his soul in the depths of those wicked, lying eyes.

She got the answer she wanted. "Let go of my wrists," she said.

He stared down at her cynically. "So you can hit me again?"

"Let go of my wrists."

He did so after only another moment of hesitation. Once released, she slid her arms around his neck, pulling him down to her, her mouth eager beneath his.

He rolled onto his back, taking her with him, and she was on fire, her hands desperate for the feel of his flesh beneath her, her mouth bold with deep, hurried kisses. He put his mouth on her breasts, and she arched her back like a cat in the intensity of her reaction, he slid his hand between her thighs and she shattered at his first gentle touch.

"Easy," he whispered. "Easy now." But she couldn't, wouldn't slow down. She was shaking all over, covered with a fine film of sweat, shivering and helpless as her needs raged out of control, unable to even say the words to beg him.

She didn't need to. He didn't bother to roll over. Instead he lifted her trembling body astride his, settling her carefully against him so that the heat of him rested at the center of her pulsing desire.

With a moan of fear and anticipation she sank down, guided by his hands on her hips, until he filled her. She let out a muffled cry at the unexpected feel of him, and the hands on her hips held her still, giving her time to accustom herself to his invasion. She bowed her head for a moment, absorbing the impact, and then she opened her eyes to meet his fierce gaze.

"I still don't trust you," she whispered, not giving an inch.

He grinned then, and his fingers dug into her hips as he slowly withdrew. "It doesn't matter." And he arched up, deep within her.

She reached out and caught his shoulders for balance, her hair a tangled curtain around her face. She rocked slightly, reveling in the sense of power it brought her, the way it made her insides clench and vibrate. She tried it again, this time more forcefully, and Sandy reacted, driving into her.

Reaching up, he put his hand behind her neck and brought her mouth down to meet his. His other hand moved between their bodies, touching her, and suddenly everything dissolved, her body, the night, the ocean air, until she was nothing but a shimmering mass of sensation.

From a long distance she felt him tense beneath her, heard the hoarse cry against her mouth, but she was past all conscious thought. She slumped against him in a welter of sweat and tears, unbearably exhausted.

Sometime later she felt his hand brush the hair from her tear-streaked face. She waited in an odd state of nerveless, lethargic tension, for him to say, "I told you so."

He said nothing at all. His hands were impossibly gentle as they moved her to his side, his lips were warm and lingering as they brushed her mouth, her eyelids, her tear-drenched cheeks. His warm, strong body wrapped around hers, tucking her into his shoulder, protecting her. And when she heard the even cadence of his breathing, sure that he had fallen asleep, she finally gave up, nestling against him, and slept, too.

WHEN JANE WOKE UP hours later, she was chilled. Sandy had managed to find a blanket to pull around them on the stripped bed, but the open window blew in a stiff, northerly breeze off the ocean, and Jane knew Indian summer had gone.

It was getting light. There was no clock in sight, and it probably wouldn't have done her much good if there'd been one. Sometime in the debacle of last night she'd been divested of her glasses, and the world was the tiniest bit fuzzy about the edges.

She only wished it could stay that way, but she knew better. Sandy was deeply asleep, protesting only faintly when she carefully slipped out of his arms. His forehead showed a fairly sizable lump beneath his tousled hair and the matted blood, and she stifled her overwhelming guilt. Their relationship had been fraught with danger from the very beginning, it was no wonder that things had escalated to full-scale disaster.

She scooped up her clothes from the floor and crept downstairs, past the debris-littered living room, on into the trashed kitchen. She surveyed the results of her fury with mixed emotions. On the one hand, she was horrified at the destruction she had wrought. On the other, she was gratified that she had finally allowed herself to vent her emotions instead of being so self-controlled.

She picked up the ripped bag of groceries, dumping the melted container of Ben and Jerry's ice cream in the sink, sniffing the heavy cream to make sure it hadn't turned during its sojourn on the chilly floor, finding the French Roast coffee Sandy had bought. Her glasses were sitting on the counter—she had no idea how they got there, but she placed them on her nose with a sigh of relief as the world came into focus. Maybe everything would become clearer.

The porch was chilly when she stepped outside, a cup of strong brewed coffee in one hand, a handful of papers in the other. She opened the sagging screen door and went out onto the beach, digging her bare feet into the sand. The wind was whipping the waves into foaming whitecaps, the day was gray and stormy in the early-dawn light, and it matched her mood.

Sinking down on the step, she took a warming sip of coffee, opened the first scrap of paper, and started to reread how Stephen Tremaine attempted, and eventually succeeded, in murdering her brother.

And that was where Sandy found her, two hours later.

Chapter Fifteen

Sandy had pulled on his jeans and a cotton sweater against the early-morning chill, and he'd washed the blood from his forehead, but he still looked half-asleep. Jane could see the coffee steaming from his mug, and she wished she could ask him for a refill. But right then and there she was determined never to ask him for anything again.

Her expression must have made her feelings clear. He skirted the doorway, his face wary, and sank down cross-legged in the sand. The day had warmed up slightly, but the gray mist proved stubborn against the encroaching sun, and the chill in the air had more to do with winter than a balmy autumn.

She waited, tense, for him to say something about last night. Chances were he had a killer of a headache, chances were he wasn't going to let things pass without making some sort of comment.

He took a sip of coffee, and the lines in his brow relaxed a bit beneath the tousled blond hair. "You said something about Stephen Tremaine killing Richard," he said, peering out at the horizon. "What did you mean?"

She was both relieved and miffed. While she wanted last night over and forgotten, a momentary aberration in an otherwise well-regulated life, she wanted it to be her decision, not his. Nevertheless, she couldn't afford to be choosy. "I went through all the trash. There was a letter from Richard to his lawyer. He must have changed his mind and decided to call him instead of sending it, but he never got the chance.''

''What did the letter say?''

''That he didn't trust Tremaine. That there'd already been an accident at Technocracies that was just a bit too coincidental, and that he wouldn't put it past Tremaine to try it again.''

''Did he know what Tremaine wanted?''

''Apparently. My brother had a fairly cynical view of the mankind he professed to love so much. If Tremaine was trying to sell the titanium coating process to an unfriendly government, Richard would have found out. And he would have done anything, absolutely anything, to stop him. Richard could be a royal nuisance when he made up his mind about something. Tremaine wouldn't have had any way to stop him, short of murder.''

Without a word Sandy leaned over and poured half of his still-steaming cup of coffee into her empty mug. She usually drank it back, while he laced his with cream and sugar, but still she was reluctantly grateful, gulping it down with a muttered ''Thanks.''

''Show me the letter,'' he said, finishing off his coffee.

She held up a crumpled, grease-stained piece of paper. ''It's taken me a while to decipher it. He said he'd call Bennett, his lawyer, from the house in Vermont. That he was going to be up there to do a little work, and to figure out how to put a spoke in Tremaine's wheels. Which answers our question. The lab must be somewhere on our grandmother's property in Newfield.''

''Seems logical,'' Sandy said.

''But he never made it there. And when I talked to Bennett about Richard's will he said he hadn't heard from him in months. He must have died before he made the phone call.''

''Exactly how did Richard die?''

She glanced at him, then looked determinedly out at the rushing waves. For all the danger of her feelings for him, for all the perfidy he'd shown, she still felt pulled with an intensity she could barely fight. ''His brakes failed. His car plunged over a cliff in upstate New York and ended up five miles downstream.''

''Were the brakes tampered with?''

''I wouldn't take any bets that they weren't. No one bothered to check. At the time it just seemed like a tragic accident. Richard wasn't capable of simple car maintenance. He hadn't registered or inspected his car in more than three years. It was entirely possible that he could have run out of break fluid and never noticed that his brakes were losing power.''

''What was the official cause of death?''

''I beg your pardon?'' She turned her gaze from the ocean, blinking slightly. He had a red mark under his stubby jaw, a mark that could only have come from her voracious mouth. She stared down at the sand, at two pairs of bare feet.

''On the autopsy,'' he said patiently. ''Was his neck broken? Any chance he was dead before he went over the cliff? We'd have a better chance of pinning something on Tremaine if we could wipe out all possibility of an accident.''

''I thought you knew,'' she said, still staring at their toes.

''Knew what?''

''Richard's body was never found. It had washed away before the car was found.''

''Damn,'' Sandy muttered. ''We'll never get an indictment.''

She stirred restlessly. ''I'm not interested in an indictment— Tremaine would just get off anyway. I hate to tell you, but my plans haven't changed. The fact that you're really a lawyer has nothing to do with this. If I wanted to work with lawyers I would have talked with Bennett. At least I know I can trust him.''

''If your darling Bennett had done his homework he would have known he could have gotten a restraining order to keep Tremaine from selling off the process,'' Sandy snapped.

''My darling Bennett is one of the finest lawyers in Princeton. He was my parents' lawyer before he worked for Richard, and he's a happily married sixty-seven-year-old grandfather.''

His shoulders relaxed slightly. ''That explains it, then. He was too old.''

"He's better than a young shyster like you."

She was hoping to infuriate him, but instead he merely smiled. "All right, so we don't go about this legally. What are we going to do about it?"

"*We* aren't going to do anything," she said loftily. "I had need of a felon, not a broken-down lawyer."

"I thought everything worked pretty well last night," he said softly.

Jane could feel the color flood her face. "Forget about last night."

"Even if I wanted to, I couldn't."

"It was a mistake, an aberration. It won't happen again," she said in a fierce little voice, glaring at him.

Unmoved by her animosity, he stretched out in the sand and eyed her with nothing more than casual curiosity. "Of course it will, Jane," he said gently. "And you know it as well as I do. Maybe not right away—we've got some things to sort out first. But sooner or later we're going to have a relationship."

"Sooner or later I'm going to torch my brother's laboratory and head straight back to Baraboo, Wisconsin."

"We'll see about that."

"We'll see about nothing. I don't want your help, I don't need…"

"Too bad," he interrupted. "You're getting it. I'm too deep in this already, and I'm certainly not going to walk away without knowing the outcome. Besides, if you insist on your illegal schemes, you're going to need a qualified defense attorney by your side."

"You don't really strike me as a model of rectitude. It was your idea to break into Technocracies, wasn't it?"

"It was."

A sudden thought struck her. "What would have happened to you if we got caught?" she asked in a less strident voice.

He shrugged. "It's always possible I could have been disbarred. I imagine I would have gotten off with a reprimand."

"Uncle Stephen would have prosecuted."

"Yes, well that might have made things more difficult," he agreed.

She said nothing for a long moment. "You risked your career because of me?"

"Don't get all sentimental on me," he said with real horror. "I risked my career for the same reason I went along with your mistaken assumption that I was Jimmy the Stoolie. I was bored, miserably, fatally bored. If I'd been caught and it had gone all the way to being disbarred I would have relished the challenge."

"Of course," she said flatly. "It was silly of me to think you might have had any noble motives in mind."

"Jane…"

She rose in one fluid motion. "If you want to go straight back to the city I can find my own way to Princeton."

"I want to go back to Princeton with you, and then I want to drive to Vermont and see if we can find your brother's lab."

"And if I refuse?"

"I can always go to Tremaine and tell him where the lab is."

"You wouldn't."

"I would. If you don't let me go with you you're going to run into a whole mess of trouble. The only way I know to stop you is to tell Tremaine. So take your pick. Him or me."

She stood with her hand on the rusty door handle. "It's a hard choice."

"Not that hard, Jane. Give in gracefully. I'm coming to Vermont with you, whether you like it or not."

"I don't like it," she said. And they both knew she lied.

THE RIDE DOWN to Princeton, while devoid of the simmering, unnamed hostility of the day before, was riddled with sexual tension. He would have thought the previous night's tumultuous encounter would have taken the edge off his desire for her. It only seemed to make it worse.

Jane, however, appeared entirely unmoved by the whole thing. She kept her distance, treating him like one of those beneficial garden insects, the sort of pests you tolerate because they happen to eat slugs, or something. She accepted the fact that he was going to keep tagging along, but the few hours they spent in the darkness upstairs in the old cottage might well have never happened. And she could have carried it off, if she didn't happen to blush occasionally, for no apparent reason. And if she didn't happen to steal small, surreptitious glances in his direction when she thought he wasn't looking.

He knew, for all her year or so of married life, that she wasn't as sexually experienced as he was. He'd known it from her hesitancy, her initial passiveness, her unfeigned surprise at the depth of her own reaction. That surprise had touched him more deeply than he cared to admit. Jane got to him on all sorts of levels, conscious and unconscious, and for all his casual talk about something as trendy as a relationship, he knew he wanted more than that. For the first time he wanted to spend his life discovering all there was to know about someone. He wanted to wake up with her, fight with her, father her children and grow old with her. With a sudden, alarming intensity he knew that he wanted to marry her, and the shock of it kept him silent for most of the drive back to Princeton.

It was going to be rough going for a while. She didn't trust him, and with good reason. She hated lawyers, also with good reason. She was so tied up in knots about her brother and Stephen Tremaine's villainy that she didn't have much to spare for her unwanted suitor. What he needed to do was help her find some sort of resolution to that whole affair, preferably with Tremaine in jail and Jane still relatively law-abiding. Then he could work on regaining her trust and breaking down her prejudices.

In the meantime, the best thing he could do once they got back to the sleazy splendor of the Princeton motel was take a long, cold shower, maybe run a couple of miles, then go for another icy shower. Then maybe he'd be too tired to think about the way Jane shivered when she wrapped her beautiful legs around him.

He shifted uncomfortably in the leather seat of the Audi, and

Jane looked at him, fortunately at his face and not at his pants. "Did someone really steal your MGB?" she asked. "I assume it *was* your MGB and not Jimmy's?"

"It was mine, and yes, it was really stolen. I called my secretary and had her file a report on it. Not that I expect to ever see it again," he added mournfully.

"Don't be so sure. Any self-respecting thief would abandon it as soon as it started acting up. Tell the police to look within a couple of blocks of where we parked it."

"Very funny. That car was a classic."

"That car was a disaster." She rolled down her window, letting in some of the crisp autumn air and the recycled exhaust fumes. "You have a secretary?"

"Two, actually." He sounded apologetic, but he couldn't help it.

"Well, Mr. Hot-Shot lawyer, if you're a partner in a major law firm and you're so busy you need two secretaries, what were you doing staying in a dive like the Princeton Pike motel, and how come you can just disappear off the face of the earth and start running around with me? Or do you make a habit of doing things like this?" He could tell by the way her adorable nose wrinkled and the glasses slid down it that she didn't like that notion one tiny bit. A good sign, he thought.

"No, I don't make a habit of doing things like this," he said patiently. "Until I called yesterday they thought I was on vacation in the Canary Islands. I was all set to go once Jimmy's trial was over—I had tickets and my bags were packed."

"How could you be certain the trial would end that day? I thought trials tend to drag on and on. What if you hadn't gotten an acquittal?"

"That was unlikely."

"Okay, Mr. Perfect, why were you at such a sleazy place?"

"For the same reason I went along with your outrageous proposition instead of spending last week sunning myself and having meaningless sex," he snapped. "I told you, I was bored. Burned out, fed up and bored. The trial with Jimmy was just the last straw in a list of cop-outs and compromises and I got sick of it. I was tired of getting slimy little criminals and rotten huge corporations out of the trouble they so richly deserved. I thought for once I could put my energies into something that mattered, helping the underdog.''

''Me being the underdog?'' she questioned, but there was a blessed trace of humor in her voice.

''And there was one more overriding reason,'' he added, knowing he was pushing his luck.

''Dare I ask?''

He wanted to tell her he'd fallen in love with her the first time he saw her. In retrospect it seemed as if he had, but he knew what her reaction would be if he said any such thing. ''I took one look at you,'' he said instead, ''and developed a case of advanced lust.''

Her expression didn't change. ''Well,'' she said briskly, ''you must be well on the road to recovery after last night.''

At that point he laughed out loud. ''Lady, were we in the same bed? After last night I think it's terminal.''

''I'll send flowers.''

''No physical therapy?''

''You're on thin ice, Caldicott.''

''Yes, ma'am.'' He subsided, satisfied at having completed his objective. Once more her cheeks were stained red, and she had trouble keeping her gaze from straying toward his face, his hands, and points south. He managed to swallow his grin, but suddenly he felt a great deal more hopeful. ''Lovely weather, isn't it?''

Jane looked out at the gray sky. ''Just peachy.''

THE PRINCETON PIKE Sleep-a-While Motel looked, if possible, even sleazier. The cold gray weather didn't help, and the turquoise paint job that surely dated back to the fifties seemed to be peeling at an even faster rate. While the place had never been fully occupied, it now appeared that they were the only guests registered. Jane, already depressed, sank into a deeper gloom.

''I'm going to take a nap,'' she said outside her door, back-

ing away from him to try to minimize some of the difference
in their heights. She didn't like him towering over her—it made
her nervous and far too aware of him.

"Jane, you fell asleep at six-thirty last night, and you must
have slept at least until six this morning. Why do you need a
nap? Did I tire you out that much?"

"This will only work," she said in a fierce, angry little
voice, "if you stop reminding me about last night. I'm not
going to sit around having you throw that mistake in my face.
It's over and done with. The next time you bring it up will be
the last." She didn't know what she could threaten him with,
but at that moment she felt capable of restaging her moments
of fury from the night before. However, there wasn't anything
handy to throw at him, and the sight of his cut forehead still
had the power to make her flinch.

He must have thought better about goading her. "Yes,
ma'am," he said meekly enough, but she could see the laughter
lurking in the back of his gray eyes. She decided she could
ignore it for now.

"Maybe I'll go for a drive instead."

"You just went for a two-hour drive."

"That was with you. I find I'm feeling a little claustrophobic." She turned her back on him, heading for her parked car,
but his hand reached and caught her arm, the first time he'd
touched her since she left the bed.

She yanked her arm free, glaring at him, but he was singularly unmoved. "Listen, sweetie, we're talking about murder
here. If Tremaine has any brains at all he'll know you're getting
too close to the truth. So I'm not going to let you out of my
sight. If you want to go for a drive, I'll drive you."

"I'll drive. You can tag along if you want."

Traffic was still heavy when Jane tore out onto Route One.
She stomped on the accelerator, and the rental Escort did its
valiant best, inching its way up toward fifty. She sped along
the highway, turning off past the Mercer Mall, and the Escort
inched up toward sixty. She cast a tentative glance at her reluctant passenger, but he appeared unmoved by her maneuvers.

He did have his seat belt on, and his hands were clutching the sides of the seat, but he was keeping his expression calm and serene.

''I bet you're a good poker player,'' Jane said, pushing the car to sixty-five. The road narrowed, turning by the Delaware Canal, but she'd driven those roads for years and had no doubt that with a light touch of the brakes she could control the curve.

Sandy didn't have the same assurance. ''That's a fairly sharp turn up ahead,'' he said faintly.

''I know.'' She grinned.

''You might want to slow down a bit.''

''I might.'' She sped a little faster. The road was completely deserted—most cars either took the highways or the more direct shortcuts through the back areas outside of Princeton.

''Damn it, slow down!'' Sandy finally snapped.

She was being unforgivably childish, and suddenly she was ashamed of herself. ''Yes, sir,'' she acquiesced, stepping on the brake.

Her foot sank to the floor as the car hurtled forward on the deserted back road.

Chapter Sixteen

"This isn't funny, Jane!" Sandy shouted as they skidded around a gentle curve in the road.

"The brakes are gone!" She tried to shove the automatic transmission into a lower gear and the Escort responded with a shriek of pain and a hideous grinding noise. The road had only a gentle downhill slope, but they were fast approaching a sharp right-hand turn at a speed too high for her to cope with it. She could yank the wheel and hope they'd make it, but the alternative to the narrowing road was a thick forest on either side. Or she could go straight through the flimsy wooden barrier at the end of the road and end up in the Delaware Canal.

Neither choice was appealing, but water was a lot more forgiving than oak trees. "Get ready to jump," she muttered, steering with one hand and reaching for the door with her other.

A moment later they were soaring through the air, through the splintered fence. Jane was out of the car before it hit, landing smack in the middle of the cold brown water.

The car almost made it to the other side. It crashed into the bank, then slowly sank, tail first, into the cold, murky water.

She treaded water for a moment, dazed, scarcely noticing the icy temperature of the old canal. "Sandy?" she called, but the sound came out as only a hoarse croak. She watched in horror as the Escort sank down beneath the surface, only the headlights showing for one brief moment before it settled on its side. She could feel the pull of the suction, and she had to use all her limited strength to keep from being sucked under with it.

"Sandy!" she screamed again, the sound echoing in the sudden stillness that was broken only by the gurgling water. "Sandy!"

The water erupted beside her, and there he was, blessedly intact and mad as blazes. "Thank God you're alive," she sobbed, flinging her arms around his neck. They both sank beneath the cold brown water, only to rise again, sputtering.

With more force than tenderness he detached her clinging arms and pushed her toward shore. "Let's get out of here before we freeze to death." His voice was terse through chattering teeth, and she went obediently enough, scrambling onto the bank from the steep sides with the last ounce of her energy. She fell in the grass, and Sandy collapsed beside her. For a moment there was only the sound of their hoarse, labored breathing, mixing with the wind through the trees overhead. And then the rain began to fall: thick, fat drops of icy precipitation. Jane sat up and sneezed.

Sandy didn't move. He was soaked to the skin, covered with a brown sludge, and Jane knew she didn't look much better. The wind had picked up along with the rain, and if they didn't get warm and dry soon they were both going to die of pneumonia. "Are you just going to lie there?" she demanded with some asperity. "I know it was my fault, I know I was driving too fast. You don't have to ignore me. I admit it. If I hadn't been so furious, if I hadn't come down this back road..."

"You would have been keeping up with traffic on Route One and the first red light you came to you would have smashed into another car, probably killing all of us. That doesn't mean you weren't driving like a bat out of hell, and if you ever do that again I'll wring your neck. But it wasn't your fault." He sat up, shaking the water out of his hair like a large wet dog.

"Whose fault was it?"

He looked at her through the miserable gray drizzle. "Do you have to ask?"

She shut her eyes in horror. "Oh, no," she whispered. "Uncle Stephen."

"You told me he could be ruthless. He probably murdered your brother. It looks as if you're next in line." He rose, reaching a hand down and pulling her up beside him. "Let's get out of this godforsaken rain."

"How?"

"By standing on the road and looking forlorn. Someone's bound to take pity on us sooner or later."

It was a great deal later, fifty-three minutes by Sandy's still functioning Rolex, when a sod truck pulled to a stop. The rain had been steady the entire time, getting colder by the minute, and Jane thought that if another moment passed without getting under cover she'd dive back into the canal.

She sat huddled in the corner of the truck, barely conscious of Sandy's directions, of the effortless stream of pleasant conversation, as if it were afternoon tea and her partner in crime weren't as cold and wet and miserable as she was. When the truck stopped at a rambling split-level on Cherry Hill Road she dutifully climbed out of the cab, following Sandy's drenched figure. It was only when they were standing under the shelter of the front entryway, waiting for someone to answer the doorbell, that she roused herself enough to ask where they were.

"My ex-wife's house," Sandy said cheerfully. "It was the closest place I could think of."

Jane stared at him with complete loathing, wishing he'd stayed in the canal. She was about to tell him so when the heavy walnut door opened and a spectacularly beautiful, enormously pregnant woman appeared.

"Sandy!" she cried, her face glowing with delight as she flung the door open and enveloped her ex-husband in an embrace that showed a complete disregard for his wet muddy clothes and her designer maternity jumpsuit. "What in the world are you doing here, and looking like that?" She pulled him inside, chattering a mile a minute. "And what have you done to that poor woman?" She flung a gorgeous smile at Jane, who tried to resist its charm and found she couldn't. "You never did know how to treat a date."

"This is Jane Dexter." He disentangled himself gracefully as he made the introductions. "My sister-in-law, Margery Caldicott."

Relief swamped Jane. "I thought you were his ex-wife," she blurted, then could have cursed her thoughtless tongue.

Things could only get worse. "I am," Margery said cheerfully.

"Oh," said Jane.

"I think," Sandy said, wrapping a protective arm around Jane's drenched, shivering shoulders, "that my partner in crime needs a very hot shower, a glass of Scotch, and clean dry clothes. We came to you because we knew you were the softest touch in Princeton."

"Not to mention that Peyton would kill you if you came back to town and didn't see us. Partner in crime, eh? Sounds fascinating. We have three showers, lots of clothes, and enough Scotch to float an ocean liner, particularly now when I can't drink. Once you're feeling better you can tell me exactly how you got into whatever mess you're in."

"Later," Sandy promised, leading a benumbed Jane down the hallway with unerring instincts. "Just let me take care of my lady first."

She opened her mouth to protest, then shut it again. Right then and there she didn't have the energy to fight it. For just a short while she wanted to be taken care of, she wanted to be his lady. Later, when she was clean and dry and nicely tipsy, she'd be independent again. For now she wanted to cling.

She took her time in the huge, sybaritic shower. When she got out, there were clean clothes waiting for her, clearly pre-pregnancy clothes of Margery's. The sweatpants bagged around her ankles, the sleeves drooped over her fingers until she pushed them up, but it was warm and soft and dry and wonderfully comfortable.

She found them by their voices, and when she walked into the living room she had to work hard to stifle the sudden, irrational sweep of jealousy that threatened to reduce her to tears. Sandy and his sister-in-law cum ex-wife were sitting on the white leather sofa, looking closer than any divorced couple had the right to look. While they both rose and greeted her with seeming delight, she couldn't help feeling like an intruder in their scene of domestic bliss. She wondered how Sandy's brother would feel.

"So you've run afoul of Stephen Tremaine," Margery said, rising with cumbersome grace and pouring Jane a drink. "I can think of people I'd rather meet on a dark night in an alleyway."

Jane took a huge, warming gulp of her drink, allowing herself a furtive glance at Sandy's bland face. "I told Margery that Tremaine is trying to get hold of one of your late brother's inventions." His voice matched his face.

"Yes, I was sorry to hear about the accident." Margery's gorgeous face rumpled in real sympathy, and Jane gave up trying to hate her. It wasn't her fault she was six feet tall, spectacularly beautiful and pregnant by the man she loved. Not to mention that she had the ability to say no to Sandy, an ability Jane didn't seem to share.

"I told Margery I couldn't really go into detail." Sandy rose, crossed the room and put his hands on Jane's shoulders, pushing her gently into an overstuffed chair. "Drink your whiskey while I see about notifying the police."

She wanted to protest, but the soft leather felt too comfortable, the room too cozy, the drink too warming. "Better call the rental place, too," she said, settling back and pulling her legs underneath her.

Margery sank into the chair beside her, her face thoughtful. She waited until Sandy was out of earshot, waited until they could hear the muffled sound of his voice on the telephone, before she spoke. "He's in love with you."

Jane spilled her whiskey on her borrowed sweat suit. "I beg your pardon?"

"I said Sandy's in love with you," Margery said, sipping her Perrier and lime.

"He told you that?" The possibility was so overwhelming

that she didn't even bother to mop up the icy drink that was slowly chilling her thigh.

"Of course not. I'm not even sure he realizes it himself yet, though I suspect he does. Sandy was never slow on the uptake, and he has more than his share of intuition."

Jane began mopping up her thigh. "I'm going to smell like a distillery," she said.

"You don't believe me?"

Jane met Margery's huge blue eyes, disarmed, but fighting it. "In a word, no."

"I know him better than any human being on this earth. Better than his parents, who are too distant and polite to ever ask him a personal question, better than his own brother, who's only open with me, better maybe than he knows himself. He never loved me, even though he felt he should. But he surely loves you."

Jane ignored the latter as only a theory, impossible to prove. "If he didn't love you, why did he marry you?" she asked bluntly, draining her depleted glass of whiskey. If Margery could be outspoken, so could she.

"We were supposed to be the perfect couple," she said with a sigh, looking out the wall of windows into the rainy evening. "We met when he was at Exeter, I was at Concord. We dated through college, we got engaged when he graduated, we got married when he passed his law boards. We love each other very much, but we're not in love with each other and never were, and neither of us noticed that wasn't enough until Peyton moved back from South America. And then I realized that the things I loved in Sandy were the things that made me fall in love with Peyton. Sandy noticed before I did, Peyton was all set to move back to Buenos Aires and I was ready to enter a convent."

"And what happened?"

"Sandy flew to Haiti and got a twenty-four hour divorce, without telling either of us where he was going, without saying a word. And Peyton and I were married six months later, five years ago."

"Happy ever after," Jane murmured. "But what about Sandy?"

"He's looking forward to the birth of his nephew." She patted her swollen tummy.

"And he's had no regrets?"

"No regrets," Margery said. "I won't tell you it didn't hurt. No one likes to admit failure, no one likes it when someone chooses another person over you, even if you didn't want them in the first place. I had moments of feeling miserable because he didn't fight for me. I wanted Peyton, not Sandy, but I wanted him to put up more of a fuss. Ridiculous, isn't it?"

"A little."

Margery's smile was rueful. "I never pretended to have much more than common sense and a certain intuition. And my intuition tells me Sandy's in love with you."

Jane thought longingly of another glass of whiskey, but resisted the temptation to beg. "I think this time you're wrong," she said firmly.

"And, of course, you're in love with him."

Jane stared at her, open-mouthed in shock, just about to wreck whatever amity had sprung up between them, when Sandy strolled back in. "I've called us a taxi. The police will meet us at the motel and get our statements. Margery, thank you for giving us a port in the storm."

"Of course." She rose and waddled over to her former husband. "But what's this about a motel? Why aren't you staying with us?"

"We prefer our independence, but thanks for the offer." He raised a questioning eyebrow at Jane, who rose dutifully enough, still struggling with outrage at Margery's last announcement before Sandy came in the room.

"Where are you staying? Maybe we could have dinner together or something."

"Jane and I are leaving for Vermont tomorrow," Sandy said. "But thanks for the offer. Take care of Junior for me." He patted her belly with an affectionate air, and Jane wanted desperately to slap his hand away.

"Which motel, Sandy?" Margery demanded, undeterred.

"Princeton Pike Sleep-a-While Motel," Jane said, as Sandy shook his head.

"That dive? But why?"

"It has character," Sandy said softly.

"It has anonymity," Jane added.

"Curiouser and curiouser," Margery murmured. "You're sure I can't talk you into staying?"

"Positive," Sandy said.

"And I can't worm any more information out of either of you?"

"Absolutely not," Jane said.

Margery sighed. "Peyton will be sorry he missed you."

"We'll catch up after the baby is born." Sandy was ushering Jane toward the door. In the background she could hear the taxi honking its horn, her bare feet were wet and cold as Sandy thrust her out into the rain.

"Your clothes…" she said to Margery.

"I'll get them next time I see you," Margery said cheerfully. "I'll be closer to fitting back into them by then."

"Bye, Margery," Sandy said, giving her a casual kiss on the cheek.

"Don't dunk Jane in any more canals," she ordered. "Your nephew is going to want cousins."

Jane didn't say a word as they drove through the pouring rain back out toward Route One, and Sandy seemed similarly inclined. They used the Alexander Road route rather than pass the old canal, and Jane could only be grateful. They hadn't even come close to drowning, but for the next few months, even years, she planned to keep her distance from cold dark bodies of water.

She padded barefoot in the rain to her motel-room door while Sandy paid the taxi driver with some soggy paper money. She'd almost managed to shut the door in his face when he reached her, and he had no compunctions whatsoever about forcing it open and thrusting her inside.

"I didn't invite you in here," she said, stalking into the

bathroom and grabbing one of the threadbare white towels they replaced every three days to dry her damp, chilly feet. She sat on the bed, knowing she was asking for trouble, not giving a damn.

"I just wanted to get our stories straight." He was uncowed by her hostility. He strolled over to the connecting door and unlocked it. "How much are we going to tell the police? Everything?"

She eyed the door warily, deciding to wait until he left to relock it. "What do you think? You're the lawyer here."

"Yes, but I'm here as your coconspirator, not as your counsel," he pointed out. "I think we should tell them the truth. That your brother died in a similar accident two months ago, that you haven't any idea who could have tampered with your car if indeed it was tampered with. I don't think we need to burden them with our theories and suspicions. They're pretty smart fellows—they can add two and two and come up with four."

"Why shouldn't we tell them our suspicions?"

"For one thing, we could let ourselves in for a charge of libel. For another, there's no way we could head for Vermont tomorrow if they suspect we're involved in attempted murder. Let them work that out for themselves while we're gone. If we have to wait, Tremaine could get the jump on us, and by the time we find the lab the entire place could be cleared out."

"That makes sense." She was very cautious in her agreement.

"Then we'll deal with just the facts, ma'am," he said, heading for the door. "I'll see if I can keep them away from you entirely. They might be satisfied with my statement."

"That would be nice." She yawned, squirming on the bed, and noticed with momentary surprise that she was sore in the oddest places. And then she remembered her activities of the night before, and blushed. "I'm going to take a hot bath and go to bed," she said with studied calm. "That dunk in the canal took a lot out of me."

"Among other things," he murmured, opening the door into

the neon-lit night. She could see beyond his shoulder that the rain had finally abated, but the wind had picked up, and there was a northerly tinge to it. He paused, gazing at her, and for the first time she noticed how weary he looked. There were lines between his clear gray eyes, bracketing his sexy mouth, across his broad forehead, and she suddenly realized that his last thirty-six hours hadn't been a piece of cake, either.

Sympathy, however, would get her into nothing but trouble. She scooted up the bed, ending at the pillows. "Good night," she said in a cool, dismissive voice.

Clearly he was in no mood to fight it, and she told herself she was relieved. "One last question," he said. "What did Margery say to you just before I came in?"

If she could feel herself blush before, this time her cheeks grew positively inflamed. She said the first thing that came into her mind. "She asked me if you were still good in bed." The moment the words were out she clapped her hands over her mouth in utter horror.

But Sandy only laughed. "I don't believe a word of it, darling," he said, some of the shadow leaving his eyes. "But if she asked you, what would you have said?"

She could think of a dozen instant responses, all of which were guaranteed to have him close the door and jump on the bed with her. But she had enough self-control, or self-destructiveness, to keep those thoughts to herself. "I'll tell you when we stop Stephen Tremaine."

He shook his head in weary amusement. "I'm too tired to get it out of you tonight, Jane. Tomorrow." The words were both a threat and a promise.

"It'll be a cold day in hell."

Sandy looked out into the windy night. "It might be, at that. Good night, Jane."

She didn't say another word as he slowly closed the door behind him. She waited until she heard him unlocking his own door before she jumped up and double-locked the outside door. Then she went to the connecting door, relocking it and moving the rickety armchair under the handle for extra protection. Not that she thought she had anything to worry about—Sandy wasn't the sort to use force. Not when he had such formidable powers of persuasion.

She heard the voices of the policemen next door while she lay soaking in her hot bath. Apparently Sandy gave them more than enough information—there were no peremptory knocks on her motel room door. She stayed in the tub until the water grew tepid, then pulled on an oversize T-shirt and was heading for the dubious comfort of the motel's best mattress when she heard the connecting door rattle.

She smiled smugly at the chair blocking the doorknob. "Go away," she said. "I'm going to bed."

Sandy's reply was short and graphic, and the door rattled with the force of his shaking it. She decided to ignore him, climbing into bed and turning off the light, prepared to enjoy the sound of his futile struggles.

A second later there was a huge, crashing noise, the chair went flying across the room, the door frame splintered, and the room was flooded with light outlining a very angry man.

"Don't," he said with deceptive calm, "lock the door again."

Jane raised her head off the pillow, matching his even tone. "I don't think that's possible anymore."

"We'll leave at six tomorrow morning. Is that all right with you?" He didn't make any effort to come into the room, and somehow she knew he wouldn't.

"Just dandy," she said. "Am I allowed to close the door?"

"Certainly," he replied with great courtesy. "I'll even do it for you." And without another word he pulled the splintered door closed, shutting out the light.

Jane lay on the sagging mattress, listening to the sounds of her accomplice as he moved about his bedroom. He was whistling softly, apparently well pleased with his brief act of violence.

At least, Jane thought, she wouldn't have Margery's problem. Alexander Caldicott wasn't going to give up without one hell of a fight. And with that thought, Jane fell asleep. Smiling.

Chapter Seventeen

Jane Dexter had to be the most infuriating, pigheaded, cold-hearted, sexless woman in the entire world, Sandy told himself. And then he quickly amended his judgment. Sexless, she wasn't; she'd simply prefer to be. No woman had ever melted in his arms the way she had, had ever turned as hot and demanding, as overwhelmed and overwhelming as she had during that too-short night in the old house in Bay Head.

He wanted her again. He'd wanted her last night when he'd given in to a childish fit of pique and smashed open the connecting door. One word, one sign of softening on her part and they could have spent the night a lot more profitably than he had, alternating between tossing and turning and taking cold showers. But she hadn't exhibited any signs of relenting, and he'd felt like a damned fool smashing through the door like that, and so he'd spent the night in misery. His only consolation was the certain knowledge that she'd had just as wakeful a night. The paper-thin walls carried every creak of the mattress, every weary sigh. He lay there in his bed, staring at the clock, wondering how much longer he could reasonably wait before he could get up. Wondering how much longer it would be till Jane came back to his bed.

He groaned, punching his pillow and rolling over. He was going to have a hell of a time driving four hundred miles on approximately fifteen minutes of sleep. Maybe he could catch just a few more minutes. Maybe he could blot Jane out of his mind long enough so he could get a short nap. He pulled the pillow over his head, nestling his face into the scratchy sheets. If he could just blot out the evocative sound of her mattress creaking, he might have a chance.

THE FIRST COOL GRAY LIGHT of dawn was filtering through the lime-green curtains of the motel room when Jane awoke. She squinted at her watch, moaned, and shut her eyes again. It was 4:45 a.m. Too early to get up, even if they were planning to leave by six. She wouldn't need to pack—everything was still jumbled in her suitcase anyway. All she had to do was stumble through her morning ablutions and climb into that sinfully comfortable Audi. There was nothing to keep her awake.

Except the certainty that Stephen Tremaine, the bluff, avuncular figure from a distant past, had murdered her brother. She still couldn't comprehend, couldn't accept the fact that her brother died from someone else's act of violence. Had he known when the car went over the embankment? Was he afraid of dying?

She shivered, sitting up in bed. Horrible, nightmare thoughts. Richard had never been afraid of anything in his life, not draft boards or the national guard or rural, reactionary sheriffs or dying for a cause. She'd seen him lie down in front of a bulldozer that was trying to raze a building Richard considered a historic monument. She'd known him to walk in front of snarling police dogs, to starve himself down below a hundred pounds, to risk death in numerous ways, and he'd never been frightened. When it came right down to it, he was too self-absorbed to consider himself mortal. When death came he probably reacted with no more than surprise and mild outrage.

She found herself smiling in the darkened bedroom, and a small part of the clutching around her heart eased a bit. For the first time some of her brother's noble, infuriating characteristics seemed to have some side benefits. At least they might have made death easier.

She only wished she were blessed with a similar self-absorption. It was always possible that the brakes on the Escort had failed normally. And it was remotely possible the moon was made of green cheese and the astronauts who landed there didn't happen to notice.

She supposed she ought to be more frightened. If she were alone she would be. But the knowledge that Sandy was beside her, that another living, breathing soul was stuck in the mess along with her, gave her enough courage to face even another case of tampered brakes. If she'd had any plans to sever her relationship with her duplicitous partner, those plans had vanished after their dip in the canal. She needed all the help she could get, and no matter how mad she was, she preferred to have that help from Sandy.

Besides, it was clear Uncle Stephen hadn't the nerve for a direct attack. He could tamper with someone's automobile with impunity, and given his background that was understandable. Stephen Tremaine was a self-made man, and he just happened to have paid his way through undergraduate school by working at a local auto repair shop.

In the past thirty years he'd been involved in too many things for Jane to even contemplate, if she had to guess where the next attack might come from. As far as she knew, after college none of his work had been particularly hands-on. Maybe his murderous expertise was limited to cars. They'd better go over the Audi with a fine-tooth comb.

These thoughts weren't conducive to going back to sleep, she thought, climbing out of bed and pulling back the hideous nylon curtain. The gray-blue light of early dawn bounced off the glaring streetlights, and there was frost on the Audi. Trucks rumbled past on Route One, but the rest of New Jersey was asleep.

She could stay in the room and brood, or she could get her last chance for a little exercise before being cooped up in a car for eight or nine hours, depending on how fast Sandy drove. While she thought jogging was a sign of insanity, she missed her early-morning walks that used to start her day in Baraboo. The parking lot of the motel lacked a certain jungle charm, but it was better than nothing. A little fresh air, even laden with chemicals and exhaust fumes, was better than nothing.

She pulled on Margery's designer sweat suit, which had to be the most comfortable thing she'd worn in years, slipped on her Nikes, tied her long hair back with a scarf, and stepped outside into the early-morning chill. She closed the door behind her, taking a deep breath and watching the ice crystals on the air as she exhaled. Stuffing the keys in her pocket, she stepped out past the silver Audi, onto the pitted tarmac.

Her only warning was the sound of gravel beneath a noiseless tread. An arm snaked around her neck, a hand clamped over her mouth, shutting her scream off before it got past her throat, and something sharp jabbed into her ribs, something that could only be a knife.

She had a faint, panicked hope that it was Sandy trying to scare her. But the solid body behind her was too tall, even for Sandy, the arm across her throat was too thick and burly, the voice rasping in her ear too hoarse and obscene.

"Shut up," he hissed in her ear. "You try to scream, lady, and you'll be dealing with a heart transplant the hard way. Understand?"

She nodded, trying to swallow her terror along with her scream, hoping the pressure of the knife against her ribs would lessen. It didn't.

The man began dragging her back toward the motel, back into the shadows. She wanted to beg him not to hurt her, but his hand was still tight over her mouth, and it took all her concentration to breathe through her nose, to keep calm, to keep from kicking and screaming and crying in sheer, childish terror.

Was he going to rape her? Kill her? Simply rob her? She'd come out without her wallet, with nothing but the keys to her room. Even if she were able to get away from him, she wouldn't be able to unlatch the ancient lock on her door before he caught her again. Maybe she could reason with the man.

She felt the sharp point of the knife leave her rib cage, and she breathed a sigh of relief, only to experience the even greater horror of having the cold, sharp steel pressed up against the fragile underside of her jaw, just above the man's arm.

"That's right, honey. You know I mean business, don't you? Jabba told you about Lenny the Rip, didn't he? But you don't learn too quickly, do you? First your brother's car, then yours, and you still go around asking questions, talking to the police. My employer doesn't like that. He wants you to butt out of his business. You'd like to do that, wouldn't you?" He gave her a rough little shake, and the tip of the knife grazed her skin. "Just nod if you agree."

She didn't have much choice. She nodded, very carefully, so as not to impale herself on the tip of the knife. "So you tell your lawyer friend that you aren't interested in your brother anymore. That he should go on back to New York, and keep out of places in the East Village where he doesn't belong. And you go back to Nebraska or wherever it was you came from, and in a few months a nice fat check will arrive. Now isn't that better than driving a car with crummy brakes? Just nod."

She nodded, but the knife still bit into the tender skin. "I'm glad we had this little discussion. I'd be more than happy to go into detail, but I think you get my drift. Don't you, honey?"

Once more she nodded, and she felt her body propelled along the walkway, back toward her room. "Reach in your pocket for the keys, lady," he said in that same, hoarsely affable voice. "And unlock your door."

Her hands were shaking so hard she could barely find the keys. Finding the lock without being able to look for it was even harder, but he was still holding her in that vicelike grip, and when she tried to move her head downward the knife jabbed deeper.

"Come on, lady, you can do it without looking, I know you can. A smart girl like you," he sneered gently.

Getting the key in the lock was only half the battle. The lock was old and rusty and usually required careful handling and just the right amount of jiggling. She wasn't going to stand and jiggle while her backside was pressed up against someone named Lenny the Rip.

Finally the lock gave, and the door opened in front of her. She didn't move, terrified to precipitate something she couldn't fight. Would he follow her in, out of sight of possible witnesses, and make his point more violently and more effectively?

"We're agreed on this, aren't we, lady?" he muttered in her ear. "You're going back to Kansas, right?" He moved his hand a fraction of an inch away from her mouth, ready to slap it down again if she made the wrong sound, and the knife still rested against her throat.

"Right," she said, her voice a thin croak of sound.

"Good," he said cheerfully. And then she felt herself propelled forward, sprawling full-length on the seedy carpet, as the door slammed shut behind them.

She lay without moving, shivering in reaction as she listened to the sound of a car gun its engine and tear away. She heard the slamming of doors, the pounding of footsteps, and then her room was flooded with light from the connecting door, and she was no longer alone.

Sandy was on the floor beside her, pulling her into his arms, his hands gentle, reassuring, as they pushed the hair away from her face. It wasn't until she felt his arms around her that she started crying, great, gasping sobs of reaction and relief.

He held her tightly, murmuring to her, meaningless words of comfort as he stroked her face. She could see streaks of darkness on his hand, and knew with a sort of benumbed horror that it was her blood on his hand. Instead of calming down, she could feel the tension building inside her, bubbling forth into what might very well turn into hysterics, when she heard Sandy's prosaic voice in her ear.

"Thank God he left when he did. I was afraid I might have had to rescue you."

Jane's tears halted abruptly. She stiffened in his arms, pulling back the few inches he'd let her, and stared up into his bland face. "You knew he was attacking me?"

"I could hear every sound you made during the night, every toss and turn. As a matter of fact, I didn't sleep too well, either.

When I heard you get up and go outside I decided to join you. I was just getting my clothes on when I heard Lenny grab you.''

She just stared at him, her hysterics forgotten. "And you didn't want to step outside without your pants on, is that it?''

"It is cold,'' he agreed. "But even more important is the fact that Lenny has had a great deal of experience with that nasty knife of his, and I had no weapon at all. Not to mention the fact that he's about half a foot taller than I am and a hundred pounds heavier.''

Jane could feel outrage and loathing bubbling up inside her. "But he could have raped me,'' she said furiously. "He could have murdered me.''

"Unlikely. Jimmy told me that Lenny's gay. And he charges too much for murders—I don't think Tremaine would be willing to pay that much just for an inconvenience like you.''

His arms were still around her. She whirled out of them, scrambling across the floor out of reach as the words tumbled forth, epithets she hadn't used since she was fourteen and on the tough girls' softball team. "You rotten, degenerate, low-living coward,'' she snarled. "You self-centered, dishonorable, lily-livered, chicken-hearted pig. You…''

"Chicken-hearted pig?'' Sandy echoed, unmoved by her fury. "Aren't you getting your metaphors mixed? And I'm not the slightest bit degenerate, as you should know by now. I'm very healthy in my wants and desires. And I may be a coward, but I'm not stupid. It didn't make any sense to make a heroic stand and risk getting myself knifed if there was no need to.''

She could feel the warm, sticky dampness of blood on her neck. "So instead you let me get knifed,'' she said, her voice very quiet.

"Don't be melodramatic, Jane,'' Sandy said wearily. "He didn't knife you. Lenny's too smart for that.''

"What's that on your hand, then? Ketchup?''

He froze. He stood up with one swift movement, and turned on the dim bedside light.

If Jane had been surreptitiously proud of her cursing a few

moments earlier, it was nothing compared to Sandy. She didn't even have time to duck before he swooped down on her, scooping her up in his arms and heading for the door.

"Put me down, dammit," she demanded, squirming fruitlessly. She hadn't realized Sandy was quite so strong. "Where do you think you're going?"

"I'm taking you to the hospital."

"It's not that bad. He only scratched me." Sandy was fumbling with the lock, and she decided it was time for more forceful action. She didn't want to go to an emergency room and have to answer a lot of unfortunate questions, she wanted to get out of New Jersey.

She rammed her elbow into Sandy's unprotected stomach. He dropped her with a thud, doubling over in pain as he tried to catch his breath. She tried not to feel guilty as she dashed across the shadowy room for the bathroom. "I don't want to go to the hospital," she said as she switched on the fluorescent light and stared at her pale, bloody reflection. "It's not nearly as bad as it looks, and I always hated Princeton Hospital ever since I had my tonsils out." She began daubing at her bloody neck with a wet washcloth, wincing slightly as she cleaned it. There were two long, shallow scratches, and the bleeding had slowed down to a mere trickle.

Sandy pulled himself to his feet, staggered across the room and collapsed on her unmade bed. "You could have said something," he groaned, still clutching his belly like a man in mortal pain. She hadn't elbowed him that hard, she thought, grimacing at his reflection in the mirror.

"I believe I did," she said. "Consider it my thanks for so gallantly coming to my rescue." The bleeding had stopped, and now that the first stages of reaction had passed she was no longer hysterical, she was blazingly mad.

"Sorry," Sandy said, sliding up and propping himself on her pillows. "Next time I'll be more than happy to be virgin sacrifice for your bloodthirsty visitors."

"It's a little late for the virgin part, isn't it?" She came and leaned in the bathroom doorway.

"You should know the answer to that as well as I do." Suddenly he dropped his indolent air. "If I'd known he was hurting you I would have stopped him."

She thought about it for a moment, then shrugged. The gesture was a mistake, causing her to wince in pain, but she did her best to cover her flinching. As usual, nothing escaped Sandy. "If you'd done anything he might very well have killed me," she said. "It's probably just as well you waited. What it lacks in romance it makes up for in common sense. I'd rather be mad and have a tiny scratch on my neck than be lying in Intensive Care right now."

"I guess I can't be your knight in shining armor."

"I wasn't looking for one."

He sat up, looking suddenly cheerful. "True enough. You were looking for a cowardly sleaze. Maybe you didn't do so badly after all."

She looked at him for a long, thoughtful moment. His long, lean body was stretched out on her bed, his hands were still stained with her blood, his face, despite the jaunty grin, showed that he'd been far from untouched by Lenny's attack. Even she wasn't too self-absorbed to see the guilt and worry shadowing his eyes. It was dangerous, but she couldn't resist it.

"Maybe I didn't," she said softly. And quickly closed herself in the bathroom before he could react. "It's getting close to six," she called out, reaching for the bloody washcloth and rinsing it in the sink. "Are you almost ready to leave?"

There was a long silence. "Give me ten minutes," he said finally. And she could hear the connecting door shut quietly.

She stared at her reflection in the mirror. Her brown hair was a witchy mass around her pale face, her eyes were huge and shadowed, her mouth pale and tremulous. Maybe once she put on makeup, wound her hair back in a bun and found her glasses she'd look more normal. But she knew she wouldn't be able to wipe away the truth.

Margery Caldicott was right. Jane was in love with her partner in crime. And all her own common sense, all the common sense in the world couldn't talk her out of it.

THEY WERE ON THE ROAD in fifteen minutes, stopping at McDonald's for a fast-food breakfast and three cups of coffee each before heading up the turnpike. The weather stayed cool and crisp, and Sandy kept the heater on low and the tape player on medium. "You sure you don't want to tell the police?" he asked for the final time as they were heading over the George Washington Bridge.

"Positive," she said sleepily, curled up against the leather-lined door. "They'd only hold us up. We don't know where Stephen is right now, but I bet if he isn't heading for Vermont already, he'll be there soon enough. You pointed it out yourself, we don't have any proof, just suspicions."

"We might be heading into more danger," he felt compelled to point out. Guilt was still riding him hard—every time he saw the long, shallow scratches on Jane's neck his hands would clench around the steering wheel.

"I know," she murmured.

"Aren't you worried?"

"Nope." She gave him a sleepy smile. "You'll keep the bad guys at bay. You've got enough guilt to keep you on your toes for the next ten years."

"It shows that bad, eh?"

"Sure does. And you deserve every rotten pang of it."

"Jane," he said sweetly, "that's what I love about you. Your generous, forgiving nature."

"Drive on, Sandy," she said, closing her eyes again. "And remember, next time you're attacked by Elinor Peabody don't look to me to save you."

"Promises, promises," he muttered. But Jane was already sound asleep.

Chapter Eighteen

The weather, already a bit brisk in New Jersey, turned sharply colder by the time they reached Connecticut. A cold hard drizzle was falling by the Vermont border, and the road grew slick and icy as the sun began to sink.

All the glorious color of Vermont in autumn was long past. The trees were bare, the ground brown and hard, the sky and the mountains bleak and gray. The Audi shook a bit as the wind buffeted it along the deserted highways, and Jane shivered as she thought about her grandmother's old house on the lake.

"I hope you brought some warm clothes," she said, breaking one of the long silences that were surprisingly comfortable.

He turned to look at her. "That sounds ominous. Doesn't your grandmother's heating system work very well?"

"My grandmother's cottage doesn't have a heating system."

"Oh, God."

"Was that a curse of a prayer?"

"A little bit of both. I hope there are motels in Newfield, Vermont."

"Nary a one. Don't worry, though. Nana's cottage has a huge fieldstone fireplace. If we just put our sleeping bags on the floor in front of it we should do all right."

"Sleeping bags?" Sandy's voice was rich with horror. "You're asking me to sleep in a sleeping bag? Inside?"

"Nana's cottage won't feel much like inside this time of year," Jane assured him.

"Small comfort."

"In more ways than one."

"I don't suppose I get to share my sleeping bag?" Sandy asked in a hopeful tone.

"Well," she said doubtfully, "sometimes squirrels get in and make their nests in the house. You could always ask one of them."

"Thanks, I think I'll pass. I presume you can provide the sleeping bags?" He sounded resigned but gloomy.

She thought about the big brass bed up under the eaves, piled high with quilts and handwoven coverlets, and sighed. She had to gather her self-preservation about her, not give in to her baser instincts. "I can provide the sleeping bags."

The snow started some fifteen miles south of Newfield, in the slightly larger town of Hardwick. Jane wasn't surprised. If the weather was going to be bad, it was going to be worse heading out of Hardwick toward Newfield. The steep hill out of the bustling little village was already slick with sleet, and by the time they reached the first dip in the road the sleet had turned into hard white pellets, halfway between snow and ice.

"I'm not crazy about the driving conditions," Sandy said between his teeth. "For heaven's sake, it's still October."

"They often get a first snow by October tenth. I will admit this seems a little intense for this time of year." She peered out through the whirling whiteness. "I suppose we should have checked the weather report before we took off. I'd forgotten how bad things could be."

The Audi's sideways skid immediately gave a perfect demonstration of just how bad things could be. Sandy proved himself more than capable, however, turning into the skid and bringing the car back under control with seemingly no effort at all. The snow was getting thicker, spattering the windshield between each swipe of the wipers, and Sandy slowed their headlong pace.

"Lovely weather," Sandy muttered.

"You're handling it perfectly," she said with only the slightest bit of resentment in her voice.

"I was on the ski team in college. If you like to ski, you get used to driving through new snow. However, I usually had snow tires."

Jane gave him a look of pure, unadulterated horror as they crested another icy hill and began sliding down the other side. Fortunately all Sandy's attention was on the slippery road and not on his companion's sudden lack of confidence. "No snow tires?" she managed in a sickly gasp. The snow was sticking to the roads now, a thin layer of white on top of the icy scum.

"No snow tires," he verified. "Look at it this way, Jane. You wanted adventure."

"I didn't want adventure, I wanted justice. You're the one who was terminally bored."

"Well," said Sandy, as the car began traveling sideways toward the bank on the side of the road, "I'm not bored now." He touched the accelerator, nudged the wheel, and averted disaster once more.

Jane leaned back against the seat and shut her eyes. If she had to die she didn't want to watch. She'd been brave enough for the past seventy-two hours, facing gangsters and near drownings and knife attacks. A snowy drive was suddenly her limit. "Neither am I," she said faintly. "I only wish I were."

NEWFIELD HADN'T CHANGED MUCH in the years since Jane had been there. The snow slackened a bit as they drove into the village, and the light flurries only enhanced its perfect New England charm. From the white-spired church to the charming general store, from the barn-red mill that had been converted into a gift shop to the rows of perfect white clapboard houses, the place reeked of photo opportunities. The village was shutting down for the night when they drove through at just after five, and they had barely enough time to grab something for dinner before they headed up the road to the old Dexter cottage.

It had been snowing longer in Newfield, probably since early afternoon, and no one had bothered to plow the long, winding drive up to the house. Sandy tried twice, gunning the motor and taking a running start, but even he had to admit defeat.

This time he wasn't able to regain control, and the Audi ended up in a shallow ditch, the headlights pointing crazily at the old cottage.

"We're here," Jane said faintly. Sandy only snarled, as the two of them scrambled out of the lopsided Audi and headed up the embankment toward the house.

Even in the fading light Jane could see it, still unchanged after almost seventy-five years. It was the perfect prewar summer cottage, with weathered shingles, porches surrounding three sides, gables and dormers and multipaned windows looking blankly out into the snowy evening. Sandy stood there, ankle-deep in the snow, staring up at the old place, and his expression wasn't encouraging.

"No heat, eh?" he said gloomily.

"The sooner we get a fire going the sooner we'll be warm." She sounded disgustingly hearty, even to her own ears, as she trudged up the broad front steps. She stopped for a moment, looking down. For an instant it had looked as if someone had walked up those steps before the snow had gotten so deep. She thought she could see the faint trace of a man's boots beneath the fresh layer of snow. She peered down, but she couldn't be certain. It was probably just Ephraim, checking the empty summer cottages as he'd been hired to do. If anyone had come up to the old house, they were certainly long gone.

It was about thirty degrees in the autumn night air. It was about twenty in the house, the high ceilings and curtainless windows keeping the air icy. Sandy dumped his suitcase on the floor and headed straight for the fireplace as Jane went around turning on lights. At least someone had left a fresh supply of wood and kindling. She listened to Sandy curse, a low, steady stream of profanity beneath his breath, as she wandered through the old place, turning on lights and looking back over her past.

She hadn't been there in three years, not since Sally had brought her kids back East for a stilted summer reunion. Things had been too hectic then, chasing around after Sally's hellions, dealing with Richard's absentmindedness, all the while trying to use her time away from Baraboo to make up her mind whether she should marry Frank or not. No wonder she'd made the wrong decision.

Richard's idea of a family reunion was to sit in the old Morris chair, smoking his pipe and telling everyone to be quiet. Sally's idea was to dump the kids on Jane and go off to visit with her childhood friends. And Jane's idea was to do all the cooking, all the cleaning, all the child-care, and then simply walk out halfway through the allotted vacation time.

She hadn't seen Richard since, though she'd spoken to him on the phone. Suddenly she missed him, missed him terribly. She could almost picture him sitting in that chair, scowling at everyone over his thick glasses. She could practically smell the rich, pungent smell of his pipe tobacco lingering in the chilly air.

By the time she finished her tour of the house and returned to the cavernous living room, laden with sleeping bags and pillows, Sandy had managed to start a decent fire. The heat penetrated a few feet into the icy vastness of the room, and her accomplice looked well pleased with himself.

He looked up at her, and the flickering firelight danced across his face. "Why don't we use the electric space heater? It's going to take a long time for this fireplace to warm the room."

"We don't have any electric heaters. The wiring's too old to take it. We were going to upgrade it but we never got around to it. The three of us inherited the place equally, and no one's got enough of a stake in it to make any sort of push."

Sandy rose, stretching his limber body. "Then what's that in the corner?"

Jane stared. "An electric heater," she said, suddenly uneasy.

"Looks like there are some new outlets, too. Want to risk it?" Sandy had already crossed the room and picked up the portable baseboard heater.

Jane shivered, but whether it was from the cold or something else she wasn't sure. "All right," she said, concentrating on unpacking the groceries.

"What's wrong?"

She shook her head. "I'm not sure. That heater shouldn't be here, for one thing. For another, I thought there were footprints on the front steps. The refrigerator is on, when the last person here would have been sure to turn it off. And I have the oddest feeling that someone's been here."

"Tremaine?"

She shrugged. "I guess so. Who else would come up here without saying anything? Except that I can't imagine Uncle Stephen hiding out in any place as cold and uncomfortable as this. He'd be staying in a first-class motel in Stowe, not lurking in a deserted summer cottage."

"Do me a favor, Jane," Sandy said suddenly, his voice tight with tension. "This man is apparently a conscienceless murderer, a man who not only killed your brother but has done his best to kill or terrorize you. For God's sake stop calling him Uncle Stephen!"

"Excuse me," Jane said stiffly, pressing a hand against her throbbing neck.

"And stop doing that!" Sandy snapped.

"Doing what?"

"Rubbing your neck. I feel guilty enough—you don't have to remind me."

"I hate to tell you this, Alexander 'the Sleaze' Caldicott, but I'm not doing it to make you feel guilty. All my actions are not motivated by how you're going to react. My neck happens to sting!"

Sandy's mouth compressed in a thin, angry line that still managed to be sexy. "Are we going to spend our entire time arguing?"

"Probably."

He glared at her for another long moment. And then a slow, reluctant smile started, first in his gray eyes, then traveling to his mouth, relaxing that tight, tense line. "Well, I guess I'd rather fight with you than be peaceful with anyone else."

"Anyone else?" She was momentarily disarmed, a danger she recognized and decided to ignore.

"Anyone else. What's for dinner?"

"Steak and baked potatoes and salad. Except that I don't want to go out to the kitchen and make it. It's too cold."

"We can cook the steak over the fire if you have a grill. And we can roast the potatoes in the ashes. I'm afraid one of us will have to freeze to make the salad." His smile was just a bit too ingenuous.

Jane sighed. "You know no woman in her right mind likes to cook over a fire. We had too much of it five million years ago. I'll make the salad."

"I don't suppose this house comes with a liquor supply?"

Jane smiled sweetly. "Treat me nice and maybe I'll break it out. I like my steak practically raw."

"Savage," he muttered. "I like my Scotch practically straight."

"Yes, sir."

By the time she came back into the living room with a hastily tossed-together salad, two glasses and a half-empty bottle of Johnny Walker Red she was shivering, chilled to the bone. The living room was redolent of broiling steak and wood smoke, and the heat had finally penetrated even the chilliest corners of the room.

Sandy had spread the sleeping bags out on the floor, one on top of the other, and Jane contented herself with a skeptical glance before seating herself cross-legged on them. It certainly wasn't the softest surface she ever hoped to sleep on, and once she made Sandy take his sleeping bag and move a decent distance away it was going to be even harder. She allowed herself a moment of delicious indecision, and then hardened her heart. She couldn't afford to get any closer to him than she already had, not until she decided she could trust him, not until she had some sign, other than his ex-wife's fantasy, that he was involved with her for any other reason than to alleviate boredom.

She had to make one more icy dash into the kitchen for plates and silverware, but the steak was well worth it. Sandy had managed to simply sear it on one end and cook it to his own tastes on the other, a talent Jane properly appreciated. The potatoes were a little uneven, but absolutely delicious with Vermont butter, and the Scotch, without ice and only a trace of water, did a great deal toward advancing the truce.

"Where are we going to look for the lab?" Sandy said once they were finished and the dirty dishes stuffed unhygienically and aesthetically under the sofa until tomorrow. "I presume it's not in the house?"

"I checked when we got here. Not that I thought he'd bother. This place is impossible to heat when it gets much colder. The lab could be any one of a number of places. There's a boathouse down by the lake, a garage, a couple of hay barns, even an old icehouse out back by the pond. We'll just have to check them out one by one." She reached up to touch her stinging neck, then caught his eyes watching her hand and instead pushed her hair away from her face.

He said nothing. He was stretched out on the sleeping bags, his second glass of Scotch in his hand, and his eyes were hooded, watchful. He was wearing faded jeans which clung to his long legs, and he'd dispensed with his sweater an hour ago. His navy blue corduroy shirt looked worn and soft to touch, and she had to remind herself that she shouldn't touch, didn't dare to touch.

"There's some long winter underwear upstairs in one of the drawers," she said, knowing she was babbling slightly. "Even in the summer Vermont can get cold enough to need them. We can put them on tomorrow before we go out looking." She'd taken off her own sweater and unbuttoned her cotton knit shirt, pulling it away from her sore neck.

"All right." His voice was deep, slumberous, almost erotically soothing.

Fight it, Jane, she ordered herself. *Fight it.* "I tend to think he would have chosen one of the hay barns," she said, reaching for her neck again. It was stinging, and a cold wet washcloth would have felt wonderful, but she didn't want to call attention to it. She no longer wanted Sandy to feel guilty. She didn't know what she wanted.

She dropped her hand on the sleeping bag between them, staring down at it. There was no mark where her wedding ring had rested, no sign of that tumultuous, painful period in her life. No sign either that she'd used that hand to fling things at the man lying so close to her. His forehead still bore the mark of the few times she'd connected, and then it was her turn to feel guilty. She'd almost gotten him killed in the canal—if it weren't for her he'd be safely away in the Canary Islands or wherever he'd been planning to go.

And if Lenny the Rip found out she ignored his warning, ignored the warning lightly etched on her neck, he might very well follow them and make his point a little clearer. And if Sandy got in the way this time…

She shivered. "Maybe you should go back to New York," she said abruptly. "I can rent a car, take over from here."

She could feel the sudden tension in his body. "I thought you forgave me for not coming to your rescue."

"It's not that." Her voice sounded desperate. "I don't want to be responsible for your getting hurt. Getting killed." She tugged at her shirt, pulling it up around her stinging neck.

He reached out and stopped her hand, pulling it away. "No one's going to kill me," he said. "No one's going to kill you, either. And if anyone lays a hand on you again I'm going to be the one who does the killing."

She lay perfectly motionless, staring into his eyes, and she knew he was absolutely serious. And she knew he would do just that.

"In the meantime," he continued, his voice low and beguiling, "we need to see about your battle scars. You've been tugging at your collar all day." His hand, deft and strong and warm, reached into her shirt.

"I'm fine." She tried to push him away, but he was too fast for her, capturing her combative hand in his while he pushed her back on the sleeping bags.

"We can turn this into a wrestling match," he said, leaning over her, a glint of laughter in his eyes, "and you know I'd prefer that. Or you can humor me. I should have insisted you go to the hospital this morning, but I'm sure we could still find one…''

''Thirty miles away,'' she said. ''All right, you can check it out. I hate to admit it, but it stings like crazy.''

She tried to look anywhere but into his face as he leaned over her, pushing her shirt back over her shoulders to expose the long scratches on her throat. She heard his swift intake of breath, and she tried to sit up. He simply pushed her back down.

''What is it?'' she demanded. ''Why did you make that sound? Does it look infected?''

''Don't be such a sissy. I wasn't reacting to your neck,'' he said calmly, and belatedly Jane realized that the bra she was wearing, now fully exposed to his interested gaze, consisted of not much more than two triangles of white lace.

She tried to pull her shirt back around her, but he pushed her hands out of the way. ''Stop leering,'' she said grumpily, giving up the fight.

''I'm not leering. I'm just being properly appreciative. Your neck does look painful. What did you put on it?''

''Earlier? Just water.''

''I think it needs some disinfectant.'' He sat up and reached for the bottle of Scotch. ''This is the best I can do at the moment. Relax, Jane. This will hurt you more than it does me.'' He poured a generous amount on the dish towel Jane had found to serve as a napkin and pressed it gently to the side of her neck.

She let out a loud, piercing scream, more of surprise than actual pain. The sting of the whiskey wasn't much worse than the scratches themselves had been, and she'd barely noticed when they'd been inflicted.

''It's not that bad,'' Sandy muttered, pouring a little more Scotch onto the dish towel as he held it against her skin. The cold whiskey trickled down her neck, sliding over her shoulder and down between her breasts. ''Now who's being a coward?''

She took a deep intake of breath as the burning liquid slid over her flesh, and from her supine position she looked up at him, into his hooded eyes. "I am," she said, her voice husky, and they both knew she wasn't talking about the pain.

For a long moment he didn't move. The flickering firelight danced across his face, and the hiss and pop of the burning pine was the only sound in the huge room. Then he leaned forward, his voice low and husky, his breath warm and sweet on her skin. "It would be a sin to waste good Scotch, don't you think?" he whispered, moving the saturated cloth away. And he kissed her neck, his lips feather soft, and his tongue snaked out to taste the trickle of whiskey along the slender white column of her neck.

Chapter Nineteen

Jane lifted her hands to his shoulders, to push him away. Instead her fingers dug into the faded corduroy, feeling the bone and muscle and sinew beneath, and she was lost. Lost as she'd been since the night in Bay Head, lost as she'd been since she first got up enough nerve to knock on a stranger's door and ask him to commit arson with her.

His tongue slid across her jaw, down her chest, to the vee between her breasts, tickling her, sipping at the spilled whiskey. Her shirt was spread around her, and suddenly the front clasp of her bra was free. Some small part of sanity, of self-preservation, reared its ugly head, and she said in her most prosaic voice, "Are you really going to do this?"

If the result came out sounding rather breathless, it was only to be expected, since his tongue had abandoned the quest for spilled Scotch and was now concentrating on the tightly budded nipple beneath his mouth.

He raised his head for a moment, his eyes gleaming darkly in the firelight. "Yes," he said. "Unless you have any objections?"

She had a thousand, but right now she couldn't bring a single one to mind. She was lying on her back in her grandparents' living room, about to be seduced in the same room where she'd once played jacks. The sleeping bags beneath her had seen many a teenage slumber party—she should feel hopelessly decadent.

What she felt was hopelessly in love. "No objection, counselor," she said. And then he kissed her.

Her arms slid around his neck, pulling him down to her, and her mouth opened beneath his, sweetly, generously, kissing him back with all the passionate enthusiasm she had in her. His mouth slanted across hers, nibbling, teasing, and she could taste the whiskey, the saltiness of her skin, on his tongue. She kissed him back, reveling in her sudden freedom, reveling in the dizzying wonder of it, so caught up with the mingling of their mouths that she was scarcely aware of his deft hands on her zipper, unfastening her jeans and sliding them down over her hips. He broke the kiss for a moment, long enough to toss the jeans into a corner, and then just as quickly divested her of her shirt and bra, with the same deft grace.

His eyes were dark with desire, and there was an expression of almost smug possession on his face as he sat back to unbutton his shirt. It was an expression she knew she should hate, and yet somehow she found it deeply flattering. The shirt joined her clothes in a pile, followed by his jeans, and his flesh was gilded by the firelight, a golden bronze color glowing with heat and desire. He sank down beside her, taking her willing hands in his and pressing them against his smoothly muscled chest, and the tips of her fingers caressed him, absorbing the feel of him.

"You aren't going to change your mind?" he asked, his voice a husky rasp. "I don't think I could stand it if you changed your mind."

"You could always change it back for me," she said, her hands drifting along his torso, the smooth, sleek hide of him.

"I don't want to do that. I want you to want me." He wasn't touching her now, instead he was letting her touch him, letting her fingertips dance over his gilded flesh, explore the smooth muscles, the trace of hair, the ribs, drifting downward with inexorable purpose.

She touched him, the hard, wanting part of him, and listened with sensuous gratification to his sharp intake of breath. "I want you," she said, using the same delicate, arousing touch on that most sensitive part of him. "I never said I didn't. I just thought I shouldn't."

"Why?" he groaned.

She shook her head. "I can't remember. Maybe it will come to me."

"Don't," he whispered. "Don't remember. Just feel." He reached for her, his hands strong and certain, cupping her full breasts, holding them, arousing them as he brought his mouth back.

She released him, reluctantly, sinking back on the sleeping bag and arching her back with a moan of pleasure. She didn't know when she'd had such a barrage of delight assaulting her senses. The heat from the fire, the smell of wood smoke and whiskey, the flickering firelight and the softness of the old flannel sleeping bag beneath her, all combined to make her feel almost drunk with sensation. She opened her eyes to look over Sandy's golden head, and outside the frosty window she could see snow swirling down. She closed her eyes again, feeling safe and warm in Sandy's arms.

Except that safety and comfort were fast disappearing beneath his practiced mouth. Her breasts felt swollen, burning against his mouth as he suckled them, giving each lingering, devouring attention. His hand slid between her thighs, touching the heated center of her, and she whimpered slightly in the back of her throat, a sound of longing and instinctive wariness. She reached out a hand to stop him, to slow him down, to hurry him up, but he ignored it, sliding his mouth down her body, glancing off her flat stomach, down to the juncture of her thighs.

"Sandy!" she gasped, trying to jackknife up in sudden panic, but he simply pushed her back down on the padded floor, his hands cradling her hips.

"Objection noted and overruled," he murmured, and his mouth found her.

She shivered in helpless delight, reaching down to push at his shoulders. Instead her nails dug in as she writhed beneath his practiced mouth, afraid to let go. Her body felt coated with a sheet of burning ice, her heart was pounding so hard and fast she thought it would explode from her chest, and all she knew was his mouth on her, his tongue, and a delight she wanted to fight and then suddenly no longer could, as wave after wave of sensation smashed over her.

Vaguely she could hear her voice, sobbing in helpless reaction. She could see him move up and cover her, sliding into her with a deep, sure, hard thrust that sent her spiraling out of control. The ice had melted, they were both covered with a film of sweat, and through the dizzying firelight she thought she could see their bodies, locked together in an undulating dance of love.

He reached down and held her hips, striving with unquestionable intent, and his mouth covered hers, his tongue in her mouth, a dual invasion. She was crying, she knew she was, she could feel her face wet with tears, but all she could feel was the man within her body, carrying her places she hadn't even dreamed existed.

Suddenly his body tensed, and he lifted his head, his eyes glittering down into hers with a fierce intensity. She could feel the life, the love pumping into her, and then everything shattered around her, dissolving into a maelstrom of sensation and dark, dangerous release.

It went on forever, wave after wave of delight wringing a convulsive reaction from her exhausted body. Her mind had long ago stopped working, and for a moment she could feel herself slipping into some sort of alternative reality, a place of infinite rest. The last bit of tension left her body, and she sank back, floating for a bit, entirely at peace.

The pop and crackle of the fire brought her awake. Her eyes shot open, and she knew why she felt so warm and so lethargic. Sandy's one hundred and eighty-some pounds were still stretched across her like a deadweight.

He must have felt her stir, for suddenly his muscles tightened, and he lifted his head from its place on her shoulder and looked down at her.

She waited for him to say something, but he just looked at

her, an odd, indecipherable expression on his face. She could feel the dried tears on her face, and her body still thrummed with latent tremors. She might as well end these games, she thought briefly. There was no way he couldn't know.

"Did I just die and go to heaven?" she whispered in a hoarse voice. "Or did I just faint?"

She managed to get a small, wary smile from him. "I'm not sure," he said. "I was on cloud nine myself. Weren't you with me?"

"Oh, is that where we were? I wasn't sure," she murmured lazily. He was still looking very serious, whereas she felt positively buoyant. She resisted the urge to tickle him, but just barely. Instead she brought her hands up over his back, stroking his still-damp skin.

His shiver of reaction brought a small, secret smile to her face. "Be careful," he warned, not moving. "The next time might just kill us."

She kept stroking, moving her sensitive fingertips down his sides. "It might be worth it."

His hands reached up and cupped her face, holding her still. "We have plenty of time."

"Do we?"

"We have the rest of our lives."

"Do we?" She held her breath, waiting. She wasn't sure for what. Not something as formal as a proposal. She wanted a promise, a commitment.

But Sandy only moved to lie beside her, and while the loss of his body heat and weight should have been a relief, she felt cold and lonely and bereft.

"Yes," he said, drawing her into the shelter of his arms.

For a moment she wanted to fight, but she was too weary, to sated to hold out for what she still needed. "Yes," would have to be good enough. For now.

WHEN SHE AWOKE she was very, very cold. Sometime during the night Sandy had managed to wrap one of the sleeping bags around them, and he must have stoked the fire at least once, but now, as an eerie gray-white dawn crept through the windows the coals were an orange-red memory and Jane could see her breath.

She was also naked beneath the sleeping bag, and even Sandy's strong, warm body wasn't enough to keep the chill at bay. She slid out from under the covers, but her accomplice, her lover, she reminded herself, didn't stir. Scrambling across the room, it took her too long to find all her clothes. She settled for his sweater since he'd ended up using hers as an extra pillow, and she stuck her bare feet in his shoes as she headed for the great outdoors and the use of nature's plumbing since the cottage water had been turned off for the winter.

The moment she stepped out onto the broad front porch she realized why the light was strange. It was just after dawn, and the entire world, or at least Newfield, Vermont, was covered with almost a foot of freshly fallen snow.

She stopped, daunted. "For crying out loud," she said, her voice loud in the hushed stillness, "it's only October!"

Not even the birds were awake. In the distance she could see wood smoke rising from some of the village houses and from the farms lying on the outer edges of the hills. They needed a little wood smoke of their own, she thought, biting her lip and trudging out into the snow for the convenient patch of woods. Not to mention some water for washing—maybe if she could wash away the remnants of last night she might be able to rid herself of her sudden vulnerability.

Sandy was blessed with the gift of heavy sleep. He barely stirred when she came back in and stoked the fire into a roaring inferno that threatened the safety of the old fieldstone chimney. He only turned over and began snoring as she came back in with two buckets of lake water and began heating them. It wasn't until she'd managed to wash, change into fresh clothes, and was just beginning to think about breakfast when his hand snagged her ankle as she tiptoed by, and he pulled her down on top of him.

"Don't give me that look, partner," Sandy muttered, flipping her on her back and looming over her.

"What look?"

"That wary, I-don't-know-what-I'm-going-to-do-with-you-but-I-know-it-won't-be-much kind of look," he said.

She thought about it for a moment. "All right," she said, reaching up and pulling his face down to hers. "I won't." And she kissed him, full on the mouth, a slow, lingering good-morning kiss that had him flipping up the edge of the sleeping bag and trying to pull her back in.

She escaped, rolling out of his reach before he had time to react. "You slept too late. And unless you want to spend another night in this icebox you'd better get dressed. It's going to take some time to find Richard's lab, and a fair amount of time to burn it."

"I wouldn't mind spending another night here," he said quietly, sitting up and scratching his shaggy head. "If we could spend it the same way."

"I don't know if I'd survive another night like the last one," she said, busying herself with the fire, afraid to look at him.

She didn't hear him move, didn't know he was behind her until she felt herself caught and turned, wrapped in his arms. "But what a way to go," he whispered against her mouth.

It was sorely tempting. He wasn't wearing any clothes, of course, and even without her glasses she could see how much he wanted her. There was nothing she wanted more than to sink back onto the pile of sleeping bags with him and wait for the snow to melt, but she couldn't. She had to pay her debt to her brother, and for now her own considerable desires would have to wait.

Of course, she'd already plastered herself against his body and kissed him back with mindless enthusiasm. And she wasn't saying a word as he was lowering her back onto the floor. Maybe family debts could wait a few hours, she thought. Maybe everything unimportant could wait a few hours. Maybe all that really mattered was Sandy.

SHE MANAGED TO FIND a half-frozen bottle of Deer Park water in the kitchen, so they were able to have coffee. Sandy had to make an extra trip to the lake for more wash water, and it took him far too long to find the dishes they'd stashed under the sofa. The sleeping bag was a mess, and Jane considered tossing it out, then changed her mind. When it was over, when she came back here alone, maybe she'd wrap herself up in it and remember. She didn't have much faith in happily ever after.

The snow was melting to a freezing slush when they were finally ready to start their quest. In the light of day the Audi proved to be only slightly mired, and it took a push from Jane and clever driving from Sandy to get it back on the narrow driveway.

"Where to now?" Sandy asked, climbing out of the car and wincing as his soaked running shoes settled into the snow.

"We look for the lab. We can start with the boathouse. I didn't see anything interesting when I went down to get water but I didn't look all that carefully. Then we'll head for the hay barns. Once the store opens we can get you a decent pair of boots and some kerosene."

"Jane, we're not going to burn the laboratory unless we have to."

"We have to," she said flatly, heading toward the lake. Her own boots were only ankle high, and the snow had already soaked them, but she was determined to ignore physical discomfort. She had already paid far too much attention to physical pleasure in the past twelve hours.

"Jane, arson is a crime." He headed after her through the snow, cursing under his breath.

"So I'll get a fire permit."

"No one's going to give you a fire permit on such short notice. Not to burn an existing structure," he argued.

"Then I guess I'll just have to break the law."

"Jane, as your lawyer I have to tell you—"

She stopped, whirling around in the snow, and he almost barreled into her. "You're not my lawyer, Sandy," she said with great reasonableness. "You're my partner in crime. If you don't want to aid and abet this particular endeavor, go back to the cottage."

He looked at her for a moment, and then he sighed. The cool crisp air brightened his eyes and brought color to his cheeks, and for one rash moment she was tempted to tackle him and roll in the snow with him.

A slow smile lit his face. "I can read your mind."

"Don't. I have work to do."

Sandy sighed, resigned. "We have work to do. Lead on, Macduff. I'll just have to do a hell of a job defending you."

The boathouse held nothing but boats, fishing tackle, aging outboard motors and bird droppings. For years it had been a favorite nesting spot for swallows, and as far as Jane could see the population during the summer had only increased.

The hay barns held nothing but hay. The family leased them to a local farmer in return for keeping them reasonably intact, and they were full of neat bales, ready for winter feeding.

The garage held nothing but broken, rusty tools that no one would ever possibly use. Richard's brilliance hadn't extended to earthly matters, and it was unlikely anyone had worked in the building since the early sixties.

Which left the icehouse. It was a small wood structure out by the ice pond, near the edge of the property adjoining the old Wilson place, and it hadn't been used for anything other than kids' games and teenage necking since electricity had come to Newfield in 1922 and people had discovered the wonders of refrigeration.

As long as Jane could remember the entryway had been a splintered pine door on one rusty iron hinge. They weren't within twenty feet of the place before she noticed the heavy steel door, the steel locks. "Eureka," she said softly, trudging through the woods at a faster pace.

Now that she bothered to look, she could see the new power box on the side of the building. Richard had had electricity and running water brought to the small, seemingly ramshackle structure, and the new roof was made of rustic-looking cedar shakes. Nice and inflammable, Jane thought.

Sandy stood there surveying the building. "Don't bother

asking me to pick the locks," he said. "That time at Technocracies was merely a fluke."

"That's what I thought." She made a halfhearted attempt at forcing the door, then stepped back. "We'll head back to the store and get some kerosene."

"No."

"Yes," she said firmly. "Have you bothered looking down? Someone's been here recently. Someone with large feet and expensive boots, the kind you get at upscale New Jersey malls, not the Newfield General Store. I can think of only one other person left alive who has any stake in this place, and that's Stephen Tremaine. If we don't burn it now he's going to win, and I'm damned if I'm going to let him. I'll do it with you or without you, but I'm going to do it."

He just stared at the building for a long, contemplative moment. "I guess you do it with me," he said finally. "I just hope we can find me some better shoes at your general store."

She moved fast, flinging her arms around his neck and smiling up at him. "Thank you," she said, her voice soft in the morning air.

"Anytime," he said, the wary expression almost leaving his eyes. "That's what you hired me for."

YOU'RE CRAZY TO DO THIS, Sandy told himself as he circled the old building, splashing kerosene against the foundations. Arson was a felony, and it would take all his powers of persuasion to get her off. Hell, he was aiding and abetting—maybe he wouldn't even be able to defend her, he'd be standing trial alongside her.

It wasn't as if she didn't own the place—she was Richard Dexter's sole heir. And it wasn't as if she was going to make an insurance claim. The blaze would provide no danger to other structures—the slowly melting snow would keep the fire from spreading, and the nearest structure was an old white farmhouse barely visible through the woods. A young widow lived there with her twin sons, Jane said. Doubtless they kept her too busy to even look out her windows, much less notice a suspicious fire.

Jane was staring at the wooden roof of the icehouse, biting her lower lip as she pondered how best to use her five gallons of liquid. He wished he could be the one to bite her lower lip, and not spend his time worrying about her criminal tendencies. He ended up pouring the last of his kerosene around the window frame, stepped back, and waited for Jane.

The icehouse was set into a hillside. Jane had climbed up the bank and bathed the entire rooftop with kerosene. It was already soaked with melted snow, and Sandy had grave doubts about the inflammability of the whole thing. If he was lucky it would simply refuse to ignite, and Jane would have to consider more reasonable alternatives.

She jumped back, rubbing her hands against her jean-covered thighs, and stared at the structure. It was midafternoon by then, already well past full sunlight, and the area stank of kerosene.

"Got a match?" she inquired cheerfully.

Sandy reached in his pocket, handed her the box of kitchen matches, and stepped back. Directly into a solid figure.

He whirled around, only to look into a pair of chilly brown eyes. The man in front of him looked like a cross between a Vermont hermit and an aging hippie, with a bald pate, long stringy brown hair hanging to his shoulders, a full beard, and wire-rimmed glasses with a Band-Aid securing one corner. He was wearing well-aged denims, and the expression on his face was extremely disgruntled.

"What the hell do you think you're doing?" he demanded.

Sandy turned to Jane. She was staring at the apparition, open-mouthed, the lit match burning her fingers.

Sandy turned back to the newcomer. "Richard Dexter, I presume?"

Chapter Twenty

Sandy stood there, waiting for Jane to fling herself in her brother's arms in joy and relief, but she did no such thing and merely stood, staring, in shock.

And then she turned to Sandy. "You knew!" Her voice was richly accusing.

He shook his head. "Of course, I didn't. I won't say I didn't consider the possibility though."

"And you didn't say a word."

"I didn't want to get your hopes up," he said in what he felt was his most reasonable voice. Jane, however, wasn't in the mood to be reasonable.

Fortunately Richard distracted her. "What in hell are you doing with the kerosene, Jane?" he demanded in righteous indignation. "Do you realize the years of work you were about to burn?"

"What the hell would it matter to you—you're dead!" she shot back.

Richard Dexter appeared only slightly abashed. "I'm sorry if you were upset at the thought of my death. We were never particularly close...."

"Never particularly close?" Jane echoed, her voice a furious shriek in the chilly air. "I thought you'd been murdered."

"So did Stephen Tremaine," said Richard with satisfaction.

Jane's fury died abruptly. "Did he try to kill you, Richard?"

"Oh, probably not," Richard said with an airy wave of his

hand. "Stephen's not quite that cold-blooded. I think he only intended to incapacitate me a little. He knew I never drove fast—I think he figured I'd get a little banged up and not pay any attention to his Salambian schemes. Little did he know I'd already spiked his guns."

"He knows now," Sandy said. "Do you have the missing part of the formula?"

Richard stared at him out of disgruntled brown eyes that were eerily akin to Jane's at her most distrustful. "Who is he?" he asked his sister. "And what was he doing setting fire to my laboratory?"

Jane turned to look at him and Sandy had the uncomfortable feeling she was considering him from a fresh viewpoint. "Oh, him," she said dismissingly, "he's my lawyer."

"Some lawyer," Richard snorted as Sandy swallowed a choked laugh. "Does he make a practice of committing arson?"

"Only with the woman I love," Sandy said smoothly, noting with pleasure Jane's look of complete shock. He left it at that, deliberately. If she didn't know he was in love with her, if she hadn't caught on to that very apparent fact, he'd have to explain it in more intimate detail later. Next time they got a few moments alone, with or without a sleeping bag beneath them.

"Put the matches away, Jane," Richard said sternly, and Jane meekly complied. "Come back to the house with me and we can talk about our mutual godfather. Any chance you can leave *him* behind?"

"*Him* is Sandy Caldicott," Jane said, her meekness gone. "And he goes where I go."

"Can you trust him?" Richard demanded, and Sandy found himself holding his breath, waiting for the all-important answer.

"More than I trust you, my dear departed brother," she snapped back, and if it wasn't quite the declaration Sandy had in mind, it would do for now.

Richard headed off toward the woods, his narrow shoulders slightly hunched, his long stringy hair floating in the wind.

"Where are you going?" Jane demanded. "The house is back the other way."

"Not that house," Richard said loftily. "I haven't been to the old cottage in weeks. It's too cold to stay there in October." He didn't bother to slow his deliberate pace through the snow.

"Oh, I don't know," Sandy murmured. "We managed to heat it up last night."

Jane tried to glare at him, and failed miserably. "What did you mean by that?" she asked in a low voice, making no effort to follow her brother's lanky figure.

"Well, what with the fireplace and the selected use of body heat..."

"I'm not talking about that," she said stubbornly. "Why did you tell Richard I'm the woman you love?"

She wasn't about to move until he said something. On impulse he reached down, scooped up a handful of fresh snow and advanced on her.

She looked at him warily, standing her ground when he reached her. "Not down my neck," she warned.

"I wouldn't think of it." Very gently he placed some of the icy whiteness against her mouth. And then he followed it with his own, dissolving the crystals between them, and her mouth was cold and delicious and hot and melting as her arms wrapped around him.

"You're as bad as your sister," Richard's disapproving voice floated back to them. "Come along now. I haven't got all day."

Reluctantly Sandy released her. "Exactly where are we going?" he questioned, taking Jane's hand and following Richard through the woods.

"Who knows? Richard's not going to explain until he's good and ready. If we want answers we'll have to follow him. Besides, we've got a little problem."

"Which is?"

"Richard said he hasn't been back to Nana's cottage in weeks. There were fresh footprints on the steps, remember? If it wasn't Richard it has to be..."

"Don't say Uncle Stephen," he warned.

"I was going to say Tremaine." She glared at him. "I wish you wouldn't…"

"What the hell is that?" Sandy demanded, interrupting her mid-tirade. They'd come through the other side of the woods and were approaching a brightly lit farmhouse. In the twilight he could see signs of dereliction, of a badly needed paint job and a roof in need of repair. Hanging from a hook on the front porch was what appeared to be the body of a hobo. Two small hooligans were dancing around the grisly figure, whooping wildly. Richard walked past them without seeming to notice them, disappearing into the house without a backward glance.

Even Jane looked momentarily startled at the macabre apparition. "It's a Guy Fawkes," she said. "I'd forgotten it was almost Halloween. Around here they stuff old clothes with dead leaves and leave them around—on front lawns, rooftops, hanging from trees. They're creepy but basically harmless—it's an interesting ethnological phenomenon."

"That doesn't explain the two demons." They'd reached the sagging porch by then, and he was relieved to see that it was indeed a dummy hanging from a noose. The two demons, on closer inspection turned out to be two red-headed boys so exact that they could only be twins. They were approximately six years old and making enough noise for a score of children as they danced around their macabre plaything.

Jane smiled at them cheerfully enough, unmoved by their bloodthirsty demeanor, and headed toward the door, Sandy in tow. He knew his own smile was more of the sickly variety, but at least he had the immediate and happy certainty that Jane would be a great mother. Only someone who truly loved children could have reacted to those two monsters with such unaffected friendliness.

As night had fallen, the temperature had also dropped, and while they had attempted to dress for it, the warmth of the house was welcome. They followed the noise and light down the narrow hallway to a huge old kitchen. A woman stood at the sink, watching their approach with friendly interest.

Richard was already slumped down at the table, drinking coffee, completely immersed in an issue of *Organic Gardening*, and his introductions were cursory at best. "This is my sister," he announced, leaving it at that.

The woman, a hefty, dark-haired lady in her late thirties with a smile as warm as the wood cook stove, held out a rough, work-worn hand and cast a cheerfully disparaging look at Richard's preoccupied figure. "Not much for the social graces, is he?" she said with an unexpected Southern accent. "But I guess you know that better than I do. I'm Hazel Dexter, and those are my two boys out there, Derek and Erik. You must be Jane."

Jane managed a weak smile. "Dexter?"

"We were married last month," Richard roused himself long enough to answer. "Figured I'd let you know once I decided what to do about Tremaine."

Jane glared at her brother, dropped Hazel's polite hand and pulled her into her arms to give her a hug. "Welcome to the family," she said. "I'm not sure if you got the better part of the deal."

"Oh, Richard and I get along just fine. And the boys mind him, which is more than I can say for me. They just ride roughshod over me."

"Really?" Jane said faintly. "I never pictured Richard as much of a disciplinarian."

"Self-defense," Richard said cryptically, not raising his eyes.

"Are you Jane's husband?"

Richard raised his head to that. "Yes, what happened to your husband, Jane? Doesn't he mind you running around with an arsonist?"

"I've been divorced for more than a year, Richard," she said patiently. "I told you at the time."

"I can't remember every little detail of my sisters' lives," he said loftily, putting down his magazine. "Come and sit down and tell me what Stephen Tremaine's been doing since my unfortunate demise."

Jane seated herself in one of the pressed-oak chairs and took a mug of coffee from Hazel's hands. "Apart from trying to find the missing part of the formula?"

"He'll never do that," Richard said smugly. "I've got it up here."

"For your information, Dexter, we think Tremaine's up here, too," Sandy said. His instincts had been right, he didn't like Richard Dexter one tiny bit, and the more he saw of him with his sister the more he wanted to smash his teeth in. He was doubly grateful for his own cup of coffee. Not only did it warm his chilled hands but it kept him from knocking Richard off his chair.

For once Richard showed some consternation. "You idiot," he said to Jane. "You must have led him up here. If it weren't for you…"

Sandy set the coffee down and advanced on the soon-to-be-unfortunate Richard Dexter. "Your sister has been busting her buns trying to keep Stephen Tremaine from soiling your stained legacy," he said in a light voice. "I'd suggest you show a little gratitude for all she's done for your sake."

"I don't see that she's done that much," Richard said in a snooty voice, then backed down hastily as he recognized the menace in Sandy's eyes. "Not that I don't appreciate it, Jane," he added. "But I could have taken care of it myself."

"I don't think you could take care of a housefly by yourself, much less a scorpion like Stephen Tremaine," Sandy snapped.

"Where did you get this young man, Jane? Are you certain he's a lawyer? He seems more like a thug to me."

"Richard," Hazel said reproving, stirring a large pot of some divine-smelling concoction on the back of the cook stove. "Watch your manners."

And to both Sandy's and Jane's amazement, Richard nodded sheepishly. "Yes, dear."

"What are we going to do about Stephen? Someone was lurking around the cottage before we got there. He's had his own cadre of hired thugs that make Sandy seem like a lamb in comparison. I wouldn't put anything past him."

"Neither would I," Richard said. "I guess I've been sentimental. That's what country living and a sensible life-style will do for you. Makes you forget what a dog-eat-dog world it is out there. If I were you, Jane, I'd leave Michigan and move up here to Vermont, where the air is clean and men are men."

"Wisconsin," Jane corrected absently. "And I'm not about to live anyplace where it snows in October. And I'm not looking for a man."

"I do think you should trade in your current model," Richard said, ignoring Sandy's presence. "And you get used to a little snow."

"No thanks."

"At least keep out of New York. It's a cesspool of danger, toxic wastes and perversion."

"I live in New York," Sandy announced in a dangerous voice.

"I rest my case." Richard gave Jane his most angelic smile, and Sandy wondered whether she was gullible enough to be won over by it.

"I appreciate your concern," was all she said, looking at neither of the two quarreling men in her life. "What are you working on in your laboratory? Is it something Uncle Tremaine will want to get his hands on? You're still under contract to him, aren't you?"

"I'm dead. The contract is null and void."

"It doesn't work that way," Sandy volunteered.

Richard ignored him. "Anyway, I've changed my area of interest. I don't think Stephen Tremaine will have the slightest use for my latest research, even though it has the potential to change the free world as we know it."

Jane stared at him, her eyes round behind the wire-rimmed glasses. "What is it?" she breathed, suitably impressed.

"Carrots," Richard said triumphantly.

"Carrots?" His sister's reaction wasn't quite what he would have hoped, but Richard charged on.

"A new strain of organic carrots," he announced, beaming. "Resistant to carrot weevils, crown rot, scab..."

"Yuck," Jane said. "I'm never going to eat carrots again."

"You certainly are. Tonight, as a matter of fact. Hazel's making carrot chowder, aren't you, my dear? Along with carrot bread, carrot salad and carrot cake for dessert. And it will all taste wonderful. Besides, the new strain of carrots is a miraculous source of protein, calcium, and vitamin A. Not to mention they're a natural laxative."

Hazel was still placidly stirring her pot on the stove, the delicious odor now taking on a definitely carroty scent. "Did your kids start out with that color hair," Sandy drawled, "or is Richard's research responsible?"

"Their father was a redhead," Hazel said. "And the boys hate carrots."

"They'll learn," Richard said firmly. "Anyway, they can't grow carrots in Salambia, even my carrots, and I don't think the profit will be enough to excite old Stephen. He's just going to have to sit and watch Technocracies go under. Serve him right, running a death factory under our very noses."

"He won't give up without a fight," Sandy pointed out.

Richard nodded, clearly reluctant to agree with him on anything. "I've known him long enough to realize he can be completely ruthless. I've been much too remiss. I should have destroyed the formula weeks ago." He rose, dropping the magazine on the scrubbed wooden table. "I'll do it now."

"Dinner's almost ready," Hazel said in a slow, tranquil voice. "You two are staying." It was a statement, not a question, and Jane nodded.

"It won't take long, dear," Richard said meekly. "Just back at the lab."

She nodded. "Don't take the boys. We'll never get them out of there before Thanksgiving, and that's a fact."

"We'll come with you," Sandy announced.

Richard stared at him, deeply affronted. "Don't you trust me? It doesn't matter whether I destroyed it or not, I still have the formula in my brain."

"Great," Sandy muttered. "That means Tremaine will have to kill you."

"Nice of you to be so concerned," Richard said, glaring.

"I'm not concerned. If it were up to me Stephen Tremaine could sell *you* as a secret weapon to Salambia. I'm merely looking after Jane."

"Jane's never needed looking after before." Dexter bristled.

"Everyone needs looking after now and then," he snapped back. "If you could see farther than the tip of your nose…"

"Let's go back to the lab and watch Richard burn the formula," Jane interrupted hastily. "Unless you need some help, Hazel?"

"Everything's just fine. I just have to feed the boys their hot dogs and potato chips. You two go ahead and keep Richard from falling into a snowbank or getting involved in some project. He has a habit of forgetting what he was doing in the first place."

"I can believe that," Sandy muttered.

"And I'll get some fresh sheets for your bed. You'll be spending the night. It's going to get down into the single numbers tonight, and that old summer cottage is too cold."

"Sheets for their beds," Richard corrected. "Separate rooms. I won't have my sister cohabiting under my roof."

"It's under my roof," Hazel said, "and you and I cohabited before we were married."

"That's different."

"No," said Hazel firmly, "it's not. Go burn your formula. When you come back supper will be on the table."

"Yes, dear."

The night had grown colder when the three of them stepped back out on the porch. The twin demons of the night had disappeared, and from deep within the house Sandy could hear the echo of a violent television show. A light snow had begun to fall again, and Jane shivered.

"Lovely climate," he said, taking her arm and heading down the sagging steps.

She looked up at him. He could read everything in her eyes, her irritation, relief, and concern for her brother, her fear of the unknown. Her love for him. "Lovely," she said, huddling up against his body for warmth and maybe something else. "I think I prefer Baraboo."

"What about that cesspool of danger, toxic wastes and perversion?" he countered softly, wrapping his arms around her slender body.

She held herself very still. "What about it?"

"It's where I live."

"I know that, Jimmy."

He winced at the deliberate taunt. "I like living there. The Upper East Side is beautiful, I inherited the apartment, and I like the energy in New York."

"So do I."

"It's not a good place for children, I suppose," he continued in a musing voice. "Maybe we should move out to some sort of yuppie suburb in a few years. Buy a place with lots of land and maybe some apple trees. Would you like that?"

She didn't move, she didn't say a word. He could no longer read the expression on her face, it was one of blank incomprehension. "I'm not doing this very well," he said. "But then I haven't had a whole lot of practice. I'm asking if you could find happiness with a sneaking, lying sleaze of a lawyer?" He threw her own words back at her, gently.

"No," she said. "But I could find happiness with you."

He smiled, a wide, mouth-splitting grin of sheer joy and relief. "You'll marry me? I don't know if that gun-toting brother of yours will let us sleep together unless we're at least engaged."

"Sandy, great sex is not a good enough reason for marriage," she warned, putting her hands against his shoulders to keep him from kissing her.

"No, it's not," he agreed. "And maybe being desperately in love with you isn't enough, and maybe sharing the same ridiculous interests isn't enough, and maybe just having a good time together isn't enough. But if you put them all together they make a pretty good case."

"Yes, counselor." She wasn't pushing quite as hard. "But

aren't you taking something for granted? What if I'm not in love with you?"

He laughed softly. "Jane, my precious, do you have any idea how transparent you are? Of course you're in love with me."

The hands started pushing again. "In that case," she said sweetly, "there's no need for me to say it, is there? Let's catch up with Richard."

Sandy suddenly knew he'd made a very grave error. He was so happy, so sure of her and him, that he'd been a little too hasty. "Jane…"

"Let's go." She gave him a shove, sharp enough so that he stumbled backward, landing in a pile of snow. "I'll meet you at the lab."

She was moving after her brother's ungainly figure at a swift pace, and Sandy sat in the wet snow for a moment, watching her with mingled admiration and dismay. "Does this mean you won't marry me?" he called after her.

"Not at all," she answered from a distance. "I'll marry you. But I'll make your life holy hell for a while."

He watched her go, then pulled himself out of the wet slush, brushing at the soaked seat of his jeans. "I just bet you will," he muttered. And he started after her.

JANE CAUGHT UP with her brother when he reached the edge of the woods. The huddled shape of the old icehouse was partially obscured by darkness and the lightly falling snow.

"Lover's quarrel?" Richard asked in a cheerful tone of voice.

"Don't get your hopes up. We just got engaged," Jane snapped.

"You don't look like a woman who just got engaged."

"How would you know? Maybe engagements don't agree with me." Sandy was catching up with them, his long legs eating the distance between them. Jane watched his approach with absent longing. Sooner or later the man was going to have to learn tact in his declarations of love.

They could smell the kerosene from halfway across the field, and Richard wrinkled his aristocratic nose. "I really wish I'd come across you two arsonists before you had a chance to make such a mess. It'll be weeks before I can get rid of the smell, not to mention…" His words trailed off in sudden horror, and some distinctly un-Richard-like cursing tumbled from his mouth.

Jane felt her stomach cramp in sudden dread. "What is it?"

"Someone's broken into the lab." Richard's voice was bitter as he took off in a dead run across the stubbled field. "Damn, damn, damn."

The heavy metal door was hanging open. Without hesitation Richard dashed into the darkened interior, with Jane and Sandy close at his heel.

Even in the inky darkness Jane could tell that the place had been trashed. She stumbled over piles of paper on the floor, peering through the blackness, Sandy close behind her, as Richard fumbled for the light switch.

"Do you think he found it?" she questioned anxiously.

The room was flooded with light, illuminating the three of them, illuminating Stephen Tremaine blocking the doorway, impeccably dressed in Abercrombie and Fitch country wear, a nasty-looking black gun in his hand.

"Oh, most definitely," he said in a smooth voice. "Most definitely, indeed."

Chapter Twenty-One

"I do regret doing this," Stephen continued, backing toward the door. "Normally I like to keep things a bit more civilized. But my dear Richard, you have always been the consummate pain in the rear. You even had the lack of consideration to die when I only meant for you to be injured, and then the audacity not to be dead after all. I doubt I would have gone so far down this particular road of illegality if I hadn't thought I was already guilty of murder."

"But you're not," Jane pointed out, staring at the gun as if mesmerized.

"Not yet," said Tremaine. "But there's really no turning back at this point. The Sultan of Salambia has ready cash, and I am in dire need of that cash. And the three of you are quite expendable. Even you…I'm sorry, I don't know your name," he said to Sandy.

"Alexander Caldicott," Jane supplied politely. "You wouldn't want to shoot a stranger."

"My dear Jane, you're almost as big a pain as your brother," Stephen announced with mild distaste. "As a matter of fact, I'm not going to shoot anyone. The police can trace bullets, you know. I'm afraid the three of you are going to burn to death in this old firetrap. I imagine they'll remember who bought the kerosene this morning, if anyone bothers to investigate. They might think it a bizarre ménage à trois. Or they might blame the two little monsters, who kept throwing rocks at me every time I tried spying, for the fire. I really don't care.''

"They'll blame Derek and Erik, all right," Richard announced gloomily. "They already set fire to the old Grange hall last April."

"Richard!" Jane warned.

Tremaine merely smiled. "You see how tidy everything will be? And trust an old veteran of the divorce wars, Jane. You wouldn't want to marry the man. This way you'll never have to be disillusioned." He stepped out into the darkness.

"You can't do this," Jane cried.

"Yes, my dear, I can." The door shut in their faces, and without hesitation Sandy flung himself at it. It was already tightly locked, and the smell of kerosene was thick in the air.

With great aplomb Jane began screaming and beating on the door. They could smell smoke, and the first evil tendrils of it began snaking under the doorway.

"We stand a pretty good chance," Richard announced calmly. He'd taken a seat on a stool by his workbench and was sorting through his papers at a leisurely rate. "Kerosene isn't that efficient for burning places—gasoline would have done a faster job. And it's been a very wet autumn. The wood in this place is old, but snow's been sitting on it for several days. Someone may see the smoke before it really catches." He picked up a pencil, made a little note, and then continued reading.

Jane looked at Sandy as the first wave of smoke hit her lungs. She started coughing, tears coming to her eyes, and she took the handkerchief he offered with gratitude, covering her mouth with it.

"Normally we should get down on the floor to get away from the smoke," Sandy said, his own voice similarly muffled, "but that's where the smoke is coming from, and this place isn't big enough to get away from it." He was coughing now, too, tears pouring down his face from the smoke.

Jane began pounding again, not bothering to cover her mouth. "Uncle Stephen, you get the hell back here," she shrieked through her spasms of coughing. "You can't leave us to die in here, damn it. Unlock the door! Unlock the damned door!"

Her furious voice faded in a paroxysm of coughing, and she sank against the door in defeat.

"Maybe I can break it down," Sandy muttered. "Move out of the way."

"For God's sake, Richard, help him!" Jane pleaded.

Richard looked up from the abstract he was perusing. "Let your fiancé be a hero," he said. "Stephen will relent eventually. If he doesn't, there's nothing we can do about it. I had the door installed to keep everything out. Your young man won't be able to do a thing about this." He coughed a bit, then lifted his glasses from his streaming eyes. "And I must say, Jane," he added sternly, "I blame you for all this. If you hadn't doused the place with kerosene I doubt Stephen would ever have thought of burning us. He never was the creative sort— he worked best in a managerial capacity."

"I'm not interested in Stephen's talents!" Jane shrieked between fits of coughing. "I'm interested in getting out of here."

"Just wait," Richard said, replacing his glasses as Sandy kept hurling himself at the door.

"Just wait?" Jane echoed in a furious croak. "Wait for what? For hell to freeze over? That's where you're going to be in a few minutes, brother dear, and I can't think of anyone who deserves it more...."

"Wait a minute." Sandy stopped his useless assault. "Someone's unlocking the door."

A moment later the door opened, filling the tiny room with acrid, blinding smoke. Someone took her hand, it had to be Sandy, and together they stumbled out into the snowy night. She landed in the snow, on top of his large, warm body, and she just lay there, taking deep, wonderful lungfuls of cold night air.

It took a moment for her eyes to clear. Stephen Tremaine was standing over them, an expression of extreme self-disgust on his face. "I couldn't do it," he said, his voice rich with regret. "I'm afraid I couldn't kill you. Just don't have what it takes after all."

"I hate to interrupt this soul searching," croaked Jane, looking around her, "but Richard's still trapped inside."

"He would be," Tremaine said gloomily. Without hesitation he dashed through the sheet of flames obscuring the doorway, and moments later came back out with Richard's semiconscious body slung around his shoulder. He dumped him in the snow, rubbing his hands together in the age old gesture of one getting rid of a nasty project.

Richard lay in the snow coughing for a moment, then managed to pull himself to a sitting position. "I didn't finish the article," he said accusingly. "Now it's in cinders. You're going to have to get me another copy, Stephen."

"Richard," said Stephen Tremaine, "you always were a pain in the rear, and you always will be."

Richard only waved an airy hand at him. Tremaine turned his back to look at Jane. She still hadn't moved. Sandy felt too good, too strong and solid and comforting beneath her, for her to be noble. "I suppose you want to call the police," he said in a resigned voice. "I won't fight it. There's not much I can do—this was a last-ditch effort and it failed. It appears," he said wearily, "that I am simply too damned civilized for murder."

"It's quite a failing," Sandy agreed from beneath Jane.

Reluctantly she got to her feet, her knees still a bit wobbly in the aftermath. "Are we going to call the police?" she asked Sandy, giving him a hand to help him up and wincing in sympathy as she realized his back was soaked with melted snow.

"We might be open to other possibilities," Sandy agreed, correctly reading her tone of voice.

"Police?" Richard roused himself from his perusal of the burning lab. "I don't want the police involved. Come back to the house, Stephen. Hazel has plenty for dinner, and you deserve to spend some time with my stepchildren. I'm sure we can come up with something mutually agreeable. Something not involving Salambia."

"Your stepchildren?" Stephen echoed. "The twins? I think I might prefer jail."

"Your preferences are not the issue right now," Sandy said. "I'm feeling cold and wet and quite angry, and I would love to take out that anger on someone who richly deserves it. Get back to the house. Now."

Richard pulled himself upright, strolled over to Stephen Tremaine and took the gun that was resting loosely in the older man's hand. "Nasty business," he said, tossing the weapon toward Sandy. He missed, it landed in the snow, and Sandy left it there, stepping over it and taking Jane's arm in his. "You know, Stephen," Richard said in a musing voice, "I can think of two things responsible for your aberrant behavior. First, you must have been given war toys when you were a child to encourage this hostile streak of yours. And you eat too much red meat. It messes up the bowels and makes people quite savage. Less animal flesh, Stephen, that's the ticket. Do you like carrots?" They wandered off, Richard chattering a mile a minute in his inanely cheerful voice.

Sandy and Jane watched them go. "I don't suppose we can just go home?" she questioned hopefully.

He shook his head. "Tremaine might murder them all in their sleep." He reached down and picked up the gun, tucking it in his pocket.

"With someone like Richard, who could blame him? Is he really going to stay for dinner with us?" Her voice was still raw from the inhaled smoke, and Sandy's beautiful gray eyes were puffy and red.

"Probably the night, too, if I read Hazel's hospitable tendencies properly," Sandy said.

"Let's go to bed early."

"Sounds like an excellent idea. I love you, you know. Even with your demented brother, I still want to marry you."

She cocked her head to one side, looking up at him. "I won't bother telling you anything you already know," she murmured. "Besides, you're no prize yourself. You may not have a loony brother but you're a pathological liar..."

"Jane…"

"You're going to have to earn it," she said fiercely. "You took my declaration of love before I offered it, so you're just going to have to wait until I'm ready."

"Jane, I'm freezing. Couldn't you…?"

"No. But I can take you back and strip off your clothes and warm you up."

He smiled down at her, and there was nothing but heat between them. "I'll settle for that. For now."

IT WAS LATE when they finally got to bed. Hazel put them in an old Victorian sleigh bed up under the eaves. The mattress sagged, but the sheets were ironed, the blankets wool, and the quilts were made by hand. Jane was wearing an old flannel nightie of Hazel's, the sleeves drooped over her wrists, the hem hit the floor and the neckline floundered around her shoulders, but it was soft and warm and much more welcome than a negligee.

Sandy had to make do with long winter underwear. When Richard had first presented him with it he'd refused, but five minutes in the icy confines of the upstairs bedroom and he changed his mind.

"This isn't what I had in mind for tonight," he said, climbing into the high bed, his teeth chattering. "I don't think I'll ever get warm again."

"You should have stayed up with Richard and Stephen. When I left they were taking off their sweaters."

"There are two reasons for that," Sandy said, pulling her into his arms and wrapping his shivering body around her. "One, they're sitting by the wood stove hogging all the heat that doesn't seem to get much farther than the kitchen. Number two, they've polished off one bottle of Scotch and they're well into their second."

"They were very drunk, weren't they?" Jane said, rubbing her face against the soft thermal cotton covering his shoulder. He still smelled faintly of smoke, despite the icy shower he'd insisted on suffering, and she felt a momentary apprehension.

"They're safe down there, aren't they? Uncle Stephen isn't going to murder us all in our beds?"

"Dear old Uncle Stephen has given up. He managed to agree to our terms in writing, and there's not much he can do about it without the whole mess coming out in the open. Whether he likes it or not he's going to have to sell the process to a peaceful, emerging nation of Richard's choice. He won't make much money on it, neither will your brother, but at least it'll be used for the good of mankind."

"What I particularly like," Jane admitted, sliding her hand up under the thermal shirt, "is the mess Uncle Stephen made of his future. Here he thought he was safeguarding the company by putting it in Elinor Peabody's hands, and she goes behind his back to the board of trustees and stages a palace coup. Uncle Stephen gets kicked upstairs and Elinor takes over. It serves him right—he always thought the trustees were just a formality."

"He shouldn't have underestimated Elinor," Sandy said, emitting a small groan of pleasure as her hand moved across his chest underneath the shirt. "I could have told him she was a man-eater."

"Humph," said Jane. "Why don't we lie here and *not* talk about Elinor Peabody?"

"Sounds good to me," he said, moving a thick strand of her hair away from her neck and nuzzling her ear. She shivered, and he knew for a fact she wasn't cold. "What do you want to talk about? Your godfather's future travel plans? Around the world with his long-suffering wife?"

"She'll probably push him overboard somewhere in the Orient," Jane said, letting her hand run down his flat stomach. "Maybe in Australia, where they still have great white sharks."

"I've tried to curb this bloodthirsty streak of yours," he said with a long-suffering sigh.

"I'm impossible to curb."

"Thank God."

Her hand slid beneath the elastic waistband of the thermal

long johns, but before she could reach her destination his hand shot out and caught hers, stopping her.

"Wait a moment," he said with mock sternness.

"Don't worry, Sandy, I'll respect you in the morning," she assured him with an impish smile.

"It is the morning," he pointed out. "It's after two, and I'm exhausted."

"Too tired for me? That doesn't sound like a promising beginning for our life together. Maybe I'd be better off with the real Jimmy the Stoolie."

"Come here, Jane," he growled, "and stop teasing me." He released her hand, caught her shoulders and hauled her up so that her face was level with his.

"It's fun to tease." She kept her voice light, waiting.

"Not at two-something in the morning, after we've been through hell and back at the hands of that drunken old man downstairs. You owe me, lady."

"What do I owe you?"

He caught her face between his hands, his thumbs smoothing her taut cheekbones and he looked into her eyes. "Anything you want to give me," he whispered. "Whatever it is, I'll take it."

She couldn't play games anymore, she couldn't summon up any lingering vestiges of outrage or hurt pride, she couldn't feel anything more except what she had to tell him. "Okay, you win," she said. "I'm in love with you."

He shook his head. "We both win, Jane," he said softly, placing his lips on hers in a featherlight kiss. "We both win."

IT WAS AFTER MIDNIGHT two days later when they arrived back at the Park Avenue apartment. Sandy insisted on carrying her over the threshold, even though they weren't officially married yet, and Jane went willingly, losing her shoes in the hallway, dropping pieces of clothing as she headed for the master bedroom. She stopped halfway down the hall, wearing nothing but a pair of lace bikini panties and her glasses, and turned to look at Sandy.

His shirt was off, his pants were unzipped, and he was hopping on one foot while he was trying to take off his other sock. In the background the phone rang and his answering machine clicked on.

"Are your calls more important than me?" Jane demanded. "Whoever it is can wait."

"You're right," he said, reaching to turn it off, when Jimmy the Stoolie's nasal tones stopped him.

"Listen, pal, you owe me. I'm calling from the twelfth precinct. They've got me on a charge of grand theft, auto, and I need you to bail me out of here, pronto. There's an old friend of mine in here who's got no reason to feel too friendly, and a person of indeterminate sex who's fallen in love with me. Get me out of here, Caldicott, and I won't say a word to the little lady about who you really are. Come on, what's a car between friends? The MGB was a piece of crap, I'm sorry I totaled it, but you owed me for getting you in to see Jabba. Save me, pal." The answering machine clicked off.

Jane just looked at Sandy. "Are you going to leave that poor man rotting in jail? After all, he brought us together."

Sandy pulled off his other sock and stripped off his pants. "Does that mean he gets to be best man?"

"At least we don't have to leave the church in an MGB," Jane said brightly. "We wouldn't have gotten two blocks in that car."

"Don't speak ill of the dead," Sandy said, stalking her down the long dark hallway, "or I'll buy another."

"How about an Edsel? Or maybe a nice little Chevy Vega? Mavericks had a certain *je ne sais quoi*...or we could—"

He caught up with her by the door, scooped her up in his arms and carried her into the bedroom. "We'll use taxis," he said. "Or walk." He dumped her on the king-size bed and followed her down.

"Or maybe," she said, "we'll stay right here and not go anyplace at all."

"Now that sounds like the best idea I've heard in a long time," Sandy said.

"And if I get bored I can always burn down the apartment. I still haven't had my chance to commit a crime. You were always so repressive."

"Someone has to keep you in line. That's what a partner in crime is for."

"I thought it was for aiding and abetting."

"There's that, too." He ran a string of kisses down her neck. "And at least I'll give you a discount on my fees if I have to defend you on a charge of arson."

"Big of you."

"Indeed."

"You're indecent, you know that?"

"I try my best."

"And you get spectacular results," she said fervently.

"What can I say?" He was all modesty.

"Say good-night, Sandy."

"Good night, Sandy."

"Indecent," breathed Jane in a pleased voice. And then all was silence, but the sound of the phone ringing and the plaintive voice of Jimmy the Stoolie wailing away on the answering machine.